WITHDRAWN

2 5 AUG 2020

FERBANE

ASH

JH

D0228464

Also by James Herbert

The Rats
The Fog
The Survivor
Fluke
The Spear
The Dark
Lair
The Jonah
Shrine
Domain
Moon
The Magic Cottage
Sepulchre
Haunted
Creed
Portent
The Ghosts of Sleath
'48
Others
Once
Nobody True
The Secret of Crickley Hall

Graphic Novels

The City
(Illustrated by Ian Miller)

Non-fiction

By Horror Haunted
(Edited by Stephen Jones)

James Herbert's Dark Places
(Photographs by Paul Barkshire)

JAMES HERBERT

ASH

MACMILLAN

Leabharlann
Chontae

Class: F
Acc: 12/1063
Inv: 12/160

First published 2012 by Macmillan
an imprint of Pan Macmillan, a division of Macmillan Publishers Limited
Pan Macmillan, 20 New Wharf Road, London N1 9RR
Basingstoke and Oxford
Associated companies throughout the world
www.panmacmillan.com

ISBN 978-0-230-70695-8 HB
ISBN 978-0-230-71126-6 TPB

Copyright © James Herbert 2012

The right of James Herbert to be identified as the
author of this work has been asserted by him in accordance
with the Copyright, Designs and Patents Act 1988.

This book is a work of fiction. Names, characters, places and incidents are the product of
the author's imagination or are used fictitiously. Any resemblance to actual events,
locales, or persons, living or dead, is coincidental.

The references to pharmaceuticals in this book are not to be relied on as medical, healthcare,
pharmaceutical or other professional advice. So far as the author is aware the information given is
correct and up to date as of January 2012, but practice, laws and regulations all change, and the reader
should seek up-to-date medical advice if considering the use of any of the pharmaceuticals mentioned.
The author and publishers disclaim, as far as the law allows, any liability arising directly or indirectly
from the use, or misuse, of the information contained in this book.

All rights reserved. No part of this publication may be reproduced,
stored in or introduced into a retrieval system, or transmitted, in any form,
or by any means (electronic, mechanical, photocopying, recording or otherwise)
without the prior written permission of the publisher. Any person who does
any unauthorized act in relation to this publication may be liable to
criminal prosecution and civil claims for damages.

1 3 5 7 9 8 6 4 2

A CIP catalogue record for this book is available from the British Library.

Typeset by SetSystems Ltd, Saffron Walden, Essex
Printed and bound by CPI Group (UK) Ltd, Croydon, CR0 4YY

This book is sold subject to the condition that it shall not, by way
of trade or otherwise, be lent, re-sold, hired out, or otherwise circulated
without the publisher's prior consent in any form of binding or cover other than
that in which it is published and without a similar condition including
this condition being imposed on the subsequent purchaser.

Visit **www.panmacmillan.com** to read more about all our books
and to buy them. You will also find features, author interviews and
news of any author events, and you can sign up for e-newsletters
so that you're always first to hear about our new releases.

All my stories begin with the premise: What if . . . ?
This has never been more so than with *Ash*. However, let me
plead that there are some basic truths among the fiction.
Have fun deciding which are which.

JAMES HERBERT

*'There are dark forces at work in this country
about which we know little.'*

QUEEN ELIZABETH II (allegedly)

Pont D'Alma tunnel, Paris
31 August 1997
12.59 a.m.

As her life ebbed away in the crumpled Mercedes she thought of her two sons.

Who would take care of them? Who would guide them through their early years?

Not their father. Oh God, not him and all he stood for. How could their lives be normal?

Now her mind, along with her flesh, was becoming cold. She could feel herself drifting away, far, far away from this ruined metal shell that entrapped and hurt her body so.

She was aware, vaguely, of incessant bright flashes, a gabble of shocked, greedy voices – the last sounds she would ever hear – as closure softened her remaining moments in this intrusive world.

Even as her life faded, her final concerns returned to those of the living. Her two sons – who would be there for them?

For the briefest of moments, their images followed her into the painless, velvet void, but then they were gone, leaving her to wonder for a second if in death she would find the soul of the barely born child she had lost.

Oblivion took her just as hands reached in to help.

PART ONE: THE JOURNEY

PRESENT DAY

1

The untidy little man peered out from the bookshop's window display, squinting to sharpen his vision.

He was watching the doors of the huge grey building that housed the BBC World Service offices and studios: those doors were in constant use, drawing in and disgorging a ceaseless stream of visitors and staff. The mark was still inside, but Cedric Twigg was patient as always, comfortable in his assumed role of book browser in the Kingsway WHSmith, pretending to be interested in the lofty novel he held in his hands. He had idled here for the last twenty minutes, having arrived half an hour earlier, picking up a hardback here and there to peruse its contents, replacing each volume, then choosing another.

The phoney shelf cruising had led him from the back of the store to the large plate-glass windows overlooking the busy street beyond and from where he chose a final volume entitled *Flat Earth News*, which he opened and brought up close to his face as if absorbed.

But every few minutes he would gaze distractedly through the windows as if considering the text while, in truth, he was contemplating the impressive edifice of the Aldwych building at the end of the broad and bustling Kingsway. There was another entrance/exit in the discreet courtyard at the back of Bush House, but he had an associate covering that. A call to Twigg's Samsung would inform him if their mark had left the building that way.

His pretended attention returned to the book again and he turned a page, appearing to be engrossed in its warnings about the world's news media.

Twigg was a fastidious individual who had once enjoyed the subterfuge involved in surveillance and tracking, learning the mark's habits and regularly visited haunts. But these days he found the chase less agreeable; the long stakeouts tedious, the satisfaction coming only with the final dispatch.

Small in stature and unremarkable in appearance – he could reasonably have been taken for a poorly paid accounts clerk on his lunch break – which suited his role perfectly. Although Twigg appeared commonplace, his unblinking grey-eyed stare could be quite unsettling if directed your way. And although his shoulders were narrow, they were strong and capable of exerting great force through his deceptively dainty hands. With a pot-belly recently beginning to swell over his belt buckle, the assumed image was complete.

Now the mobile phone in his trouser pocket vibrated against his upper thigh, its ringtone switched off; he reached for it. The tiny screen showed the caller's code name – Kincade – and Twigg thumbed the accept key.

'Mark leaving the building now,' the thin excitable voice of his apprentice blurted. 'Rear exit, heading up the Strand. Alone.'

'Right.' Twigg broke the connection and slid the neat little instrument back into his pocket. He returned the book to its shelf and made his way out of the store.

He walked quickly along the pavement, almost invisible among the lunchtime throng, making his way towards the even busier Strand, searching ahead for his prey. He only caught the attention of one person, a pretty young office worker on her way to have lunch with a friend, and that was only because he reminded her of someone as he strode purposefully towards her. She couldn't quite place the name, but the little man in his old-fashioned raincoat looked like the creepy actor who was in all those slasher movies a few years back. What *was* his name?

Then he'd passed her and the moment was gone. Now what puzzled her was why the little man with freaky eyes was carrying a furled umbrella under his arm on such a chilly but bright, cloudless day.

2

Lucy Duncan looked up from her receptionist's desk as the heavy, black-painted entrance door was pushed open, allowing cold air to impinge on the comfortable warmth of the lobby.

David Ash, unshaven and weary-looking, hurried through, the front door slowly closing of its own accord behind him. He strode towards the desk, making for the carpeted staircase. As usual, he ignored the building's claustrophobically small lift, preferring to take the stairs to the first floor where Kate McCarrick's office was located.

He managed a brief smile at Lucy, but the smile didn't quite make it to his eyes.

'You're late, David,' the receptionist scolded him lightly. 'The meeting started twenty minutes ago.'

Lucy watched as Ash climbed the stairs, two at a time, and gave an inward sigh. Such an attractive man, with his thick, tousled dark hair, flecked slightly with grey, and his deep blue but ever-melancholy eyes. This morning his chin was stubbled. Somehow it made him look sexier, though usually she preferred her men clean-shaven.

Lucy had replaced the previous receptionist called Jenny, who had left 'to have babies', although staying on an extra month to show Lucy the ropes and how to deal with some of the more questionable – and often distraught – phone calls that sometimes came through. Jenny had told her that Ash had been through some difficult times over the past few years, with two particularly unfortunate cases that appeared to weigh heavily on him. Perhaps they still did: he always seemed to be so downcast. Or 'brooding' might be more apt.

The phone rang as David Ash disappeared up the stairs and Lucy quickly picked up the receiver.

'Psychical Research Institute. How may I help you?'

Ash reached the first-floor landing and paused to take a breath. The meeting with Kate and the prospective client had been due to start at 9.30 a.m., and he, as Lucy had already told him, was late. If only he could sleep peacefully at night in the darkness of his room. If only the nightmares that always culminated in his eyes snapping open, his body in a sweat, would stop. Dawn was always a relief. Only then could he sink into oblivion in the knowledge that he was safe now that the night terrors had expunged themselves.

Kate McCarrick's office door was closed and he knocked before entering.

Kate, who was head of the Psychical Research Institute, looked past the shoulder of the person seated across the desk from her. She frowned slightly.

'Sorry I'm late,' Ash apologized both to Kate and the trim, dark-suited man, who had turned in his chair to appraise the new arrival. His expression was neutral.

'David, this is Simon Maseby. Simon . . .' her hand indicated Ash. 'David Ash, the investigator we were just discussing.'

Ash raised his eyebrows at Kate as Maseby rose and extended a hand towards him. He was a short, smartly dressed man, somewhere in his forties, his dark hair slicked back from his forehead, his chin clean-shaven (unlike his own, Ash thought), and his eyes were a very pale shade of green in his fresh roundish race.

'You've had some interesting times, Mr Ash,' Maseby said with a faint smile.

Again the parapsychologist glanced at Kate, who gave him

a slight but reassuring nod of her head. He shook the proffered hand, which was dry and firm to the touch.

'I've just filled in your background a little for Simon,' Kate said. 'Your experiences are of great interest to him.'

Maseby sat, eyes on Ash, a hint of curiosity and – no, not humour, Ash decided, but a kind of bemusement in his expression.

'So you believe in the supernatural, Mr Maseby,' Ash asked as he took the other chair facing Kate McCarrick's desk.

'Well now, that's a difficult question to answer.' Maseby crossed his legs, and Ash saw that the dark-suited man's shoes were polished to perfection, his grey socks made from some silky material. 'I have to say that I haven't given such, er, such things much thought in the past.'

'But now you have, for some reason.'

'Quite. For the moment, let's say that my eyes have been opened to what I would have thought unbelievable only a short time ago.'

'Shall I explain, Simon?' Kate leaned forward on her crowded desk, at one side of which was a computer screen and keyboard. Bookshelves were filled with studies on psychic phenomena and the paranormal, with titles such as *The Vertical Plane*, *Telluric Energy*, *Radiotelethesis* and *Genius Loci*. Grey, chest-high filing cabinets overspilling with case-history folders took up one side of the room. Two tall windows behind Kate's desk overlooked the busy city street below.

Maseby acquiesced with a bow of his head. He smiled at Ash, wrinkles appearing at the corners of his eyes.

But before Kate could begin, Ash jumped in with a question. 'Can I ask you something, Mr Maseby?'

'Of course.' Maseby glanced enquiringly at Kate.

She anticipated Ash's question. 'David is always interested in why a prospective client should choose this particular institute and not one of the equally respected organizations such as The Spiritualist Association or The College of Psychic Studies.'

'It's very simple,' said Maseby, his patronizing smile beginning to irritate Ash. 'Katie and I go way back. We met when we were students up at Oxford, she at St Hilda's College and I at Magdalen. All the colleges hold a weekly "formal hall" – a dinner for students to which guests from other colleges are invited. At that time, St Hilda's was an all-female establishment, so the girls there were particularly keen to welcome young men to their social evenings. That was how I met Kate, and we became firm friends – of the platonic kind, I might add.'

'Okay. I just wondered.' Ash looked across the desk at Kate McCarrick, who smiled back, giving nothing away. She guessed Ash suspected that she and Maseby had been lovers in the past despite her old friend's comment to the contrary.

In fact, she and Simon had slept together only once when they were students, both quickly deciding they were not suited to a drawn-out affair. Even then, Simon was a little too much in love with himself to sustain an equal partnership.

Maseby continued to answer Ash's question. 'Kate and I have kept in touch over the years and I admit, while I couldn't quite accept the strange profession she'd chosen, I've always had high regard for her intellect. When events that could only be described as paranormal began to occur in an establishment with which I'm associated, she was the first person I thought of turning to. Ghosts and hauntings are not something I've experienced before.'

Kate took over from him. 'Simon represents a group of influential people who have an interest in a particular Scottish castle.'

Ash caught the sharp glance Maseby suddenly gave Kate so he dug deeper. 'And who are these influential people?'

'That really doesn't matter at this point,' Maseby all but snapped back. 'All you need to know is that the castle is currently having problems that are unaccountable.'

'Hauntings?'

'We think so.'

Kate spoke up again; she knew David had lost none of his surface cynicism, despite the shocking experiences he'd suffered over the past few years. It was his way of testing potential clients: he never wasted time on neurotics with over-imaginative and often misguided claims of supernatural activity. 'Comraich Castle is used as a kind of, well, a kind of sanitarium. Would you call it that, Simon?'

'I'd prefer to say it's a retreat.'

'A religious retreat?' asked Ash.

Maseby gave a sharp bark of derision. 'No, it has nothing to do with religion, even though one of our residents was an archbishop in his better years. When his mind wasn't so addled.'

'It's a mental institution?' Ash refrained from calling it an asylum.

'As I said, we refer to it as a retreat.'

'But a retreat from what?' Ash persisted.

'From the world, Mr Ash,' Maseby said simply. His smile this time was thin-lipped.

3

Maseby spoke to Kate McCarrick. 'Perhaps from this moment on we should have Mr Ash's assurance that whatever else we discuss this morning will not be mentioned beyond these four walls.'

'All our cases are confidential, you know that, Simon.'

'Mr Ash?' There was something hard in Maseby's stare.

Ash gave a shrug. 'It's fine by me. Victims of haunting often demand the utmost discretion.'

'Kate tells me you have had a drink problem.' It was bluntly put and, to Ash, irrelevant. He frowned at his employer, who had the grace to look apologetic.

'Simon needs to have every confidence in you before engaging the Institute,' she explained. 'I've told him your drinking is no longer an issue.'

'Vodka, wasn't it?' Maseby enquired, his face a mask of indifference. Ash knew he was probing, looking for weakness.

'Kate's right – I've given up the vodka.'

'Then I hope there'll be no relapse during this assignment,' the other man said grimly. 'I have to answer for any mistakes, so I must be sure of you.'

'I haven't tasted a drop of the stuff for over a year now. But I'd still like to know who it is *you* answer to.'

'As I explained, that's irrelevant for the moment. However, I *can* tell you that it's an alliance of like-minded and extremely wealthy individuals. People of influence, as Kate has already informed you.'

15

Kate spoke. 'So let's move on and tell David of the strange – and terrifying – incidents that are happening at Comraich. You already know I have absolute trust in him.'

Maseby acknowledged the firmness of his old friend's tone with a small nod of his head. 'Well now,' he said briskly, turning round in his seat to face Ash more easily. 'The organization I represent owns a large but necessarily remote castle in Scotland. Its residents are only accepted on the understanding that no outsider can ever know its precise location, not even the people who have placed them there and pay their fees. I should add that those fees are extremely high, with a harsh financial penalty for betrayal of trust.'

'Betrayal?' Ash was surprised. It seemed a potent word to use.

'You'll understand after you've countersigned the contract drawn up between myself and Kate. The Institute would be liable should you break our agreement.'

'It would wipe us out,' Kate told Ash grimly.

'Then why take it on? Why risk everything?' Ash stared at Kate.

It was Maseby who answered him. 'Because the reward for success would mean that the Psychical Research Institute would never be under financial pressure again.'

For a second or two, Ash was lost for words.

'It's true, David,' Kate said. 'You know our cash flow has always been borderline, but if we accept this contract and are successful we'll be secure for a long time to come. Trust me on this.'

Ash hesitated before expressing his thoughts. 'And if we're not successful with this case, if we're unable to discover the root cause of these alleged hauntings?'

His question was directed at Kate, but it was Maseby who responded. 'You haven't yet heard the nature of the phenomena.'

'True. But from what you imply you could need a spiritualist rather than a research team.'

'There'll be no team, David,' Kate informed him. 'It's just you initially; no one else will be involved at this stage.'

'A castle will be impossible for one person to cover.'

Maseby leaned forward in his seat as if to speak conspiratorially to Ash, his voice almost hushed. 'Unfortunately, the more outsiders invited there, the higher the risk of exposure. Comraich Castle is intentionally private and I reaffirm, even its location must remain secret. Strangers are never allowed inside the grounds, not even tradesmen.'

Ash was perplexed. 'How can you keep that kind of landmark secret? How about the locals – they must be aware of its existence?'

'Oh, they know Comraich is there all right, but they have no idea of its purpose. We encourage them to believe it's been turned into a private and very expensive health spa. In some ways it is just that. As for tradesmen and deliveries of any kind, there is a dropping-off point at the estate's boundary. Mr Ash, once you're there, you'll appreciate its need for secrecy.'

The parapsychologist shifted uncomfortably in his chair. Absent-mindedly, he fingered the short scar on his cheek.

'David, again, you must trust me,' Kate urged. 'I chose you because you've always worked best alone.' *And you also have some psychic ability, even though you won't admit it to yourself,* she thought. 'Let's not be modest, you are the Institute's leading, as well as the most experienced, investigator.'

'But I can't handle the latest technology on my own. Monitors, cameras, capacity-change recorders, anemometers, ventimeters, air meters, CCTV – the list goes on and—'

'We already have a closed-circuit television facility,' Maseby interrupted, 'and, of course, a monitoring area with full-time security observation.'

'Besides, David, yours will only be a preliminary investigation,' added Kate.

'But a castle? There have got to be so many rooms, corridors, underground chambers, halls and passageways, not to mention *secret* passageways. I can't cover them all.'

'That isn't being asked of you, Mr Ash. First we need to establish if Comraich is – and as a sceptic myself, it's difficult for me to say this – truly being haunted, and that whatever's happening is not just some weird but accountable phenomena. No doubt you remember in 2008 when there were twenty or more suicides of young people, all around the area of Bridgend in Wales within weeks of each other. Nobody has explained the catalyst for such tragic self-inflicted deaths. I've also heard that one schoolgirl fainting can cause others around them to faint.'

Ash frowned. 'If you think there's a kind of collective hysteria among your castle residents, then maybe it's not a parapsychologist you need, but a psychologist.'

'We already have one and she is as perplexed as everybody else. If we can agree to the terms of the contract, you'll meet her on the plane tomorrow.'

'I'd have to fly to Scotland? I could easily drive or take the train.'

Maseby shook his head. 'You'll go by jet from London City Airport. It isn't a long journey, an hour or so. You'll join Dr Wyatt, our resident psychologist, who is accompanying a new client to Comraich. Interestingly, Dr Wyatt practised psychiatry before psychology, the former being how she gained her MD.'

Ash was unwilling to debate the point. 'So you have two for the price of one.'

'No, no. We also have a resident psychiatrist at Comraich. A Dr Singh.'

'The people you represent *must* be wealthy, especially if they have their own jet.'

'I thought I'd made that clear.'

'Freemasons?' It was a wild guess that was met with disdain. The next guess was even wilder. 'The Illuminati?'

'No,' Maseby said brusquely, ignoring the investigator's deliberate facetiousness. 'You'll receive more information when it's considered necessary. And of course, the first thing you must do is sign both the confidentiality agreement and the contract between the Institute and Maseby Associates on behalf of Comraich Castle.'

'You didn't mention there were two contracts.'

'Yes, the Institute's and also your own personal agreement.'

Kate intervened. 'I think it's time you told David exactly what has happened at Comraich so far. Then he can either accept the assignment or walk away. Agreed? David, if you decline, you can never tell anyone of this meeting.'

'We hope you will come on board, Mr Ash.'

Mystified but intrigued, Ash nodded in acquiescence and Kate breathed a sigh of relief. Despite her recommendation to Maseby, she hadn't been sure that David Ash had truly recovered his nerve.

4

Maseby now shifted his chair so that he could look straight into Ash's eyes without the discomfort of twisting his body.

'Apparently it started a couple of months ago,' he began, 'around the end of July or beginning of August, or so I'm told. One of my duties is to visit Comraich Castle at certain intervals just to see how it's running, to note any problems, sometimes to accompany new clients, get them settled in – that sort of thing. Problems are generally minor, but with others I need to spend a week or so up there.'

Kate leaned back in her seat, her eyes flitting between Ash and Maseby, but mostly her attention staying with the former; having already heard Maseby's account, she was now interested in Ash's reaction to it.

Maseby continued. 'It was after supper, late enough for the castle lights to be switched on. As was customary, many of our guests had gathered in one of the larger rooms used as a lounge area, where they could relax with a coffee, or brandy. It's all part of the service. There was nothing amiss, and although it was summer, a fire had been lit in the room's big open hearth. In a place as huge as Comraich, with stonework and wooden beams dating back to the fourteenth century, there are always draughts coming from somewhere. I think there were twenty or thirty guests and staff in the room at that time and everything appeared normal enough, but some of the residents started complaining about the chill that had set in.

'The staff were perplexed. Despite the roaring fire and heat from the radiators, which are always left on whatever the season, the place really was cold and becoming colder by the minute – and it was still summertime, remember. In fact, everybody there could see the vapour of their own breath, that's how cold it was. Then all the lights slowly began to dim; apparently it was the same in every hall and passageway where there were ceiling and wall lights. Soon, the castle was almost in darkness.'

'Do you have a back-up generator for when the power supply from the main grid goes down?' Ash enquired.

'There are more than one, in fact, for different areas of the castle, and they're always set to kick in automatically whenever there's a power failure.'

'Then maybe you need a qualified electrician.'

'David . . .' Kate warned.

Maseby smiled coldly. 'Besides a psychologist, we have top-rated electricians *and* engineers at our disposal. We also have a doctor, two general surgeons – specialist surgeons can always be flown in – several nurses, both male and female, an estate general manager and several wardens . . . I could go on, but is it necessary?'

Ash shook his head.

'In any case, an electrician wasn't required. In a matter of moments, the lights came back on.'

'And the heating?'

'Yes, everything was normal again.'

'You said the room also had a fireplace as well as hot radiators. What happened to the fire?'

'Ah. The fire itself somehow lost its heat; the flames died even though it was stacked with burning logs and coal. It still shimmered, but gave out no heat. When the lights returned, so did the flames. It was very disconcerting for everyone, both clients and resident staff. But worse for the clients in the special unit below.'

'Below?'

'Some of our medical facilities extend to the castle's

basement area. A long time ago, these rooms were cells – *oubliettes*, they used to be called – but of course now they've been converted into very comfortable suites.'

'Okay.' The word was drawn out, as if Ash were considering the information. 'So for one night the castle had a blackout. Obviously, there's something more you want to tell me.'

'Oh, believe me, Mr Ash, there's much more to be told. I want to proceed with the incidents in the order they transpired.'

Noting that her investigator still looked worse for wear, Kate broke in, turning to the prospective client first. 'I'm sure you'd like more coffee, Simon.'

Ash guessed the coffee was really meant for him. Did he honestly look that bad this morning?

Maseby declined the offer, but Ash nodded his head gratefully. 'Yeah, I could use a refresher. You know I'm not at my best this time of day.'

He meant the last remark as a self-deprecatory comment, but Kate didn't smile. Instead, she pushed a button on the desk's intercom and spoke to her secretary.

What Ash really needed was a cigarette, but ridiculously that would be illegal now that smoking in offices, restaurants, pubs and theatres was banned. The lack left him a little shaky at times. Like now, even though he'd made the decision that tomorrow he would give them up.

Releasing the button, Kate said to her old friend, 'Please continue, Simon.'

Maseby's appraising eyes suggested he knew the coffee was a lifebelt thrown to this unshaven, tousle-haired individual she claimed was the Institute's best psychic investigator. But Kate really wouldn't have recommended Ash if she had any doubts about his ability.

'Now we think,' Maseby said as he gave a small tug at the trouser leg stretched too tightly over his knee, 'that was the beginning of it all. You see, the same thing happened over the following two nights, even though the castle's electrical circuits had been tested and the generators checked. No malfunctions were found in any of the systems.

'Three nights in all, Mr Ash. Now tell me nothing unnatural is going on at Comraich.'

Ash gave him a humourless grin of repentance. 'You're right. If it happened three nights running, then I'd be concerned.'

'And on the third night, a terrible stench came with the darkness, as if the air itself had been contaminated. Some of the guests, as well as members of staff, became nauseous because of it. Even when the lights returned and the fires regained their heat, the putrid odour lingered so that windows had to be opened to let the sea wind sweep through and cleanse the place of its stench.'

'I admit, it's puzzling,' commented Ash, 'but it isn't necessarily proof of a haunting.'

The office's side door opened and a young man entered carrying a tray bearing two cups and saucers, a tiny jug of milk and a cafetière. He gave Ash a quick nod hello and settled the tray on Kate's desk where she'd cleared a space.

'Thank you, Tom.' She passed the used cups to her PA and he left the room, heeling the connecting door shut behind him.

Ash gratefully accepted his coffee and burned his top lip taking a sip too soon. Nevertheless, he took another sip, the heat and caffeine working its way into his system. He picked up from where the conversation had left off. 'I assume the castle drains were inspected as well as the electrical circuits?'

Maseby was emphatic. 'Everything that could be checked *was* checked. No fault was found in either utility. There was nothing to explain the stench, and the castle's wiring was functioning properly.'

He lowered his voice, controlling his sudden exasperation. The investigator was meant to pose questions and hopefully *rationalize* what he heard. When neither happened, Maseby ploughed on. 'I was called up to Comraich and I witnessed the next incident myself.'

Ash froze with his cup halfway to his lips. He was interested in hearing Maseby's personal viewpoint on what was happening in the Scottish castle and whether or not it could be defined as a 'haunting'.

Kate studied Ash's face, waiting for some kind of reaction. But, as always, the investigator gave nothing away.

'On this occasion,' Maseby was continuing, 'the castle's CEO, Sir Victor Haelstrom, and I were in his ground-floor office when we heard a terrible racket coming from next door, where his secretarial staff are. It sounded like somebody was trying to wreck the place. There were bangs and crashes and one of the women was screaming. We rushed through the connecting door and we both ducked instinctively as a chair came flying towards our heads. Fortunately it missed, but the sight that we came upon was alarming to say the least. The three typists and Sir Victor's PA – it was she who was screaming – were huddled together in a corner of the room, while the general manager Andrew Derriman was sprawled on the floor, blood spilling from a wound to his head. He was trying to rise but every time he was on one knee, a heavy piece of furniture skimmed across the room as though purposely aimed at him. He was knocked down again and again. Furthermore there were some black orbs flying around the room. Where they came from we're not sure. They're not part of the office furniture.'

Kate and Ash glanced at each other.

'Paintings and photographs were dropping from the walls as if caused by a seismic shock. A computer on another desk kept switching itself on and off, even though its plug had been yanked from the wall socket. The fax machine was spewing out plain paper and, even when emptied, the mechanical process continued. It was the same with the copier, light constantly flashing on and off.'

'Poltergeists?' Ash aimed the suggestion at Kate, who shook her head.

'There's more to tell,' she said quietly.

Maseby took his cue. 'I stayed on at Comraich for a further week, just to be around should there be any more incidents. There weren't. Everything became normal again, so I left, only to be called back the very next week. The lights had begun dimming again, but this time it was different.'

'In what way?' Ash enquired.

'This time the lights, having almost faded to darkness, suddenly grew bright, then brighter, until it was impossible to look at them for more than a split second. In less than a minute the lights radiated so much power that the bulbs began to pop, showering the people below with fragments of hot glass.'

Ash frowned. 'Anyone badly hurt?'

'Some of the clients and a couple of maids suffered minor cuts to their faces, but no one was seriously injured. It was a miracle no one was blinded; they had instinctively closed their eyes when the bulbs exploded.'

'I've already suggested to Simon,' said Kate, 'that it might be a paranormal storm, with so many bizarre episodes happening one after the other.'

'Possibly. But what instigated it if that were the case?' Ash looked to Maseby for an answer.

'I have no idea, and I'm surprised you'd think I would know. Nothing's changed at Comraich Castle recently, and there haven't been any new guests for quite some time.' He avoided Ash's eyes. 'Except for one,' he finished quietly.

'Has anyone – residents or staff – witnessed manifestations of any kind, aside from those that you've mentioned?'

'Ghosts, you mean.'

'Not necessarily. It could be anything from a floating mist inside the building to noises, banging, knocking, tapping, voices. Hazy, or even solid, figures that suddenly appear and then disappear, or pass through walls, or float up or down rooms or corridors. Shouts, screams. Disembodied hands, heads, and torsos. There can be any manner of anomalous

25

disturbances created by other-worldly influences. But what I really want to know is, has anybody at Comraich Castle actually encountered the spirit of someone supposedly dead?'

Maseby considered the question for a few moments. 'It seems not,' he said at last. 'But I myself have definitely felt cold spots, especially in the rooms and passageways beneath the castle.'

'Old dungeons?'

'As I told you before, old dungeons converted into comfortable quarters for some of our guests. We also have medical facilities down there.'

Ash regarded him curiously.

Maseby explained. 'Several of our guests are not quite sound of mind, and we tend to keep them apart from our other residents. But getting back to the point: yes, I have experienced so-called cold spots in areas below ground and that doesn't surprise me, because the castle is built on top of a promontory over the sea, and there is supposed to be a network of tunnels leading down to caves on the shoreline.'

'Okay, so that's easily explained. There can be any number of reasons for cold zones in the main part of buildings. A lot of structures, particularly *ancient* ones, and especially stone-built castles, have perfectly natural cold spots caused by draughts through the cracks in the masonry, or poor joints and crooked doors, gaps in the flooring, bricked-up chimneys or those still open, worn woodwork around windows, and leaky roofs. The list goes on.'

'I understand that. But in one or two, there . . .' Maseby considered his own words. 'Well, there is a . . .' Now he shook his head, a pragmatist searching for a way to describe the improbable. 'I suppose you might call it an "atmosphere".'

'A presence?' Kate prompted.

'I'm not sure. Something even more intangible than that. It left me feeling very uneasy, you know, like icy spiders' legs down the spine.'

'Just a feeling, though,' said Ash. 'You didn't actually see anything odd, anything out of place?'

Maseby bit down on his lower lip like a child thinking on a problem. 'No. No I didn't. But others have.'

Both Kate and Ash straightened a little, as if suddenly more alert.

'You didn't tell me, Simon,' Kate reproved him.

'I was about to when Mr Ash arrived. Besides, I haven't given it much credence. The eyewitness is – how should I put it? uh, a less than reliable witness at present.'

'In what way?' Ash enquired.

'If I'm to answer that, I must remind you yet again that this is all highly confidential.'

Although intrigued by the man's caution, Ash nodded agreement. 'That's already understood.'

'I mentioned Comraich has lower-level units for certain guests who necessarily have to be segregated from the rest of the residents for a while. Their mental state is too delicate to have them mix with others in the castle. It was one such confined person who claimed to have been visited by a ghost in his room for several nights running.'

'If by less than reliable you mean this person is insane, he might even be seeing pink elephants dancing on the ceiling.'

Maseby made it clear from his expression that he didn't appreciate the flippancy, even though Ash hadn't meant his comment to be taken that way. If someone was crazy, then obviously they might imagine crazy things.

'Can you let me have his name for my notes?' Ash reached for the microcassette player he always kept handy in his jacket pocket. 'And can I record this conversation?'

Maseby seemed to bridle, as if both requests were an impertinence.

'There will be no record of our conversation. Even if you accept the assignment – which I gather you will by those two questions – nothing is to be put down on tape.'

27

'I'll need to use it when I begin my investigation.'

'I understand that. But Kate and I have agreed all such recordings will be the property of the organization I represent. That will also include written reports.'

Ash stared at Kate in amazement, as if she'd made a false promise to this irritating friend of hers.

'Simon is correct,' she concurred. 'We won't even keep a written report for our own files.'

'But that can't be right,' Ash protested. 'It's not what the Institute is about.'

'Must we go through all this again?' Maseby had directed his impatience towards Kate.

She sighed. Before Ash's arrival, the meeting with Simon had stalled precisely on this point. The Institute documented *every* investigation, whether successful or not, but her old friend had eventually persuaded her that this must be an exception, and with further revelations she understood why. Besides, the reward for the venture, satisfactory or not, really was *too* good to be dismissed.

She addressed her senior investigator, her voice as firm as her expression. 'David, once the investigation is underway you'll understand why the secrecy. I can assure you, when you visit Comraich Castle, you'll be told everything you need to know. Isn't that right, Simon?'

Ash wondered why Kate appeared to need further assurances from Maseby.

'Absolutely.' Maseby tentatively clasped his hands together as if a deal had already been struck.

Slipping the microcassette player back into his pocket, Ash gave a short nod of his head. 'All right, no names for now and all notes and reports to be handed over to you, Mr Maseby.'

'Please, call me Simon.' The smart-suited consultant seemed satisfied.

Ash didn't accept the familiarity. 'So, Mr Maseby, this unnamed guest kept in the rooms below ground claims he saw a ghost several nights running?'

'That's right.'

'And he still maintains it's true. I assume he was thoroughly questioned after each occasion?'

'He was indeed.'

'Obviously I'll have to talk to him myself.'

'Unfortunately, he is no longer capable of answering questions.'

Once more Ash raised his eyebrows. His next question was deliberately blunt. 'He's out of his head? Have these alleged hauntings tipped him over the edge or was he already insane?'

'It's even more serious than that,' the reply came back instantly. 'The poor man has been physically injured and is now in a catatonic state of shock.'

'Are you saying he has self-harmed?' asked Kate. She and Ash had shared glances.

'If only it were that simple.' Maseby slowly shook his head as if from sadness. 'His injuries are not of his own making. There's the mystery, you see.'

He held up a hand, palm forward, to ward off further questions. 'Let me elucidate – *if* I can.'

Ash leaned back in his chair and said nothing. Kate, too, kept silent.

Maseby's voice was sombre as he began to explain.

5

'A week ago, Comraich Castle's senior nurse, Rachael Krantz, was on her early-morning rounds, checking the special units below ground level.

'All the code-locked doors down there are metal, each with a small toughened-glass viewing window so that patients can be observed without the observer entering the room.

'There was nothing amiss in the first few rooms – the patients inside were either sleeping or sitting quietly – but the fourth appeared to be empty.

'Nurse Krantz was not too concerned initially, because the occupant might have been in a blind spot beside the door itself. But she noticed a pool of blood seeping out from under the door and heard an agonized moaning coming from within that had her punching in the door's key code. Most of the nurses and other ancillary staff have radio transmitters attached to the lapels of their uniforms, but Krantz decided not to waste time alerting others before assessing the full nature of the situation.

'She pushed open the door, but waited a second or two before going through – and who could blame her for that? There was so much blood pooling over the floor she said she could smell its coppery odour. The moaning she'd heard was, of course, louder now that the door was wide open, but it remained low and muted, as if it came from someone barely conscious.

'She went in, careful not to tread in the blood-soaked

30

section of carpet. Then she turned to see what had been hidden from view beyond the observation window.

'Any other person, male or female, might have screamed and run from the room, but Nurse Krantz is made of sterner stuff. Instead of fleeing or calling for assistance, she moved closer to the mutilated man who was pinned to the wall several feet above the floor.

'She knew who the man was, of course, but barely recognized him beneath the thick mask of blood. It was running from his eyes, ears, nose and mouth onto his chest and stomach. His genitals had been cut off. He was naked and spread-eagled on the stone wall, his arms outstretched, the blood streaming onto the carpet below, soaking in and spreading.

'She assumed he'd been somehow physically pinned there, but when she looked at his hands and feet she saw there was nothing to hold him, no wounds, no marks, no deep cuts.

'It was a crucifixion without nails.'

'And without death, it seems,' Ash murmured.

6

Kate McCarrick stepped out of the shower, her auburn hair hanging limp and almost straight against her neck and scalp. She took a thick white bath towel from the heated rail and quickly rubbed her body down, leaving her hair till last, patting it gently, the towel absorbing surface dampness.

Kate studied her naked body in the full-length mirror mounted on the back of the bathroom door. The glass was steamed up just enough to blur her image, but as she turned sideways for a different view she sighed, not in despair but in rueful resignation.

Breasts that had been full since puberty had lost their 'lift', and her tummy bulge seemed a little more prominent than only a few months ago (the tightness of the waistband in her skirts and slacks gave independent testimony to that!). But her legs were still good, if slightly heavier round the thighs. For a woman in her mid-forties, she was in good shape overall, even though her hair, presently damply dark, needed help from a bottle to disguise the encroaching grey threads.

Slipping into her luxurious white robe, Kate left the bathroom, intending to blow-dry her hair before it got too lank to shape, but decided she needed a preparatory drink before her dinner date arrived. She'd accepted Simon's invitation on the understanding that it was merely a reunion dinner with an old friend, no strings attached. If Simon expected more, then he was sadly deluded; she was no longer young and capricious, nor was she quite middle-aged and desperate. There were other men in her life, but no one special, nobody she wished to grow old – older – with.

At one time, David had certainly been a consideration, even though she was ahead of him in years. That was long ago though, and both of them had wandered off along their separate paths since – only the Institute itself sustaining their relationship. Sometimes she regretted not having become more serious with him. Certainly, she'd tried, but it would always come back to the truth of the situation: in essence, David Ash was a loner, and in all probability he would remain so. Instead of advancing years mellowing his temperament, David had become even more detached. Some women might find it attractive in a man, feel that his brooding manner and dark good looks somehow made him interesting, gave him a Heathcliffian allure. But Kate knew his self-containment and complexity of mind would eventually wear them down, even prove tiresome, if not vexatious. After a while, it would sap any serious partner's devotion.

Two previous investigations had taken their toll on him: the last one, concerning a village in the Chilterns called Sleath, had almost destroyed him. He'd needed weeks of special care and recuperation afterwards in the psychiatric wing of a private hospital a few miles outside London and, although he'd been patched up mentally, Kate had wondered if he would ever really be the same again. That had been two years ago, and he was still unable to explain precisely what had happened in Sleath.

Years of repressed guilt had come to the fore, its origins a tragic accident that had occurred when he was just a child. He'd told her of it in intimate conversations during their brief spell as lovers, and it had helped her understand him a little more.

When they were children, David and his older sister, Juliet, had fallen into a dangerous river, whose strong mid-stream current had swept Juliet away. He too would have been carried off but for his father, who had jumped in after them. David was hauled back to the bank, but Juliet had drowned, their father unable to find her in the murky, fast-flowing river. And for some reason, David had blamed himself ever since; perhaps he felt guilt because he'd been saved while she had drowned.

Some years before the Sleath case he'd been involved in an investigation concerning an alleged haunting of an old mansion called Edbrook. He told Kate that the ghost of his sister, Juliet, had returned to haunt him there. And she had not been alone.

Even now, it was difficult to make sense of David's claim, but he'd come back from that place a changed man with a short but deep gash on his cheek. Always somewhat cynical (that was what made him so good as a psychic investigator: he was never fooled by a phoney haunting or fake mediums) he was now even more guarded.

It was as if those deep mental scars had been raked open again when he'd visited the little village of Sleath some years later. It had taken some time to bring him back from the brink of madness.

But she'd never truly unravelled the traumatic events that had occurred in Sleath, a bizarre haunting that had involved the whole village and centred on David. She was aware that a woman called Grace Lockwood had died when the walls of an old ruined manor house had collapsed and crushed her. Kate guessed that she had been very special to David, but he'd refused to discuss their relationship.

Typical Ash: suppress all true feelings; keep them at bay, especially away from himself, lest they render him even more vulnerable.

Kate poured herself a gin and tonic and went to sit on the sofa facing the apartment's floor-to-ceiling window overlooking the dark waters of the River Thames. Simon would be collecting her within the hour, but she was content to dwell on her thoughts for a while. Twenty years ago, maybe even less, she would have been rushing around to get ready for a date: varnishing her nails, fingers *and* toes, choosing the right underwear (one never knew how the evening might end) and tights, applying make-up, drying and styling her hair then choosing her outfit. Including bath or shower, it would take a couple of hours. Was she getting too old for such fuss? It seemed so.

Then again, her dinner date with Simon Maseby definitely didn't fall into the 'special' bracket. But at least she might learn a bit more about this covert organization he represented.

7

The private jet's stewardess welcomed Ash aboard with a beaming smile and bright blue eyes that were almost sincere. She led Ash along the Gulfstream G450's short cabin, turning to ask which seat he would like to take. As he was the only passenger so far, the investigator had plenty of choice; he opted for a beautifully designed single armchair which faced another that was identical. Both were made of soft grey suede with charcoal-black cushions, broad with high headrests.

In fact, the whole cabin, with room for up to eight passengers, was decked out in the same muted greys. The ambience was of stylized (and reassuring) comfort.

Ash settled into his seat, noticing that across the narrow aisle from him, its backrest against the curved cabin wall, was a sofa-type seat with room enough for three people. He dropped his leather shoulder bag onto the floor beside him.

'I'm Ginny,' the slim stewardess announced. (*No plastic name tag for you, then*, thought Ash.) 'Can I get you something to drink, Mr Ash?' She was leaning over him, professionally manicured hands clasped together against her knees. She had light brown hair pulled back into a neat ponytail and was without the usual hostess's cap.

Foolishly pleased she knew his name without asking, Ash said with a returned smile, 'That would be nice.'

'We've a choice of teas and coffees: Jamaican Blue Mountain, Columbian, Arabic coffee, not too strongly roasted. Or I can make you a blend of Robusta and Arabica. Teas are Twinings Lapsang, herbal – a blend of rosehip, hibiscus – Twinings or Jackson's Earl Grey, Black Russian or English breakfast tea. Unless you'd prefer something stronger? We're still waiting for the arrival of three more passengers on this morning's flight, so there's time to relax before take-off.'

Three more? Maseby had only mentioned two other passengers – the psychologist Wyatt and a new client. Ash wondered who the third person might be.

'Mr Ash . . . ?'

'Uh, sorry.' He glanced at his wristwatch. 'Eight-thirty in the morning is a little too early for alcohol.' He briefly wondered if Ginny had been instructed by Maseby to offer him booze as a test, then quickly dismissed the thought as paranoid. 'Yeah, coffee could be good. Black, two sugars?' The sugar should jimmie up the caffeine to get his brain functioning this early in the morning.

Ginny, whose lovely smile had never once wavered, nodded her head as though he'd made a brilliant choice.

'What kind of coffee?'

'Oh, just regular. Strong and hot. I'm no connoisseur.'

'Be right back.'

She straightened and turned away. Ash watched her trim figure make its way to the aircraft's galley. Her mid-grey suit – designed to match the cabin's interior decor, obviously – was not quite a uniform, with its elegant cut and quality material, the skirt reaching just above her knees, the three-button jacket with lightly padded square shoulders. It gave her an air of calm authority; she could easily have been on her way to a business meeting at an exalted fashion house. And no standard stewardess's silk scarf to cover her chest, the jacket's plunging neckline teasingly arrested by the top button he'd noticed when she'd leaned over him. Just a glimpse of her bra's black lacy edging was enough to excite the attention of any warm-blooded male. It had been a long time since . . . he stopped the thoughts dead in their tracks because he knew they would only bring on regret and anguish.

Fortunately, the mobile phone began to vibrate silently inside the deep pocket of his jacket, distracting him. Angling his body in the plush soft-suede seat, Ash took out the phone and checked the caller's ID. Ginny was on her way back to him, bearing a tiny silver tray with a bone china cup and saucer, a sugar bowl and a small array of unwrapped biscuits on a tiny plate, the pleasing aroma of roasted coffee beans preceding her along the deck. He held up the neat little phone in the palm of his right hand, pointing at it with his left; he wasn't sure of the regulations regarding the use of mobile phones on aeroplanes nowadays.

'Of course,' she reassured him with that same lovely smile. 'As long as you don't use it during take-off or landing. Just a precaution, but you're free to use it again when we're in the air.'

Ginny leaned over him again and pulled out a cleverly recessed mini-table from the arm of his chair. She left the tray with him while he took the call.

'Morning, Kate.' His voice was low and husky at this time of day.

'Where are you?'

'Where I'm supposed to be.'

'Good, you made it.'

'What did you expect?'

'Just checking, David. I know you're hopeless with mornings.'

'Daylight *burns*.'

'Enough. Sorry I doubted you. So you're on the plane?'

'Yup. Y'know, I could get used to this lifestyle. Cab I pre-booked was on time, the journey to City Airport dragged a bit because of rush-hour traffic, and the area around the airport is remarkably soulless but, with the letter of authorization

Maseby gave me yesterday, I was through check-in and on the plane inside twenty minutes. Didn't even have to carry my own suitcase; it was taken care of before I even entered the terminal building. Right now I'm sipping steaming-hot coffee and waiting for the other passengers to show.'

Even as he spoke, he glanced out the small round plexiglas window to see a shabby little man wearing an old-fashioned trench coat leave the single terminal building to hurry across the tarmac towards the jet. In one hand he carried a small case while in the other was a rolled umbrella.

'One of 'em's just turned up,' Ash told Kate.

'First, I want to thank you for accepting the assignment,' Kate said, pleased that Ash was so peppy this morning.

But his tone changed when he replied. 'I still think it's a matter for the police. We're talking serious crime here, no matter how weird and unlikely. Tell you the truth, I don't see how they can get away with not reporting it. I only accepted the job because you seemed desperate for me to do it. Is the Institute really so badly off?'

The man in the trench coat appeared in the open doorway further down the cabin. Ginny was giving him that same beaming smile, almost making Ash feel cuckolded.

'Good morning, Mr Twigg,' Ash heard her say. 'How nice to see you again.'

The response was little more than a quick grimace. He had strange, unblinking eyes that stared straight ahead rather than at the stewardess. With his bald pointed head and narrow rounded shoulders, he reminded Ash of someone, but he couldn't think who.

'Sorry, Kate. What were you saying?' The new arrival had distracted the investigator while Kate was still talking.

'I said we would soon have had money problems if it hadn't been for this deal with Simon Maseby. Oh, no doubt we could have eked things out. We'd have got through it somehow, but this investigation will pay the bills for quite some time to come, not to mention salaries. With this recession, people are just not interested in things paranormal; they have too many material problems to worry about.'

Ginny was waving a hand, inviting the man she'd addressed as Mr Twigg to pick any unoccupied seat, and as he approached, he ducked his bald head as if the cabin ceiling might be too low for him, which was a pointless exercise for a person so short.

That's it, Ash thought to himself. Mr Twigg looked similar to a certain actor, but for the life of him the investigator couldn't recall the actor's name. The little man with the pale staring eyes chose a seat that backed on to the one opposite Ash. When he'd placed his small battered suitcase and umbrella (which he'd declined to hand over to the stewardess for storage) on the floor, Twigg slid down into his seat, the tip of his head just visible to Ash above the padded headrest. Before he sat, though, he'd taken in the parapsychologist without giving any acknowledgement.

Suit yourself, thought Ash, who had given a cheery smile, and returned to his conversation with Kate.

'. . . didn't call in the police, because, well, Comraich's own senior doctor certified that it had been an accident.'

'You're kidding me.' Ash frowned disbelievingly, keeping his voice even lower so as not to be overheard by the new arrival.

'David, these people are very influential. Over dinner last night, Simon told me a little more about the organization he represents.'

'Okay, I'm listening.'

'First of all, it *is* a kind of clandestine . . .' she paused for a moment '. . . consortium, you might say. Or an association, a confederation, or just an elite body of people who quietly work for the good of the country and avoid publicity of any kind. And at any price.'

'Are they legal?'

'Well, you might look on it as an upmarket Rotarian Society. Ludicrously, massively, upmarket. Like the Freemasons, only—'

'Only more sinister,' Ash cut in.

'I don't know. And, to be honest, I don't care. With the fee they're paying, I can forget about a lot of things that aren't really important anyway.'

'Uh-huh. You're the boss. I'm intrigued, though.'

'Don't be. As far as the Institute is concerned, it's just another paranormal investigation.'

'Kate, you don't sound too convinced yourself.'

'Simon is an honest man, with great integrity. I'm sure he wouldn't be associated with anything doubtful.'

Ash shrugged, aware it was pointless to argue further: he'd signed the contract – *both* contracts, one on behalf of the Psychical Research Institute and another personal non-disclosure agreement – so he might just as well get on with the job. Nevertheless, he couldn't entirely resist pressing her.

'Just give me a little more info, Kate,' he said. 'I'm not sure I'm comfortable with this.'

'David, I can't – well, *shouldn't* – say any more. But let me give you an idea of their importance. Simon made it plain again last night that the organization has no true power. What it has, though, is immense influence. Much more than you might think possible and more than *it* would ever admit to.'

'So how does that work?'

She ignored the cynicism. 'They're a collection of high-powered individuals who call themselves—'

'Let me guess again. Scientologists? No? Okay, how about the Opus Dei? The Kabbalah, then? That could be fun.'

'The IC.'

'Icy? Is that as in ice skating? Ice hockey? Ice cream?'

She knew he would be grinning. 'No. The I-C. It's an acronym for the Inner Court.'

'So nothing to do with religion? Politics?'

'Not exactly.'

'Not exactly? What does *that* mean?'

'I only got the name from Simon because he was half-cut. He buttoned up again once he realized what he'd said.'

Ash surprised himself by hoping Kate didn't mean that literally. The thought of Maseby making love to her somehow angered him, even though he and Kate hadn't been lovers for a long time now.

She sensed his mood just as she'd sensed his grin. 'He came in for coffee after our dinner together and I plied him with a few more brandies to loosen his tongue, then I sent him on his way. Even so, he was very discreet.'

'So that was all, just a name? The contract agreement we signed was for Maseby Associates on behalf of Comraich Castle. I didn't see the title Inner Court on any of those documents. Just a name: Sir Victor Haelstrom.'

'I know. That's how covert they are. But I did learn something more.'

'About the Inner Court?' Ash was now talking in a ridiculously hushed voice.

'Sort of, but not directly. The man Nurse Krantz found pinned to the wall. He suddenly dropped, by the way, just as she was calling for help on her radio. She said he'd curled over, head first, as if peeling himself from the wall like Velcro. His body weight released his legs.'

'So we only have this nurse's word that he'd been suspended above the floor.'

'Yes, but why should she lie? Krantz is well regarded at Comraich, and apparently not one to exaggerate. She was believed even though closer examination still found no wounds to his hands and feet.'

'It's a bit hard to take. I mean, the body of a full-grown man stuck to a wall well above the floor with no visible means of support?'

'David, you've witnessed extraordinary things yourself in the past.'

He was silent for a while and Kate regretted stirring up unfortunate memories.

'David . . . ?'

'Yeah, sorry. You said this Inner Court had something to do with the man pinned to the wall at the castle?'

'Only in that the organization owns Comraich Castle and he had some kind of contract with the IC to be given refuge there.'

'Don't tell me he was punished for breaking the rules. Now *that* I'm definitely uncomfortable with.'

'No, no. We're fine.'

'We'll only know that's true if *we* break our contract with them. Are there any penalty clauses that I missed? Apart from the secrecy agreement, I mean.'

'You read through both contracts.'

'I *skimmed* through them. I didn't bother with the small print because I thought you would've gone through it with a fine-tooth comb.'

'I did, and we don't have a problem. But let me get back to the point.'

'I'm listening.'

'Simon told me – and he regretted it afterwards, making me swear to keep it to myself – he told me the name of the poor victim at the castle.'

'Someone I should know?'

'You might have a year or so ago. D'you remember the front-page reports about the millionaire venture capitalist who killed himself by walking off into the North Sea? He'd left his wallet with credit cards, driving licence, and his car, with the keys still in the ignition, on the shoreline?'

Ash racked his brain. 'Yeah . . . yeah, I seem to recollect . . . when the business almost bankrupted the country. Didn't a few financiers top themselves because they'd lost everything, including their high-maintenance wives and mistresses?'

'Ever the cynic.'

'It's in my nature. But yeah, I remember the story; it made the news worldwide because it was happening globally, especially in America.'

'It was because he was the first case in this country. His name was Douglas Hoyle.'

Ash drew in a short breath. 'You're not telling me the victim in Comraich and Hoyle are one and the same man. The so-called financial genius who gambled wildly with other people's money and lost it all?'

'The same. His high-profile and once highly respected company lost millions of its clients' money.'

'And Hoyle led the way,' breathed Ash.

'Yes, David. Douglas Hoyle, the supposedly dead financial genius who didn't commit suicide by drowning in the sea as everybody believed – which is why his body was never recovered – but went into hiding at Comraich Castle.'

'Jesus. Wait. Wouldn't the police have investigated a bit further than a wallet and car and its keys left on a beach? It's been tried before. Then there was his wife and family, business associates even – wouldn't the authorities have found him through them?'

'He hasn't had contact with his family from the day he went missing. That apparently is a strict condition imposed on Comraich clientele. He knew he would never see his loved ones and friends again. Oh, and the price of refuge is stagger-ingly high.'

'I thought Hoyle was bankrupted.'

'As far as City assessors and his own investors were aware, he was.'

'No wonder Simon Maseby was coy about his employers.'

'I told you the Inner Court members are immensely influ-ential, powerful people. And they're incredibly rich. And *very* secretive. That's why you and millions of others have never heard of them.'

'So they *are* illegal?'

'I'd say they're above the law.'

'Nobody's above the law.'

'Keep assuming that, David: it'll make you feel better. Now look, what they are, who they are, and where they are, is not important. We – mainly you – will carry on with our commission.'

'God, I was uneasy before . . .'

'Perhaps I shouldn't have told you.'

'Why did you, Kate?'

'Because Simon Maseby is an old acquaintance; you're something more to me. I didn't want you going in blind.'

'I can get off the plane right now.'

'No, we're committed. If you did renege on the deal, there'd be too high a price to pay. Believe me on that. Besides, Simon would be in big trouble if it was discovered he'd been such a blabbermouth. I called him an old acquaintance a moment ago, but the IC wouldn't make allowances for even that.'

'Okay. I'll go on as planned.'

'And you won't let on what you now know?'

'No, of course I won't. Anyway, once I'm up at the castle I'll probably find out a lot more. I'll try to look surprised. You think there might be others like Douglas Hoyle at Comraich?'

'I'd bank on it. Excuse the pun. But hiding wealthy fugitives could be what the Inner Court is all about. The reward could be fantastically high if they only favour very wealthy runaways. It costs the client or their patrons £2 million per year just to stay at Comraich and a £5 million penalty should the client abscond.'

'*How much?*' Ash gasped incredulously.

'You heard. And once you're a guest – that's the term used: "guest" – then you leave the outside world for ever. No exemptions, no exceptions.'

'So they become prisoners.'

'Very well-looked-after prisoners. According to Simon, they live the rest of their life in absolute luxury.' Kate paused, then added, 'When Simon realized how much information he'd given away he practically begged me never to tell another living soul about the Inner Court and Comraich Castle.' She didn't say that plea had come from Simon Maseby when he woke sober in her bed at dawn that morning and realized just how much he'd divulged during the night. Alcohol and sex: sometimes a lethal combination.

Ash had been leaning forward, hunched over the phone, elbows on knees, his voice low, when a movement outside the thick window caught his eye again. A sleek black limousine had drawn up beside the aircraft and, as he watched, a grey-suited chauffeur stepped out and marched briskly round the long bonnet to a rear passenger door. Moving closer to the plexiglas, Ash looked down to see the opposite rear door open to reveal a dark-haired woman wearing a smart black wool business jacket and a knee-length skirt over black tights and ankle boots. He just caught a glimpse of a crisp white shirt collar against a light coffee-coloured neck, her chin tucked in as she bent forward, getting out of the vehicle and hurrying round to the other rear door, which the driver had already opened. He was now standing at loose attention, waiting for his other passenger – obviously the more important of the two – to emerge.

The dark-haired woman had reached the open door and was leaning in to help the person now climbing awkwardly from the limousine.

From his elevated position inside the jet, Ash just saw the top of the other passenger's head emerging, a mass of unruly blonde hair, dark at the roots, when Kate's voice drew him back to the phone.

'Still with me, David?'

He settled back into his seat. 'Yeah, sorry. Looks like the late arrivals are here. We should be taking off quite soon.'

'The psychiatrist, Dr Wyatt?'

'Psychologist these days, Maseby said. There's a difference. Psychology's the study of human development and behaviour, and it's classified as a social science, whereas psychiatry's more to do with abnormal mental or emotional condition and disorders. Naturally, they can overlap,' Ash said.

'I already knew that, professor. I am ex-uni.'

'Well, I had to look it up. Anyway, I presume it's her, and the client appears to be a young woman.' He took a quick peek out the window again and noticed that the chauffeur, who had obviously popped the boot from inside before alighting from the limo, was hauling out two distinctively styled Louis Vuitton suitcases. Expensive, but no surprise there. The two women were no longer in sight and Ash assumed they were on the short flight of steps leading into the aircraft.

'Good morning,' he heard the air stewardess greet the young girl as she entered the cabin with her shoulders hunched, head bent. 'Hello again, Dr Wyatt,' Ginny said to the woman following close behind.

It struck Ash that the vivacious stewardess hadn't used the blonde girl's name and he wondered if that was company policy with pre-guests. Maybe Ginny didn't even know what it was. He remembered he still had Kate on the line.

'Kate, I'll phone you when I get to Comraich, but if you need to, you can call me again mid-air.'

'Shouldn't be necessary. I'll be interested in your take on the castle, though.'

'Okay. Later.' He closed the mobile phone and returned it to his jacket pocket.

The girl with the mussed-up blonde hair plodded her way down the cabin, the sulky, sullen look of a Geldof daughter spoiling her otherwise pretty face. She barely glanced at Ash as Dr Wyatt guided her from behind to the sofa seat across the aisle from him. In contrast to the psychologist's modish outfit, her charge wore an odd match of clothes that seemed thrown on rather than carefully chosen when she'd stirred (probably reluctantly) from her bed to make the morning flight. She wore a deep-mauve open blazer that was longer than her high-waisted dotted skirt, which was loosely tied with a cloth belt. A white T-shirt was tucked into the skirt's high waist and three silver chains of different lengths hung down around her neck. She was slight of stature (worsened by the hunching of her shoulders). Her fishnet tights, slightly torn at one knee, ran down into chunky wedge heels, and clutched in both hands was a brown overfilled Mulberry bag. Pretty though she was, the girl's over-kohled, downcast eyes only added to her air of sulky recalcitrance.

'We'll sit here, Petra,' said Dr Wyatt, easing the girl into the seat, 'then after take-off you can lie down and sleep for a little while.'

Settling herself beside Petra, the psychologist tucked her own crinkled leather satchel behind her ankles and beamed a smile towards Ash.

He returned the smile but it faltered in surprise, for her dark eyes, her finely etched lips, the light tan of her smooth skin . . .

Well, she wasn't quite what he'd expected.

8

Kate sat at her desk, her swivel chair turned to face one of the tall windows of her office. Beyond the glass it was yet another fine early autumnal day, although nippy in the streets. She usually got to the Institute around 8 a.m., which gave her quiet time to deal with the paperwork – the government rules, red tape and health-and-safety directives – that was every employer's bane. By the time other staff arrived and things started to get busy, she would be able to concentrate on her proper duties, which meant sending and checking emails, making and receiving phone calls, writing reports on any supernatural or paranormal activities that had come to the Institute's notice, genuine or suspect, which would then be filed and copies sent to other psychical research establishments around the world (she believed in sharing information with those who were both friendly and legitimate), while taking on board any new accounts of phenomena and interviewing prospective clients (she'd no idea why, but people seemed more susceptible to hauntings when the days grew colder and the darkness earlier).

But this morning Kate was spending more time on reflection.

Had she done the right thing in sending David up to Scotland? Was he mentally strong enough to handle a genuine and apparently vicious haunting? And had she been right in accepting this commission when the organization that Simon Maseby represented was so shadowy, even if so lucrative for the Institute?

In less than five months' time the lease on the building would be up and the rent, plus management fees, ground rent and service charge, were bound to be increased. Where the money would come from Kate had no idea; not until Simon Maseby had contacted her, that is. She'd been about to warn her workforce and consultants (spiritualists, mediums, clairvoyants – even exorcists) of the impending problem when Simon had called her from out of the blue.

Kate was pleased to hear from an old friend after such a long time and, because he'd said the matter was urgent, she'd arranged a meeting for later that afternoon. That had been a few days ago, just before the weekend, and Kate was intrigued by Simon's story and mystified by his reluctance to divulge details of the people or organization that employed him. Nevertheless, the amount they were prepared to pay for an investigation into this supposedly haunted Scottish castle had blown away all reservations on her part; considering the Institute's looming financial situation, she would have been foolish not to have accepted his offer.

One of the contract's conditions did concern her, though: Simon was adamant that only a single psychic investigator should be assigned to the case. Kate had argued – as had David at the subsequent meeting with Simon – that such a huge building would require a team of investigators – at least three or four people – to cover the area, but Simon remained inflexible. Eventually they had agreed on a compromise: one investigator initially, then a proper team if necessary afterwards. And as far as she was concerned, that one person had to be David Ash. Simon agreed, although he insisted on knowing more about this particular parapsychologist.

Kate had given a brief summary of Ash's career so far (although she avoided giving too many details of David's previous investigations). She'd also sent over a couple of copies of David's treatise on the supernatural when Maseby had first contacted her.

The side door of her office opened and her PA poked his head through the opening. 'Morning, Kate. Coffee?'

She swung the chair round to face him and pointed at the empty jumbo mug on the desk – dainty crockery was only used when clients were present.

'Had some already, Tom,' she told him.

'Right. Anything special you want me to get on to?'

'I'll dictate some letters later. Can you file the stuff I've already left on your desk? Oh, and will you spend a little time on your computer for me this morning?' Tom was a master of Google.

'Sure, no problem. What d'you want me to look for?'

Kate hesitated. Was it right to involve her young assistant in this affair? After all, she herself was sworn to secrecy. Bringing in another person at this stage might be unwise and a breach of the contract she'd signed. She quickly changed her mind, not prepared to jeopardize the agreement.

'Sorry, Tom. Forget about that last bit.'

She would search the net herself. It would take her longer, but at least it wouldn't involve another person from the Institute, just as Simon had stipulated again after they had made unsatisfactory love.

Today she felt guilty. Not because she'd slept with Simon – regret would have been ridiculous – but because she'd lied to David, and she knew he'd sensed it. His psychic abilities were more than just a focused intuition.

With a sigh that was almost a groan, Kate logged on and got ready to Google.

She already knew it would be a difficult search and, possibly, a fruitless one.

9

Cedric Twigg had been looking through the Gulfstream's window, but taking nothing in, when the stewardess's voice interrupted his reverie. As he peered up at her, he realized his heart was beating like a jackhammer, too fast and too hard. He forced himself to control the palpitations, something he used to do with ease a year or so ago, but not nowadays. Even though the surprise was quickly dealt with, he realized it took a little longer to compose himself each time he was caught day-dreaming.

'Sorry, Mr Twigg, I think I startled you.'

Balanced skilfully on one arm, she held the daily newspapers, fanned out like a magician's giant deck of cards.

He skimmed the titles. '*Telegraph,*' he said.

Ginny's smile was unaltered, but he noticed her eyes had hardened at his rudeness. With her free hand she pulled out the requested broadsheet and handed it to him. He accepted it without thanks.

Twigg immediately saw the headline he was expecting, and while the story didn't take up the whole front page, it was prominent enough to satisfy the assassin's perverse ego. It surprised him that they had already made the connection between yesterday's killing and the one carried out more than thirty years ago. He remembered with relish.

In September 1978, the Bulgarian dissident Georgi Markov, who used the BBC's World Service to broadcast damaging diatribes against his mother country's communist regime, was marked out to be 'liquidated'. The Bulgarian Secret Service had sought help from Russia's KGB – nowadays known as the SVR – and they had suggested using a young Englishman who lived in London, and who had carried out three successful 'closures' for them already.

Twigg smiled as he recalled the method chosen to eliminate Markov. A simple umbrella had been fitted with a hidden cylinder of compressed gas that fired a single pellet filled with the biotoxin ricin, the deadly derivative of castor oil. He had followed the dissident onto Waterloo Bridge, and when Markov waited at a bus stop, the young assassin had pushed the umbrella's tip into the Bulgarian's calf muscle. An innocent accident that Markov gave little attention to. Three days later he was dead.

That was many years ago and Twigg almost chuckled to himself, for New Scotland Yard was *still* investigating the murder. A British counter-terrorism team had even paid a visit to Bulgaria in 2008, and continued to work with the 'appropriate international authorities', as they put it, hoping to draw a satisfactory conclusion to the investigation. As yet, nobody had been charged with Markov's murder.

Monday's assassination of the Russian broadcaster Boris Dubchenski, who constantly railed against the influence of certain billionaire oligarchs over his country's political leaders, was practically a replica of Markov's murder more than three decades ago. Except this time, Twigg had use of a 'spotter', waiting on the other side of Bush House, whereas before he'd worked alone; also, Twigg had used a faster-acting dose of ricin, which had killed even more expeditiously. To this day, Cedric Twigg was uncertain exactly how the Inner Court had discovered he was the original dissident's assassin (a Russian informer, he guessed), but they were swift to appreciate his skill and just as swift to recruit him for themselves. Their inducements of high financial rewards and 'lifetime' security (unusual for a hit man) were enough to win his loyalty, a loyalty he'd always assumed was mutual. But now he was sixty-one years old and there was something not quite right with him physically: occasionally his whole body, especially his hands, gave in to small though, as yet, unremarked tremors.

He laid the newspaper across his lap and dropped both hands to clutch the edge of his seat. It seemed that just thinking of the slow but merciless onset of illness was enough to incite those tiny tremors again.

A thin, almost invisible, drool of saliva seeped from one side of his mouth.

10

Ash had known that Dr Wyatt would be female, but he'd expected someone older and less – well, less alluring. Ash found it hard not to stare across the plane's narrow aisle at the stunningly beautiful woman who shared the sofa seat with the young blonde girl.

Dr Wyatt acknowledged him with a quick smile before returning her attention to the girl in her charge. The psychologist spoke in hushed tones, as if to calm her before the flight, and soon the patient was lolling back, her tousled head resting on the psychologist's shoulder. When Ginny came by with the daily newspapers, Dr Wyatt gave a small shake of her head accompanied by a sweet smile.

'Can I get you something to drink after take-off?' Ginny asked.

'I'll have some tea,' replied the psychologist. 'English breakfast tea?'

'Not a problem.'

Ash was surprised at her preference: with her Mediterranean looks, he'd expected her to request something more *exotic*, especially when the aircraft carried such a richly distinctive choice of beverage.

And then she glanced at him again, but this time – and with no effort on his part – he held her gaze. Her cheeks blushed red even through the natural tan of her skin, and her eyelashes fluttered (not through coyness, he was sure, but involuntarily) before she broke away. Yet in those few seconds, Ash had felt a confusing kind of frisson between them, as if they already knew each other – no, that wasn't it; it was as if they were both suddenly aware that their futures were tethered together. It was crazy. How could he possibly know what *she* felt when he was so bewildered by his own reaction? Surely he'd misread the mood. But the feeling had begun to form the moment she'd entered the plane, and just now had asserted itself so profoundly that it left him dazed. With something like despair, he remembered having a similar reaction once before, a time best forgotten. The cause then had been a woman named Grace; a woman he'd loved so very much.

The stewardess's voice penetrated the awful memory. 'Would you like today's paper, Mr Ash?'

'Sorry . . . ?'

She lifted the fan of newspapers slightly to bring them to her passenger's attention.

'Oh. Er, no. I'm fine, thank you.' He rested his head back against the top of his seat and closed his eyes.

'It's only a short flight, sir. Just outside an hour.' She'd misunderstood his reaction, thinking him nervous of flying. 'We'll be in Scotland in no time at all.'

He opened his eyes again, if only to reassure Ginny. 'It's a nice way to travel,' was all he could think of to say.

'Yes, the interior designs of private planes can be made to suit the client's specifications. Corporations like to see their insignia inside and outside the aircraft. Some very wealthy individuals like works of art on the cabin walls, or even chandeliers, would you believe? Not made of glass though – that would be foolish.' She giggled at that.

Ginny reached for his now-empty coffee cup. 'I'll clear this away for you. Perhaps you'd like something stronger when we're in the air?'

Again that irrational notion. Was he being tested over alcohol? No. Paranoia, he told himself again.

Looking up into her clear blue eyes, he asked, 'Who actually owns this jet? Is it chartered?'

'Oh, no. It's Sir Victor's. Sir Victor Haelstrom? That's who you're going up to see, aren't you?'

'Yeah, of course I am. I'm looking forward to it.'

So it wasn't a company plane, nor chartered, but privately owned. He decided that when he had a chance, he'd use his laptop to do a bit more detailed research on Sir Victor Haelstrom.

Once again he glanced across the aisle to see Dr Wyatt tying her deep-black shoulder-length hair into a bunch at the back of her neck. She suddenly looked more serious and a little older. Instead of late twenties, Ash now thought she was probably in her very early thirties. She reached into her shoulder bag and donned a pair of dark-framed glasses. When she took out a notebook and pen from the bag, she caught his appreciative eyes on her.

Ash felt as though *he* was blushing, although he knew from experience that his face remained pale. Pale and worn, he told himself. And probably older than his thirty-eight years.

This time the psychologist didn't smile back at him, but consulted her wristwatch, then flipped open the notebook and jotted down a note. From the way she quickly checked the sleepy-eyed girl at her side, Ash guessed it was about her patient's medication and the reaction to it.

'You can lie down once we're in the air, Petra,' he heard her say in a soft but clear voice.

The blonde girl merely yawned and rested her head on the psychologist's shoulder again. She was bleary-eyed and sluggish, and Ash thought it seemed due to sedation rather than early-morning tiredness. Possibly Dr Wyatt had given her something to calm her nerves before flying. He was still pondering his own reaction to the psychologist when the pilot's voice came over the intercom.

'Good morning, ladies and gentlemen. Despite our late arrivals, we're still on for our scheduled slot.'

His manner was relaxed yet authoritative, a perfect pilot's voice.

57

'For those of you who haven't had the good fortune to fly with us before, my name is Mike Roberts and I'm your captain for this flight. My first officer, and sitting by my side as co-pilot, is Marty "Chuckles" Collins. We call him "Chuckles" because he seldom laughs. He's the spirit of gloom, but don't let that put you off.'

A muffled groan came over the intercom and Ash guessed that Collins was growing weary of his captain's obviously frequent put-downs.

'Fortunately,' the captain continued, 'it's only a short hop to Scotland, so I won't have to put up with his lugubrious presence for too long.'

It occurred to Ash that while the plane was still on the tarmac warming up, the pilot could have just as easily opened the cockpit door which had been closed, unnoticed by Ash, and made his pre-flight patter even more personal.

Captain Roberts finished the rest of his spiel in the same breezy manner. Ash rested back in his seat again, letting his eyelids droop; he'd never been afraid of flying, but found the pilot's easy, laid-back style reassuring all the same.

Just a couple of feet or so from Ash, Dr Wyatt had persuaded the girl called Petra to sit up while her seatbelt was adjusted round her waist, and he couldn't resist another sneaky look at the psychologist as she then fastened herself in. She met his gaze, although again she didn't return his smile.

Instead she frowned, as though something about Ash concerned her.

He quickly looked away and clicked in his own belt.

11

Ash had almost drifted off to sleep when he sensed movement in front of him. Opening his eyes, he found Dr Wyatt settling into the opposite seat.

'So sorry. Did I disturb you?' She placed her soft leather satchel behind her ankles. Her black-rimmed glasses had been put away, but her raven-black hair was still tied at the back.

'No,' he assured her, 'I wasn't asleep.' He smiled at her warmly.

'Good. I've left our new guest, Petra, to rest on the couch.'

Across the aisle, the young blonde girl was stretched out on the three-seater. Her knees were bent and her head rested on a plush charcoal-grey cushion; a blanket of the same colour had been placed over her. She seemed to be out for the count, a thumb resting against her lips; a fraction more and she would have been sucking her thumb like a baby.

'You're the investigator, aren't you?' Dr Wyatt had leaned forward, clasped hands resting on her knees, as if she wanted to talk to him in confidence.

She spoke softly, but as the genial Mike Roberts had told them, the acoustical insulation was excellent, so every word was clear. Because of the light-coffee colour of Dr Wyatt's skin, and the deepest ebony of her hair, he'd half expected her to speak with an accent – Spanish; or South American, maybe? – but her words had no foreign inflection whatsoever.

'Oh, yeah,' he replied, unconsciously straightening himself

in the seat. 'Psychic investigator, that is. Or, if I'm being pompous, parapsychologist.'

'A ghost hunter,' she responded.

'Well, that's the popular name for it. And you're Dr Wyatt, I presume.'

She put forward a hand and he only had to lean forward slightly to shake it. It was a one-shake, but for some reason, neither let go. They stared at each other, and Ash could plainly see the confusion in her wonderfully seductive deep brown eyes.

He felt a similar confusion himself, although he tried to conceal it. The moment passed and then, as if by mutual consent, they let their hands drop.

It took her a little while to compose herself and he looked away to give her time. Through the small window the white tops of the clouds stretched into the distance like a huge rumpled white duvet, and the brightness as they flew above the weather cheered him. He turned back to the psychologist.

'Are you permanently based in Scotland, or are you some kind of flying consultant?' he enquired, anxious to prolong their conversation.

'I'm based at Comraich Castle, but I take frequent trips away. Sometimes it helps if I can accompany new guests to the castle just to reassure them. It's a big step for a client to take.'

Her voice was pleasant but subdued, as if she were a touch nervous of him. At least, that was how he read it, and he was good at picking up on the mindset of others. Years of determining honesty and dishonesty, bravura or restraint, fear or courage, had honed him sharply to the nuances of those his profession had compelled him to interview. Or was Dr Wyatt merely chary of what she might unconsciously reveal about the Inner Court?

'So, the girl . . .' he indicated the sleeping blonde across the aisle '. . . is obviously in your charge.'

The psychologist nodded but said no more.

'You implied she was a guest,' Ash insisted politely. 'Isn't she really a patient?'

'Yes, but at Comraich we prefer to regard patients as guests, otherwise it might suggest they had mental health problems, or some contagious illness, which isn't necessarily the case.'

'Yesterday I met Simon Maseby, who called Comraich a retreat.'

'Well, then,' Dr Wyatt replied. 'I think retreat is an ideal way of describing the castle, even though we're licensed to carry out medical procedures there.'

'Like what?'

She wasn't fazed by his blunt question. The psychologist smiled at him. 'Like major and minor operations, counselling, and the use of new, superior medication for those who need it. We use the most up-to-date treatments for all kinds of ailments, including mental instability.'

'And all in luxurious surroundings, going by the hefty fees your guests or their benefactors have to pay.'

'Yes,' she replied simply.

'Paid to the Inner Court?'

Her dark eyes skittered to one side.

'I'm sorry, Mr Ash,' she said, 'that's privileged information. May I ask where you heard it?'

He smiled pleasantly. 'Why does everything have to be so covert?' He was gently pressing her, genuinely interested, but he also had a mischievous desire to rock the boat.

'I'm sorry,' she repeated, and she looked truly apologetic as she swung her eyes back to meet his. 'I have to keep to the code.'

'The code?' This was becoming even more interesting.

'Oh, it's nothing formalized, just a general rule, but we are expected to be discreet. Why don't you tell me more about yourself? I knew you were coming to Comraich Castle to investigate the strange goings-on there. Being a parapsychologist must be fascinating.'

She was deliberately changing the subject, and Ash had no wish to push his luck. 'It is sometimes,' he responded to help her out. 'What have you been told about this investigation?'

She was immediately more relaxed now that he'd changed tack. 'Just that you'd be with us for possibly up to a week and that we were to keep out of your way while you explored the castle.'

'A week or so?' Ash was dismayed: he'd hoped to draw conclusions within a couple of days.

Dr Wyatt nodded affirmation. 'It's a huge place.'

'So I gathered. But I'd hoped to finish my job sooner than that. Tell me, have you personally had any strange or unaccountable experiences at Comraich?'

'You mean have I seen a ghost, heard footsteps when there's nobody there? Screams in the night, rattling chains, freezing areas, that kind of thing?' She was joking, her voice low and eerie.

'Not necessarily.' He ignored the exaggerated dark humour.

'Oh, Mr Ash, you don't know Comraich.'

He grinned back at her. 'How old is the castle, by the way?' Maseby had already told him, but now Ash was only making conversation.

'I think it dates back to the fourteenth century but it was considerably enlarged and improved on over the years. It was built on a clifftop, which makes it look very dramatic.'

He changed the subject again. 'How long have you been with Comraich?' He'd nearly said *with the Inner Court*, the answer to which might have proved more interesting; instead he put his question less obviously.

'Almost three years,' she answered without hesitation. 'My father knew Sir Victor and some of his associates and I think he wanted me to be taken care of before he died.'

'I'm sorry. I mean, about your father.'

'Don't be. It was a blessed relief when he was released from all the months of pain. The end for him was swift, mercifully so, and frankly it came as a relief. It's hard to watch someone you love suffer.'

She lowered her eyes and her grief was palpable.

To move on, Ash asked, 'Where are you from, Dr Wyatt?'

'My mother was Brazilian, and Brazil was where I was born. My father was an English diplomat and he met my mother in São Paulo, the country's largest city rather than Rio de Janeiro, as many foreigners seem to think. Rio is the playground that entices the tourists – and criminals – and Brasilia is the seat of government, but São Paulo is Brazil's financial centre.'

She cocked her head sideways and stared into Ash's eyes as if to see whether he was interested.

He was. 'You were born in São Paulo?'

'My mother was a *Paulistano*; that's what people who live in the city are known as. Ambitious Brazilians flock there for the chance of a better life. It's a modern city, expanding all the time. My mother was a translator working at the British Embassy, which was how my father got to know her. I'm the only consequence of their marriage.' She said this with a hint of regret.

'They divorced?' The question was carefully put, and not, he hoped, intrusively.

'No, my mother died when I was three.'

Ash could have kicked himself. 'I've put my foot in it, haven't I? I'm sorry. I didn't mean to . . .'

'Pry?' she finished for him, smiling so that he could see his curiosity didn't trouble her. 'As I told you, I was barely three years old and now I can hardly remember her.' She paused, as if in thought. 'Although,' she went on, 'I sometimes see her in dreams. I've only a few faded photographs of her, but they're enough for me to recognize her in those sleeping moments. At least, I think I do.'

She gave an embarrassed laugh. 'Listen to me, and *I'm* a psychologist! It isn't hard to understand why I choose to identify this woman as my mother, despite having no real knowledge of her.'

'I guess Freud would have the answer,' Ash commented lamely.

'Don't be so sure. Many psychologists today are not in total agreement with all of Sigmund Freud's tenets. Even Jung disagreed with certain Freudian precepts, especially with their constant emphasis on infantile sexuality.'

'So which are you – Freudian or Jungian?'

'It isn't that simple: both have theories that are perfectly sound. Besides, they're not the only psychologists worthy of study. *And . . .*' she emphasized the word, 'there's a lot of overlapping going on in so many areas of different theories. Then there's another approach called gestalt psychology, founded by Max Wertheimer, whereby it's claimed that every aspect of thinking can have a gestalt character – emotional, interpersonal and social. I'm beginning to bore you, aren't I?'

He was taken aback and raised his eyebrows at her.

Her chuckle was throaty and her face lit up at his embarrassment.

'I'm sorry,' she said, still smiling. 'I thought I saw your eyes glazing over.'

Ash grinned back. 'You know, parapsychology is sometimes – no, often – linked with psychology.'

'Of course. It's why I wanted to have this conversation with you. Wouldn't you accept that a good number of so-called hauntings are caused by the psychological make-up of their victims or observers, whatever you'd call them?'

'Well, I couldn't disagree with that.'

'I know. You said much the same in your book.'

'You've read it?' Ash was genuinely pleased. 'It was written some time ago.'

'You've changed your opinions?'

'Not completely. Let's just say I've learned a lot more about the paranormal and supernatural.'

'Does that mean you no longer dismiss the supposition of ghosts and disembodied souls? In your book – which, by the way, has been required reading for myself and Dr Singh, my psychiatric counterpart at Comraich, over the last few days – you're very cynical regarding spiritualists and clairvoyants, branding many as no more than charlatans who are either in it for the money, or who truly believe in what they do but are misguided, even somewhat eccentric, if not deranged.'

'As I said, I know a lot more about the phenomena than I did then. So how did you get a copy of the book? It's been out of print for years.'

'Simon Maseby obtained a couple of copies from Kate McCarrick at your own Psychical Research Institute. He passed them on to us a few days ago. I'm surprised you haven't written more on the subject.'

Ash was surprised Kate hadn't mentioned giving copies of his book to Maseby earlier. 'One book was enough. The fact is, I've experienced too many genuine – or let's say, inexplicable – cases that have led me to doubt most of my original conjectures. I've learned to approach each new case with an open mind.'

'Is that possible?' she asked.

'No, of course not.' He smiled. 'But these days I try to keep my natural scepticism in check. Tell me, though, what's your take on the alleged haunting at Comraich Castle?'

'I'm just not sure about anything that's happening there. My own common sense keeps me grounded, but . . .'

Ash's ears suddenly popped and he turned away to look through the window on his left. It was pure grey out there now and growing darker as the plane began its descent.

'It's just normal procedure, Mr Ash. We won't be landing for a while yet.'

This time it was she who turned to the plexiglas window by her seat. He watched as she strained to get a view of the land below. Her neck was elegant, finely shaped, and her profile added to her allure. He thought he could sense a barely repressed passion hidden beneath the formal yet chic outfit and her calm manner.

'We're deep in cloud,' she remarked superfluously as she

tried to see through the mist. 'At this point in the flight we're usually somewhere over Comraich. When the weather is clear it's a wonderful sight. Sometimes I—'

The cabin lights failed as the jet suddenly lurched, then began to free-fall.

Ash clutched the arms of his seat, his fingers clawing to grip them hard as he found his body was almost weightless.

The girl, Petra, shrieked as she was tossed from the three-seater. Then everything darkened as the plane plummeted towards the earth.

12

Luckily, Ash was still wearing his seatbelt, which had been
such a comfortable fit he'd forgotten to unfasten it. Nevertheless, as the plane dropped with such suddenness, he felt as if
he'd left his stomach behind. The cabin lights were not functioning and neither was anything else on the jet: there was no
background hum of the engines and no seatbelt or emergency
warning lights. He might have cried out, such was the fear that
suddenly swept through him, but in the dim grey light coming
through the windows he saw the psychologist rising weight-
lessly before him.

Instinctively, he grabbed her with both hands and pulled
her down to him. He heard screaming, but it wasn't coming
from her. Petra had spilled from her makeshift bed to be
thrown upwards almost to the ceiling as the Gulfstream jet had
entered its steep dive.

Ash had managed to get his hands round the doctor's back
and he hugged her tightly, the side of her head pressed against
his shoulder. Oddly, for such a perilous situation, he was aware
of the sweet light scent she wore, and even under that, the
faint fragrance of the herbal shampoo she must have used to
wash her hair that morning. He felt her panic and heard her
soft moaning even over the screams coming from her patient.

'It's okay,' he told her, speaking loudly with all the calmness
he could muster. 'We've hit an air pocket, that's all.'

But the plane went into a deeper dive which sent Petra
sliding down the cabin. Ash knew a simple air pocket wouldn't

interfere with the aircraft's mechanical and electrical systems, but there was no other explanation he could give to reassure the doctor.

She buried her face into the corner of his neck and shoulder and clutched him for dear life, her body trembling, her breath coming in short sharp gasps. He could feel her tears on his neck and he brought up a hand to press her head into him. The Gulfstream 450 dropped even further into the darkness of rain-filled clouds, and Ash, now sure they were all going to die, held on to the psychologist for his own sake as much as hers. Pressure built up in the cabin, sending terrible mind-numbing pain through his head. He wanted to release the quaking woman from his embrace and clamp his hands over his ears for relief, but he fought the urge and held her even more tightly in his arms. All noise seemed far away until his ears unexpectedly popped and Petra's screams came back full-throttle.

Then the darkness gave way to daylight again, the row of windows quickly growing brighter, so that he was able to see around the cabin as before. But the jet continued to plummet and the screams from Petra hadn't ceased.

Then the lights in the cabin suddenly returned and Ash heard the jet's engines roar back into life. It took several terrifying seconds for the pilot to regain control of his aircraft, but soon the plane began to level out and resume its course. Captain Roberts's steady voice came over the intercom.

'Sorry about that, ladies and gentlemen. We've no idea why that little problem occurred, but I can assure you that every-thing's shipshape again.'

Ash could imagine the pilot crossing his fingers as he spoke.

'Everything's running smoothly now and you can see for yourselves we're below the clouds. We'll maintain this height until our final descent to Prestwick in a few minutes. Please keep your seatbelts fastened until we land. Our landing will be fine, believe me. As far as we can tell, we have no faults, significant or otherwise, so please try to relax until we're on the ground. When we do land, I recommend a fine Scotch or brandy, then another. I'm only sorry I won't be able to join you – I've two more flights later today. "Chuckles" here has a grin on his face you wouldn't believe, although I'm not sure he hasn't wet himself.'

His voice was crisper when he addressed the air steward-ess. 'Ginny, will you make sure everyone's comfortable back there, then report to the cockpit.' His voice became less formal again. 'First Officer Collins will join you to explain our unpleasant but mercifully brief interlude once we've run through a few more minor checks.'

The intercom went silent.

Ash felt Dr Wyatt slump in his arms, not in a faint, he was sure, but with relief. His hold on her became more tender, comforting, but still she trembled. He could hear sobs from Petra, who now lay in the aisle by his side.

'Dr Wyatt,' Ash said softly, 'everything's fine. We're out of danger now. The pilot has control of the plane; there's no need to be afraid any longer.' *Unless the same thing happens again as we approach Prestwick*, he thought sombrely.

Rivulets of rain were driven diagonally across the row of small windows by the aircraft's speed, but at least the grey daylight worked with the cabin lights to make everything visible again.

The woman in his arms gently pulled away from him so that she could look into his face. He relaxed his grip but didn't entirely let go. Her deep brown eyes were softened by tears, but as they stared into his, he detected a trace of uncertainty in them. Somehow, the shared near-death experience and the intimacy it created between them had confused her even more.

'Thank you,' she whispered, her face so close, her lips so near, her very scent so enticing, that he was reluctant to give her up.

'It was my pleasure,' he said glibly, stupidly. 'I—'

Too late. She'd regained some of her composure.

She pushed against his chest to steady herself as she rose to her feet. 'I have to see to Petra,' she said, and he became aware of the girl's cries of fear once more.

Dr Wyatt moved away from Ash and knelt to attend to her patient. 'It's all right, Petra, everything's okay,' Ash heard her say soothingly.

But the young girl was still in panic and she thrashed at the air around her as if the plane were still in free-fall.

'Petra, Petra, please.' The psychologist held the quaking girl's wrists to avoid being struck herself.

'Can I help?'

Dr Wyatt motioned her head towards the seat she'd occupied before the Gulfstream's loss of power. 'If you could get my bag . . .' She hardly glanced at Ash, concerned that her hysterical patient might injure herself.

'Sure.' Ash reached for the leather strap-bag that was now wedged beneath the seat opposite, but he was restrained by his own safety belt. He quickly released the metal clasp and reached again for the bag. Pulling it free, he turned and thrust it towards the doctor.

'Please, open it for me,' she said evenly, her hands still around the girl's wrists.

Ash fumbled with the bag's two buckles and opened it up. Finally releasing Petra, the doctor took the crinkled leather bag and reached inside.

'I have to sedate her,' she said briskly. 'I gave her a mild sedative before we boarded, but she needs something a lot stronger. It means an injection if it's to have an immediate effect.'

'Anything I can do? Hold her down, maybe?'

'No, I can manage. She'd only fight against you, but she trusts me.' Now the psychologist turned her head his way. No confusion this time: she was all efficiency, emotions put aside for a while. 'You could see if anyone else is hurt. The stewardess might be injured if she wasn't wearing a belt.'

Ash levered himself off the seat. 'Call me if you need a hand with Petra.'

But Dr Wyatt was already drawing out a small medical box from the open bag, all her concentration on treating her distressed patient.

Ash made his way down the cabin, walking unsteadily, and not just because he was on a moving plane. His first stop was by the shabby little man with the bald head. He was frozen in his seat, hands gripping the armrests on either side, his eyes closed. He could have been unconscious.

Leaning closer to the man, Ash said, 'You okay? Can I get you anything? A drink, maybe? The plane's fine, there's no more danger.'

The man's eyes opened, and they were cold as he stared up at Ash. 'You might see to the stewardess,' he said quietly. 'I think she took a fall.'

Ash left him, wondering why this guy hadn't gone to Ginny's aid himself. He found her on the floor by the exit door, the seat in front hiding her from view. She seemed to have hit the back of her head when the Gulfstream had taken the dive, for one hand was stretched behind her neck as if feeling for a wound. At least her eyes were open, Ash noted as he knelt beside her. Her eyelids fluttered, but she recognized him immediately.

'You must have cracked your head when the plane dropped,' he said.

Ginny blinked several times more before responding. 'I think I'm okay,' she assured him weakly. 'No real damage, just a knock to the head.' She tried to rub the spot, but it was awkward for her.

'Let me take a look.' Ash put a hand around her neck and gently pulled her head away from the door. He peered over her shoulder and felt her scalp through her thick hair. 'No blood. You might have a bump there soon. D'you hurt anywhere else?'

71

'The – the other passengers,' she managed to stammer. 'Is everyone all right?' She seemed genuinely anxious and Ash was impressed.

'They're all fine, just a bit shaken,' he reassured her. 'The young girl, though – Petra – is in shock. Dr Wyatt's treating her right now.'

'And – and you, Mr Ash. Any injuries?'

'No, I was lucky. Still strapped in.'

'We always recommend passengers keep their seatbelt on throughout the flight.'

'Well, people don't like to think they're in mortal danger. Seems kind of wimpish to stay buckled in.'

'If you could help me up, I'll go and see if I can do anything for them. We'll be landing in a few minutes, but I think we've got time to settle their nerves with a large double of whatever's their preference.'

'Captain Roberts recommends we hit the bar once we've landed.'

'Oh, I'd better get into the cockpit to report the situation back here.'

'I don't think you should try to walk just yet, Ginny. Look at your leg.' Her right ankle was beginning to bloom into a watery swelling. The air stewardess groaned more in irritation than pain.

'I don't think it's broken,' Ash advised, 'but you must have sprained it badly.'

'Can you – can you help me up? I have to make some checks.'

'Ginny, with that inflating bulge you won't be checking anything for a while.'

As he put his hands under her armpits and began lifting her on to the seats, Ginny wincing as she rose, the cockpit door opened behind him and First Officer Collins stepped out.

'A little help here?' Ash asked mid-lift.

'Ginny, what damage?' Collins's voice was tense.

Ash answered for her. 'A nasty blow on the back of her

head – no blood, though – and an even nastier sprained ankle. Nothing too serious as far as I can tell, no broken bones. Help me get her on facing seats, will you?'

First Officer Collins hurriedly slid one arm around the stewardess's shoulders and the other under her knees. Ash followed suit on the opposite side and between them they manoeuvred Ginny into a seat. Apart from some sharp intakes of breath, she seemed all right.

Ash straightened and addressed Collins. 'Are we okay now? D'you know what happened to the jet's power?'

'I could tell you we hit an air pocket, which caused the plane to drop, but I know you wouldn't believe me.' His voice was low, keeping the conversation strictly between Ash and himself. 'In all my experience with different planes, I've never once gone through anything like that before. All power, all electrics, just packed up. We couldn't even put out a Mayday. It's a goddamn mystery to us. We can only pray it doesn't happen again, although, with all power back on we've sent out a distress signal to Prestwick so they'll be on full alert when we land. But look, I mean it: everything in the plane is functioning normally.'

'I'll take your word for it. Why don't you look after Ginny here while I go back to give Dr Wyatt a hand? The girl with her is in a bad way, but as far as we can tell she hasn't sustained any serious injury.'

'Thank you, sir. Your help is appreciated. I'll be along myself shortly.'

The investigator retraced his steps down the cabin, taking a quick peek at the person Ash had heard called Twigg.

The small man, in his oversized trench coat, sat in exactly the same position as before and, although his pale eyes were open, he didn't bother to acknowledge Ash.

The psychic investigator reached Dr Wyatt, who was dropping a syrette into a plastic bag. Petra lay still on the floor, an occasional twitch of her limbs suggesting she was not too deeply unconscious.

JAMES HERBERT

Ash knelt down beside the doctor. 'She going to be okay?'

'Yes, I gave her a shot of lorazepam to relax her. It's not usual, but works fast. To carry disposable syrettes isn't strictly legal, but we work somewhat differently at Comraich.'

It was a telling remark that Ash was to remember.

'Each contains a single dose of tranquillizer. She'll probably have to be helped off the plane when we land, though. She was already medicated before we boarded, so the combination of that with what I've just given her should put her into a peaceful sleep shortly.'

Remaining on one knee, Ash examined the girl's face. She flinched and Ash pulled back in surprise.

'No problems,' Dr Wyatt began to say. 'She'll—'

The girl suddenly sat up so abruptly that Ash and the psychologist recoiled from her in alarm.

Petra's body was as stiff as a board, and her bleak eyes stared solely at Ash.

In a low, rasping voice, she said to him, *'They know you're coming!'*

Eyes rolling back inside her head, Petra went limp and slumped to the floor again.

13

Ash was trembling as he stood at the bottom of the short flight of steps on the aircraft's port side. A strong gust of wind ruffled his hair, bringing with it an intimation of fresh sea air under the usual blanket airstrip-smell of oil fumes.

He felt chilled to the bone, and it had little to do with Scotland's climate. No, it was the young girl's strange other-worldly warning.

Petra was clearly in shock from the fright she'd had when it seemed they were all about to die. Had the horror of their assumed fate sharpened her sensibilities to the extent that she'd perceived some kind of subliminal threat meant for him? But then, why the warning? What could be waiting for him at Comraich Castle?

He put a hold on these thoughts when movement and a soft soothing voice came from behind him. Ash turned to see Dr Wyatt carefully guiding the puffy-faced girl down the air-craft's steps, the co-pilot following with their hand luggage.

'Can I do anything?' Ash asked, reaching up to take Petra's other arm.

The raven-haired psychologist gave him a faltering smile. 'No, we're doing fine,' she said uncertainly.

The girl she was helping was visibly shaking despite the drug that had been injected into her system. He was a little shaky himself.

'She going to be okay?' Ash asked with a nod towards the doped-up teenager.

'She'll be all right once she's over the fright,' the psychologist told him. With a protective arm around Petra, she inclined her head towards a clear stretch of tarmac well away from the runway and docking areas where a Gazelle helicopter was warming up. It was decked out in the corporate livery of black and charcoal grey, a combination that Ash was beginning to dislike. Its rotating blades were individually visible, not yet having reached take-off speed. 'That's for us,' Dr Wyatt said. 'We'll be at Comraich in minutes.'

One of the ground crew was wheeling a trolley laden with suitcases and a few labelled boxes taken from the plane towards the helicopter. Ash caught a glimpse of his own luggage among them: a big, black case with battered corners, which carried most of the equipment he planned to use initially at Comraich, and a sizeable leather travelling bag, distressed by wear rather than fashion, containing changes of clothing, books and a few other personal items.

Glad to be safely on the ground, Ash didn't relish another flight so soon, and especially not by helicopter, no matter how short the journey.

Without enthusiasm he said, 'Great. I'm looking forward to seeing the castle.'

Dr Wyatt looked surprised. 'Oh, I'm sorry. They didn't tell you?'

'Tell me what?'

'I'm afraid you won't be coming with us in the chopper. It's carrying pharmaceuticals to Comraich as well as Petra, myself and Mr Twigg. There isn't room for another passenger.'

The small bald-headed Mr Twigg had been first off the jet and Ash saw him striding towards the Gazelle ahead of the baggage handler.

'Really?' Ash said to the psychologist, only mildly disappointed.

Petra, leaning heavily against Dr Wyatt, slowly raised her head to peer up at him.

'Who's he? What's happening?' she demanded petulantly.

'It's all right, Petra. This is Mr Ash. He'll be joining us at Comraich later.'

The girl immediately lost interest in the investigator. 'I'm tired, I want to sleep,' she whined.

'Not long, Petra,' the doctor reassured her. 'We'll soon be there. Then you can go straight to bed and sleep it off.'

'I want to see Peter,' the girl complained, now sullen.

'You will. He'll be waiting for you, I'm sure.' Dr Wyatt addressed Ash. 'Peter is her twin brother. He's been at Comraich a few months and they've really missed one another. Well, I'll see you there, Mr Ash.'

The last remark sounded like a pledge and he hoped it was. 'It's David,' he told her. Then he said, 'I might need to consult you with regard to some of your patients.' He stopped her before she imposed client confidentiality. 'Only those who claim to have witnessed or have been directly affected by the so-called haunting, of course.' He noticed, not for the first time, she had a habit of facing him full-on while her eyes switched to one side, like an actor looking for a prompt. Maybe it was her way of avoiding direct confrontation.

'Dr Wyatt is kind of formal,' he said, with different thoughts running through his head. 'Can I know your first name?'

'Delphine. My mother's choice.'

'Does it mean anything in particular? I've not heard the name before. Brazilian, maybe?'

'No. My mother took it from a book she'd loved. But perhaps we'll be able to talk more at Comraich.'

Yes, I'd like that, Ash thought to himself. He hadn't been attracted to any woman for a long time – deliberately so. For him, emotional attachment had never been a safe option: in fact, it was something to be avoided, given his track record. Yet he was already feeling captivated by Dr Delphine Wyatt . . .

Ash saw that Twigg was already aboard, safety-belt buckled, headphones in place to soften the noise. The helicopter's rotors began to pick up even more speed, becoming a blur.

Still supporting Petra, Delphine managed to look back over her shoulder. '*Adeus*,' she called out. '*Até logo.*'

He half raised his hands towards her, palms upwards to let her know he didn't understand. 'Is that Portuguese?'

'It's almost all I know,' she shouted over the increasing noise of the helicopter. '*Se cuida!* Take care!'

He waved, but her attention was focused on Petra once again, the girl plodding alongside her as if her boots were filled with lead. One of the ground crew helped them into the Gazelle, virtually having to lift Petra into her seat.

Ash watched the machine rise into the air, nose tilted initially for direction. The Gazelle picked up speed and headed south, as far as Ash could tell with the sun hidden behind thick cloud.

He was jolted from his thoughts by a voice calling to him. '*Fàilte oirbh*, Mr Ash!'

14

The sleek black Mercedes-Benz had almost silently crept up on him while he was otherwise distracted. The driver's side window was fully open and a youthful face with bright blond hair and a cheerful grin shone out at him.

'*Dè an doigh?*' the young Scot called out and grinned again when Ash shrugged his shoulders and shook his head in non-comprehension.

'I'm sorry, Mr Ash,' the driver apologized as he pushed open the car door. 'I just like visitors from the south to be aware they've entered another country.' He chuckled, mostly to himself, and Ash stood his ground so that the driver had to come to him.

The car itself was beautiful, with smooth aerodynamic contours that suggested it was as much a racer as a six-seater people-carrier. Its driver, still smiling broadly, strode towards him, one hand outstretched to be shaken. Ash was surprised to see he wore a plain, charcoal-coloured woollen kilt rather than a tartan, but that and the thick black crewneck jumper and sporran he was also sporting obviously reflected the corporate identity: it was a variation of the stewardess's uniform, which itself blended with the Gulfstream's interior decor. Long thick socks ended at a point just below the driver's knees and, to Ash's amusement, instead of the short dagger (known formally as the *sgian dubh*) the Scottish Highlanders wore protruding from the top of one sock when in full clan dress, this man had a small mobile phone in a leather carrier strapped to his leg.

'*Fàilte* – welcome,' the driver said, coming to a halt before the parapsychologist.

At close quarters, Ash could see that the cheerful driver was somewhat older than he'd first assumed from a distance, the crinkles around his eyes and furrowed brow giving honest evidence of some good living gone by. He was handsome though, with blue-grey eyes and, Ash suspected, bleached highlights had been worked into his thick short hair.

By now, the helicopter had gone so that Ash no longer had to raise his voice to be heard.

'I thought most Scots spoke English,' he said, smiling so that no offence would be taken. 'You still use the Gaelic, then?'

'Aye, some of us do, but it's mainly the Highlanders who keep the tongue, y'know, among the clans? I'm from the Highlands, so I like to remind myself of my heritage. And I tend to use it sometimes to please my grandpa. He's ninety-eight and still insists on sticking to the mother-tongue, the *aulde* dialect. He always gives me a quick lesson when I visit, because he's proud we're descended from the Celts. I'm inclined to use it when I'm stressed or, like I said, to welcome new clients.' The kilted man chuckled so that the response wouldn't sound discourteous.

'Scotland's always been a different country to me.'

'Ach, so we see eye t'eye, sir.' He was still smiling genially.

'Or aye to aye. Sorry, weak joke.' Ash had attempted a Scottish accent, but it was pretty lame.

'Indeed it was, sir, but not totally without humour. M'name's Gordon Dalzell, by the way.'

Ash found himself warming to the man despite – or maybe because of – the teasing banter. 'Mine's David, and I'm not a client, so no need for sir.'

'Right y'are, but my employer would frown at such familiarity, so best make it Mr Ash, if that's okay wi' you. It's a pity our other helicopter is being used elsewhere this week; it could have brought you directly from London to Comraich.'

'They have *two* helicopters?'

'An Agusta 109 Grand. The name speaks for itself. Executive use mainly. Beautiful job, inside and out, and it'll carry up
to six passengers with light luggage. Shame you couldn't use
it today – y'could've avoided the little mishap with the jet.
Unfortunately, it's being used in the Home Counties ferrying
various buyers back and forth to this week's Arms Fair.'

'Your employer's involved in the arms trade?' It was a
surprise to Ash.

'Aye, and other things besides. Investment is its main
priority, though.' He gave the investigator a quick scan. 'Sorry
you were, uh, inconvenienced on the Gulfstream.' He sounded
sincere, even though he made light of it.

'You heard about that?'

'Aye, it was radioed through and I was informed. My
instructions are to help settle y'nerves.'

'I'm fine. Flying doesn't bother me.' *Neither does dying*, Ash
might have added if he was being frank.

'Well, if y'want to stop for a wee dram I know several very
pleasant hostelries on our route. Oh, and please feel free to
smoke – there's no ban in this car.'

'I gave them up.'

'When was that?'

'This morning.'

Dalzell shot a look at Ash and saw he wasn't joking. 'Now
y'll find that brutal, sir.'

'Tell me about it. This is the third time I've tried. Last time
I quit for all of two weeks. And I could certainly have used a
cigarette earlier.' He closed his mind to it.

'Well if you change y'mind about that dram along the way,
just gi' me the nod.'

'No,' Ash responded firmly. 'I'd like to get straight on to the
castle. There's a lot for me to check out and daylight is more
practical at this stage. Shall we go?' Ash wasn't particularly
impatient to reach Comraich, but he was methodical in his

approach to alleged hauntings. As he expected to spend no more than three days and nights at the castle, it would be foolish to waste time this early in the game.

'As y'wish, Mr Ash.'

Taking the investigator's shoulder bag, the amiable driver walked to the rear passenger door of the Mercedes and opened it for Ash.

The investigator shook his head once. 'I'll sit up front alongside you. That okay?'

'Certainly. But y'do have a telly and DVD screen set into the back of the headrest in front of you there. It might fill in some of the time for you on the journey?' The driver raised his eyebrows questioningly.

'I thought Comraich was close by.'

'Nae. Y'll find it'll take some time along the narrow and twisting country roads.'

'All the same – I'll ride up front.'

'Then shotgun it is.'

The Scot opened the rear door and put Ash's bag on a seat, then went to the front passenger door and opened it smoothly. As Ash ducked his head to enter the Mercedes he thought Dalzell looked as if he could take care of himself and his passenger in any road-rage brawl. He couldn't think why, but it gave him an odd sense of security.

'Nice car,' Ash remarked appreciatively as he settled into the soft charcoal-grey leather seat and took note of the panoramic glass roof.

'Mercedes-Benz Grand Sports Tourer,' the driver informed him proudly as he opened the opposite door and got behind the steering wheel. 'Smooth ride and plenty o'power. Makes m'job easier.'

He strapped himself in and gunned the engine, deliberately heavy-footing the accelerator pedal to achieve an engine roar. He grinned at Ash like a boy performing his first party trick.

'Okay, I'm impressed,' said Ash, taking in the complex hi-tech centre console with its navigation display and rows of multi-functional control buttons. 'But let's get going.'

'Right, Mr Ash. Lock 'n' load. I've always wanted t'say that.'

They were out of the airport in less than a minute, Ash already relaxing into the sumptuous interior of the high-powered vehicle as it swept through the gates. He caught the driver giving him a quick once-over when they were on their way.

'Is the heating all right for you, Mr Ash? Too warm, too cold?'

'It's just fine. Don't change a thing.'

'Some music then? Or local news?'

'No, I'll just enjoy the drive.'

He sank further into his seat.

'How long have you been driving for Comraich Castle?' he asked Dalzell.

The car slowed to turn off the main artery into a narrow hedge-lined lane.

'Oh, now there's a question.' The driver squinted his eyes as if the answer lay beyond the windscreen. 'Let's see. It must've been four years now. M'partner and me, we were running our own chauffeur-drive service in and around Edinburgh when a representative for Comraich Castle approached us. Just in time, too – business was dire and getting worse. Tourism was bleak, particularly where the Americans were concerned.'

He shook his head regretfully as if the memory still irked him. 'We depended mainly on USA tourists to keep us afloat, not just in summer, but during the cold months as well. Unfortunately, they were staying home, reluctant to risk air travel for a while. And who could blame them? That's why it was good luck when Mr Maseby turned up with an offer we couldn't turn down. We'd driven him once or twice before, so we weren't unknown t'him.'

'Simon Maseby?'

'Aye, that's the feller.'

'And your contract's with his entire company, not just with the part that runs Comraich Castle?' Ash guessed.

'That's right. One of the conditions, though, was that we had to drive exclusively for Comraich. No other clients, just the Comraich and Maseby people. And we had to live there to be on call, night or day. There's quite a community of them – servants, maids, chefs, office staff and groundskeepers as well as doctors and nurses. It's a little world of its own. And sometimes, we have visits from very special VIPs, but that's kept all very hush-hush.'

Ash was even more curious. 'Why would that be?'

'I really don't know. We collect 'em from the airport or sometimes we make the trip to London or elsewhere to bring them up, or we travel down to bring things back. Documents and the like. We're kept busy, no two ways about that.'

'I suppose the patients – sorry, "guests" – get quite a few visitors?'

'Nae, nary a one. None allowed. That's another condition of Comraich.'

Ash looked at him in surprise. Then he rested back in his seat again, deep in thought.

Although the day was overcast with a low blanket of metal-grey cloud, the landscape remained vivid in autumnal colours, the leaves of the trees gradually giving way to reds, browns and golden yellows, while among them, hardy evergreens declined to give up their year-round tones to the oncoming season. In the fields beyond the trees, cattle and sheep steadily munched their God-given grass and any tasty morsel found in the soil with it, instinctively aware that the cold season was fast approaching and inches-deep snow might soon cover nature's usual sustenance so that they would have to rely solely on trough fodder.

The peace of gentle glens and distant hills, together with the car's comfortable air-conditioned warmth, slowly lulled Ash into a soporific mood, with the driver's incessant but softly spoken commentary on all they passed fostering the investigator's drowsiness. Adrenaline flow caused by the morning's near-fatal incident had slowly drained away to be replaced by a tempered sense of well-being.

Dalzell's easy chatter ranged from the vernacular aspect of several single-storey roadside houses with hipped roofs, some of which were thatched with heather, to long-since abandoned vaulted tower mills. Then there were the weavers' cottages, the open moorlands and more deep glens. The journey to Comraich was taking longer than he'd expected, and the route seemed unusually complex, with twists and turns, the main roads avoided for quieter narrow lanes.

Not for the first time during the drive, Ash's thoughts returned to Delphine Wyatt.

'How much further?' he eventually asked, cutting through the driver's jabber.

'To Comraich? Oh, we'll be there in no time at all,' Dalzell responded. 'I was instructed to bring you by the scenic route.'

'Really? Any reason why?'

The chauffeur gave a small shrug of his shoulders. 'I just do as I'm told. They probably wanted t'make the journey more pleasant for you. *Rach air muin*!'

Ash had no idea what they meant, but the driver's last words sounded like an expletive. Then he saw what might have caused Dalzell's sudden and unexpected ire.

The predominately white police car that had just rounded a bend ahead began slowing down so that both vehicles could squeeze past one another in the narrow lane.

Dalzell gave the two policemen in the other car a cheerful wave which was not reciprocated. Both policemen stared long and hard at Ash as their car eased by. The police car's insignia was yellow and blue, and he noticed that on the bonnet was a logo with sans-serif lettering next to it. Out of curiosity, he leaned forward in his seat, angling his head to read the wording: STRATHCLYDE POLICE.

'Friends of yours?' he asked the blond chauffeur drily.

Dalzell scoffed good-humouredly. 'Ach, no. They're okay,

unless they catch you doing the ton or weaving with the hooch.'
He snatched a look at Ash. 'And I do neither – at least, not
when I'm working. We call them *polis*, by the way,' Dalzell
added.

'*Po-lis*. I like it. Less forbidding.'

'Normally, we don't see much of 'em – the area they cover
is too far stretched. So if you're thinking of calling 'em for
some reason, be prepared for a long wait.'

'I'll keep it in mind,' Ash answered flatly.

Foliage lightly brushed the glass and bodywork, so close
was the Mercedes to the edge of the lane, and the Scot steered
back into the middle.

Again Ash considered the length of the journey to Comraich.
Because the sun was invisible behind leaden clouds, he'd lost
all sense of direction a while back, and it was tempting to believe
this was a deliberate ploy to confuse him and not paranoia on
his part. Had his problem with alcohol (Simon Maseby was
certainly aware of it at yesterday's meeting) been tested, first
by Ginny, the air hostess, then by Dalzell during their journey
by road? Maybe the idea was to dull his wits so that this
roundabout route to Comraich would confuse him. A couple of
times he thought he recognized the same landmark, although
approached from a different direction.

But why? It seemed pointless and simple-minded subterfuge to him. What could be gained from it?

Additionally, there had been no mention of Comraich Castle
or its location on either of the two documents he'd signed with
Kate: the contractor was Simon Maseby of Maseby Associates,
and only the company's London address was given. As far as
the agreements were concerned, they were between the Psychical Research Institute and Maseby Associates, and discretion – no, *secrecy* – was a special feature of the deal.

He straightened his shoulders and stretched his arms out
in front of him so that his fingers almost touched the dash-
board. He rolled his head twice to loosen tension in his neck

and shoulders, then, dropping his hands into his lap, he turned to the Scot.

'Okay,' he said to Dalzell. 'Tell me about Comraich.'

The driver glanced his way and Ash thought he seemed a little put out. Maybe he really had expected Ash to have dozed off by now.

'Comraich?' the investigator reminded him meaningfully.

'Y'mean its history?' Dalzell asked, his attention on the road again.

'Anything you'd like to tell me, except what's happened recently.'

'Well now, I cannae tell you too much about the place – it's nae permitted. Every person employed there has signed a confidentiality agreement.'

'But you've worked for the castle for – how many years did you say?'

'Nigh on four. But y'see, m'partner and me, we don't get too involved, we just drive.'

'I'm sure you talk to other staff members,' Ash said pointedly. 'But look, I'm not concerned with any of that. What I'd like to know is something of the castle's history.' He couldn't be sure, but he thought Dalzell seemed relieved.

'Oh aye, I can tell y'about that, although you'll nae be surprised if it's nae too much. The castle has always been a kind of enigma in these parts. Its way off the beaten track, as y'll see, and interlopers are made to feel unwelcome. Local people assume the castle's some kind of ultra-discreet and very expensive sanitarium for the wealthy, and in a way that's correct. It's very inaccessible, and would-be trespassers rarely get near the castle itself.'

'Tight security?'

'And then some. But m'partner and me, we're nae curious, y'ken? The wages are high and conditions are good. We were grateful for the opportunity to work there. We've ne'er looked back since.'

A little weary of being told how generous Comraich – or Maseby Associates – was to its employees, Ash came straight to the point. 'How old is the castle? Has it any history of early hauntings?'

'Hauntings, you say? Well now, that's an interesting area for discussion. Did y'hear Comraich has a curse on it?'

Ash almost groaned aloud. What ancient bloody castle or mansion *wasn't* cursed? As a ghost hunter he'd been assailed with such stories of curses on age-old buildings, including churches and pubs.

'All right,' he said wryly, 'tell me about it.'

'Ach, I dinnae ken the full story, but it was when the true clans were taking their revenge on the Scottish noblemen that had allied themselves with Edward I of England against Robert the Bruce, who was twice defeated in battle. That was near the beginning of the fourteenth century, a very troublesome time for Scotland.

'It was the Laird Duncan McKinnon who owned Falaich Caisteal, as Comraich was known in those days. Hidden or concealed, it meant, because it was devilish to find unless you approached it from the sea. To this day, that's where you'll see the castle in its full glory, there on top of the *creag*, the cliff.

'Anyway, Robert the Bruce eventually returned from hiding on a remote island off the Irish coast. He gathered his forces again and this time... oh, this time, he did battle with Edward II, who he defeated at the Battle of Bannockburn! That was in 1314, but it was only when Edward III was on the English throne that Scottish independence was declared. The year was 1328, and nae have we e'er forgotten it.'

Ash smiled as Dalzell chuckled. 'So what was the curse?'

'Aye. The Mullachd. I'm not sure of the details, but it's the stuff of legend in these parts. The Laird McKinnon's wife and daughters were flung from the castle battlements, to be dashed on the rocks below and their bodies swept out to sea. It was McKinnon himself who spat out the curse, just before he jumped of his own accord.'

The Mercedes was approaching a road junction, and Dalzell frowned as if worried he was giving away too much information on the castle. He turned right, joining other traffic travelling in the same direction.

'So do you know why I'm going to Comraich?'

'As I said, it's an enclosed community. Word gets around, even though Sir Victor tried to keep a cap on it. Too many rummy things going on at the castle to hush them all up, though.'

'Have you ever experienced anything unusual?'

The driver smiled grimly as he overtook a heavily loaded flatbed truck.

'Nae,' he said, as if disappointed. 'But I've heard some peculiar stories from others who have. The whole bliddy place is full of such nonsense, and the medics have been dishing out tranquillizers like candy.'

'They drug the patients?'

The Mercedes picked up speed on the broader stretch of road. 'I cannae say any more, Mr Ash. It's agin' orders. Hope y'don't mind, but it's more than the job's worth. And y'did say you didnae want to hear about the haunting.'

Of course, Dalzell was right. 'Well, at least tell me about McKinnon's curse,' Ash prompted. 'You can do that, can't you?'

'Oh, there was sommat about sending the fires of Hell to burn the castle to the ground.'

'Not a very accurate curse, then.'

'I'm not so sure. There was a fire in Falaich Caisteal sometime *after* the laird who'd had McKinnon and his family killed was long since dead, having peacefully passed away in his bed, at that. But the curse didnae die with him; the place was nearly destroyed by fire once and then again years later, when the castle had been restored. It's why the castle has changed its name over the centuries.'

'As you said.'

'Another time it was known as Air Leth Caisteal, meaning isolated castle, which it certainly is to this day. But it seems bad things were always happening there; one time, for instance, the next owner had to flee with his family in the dead of night to escape its spite.'

'Spite?'

'Aye, I ken. Sounds ridiculous, doesn't it? But that's how they had it pegged in them days. After a few years, the castle was rebuilt yet again, or at least, the parts that had been ruined were. Some of the main rooms were brightened up too; cold and dark, it used to be, so I'm told. And of course, there was yet another name change, all in an effort to shake off the curse. It was called Uaigneach Caisteal this time, which means lonely, solitary, secluded, private, secret – take your pick. It was fine for a while, although the story is that nae tenants were ever happy there.'

'That doesn't surprise me,' said Ash. Half-jokingly, he added, 'I think I see a pattern emerging here.'

'Huh! But if y'saw it in the evening of a sunny day, when there's a glorious sunset and the grey sandstone walls turn a mellow shade of pink, y'd never believe there was anything sinister about the place.'

The description sounded like a tour guide's rehearsed patter.

'And the name changed yet again,' he remarked. 'What happened this time?'

'Ach, to tell you the truth, I dinnae ken much more, but the castle eventually became a kind of rich person's refuge. As it is to this day. And that's why it's called Comraich.'

'*Comraich* meaning . . . ?'

'Sanctuary,' came Dalzell's emphatic reply.

The investigator regarded the chauffeur curiously, but the Scot was concentrating on the road ahead. They reached a T-junction and stopped; for a moment the driver seemed as uncertain as before.

'Lost your way?' Ash enquired drily.

'Ah, nae, nae. Just thought of something you might like t'see.'

'Okay, why not?'

Dalzell indicated left and turned onto the broader thorough-fare, where conversely there was little traffic.

A large white bird flew low over their heads.

'A seagull?' Ash asked Dalzell. 'So we're near the coast?'

'A gannet, sir. Aye, the sea's not far away t'the right. You'll see fulmars, cormorants, all sorts of seabirds along the way. Kittiwakes nest on the sea cliffs.'

'So we'll soon reach Comraich?'

'Not far, Mr Ash. Not far at all now. From the castle's ramparts and on a clear day, you might just see the grey seals that spend time on the rocky shores. We're not short of wildlife in Scotland, y'ken? In the castle grounds y'll come across deer and red squirrels; then there's the kestrels, and we've even had the odd golden eagle come down from the north. If you're a nature-lover at heart, you'd have a bonny time in this little corner of the world. That goes for all of Scotland, of course. Not *too* many regions have been wholly urbanized and if y'want to see nature at its awesome best, y'd do well to spend a month in the Highlands.'

'The Scottish Tourist Board must love you. D'you tell all your pick-ups this?'

Dalzell laughed. 'Y'cannae blame a man for loving his country. How long d'you think y'll stay?'

Ash frowned. 'I'm hoping it won't take longer than three days at most.'

'To do what, if you don't mind me asking, Mr Ash?'

'You honestly don't know why I'm up here?'

'Haven't been briefed on all of it, but I'm aware y'not on a pleasure trip. I ken y're a ghost hunter, but is it anything to do specifically with what happened to one of the castle's clients the other day?'

'What have you heard?'

91

'Nothing that makes any sense. There's talk of a badly injured— *A bhidse!*'

That sudden word, followed by a sharp release of breath, sounded like another Gaelic expletive to Ash.

'Something I've got to check,' the chauffeur said.

They had been travelling up a hill, the road lined with trees and bushes, and now they were over its crest, looking down the road ahead. Ash was puzzled when Dalzell stopped the car and stepped out, apologizing as he did so. 'Won't be a tick,' the driver said before closing his door. 'Just enjoy the scenery for a minute or two.'

Ash looked down the hill, contemplating the view. The dampness in the air gave the greenery all around a darker lushness and, as he savoured the peace of it all, the horizon began to move away from him. The car, impossibly, was rolling backwards *uphill*.

When he lunged for the handbrake, his seatbelt locked tight and restricted his movement. But in that instant he saw that the gearstick was in the P for Park mode.

Yet, as he gaped through the windscreen, the landscape continued to move inexorably away from him.

15

The opposite door suddenly opened again and there was Dalzell, leaning in with a big grin on his sunny face.

'Did y'enjoy the fright, Mr Ash? It's quite something, isn't it?'

Ash, trapped by his seatbelt, could only stare at him.

'Now dinnae worry, the car isn't moving and nor is the scenery. Y'perfectly safe.'

Dalzell eased himself back into the car, rump first. Almost chastely, he eased the hem of the grey kilt he wore back over his knees. After belting up, he grinned at Ash again.

'I didnae mean to scare you,' he said by way of an apology.

'You didn't. You got my bloody mind screwed up, is all.'

Engine running, the long car headed down the hill as normal.

'What caused it?' Ash had to admit he was fascinated. 'An optical illusion, obviously.'

'That it is. It's called the Electric Brae, although the locals hereabouts know it as Croy Brae. The configuration of the land on both sides of the road and in the distance causes the illusion. One time, they thought it was because of electric or magnetic attraction in the Brae, which is how it got its name. Seems they got it wrong – no one really understands the phenomenon – but the name stuck. When I was a boy and we got to stay in Glasgow, my pa used to bring me here for the fun of it, although I have t'confess, it always bothered me somewhat.'

'Any other weird places in the neighbourhood?'

'Apart from Comraich?' Dalzell responded.

'So you do think there's something unusual about the castle, then? Apart from the curse on it, I mean.'

The driver shrugged. 'Ach, it's centuries old and had more than its share of violence and murders over the years. It can look very haunted when the sea mist drifts in. There's bound to be stories. I can tell you some of the latest—'

'No,' Ash cut in. 'I need to be open-minded when I begin my investigation. In fact, you've already told me too much, but then I guess it's my fault for asking.'

'Ah, so *that* will be the reason you're here. M'partner said so last night, though none of the staff will admit to it. They dinnae want their guests getting more stressed than they already are. Comraich is supposed to be a haven of tranquillity.'

'But the man found—'

It was Dalzell's turn to interrupt. 'I'm sorry, Mr Ash. I almost told you before, so it's just as well we were distracted.'

'Okay, I understand that.' *Besides*, Ash thought wryly, *you were the one who caused the distraction.* 'Wouldn't want to jeopardize your job.'

'And I'm grateful t'you for that. I like my job. Now look, see, we've not much further to go.' He indicated a milestone almost concealed by overlapping foliage at the side of the road.

It was Dalzell's marker, but it meant nothing to Ash. All he saw through the windscreen was more road and more greenery.

On impulse, Ash reached inside his jacket for his tiny Samsung phone, but when he slid the top section back and pressed the ON button he was surprised to see the 'no signal' sign displayed on the small screen.

Dalzell glanced at the mobile, then briefly up at Ash, who obviously was puzzled by the message.

'Y'll nae get a reception in this area,' he told his passenger. His attention was already back on the road.

'No mast nearby?' It troubled the investigator, who had

wanted to contact Kate McCarrick to let her know he'd arrived safely (at this point he wouldn't mention the near-fatal incident with the jet) and he was disappointed not to be able to talk to her.

Dalzell nodded his head without looking at Ash again. 'It affects Comraich, too.'

'Only landline contact?' said Ash, perturbed.

'Well . . .' the driver dragged out the word, 'y'll find rules about that as well.'

'Wait a minute.' Ash was rankled. 'You're wearing a mobile phone attached to your sock.'

'Aye, but it's no use trying to contact Comraich with it. I carry it for when I'm in different parts of the country, but nae to make calls to the castle – the car has its own radio transmitter for that.'

'I assume, then, Comraich has petitioned for a local mast?'

Dalzell merely said, 'I dinnae think so,' and left it at that.

Ash consoled himself with the thought that at least they must be near the castle by now.

The journey had taken time, but they'd passed little traffic along most of the winding roads and lanes they had used. Right now, there were hardly any other vehicles at all.

Dalzell began to ease off the accelerator and the Mercedes smoothly slowed down. Alert once more, Ash searched the road on both sides for an entrance or sign, and he realized that on his own, he would have missed the opening entirely. But the chauffeur turned the steering wheel to the right and it was only when they entered the small lane with hedges and trees on either side, high branches meeting overhead to create a shaded avenue, that Ash guessed they were drawing close to their destination.

Surprised by the absence of any visible indication that the pot-holed road they were on led to Comraich Castle, Ash pressed a button situated on his left armrest and the side window slid down with barely a whisper. He breathed in the cool fragrance of mixed country and sea air. The bumpy road twisted and turned, and he wondered if this was another way of deterring unwelcome visitors or sightseers; it seemed to lead nowhere. Despite the onset of the autumn chill, which brought with it the variegation of rich colours from russet to gold, there was still enough leafy green and wild foliage to screen anything beyond on either side. The Mercedes' soft pneumatic suspension dealt easily with the dips and turns, and the breeze coming through the open window revived Ash from the languor to which he'd almost succumbed. That, and the thought that they were practically at their destination alerted his senses even more. He strained his eyes to see as far ahead as possible, expecting Comraich Castle to rise up before them round the next bend. But, for the moment anyway, he was disappointed when they came only to a set of high iron gates, and to the right, an old and neglected gatekeeper's lodge.

'Not far now,' Dalzell announced cheerily to Ash, who had expected the castle to be at least within sight of the massive gates.

The chauffeur tooted the car's horn and after a few seconds, an aged and bent man emerged from the lodge's open door. If a man could look grizzled, then this was him. He wore baggy trousers held up by braces *and* a thick leather belt, a crinkled and tired-looking collarless shirt, together with an equally wrinkled and tired-looking waistcoat, whose faded brown corduroy matched the fading of his loose trousers. Big muddy boots and the curved smoking pipe held at the corner of his thin-lipped mouth almost completed the image of an old family retainer whose duty apparently was to guard the entrance gates and warn off any intruder or busybody as well as shoot an unsuspecting rabbit or two, maybe even a wandering pheasant, for the laird's supper. And maybe a trespasser or poacher would also be fair game.

A thick thatch of grey-white hair met the thick grey-white mess of beard at the sides of his face as though the matted ensemble were all one piece. To show that he wasn't all hostility, he left the twelve-bore shotgun he carried leaning against the weather-beaten frame of the lodge door, then shuffled forward to thrust his broken-veined face against the gate's metal bars.

Ash couldn't help but think the old gatekeeper looked exactly how you'd imagine a hoary old sentinel to a venerable Scottish castle's estate would look like. Always suspicious, the investigator wondered if that was the point.

'That you, Dalzell?' the gatekeeper enquired, squinting at the Mercedes, his pipe projecting through the black, rusting bars. His eyes were rheumy, their pale blue irises lacking definition.

'Aye, y'know 'tis, y'bent old rapscallion,' Dalzell called out with a grin, his side window open fully so that he could lean out.

'I was told t'expect you wi' a passenger.' The bearded man regarded Ash suspiciously through the windscreen, his scowl implying he hadn't yet made up his mind if Ash were friend or foe.

'Yes, I told you, m'self, Angus, if y'remember correctly.'

The old man's voice was gravelly, probably from too many inhalations of strong shredded baccy. But there was nothing truly fierce about him, despite his crotchety manner. 'I'll trouble y'for y'pass, if it's all the same t'ye. Y'might be a lookalike.' He wasn't smiling.

'Yeah, and Brad Pitt might be my doppelgänger.' Dalzell had already unclipped his safety belt so that he could reach into the sporran on his lap for the evidently official pass. He held it through the window and the old boy pretended to inspect it from yards away.

Quietly, Dalzell spoke to Ash. 'The old bugger cannae see the writing nor the pic, but he likes to make a show; helps him assert his own importance but it does nae harm.'

'Come on in,' Angus grouched, waving arthritic fingers before producing a ring of keys chain-linked to his belt, the longest of which he inserted into the gate's hefty-looking lock.

It seemed to turn easily enough, as though it was always kept well oiled or well used. The bent gatekeeper swung one side of the gate open, then ambled over to the other one to repeat the performance.

Ash was surprised and, he had to admit to himself, a little disappointed. For all of Comraich Castle's secrecy and the apparent influential but shadowy consortium behind it, it was remarkably easy to gain entry. Security could hardly be described as hi-tech.

As Dalzell guided the Mercedes-Benz through the gateposts, Angus leaned close to the passenger window for better scrutiny of the intruder.

His and Ash's eyes locked for a moment as the car went by and the parapsychologist saw the weariness of many years of unappreciated servitude in the other man's watery gaze. But there was something more lurking behind those tired old eyes and Ash shivered inside a little before chiding himself for being over-imaginative. Kate would have put it down to his highly tuned intuition, but the shiver of apprehension, Ash realized, was not because of the gatekeeper's suspicious inspection and the shotgun lurking nearby: it was because now he was entering the grounds of Comraich Castle itself.

They drove in and the road soon became firmer, the bordering verdure and branches pruned severely to prevent any hindrance to wide or high-sided vehicles. And soon the road broadened into passing places along the way so that those same vehicles might make way for oncoming traffic or vice versa.

It would have been an agreeable pleasure for Ash, with the rich and varied autumnal colours all around and the very smell of nature itself mixed with the faint tang of salt breezes drifting in from the sea that must have been close by, had not a mounting trepidation spoilt the mood. Again, he was annoyed at himself. Certainly, it was a curious assignment – for a start, a human body stuck to the wall as if by its own blood (although in the past he'd investigated cases of equal peculiarity – some even more so) and these other alleged hauntings. Of course, he'd nearly died in a plane crash that very morning, so naturally he should not be feeling calm or at ease with himself, yet there was something more tormenting his psyche, a foreboding, a presentiment of – what? He had no idea.

He closed his eyes. Maybe there had been too much fear in his life; maybe over the years his resolve, his fortitude, had been sapped. Maybe he hadn't allowed sanity enough time to heal old scars. Well, Kate obviously thought he was ready to take on the vicissitudes of ghost hunting again (unless she was testing his capability in dealing with such strange and possibly damaging investigations). He knew she sensed the dread hidden beneath his veneer of cynicism and his dry manner, but her faith in him had never wavered. They hadn't been bed-partners for a long, long time, yet their affection – and their respect – for each other had endured. That alone gave him inner strength. He almost smiled at the thought of her. Sometimes she could be like a mother hen.

'*Rach air muin!*'

Those Gaelic words that sounded like an expletive again tugged Ash back from his nervous cogitations. He opened his eyes as the Mercedes' brakes were applied and his seatbelt checked his helpless lunge forward. He just had time to see a blur that could have been a fox or a medium-sized dog dash into the undergrowth on his side of the road.

'*Tha mi duilich,*' Dalzell said to him as the long car came to a halt then rocked lightly on its suspension. 'Sorry to gi' you a fright again, Mr Ash. Y've had your share today.'

Ash peered into the undergrowth. 'What was it?' he asked. 'Dog or fox?'

'Neither one. Did y'nae see its striped fur and bushy tail? It was a bliddy cat!'

'A cat? That size?'

'Aye. A wildcat. I should've run the bugger down. There's a whole tribe of 'em hereabouts and they've become an awful nuisance.'

'I wasn't aware that wildcats existed any more in the UK.'

'Oh aye, they're about. But mostly they live in the Highlands. It's only recently that we've begun to see 'em in the South. Bliddy pests, the lot of 'em!'

'Are they dangerous?'

'They can be very dangerous. They'd tear the skin off y'face if'n y'were foolish enough to corner one.'

Ash visibly blanched for the driver's warning had jolted his mind back to another case just two years ago and Grace Lockwood, whose skin had been shredded from her whole body by unseen forces while he'd looked on helplessly.

Ash forced the memory away. At least, for the moment, for it was one that would never really leave him.

Dalzell gently applied pressure on the accelerator once more and the car resumed its journey with gentle speed.

Because they were in the shade of overhead tree branches and also because, Ash assumed, they were drawing near to the coastline, the air was considerably cooler. He used the button on his armrest to close the passenger window and the glass slid upwards with barely a whisper.

'The cats,' Dalzell was saying, 'they're trying to get into the compound for some reason, and we think a lot of 'em have made it. God knows how.'

'The compound . . . ?'

'Ach, it's just something we call it. The castle grounds and land around Comraich. Fortunately, it's protected by an electric wire fence. Keeps trespassers out and inmates in.'

Ash frowned. 'Inmates?'

'They keep trying though.'

'The *inmates*?'

The driver chuckled. 'Sorry, I didnae mean to call 'em that,' he said, glancing at his passenger. 'I'd be obliged if y'd nae mention that lapse of respect to Sir Victor Haelstrom.'

'You've got my word on it. But I can't help wonder why you'd describe them that way.'

'It's just that many of 'em have been here for years – way longer than I've worked for Comraich – and none of 'em ever seem to leave, not even for a day or a couple of hours. I shouldnae say it, but sometimes m'partner an' me, we wonder about it, and none of the castle staff will gi' an opinion.'

'But an electrified fence is used to keep the, uh, guests inside the grounds?'

'Well, no. That was a little quip on my part. All the residents seem happy enough to be here. Mind you, a 100,000-volt shock would make sure of that, too.'

'Seems excessive,' Ash remarked.

'Aye, but it keeps people safe.'

'I bet.'

Dalzell suddenly looked serious. 'Y'ever heard a cat howling at night, Mr Ash?' he asked. Without waiting for an answer he went on. 'Sounds like a human baby crying. And when one starts up, then so does another. And another after that. Soon it sounds like the woods are full of 'em. It's an awful eerie sound.'

He eased up on the accelerator as they reached another bend in the road.

'What y'll see next will surprise you,' he told Ash. 'But dinnae let it intimidate you.'

Nevertheless, it did.

16

The sleek car rounded the bend, and when Ash caught sight of what lay ahead, he was taken aback. The tall, solid metal gates made an imposing and somewhat sinister barrier that completely hid whatever view lay beyond them, which, he assumed, was the castle's inner grounds. A sign on the ivy-clad brick wall beside them said ALL GOODS, with a red arrow pointing left just to clarify the message. The road itself continued in that direction, but Dalzell pulled the Mercedes Tourer over into the open space before the gates.

'Are they meant to keep callers out or guests in?' Ash asked before the driver could speak.

'Both, Mr Ash. You'll find the security at Comraich quite extreme, but y'll get used to it.'

'I don't intend to stay that long.'

Dalzell shrugged. 'Well, I hope there's nae need.'

That remark had sounded almost ominous, but Ash let it go.

Dalzell unclipped his seatbelt and then rummaged through the sporran on his lap. He brought out a small gadget that looked like a pager but with a red button beneath its text window. He pointed it at the looming black gates and pressed the button.

'That little thing's going to open *those*?' Ash asked in mild bemusement.

Tucking the gadget back into the sporran, the driver replied, 'Not exactly. You'll see . . .'

A wicket door in the right-hand gate opened and a big man stepped out. He wore the quasi-uniform now familiar to Ash. Grey shirt and black tie, black trousers and black commando boots; he also wore a black beret, and a dark radio earpiece that looked like a slug crawling from his ear. Ash had gained a fair knowledge of police armoury during the many occasions on which the Institute had loaned him out privately – *very* privately – to police forces baffled by extraordinary events which only a psychic investigator might resolve. He saw that, amazingly, the guard was fitted out with full Kessler rubberized chest armour, a Glock 17 9mm self-loading pistol holstered to his side. He also carried a Heckler and Koch L104A1 37mm single-shot rubber baton launcher and a stun gun capable of delivering 50,000 volts.

Ash assumed the big man was a guard – the *real* keeper of the gate, he mused – and his size alone made him formidable enough to substantiate the assumption. Leaving the wicket door open, the man strolled towards the car, raising a thick, indolent arm at Dalzell, who waved back, his hand barely lifted.

The driver's side window glided down and Dalzell poked his head out a fraction.

'Come on, Henry,' he called, 'y'ken it's me. Open up!' He pulled his head back in. 'Henry always goes by the book,' he said quietly to Ash, his half-smile showing no malice. 'I like to pull his chain occasionally, just to rile him. Unfortunately he's too serious about his job t'appreciate humour.'

The big man's leisurely saunter towards the car gave Ash time to notice the CCTV camera mounted high on the stone post beside the gates and almost concealed by ivy. Unexpectedly, the camera's lens slid forward a fraction and he realized its operator was taking a closer look at him. He became aware of the guard's presence at the driver's window; he was bent almost double, his broad shoulders and large beret blocking the light as he peered across to inspect the passenger.

'Morning, Henry,' Dalzell greeted.

'Your pass and ID,' was the gruff response.

'One day, Henry, you'll crack,' said the driver as he reached into his sporran, this time producing a laminated picture ID the size of a credit card.

Henry took it from him and studied it closely. He still wasn't satisfied, though. 'Who's your passenger?' he demanded, glaring at Ash as though the investigator were an unwelcome interloper.

Dalzell sighed loudly, pretending it was all too much for him. Now he produced a folded piece of paper and handed it to the louring guard. 'Y'ken what it says, Henry, I showed it to you when I left this morning. This *is* Mr David Ash.'

'Routine,' came the curt response. The guard opened the folded piece of paper and inspected it. Then he eyed Ash again. 'All right, you're both okay to enter.'

'Y'so kind,' Dalzell retorted.

The guard took a second or two longer to study Ash before straightening up and ambling back to the gate. He disappeared inside the small door set in the massive gate which, when closed, was all but invisible to a casual glance. Seconds later, one side of the huge gates began to move, followed by its partner a second or so later. The movement was slow and ponderous, as if they were reluctant to reveal the secrets that lay beyond.

Dalzell took the moment to reassure his passenger. 'Well, here y'are at last, Mr Ash, and I wish y'all success with your, uh, your mission.'

'I'm not on a mission, believe me; I'm here just to investigate.'

'Good luck wi' that, then. The guests are getting pretty spooked. On one occasion—'

Ash cut him off with a raised hand. 'I've already heard some of it. Maybe we can talk later on?'

'Of course we can. I just didnae want you to go into things blind.'

'That's normally the first step. I have to find out if anything paranormal is really happening in the castle without being told what to find. I've already had too much information, but that was necessary.'

The Mercedes drove through the now wide-open entrance and the first thing Ash saw was the small single-storey concrete office block that was hardly constructed to fit in with its rural surrounds. A wide frameless window dominated the facing wall and he could see two guards watching the Mercedes drive through; one was Henry, and his companion, who wore the same monochrome faux-uniform, was speaking into an inter-com, no doubt alerting someone further along the line that Dalzell had returned with the expected POB – passenger-on-board. Ash just caught a glimpse of a bank of monitor screens on the wall behind them.

The scenery didn't so much alter dramatically as take on a new, carefully cultivated splendour, and Ash felt he'd entered another land where everything – even the foliage and under-growth – had been carefully designed to a parkland theme. The woods on either side of the roadway were thick without being crowded. The flowers on the neatly trimmed verges still dazzled with myriad colours despite the encroaching colder months, and would have lifted the saddest heart.

He cleared his throat before he spoke. 'That, er, that blockhouse, guard post? It doesn't sit easily with the traditional lodge at the first gates. Nor do those two uniformed guards fit in well with the old feller on watch back there.'

'Know what y'mean, Mr Ash, but, as I keep advising, y'll find security is exceptionally tight at Comraich. I shouldnae be telling y'this, but those guards keep very up-to-date weapons out of sight in case of emergencies.'

The investigator was momentarily taken aback. 'What kind of emergency would warrant an armoury? Storm-troopers, religious fanatics, the Taliban?'

'Not for me to say, sir. Y'll see for y'self how the place is run.'

'Sounds like a prison camp.'

The driver laughed aloud. 'Well, I've wondered about that

m'self on occasion. But nae, y'll find Comraich is a very peaceful place. The guns are only for the protection of some very wealthy and important people here. To my knowledge, there has never been an incident requiring the use of weaponry.'

'That's good to know.'

Dalzell gave another sideways look at his passenger. Ash kept his expression grim to show him he wasn't joking. 'Enjoy the scenery, Mr Ash. Its tranquillity will reassure you.'

Ash let it ride and took in the panoramic view opening up before them. Through the neat trees that were now becoming sparser, he could see green parkland with several grazing deer. Even from a distance, they appeared magnificent creatures, their sleek pelts a reddish brown, and among them were taller beasts with majestic antlers. Beyond them, there was thick forestry where artificial symmetry had no place. The woods were dark and seemed impenetrable, although Ash guessed there would be interesting paths through them. The whole area seemed immense.

'How much land does the estate cover?' he asked Dalzell.

'Two hundred and fifty hectares,' the driver responded.

Ash noticed they were travelling uphill and Dalzell anticipated the next question.

'On this, the land side,' he pointed out, 'is a steep glen. With the rough sea and the high cliffs the castle sits atop on the other side, the *caisteal* is virtually invincible, ready to fend off a whole army. And believe me, it's done that many times since it was built as a fort.' Dalzell was once again playing the tourist guide with relish. 'On the left of the castle – our right – are the old stables and a winding wooden stairway which'll take y'down to the shoreline, and there y'll find a network of caves, one of which, so legend has it, leads up to the castle dungeons themselves. It's nae secret that the caves were used for hiding contraband from the revenue officers in the past for it's nae far across the water to the Isle of Man, and believe me, smuggling was a major activity on the island. From there they were shipped to the Ayrshire coast, as well as England and

Ireland, where they were either banned or high duties had to bc paid on thcm. But that was in centuries past – things've changed since. For the worse, if y'ask me.'

Occasionally, they passed single men wearing the same quasi-uniform as the guards on the gate, except some wore fleece gilets to keep out the chill. Each one appeared to speak into what looked like a very thick wristwatch which must have been a hi-tec RT linked to the earpiece, no doubt being used to report on the progress of the chauffeur and his passenger to some central command post.

Because they were nearer to the sea now, there was a low mist rolling in across their view. Much of the grounds were becoming difficult to see clearly, which disappointed Ash, though it didn't hinder Dalzell's flow.

'Y've glimpsed the deer park and the woodland beyond. In fact, most of the woodland is wild hereabouts and y'could mebbe get lost if y'strayed from the paths through it. There's a cottage hidden away in the woods and a swan pond further on and somewhere in there is a braw walled garden. Y'shouldnae give it a miss. It includes a lovely summerhouse. Close to that there's an aviary. An old disused railway line borders the north-west aspect—'

'With an electrified fence?' Ash interjected.

The driver nodded. 'Aye, that's right. Now, coming back there's a cliff walk where you'd need to take care if you use it. A boat house is on the beach and, above that, what we call the Battery. That's the ancient cannons facing out to sea. S'been a long time since they were used, of course; then you'll find what's known as the Fountain Court, which speaks for itself – a central ornamental fountain in the middle of a beautifully kept lawn surrounded by flower beds.'

'Sounds like heaven,' Ash said flatly.

'Oh, y'can be sure o' that. It's only recently that it's lost some of its charm.'

Ash wondered why that was but, playing by his own rules, he let it go for now.

'So what about the castle itself?'

'Be patient a little longer and y'll see for y'self.'

Ahead there was a ruined archway, the stonework that hadn't been destroyed or neglected still forming an entrance into the castle forecourt.

Dalzell brought the Mercedes to a standstill, its engine left purring, so that the investigator had a fine view through the partially demolished arch.

Ash suppressed a sudden gasp of apprehension.

There, rising from the low, drifting sea mist like some towering behemoth, stood the dark castle called Comraich.

PART TWO: COMRAICH CASTLE

17

Dr Delphine Wyatt lifted the pen she was using to add further notes about her new patient Petra Pendine. Later, when the psychologist was in her proper office on Comraich Castle's lower ground floor where the medical unit was set, she would enter them into the fresh file she'd created on her computer, which also contained individual records of all her clients. Calling patients 'clients' bemused her, but she'd become used to it.

She removed her black-framed glasses and leaned back in her cushioned chair, one wrist resting against the edge of the mahogany bureau's desk flap, a Mont Blanc fountain pen dangling between her long slender fingers.

Next to the notes was the hard-copy file on Petra's twin brother, Peter. The bond between the young man and his sister was troubling, to say the least. The brother had been waiting for the executive helicopter to arrive at the helipad not far from the castle walls. It was fortunate that the Gazelle carrying three passengers, plus the pilot and carefully packed pharmaceuticals, had reached its destination just as the mist had come rolling in from the sea otherwise landing would have been tricky, though not impossible.

Petra, who had the privilege of being in the seat next to the pilot, was completely revived since Prestwick and had virtually leapt from the machine the moment it settled. In her excited haste she'd forgotten to remove the mike and headphones that enabled passengers and pilot to speak to one another above the sounds of rotor and engine. The curled wire had jerked her head back, pulling her to a halt. She'd snatched them off and tossed them onto the Gazelle's front seat, and had then run towards her brother without even crouching below the still-turning rotor arms, an involuntary if usually needless precaution against decapitation taken by most passengers.

She'd given a short, delighted shriek as her brother, who had been waiting by the landing pad since the moment he'd heard the jet had touched down at Prestwick, scampered towards her with arms open wide. They met, they hugged each other tightly, then had kissed, kissed full and passionately on the lips.

The psychologist had been briefed on Petra only a week ago and had spent a couple of days with her in the girl's parents' luxurious home near Regent's Park; Delphine already knew Peter – he was one of her clients at Comraich. Drugs, insecurity and obsession were part of his bipolar condition, and sometimes violence was a major fault. In fact, six months ago he'd almost killed a man in Boujis, a trendy London nightclub, by smashing a bottle and then grinding the jagged end into the victim's face, leaving him scarred for life. What made the matter unaccountable, and so much worse, was that the severely injured target was one of Peter's best friends.

To avoid involving the law, even though the friend – now *ex*-friend – was left with only one good eye set in a face no longer handsome, a *huge* amount of money was paid as compensation by Peter's billionaire father, and his parents also agreed that Peter would be locked away in a non-penal institution for many years. According to the brief given to Delphine, the attack was over a girl, and that girl was Petra.

Over the months and with regular psychological probing, Delphine found it almost impossible to get to the root of her client's conscious and subconscious problems; on the face of it, Peter appeared to be a pleasant if rather arrogant young man, but one whose life so far had combined acts of extreme cruelty to others, including family pets, with more commendable traits such as extreme kindness towards people less fortunate than himself. When questioned about his relationship with Petra, he tended to be evasive. A sister who could be relied on to support her brother through thick and thin. Mutual hatred of their own father, coupled with a total disregard for their mother, had created a special bond between them. Certainly, Peter realized he would have had to serve a long prison sentence for the physical harm he'd wrought, but fortunately his father had not only extreme wealth, but power and influence too.

Arrangements had been made for Peter to disappear from society for a while (Delphine, unlike the spoilt young man, knew that it would be many, many years before he would be fit for release) and he'd agreed to be interned by people his father had had dealings with over the years, a powerful though covert association that could solve problems with the minimum amount of fuss, albeit at a high price.

Delphine still had difficulties with Peter, who, even after six months of psychoanalysis and therapy, continued to insist on one condition to ensure his co-operation in any programme of treatment: the presence of his sister. Delphine had thought it was just an example of the close bond between siblings, the uniqueness of the 'twin connection'. She had been surprised when Peter's father, whose business was in the mass production of titanium, had deemed it a favourable solution to his son's problems. And even more perplexing, Petra had jumped at the idea, perhaps because of her own psychological issues and the fact that she truly loved her twin both emotionally and physically.

That kiss between them at the helicopter landing pad – a kiss so intense it had alarmed Delphine – had also given her fresh insight into their relationship. She'd realized that a further element had entered the frame, a factor that hadn't yet emerged from her lengthy counselling sessions with Peter and one that explained his father's attitude. It seemed that the twins' parents were aware of their children's incestuous relationship and now, cold-heartedly, they wanted to rid

113

themselves of this blight, a perversity that they couldn't begin to understand, one that could have had serious, and more than moral, consequences. So, at a very high price financially, they had washed their hands of their offspring. The parents' inhibited attitude towards their degenerate progeny doubtlessly played some part in the complexity of the twins' feelings for each other.

Delphine squeezed the inner corners of her deep brown eyes between finger and thumb. She could feel the tension headache growing worse and she prayed it wouldn't turn into a serious migraine. Such attacks had once been the bane of her life, although she hadn't suffered a full-throttle migraine cluster for some time, leading her to hope – and pray – that she might finally be free of this malady. Laying the fountain pen down and pushing her chair back, she rose from the bureau. Deep in thought, she slowly walked over to the window.

When she'd got to her room after the mercifully brief helicopter flight, she'd immediately changed into black fleece pull-ons and a mauve V-neck sweater, the sleeves of which were pushed up to the elbows, the soft material ruffled around her lower arms.

Her living quarters were compact, rather than cramped, with a tiny bathroom, bedroom, and sitting room squeezed onto the castle's second floor with other renovated apartments. The bureau shared the main room with a mahogany chest of drawers on which stood a twin-branched table lamp with elegant cream shades. Despite renovation, an old brick fireplace with a green leather fender seat remained, and at one side there was a set of black Victorian fire irons. A landscape print occupied one wall. The sparsity of art was easily negated by the impressive window-framed view overlooking the sea, which was usually magnificent, with waves crashing madly against the rocky shoreline below the high vertical cliffs and great spotlessly white adult gannets plunging past the window or the slightly less impressive cormorants and shags swooping down on helpless prey. On a clear day she might see the hazy outline of the island of Arran across the Firth of Clyde, but today the sea was full of mists. Even with those mists and the greyness the wonderfully fresh, tangy air would usually have lifted her spirits, but not this time; today she felt strangely feeble. She'd assumed it was due to the sudden drop in adrenaline after the near-death incident, but now she began to wonder if it was not Comraich Castle itself. Arms folded, she closed her eyes as if to appease the gradually worsening headache by blocking the daylight. Instead, flashbacks of the almost-fatal plane crash crowded in on her.

With those images also came the memory of the man who had held her tight so that she wouldn't be tossed around the aircraft's cabin in free-fall, refusing to let go of her even though it seemed inevitable that they would all die.

Although she knew little of him, David Ash appeared to be a strange, impenetrable man, something she felt immediately when she set eyes on him after she and Petra had boarded the jet. He was certainly attractive in a dark, tousle-haired sort of way, but it was his eyes that puzzled her: they were a deep shade of blue and somehow they looked – well, they looked *haunted*, as if they'd witnessed events that were irrational, illogical. Yes, eyes that had truly *seen* ghosts, burdened with intimidating thoughts of them. A psychoanalysis would be interesting, to say the least, but she sensed that he bore secrets he would never tell.

Delphine looked out on a day that was darkened by cloud and mist and continued to wonder about the psychic investigator. She wanted to know more about him and why Petra, in her fraught state, had warned him that they – whoever *they* were – knew he was coming, presumably to Comraich. She—

There was a sudden brisk knock on the door, accompanied by the calling of her name.

'Delphine, are you in there? Can I come in?'

The visitor was not unexpected and it was a confrontation that she'd been dreading.

'You know the door isn't locked, Rachael,' the psychologist responded reluctantly. For whatever reason, none of the old-fashioned door locks on that floor had keys to lock or open them.

The panelled door opened and Rachael Krantz, Comraich's senior nurse, came through. She was a tall woman and her strong-featured face was handsome rather than beautiful. Under a certain light her long dark-red hair could look like burnished copper. Today, it was loosely tied at the back, much like Delphine's was at the moment. She wore a spotless white tunic, which reached below her knees. Her tights were also white, as were her functional, soft-leather, unscuffed shoes.

Rachael quickly crossed the carpeted floor and stopped only when she was barely two feet away from the startled psychologist, who stepped a few inches backwards to create space between them again. Rachael smiled as though she hadn't noticed the reaction, her hazel eyes, flecked with light-brown shards, looking intently at Delphine.

For a moment, Delphine thought the taller woman was about to sweep her up into her arms.

'I was worried about you,' Rachael said, keeping her distance. 'I heard about the problem with the plane and thought you might be traumatized. Why didn't you look for me when you got back?'

Those fierce hazel eyes seemed to search Delphine's mind and, not for the first time, the psychologist realized she was a little frightened of the tall nurse. Yet – and the young psychologist hated herself for accepting this – there was something undeniably seductive about Krantz, even to another woman.

'I thought we might take an early lunch together. In the staff canteen, if you like, rather than the restaurant.' Delphine often preferred the large canteen meant for nurses and the manual employees, rather than the more formal dining room inside the main part of the castle, which was usually used by heads of department and Comraich VIPs. Important clients also dined in the huge, round room, although some preferred to eat alone in their comfortable apartments, while others were kept under lock and key for the safety of all, including themselves.

'I need to write more observation notes on our new client, Petra Pendine, while they're fresh in my mind,' Delphine replied.

'It's taken you all this time?' The question was rudely challenging.

'I showered and changed before I started my notes, so I really do have to get on with them.'

The senior nurse was hardly appeased, and it showed in her tone. 'How did the girl react to the scare?'

'Well, she's already on fluoxetine hydrochloride, and I gave her one clonazepam when I collected her from home this morning,' Delphine said calmly, 'but I'm sure she'd been partying on coke or skunk last night – her last night of freedom before "incarceration", as she likes to put it. I also gave her a shot of lorazepam for shock on the plane.'

'Does she realize she'll be here for a very long time, possibly years?'

'Her parents were supposed to explain everything to her, but I don't think she understands what *internment* means, or why she and her brother Peter had to be separated in the first place. She attempted suicide twice in the absence of her twin – fake attempts to get her own way to be with him, I believe – which certainly worked. I don't think her parents were too reluctant to allow it, despite the cost, and as far as Petra knows, Comraich is the Scottish equivalent of the Priory in London, only far more expensive and with a better class of addict.'

'And I suppose, as usual, you question the legality of all this?' It could have been a sneer, or it might have been said mockingly. Delphine was never quite sure with Rachael.

'It *is* a form of imprisonment.'

Delphine turned away from the senior nurse's censorious expression and went back to the bureau, as if the notes there really required further attention.

'You need to grow up, Delphine,' came Rachael's sharp

rebuke. Then her voice softened as she followed the psychologist over to the bureau. She gently touched Delphine's upper arm. 'I'm sorry,' she said, 'but I did miss you. I thought at least we might lunch together today.'

Delphine shrugged off the offending hand and her own voice was brittle. 'I was only away for a week. For God's sake, we're not a couple.'

'We could have been. We could st—'

'No, Rachael. Not in the way you mean. To put it bluntly, I'm not that way inclined.'

'You were once.'

'Yes, *once*. When I was grief-stricken over my father's death. I just needed comfort. I had no one . . . no one to turn to.'

'It was sexual. You know it.'

Delphine angrily thumped the heel of her hand on the bureau's top. 'No! It wasn't!'

'I finger-fucked you, here, in this room. And you didn't object then. Did you?'

For a moment, Delphine was shocked by the nurse's crudity about what had taken place between them.

Rachael's face was flushed red as she moved even closer to Delphine again. Her voice was full of sly insinuation when she said, 'And let's not forget, *you* came to me later that night, and we made love, properly this time, in my bed!'

The room suddenly brightened as the sun made a late appearance, finally breaking through the overcast sky, gloomy clouds beginning to fracture and move on. But even so, the lightening of the day could do little to lift Delphine's mood.

'Yes,' she responded to Rachael's jibe, 'but only because I was afraid to be alone that night. You know I needed comforting.'

'Huh! Of course you were upset – you only learned of your father's death that morning. But listen to me, Delphine, you were passionate, wild even, and you soon lost any inhibitions. I showed you how beautiful and intense physical love could be between two women, and you were eager to learn. There was not one thing you resisted or were reluctant to try. Oh, you were close to hysteria, I grant you that, but that night with me you showed your true nature, the side of you that you'd repressed for such a long time.'

'It was an aberration! I don't regret it and I thought it would help at the time. I was hurting so much that I needed to reach out for help from someone – *anyone*! – and you were there.'

Delphine's eyes sparkled with tears that, as yet, were unshed.

She went on, 'Rachael, why can't you accept it was for one night only, when I was at my weakest, and so very lonely? For the first time in my life I was truly on my own.' The first tear trickled down the light tan of her cheek. Delphine straightened, tried to get a grip on herself. 'It – it wasn't the beginning of an affair for us. There *is* no us! Surely you must understand I'm not interested in you that way. Surely you've noticed I've avoided being alone with you ever since.'

'Or kept your distance from me because you were in denial.' Krantz's voice was cold.

Delphine was becoming angry, despite the tears that now streaked her cheeks. 'I felt ashamed of what happened that night, that's why I've kept my distance. It's been difficult because of working together, but you must have realized the same thing would never happen again.'

'You could have talked to me. I could have helped you recognize your self-abnegation.'

Delphine's words were sharp, as if there were no reasoning with Rachael, and that she, herself, had to be uncompromising. 'Whatever you say, especially about that first – and *last* – night together, it doesn't make me a lesbian. It's *not* for me.'

Rachael was growing angry. 'You can't just dismiss—'

'I *can* dismiss it,' Delphine cut in brusquely. 'I *am* dismissing it. I still regard you as a friend and colleague, someone I can talk to about our work, but nothing more than that.' For a

119

moment she regretted hurting the nurse who had been so kind to her in the past, and she lowered her voice. 'I still want you as a friend, Rachael,' she insisted.

It was a mistake, for Rachael closed the short gap between them and took Delphine back into her arms. When the smaller woman didn't resist, Rachael squeezed her tightly and kissed her hard on the lips.

Delphine broke away, furious now, no longer defensive. 'I told you, it can't be like that ever again.'

'You don't mean it. You just let me kiss you.'

'No, you forced it. Please leave, Rachael. Let's both just get on with our lives with no complications and no false expectations.' She looked up into the other woman's eyes, hoping the hardness of her own stare would help enforce the message. 'Rachael, I don't want you.' The words were measured, deliberately controlled, and she didn't let her gaze drop away.

The senior nurse remained silent, although Delphine could sense the turmoil, the resentment, and, finally, the disappointment reeling through Rachael's emotions.

Too many moments went by before Rachael, instead of sinking into herself as Delphine imagined she might, suddenly squared her broad shoulders and glacial hatred replaced the hope and confusion in her expression.

She turned and walked to the door, opened it, and took one last look at the psychologist. 'This is a bad place to be without friends, Delphine,' she murmured quietly, and that steady quietness of voice made her words sound all the more chilling. 'More goes on here at Comraich than you realize. And one of these days – possibly not before too long – you may find yourself in need of a good friend. I'm not sure I'll be there for you any more.'

With that, the senior nurse left the room, closing the door almost silently behind her.

Delphine shivered. As a psychologist, she would rather Rachael had slammed it shut.

18

The quaint little heather-thatched cottage was not quite hidden in the deeper woods of Comraich, but it was purposely hard to find. Its lime-washed walls and wallhead chimney were in need of some repair, but generally the small house was in good shape. A dormer window overlooked the flower-bordered path that led up to the stable-style front door.

The cottage had been tenanted by generations of chief groundsmen, custodians who saw to it that all was well in the woodlands, lake and glen on the grand estate belonging to the *caisteal* now known as Comraich.

But for the past thirty-odd years, a different kind of professional had occupied the place. Cedric Twigg was no groundsman or park warden, even though he loved to be in his rural retreat where he found quiet solace (apart from the twittering of birds or the rustle of leaves as an animal or two foraged in the undergrowth), and genuine tranquillity. For this was the strange dichotomy of Twigg's character: he loved nature and the animals that dwelt in his own little woodland kingdom, yet he despised people and their pathetic and selfish ways.

He'd debriefed earlier that day and Haelstrom appeared satisfied with his work. On returning to the cottage, Twigg had first dismantled the phoney umbrella, removing the now empty compressed-gas cylinder, then the injector tip that had contained the ricin poison, putting the separate parts into a wooden box which he'd hidden under the cottage's loft insulation. After that he'd changed his clothes, shedding the rumpled grey suit, the white shirt and dull tie, the shabby raincoat – all city camouflage – and donned his gardening gear: loose brown cords, wellington boots and a green collarless granddad shirt, sleeves rolled up to the elbows. Tending his garden was a comforting release from the pressures of his true occupation. Even though his missions were infrequent, each one necessitated days, weeks, sometimes *months* of planning, travelling and waiting before the final execution. Assassination was a highly skilled, highly paid profession that required steady nerves and patience. And, of course, a complete lack of compassion for the target.

Now, pulling off the thick gardening gloves that protected his dainty but surprisingly strong hands, he stood on the stone doorstep of the cottage and surveyed his tiny plot with some satisfaction. The mist that had earlier seeped through the trees to curl around the clearing hadn't been heavy enough to hinder his labours in the garden. At present it was slowly dispersing, as if the journey from the sea had finally sapped its force.

So far that morning he'd replaced the fading summer bedding with winter pansies and wallflowers, cleared the fallen leaves that had accumulated in his absence, cut down flower stems, pulled weeds, then put all the detritus into two large black plastic bags for burning later. He planned to spend the rest of the day picking off any rose leaves disfigured by black spot, checking tree ties before the autumn gales arrived and planting the new shrubs he had brought back with him. There was plenty more to do before the autumn's chill set in, but it could wait till after he'd eaten his lunch: cheese sandwich and tomato soup.

Twigg always regretted the time spent away from his countryside idyll these days, shadowing the mark through city and urban streets, noting their habits, their routines, their schedules, and time-keeping. It had become a bore over the years, and even the kill was losing its pleasure – the moment of dispatch less thrilling, the adrenaline rush not as keen, the flatness afterwards lasting longer and longer. And on top of that, he had an idiot trainee deputy to contend with. Eddy Nelson, his so-called 'apprentice', was a quick learner and had plenty of muscle (although that wasn't always necessary for the job), but he was thick, stupid, brainless – too brainless, in fact, to realize how brainless he was. Oh, he had the attitude, the physical quickness and the stamina all right, but he also had an alarming propensity to fuck things up every so often.

The death of Dr David Kelly was a case in point.

In 2003, the reputable weapons scientist and microbiologist had let slip to a journalist that Tony Blair's government had exaggerated, perhaps even lied about, Iraq's capability to attack Britain with weapons of mass destruction that could be activated within forty-five minutes.

On the day that Dr Kelly 'committed suicide', Twigg was out of the country on another and entirely different mission, so was unable to carry out the assignment himself. Catastrophically, the Inner Court gave Nelson the job instead.

Knowing that the scientist took regular afternoon strolls to the woods on Harrowdown Hill, near his Oxfordshire home, Nelson had hidden himself among the trees and waited for the mark to come to him. All he had to do was rush up behind the man and snap his neck in one swift but deadly movement. It was an efficient technique favoured by many in the same trade as Twigg and Nelson, but it required force and skill.

As a freakish if inexplicable accident, with no clear evidence of foul play, it would have been swept under the carpet and forgotten in a few months, but Nelson, instead of leaving the body where it lay, had decided to be smart and make the death look like suicide.

Foolishly, stupidly, the apprentice assassin had found a small garden knife in the scientist's own coat pocket and used it to slash the still-warm corpse's left wrist. Then – *then* – he'd discovered a packet of co-proxamol tablets in another pocket and had attempted to force them down the dead man's throat.

Finally, Nelson had, for some peculiar reason of his own,

dragged the body to a nearby tree and left it there, half-slumped against the trunk.

Suddenly, the sun brightened the landscape, though it was unable to lift Twigg's mood, for the trembling in his hands had begun again. He dropped the garden gloves on the doorstep and retreated into his sanctum, closing both halves of the door behind him. The legs of the chair screeched against the tiled floor of the tiny cottage's kitchen-cum-sitting room as he pulled it out from the old wooden table (so small was the cottage, sitting room, kitchen and scullery were all one).

He sat and laid his hands on the tabletop, palms downwards as if, with enough pressure on the hard surface, the trembling would stop. It was a forlorn hope though: his hands had a will of their own. The doctor he'd consulted had explained to him that the debility would only grow worse over the coming months and that there was little he could do to slow the disease's progress. Naturally, he would refer Twigg to a specialist, but the prognosis was bleak, the outcome inevitable. Well, Twigg had asked for a frank assessment and that was precisely what he'd got.

Sunlight ventured into the gloom, dust mites carousing in its shafts.

Realizing his head was bowed as if already in obeisance to his illness, Twigg straightened and stifled a groan of despair.

His days as an executioner would soon be over – of that there was no doubt. But he'd planned his own unforgettable swansong.

And now, despite the telltale tremors that would soon be noticed by others, he managed a quiet, bitter smile. What he had in mind would shock the world.

19

Ash sat as if transfixed, mesmerized by the strangely apocalyptic vision before him.

Because of the heavy mist that swept in from the sea, the lower walls of Comraich Castle were invisible, making the building appear rootless, as if its great darkened bulk floated in the air, unattached, like some mythical citadel that defied both natural physics and human logic. Dread seeped through him like cold black oil.

Next to him in the Mercedes, the Scottish chauffeur became concerned. The medium he'd brought to Comraich some weeks back had reacted similarly. Moira Glennon had drawn in a long gasp and her body had gone rigid. It had been dusk then, and although there had been no mist, there had been a Delphic, somehow unearthly, gloom about the place.

When he'd collected her from her Glasgow home he'd found the plump little woman disappointingly normal, with a ruddy complexion and thread-veined cheeks that suggested she'd spent long periods on the moors and beside the lochs. All such ruddiness had drained from her face when she'd finally stared through the windscreen at the dimly lit building across the broad courtyard. But it was her poor bulging eyes that had really caught his attention, for their whites had gone pink and her pupils had become so enlarged their blackness had made thin bands of the irises around them. Even in the dull light he'd seen them, and it was this that had made him reach to steady her.

Then something completely weird had happened.

The woman's body had begun to emit a coldness so intense that all the windows *frosted* inside. He'd jumped when the automatic air conditioning suddenly blasted warm air into the car. Warm air that had inexplicably turned to arctic chill.

Dalzell had quickly switched the system off so that its noise – and its added iciness – was one thing less to worry him. Then came the smell. He'd often heard of the smell of fear, but this was not the stench of loosened bowels: it was from the sweat that, despite the cold, poured from the medium's armpits and her neck, from her wrists and her lap; the light cotton of the dress she wore under her open topcoat had darkened between her ample breasts and her thighs; fluids had erupted from her skin, her forehead first, then her upper lip, and yellow mucus drained from her nostrils, to be frozen there like crusted cheese. Her cheeks had become wet with the sweat oozing through her pores, trickling down onto her double chin. He'd called her name, his own face close to hers, but there was no reaction. The woman had lost all sensibility and had merely gaped at the castle with eyes that had seemed to have frosted over so that the pupils were just faint blurs behind the whiteness.

Dalzell shuddered, thinking that Ash was about to give a repeat performance, but he was relieved to find that the investigator's reaction to Comraich was far less extreme than the medium's. Certainly, his body was rigid, and the pallor of his skin was troubling, but while obviously disturbed, Ash had maintained his composure. Perhaps, the chauffeur mused to himself, the investigator had seen things like this before.

Ash watched perturbed as the mist around them began to thin so that the castle's lower floors were slowly unveiled. The investigator sensed the queer malevolence that bled from Comraich, a corruptive leaking that, it seemed to him, sought sustenance from the observer's soul, as it had used other poor souls through the centuries. At that moment he knew that his own spirit was in danger.

The fear weighed heavily on Ash. His clawed fingers clamped tightly on his thighs as he fought mentally against the almost overwhelming force emanating from that nightmare place across the courtyard. It felt like a losing battle, though: he could feel himself being drawn towards the abyss, into the sort of black mire from where a person seldom returned sane.

It was Dalzell who brought such intense thoughts to a halt. 'Mr Ash?'

Again, with more emphasis: '*Mr Ash?*'

Ash blinked, suddenly aware that his eyes were completely dry.

'Are y'all right, sir?'

The investigator drew in a sharp breath and slouched back in his seat. He forced his eyes away from the castle, the lower floors of which were emerging like a photographic print in developing liquid.

'Yeah,' he answered weakly. Then, 'Yes . . .' this time more affirmatively. 'I'm okay.' He flexed his neck and shoulders as if to relieve stiffness.

'I thought for a moment there you'd gone . . .' Dalzell paused, then said, 'Y'know, like the other one.'

Still twisting his neck, eyes closed, Ash asked, 'What other one?'

Beyond the windscreen, the low mist was stirred onwards in untidy straggles by a stiffer breeze from the sea.

'The medium they sent for,' Dalzell told Ash, all the while staring hard into the investigator's pallid face. 'Moira Glennon, a well-thought-of but very private psychic from Glasgow. Apparently her services were only for the chosen few. I had the job to bring her here when the weird occurrences started in the castle. They were fair getting out of control and naebody here knew what to do about—'

Ash raised a shaky hand to cut him off. 'I guess, then, she didn't succeed,' he said. Usually dismissive of mediums, clairvoyants, or spiritualists in general, whatever they deigned to brand themselves, but even fake or self-deluded, experience had shown him that there *were* genuine psychics in the field of the paranormal. Yet cynicism was in his nature, and preternatural ability had to be proved to him beyond doubt (as it had in the past) before he would accept the anomalous.

Dalzell found it difficult to answer Ash's direct question. 'Succeed? Well, the poor woman didnae solve the problem, if that's what y'd be meaning. Would that she'd had the chance.'

Ash frowned. 'What does *that* mean?' he asked, curiosity trumping professionalism.

'I'm nae allowed to speak of it.'

Ash looked at him inquisitively. 'So be it,' he said finally, almost in a murmur.

He returned his attention to the castle and the sight caused him to shudder. The drifting mist almost gone, Comraich loomed forbiddingly. There wasn't anything psychic about Ash's appraisal: structurally, there appeared to be nothing sinister about the place, the fresh light now enhancing the warmth of its sandstone walls. And yet . . .

In the periphery of his vision, he could sense Dalzell's intense gaze on him.

Ash could hold his questions back no longer. 'Look, forget the rules. Forget what I said on the way here. No more runaround like the scenic route we've just taken. Whatever you say, it won't scare me off – I've already come this far. Tell me what happened,' he demanded.

Dalzell sighed and looked straight ahead, his troubled thoughts evident.

'She died, Mr Ash.'

Ash blinked. 'Died? How?'

'She died when she saw Comraich. Sitting exactly where you're sitting now.'

As he stared at the chauffeur, the sun finally broke through the thick blanket of cloud, but Ash felt no warmth from it whatsoever.

20

The sun had finally won its right to the day helped by high winds shifting and breaking up the thick cloud layers, scattering them towards the north, leaving the south-western coast of Scotland to enjoy the fine autumn burn.

It changed the face of Caisteal Comraich considerably.

Eddy Nelson had driven into the estate by another, even more secret access, two miles beyond the castle's main entrance. It was a narrow, winding road that led to private garages some distance from the castle itself. He left his red Ford, slamming the door shut but not bothering to lock it. In fact, he left the keys in the ignition; car theft was unlikely at Comraich.

A sour expression on his face, he followed the barely visible track through the woods leading to Cedric Twigg's tucked-away cottage somewhere near the woodland's centre. He was annoyed because, unlike Twigg, for whom he'd acted as look-out at the rear of the huge BBC World Service offices near the Strand, Eddy had had to make his own way back to Scotland. So while Eddy had endured the hell of getting to Heathrow itself – then queuing for a ticket, being herded onto the always busy early-morning flight to Glasgow, bumping elbows in economy with business types opening their *Financial Times* to full extent – his mentor had journeyed from London City Airport in first-class luxury.

The novice assassin trudged through the woods, resenting even the stray leafy twig that had the temerity to block his way, stamping down on it with his high-priced shoes, cursing under his breath as his fashionable and very expensive foot-wear became covered in mud and dew. His general attire was not exactly suitable for countryside rambling, but he wanted his debrief with Twigg to be over before contemplating lunch, so he hadn't bothered to change. On his visits here he usually wore strong desert boots, olive green chinos, and a thick crewneck pullover; today he was wearing a dark blue Hugo Boss suit and a white deep-collar William Hunt shirt with matching tie. Eddy enjoyed looking smart – what else would he spend his money on? – even though Twigg had chided him several times, pointing out that stylish young men would always be noticed, and not only by women, whereas shabby men were generally ignored. *Well, fuck you*, the mean little voice in Eddy's head said.

If anyone was going to look distinctive in a crowd, it would be the sad, beady-eyed little bald man who looked like the guy from the *Halloween* movies.

Eddy sniggered to himself: what a joyless creep Cedric Twigg was. And what a pitifully hilarious name! But that reminded him of his own stupid name.

He mashed a funny-looking creature with two hundred or so legs into the muddy track just for its insolence in crossing his path.

Eddy Nelson! Christ, if people knew his proper moniker they'd laugh themselves sick. His unmarried mother's surname was Eddy, and *her* mother, his granny, wanted him named after some old wrinkly crooner or bandleader or something who went by the name of Nelson Eddy. Fucking *Nelson*, for God's sake! It wasn't as if many people these days had ever heard of him; certainly no one of *his* generation had. He could still see the batty old woman chucking him under the chin, laughing like a loon as she repeated his name over and over again. *Nelson fucking Eddy!* No wonder he changed his name by deed poll to the slightly less ridiculous Eddy Nelson the day he turned sixteen.

Something moving in the undergrowth on one side of the track caught his attention. Something ginger.

'Fuck off!' he shouted towards it, and suddenly the animal was gone, with only twitching foliage to show it had ever been there. Eddy unplugged the iPod he'd been listening to by yanking the tiny earphone from his ear and pushing the wire down into his breast pocket. There had been talk in the castle about nasty creatures roaming the woods these days and, although the thought of confronting one didn't bother him, it might be better to concentrate on the path ahead rather than Bono and U-fucking-2.

Distracted for only a short while, he returned to thoughts of his rotten upbringing. Old demented Granny Eddy had been shipped off to Nutterland when Nelson was five years old, and soon after it was deemed by concerned social workers that his semi-imbecilic single mother couldn't be trusted to bring up her son properly. He was institutionalized from then on. All he remembered of his fat slut of a mother was her picking him up and handing him over to the woman who came to collect him with a sneery smile that said she was glad to be rid of him. She certainly wasn't crying, and neither was he. He'd just been glad to be away from her and in a place where he was regularly fed and there were toys to play with.

Nevertheless, relieved as he was, the damage to his personality had already been done. Other kids didn't like him, and he didn't like anyone. Every few months he was in a different home for abused or orphaned children. Finally, he arrived in a place that was quite different from all the others: discipline and chastisement were the order of the day, but there was something else going on there; it was almost as if the people in charge were monitoring him to see how far he would go. Young Nelson was a stocky boy and very strong for his age, and he not only enjoyed cruelty for pleasure, but took an almost scientific interest in how much pain he could inflict on a creature before death intervened.

The thing of it was, Nelson liked to kill things: insects,

small animals and birds, especially the sparrows and robins he managed to capture by enticing them with breadcrumbs. The smaller and the more fragile the bird the better: he would reach for the panicking prey and hold it aloft tightly in his fist. Then he'd slowly crush it to death, listening delightedly at its feeble cheeps of distress and the crack of tiny bones. Another treat for him was to catch a horsefly, pull off its wings and then detach one thread-like leg at a time until all that left was a minuscule and immobile but still living organism that could be placed near the centre of a spider's web. He would wait patiently, a Sherlock Holmes magnifying glass stolen from the biology room in one hand, the other giving a little flick to a silky strand of the web, setting off a vibration that would awaken the spider for its afternoon tea. He enjoyed the kill because it always gave him a sexual thrill and a spattered milky release, the most glorious feeling he'd ever known, even though he was not much more than a child.

The boy's instinct had been right; his progress was indeed being monitored. At sixteen years of age, the newly named Eddy Nelson was removed from this singularly idiosyncratic orphanage to a secret manor house hidden in the enormity of its own acreage, where an entirely different and harshly disciplined atmosphere reigned. He wasn't a great asset as far as training was concerned, but as he grew yet bigger and stronger, he was finally chosen from a poor crop of others for special purposes, because he had the one 'quality' that the Inner Court valued above all else in the profession set out for this obsessively inhumane young man.

Eddy Nelson was psychotic.

Twigg's cottage couldn't be very far now. The trouble with these bloody thick woods – a forest, really – was that it was so easy to get lost in it. His so-called 'mentor' (how the thought of being an apprentice to someone who looked just about ready to draw his pension stuck in Eddy's craw) had taught him many things about the assassin's trade: the ploys and ruses, the stratagems that gave the mark a false sense of security, following without being noticed, surveillance techniques, signs that meant aborting the mission, and many other ways to carry out assignments and avoid the problems that invariably cropped up from time to time.

He knew Twigg didn't like him – a feeling that was mutual – but Eddy was eager to learn the tricks of the trade. He was also receptive to the methods of killing: sniper's rifle, cheese wire, stabbing, drowning, poison, hit-and-run, shooting, strangulation, a quick shove off a platform into the path of an oncoming train. Hanging corpses in hotel wardrobes, hinting at sexual masochism, always amused him. He'd been taught about concealed cameras, lock-picking, industrial sabotage, bugging devices, moles and sleepers. There was a lot more that Eddy had to learn, but the lessons were usually interesting, if not always a bundle of fun.

The only sour note for Eddy was Twigg's mean-spirited tutelage. It seemed he could do nothing right for the older man and, for fuck's sake, Twigg had never forgiven him for the scrappy job Eddy had done on the Kelly assignment a few years ago. The old man refused to discuss it, but Eddy knew the veteran assassin still fumed about the bungled affair.

Anyway, what about Twigg's own fuck-up before Eddy was even born? The IC had helped out a senior Liberal politician called Jeremy Thorpe, who claimed he was being blackmailed by a younger man with whom Thorpe had had a homosexual affair (both a serious offence and a career killer in those days). The alleged blackmailer was a reclusive male model by the name of Norman Scott. The Inner Court arranged for someone to drive Scott onto the moors one day, where Twigg was waiting armed with a gun. Scott's dog had got yappy, so Twigg shot it in the head. Unfortunately for several people, but not for Scott, when the would-be assassin had aimed the firearm at the male model, the fucking gun had jammed, and there was nothing Twigg could do about the bullet stuck in the chamber, so he'd run off to his waiting car.

The trial in 1979 must have been one of the biggest farces in British legal history, and Thorpe, with three other cohorts, was cleared of any conspiracy to murder, and walked free – 'Scott free', said the headline writers – after the IC used its influence.

Of course, Cedric Twigg's name had gone unmentioned, as had his presence at the crime scene. But Twigg's blunder had become the stuff of legend among assassins the world over, and it had taken many more successful missions for him to regain respect. For Eddy, it was one of the first stories he'd heard when he was brought to Comraich years afterwards, but it was always told in sly whispers and never in front of Twigg. So even the mighty Cedric Twigg had disgraced himself at least once, the loony fuckwit! Eddy sniggered again as he tramped through the woods. He was determined to bring it up in Twigg's presence sometime, but not just yet. The bald-headed man was too scary for that at the moment. But the day would come – Eddy had already noticed Twigg was a bit shaky – and what a fucking glorious day that would be!

Neither the twittering birds in the trees, nor the dappled sunlight on the woodland floor, helped to raise Nelson's mood though. A squirrel, a *red* squirrel – not rare in these parts – shot up a tree trunk nearby and disappeared among the branches; from somewhere not far away came the soft sound of a muffled drill, which was in fact, the repetitive rapping of a woodpecker on tree bark. There was life all around the apprentice assassin, but his sullen state of mind allowed no joy in his awareness of it.

He plodded onwards, aware the cottage was not too far ahead by now. God, if he could live there on his own instead of the room he had at the barracks, the women Eddy would have for overnight stays. Mind you, he'd been through a good number of female staff already, but the psychologist, *oh*, the fucking sultry psychologist, she was his wildest wet-dream, with her tanned Latin looks and trim little figure. She was well fit! Unfortunately, she was also out of his league for now. But if *he* took over from Twigg, then maybe he'd be in with a chance.

Don't kid yourself, the sour little voice in the back of his brain sneered. *You know you're not good enough to suck her toes.* He gritted his teeth, angry at this little voice he knew was his very own.

Anyway, there was something going on between Wyatt and Senior Nurse Rachael Krantz. They hid it well, but he wasn't alone in being suspicious . . .

The younger nurses whispered that Krantz was a dyke who had special feelings towards the young, glamorous psychologist, and that didn't surprise Eddy at all. Mind you, Krantz was fit as well: big boobs, which he liked on a woman, not exactly pretty, but she certainly had something going for her. Great body, even in her white uniform; good legs, nice ankles despite the white brogues she wore, and nice wide hips. Maybe just a little bit too tall. A thought hit him so hard that he almost stopped in his tracks. Now Krantz and Wyatt together! Oh, what a dream! With . . . even his thoughts stumbled . . . with him in the middle!

Yeah, dream on, son.

That fucking voice again!

Eddy Nelson, aged twenty-nine, and apprentice assassin for nearly a decade now, kicked out at some pretty bluish-purple flowers in his path. Crushing them underfoot, then regretting that he'd muddied his shoes even more in the process, he stalked onwards with his temper rising a few more notches.

The welcoming smell of a wood-burning fire was drifting down the trail. *Must be getting close at last*, he thought. He slowed his pace, his footsteps becoming lighter and his breathing shallower and considerably quieter. He'd never yet managed to sneak up on Twigg without giving himself away, but *this* time Eddy had the initiative.

He also had an incentive, one provided by Sir Victor

Haelstrom himself. Just a week or so ago, when Twigg and Eddy were making arrangements for their trip to London, Sir Victor had mentioned privately to the apprentice assassin that he might just keep a watchful eye on Twigg while they were in the capital.

There had been no explanation, not even a direct order; but the message was clear enough. Sir Victor had rarely addressed him personally before. He frowned, then the corners of his mouth twitched. He smiled. Those words, he realized, had for the first time given him some authority.

Almost creeping now, Eddy spied a splash of off-white further on, and the thin curling of smoke obviously from a chimney told him he'd nearly reached the cottage. Although it was October, the apprentice was perspiring just a little, and gave himself the excuse (he was *always* clean) that Hugo Boss material wasn't good for jungle trekking. Neither was his William Hunt shirt.

He crouched as he moved forward, for once wanting to challenge Twigg before the senior assassin spotted him.

The cottage was in a forest clearing, the area around it full of flowers and neatly pruned shrubs. The heather-thatched roof, with its minuscule wall chimney, smoke lazily rising from it, would be considered enchanting by kids, newlyweds and estate agents, but to Eddy it was just a country hovel. He half expected the seven dwarfs to come marching out at any moment, the dopey one – what was his name? – tripping over the doorstep as the others whistled on into the woods. There were plenty of birds about, twittering and fussing, as if to betray his light footsteps.

Scarcely breathing, he crept through freshly turned flower beds as a magpie swooped past his left shoulder and squawked. It flew off, over the roof of the chocolate-box house, while Eddy froze on the spot. Twigg had acute hearing, the apprentice knew that, and Eddy was afraid that the alarmed squawk had given his presence away.

But no, there were no sounds from within, no scraping of a

chair, no footsteps on the hard flagstone floor. Still he waited until he was sure that the bald-headed fucker hadn't been roused. Maybe Twigg was sleeping – it had been a long day for him. Or maybe he was strolling in the woods. Either way, Twigg was too much of an old hand to leave the top half of the front door open.

Well, Eddy told himself, *you can't stand here for the rest of the day*. He thought of calling out casually, as though he expected Twigg to be inside. But then, what would Eddy be doing trampling all over Twigg's flower beds when there was a perfectly sound path of evenly spaced flagstones leading straight up to the front door? And anyway, there seemed to be no sign of activity inside the cottage, so Twigg had to be napping. Cautiously, Eddy ventured on. Could be Twigg was testing him.

When he was near one of the closed windows, the apprentice ducked low, but continued his approach. Stooping even lower, he placed both hands on the window sill and tried a sneaky look through the glass.

He immediately ducked down again, a ploy he'd been taught to save himself a bullet in the head should someone inside be expecting him. That way he instantly had the lie of the land without exposing himself long enough to have his head blown from his shoulders.

Yet he'd almost frozen in full view because of the sight that had greeted him – only rigid training made him drop instinctively. He waited out of sight while the scene beyond the glass played back in his mind.

The interior was gloomy, and even though light streamed in through the open half-door and window, Cedric Twigg was plain enough to see.

Afraid, but no coward, Eddy shifted his position, leaning his left shoulder to scuff against the whitewashed wall, and slowly raised his head again until his eyes were level with the window ledge. Dangerously, he had to raise a hand sideways against the glass pane to see inside more clearly.

Yes, as he'd thought, it was Cedric Twigg sitting there at the scarred old table in profile view. This time Eddy didn't pull away but remained as he was and watched the other man in astonishment.

Twigg was seated at the table, wearing a collarless old shirt with the sleeves rolled up, as if he'd been toiling in the garden. One of his hands was pressed against the table's scratched surface, yet twitching and jumping as if its owner had no power over it. But it was Twigg's other hand that caused Eddy even more consternation.

It was in constant fidget, a strange one at that, because it was as if it were rolling a pill or ball bearing over and over between thumb and first finger, the motion increasing in speed and becoming more jerky, Twigg, it seemed, unable to take his eyes from the movement.

Over and over the thumb and finger went, with the assassin bent over the table, his normally rigid back stooped, his head low as he watched his own shaky fingers move again and again, rolling the minute or *non-existent* object.

That disturbing hand mime refused to be still, even though Twigg stared, his thin lips moving, as if he were *commanding* the fingers to stop.

Eddy slid down below window height and squatted there, the back of his suit smeared with white dust. Never before had he been so afraid of Twigg, and that was because the senior assassin was always in strict command of himself. At this moment he wasn't, and Eddy didn't want to witness any more. Especially, he didn't want to be in the same room as the man whose eyes now bulged with craziness.

Yet sometimes fear has its own fascination.

Although scared – *hell, fucking terrified!* – Eddy just *had* to take one more peek through that wood-framed window. Almost robotically, he dug the muddy heels of his Shipton & Heneage rustic-grain calf shoes into the dirt and pushed himself haltingly up the flaking wall that dusted the back of his sharp Hugo Boss jacket.

When the back of his head rose above the window sill, he slowly turned to look directly into the room once more . . .

. . . To see Cedric Twigg, perfectly still and straight-backed at the table, his head now turned, those far-gone, crazy bulbous eyes staring directly into Eddy's own. It was the assassin's malign, thin-lipped smile that provoked the high, terrified shriek from Nelson.

The apprentice assassin struggled to his feet, stumbling twice before he made it and, mouth agape, he fled that hideous little thatched-roof cottage in the clearing deep inside the suddenly hushed autumnal woods.

21

The driver's words slowly sank in as Ash gazed at Comraich Castle. It felt as though the centuries-old fortress were revealing the towering menace of its full grandeur specifically to him – maybe as a warning after what had happened to the medium. The grey mists that had swirled around the substructure only moments before (or so it seemed), making the building appear rootless, distanced from the earth itself, had roamed onwards, thinning and dispersing as they went. The now almost-blue sky outlined the castle's ramparts and towers as if they marked the edge of the world.

The ghost hunter hadn't expected a display of this magnitude and of such proportionate design, even though it was obvious that it had gone through much renovation work and additions throughout the years.

The castle spread out before him, its high solid sandstone walls, with their crenel and merlon battlements ending in round towers, was a magnificent sight. Two more towers rose even higher in the middle section of the edifice, both projecting from the main structure itself. He expected to find arrow loops in the walls, simple vertical slits through which arrows and later, guns, could be fired in defence, but in their place were many windows of differing sizes, some tall, some low, indicating that this was no longer the age of arrows and muskets, and certainly not spears. To the right of the old building was a defensive, crenellated walkway leading to much smaller buildings and a battery of cannons, all pointing seawards. Comraich itself was too wide to see what lay beyond the far side.

Ash was impressed. The sun had made its presence known and the lower mists around the castle had faded to gossamer – but there was something inaccessible, intangible about how it made him feel. He was mesmerized.

The big arched wooden doors centred in the facade directly across the vast courtyard suddenly opened and two figures emerged to descend the short flight of steps; they strolled casually towards what Ash presumed were the castle's walled gardens.

Ash had been aware that while he studied the castle, Dalzell had been casting surreptitious looks his way as though waiting for a reaction.

'Are you okay, Mr Ash?'

Ash was surprised. 'I'm fine, although I must admit, I'm still a bit shaken by the sudden death of the medium – what was her name, Moira Glennon?'

'Aye.'

'But the sunlight makes a difference to Comraich.'

'Um, Mr Ash, we've been sitting here between ten and fifteen minutes, y'ken?'

'What?' The investigator glanced down at his wristwatch. 'That's not possible.'

''Fraid so, sir. Y'were certainly engrossed in the place. I didnae like to disturb you.' *And I didnae want to describe the circumstances of her death*, Dalzell thought. *Someone else can tell him.*

Ash let out a breath of mild exasperation. 'Sorry,' he said to Dalzell.

'Nae need. It's a wondrous vision at the right time of day and with the right kind of weather.'

You got that right, thought Ash, still stunned by his first sighting of the castle. 'Maybe you should have brought Moira Glennon along when the sun was out.' He saw Dalzell wince.

The driver's voice was serious. 'What's it to be, Mr Ash?' he asked intently, as if there were an option.

It took Ash a second or two to register the question. 'What d'you mean?'

'D'you want me to drive in? Or d'you want me to take y'straight back to the airport?'

Ash had recovered his wits by then. 'Now why in the hell would I want you to do that?'

Dalzell let out a long sigh, as though he were already having regrets.

'Right y'are,' he said and the Mercedes began to glide forward.

While Ash had been studying the castle, the car had been parked just under the arch leading into the broad courtyard, and he guessed that this had once been the main entrance – the gatehouse – to the whole castle area. Across the courtyard, more people were descending the steps and sauntering off in different directions, as if taking advantage of the late sunshine for a leisurely stroll. Most were casually well-dressed, and he wondered if they were castle residents or staff. He put the question to Dalzell as the driver guided the big car slowly around the courtyard to approach the broad steps side-on.

'Both,' came the answer, 'although most are guests. They tend to enjoy a wee bit of exercise before lunch.'

Ash eyed two people as they drove by. The pair seemed as curious about Ash as he was of them. The man was tall, hands clasped behind the back of his navy blue blazer. He wore a bold red-striped tie over a pale blue shirt, and beneath the blazer was a pair of sharply pressed grey slacks that creased where the hem met the brown suede loafers; the woman had on a sleek, fawn, unbuttoned overcoat over a grey silk pleated skirt and blouse. Both looked to be around sixty to sixty-five years old, and Ash guessed that they were a wealthy and healthy couple, perhaps retired and perhaps married.

What they thought of him, he'd no idea, but neither one

acknowledged the nod of his head in greeting. The car passed on while they stared at Ash.

'Do they all live in Comraich?' he asked the driver discreetly, as if they could hear him.

'Aye, the seriously rich ones do. Our head people occupy the classier rooms and suites mostly in the upper floors of the castle. There are also modern apartments and suites built on the side of Comraich, which y'havenae been able to see yet. The barracks are a short distance from the castle.'

'Barracks?'

'Aye, but dinnae let that put you off. It's just what we call the complex for guards, rangers and employees, including the intern doctors. Oh, and that includes our resident dentist.'

'Christ,' Ash said, almost in awe, 'it's a little self-contained kingdom.'

'It's that, all right. But the problems are inside the castle itself.'

That quickly brought the investigator back to his assignment there.

They had neared the steps to the huge, arched oak doors of Comraich Castle when a blonde, mussy-haired girl tripped down the steps arm in arm with a youth about her own age who resembled her so much that he could be no one other than her twin brother. Petra Pendine now wore a long dark loose-knit cardigan with a ruffled collar over a white sweater, the hem of the cardigan just reaching the top of the knees of her deep indigo leggings. Bulky tan Ugg boots paid mind to the air's chilly crispness. The boy – wasn't he called Peter? – wore a comfortable-looking rigger jacket over loose, casual jeans and similar to his sister's, brown laceless Ugg boots. His head was covered by a striped knitted beanie and around his neck he wore a ragged, sizeable olive-and-black patterned desert scarf.

Petra's presence surprised Ash, for he thought she would still be sleeping off the injection Delphine Wyatt had given her on the jet; he could only conclude that habitual class-A usage had made her somewhat resistant to prescription drugs. Or maybe the excitement of reuniting with her twin brother had set the adrenaline rushing once more and the crashout was yet to come.

She spied Ash in the Mercedes and elatedly pointed him out to her brother, before running forward and pressing her face to the passenger window like a juvenile fan who had just set eyes on her idol. Ash cringed in his seat and put up a hand to hide half his face, as if that would help the situation.

'Peter, Peter,' Petra cried, 'come and meet him, he's the hero that kept us calm when the plane took a dive!'

He could hardly claim that, and he slid the passenger window down a couple of inches so she could hear as he tried to explain he'd done nothing so courageous. Obviously, she'd forgotten her dire warning to him; or maybe she hadn't even been conscious of it.

'Oh yes you did!' Petra cried. 'I want you to meet my brother, please come and say hello!'

Petra yanked open the door, then grabbed at him and tried to pull him from the car. Ash realized the only thing to do was to unsnap his seatbelt before an awkward scene developed.

Reluctantly, the investigator got out and tried to extricate himself from the arms she'd thrown enthusiastically around his neck. Whatever she was on now, he thought to himself, it wasn't lorazepam. He got a clue when her brother shoved an asthma inhaler into his nostril and pressed down the plastic lever twice. Then Petra grabbed the small blue device, blatantly spraying its white powdery contents into both nostrils. Jesus, Delphine was going to have problems with this pair.

Peter came forward – lurched forward might have been a more accurate depiction – to shake Ash's hand. His wide smile revealed brilliantly white teeth, but there was a reserve in his perfectly blue eyes – matched in colour with his sister's – that long ago Ash had come to recognize as suspicion or dislike.

'It's been nice,' the young man said curtly as he grabbed his twin's elbow and began to extract her from Ash.

She let go of the investigator quite easily, although she gave her brother a sulky look. But both sets of blue eyes remained coke-wide and overexcited.

'Let's forget about the walk: I can show you round later. I've got something for you in my room,' Peter stage-whispered, and instantly Petra perked up even more.

'What about lunch?' she whined as an afterthought.

'Let's call it an appetizer,' he responded in a softer whisper that Ash only just caught.

What the hell is going on in this place? he wondered. Dr Wyatt's small case of ready-filled syrettes had already provided evidence that Comraich was lenient with regard to certain drugs, and he wondered if this was part of the regime, allowing rich folk to indulge in whatever they felt they needed. It was none of his business, of course, but he intended to confront Delphine with the suggestion sometime when they were alone.

The car was parked so near the castle's stone steps that there was no point in climbing back inside the Mercedes. Dalzell opened the rear door and brought out the investigator's leather shoulder bag. He also donned his smart charcoal-grey chauffeur's cap, which apparently had been out of sight behind the driver's seat while they were travelling.

'I'll see y'inside, Mr Ash,' he said with his customary grin, 'then y'll be looked after by the boss, I think.'

Ash fished inside his jacket to find his wallet, intending to give Dalzell a twenty-pound note.

Seeing his intention, the driver raised a hand to ward off the gratuity. 'Not necessary, sir,' he said, but obviously grateful for the gesture. 'All part of the service.'

'Just a drink on me?'

'Nae. I enjoyed y'company.' Something or someone caught his eye. 'Oh, I see the big guns are already out t'greet you.'

Ash turned back to the castle steps and once more was surprised at what he saw.

22

A man – so big in bulk that his descent of the steps should have been cumbersome, heavy, even awkward – fairly skipped towards Ash. He barely took a breath when he seized Ash's hand in his own, almost threatening to crush the investigator's fingers in a grip so hard it made Ash wince.

Ash made the excuse of looping his travel bag over a shoulder, the strap across his chest, before his hand was crushed permanently.

'Good to see you, Mr Ash. Excellent to see you.' Before Ash could reply, the big man, who was three inches taller than him, was introducing himself.

'I'm Sir Victor Haelstrom, as you may have assumed, and the CEO of Comraich Castle.'

'I expected nothing less than a laird,' Ash returned with a smile. 'Does that mean you're also the Chief Executive Officer of the Inner Court?'

Haelstrom looked at him curiously. 'What do you know about the Inner Court?'

Ash was unfazed by the other man's sudden sharpness of tone. 'Well, I understand the IC owns Comraich.'

'The castle is owned by a consortium of Inner Court members, yes. But it's run independently, like any other sanitarium or health spa, and I'm the man who runs it, no more than that. Does that satisfy your concern?'

Ash shrugged non-committally. 'Guess so,' he answered.

The big man's robust manner returned immediately, a character trait Ash was to become familiar with.

'Did you enjoy your journey here? I'm meaning the drive from Prestwick, not your uncomfortable few moments in the air. We were shocked when we heard of the Gulfstream's technical problem, and I do hope your nerves are at least a little more settled. It's a lovely drive; very calming. Did you have the chance of tasting a glass or two of Scotland's famous whiskies on the way?'

'Uh, no,' Ash told him. 'I wasn't in the mood for a drink, believe it or not.'

Haelstrom eyed him for a second or two, and Ash had no idea what he was thinking. But he saw the big man quickly shift his attention past Ash's left shoulder to the driver. Haelstrom flashed a brief glare of annoyance before his eyes came back to the new arrival.

'Perhaps we can persuade you to sup one of our single malts later. I can assure you our cabinets are well stocked at all times and for all occasions.'

Ash felt churlish for declining, but his mind was already on other things.

The CEO of Comraich was an extraordinary figure, of a kind Ash had certainly not expected. At first, when Haelstrom had appeared descending the steps from the main door, Ash had assumed his vast physique was mainly flab, but he soon realized he was wrong. When the big man stood before him, pumping Ash's hand with such vigour that the investigator almost grimaced, it had given him a moment for a reappraisal. As far as he could tell, there was hardly an ounce of spare flesh on the man.

His title was also curious, for the investigator detected the trace of an accent in his speech that definitely was not of Scottish origin: Norwegian, Germanic, Dutch – it was too slight to tell. So how could he be a knight? Born in the UK, spent years of his youth in another country, returned to Britain and earned himself a gong? Or was it an honorary title – quite common nowadays. Besides, in truth, the accent was barely noticeable; the investigator only caught a brief inflection in certain words.

But what really fascinated Ash was Haelstrom's head.

It was *huge*, the cheeks like two sides of pink ham. And so immense was that head, his reddish hair sprang only from the top, a small copse on a hill of stretched skin and stubble. With no hair on either side, both ears seemed isolated and the tops were curled over, much like an old palooka's, one who'd taken too many punches and lost too many fights. Yet, tall and as thick-bodied though Haelstrom might be, an early career as a pugilist seemed improbable.

Ash found Sir Victor's facial features even more astonishing.

It was as if his thick eyebrows, tiny, inset eyes, and short hooked nose, all above a narrow thick-lipped mouth, were drawn tightly into the centre of an excess of skin, the neck almost a part of the head itself, with no defining chin but for a vague stubbled projection. Haelstrom's expression looked as if it hurt him to smile.

The big man suddenly leaned forward and Ash felt his own head draw back a little. If he expected a change of mood, he was wrong, for Haelstrom spoke enthusiastically. 'I managed to read your book, Mr Ash. Interesting, yes, very interesting. Although I was left with the impression at the end that you personally do not believe in ghosts as such, despite your own experiences.'

'Well, the book was written a long time ago, and since then several things have happened to change my mind.'

'I see.' That great head bowed forward again, as though proximity might encourage openness. 'Then tell me why you've written nothing more on the phenomena.'

'Oh, I have. But usually for specialist journals and organizations involved in the paranormal and the supernatural.'

'Like your own – the Psychical Research Institute?'

'Right.'

'Yet no doubt you could find writing books on the subject very lucrative. Such accounts are very popular with the public, as I'm sure you know.'

'Would you believe I'm not interested in making a lot of money? I do okay with the work I do for the Institute.'

'Yes. Yes, I can honestly believe that. I think you're a very dedicated person and the reports I've had on you seem to bear that out.'

'You've had *me* investigated?'

Haelstrom gave a short laugh. 'But as a reference point, no more than that.'

Ash shrugged. 'That's reasonable.'

Haelstrom took him by the elbow. 'It'll be lunchtime soon, so why don't we find someone to show you your room first so you can freshen up, then you can come to the dining room for some lunch. You can take the tour afterwards: I think you'll find Comraich an intriguing place, with quite a violent past. I'm sure its history will interest you.'

'I thought we could have a private meeting so that you can fill me in on whatever's taken place here. Regarding para-normal events, of course.'

'"Ongoing occurrences" would be more accurate, Mr Ash,' the big man insisted. 'I'm hoping you're the man to bring them to an end.'

His little gimlet eyes bore into Ash's, and the investigator felt an inexplicable shudder run through him. He hoped the other man hadn't noticed. 'I only need a broad outline,' he managed to say.

'Right, Mr Ash, let's get you inside,' Haelstrom said briskly, already heading for the steps. It was a command rather than an invitation.

'Sure. So I call you – Sir Victor?'

Haelstrom gave a quick nod, then led the way into Comraich.

Only when he'd taken the first two steps did Ash catch a glimpse of someone tall and thin, dressed in a grey suit and pale greyish tie, watching them from just inside the large open door. Although thin, the middle button of his jacket seemed under pressure from what could only be described as a pot-belly. By the time Ash himself was inside the giant doors, however, the grey man had disappeared.

Ash and Haelstrom entered the great hall, which the investigator was surprised to find resembled an opulent hotel foyer. There was even a long polished wooden counter, behind which sat two receptionists. One was a young woman dressed, naturally, in a trim charcoal-grey uniform; the blouse she wore beneath the jacket was of black silk. She gave him a warm smile while her partner, a young man of around the same age and wearing a grey suit and black tie, continued to tap a computer keyboard just below the level of the counter.

Ash smiled back at the woman, who was awaiting instructions from Sir Victor.

'Veronica,' Haelstrom all but boomed, the sound resonating around the marble floor and tall pillars that reached the high ceiling, 'this is Mr David Ash. He shall be staying with us for . . .' He faced Ash. 'How long would you say?'

'Three days, three nights,' Ash answered promptly.

Haelstrom was momentarily taken aback. 'Really? So short a time . . . ?'

'That should cover the preliminary investigation, then we'll take it from there.'

Haelstrom hastily looked about him. There were only a few clients standing around in quiet conversation, but they were soon casting inquisitive glances in the new arrival's direction. On a chair between a marble column and the foot of the graceful round staircase leading to a natural gallery above was a uniformed, middle-aged man, whom Ash guessed was a guard of sorts. He was amused to see the man was sitting at attention, presumably because of Haelstrom's presence.

Noticing the interest Ash had stirred, Haelstrom leaned into him yet again, his voice lowered this time. 'Our guests are aware that there's strange activity going on at Comraich, and as a newcomer, you must expect to attract a certain amount of curiosity, but I'd be grateful if you kept your investigations as discreet as possible.'

Ash was bemused by the big man's dismissal of the violent events as 'strange activity'. It was a rather euphemistic assessment of a bad haunting.

Haelstrom returned his attention to the receptionist. 'Leave the departure date blank,' he instructed.

The woman tapped her own out-of-sight keyboard.

'All done, Sir Victor,' she said with the same warm smile she'd given Ash. 'And Mr Ash's room is ready for him.'

'Good. Now page Derriman for me.'

'Uh, shouldn't I sign in or something?' asked Ash.

'We rarely use paperwork here at Comraich,' Haelstrom replied. 'Gerrard here' – he pointed at the male receptionist, whose smile was less genuine than his colleague's – 'already has you entered in our very private system.'

Haelstrom seemed unaware of how furtive he was making the investigation sound; but then, Ash remembered, Comraich was a kind of sanctuary for the wealthy, so ethereal roamings of lost spirits would be almost as dire as hearing the kitchens were infested with cockroaches as far as they were concerned.

A thin, bespectacled man was hurrying towards them.

'So sorry to keep y-you waiting.' His face flushed red as if embarrassed by his own stutter. Angled across his forehead was a large, fresh-looking sticking plaster, and Ash recalled Maseby's account of the man hit by flying furniture when all hell had broken out in the castle's offices.

'Mr Ash,' Haelstrom said, his voice loud once more, 'this is Andrew Derriman, general manager of Comraich. He helps run the establishment, makes it all flow as smoothly as possible.'

Ash shook Derriman's hand, which was soft and light of touch. The physical contact lasted no more than two seconds.

The general manager might have been as tall as Ash himself, had not stooped shoulders knocked a couple of inches off his true height. He peered at the investigator through round, thin-framed bifocals, his pale blue eyes anxious, as if he'd been summoned to answer for some important error of management. At least, that was how Haelstrom treated him.

'Derriman, you should have been at the door with me to greet Mr Ash.'

'I, um, I—' Derriman wiped long, nervous fingers across his thin, silver-grey comb-over.

'Yes, yes, I know,' said the big man curtly, 'other duties kept you busy.'

'W-well, as a-a m-matter of fact . . .'

Ash squirmed inside: he disliked the underdog type Derriman seemed to represent, and *loathed* those who treated others as such.

'Y'know,' he interrupted, 'I need to freshen up, grab a snack, then begin the investigation.'

Haelstrom eyed him coolly and Ash glimpsed another side to the man's character. *Not good*, he thought.

'Show Mr Ash to his room,' Haelstrom instructed, glaring at Derriman. He turned to Ash. 'Our dining room is on the floor above this one. You're on the second floor, so come down as soon as you're ready.'

That last part sounded like an order and it rankled Ash, whose own disposition was anything *but* servile. In fact, Kate McCarrick was probably the only person he'd take an order or reprimand from.

Haelstrom was turning away, heading towards the curved staircase.

'Oh, I'll need architectural drawings of the building, and a brief history of Comraich,' the investigator said, then smiled when Haelstrom wheeled round to face him. The tiny features in the sizeable head drew into themselves again, so that his expression seemed pained. Ash decided there was something unwholesome about Sir Victor Haelstrom, from his sweat-stained shirt collar to his abrupt manner.

'I'll also need a summary of any out-of-the-ordinary activity, although not just yet. Tomorrow morning will do.' Ash had spoken at a natural volume to the big man, but even so, Haelstrom was plainly annoyed.

'Keep it down, will you,' he almost hissed at the parapsychologist. 'I told you to be as discreet as possible. As I said before, our guests are aware that currently all is not well in Comraich, but so far there is only silly gossip and rumours. They don't understand what it all means.'

Ash was taken aback. 'What it means? You're telling – ' he'd caught himself raising his own voice, so lowered it again. 'You're telling me *you* know the reasons for the alleged haunting.'

By now, both men were almost whispering. 'No, no, I'm not even suggesting they have a cause; but then, Comraich does have a history of bloodshed and violence. There are bound to be incorporeal repercussions of some kind. You say as much in your own book, don't you?'

'If I remember correctly, I suggested there could be *normal* causations for apparent *abnormal* events. Seems to me you skimmed through the text and missed out on some relevant points.'

'Unfortunately, I only received a copy a couple of days ago,' said Haelstrom, clearly irritated by the reproof. 'You were a last-minute replacement; we had intended to use someone local.'

'Moira Glennon?'

The big man's eyes narrowed. 'I see you've had a nice long chat with the chauffeur on your way here.' Haelstrom looked down at the floor and gave a single shake of his head. 'We made a bad decision with the medium; we engaged someone who was weak of mind as well as weak of body.' He lifted his head again and stared at Ash almost contritely. 'I saw then that we needed someone with *strength* as well as experience. Someone knowledgeable in this peculiar business, but also someone sceptical enough to give an honest and unequivocal view. I'm sure you'll agree there are many crackpots and charlatans only too ready to take advantage of vulnerable people who've lost all common sense. But I'm informed you're different, that your expertise is second to none. That's why you were chosen, Mr Ash.'

Ash was bewildered by this big, unusual man before him, one moment garrulous and welcoming, the next a bullying tyrant and then practically contrite. Now he was paying Ash compliments.

'Look,' Ash said, 'over the years I've come to realize that the supernatural and the paranormal have validity. *Real* validity. I've experienced things that can only be described as unearthly. And dangerous.'

Haelstrom gave that grimace of a smile again, as though he had a bad headache but was enjoying the torment of it. 'Mr Ash,' he said, 'you and I can discuss this later, after we've given you a proper briefing.'

The investigator wondered who the other part of 'we' was. The mysterious tall thin man watching from the castle's doorway while Haelstrom was greeting Ash? Or were there other 'advisors' he had yet to meet? Then again, the CEO may have merely included Derriman, who hadn't had much to say so far.

'I guess that suits me, Sir Victor. But let me look round first, get a general overview of the building itself. The castle is centuries old and built on top of a promontory with rough seas and caverns below. That can cause all kinds of strange anomalies in the structure of the building above. You can rest assured that I'll do my very best to discover the source of any disturbances that are troubling you – natural or unnatural.'

Haelstrom appeared satisfied with the statement of intent and grimaced at Ash, who took it as a smile.

'Very well, Mr Ash. From here on it's in your capable hands.'

With that Haelstrom wheeled round and made for the stairs again, this time nodding and exchanging short pleasantries with guests as he went.

Derriman touched Ash lightly on the arm. 'Well, Mr Ash, shall I show you to your room?' he asked deferentially.

Ash noticed the apparent change in the thin stooped man now that Haelstrom had left them, but nonetheless, the bespectacled manager remained edgy, his long-fingered hands clasped together as if in appeasement; but the redness had left his face and, for the moment at least, he seemed to have lost his stutter. Was he really that intimidated by his employer?

Ash did his best to put him at his ease. 'Tell you what – you call me David and I'll call you Andrew, if that's okay.'

Derriman managed a courteous smile and immediately became less skittish.

'That would be fine,' he agreed. 'Sir Victor enjoys formality, but sometimes I think it gets in the way of mutual understanding.'

Ash wouldn't have gone as far as that, but it was a sound idea and if it made his investigation go more smoothly, then he was all for it. Together, they began to walk towards the far end of the reception hall. The investigator's boots clattered on the marble flooring and he had to endure the naked stares of apprehension from separate groups of residents.

Derriman spoke as mildly as his manner would suggest. 'Do you know *anything* about Comraich Castle, Mr— sorry, David?'

'Only that it has a curse on it.'

'Ah yes, the legendary castle curse.' Derriman smiled to himself, while sweeping his fingers across his sparse silver-grey hair.

On the way down a cavernous marble hallway, the general manager pointed out early works of art on the walls, paintings and tapestries, as well as statues and busts of long-dead dignitaries displayed on plinths.

Derriman and Ash soon reached a broad lift-door with a sturdy-looking vertical brass handle. 'The lift's at the top of the building,' he told Ash, who had already gathered as much from the old-fashioned floor indicator above the closed door. 'It was put in sometime around the early fifties when the castle was renovated. I'm afraid it's rather slow and clunky.' Derriman stabbed twice at the brass button on the slim metal panel beside the door as if it might make the lift's descent a little quicker.

Biding his time while they waited, Ash took the opportunity to peek through a wide doorless entrance. Curious, he stepped inside. There were similar wide entrances directly opposite each other all along the corridor.

He found himself within a large, high-ceilinged armoury with flagstone flooring and sandstone walls. It had the musty smell of ancient iron. Antique weaponry was mounted on all four walls, arranged in menacing though somehow eye-pleasing symmetry. Old British Army flintlock pistols were displayed in two circles, one set of guns inside the second, while other obsolete weapons were held on wooden mountings. A lattice on the left-hand wall was made up of cut and shaped sword hilts. Full swords hung horizontally over a second entrance to the room, while more sword blades were arranged in criss-cross patterns; a circular arrangement of pistols and swords graced the wall over the fireplace mantle, and miniature polished cannons occupied a space before the incongruously white fireplace itself, its grate filled with rough-hewn logs.

It was all immensely impressive and left Ash open-mouthed in admiration. Then something on the far side of the armoury caught his attention. He was sure he'd seen a slight movement among what must have been the most venerable of the room's weapons: long pikes, iron axes and claymores filled one particular wall, among them halberds and lethal iron maces, longbows and deadly crossbows. While the rest of the chilling collection looked pristine, this last miscellany of weapons was made even more fearsome by being so obviously time-worn, the blades of the claymores and the halberds dark-stained and dented, the crossbows and pikes scratched and scarred.

Ash felt sure that whatever had caught his attention had come from this area of the room. But now everything was still, motionless, just historical icons that had outlasted their use. But then it came again. A sudden vibration, as though

157

something lived among the ancient armoury, perhaps an echo of its violent past.

Then he saw it.

It was the solid iron mace, with its evil-looking spiked, round head. His eyes were drawn to it, although it was now still. He was about to give up, telling himself it had been an illusion, that the mace was firmly mounted on its brackets and what he'd seen was merely a trick of the light. But then it came again. A slight twitching of its length and spiked head. And as he stared, aghast, it twitched once more. Then again, and again, until it was vibrating on its mounting, scratching the wall behind.

It seemed infectious, for the other weapons – the pikes, the halberds, the bows – now were all vibrating so that they made a rattling sound against the stone wall on which they hung. Ash stared, and retreated backwards as if the lethal implements of old wars could fly across the room to impale him.

'Mr Ash. David?'

Derriman stood at his side, his expression a mixture of anxiety and confusion.

Ash looked at him swiftly, then back to the armoury . . . where all was quiet and inert.

'Did you . . . ?' He'd been about to ask the general manager if he'd witnessed what Ash himself had seen. And heard. But the room was now peaceful. Even the weapons had lost their sinister aspect.

'Are you all right, David?' Derriman asked with genuine concern. 'Perhaps the atmosphere of the place has . . .' Has what? The armoury looked perfectly normal to him, despite the nature of its exhibits. Perhaps the parapsychologist sensed what ordinary men and women couldn't. How pale he looked.

'David, you seemed shocked,' Derriman said gently.

Ash groaned inwardly. Cynicism made him wonder if the scene just played out had been deliberately rigged to test his nerve. But no, that would be absurd. Such an elaborate trick would be a waste of time for everyone concerned.

'Sorry, Andrew,' he responded, silently cursing his own paranoia. Haelstrom himself had said the castle had a history of bloodshed and violence. A malign haunting was definitely feasible. 'I've just got a bad feeling about that particular room,' he tried to explain to the anxious general manager as they returned to the lift. 'It happens from time to time.'

'Because you're psychic?'

'Let's just say I've been in the business of ghost hunting for some time. It tends to rub off on you in certain ways.'

'But you saw no apparition?'

'No, none at all. Just a bad feeling.'

With a heavy thud, the old-fashioned elevator arrived and distracted Derriman from asking more questions.

The thin, stooped man, with his long angular body and silver-grey hair, bore a worried expression as he pulled open the hefty wooden door to reveal a latticework iron safety door behind it. The gloomy cabin was empty of passengers.

'Many of our clients are nervous of the lift,' Derriman told Ash as he yanked the safety door aside. 'Even Sir Victor prefers to take the stairs. Good exercise, he always says, but I think he's a mite c-claustrophobic in small spaces.'

Ash could see why as he entered the dimly lit lift cage. As he leaned against the panel-sized mottled mirror on its back wall, the investigator realized how tired he was. Maybe the incident during the flight had scared him more than he cared to admit, its aftermath a depletion of energy.

His throat felt suddenly very dry.

Derriman had climbed aboard and was closing both doors, the heavy wooden one swinging shut almost by itself, the iron safety door having to be pulled across hard until its latch locked into its niche. Ash thought the old lift might hold three people comfortably, but more that that would be a squeeze.

The older man firmly pressed a button for the second floor and the lift juddered disconcertingly before ascending smoothly enough past the first floor.

'Who's at the top?' Ash asked, settling his shoulder bag at

his feet for the ride, defusing the unease caused by the sudden incident in the armoury.

'Ah, the fifth floor,' Derriman responded, turning to face him in the slow-rising lift car. 'Only two people occupy that floor. One is Sir Victor himself, and the other . . .' he hesitated, nervous again. 'Well, let's just say he's a k-kind of overseer.'

Ash wondered whether the 'overseer' was the thin man with the pot-belly he'd noticed on his arrival at Comraich. 'The latter has a name, I take it?' he said a little caustically, tired of the runaround he'd been given for asking simple questions, not to mention the literal runaround on the car journey to Comraich.

'Lord Edgar Shawcroft-Draker uses a suite when he stays, which isn't very often. Other rooms on the fifth are generally used for meetings and such like; and, oh yes, you'll find a small chapel there.'

Ash tried a long shot. 'Is Shawcroft-Draker head of the IC?'

'The IC?' Derriman blinked nervously. 'I'm sorry but, um, we rarely s-speak of the Inner Court to outsiders. I don't want you t-to think I'm being evasive, but please understand.' He stared curiously at the investigator, obviously uncomfortable.

Ash could tell that Derriman would prefer not to continue this line of questioning so he pressed him no further.

The lift juddered to a clanking halt and the pair stepped out into a long corridor, its carpet worn and faded with age, in direct contrast to the opulence below.

'This way, David,' Derriman said, gently offering a guiding hand.

Ash hoisted his bag over his shoulder and followed Derriman down the corridor. Despite the lack of luxury, the wide hall was still well maintained, he noticed, even if parts of the carpet were somewhat threadbare. Although it was still daytime, the wall lights were on and they gave out a softening glow. Ash guessed that the rooms on this, the second floor, were not for guests but for senior staff members and, perhaps, contractees such as himself.

'This room is yours,' Derriman announced, coming to a halt halfway down the corridor. He leaned towards the round brass handle and pushed the door open, then stood aside, allowing the investigator to enter first.

Ash was pleasantly surprised. The rooms along the second floor may have been staff quarters, but they had been well maintained, and the sight of an old-fashioned bed with clawed mahogany feet and a feather mattress delighted him. The view from the window overlooking the courtyard and the gardens beyond was beautiful, especially against the greens and golds of the woodland that stretched into the glen some distance away. A second window afforded a partial view of the sea.

He turned back to Derriman, noticing that his own large battered suitcase was laid on a rest at the foot of the invitingly soft-looking bed.

'I hope this will be all right for you,' said Derriman solicitously.

Ash eyed the old bureau of polished yew against one wall with a cushioned chair before it. A tallboy made from oak stood by the wall next to the open door, where the general manager waited with a self-satisfied smile on his long face. Ash's own delight as he'd entered had obviously pleased Derriman too.

'You do have a very small bathroom through there.' Derriman pointed to the lesser door next to the splendid writing desk. 'No bath, though; just a small sink and shower, I'm afraid.'

'I'll cope,' Ash replied with a grin.

Then he looked around, puzzled.

'Where's the telephone?' he queried.

'None of the rooms have private telephones,' the thin man told him apologetically. 'In fact, you'll find the only telephones are in the ground-floor offices. Of course, you're welcome to use them at any time.'

Ash wondered why the hell the castle's upper rooms had no means of phoning out.

'Comraich is a very private estate, you see,' the manager continued. 'We find it best for our guests to be cut off from society in general. After all, it's problems in the outside world that bring them to this sanctuary in the first place. Our therapy demands there'll be no such contact.'

'I'm no guest.'

'N-no, of course not. But it's a rule of the establishment – no unmonitored external communication for guests and visitors alike. It *was* in the contracts you signed with Simon Maseby,' he added apologetically.

Ash regretted not having read the agreements fully. But Kate McCarrick would have done so, so it must have been okay with her. Maybe she'd objected at first, and Slimy Simon had talked her round. Ash wondered if Maseby had been fully aware of the Institute's financial crisis before he'd contacted Kate. The thought rankled the investigator.

'There's no Wi-Fi, I take it?' Ash asked, already knowing the answer.

'No, I'm sorry, Mr Ash.'

'D'you use carrier pigeon at all?'

That brought the ghost of a smile to Derriman's lips. 'It sounds odd, I know,' he said, 'but we do have some very important guests staying with us, and if their whereabouts became known, I fear Comraich would no longer be the peaceful haven that it is today. The press alone would be all over us.'

'And the VIP guests, they can only phone out from your offices as well?'

'Oh no, our clients are never allowed to use the telephones. That would be entirely against the Comraich rules.' His nervousness had once again been overcome, although he was choosing his words carefully. 'It's also the reason the contract you signed was s-so, er, watertight. We demand the utmost duty of care and a guarantee of complete secrecy from all our employees, and, naturally, a binding agreement of silence from those we contract.'

'What if I really *need* to get in touch with my boss at the Institute?'

'Then, by all means, use the office telephone. You just have to play by our rules.'

Which meant that someone would be listening in, Ash supposed. He felt both angry and frustrated, but his expression remained neutral.

Derriman did his best to appease the investigator. 'Of course, you can always write a letter.'

Yeah, right, thought Ash, and anything detrimental to Comraich would be heavily censored or even destroyed.

'I take it I'm allowed to leave whenever I choose?' he muttered.

'Yes, indeed!' It sounded as if Ash had touched on a happier note. But then, as if he were the bearer of bad tidings, Derriman grew anxious again. 'There's something else: during your stay here, you mustn't leave the grounds, not that you would have to; I think you'll find everything you need is here.'

Christ, Ash silently exclaimed, *it's like being sentenced to a term in prison, without the normal niceties.*

Derriman perked up, or at least forced himself to lift the mood again. 'I'm sure that once you've been here a few days and enjoyed our hospitality, you'll have a better understanding of our rules, draconian though they must seem to you at present.'

Ash failed to return his smile. 'I'll take your word for it. Uh, I need to freshen up and have some lunch.'

The general manager immediately made for the door, still smiling wanly as if only partially satisfied that he'd appeased Ash. As he was closing the door behind him, Ash remarked, 'There doesn't appear to be a key in the door.'

Derriman, halfway out, looked back at Ash with another embarrassed smile. 'None of the rooms on this floor are ever locked, David. Where necessary, we maintain code-locks.'

Beyond surprise by this stage, Ash just waved a weary

hand in response. Derriman left, closing the door quietly behind him.

The investigator stood watching the closed door, listening to the fading footsteps of Andrew Derriman as he trod down the threadbare carpet towards the lift. He remained there until the footsteps had gone completely, wondering just what Kate McCarrick had let him in for. What *he* had let himself in for. Eventually, he went to the window.

The sun had reclaimed its rightful place in the sky, and he scanned the scenery, relishing the glorious autumnal colours of the landscape. He could see the ruined arch across the broad courtyard where he'd sat in the Mercedes, in awe of the castle that had seemed to float eerily on the low mist.

He went to his old and battered suitcase on the luggage-rest at the end of the bed and, taking a small key from his trouser pocket, he unlocked it. The suitcase was filled mainly with the instruments of his trade: two cameras, wall thermometers, spectrometer and other devices that would help him in his nocturnal vigil later that night. Lifting some of the change of clothing piled on top of the equipment, he reached deep into the right-hand side of the suitcase and drew out a slim chrome-and-leather flask.

He undid the screw top which also served as a tiny cup for the green liquid inside.

Usually, he would have filled the cup half with water, half with the green stuff, but not today.

His hand trembling only slightly, he downed the absinthe in one greedy gulp.

23

Eddy Nelson ran from the cottage as fast as his strong stocky legs would carry him into the wild (and now, it seemed to him, hostile) forest. Twice he stumbled over hidden tree roots, and supple branches from overgrown foliage whipped his face, forcing him to raise an arm to protect his already watery eyes. His face flushed, his shirt stained and stuck to his body with sweat, he barged onwards, hopelessly straying from the given but indistinct path. His only ambition was, at that moment, to get as far away as possible from Twigg's 'chocolate-box' abode.

What the fuck was wrong with the man? he asked himself breathlessly. Those eyes that had been expecting him as he'd raised his face over the window ledge to peek in again, those *fucking cold malign eyes*, staring from that shadowed, evil-distorted face. Had Twigg been waiting for him this whole time, as though he knew when to expect Eddy? If a word like hate somehow had a physical embodiment, then that face was it.

The apprentice assassin sobbed as he hit a tree, earning a bruised shoulder as he fell to the ground.

Twigg had finally flipped, Eddy was sure of that. Even though the man – *his boss, his own fucking boss!* – had never seemed quite sane to him anyway, with his detached, joyless manner, barely speaking a few words to him even when briefing a new assignment, never smiling, never congratulating him on the success of a fresh mission, only ever giving him a quick nod of the pointy bald head as though a satisfactory completion was only to be expected. And even then, there was always some niggly little thing that hadn't been carried out to Twigg's satisfaction. Eddy had always known that the shabby, stiff-limbed murderer was not quite right in the head, but Haelstrom had continued to support the stunted git.

But not so much nowadays though, not when Eddy had been instructed to trail Twigg around the streets of London, or wherever a job had to be carried out. And when Twigg visited certain shops – a clock-maker's or newsagent's or small back-street tobacconist (and Twigg didn't even smoke) – he would always emerge with a package of some kind which he'd tuck into his grubby old raincoat pockets. What was *that* about?

Eddy bit into his knuckle to stifle a further sob and peered up from where he lay on the leaf-littered ground, the knees of his once-smart Hugo Boss trousers digging into the soil beneath the dead leaves, the once brilliantly shined rustic-grain calf-leather footwear now scuffed and dirty, and his tie askew and loose from his buttoned jacket.

The other day in London – the day they'd carried out the poison-umbrella stunt, in fact – Nelson had followed Twigg to a new place. Special employees were sent annually to Harley Street for a full physical check-up, the results of which were then sent to Sir Victor Haelstrom or Comraich's senior doctor. But this time, Twigg had gone to a medical practice in a different street, though one that was probably just as expensive. This was a significant departure from the norm.

The young apprentice had strolled up to the prestigious shiny black front door and read the polished brass nameplate. Several practitioners' names were displayed and they all had one thing in common: all were neurologists.

It didn't take much to work out that Twigg was very sick, symptoms of his disorder already noticed by Sir Victor, who would certainly have reported it to his Inner Court superiors. Eddy supposed the idea was to let the illness develop before jumping to the wrong conclusion. After all, Twigg had been a loyal servant for many years and was, Eddy hated to admit, a superbly professional operative.

Had Eddy not been swallowing so hard, he might have been capable of raising a jubilant cheer. Now he, Eddy, the bloody *apprentice*, no less, would be able to convince Hael-strom that Twigg had finally gone loony, that he'd become a danger to the organization itself. Twigg had gone beyond psychotic: he was a menace to them all.

Had the old bald-headed coot thought no one had noticed the trembling of his once-steady and deadly hands? And this was all but confirmed by Twigg's furtive consultation with a Wimpole Street neurologist. *Oh boy, he really had the fucker now!*

He shuddered as he remembered the white staring eyes that were waiting for him as he raised his head above the window sill and the sick madness of Twigg's horrible smile. The malevolent look that bore straight through to Eddy's horrified soul.

He drew in great draughts of fresh air, but stopped halfway through the next breath. Something had stirred the under-growth close by. He squinted his eyes as he looked first to the right, then to the left and then behind. Back to the front again. All perfectly still now. Twigg couldn't have got ahead of him, surely? No, his own muscled legs would carry him faster than a man twice his age. Then again, Twigg knew these woods better than him. For all Eddy knew, he could have been running round in circles, the noise he made as he thrashed through the trees and undergrowth giving his position away; his sobs alone were loud enough to be heard from a distance. Maybe the bald-headed assassin was ahead of him, just waiting for Eddy to run straight into his deadly, if shaky, arms.

But hold up, Eddy chided himself, *be logical*. Surely he could beat the older man in a fair fight. Then who said it would be fair? Nelson had left his weapons of choice behind – the Stasi cosh, with its flexible tip and telescopic, compressed, rubber stem and plastic grip, or the iron knuckleduster, which could be carried in the side pocket of his jacket, both priceless in close-quarters combat. All had been left in his barracks apartment when he'd gone down to London, airline security not being fond of passengers including weaponry in their hand luggage. Similarly, the neat Walther PPK pistol he favoured and which, ironically, was a firearm that Twigg had trained him to use, was locked away in a grey metal cabinet inside his wardrobe.

As he assembled all these pointless thoughts, something stirred the forest foliage again.

He became aware of his location: surrounded by trees and undergrowth, and the forest floor so shady that it could be dusk. He felt vulnerable; he felt shit-in-his-pants scared.

But it couldn't be Twigg sneaking up on him because there wasn't enough cover for a full-grown man. He'd startled an animal. Yep, that's what it was: all the noise he'd made had startled some kind of animal in the woods. A small deer, maybe? There were a lot of them roaming the estate. It could be anything, the estate was stuffed with them: badgers, foxes, rabbits, mice and rats, not to mention the many species of bird life.

With a long sigh of relief, he told himself that was the answer: he'd frightened some shy creature by blundering across its path. He changed his mind when a peculiar sound came from the bushes in front of him. It was like – no, he didn't know what it was like. A soft hissing noise at first that soon grew in pitch, only to give way to a snarling of a kind he'd never heard outside a zoo.

Then he saw a pair of yellow-and-black eyes watching him from under a fern.

'*Shoo!*' he hissed sharply, but not too loudly; he didn't want Twigg to hear him.

The animal, whatever it was, refused to be bullied by Eddy's voice. Instead, it came further forward, its eyes unblinking and revealing no fear.

The apprentice picked up a small branch and threw it in the general direction of this unknown threat.

The animal was unfazed by the light projectile that had landed inches away from its front paws and slowly, like a stalking predator, it came into the open, unveiling its true nature.

'A cat!' Nelson cried out. 'A bloody mog!' and here was he on hands and knees, terrified by a bloody cat!

But wait – this was a different kind of cat. This big bugger now thumping the ground with one paw, its haunches high, its head and shoulders low, a brittle kind of tenseness in its manner, was slowly creeping towards him. As it came into full view, striped fur bristling, its bushy tail oddly waving with short, sharp flicks, a new fear took hold of Eddy.

One of the park rangers had told him there were wildcats prowling the woods. Don't ever think of them as pets, he was warned, because they weren't dubbed the Tigers of the Highlands for nothing. No one, as yet, could understand why and how they had immigrated from the north to take up residence in the woods of Comraich, but the occasional sightings and the discovery of riven carcasses of smaller animals and birds gave evidence of their presence. What was not known was how many of them were presently living in the woodland.

The ranger had also told him that they were solitary animals, rarely hunting in packs. That was at least some comfort to Eddy as he remained frozen on all fours. Just back away slowly, he advised himself. Very slowly.

He shuffled backwards, horribly frightened by this huge untamed animal that snarled and hissed at him, a fine spray of spit shooting from its fanged mouth.

Solitary animals, he remembered. Well, he could deal with one, no matter how big the fucker was. One on one. He wished that he was armed with the cosh at least; he could easily have handled the beast with that. A good hard crack would have sent it staggering senseless back into the undergrowth. But

Eddy found it was he who was retreating from the now *growling* cat. *Could cats even growl?* This one bloody could.

Another thought came to him as he forced himself to move cautiously away. Who would he prefer to fight: Twigg – who might be sneaking up on him at this very moment – or the wildcat, which only had claws to fight with, and teeth to bite? Yet he never underestimated the bald assassin, whose frame belied his strength. He recalled how Twigg had snapped the neck of a watchman who'd had the nerve to challenge them as they'd primed incendiary devices in a certain French armaments factory.

The big cat continued to creep towards him, its whole body lowered close to the ground in a way that a normal cat might sneak up on an unsuspecting mouse or small bird before pouncing; its powerful-looking jaws were stretched wide and emitting those peculiar hissing-snarls again, its fur erect and spiky, swelling its body to a frightening size, tail suddenly still, its shoulder muscles bunched, haunches quivering as it prepared to launch itself at its human prey.

But to Eddy's further horror and dismay, other wildcats were emerging from the undergrowth, their movement smooth and fearless. They shouldn't have been there, the park ranger had said they were solitary creatures that usually hunted alone. This wildcat was mob-handed with at least a dozen others behind it, all slinking around trees, moving through the ferns and bushes, in a smoothly choreographed hunt. And he was the prey! It was as though they had been told he would be here, as though they were expecting him.

The apprentice assassin felt warm liquid trickle down his thigh, soaking his already mud-soiled Hugo Boss trousers with urine he could no longer hold in.

Eddy half rose and faced the advance, his face screwed up in anguish, tears blurring his vision and running down his cheeks as he mumbled words that even he didn't understand. Maybe words of prayer . . .

As the pack of wildcats surged forward, fangs bared, their

movement was so swift that he was unprepared for the claws that rent the back of his hands now hiding his face. Then came the tearing bites and deep scratches that shredded his quality suit, reaching the flesh below and raking it with knife-like claws as he curled his body into a foetal position on the leaf-strewn ground, arms trying to protect the back of his neck and head from the tearing and slashing of vicious lacerating claws that drew blood and pulled strips of flesh from their humbled prey, hungry jaws beginning to eat the very meat of him and gulping down his spilled blood as he shrieked . . .

Those shrieks echoed through the otherwise silent woods, causing birds to take wing and smaller creatures to scurry back to their secret, safe hideaways.

24

Having shaved, and washed his hands and face in the tiny bathroom, Ash wandered back into the pleasingly appointed bedroom-cum-sitting room, once again finding himself looking out of the window. There were more people in the courtyard below, in groups or alone, enjoying the suddenly clement weather. As before, he directed his gaze towards the far side of the courtyard and the ruined arch from where he'd been given his first view of the castle; at present, a single uniformed guard stood beneath it, as if to dissuade any drifters from taking that route.

As he watched, Ash saw the guard turn his head to speak into his wrist radio. The investigator wondered what his message would be: all quiet on the home front? No trespassers and no escapees? Despite the grandeur and the plushness of its interior, Ash couldn't help thinking of Comraich as a luxurious Colditz, with its extensive electrified and razor-wired fence, patrolling guards and strategically placed CCTV cameras. Sir Victor Haelstrom could almost be the Kommandant. Or . . . his thoughts lingered on this . . . or maybe the thin man with the grim face and the pot-belly, who seemed to have deliberately avoided meeting Ash this morning, was in charge.

He was being over-imaginative, not to say paranoid; although, as Kate was always telling him, he did have an instinct for certain things, certain situations, and certain people.

'*Enough!*' he muttered sharply. He was there to do a job and he would do it to the best of his ability.

The upkeep of Comraich Castle – and he hadn't as yet even perused the grounds – must be astronomical, and the fee paid to his own Institute was beyond reasonable. In fact it was more than exorbitant. But then, it also bought complete secrecy. They weren't even allowed to keep copies of the reports they submitted to the Inner Court, let alone disclose their contents to anyone. It was an unusual arrangement, all right.

Even so, Ash had decided he would keep his own handwritten notes for himself. He wondered if he and his luggage would be searched before leaving Comraich when the investigation had been completed. In the distance, in what looked like the densest part of the woodland, his attention was caught by a sudden flurry of birds that rose excitedly into the air and flew off in all directions. He wondered what had disturbed them.

Turning from the window and his private thoughts, he reached round the bathroom door and dropped the damp towel into the small sink, then quickly donned a fresh blue denim shirt and a houndstooth jacket. He imagined lunch at the castle would be a semi-formal affair.

For just one moment, he was undecided whether or not to take another slug of absinthe, but on reflection he decided against it. The pocket-sized chrome-and-leather flask didn't hold much, although one shot was as effective as two whiskies. Saving it for the three nights of his stay was a more practical alternative.

Ash went to the door and pulled it open; its hinges made barely a squeak. As he was closing it behind him, he heard a noise further down the corridor, and when he looked he saw the psychologist, Delphine Wyatt, just closing her own door. *Synchronicity*, he thought, with a small smile.

When she glanced up and saw him, Ash was sure a look of alarm shadowed her face for an instant.

'Mr Ash,' she acknowledged. 'Are you on your way to lunch too?'

As she walked towards him, her step unconsciously graceful, he saw that she'd also changed her clothes. She wore a crocheted tie-front jumper, deep aubergine with a V-neck, and a gypsy-type skirt that reached just below her knees, black tights sinking into calf-length high-heeled boots.

Once again, Ash was almost speechless at this vision coming towards him, her black hair let loose from the back so that those dark curls framed her tanned face. If she'd spoken in Portuguese then he wouldn't have been surprised.

'Lunch?' she prompted, confused by his hesitancy.

He briefly wondered if she knew the effect she had on him, the cause of his hesitation.

'Uh, yeah,' he said when she was almost within reach. 'I was just wondering if I was smart enough for the dining room.' He waved a hand at her apparel.

She gave a short laugh, and her eyes, almost black in the dimness of the corridor, half-mockingly looked him up and down.

'I think you'll pass muster, as my father used to say.' Her full red lips continued to smile.

'I could eat a horse,' he said, grinning foolishly.

'I'm famished too,' she replied. 'I think it's the aftermath of the adrenaline rush we had earlier.'

Yes, he thought to himself, *and I seem to get a different kind of adrenaline rush each time I see you*. He couldn't help but wonder if she sensed his feelings, if she was somehow aware of the mixed emotions he tried to conceal. After Grace, he had vowed never to risk such intense passion ever again. Now he felt that once-firm wall of resolve gradually breaking down, brick by brick.

He found himself saying mundanely, 'Shall we take the lift?'

'I'd rather take the stairs; I don't trust that antiquated piece of machinery.'

She began leading the way along the dim corridor, with its patchy carpeting and picture-lined walls.

'Why don't they do something about it, then? The lift, I mean,' he asked as they walked side by side.

'Oh, there is another one – another two, in fact,' she replied as they came to the oval colonnaded staircase. 'One of them is rather grand and used exclusively by Lord Shawcroft-Draker and certain VIPs who visit Comraich from time to time.'

They began to descend the wide red-carpeted stairway, with Delphine allowing her hand to slide down the broad variegated marble balustrade and with Ash on the narrower section of the rounded staircase. Elegant hanging lights brightened the way. The carpet was plush and springy under Ash's boots.

'I take it,' he said to Delphine as they made their way to the first floor, 'that Lord Shawcroft-Draker is the tall thin man I saw when I arrived, who disappeared before Sir Victor could introduce us. The man with the rather obvious pot-belly.'

'That sounds like him,' the psychologist replied. 'He keeps very much to himself, so we rarely see him, let alone speak to him. He was – *is* – the actual owner of the castle. I suppose you would describe him as Comraich's patron, the Big Chief. Lord Edgar is what we usually call him.'

Ash digested the information, then said, 'You said there were two more lifts. What's the third one for? A service lift?'

'You could say that,' Delphine replied. 'But it's regularly scrubbed clean and takes patients down to the operating theatre. There are two general surgeons, and specialist surgeons are brought in as required. Our personal senior doctor oversees everything medical.'

'Presumably these specialists are sworn to secrecy, and paid a hefty fee for their silence.' He glanced at her and, in some way, was pleased to see her anxious expression; maybe she was uneasy about some of the 'rules' of this place too.

'It's for their own good, David,' she said after a beat or two. 'Some of the guests would be unacceptable beyond the boundaries of Comraich.'

'You do realize that sounds sinister, Delphine.'

She managed – but only just – to smile back at him. 'What *is* sinister, David, is the strange things that have been going on here lately.'

They passed a niche in the wall containing the bronze bust of some nobleman or other, who obviously had relevance to the castle's history. Ash had no interest in it whatsoever; his concern was for the beautiful woman at his side. The sense that she, herself, had misgivings about Comraich grew stronger.

They had reached the first-floor landing and she stopped to face him squarely. But once again her eyes failed to meet his.

'David,' she said almost passionately, 'if you knew the fine medical work carried out here, you wouldn't be so suspicious. Nor so critical.'

Was she trying to convince herself? he wondered. The way her eyes avoided his suggested it might be so.

'Maybe you can show me where you work later,' he said.

'I'd need to get permission first, but I'm happy to do just that.' Her gaze had returned to him.

As one, they continued to the next flight of stairs, a silence hanging between them.

Ash was even more impressed with the castle when he and Delphine entered the imposing circular dining room, which was busy with people. There was a hush when heads turned in their direction as Ash and his companion stood in the wide double-doored entrance. Either they seldom had new arrivals at Comraich, Ash reflected, or they already knew a ghost hunter had come into their midst. He felt uneasy. He casually looked around and could almost *smell* the affluence in the room.

The guests were seated at round tables, the tablecloths immaculately white, fresh flowers in the centre of each, bright, crystal-like chandeliers high above their heads. Even the gleaming cutlery appeared to be silver. Ash was hungry: he hadn't had time for breakfast and had been offered only tea, coffee or alcohol since. Alcohol, on the plane, at that time of the morning? On an empty stomach? Once more, suspicion vexed him. Had they *wanted* him to arrive at Comraich half-cut?

Next to him, Delphine was scanning the dining room as if looking for something. She said a quiet 'ah' of satisfaction and pointed.

'Over there,' she said her voice all but a whisper. 'There's someone I'd like you to meet.'

She led the way through the diners, heading towards one of the smaller tables in a comparatively empty part of the dining room. A man sat there alone, reading a magazine propped up against the flower vase while he ate.

Eyes followed Ash's progress through the room until the chatter of voices resumed, the guests' curiosity evidently waning. He caught sight of Haelstrom at a centre table, the ever-anxious Derriman sitting next to him, two other people that Ash hadn't yet met filling the other two seats. The big man noticed the parapsychologist and gave a brief wave of his hand, which Ash acknowledged with a casual nod of his head.

He took in the two unrecognized diners at Haelstrom's table. The one closest to Comraich's CEO was a female in hospital whites: a spotless tunic, which was in contrast to her drawn back lustrous auburn-red hair. As she stared his way, he noticed a particular glint in her hazel eyes and wondered why she appeared so interested in him, for she made no attempt to look away. Although not pretty, her face had attained that rare handsomeness of features that few women in early middle age managed to achieve. Her attractiveness was spoilt only by the hostility in those eyes.

The fourth member at the table had his back to Ash and he peered round to see what had captured his fellow diners' attention.

Ash glimpsed only a hard face with buzz-cut hair and broad shoulders. It was difficult to judge when the man was sitting, but the psychic investigator guessed he was short but stocky; he certainly had the features of a bruiser. It was no more than a glance, but the man's small, calculating eyes seemed to assess Ash in an instant.

'David . . .'

The investigator immediately turned back to Delphine.

'David,' she repeated, smiling at the man, who had looked up from his copy of the *Lancet,* and who now turned his attention from her to Ash, his eyebrows raised but with a clear smile showing in his neatly trimmed goatee. 'This is our senior surgeon, Dr Vernon Pritchard, who is in charge of the medical unit.'

Pritchard didn't rise but extended a hand across the able. Ash shook it and noted its natural firmness.

The senior doctor was a smallish man, no more than five foot nine, Ash guessed, and stylishly dressed: fawn herring-bone jacket, dark brown waistcoat, light blue shirt and natty blue-spotted bow tie. Ash put him in his early fifties, and although there was a casual air about him, his brown eyes were searching, almost questioning. One eyebrow was raised above his tortoiseshell bifocals, as if appraising the newcomer, and grey hair at his temples helped bestow upon him the necessary gravitas for someone of his status. That and the neat goatee he wore, which, suspiciously, hadn't a single grey hair in it.

Before Delphine could introduce Ash, Pritchard said with a note of satisfaction, 'Ah, you're our parapsychologist, I take it.' His grin was wolfish.

'Ash,' the investigator acknowledged.

'Yes, David Ash. Correct?'

Ash nodded and returned the smile.

Delphine broke in. 'I'm sorry to disturb you Dr Pritchard, but I felt David should know a little about our work here at Comraich.'

'Oh, I'm sure you could have done just as well yourself.' There was no criticism in the senior doctor's remark. 'But please, take a seat, won't you both? My lunch is over and I was just about to order an Armagnac and a coffee to complete it. Have you eaten yet?'

'No,' replied Delphine. 'I'm sure David is ravenous by now.'

'Yes, I heard you had a rather harrowing ordeal on the

plane. Strange how such an adrenaline rush can often leave you a bit peckish afterwards. And your body becomes unconsciously delighted to be alive, or so I'm told. Survival instinct kicks in, furtherance of the race and all that. As a psychologist, I'm sure Dr Wyatt can tell you more about that than I.' He cast a mischievous grin at Delphine, whose cheeks reddened slightly.

Ash covered her embarrassment. 'All I wanted afterwards was a stiff drink and a cigarette. Fact is, I had neither.'

'Commendable,' said Dr Pritchard as he leaned back in his seat. Although the doctor's smile was relaxed, Ash couldn't be sure if the older man was teasing. Still, he seemed amiable enough.

Pritchard barely waved a hand and a waitress, dressed in a creamy white blouse and a slim black skirt with dark tights, appeared before them.

'Chloe, my darling,' the doctor drawled smoothly, 'the usual coffee for me with a Bas Armagnac. Domaine Boingnères, of course. And could you bring menus for my two colleagues?'

Ash felt the girl might curtsey, but she only smiled at Dr Pritchard before leaving the table.

'You'll find the cuisine here splendid, Mr Ash,' the senior doctor remarked, indicating a chair opposite him across the spotlessly white tablecloth. He placed his copy of the *Lancet* to one side with a muttered 'Only bloody magazine I can get here,' while Delphine took the seat on his right. Ash's back was to the room, but he was even more aware of the too-soft drone of conversation behind him. Something had been bothering him since he and Delphine had entered the room.

The general hum of voices, apart from when he and the psychologist had made their appearance and conversation had been momentarily suspended, was low, with no peaks of volume, no sudden laughter, and certainly no raised voices. He realized it was this that had caused his disquiet when entering the oval room. All the voices were low as if . . . as if the clients were sedated. He tried to shrug off the idea, yet the thought lingered that they had all been mildly tranquillized. He was trying to decide how he could diplomatically put the idea to Dr Pritchard and Delphine when the senior doctor spoke again.

'Now, my darling Delphine,' he said smoothly, 'what is it I can tell Mr Ash that you feel unable to?'

Delphine smiled but Ash noticed her underlying discomfort. 'I'm sorry, Vernon, I noticed you had almost finished your lunch and thought you wouldn't mind my interruption.'

'And right you are,' Pritchard said with a small laugh. 'It's always interesting to meet someone new in Comraich. Mr Ash, then, what can I do?' He'd turned his attention to Ash opposite him.

'Well,' said the investigator, unfazed by Pritchard's seniority or grandiloquent manner, 'I was curious about the medical practices here. I mean are you really geared up for surgery? Do you have a cardiac unit, for example?' he added, remembering Moira Glennon.

'Oh, we manage much more than just that, Mr Ash. We also maintain a research department of a very high standard. In fact, we pioneer many treatments.'

He paused as the waitress put a balloon glass of amber liquid before him and a small cafetière to one side. Chloe produced two menus from under her elbow.

'Might I suggest,' interposed the senior doctor, 'that you order now.' He lifted his wrist to check his watch. 'Yes, Chloe will bring it in ten minutes' time. By then I shall have finished my discourse on Comraich Castle's medical facilities as well as having imbibed my after-lunch Armagnac and coffee.'

He'd noticed Ash's admiring interest in the ornate timepiece he wore and lifted his wrist again to give the investigator another sight of it. All Ash really knew was that the wristwatch looked old and very expensive. 'Vintage Rolex, 1936,' he told Ash proudly. 'Worth about sixteen K on today's market. Had it several years, a little guilt-gift to myself.' He shot his shirt cuff with practised ease, concealing the small treasure again.

While Delphine and Ash turned their attention to their

menus, Dr Pritchard withdrew a metal cigar tube from his inside breast pocket, unscrewed its flat end and slid its content into his open palm. Ash reflected wryly that, despite its plethora of rules for outsiders, Comraich was probably the only institution in the country not to have imposed a smoking ban.

'Hope neither of you minds,' he said, smiling first at Delphine, then at Ash. Without waiting for a response, he told them, 'This is a rather fine cigar, which I'm very partial to. Cohiba, from Cuba.' He struck a match and puffed the cigar into life, drawing in deeply before exhaling a dense stream of smoke across the table towards Ash. With a grin, in a mock theatrical whisper, he confided, 'As a doctor, I know I'm a bad example to some of our guests, and that's why I always lunch alone in this deserted corner of the room.'

At first Ash had thought Pritchard had directed the smoke at him purposely as a sign of disguised contempt, or at least disdain for his kind of trespasser, but when he breathed in the rich scent of tobacco, he changed his mind: the other man had wanted him to appreciate the cigar's quality. The senior doctor was obviously a man who enjoyed the rewards of his elevated profession.

He regarded Ash and his inflection was a little more brisk, although unequivocally genial. 'Actually, as a psychic researcher, I would've thought you were more interested in the dead than how we preserve the living.'

He stared into Ash's eyes, humour – or mockery – still evident in his expression. The investigator was confused: he didn't know whether to like the man or not. Whatever, he didn't like the soft-voiced teasing.

'I thought we were going to order lunch first, Vernon,' Delphine cut in, sensing the investigator's uncertainty.

'Of course, my dear,' Pritchard said, as if surprised. 'You go ahead and order while I brew myself a coffee.'

The smell of the coffee complemented the cigar's aroma perfectly and Dr Pritchard couldn't help but boast as he poured the steaming liquid into his cup, 'Above all, my favourite.

Jamaican Blue Mountain, considered one of the rarest and most expensive of all coffees.'

Like I would know, thought Ash as he studied his menu. *What next – the glorious merits of the bloody Armagnac?* Ash was surprised at the wide choice offered. Food had never been a priority in his life – he ate to live, not vice versa – but when he read the selections, his mouth began to salivate.

'Oh, just the Arran smoked salmon for me,' Delphine told the waitress who hovered between her and Ash. Chloe scribbled the order on her pad and said, 'And the main course?'

'Nothing more, thank you. Just the starter.'

The waitress addressed Ash. 'And for you, sir?' Her Scottish accent had a pleasant lilt to it.

Despite himself, for the menu had certainly looked appetizing, Ash showed restraint. 'Uh, just a main course for me, then. I'll have the fillet steak, medium rare, with the hollandaise sauce rather than the peppercorn.'

'Gratin of vegetables, the garlic barley risotto?'

'Some new potatoes and that'll be it.'

Chloe dipped her head and made her way back to the kitchen.

Ash spoke. 'You were wondering why I was interested in your medical department.'

'Yes, so I was. But it isn't just a department, you know. It's rather grander then that. I suppose you could say it's the size of a small cottage hospital in square footage but with hi-tech equipment and state-of-the-art laboratory apparatus, pioneering research, and the best proven drugs to date. We treat conditions as varied as heart dysfunction and cancer. And from, say, motor neurone disease to food allergies. We've made inroads with manic depression, which Dr Wyatt and Dr Singh would, I'm sure, be only too happy to explain to you.' He leaned towards Delphine, rather leerily, Ash thought. 'By the way, my pet, you look a mite fretful. Has your migraine come back to torment you again?'

'It's just a headache.'

'Perhaps it is now, but I wouldn't like it to develop into a migraine cluster; you know how they bring you down.' His voice was syrupy with concern. 'Now why don't you follow the advice I gave you last time? Botox will clear it up in no time at all.'

Ash was surprised by the information and he stared at Pritchard incredulously. *Botox? For migraine?*

'I told you before, Vernon,' said Delphine, mock-scoldingly, 'I'm too young for that kind of procedure and not yet vain enough.'

'Well, it's up to you, precious, but you should give it some serious thought.'

'That *would* give me a headache.'

Both of them laughed and Dr Pritchard dropped the subject.

'Well, then, Mr Ash,' he went on, 'other treatments here are for disorders as diverse as hypertension, Alzheimer's, strokes and meningitis. We have extremely efficient screening equipment that will show early signs of any number of diseases.'

He tilted his chair back, drawing deeply on the exalted cigar as he reflected.

'Let's take cancer, for instance,' the doctor said after a moment's further thought. 'You see, there are new drugs not yet on the market simply because in England NICE – the preposterous acronym for the National Institution for Health and Clinical Excellence – was reluctant to fund treatments for various cancers before it was satisfied beyond all possibility of doubt that they were safe and their efficacy proven. It is, of course, limited by financial restraints from the government.

'The trustees of Comraich have neither NICE's timidity, nor its monetary constraints. We are happy to use these so-called "unapproved" drugs to the benefit of our guests. We began to use Revlimid, for instance, long before its approval by NICE in 2009 because it is particularly useful in the treatment of bone marrow cancer, and its effect provides an insight into other forms of the disease. As well as Revlimid, NICE also rejected the use of various drugs for advanced kidney cancer because it found interferon is as effective – though studies suggest otherwise – and far cheaper to use. In fact, interferon is of such limited use that only one in ten sufferers are treated with it.'

Pritchard gently swirled the Armagnac in its balloon, creases between the inner corners of his eyebrows forming vertical ridges on his forehead. It seemed that poor government funding for the health of British citizens roused his ire. He further underlined this by exclaiming, but quietly, 'God, we're so far behind Western European countries and the United States that they're beginning to regard us as medical primitives. British oncologists were up in arms when they weren't able to use Sutent to treat advanced kidney and liver cancers until 2009, because the health service in Britain declared the cost is too great to bear!

'You know,' Pritchard continued with a faux-hopeless sigh, 'NICE even vetoed marvellous drugs such as the anti-TNF for rheumatoid arthritis and Aricept for Alzheimer's because it talks in terms of "evaluation according to their excellence", but no, it's a lie! What it means is drugs are not truly assessed by their excellence, but by their cost-effectiveness! The government does not think in terms of life extension and reductive pain, but believes in palliative care, using drugs that only make patients drowsy and so less complaining. I tell you, it's all down to budgetary restraint and therefore, politics.'

'Isn't it always?' Ash put in, mostly because he felt it was expected of him.

The sympathetic agreement seemed to raise the senior doctor's spirits again. He sipped his Armagnac, then his coffee, and finally drew on the cigar which was rapidly decreasing in length.

'Well let me tell you this,' he said, happily jabbing the remaining half of the cigar at Ash. 'We at Comraich buy in the best drugs available rather than wait for the results of some long drawn-out assessment policy. Reolysin, for instance, probably won't be approved for another five years, but we're curing people with it today. It works where chemotherapy doesn't. It's a kind of magic bullet that shrinks tumours and in some cases has made them vanish.'

Dr Pritchard leaned back in his chair and regarded Ash, deep satisfaction broadening his smile. 'We're very proud of our work at Comraich,' he said smugly.

The investigator nodded sagely, not knowing what else to do. But he was beginning to wonder if Comraich was actually just a research institute working in an unholy alliance with big pharmaceutical companies and the 'guests' acting as guinea pigs.

'Are you as advanced in areas of health care other than cancer?' he asked, genuinely curious.

'Oh, yes, we certainly are.' The senior doctor looked up and saw the waitress approaching with Delphine's and the investigator's lunch. 'But look, I've taken up enough of your time – your fault for getting me on to my old hobby horse. Here's Chloe with your lunch, so I'll leave you in peace. I expect you're tired of the diatribe by now, in any case.'

He drained the last of his Armagnac with relish, then the rest of his coffee. He pushed back his chair, the stub of his cigar still burning between his fingers, stood and reached across the table to shake the investigator's hand.

'There's plenty more to know about our various treatments and cures for our guests here at the castle, but I'll let Delphine fill you in with more details. Much more pleasurable for you, wouldn't you say?'

Also standing, Ash smiled at the brashly elegant (if such a description were possible) senior doctor.

'Thank you for taking the time,' Ash said appreciatively, but not too humbly.

'Been a pleasure, old boy. Now, if there's anything I can help you with, just let me know, all right? And I'd like to have a chat to you sometime, about your business and what crazy things you've witnessed. I think you might call me a sceptic, but I am, nevertheless, interested in the sort of thing you get up to.'

With a touch on Delphine's shoulder, Pritchard moved around the table and eased himself past Chloe.

Ash caught the senior doctor before he could go on his way. It was the investigator who moved closer to him, realizing he'd been wrong about the physician's height – Pritchard barely scratched five foot six. The girl laid both full plates at their settings on the table, her hands shaking a little.

'Tell me, Dr Pritchard,' Ash said quietly, leaning down towards the other man's ear. 'D'you keep your, uh, your *guests* . . .' he emphasized the word '. . . under sedation *all* the time?'

The dandified doctor pulled his head away from Ash to regard him quizzically. Then, his voice also low, he replied, 'Is it that obvious?'

Ash nodded with a bland smile, but caught the brief exchange as Pritchard looked past his shoulder at Delphine, who had remained seated.

'Well you see, old boy,' said Pritchard confidentially, 'we like to keep them happy – and peaceable,' he added. 'Oh, they're not under any "chemical cosh", if that's what you're driving at. Absolutely not. No, we use a group of drugs called benzodiazepines – Valium and the like. And, of course, our old friend Prozac. Perhaps something a little stronger for those who require it most. But our guests are kept healthy and happy. That's our agreement with them, or with whoever is footing their bill. It's why we're so anxious to clear up this present nonsense about ghosts – it isn't good for their well-being!' He managed a quiet chuckle as he placed a manicured hand on the investigator's shoulder. 'It's nothing for you to worry about, old boy. They aren't aware of the mysterious crucifixion of Douglas Hoyle' – *He's making it sound like a TV drama*, thought Ash – 'but rumours do tend to abound and become exaggerated in a confined location such as this. You just solve our temporary problem as quickly as possible, then all will be as it should – a peaceful, benign inner sanctum.'

He patted Ash's shoulder, then smoothly made his way out of the restaurant, stopping only occasionally to charm a guest or two before moving on.

The investigator came back to the table from where Delphine had been watching him, her brown eyes anxious.

He grinned at her and took the seat just vacated by the senior doctor. 'Well,' he said, 'that was informative.'

The investigator had moved his position so that his back was to the wall, giving him an unrestricted view of the high-ceilinged room and its occupants. He remembered that when he removed himself from the mental health wing of a London hospital a couple of years ago, they had insisted that he remain on Fluoxetine, which was just another brand of Prozac, apparently, and amitriptyline hydrochloride; just, at least, till the night terrors had stopped. Those nightmare attacks continued to plague him, but only occasionally.

'Are you all right, David?' Delphine had placed her hand over his, causing him to flinch involuntarily.

'Sorry,' he apologized when he saw the hurt in her eyes. She'd hastily withdrawn her hand. 'I just had a couple of flashbacks. Memories I should have laid to rest by now. It isn't you, Delphine.'

'Bad memories?' she asked, looking concerned.

'Yeah,' he admitted bitterly. 'Maybe I should've stuck with the sedatives they put me on, but I ditched them long ago. I don't like my senses dulled by medication of any kind.'

'Do you want to talk about it?'

The question was asked tenderly, and he had to remind himself that this beautiful woman was a psychologist. He was afraid of misinterpreting the signs. And yet, he was sure there was a bond between them, probably engendered by the near-death experience they had shared that same morning. He felt it may have been the catalyst that had drawn them together without the usual rituals of courtship.

This time it was he who reached for her hand, which had dropped to her lap, and she didn't resist when he brought it back to the table and continued to press softly with his own.

'There are things I'd like to tell you, Delphine, but not now, and certainly not on a professional basis. You understand, don't you?' It was a deliberately loaded question and he breathed an inner sigh of relief when she nodded and cast her eyes almost demurely down at her lap.

The moment passed and Ash attacked his medium-rare steak and soft-as-butter new potatoes with relish, wondering at his own hunger, while Delphine picked at her smoked salmon. And as they ate, the psychologist continued to tell him of other medical facilities, cures and procedures for the sick and the elderly at Comraich Castle, as if she felt it important to extol its virtues. He listened attentively, while also taking the opportunity to study this lovely, raven-haired woman. Occasionally he put in a question for clarification, but mainly he absorbed her words and was touched by the intensity of her passion for Comraich's medically advanced accomplishments, such as a postage-stamp-sized sponge infused with a pain-killing drug that gave post-operative internal relief for up to four days, or the use of stem cells as a permanent cure for congenital glaucoma, angina and other chronic cardiac problems.

Delphine eventually noticed the slightly glazed look in Ash's eyes.

She laughed. 'I'm so sorry. Once I get started on our medical treatments here I get carried away with enthusiasm. Forgive me?'

He blinked twice and grinned at her, hiding his own embarrassment. Certainly he could have watched her animated face and keen but beguiling eyes for ever, but he had to admit the medical jargon, fused with her unrelenting earnestness, had proved his spirit willing but his flesh weak. Or was it the other way round?

'You did your best.' She was still smiling. 'And I appreciate it. But let me give you just one last example of how far advanced our medical practices are at Comraich. You probably know about warfarin, a drug commonly used today on patients at risk of strokes and heart disorders. It thins the blood, thereby reducing the risk of clotting.'

'It's also used to kill rats, isn't it?' he asked.

'That's right,' Delphine went on, 'but here we use a new drug called Pradaxa. Its advantages over warfarin are too many for me to go into now, but believe me, they are many. Yet, until recently Pradaxa was considered too expensive by the NHS.'

'Same old story,' Ash concluded.

'Same old story,' Delphine agreed. 'Of course, that problem doesn't exist at Comraich, thanks to the funds we have at our disposal.'

'Okay, okay,' he protested lightly. 'It's interesting – I had no idea such medical procedures and curatives were available here. But, well, you know, it's been a long day so far.'

'I'm with you there. There's so much more I could tell you, things that might surprise even a cynic like you.'

'You think I'm cynical?' Now that did surprise Ash: they'd known each other less than a day.

'I think you're . . . complex.'

He averted his gaze, looking sideways through the window. From their secluded spot in the dining room he could see a faint grey land mass that might have been an island across the sun-sparkled sea. Delphine's perspective on him had made him feel uncomfortable.

He turned back to her. 'You've got me wrong: I'm a simple man.'

She laughed again, a lovely sound without a hint of derision. And this time, his own grin was less tight.

'I would guess you're determined, David,' she told him, 'yet I know there's a tender side to you because you demonstrated that on the plane this morning. And there's your interest in the supernatural, not as a game, not as something to wonder at, but as a feasible subject for exploration or even denunciation. I sense you're reluctant to dismiss the idea of life after death just

189

as much as you hope to discount the notion. I think it's something that lies in your past, David. I can't help but wonder if there is some guilt involved.'

'Delphine,' he said softly but firmly, 'I'm not here to be psychoanalysed. I've a job to do and even before I've started I know there's something wrong and something vile here at Comraich Castle. I believe you feel the same. My past, my background, doesn't come into it.'

'Not yet,' she said, staring intently at him.

He stiffened in his chair, then pushed back his empty plate so that he could lean his elbows on the table. He rested his chin on his knuckles.

Though he was silent for a while, his body language was speaking volumes: the raised arms protecting his exposed chest and upper stomach, the hands with interwoven fingers supporting his chin, and the grim stone-like expression of his face. David had erected his own mental barrier with a tell-tale physical posture; one that a psychologist such as Delphine Wyatt could see through instantly.

Ash raised his head as Sir Victor Haelstrom approached them through the now mostly empty tables, his strangely large head with pinched features fixed on the investigator. With him were his three dining companions.

Haelstrom was breathing heavily from the exertion, no doubt after consuming a substantial lunch, as he reached the table where the investigator and the psychologist sat. He glowered down at them both as the white-garbed, red-haired nurse, the hefty-looking guy and the gaunt Derriman caught up with him.

'I take it you enjoyed your lunch, Ash?' Haelstrom said as he slowly regained his breath.

Well, well, no 'Mr' this time, Ash thought, guessing he was now just another employee. Well, he hadn't journeyed to Scotland to make friends.

'Yes, Sir Victor,' replied Ash with the sort of smile he kept only for those he instantly disliked. It was just a wide, up-turned movement of his closed mouth accompanied by dead-pan eyes. 'The steak was delicious. I thought I'd skip dessert, but have one of your fine Armagnacs.'

'I thought you had a lot to do this afternoon,' Haelstrom grumbled. 'And Dr Wyatt, haven't you got patients to see?'

The charm hadn't lasted long, then, thought Ash without animosity. Whatever his own feelings, Sir Victor Haelstrom was a client – a 'client' in the proper sense of the word – as Kate always liked to warn him whenever he came up against an awkward customer.

Delphine looked startled, like Bambi frozen in the powerful headlights of a speeding car.

'Dr Wyatt was informing me of just some of the medical procedures and client care here at Comraich Castle,' he said for her sake as he looked up at Haelstrom from his comfortable chair. 'Fantastic,' he added, nodding his head as if reflecting on the hospital unit's achievements.

'Yes, well, that's all to the good, but you're not here to admire the castle's medical expertise.'

'Nor its grandeur, I agree.' The investigator had allowed a pleasant smile to temper the situation. 'I think I'll try one of your splendid coffees, and then get down to some serious work. Only kidding about the Armagnac.'

Haelstrom swivelled his odd, large head, looking for a waitress. Chloe was clearing a nearby table.

'Waitress!' He barked. 'Coffee for Mr Ash here, and Dr Wyatt . . . ?'

Delphine nodded almost guiltily.

'Two coffees,' the big man ordered. Then, back to Ash, 'I hope you're not going to waste time on a cigar, too?'

'I gave up today. Although one of Dr Pritchard's fine Cubans is tempting.' He added playfully, 'Cohiba, I think they were called.'

Four sets of cold eyes glared down at him as if their owners were all aware the investigator was toying with Haelstrom. But to Ash, the red-haired nurse glared hardest of all, and he wondered why. Why she seemed so hostile.

'Your plan is to get an overall view of the castle to begin with, I believe you told me,' Haelstrom almost growled.

'That's right. I think that'll take most of what's left of the afternoon, but I may get the chance to lay out some detection equipment.' He paused. 'You and I, Sir Victor, will have to agree on what areas can be kept out of bounds for everyone at that stage.'

'Hm.' It was a gruff noise, indicating nothing in particular. Then Haelstrom waved generally at the group who had followed him across the dining room.

'You met Derriman earlier and I think he should accompany you through the building,' Haelstrom all but ordered, then added by way of introduction, 'This is Comraich's Senior Nurse, Rachael Krantz, who insists on the seventeenth-century spelling of her Christian name – Rach*ae*l.' He'd emphasized the second *a* as if it offended him as a trivial pretension.

Without bothering to stand, Ash gave the white-clad nurse a casual but nevertheless courteous bow of his head. As she turned away from watching Delphine, her hazel eyes took on another, entirely different gaze. It was subtle, if hardness could be so termed, and its hostility might have intimidated a meeker person than David Ash.

In a way, she reminded him of the head nurse in *One Flew Over the Cuckoo's Nest*, whose odious Nurse Ratched (great name, he mused) ruled the asylum wards with cruel zealousness. But with her fine features and lush darkish red hair beneath the small nurse's cap Krantz would be a good choice for the movie remake just on presence alone. There was a stern beauty about her and her body had attractive, sturdy curves that were not diminished by her uniform.

She made him feel uneasy, and it wasn't because of the wintry look she gave him. No, it was the way her and Delphine's eyes had connected a moment or two ago. He stopped his imagination there, unwilling to go further. Unfortunately he couldn't as easily ignore the barely disguised animosity Krantz held for him at that moment, her attention drawn from Delphine.

'And this is Senior Security Officer Kevin Babbage,' Haelstrom's voice boomed across the table now that the restaurant was virtually empty. 'I doubt you've come across him yet; he likes to work in the shadows.'

The stocky man moved around the table towards Ash, offering him his thick-fingered hand. His grip was a little stronger than necessary as Ash half rose to extend his own hand. Their eyes met squarely and neither man blinked. Or smiled.

'We may have to work together at times,' Ash told him, relieved to be distracted from Delphine and Krantz.

'Anything I can do, please ask,' was the welcome, if cold, response. 'I'm anxious to deal with this problem. Hope you're not gonna let us down.'

'I'll try not to.' Ash detected an accent from the States.

'It's been going on too long and it's getting worse.'

'So I've heard.'

'Yeah, well, we gotta do something about it. Guests are getting spooked.'

'I'm not surprised.'

'They don't even know the half of it.'

Like what happened to the big-deal financier Douglas Hoyle, for instance? Ash thought to himself. *And as chief of security at Comraich Castle, surely Babbage should have brought in the police.*

'Any clues?' Babbage asked unexpectedly.

'Clues?'

'Stupid question – you just got here. I just kinda wondered if you've, uh, you know, picked up any vibes from the place?'

'Oh, I'm getting plenty of vibes.'

They all looked alarmed.

'Already?' said Haelstrom, his frown more like a scowl because of his oddly compressed features.

'Well, it's more of an uneasy feeling deep down. You get to sense things if you've been in the job as long as I have. You get it particularly in older buildings such as Comraich, mainly because they have long histories, and often terrible and violent things have taken place within their walls. If you can imagine that the very fabric of the structure – the stonework, the wooden beams, any of the original materials used – acts like a sort of tape-recorder, or camera: from time to time, someone or something triggers the release of the recording. It could be a centuries-old murder, or, more often, just a routine activity such as a person, a servant, maybe, habitually using a certain staircase or corridor which has become imprinted on the building itself.'

He paused to look at each face in turn: Haelstrom still wore his scowl, Babbage looked at Ash as if he were a lunatic, Derriman just appeared frightened, and Senior Nurse Krantz regarded him with undisguised distaste. For relief, he peered round at Delphine, whose expression was at least one of encouragement.

'Not only that,' Ash continued quizzically, 'your clients – or guests – seem unnaturally subdued, yet remain, uh, apprehensive. I'm informed by Dr Pritchard they're kept lightly sedated anyway, but still a peculiar feeling of disquiet seems to be getting through to them. And your staff are kind of jittery too. Our waitress, for example.'

'Chloe? She's very young and highly strung, as well as being mindful of your occupation. As are all of our staff by now. Word of your arrival was bound to circulate among our employees and then, because of silly rumours that spread, to our guests also. But what's your point, Ash?'

'No point, really. Just trying to get the full picture.'

'Then you will get that this evening, after you've finished your initial reconnoitre. Babbage here will accompany you part way, and Derriman will be your guide to every nook and cranny of the castle. I'll expect you in my office – no, make that in my quarters upstairs – at six thirty, when you can make your first report and advise me on what you expect to be done about the situation.'

With that, Haelstrom turned and headed towards the restaurant's double doors. Senior Nurse Krantz followed in his wake, but not before she'd given Delphine a lingering look, and then cast another spiteful glare at Ash.

What was it between Krantz and Delphine? Professional rivalry? The nurse's contempt for psychologists in general?

He shrugged it off and pointed at the two empty chairs at his table. 'Why not join us for coffee,' he invited Derriman and Babbage, 'and we can discuss the places I should investigate first.'

Babbage declined. 'I'll be in my office, so you can pick me up when you're done here. Mr Derriman will bring you to me.'

'Fine,' agreed Ash.

Babbage half turned, but thought of something more to say. 'Where d'you intend to begin your tour?' The question seemed of particular interest to the security chief.

'Hm. I hope to visit every part of Comraich,' Ash told him. 'But first, I'd like to see Douglas Hoyle, even if he's still in shock.'

He couldn't help but notice how pale Derriman became. For a moment, he thought the man might faint. 'Something I've missed here?' he asked.

It was Babbage who answered him. 'Mr Hoyle passed away this morning,' he said flatly. 'Probably around the same time your plane was making its descent into Prestwick.'

PART THREE: THE HAUNTINGS

25

It wasn't a pleasant sight, but it pleased Cedric Twigg as he looked down on Nelson's shredded body.

The late apprentice's once-sharp blue suit was nothing but tattered rags and one of his expensive shoes was missing, as were the toes on the exposed sockless foot.

Twigg bent over the lacerated corpse, his stiffened face set in a satanic grin, aware that his stoop and the malign expression were as much symptoms of his own disease as of his delectation. He'd tried to chase Nelson from the cottage but his worsening illness had meant he could only shuffle after his prey rather than catch him and cleave the younger man's head with the axe he used for chopping wood. The symptoms were growing increasingly noticeable – the flight from London had been gruelling.

Drool seeped from his open grin to drop from his chin like a slow-leaking tap – more evidence of his deterioration which he accepted now but still railed against. The specialist he'd visited in London had assured him that drugs such as Pergolide would slow his decline, but the physician hadn't offered any hope of a cure, which was why Twigg was in a hurry to finalize things himself, rather than allow the Inner Court to engineer his end for him.

He knew assassins like himself rarely lived out their retirement till its natural end; he knew his masters always made other 'arrangements' for those who were no longer of any practical use for them. He had played the Grim Reaper himself for more than one aged or debilitated assassin.

So why had he let himself fall into the same situation? Because he'd made other plans. Not for him to grow old and lose the keenness of eye and sharpness of wit required for the job; no, when the time was right, he would simply disappear and collect the money he'd salted away in many different countries and islands, banks all over the world, and find the utopia of his own choosing, not one the IC had always falsely promised him.

He would simply vanish.

But contracting Parkinson's disease had disrupted those plans for good.

To make matters worse, it was taking hold more rapidly than the Wimpole Street specialists' prognosis. Twigg could only hope that nobody at Comraich – especially the medics – had yet noticed his deterioration. But when they did – and it would be soon – he knew exactly what action the Inner Court would take. Before they could do that, however, he was going to take some action of his own.

It was just as well he was a loner (as all assassins should be), living in isolation, interacting with other people as little as possible, the debriefings to his masters short to the point of curtness. He'd never tried to be popular.

How he despised these rich, pampered clients who resided at Comraich, all guilty of things most ordinary people would have been condemned or punished for. Just because they had untold wealth, or their benefactors were rich beyond compare, these guilty people lived in quiet luxury instead of ending their days in the harsh surroundings of prison or, at the least, as pariahs. But mostly, he hated his own masters, those who sent him to assassinate men and women they feared or distrusted, outsiders who could damage or inform on the Inner Court, which was the most powerful, most sinister, and most influential secret organization in the kingdom.

Eventually – no, *soon* – he would strike out at this nefarious and influential cabal, as well as their hirelings such as Sir Victor Haelstrom, who would never deign to share a normal conversation with him, let alone eat a meal together. Haelstrom gave Twigg his orders, his missions, and only the man's own arrogance prevented him from being afraid of the professional killer.

And then there were the underlings, young fledglings, abhorrences all, sent to Twigg so that he could teach them the dark art and practicalities of assassination. Men like Eddy Nelson.

Nelson . . .

Twigg, his heavy breathing beginning to subside, stared down at the torn, mutilated figure of his most recent, despicable trainee. Once, Eddy Nelson had been about five foot ten tall; now his body had been shredded and tugged until – if he could have done the impossible by standing on his own two feet – he would have been at least six foot six, his body had been pulled apart and stretched so vigorously. It was as if the wildcats had played tug of war with the carcass. (Or had it been a carcass? Maybe Nelson had still been alive when it happened.)

The young man's belly had split in two, exposing the slithery innards that steamed in the open air, chunks of good soft meat pulled free to be eaten at leisure. The intestines popped and wriggled as if still alive, though their host was clearly dead and strings of arterial veins that had led to the missing heart still seeped deep-red blood as if the kill had only just occurred.

Cats like to play with their victims, Twigg recalled, and it seemed it was no different with these wildcats, who made up for size in numbers. They had mauled poor old Nelson (even Twigg had the smallest spark of humanity) and the assassin shuddered at the sight of his half-eaten and drawn apprentice. The odd thing was – odd because it drew attention away from the naked and disturbingly twitching guts – that Nelson's whole lower jaw was missing.

His upper set of teeth grinned up bloodily at Twigg, but below was just bright gory meat down to the exposed throat. Above that monstrous invasion, Nelson's eyes were still open. Open wide and staring. Except one eyeball looked up as if to see what was inside its own head, while the other one peered downwards as if it couldn't believe the lower jaw had gone.

Cedric Twigg did his best to stand upright against the constraints of his debility, and he looked left and then right, strangely unafraid of the wildcats.

He felt an affinity with them, because they, like him, were assassins too.

26

Back in his room on the second floor and after closing the door firmly behind him, Ash headed straight for his big suitcase on the carrier at the foot of the bed. He'd returned to his quarters not to collect any of the equipment of his profession, but to dig down into one corner and remove the chrome-and-leather flask secreted there.

Then he turned to the little round table on which a thoughtful maid had placed a jug of fresh water and two small tumblers. First, he poured two finger-widths of absinthe into one tumbler, then an equal amount of water. (Not for Ash the ritualistic pouring of the liquor over a spoonful of melted sugar; an unnecessary affectation, he always told himself.)

He watched the liquid turn a cloudy green, then picked up the glass and swallowed half its contents. The liqueur was sufficiently diluted not to scour his throat, but nevertheless strong enough to have an effect. He felt the warmth bloom in his chest and already the shocking news of Douglas Hoyle's death was becoming acceptable. It wasn't the death itself that had so jolted Ash, it was the timing: the financier had died at the exact moment the Gulfstream's engines had malfunctioned.

Was there – could there be – a connection? Ash sipped the rest of the absinthe and water, walking over to the small window again. Looking down he saw people – *ordinary* people who looked neither mad nor unwell – strolling through the gardens, wandering around the immense courtyard, some perhaps making for the castle walkway for a view of the ruffled sea. They moved in groups of three or four while some were solitary figures, lost in their own thoughts. They were too far away to distinguish features, but even so, some of them felt familiar to him.

Ash was about to reach into his luggage once more, this time for binoculars, when he realized time was marching on and Derriman was waiting downstairs for him, no doubt becoming a little impatient. Replacing the tumbler on the small table, Ash removed his jacket and donned what he referred to as his 'field jacket', which was olive green and had many deep and useful pockets as well as a collar he could use to shield his neck against chilly draughts. Mindful that he would first be checking out the lower regions of the castle, he also pulled a dark biker's muffler over his head so that it crinkled around his throat. It could also be pulled up over his mouth and nose if necessary. He then picked up his leather shoulder bag, the contents of which included two cameras, one a tiny digital model, the other a bigger Polaroid type. The latter he hung round his neck by its strap, the former he placed into one of the deeper pockets of his field jacket. *Time to go to work*, he told himself. *Time to earn a living. Time to engage whatever paranormal evil dwells in this huge ancient pile.*

When he met Derriman, whose face had mercifully regained some of its natural colour, outside his office on the ground floor, the general manager was wearing a buttoned-up jumper under his coat and a short, bright tartan scarf around his neck. The lower we go, he'd explained to Ash, the colder it gets. The investigator pointed at his own apparel to indicate he'd had the same thought. Somehow, it broke the ice between them.

'Will you call in a coroner to ascertain how Douglas Hoyle died?' Ash said as they prepared to begin their exploration.

'You're f-forgetting one thing,' Derriman stuttered. 'Mr Hoyle died over a year ago as far as the public and the authorities are aware. He no longer officially existed, and now I'm afraid he t-truly doesn't, so why would we call in a coroner?'

Ash appreciated the logic, but it didn't make things right. He decided it was pointless to pursue the matter.

'W-when death occurs, of course close relatives are in-informed, but our contract with them allows us to dispose of the body as we see fit.'

'Don't people ask to see the body, or at least attend the funeral?'

'That's at our d discretion, and they're well aware of this when they sign the contract. To tell you the truth, Mr Ash, some are relieved that they no longer have to bear the fees.'

The stutter disappeared as Derriman became more sanguine.

'Okay,' said Ash resignedly. 'And, please, it's David,' he told the general manager again.

'Yes, of course. With so many distinguished guests, we tend to keep up the formality. Think that's what's expected of us.'

Not quite 'distinguished' if they'd had to go into hiding, Ash thought to himself, but naturally, he let it drop.

'What about an autopsy?'

'We have our own pathology department and I believe the corpse is under examination as we speak. We expect a written report either tomorrow or the day after.'

Derriman pointed to a closed door further down the hall. 'We'll collect Babbage first, then we can make a start.'

Together they walked down the marble floor of the long, pillared hall and Ash noticed the guard who sat by the broad curving stairway stiffened and gave Derriman a half-salute as they passed. *Someone doesn't want to lose his job*, thought Ash.

Striding forcefully towards them came a tall, slightly portly, grey-haired man dressed wholly in black, except for the clerical collar at his throat. Following behind, and hurrying to keep up, was a tiny woman wearing a nun's black habit and white bib, which cast a waxy light over her already pale, plump-cheeked face. The loose black gown was so long it flowed behind her and almost covered her shoes. Her head was covered by a wimple and around her waist was a woven woollen belt with a beaded rosary linked to it. A silver cross hung from a cord around her neck. She had a smooth, unblemished, pretty face, which at that moment was anxious, her eyes on the back of the cleric she strove to keep up with.

The man in black came to a sudden halt two paces in front of Ash, the earnest nun almost stumbling into him.

'A newcomer, I see,' the man boomed. 'Have you sinned, my son?' Ash held his stance, despite the temptation to step back and recover his own space. Ash thought the sudden confrontation amusing, especially the 'my son', which he thought was an endearment no longer used by the modern clergy.

Derriman quickly stepped in to avoid further embarrassment for them all. 'L-let me i-introduce you,' he said, and Ash realized the general manager's stutter had returned again, due to unease. 'This is the Reverend Archbishop Carsely,' Derriman told Ash. 'And his, uh, acolyte, I suppose you'd say, is Sister Thimble. She acts as the archbishop's PA and devotee.'

The nun smiled at Ash around the archbishop's left elbow, while the clergyman drew his head back almost as if deliberately to look down his nose at this newly arrived interloper. 'Well, my boy, have you?'

'Have I what?'

'Sinned. Didn't you hear me the first time?'

For a man of the cloth, Ash considered, this guy was pretty pompous as well as brusque.

'I guess I have,' he admitted, playing along.

'Would you like me to hear your confession?'

It didn't sound like an invitation.

Derriman stepped in again. 'Mr Ash is a psychic investigator, here to help us with a small problem, Your Grace. He isn't a guest.'

Archbishop Carsely looked imperiously at the diplomatic general manager. 'To rid us of these evil spirits?' he demanded.

'I've already informed you that I'm able to perform an exorcism.'

'You feel dark forces have manifested themselves in this place?' Ash asked. It was a pointed question and he hoped for an apt reply.

'The whole *world* is governed by malign forces, Mr Ash. Why should this castle be any different? Nevertheless, I have offered my services to Sir Victor, but he insists that I remain silent about the recent spiritual disruption within these walls. He's afraid of alarming the other residents. But hear me now; these loathsome unseen entities are growing in number. It's as if a dark oppressive legion has been drawn here to seek allegiance with the evil that dwells in Comraich.'

Like these dangerous Highland wildcats have been drawn here? Ash silently mused, suddenly reminded of his drive through the grounds.

'Wickedness abounds at Comraich,' the archbishop went on, 'and there must be a reason. Whatever it may be, you can be sure it will soon reveal itself. And only the Devil will rejoice in the revelation.'

Without warning, the cleric reached out and laid his hand on top of Ash's head, firmly pushing it down so that the parapsychologist was left looking at the marble floor. Archbishop Carsely then mumbled an unintelligible stream of words that Ash supposed were Latin.

Too startled to pull away, even though he felt awkward and embarrassed, as if he were abasing himself before this eccentric man of God, Ash remained still, waiting for the clergyman to finish. Fortunately, that wasn't long.

The archbishop removed his hand, gave his imagined supplicant a swift blessing with two straightened fingers and then, with a short bow of his head, went on his way.

The nun's eyes met Ash's with a note of anxiety before she scurried after her ecclesiastical master, leaving the investigator looking after them in wonder and metaphorically scratching his head.

He turned to Derriman. 'What the hell was that about?'

Guests around them went back to their conversations as if nothing untoward had happened.

'I'm s-s-so sorry.' His face had flushed red again. 'Perhaps someone should have told you before.'

'About the archbishop?'

'Yes, and other people you might meet here.'

'I'm intrigued.'

'Don't be. You signed a binding contract.'

'I signed two, actually. It doesn't mean I can't be interested though.'

Derriman accepted his point with a sigh. 'I suppose not.'

'Naturally, I'll use discretion, but right now I have to be fed *some* information. I promise my lips are sealed.'

'I can only implore you for restraint. Do we have an agreement that whatever you learn never escapes these walls?'

'As I said, I've signed two contracts to that effect and I'm not about to break either one. It would be too costly.'

Ash didn't like Derriman's sudden silent stare. The general manager seemed to ponder an inner conflict.

'You need to ask Sir Victor?' Ash asked helpfully.

A second or two, then Derriman gave a slow shake of his head. 'No, I'll put my trust in you, David. All I ask is that you keep me fully informed of your activities in the castle, and that you'll seek me out for any answers you might require.'

'Deal.' Ash gave one shake of the other man's proffered hand and tried to convey trust in his expression. 'Let's start with the archbishop and his nun, shall we?'

'Yes, Archbishop Carsely and his votary, Sister Thimble.' Andrew Derriman ruminated for a few seconds more. Then, he appeared to have made up his mind. 'There shouldn't be any harm in explaining the man's personal circumstances to you. After all, you may come upon others that you'll recognize, or at least be familiar with, and – who knows? – they might be involved in deeds that have attracted, in the archbishop's words, "a dark oppressive legion". Who can truly know?'

Derriman leaned in closer to Ash and his words were hard to catch under the drone of other conversations in the great hall.

'When he was just a bishop, Carsely's diocese was in London's East End. Priests who knew him then and had worked with him in deprived areas were aware that he was abusing children of both sexes. Carsely would tell the children it would be a mortal sin to speak of what happened between them and that if they did so, their souls would be banished to the fiery depths of Hell. He went on pilgrimages to Lourdes with many sick children. Carsely was a learned and respected member of the priesthood and other priests were frightened to expose him. Nevertheless, every so often a priest would try to denounce him, and the Church, fearful of yet more bad publicity, would either move them on to different parishes or abroad on missionary work.'

Derriman shook his head wearily, as if the problem was bearing down on his own shoulders.

'You may remember the scandal in the Roman Catholic Church when correspondence between American bishops and a future pontiff was made public in the 1990s. The bishops had condemned an American curate who had allegedly abused two hundred deaf children. At the time, the disciplinary division in Rome, the Congregation for the Doctrine of the Faith, was led by Cardinal Ratzinger, later elevated to Pope. As Cardinal, he failed to respond to the American senior clergy. Eventually the accused priest, Father Lawrence Murphy, died of natural causes and the affair itself was allowed to die.'

Ash hadn't wanted to interrupt, but he was way ahead of Derriman. 'You're going to tell me that Carsely, eventually elevated to archbishop, was a paedophile, so they sent him here to avoid further scandal.'

'I'm afraid so. Such a high-profile case, you see. It was much, much more damaging that it was an archbishop rather than a mere priest. This was before the problems of paedophilia in the Church became much more notorious. Carsely was brought here to keep a tight lid on his indiscretions. And it worked – he was contained.'

'I don't understand why the nun is with him. Sister Thimble?'

Derriman shrugged his narrow shoulders. 'She served him in his parish when he was just a priest, then followed on when he was promoted. She's devoted to him, even if he is perverted. I think her vocation is to bring him back to God and have him repent his transgressions. Besides, Archbishop Carsely refused to enter Comraich without her. She'd become his faithful servant and remains so.'

'Sounds kind of creepy.'

The general manager nodded his head. 'Yes, I suppose it does. But it works.'

Ash watched the ex-archbishop as he made his self-important way down the lengthy marble hall, making a straight path through other guests, blessing them with an imperious sign of the cross as he went. Sister Thimble followed close behind, almost running to keep up with what to her was obviously deity made flesh.

Ash looked questioningly at Derriman. 'You don't think . . . ?'

It was as if the stooped general manager had read his thoughts. 'That she devotes her whole body to the defrocked archbishop if only to keep him appeased? Or perhaps I should say "satiated"?'

'Well . . .' Ash let the word hang.

'No. Our absolute condition of admission was that he be chemically castrated at Comraich to avoid more problems of a sexual nature. Although his preference was for the very young, who knew what substitute he might use once he was here? Sister Thimble acts both as his acolyte and his nurse, administering his medication.'

Ash opened his mouth to speak, but found he had nothing to say. He was too stunned. And he felt sorry for the nun. What had she ever done to be incarcerated, apart from being too loyal for her own good?

'When the archbishop arrived,' Derriman went on, disregarding the astonished look on the ghost hunter's face, 'he was given a choice of two methods to check hyperarousal and intrusive sexual fantasies. The third method, the complete removal of the testicles, was not even offered as a choice. We're not barbarians here at Comraich.

'The first offer was a twice-daily intake of tablets called Androcur, an anti-libidinal drug which opposes the action of testosterone rather than interfering with its production.

'The second choice was Leuprorelin, which acts on the pituitary gland to halt the production of testosterone. This drug takes the form of a monthly injection.'

'Is it legal in this country?' enquired a dismayed Ash.

'It is now,' came the swift response. 'It's voluntary here. Archbishop Carsely volunteered for the first option. Sister Thimble ensures he takes an Androcur tablet twice a day, and so far they appear to have been effective. There are some side effects, as one would expect from any drug, but none has actually caused the archbishop any distress. Not the best of solutions, I admit, but the best we have at present.'

Both men started walking again until Derriman stopped by a solid-looking door on their left. He knocked loudly, then entered a code on a keypad beside the door. A voice from within called out '*Okay*,' and the lock clicked before the door was opened.

Ash entered behind Derriman, and in a day of shocks, some good, some bad, some confusing, he was taken by surprise yet again.

27

'Awesome,' Ash murmured quietly to himself.

It wasn't the size of the high-ceilinged room that astonished him, but the sophisticated hi-tech equipment that filled it. It was completely out of context with the venerable building in which it was housed.

This might well have been a mini-control complex for the space shuttle at NASA, but for the juxtaposition of new with old, and that, to Ash, was the shock of it.

Banks of CCTV time- and date-stamped screens filled one wall entirely; three observers sat before them at a long desk filled with computer workstations and joysticks to control the cameras that monitored the entire castle and its grounds. At a second desk uniformed men and women typed and Skyped in various languages. Above a door across the wide room a red warning light shone, while below, on the door itself, bold capital letters announced PROCESSING ROOM. Looking around, Ash took in computers and laptops, more desks occupied by data processors, large flat-screen televisions showing CNN, Bloomberg, Al Jazeera and BBC News 24.

A separate television monitor showed the monochrome interior of the guardroom by the estate's second set of gates that Ash had passed through earlier that day. Another single monitor revealed the area just outside the first gate by the lodge at Comraich's initial, innocent-looking first entrance where he'd caught the camera zooming in on him. A third monitor displayed what looked like a docking area for both large and small vehicles and Ash guessed this had to be the castle's delivery point where vans, lorries and transporters unloaded goods. In fact, there was already an articulated lorry backed up there with several uniformed men transferring cardboard boxes of various sizes onto a raised loading bay.

Ash spotted Kevin Babbage sitting at a desk on a long dais in front of a whiteboard that ran the length of one wall. He was in shirtsleeves, his tie loosened. Babbage's shoulders somehow looked even broader without his jacket, the shirt stretched as if the muscles beneath were striving to break through. His buzz-cut hairstyle was perfectly suited to the launch-pad activity among his staff, and his granite expression looked as if he would break legs if annoyed.

He stood, pulled on his jacket, straightened his tie and hopped off the dais. Babbage headed straight for Derriman and Ash, ignoring a young, bespectacled man who tried to catch his attention as he went by. Babbage came to a halt directly in front of Ash, ignoring Derriman entirely.

'You ready to get your hands dirty?' Babbage's voice was gruff, suiting his appearance perfectly. He lowered his voice and continued, 'I suppose you'll want to see Hoyle's room first?'

He nodded. 'Maybe I can pick up some clues there.'

'This isn't a detective story,' Babbage said brusquely, surreptitiously glancing round. 'We don't have a murderer here in Comraich.'

'Maybe not. But *something* killed him and I'd like to find out what. There may be a clue – or a *sensing* – in his room.'

Babbage looked sceptically at Ash.

'Then the sooner we start the quicker we might achieve a result,' Derriman interceded, obviously conscious of the friction that was building between the two men.

'Fine by me.' Ash gave Babbage a broad but humourless smile and the security chief just offered a grunt.

*

As the trio descended the steps leading down from the ground floor, Derriman eagerly explained the castle's different levels and layout. Ash felt the stooped man, bundled up as he was in scarf and thick pullover beneath his coat, might have served better as a professor of history rather than a manager in a covert world of high stakes and nefarious dealings. The Inner Court regime he was part of didn't seem quite right for a man of his apparent sensibilities.

His guide's voice sounded more hollow with every step they took down the spiral of worn stone steps, and the air was cooler the lower they went. Ash was glad of his jacket, the collar of which he pulled tight around his neck. Babbage seemed unaffected by the chill.

The castle had six levels above ground, Derriman explained, with many confusing chambers, passageways and turret rooms. The very top rooms, which had access to the battlements, contained the living quarters of Lord Edgar Shawcroft-Draker and Sir Victor. Also the fifth floor was the castle's chapel which was presided over by the defrocked Archbishop Carsely. VIP guests were also accommodated on the third and fourth floors.

For such exalted guests the apartments were more like five-star hotel suites; practically all were full at present, or soon would be. The second floor housed the senior staff and visitors. The first floor was where the dining room, reading rooms and libraries, viewing rooms, cinema (television and radio were not available – Comraich was deliberately isolated from the rest of the world, after all), games and card room were all situated. Also on that floor were the kitchens, the first of which served only the main restaurant, while another smaller one catered mainly for the estate rangers, wardens, guards, gardeners, manual labourers, nurses and others who worked within the complex.

On the ground floor was the long reception hall with various offices along the way. At the rear of the massive property was a gymnasium, health club and small indoor swimming pool. And, of course, there were many, many display rooms exhibiting all manner of fascinating items from the past.

Suits of armour guarded several hallways and there was more than one armoury full of violent-looking weapons of destruction. Displayed in many rooms roped off out of necessity, although the contents of each were in plain view, were four-poster beds, genuine crystal chandeliers, in one a long refectory table, a pair of serpentine marquetry commodes, in others rosewood bookcases, silver cutlery and wine coolers, paintings, marble statues and busts, hand-painted and silk wallpaper as well as tapestries, elegant cabinets, exquisite clocks – all manner of precious antiquities that could keep a serious historian interested for months.

Beneath Comraich there were three subterranean levels. The one they were currently descending to was the hospital unit, where Ash was somewhat perfunctorily shown around; he was amazed at the state-of-the-art equipment kept in different surgeries or operating theatres. He was also impressed by all of the hi-tech medical paraphernalia on view and the lavishly furnished wards and single rooms.

'Is this where Douglas Hoyle's body is being held for the autopsy?' Ash had asked, only to be assured that there was a discreet mortuary on this floor that was kept well away from the general hospital section. This was where Hoyle was undergoing a post-mortem at that very moment. Below this lower floor was a place specially kept for newcomers, where they could recover from the trauma of leaving behind the world they had known for this new environment. Here they were kept in luxurious but solitary confinement where they could be physically examined by a doctor and counselled by both psychiatrist and psychologist until they were deemed fit to join the general Comraich community. It was a kind of limbo, Ash thought.

'I take it, then, that guests here are watched by cameras day and night,' Ash pressed. 'So whatever happened to Hoyle would have been captured on film.'

It was Babbage who answered. 'There are CCTV cameras in every important room in the castle, including Douglas Hoyle's, but when we examined the observation tape the morning after the incident, all the video file was blanked. And I mean *all* the CCTV files were blank, as if somehow they had been overexposed. Not a single image on any of 'em. That same night practically all staff members and guests felt nauseous. At first, we thought food poisoning was to blame, but all the kitchens were spotless and what was left of the food was subsequently analysed in our own lab. No dodgy bacteria or poison was found in any of it. All normal.' He paused on the stairs and faced Ash. 'I'll say this – it was a night none of us, staff or guests, ever want to go through again.'

Little else was said on the subject as Ash was led down to the next level. On the stairs, they met Rachael Krantz, on her way up. She carried a clipboard on which was a graph of some kind.

Derriman, who had been leading the way, stopped and looked anxiously at her. 'Is-is everything all right?' he asked timidly.

She gave him an unpleasant look, then switched her eyes to Ash.

'Everything is as it should be,' she answered curtly, as if to Ash alone.

'Yes, yes, of course,' Derriman stammered, as if realizing he might have made a mistake in questioning the nurse's ability to run a tight ship. 'We-we're just showing Mr Ash the different levels of Comraich.'

Krantz looked alarmed, as did Babbage, Ash noticed. Derriman looked terrified, and Ash wondered who he was more scared of, Haelstrom or Krantz?

'We're taking Mr Ash to Douglas Hoyle's room,' Babbage intervened. 'Seems it's important to him.' The last comment sounded like a rebuke. Ash had come to expect hostility from the chief of security by now. He expected nothing less of a man who must have felt this parapsychological investigation was a waste of everyone's time and money, even though Babbage could offer no feasible explanation for the bizarre events himself. On the other hand, Krantz's obvious dislike of him remained a mystery. Unless she, like many other 'normal' people, thought he was a crackpot who shouldn't be allowed near her patients.

'I haven't had time to get Mr Hoyle's room cleaned up yet,' Krantz said discourteously.

'All the better,' Ash responded. 'I need to see the scene as it was.'

With a cold stare, she stepped aside to let them pass, but she never took her eyes off Ash as he went by.

Outside the room messily vacated by the unfortunate Douglas Hoyle, opposite the lift, the three men paused.

'If neither of you minds, I'd like to go in alone to begin with. Just to get the feel of the place. What I don't want is your own emotions interfering with whatever psychic field or subliminal intimation has been left in there.'

Babbage stared at him as if he were crazy and Derriman started fidgeting with his fingers.

Ash grinned, but it was a hard expression, for he could already feel some kind of presence beyond this closed door. Years ago he might have ignored it, but for him, life – *and* death – had changed.

He pulled himself together, looked at Derriman, and waited.

'W-what?' the general manager stuttered.

Ash pointed at the keypad fixed to the door. He'd already peeked through the small observation panel.

'Of course. I'm sorry.' Derriman reached into his inside breast pocket and drew out a small plastic-covered notebook and quickly scanned through the pages, his hands now trembling instead of fidgeting. 'Ah.' He stopped at a page. 'Subroom 3a,' he murmured. To Ash, he said, 'Four numbers. Two, six, four and eight.'

The investigator tapped them in, mindful of his own hand trembling slightly. Something clicked and the door shifted a fraction as if freed from its surrounding frame. Ash pushed the door open wide and walked through.

He cried out as he was immediately thrown back into the corridor by some fierce, invisible force.

28

Babbage caught him before he went down.

'Jesus, feller . . .' the security boss spluttered.

Derriman had backed away from the room, the expression of alarm on his face almost comical.

But Ash wasn't laughing. Still held by Babbage, he struggled to regain his balance.

'Somebody – some*thing* – doesn't want me in there.'

The chief of security muttered another blasphemy 'That wasn't you? You didn't throw yourself backwards?' he growled in disbelief.

'Believe me,' said a shaken Ash, 'something *really* doesn't want me in there.'

'So what do we do?'

'We try again.'

But this time the investigator entered more cautiously. Although he still felt pressure pushing against him, it had weakened considerably, as though whatever unseen psychic force was present had become depleted.

Vapour escaped his mouth and he shivered against the deep, frigid atmosphere inside the room. Babbage waited on the threshold while Derriman peered fearfully over the thickset man's shoulder.

'It's here,' Ash announced calmly. 'But it's fading, taking the chill with it.'

'You gotta be kidding,' rasped Babbage. 'There's no one else in the room.'

'Feel it,' Ash told him. 'Feel it draining away. Come on in, it can't hurt you any more. I think all its energy was used up when it tossed me out.'

The security chief walked in, but Derriman remained by the door.

The room contained one large bed, at the foot of which were its rumpled bedclothes. As it was an underground bedroom, there were no windows to the outside world, but there were paintings, all of them peaceful landscapes, presumably to take away the starkness of the walls. Some were tilted, while others had fallen to the floor. Across the room was an upturned armchair, and a sofa leaning almost upright in a corner, cushions scattered around it. A bedside cabinet had been turned over, its contents strewn across the carpet.

And on one wall, to the investigator's right, was the definite imprint of a man's figure, formed by hundreds of dark red spots and smears. Bigger patches of blood shone dully.

The silhouette of gore ended at least two feet from the floor, although rivulets of blood had run down to the skirting board, and Ash imagined the helpless man transfixed there, crucified without nails.

The room also reeked of the coppery scent of blood that mingled with the nauseating stink of excrement. Fortunately, this too, was swiftly fading.

'Was Hoyle conscious when he was taken away?' Ash asked the security chief, taking a thermometer from his shoulder bag.

'Nurse Krantz said he was delirious,' replied Babbage, 'mumbling words she could only just hear, but couldn't understand.'

Still partly shielded by the security chief's muscled body, Derriman, his voice querulous, spoke up. 'B-by the time they reached the surgery above us, he w-was making no sound whatsoever. Nurse Krantz said his eyes were open and there was a look of sheer terror in them. He never woke from his catatonic state.'

'Caused by loss of blood?'

It was Babbage who answered Ash. 'We'll know more after the post-mortem, but our pathologist's initial opinion was that it wasn't his wounds or loss of blood that killed him, but myocardial infarction. Heart attack.'

'Like the medium, Moira Glennon.'

'Yeah, like her. Scared to death.'

29

Breathless, Twigg stood back to survey his work. He leaned on his shovel to steady himself.

The six-foot-long trench he'd dug in the peaceful woods should easily be deep enough to accommodate what was left of Nelson's corpse. When Twigg backfilled it, the dead apprentice would easily be covered. A scattering of fallen leaves over the patted-down bump should conceal the grave from any warden or rambling guest.

Now to move the body. It was a good thing he wasn't squeamish, Twigg told himself, because just the sight of the eviscerated body when it was dragged out of the heap of dead leaves and forest ferns he'd partially hidden it under would be enough to turn a normal person's stomach. Most people wouldn't go near the wreck of a corpse, let alone touch it.

He straightened, wiping drool from his chin as he did so. But once he took his hand off the embedded shovel's handle his fingers began to shake again. He tried to hold them still, but could only do so by pressing his hand against his upper thigh.

The assassin drew in deep breaths, slowly letting go of them until he felt well enough to finish the chore. Twigg cursed. He used to be so much stronger than he looked – which on some occasions seemed to surprise his victims – but he knew his age as much as his illness contributed to his breathlessness. Even so, despite his years, he would have remained a valuable asset to the organization, because killing someone these days rarely depended on strength. There were more subtle methods, such as poison or even the garrotte, which no mark could fight against so long as the wire was sharp and the positioning around the throat swift and accurate. Blades were good, providing they went in deep and cut the correct arteries or destroyed the right organs.

The reason he'd decided to hide Nelson's mutilated corpse would seem crazy to most. It was because he felt in league with the wildcats. Of course, no love would ever exist between himself and the vicious felines, but he felt an indefinable affinity with them, and he somehow knew that he was their protector. Otherwise, the woods would be swept by gun-toting guards until the problem had been eradicated. Maybe his affiliation was fanciful, illusory, but it felt real.

The assassin went over to the body secreted beneath the woodland detritus of crispy leaves and damp ferns and reached for its one shod foot – the other was bare, although the caked blood resembled a red sock (not at all to Nelson's taste, but then it didn't really matter any more). Twigg pulled both feet towards him and the now-loosely constructed body slithered from its hiding place.

Oddly, the body looked in an even worse state than before; either that or the time spent bringing quicklime and water, not forgetting the shovel, back to the spot had deadened the shock of its image slightly. He pulled again and, the covering leaves disturbed, Twigg saw and felt the still-soft body stretching, only strands of skin and the spine managing to keep it in one piece. With less force, Twigg eased the pieces towards the shallow hole in the ground, and when grave and corpse were more or less adjacent he knelt and rolled the body in. Jawless head and torso first, then the hips and legs, still joined tenuously to the whole by the spine, skin, and some flesh.

Twigg found it difficult to rise to his feet again, for it had been a long and difficult day so far, and he comforted himself that any man would have been near exhaustion by now. But he made it, smacking the palms of his hands together to dislodge dirt and bits of bloody debris.

He surveyed his work for a moment or two before dragging the sack of lumpy quicklime over to the grave. He pondered on the stupidity of some murderers, those who simply poured ordinary garden or chlorinated lime over the victim, expecting to hide the smell of putrefaction. Smugly, he picked up the quicklime sack and spread the white powder over the body in the grave, then quickly used the water in the bucket to slake the lime. This method would keep the flesh dry and firm, avoiding the worst of the corruption and hence creating little stench once the earth was replaced. If Eddy Nelson's cadaver were to be discovered in, say, six months' time, then, apart from the foulness of his shredded parts, it would be in good condition: the flesh would be dry and firm, if a little shrunken, and there'd be no further rupturing of skin beyond that caused by the malicious ferocity of the wildcats.

With his grin drooling more saliva, the assassin picked up the standing shovel and covered his dead apprentice with dirt, remembering to scatter more fallen leaves and forest ferns over the low bump in the ground before he returned to his own sanctuary, the little cottage lost in the heart of the woodland paradise.

30

The breeze coming off the darkened sea was icy, but at least the air was fresh and cleansing. Which was how David Ash wanted to feel – cleansed from the dank mustiness and dirt in so many neglected regions of the huge castle.

He sat on a bench that was thoughtfully situated on the long walkway leading from Comraich overlooking the great Scottish waters. The red sun was low on the horizon, helping to warm the greyness of the land mass in the far distance, this just visible through a soft sanguine mist. The peaceful view at least helped Ash shed some of the tension he'd felt during his searches, a tension he knew was shared with Derriman, while Babbage seemed oblivious to the unease of his companions, as well as to the gloomy tenseness in the atmosphere. Ash, of course, was seasoned enough to differentiate imagination from sensing, and he was sufficiently attuned to know paranormal activity was present in this place. With the nature of Hoyle's death, how could it be otherwise?

And it was not just the coldness of certain corridors and stairways, not even the draughts that swept or drifted through the old refurbished chambers. At times, when Ash had asked the others to pause so that he could consider whether a 'mood' was either static or transient through a location, Babbage would stand there, thick legs braced apart, arms folded, as if challenging any hint of spectral presence in the room or hallway. Ash knew that such stubborn scepticism was not conducive to supernatural revelation, but he couldn't forget that a few years ago he would probably have adopted the same negative stance.

From his shoulder bag, he took out a journalist's notebook and began to read through the brief observations he'd made during the tour of the castle's lower floors. He also studied rough sketches he'd made of certain locations. Later, in the privacy of his own room, he would transfer the notes into his laptop, perhaps making more sense of them to gain an overview.

Although there hadn't been time to assess the upper floors, he and the two guides, with Babbage acting as a resentful malcontent, had scoured several levels of the ancient building, including the kitchens, drawing rooms, libraries and armouries (including the one that had given Ash a fright earlier that day), as well as stairs, hallways and corridors. The investigator had marked a few locations that warranted further research, places where he would later instal cameras and sensors. More complicated equipment might be brought in after this initial search, but that was for another day – or night.

Ash had been both frustrated and angered by Babbage's refusal to grant full access to the levels beneath Douglas Hoyle's wrecked apartment. The security chief had been adamant that the lowest reaches were out of bounds to the investigator, and Derriman had apologetically concurred. Strict orders from Sir Victor Haelstrom had already vetoed any request to descend further than the second lower level, and neither Babbage nor Derriman was prepared to overrule him, even after witnessing Ash's startling ejection into the corridor.

Ash was convinced that the haunting, and he had no doubts it was a haunting, emanated from the depths of Comraich, and during his meeting with Haelstrom in – he consulted his wristwatch – just over forty minutes, he would insist he be allowed down there. If not, then the deal was off: he would leave and return to London, even if it meant getting there under his own steam.

As he scribbled in the notepad resting on the flattened

leather shoulder bag laid across his lap, a shadow fell over the page.

'Mind if I sit with you a moment, old son?' a crisp yet somehow weary voice said.

Ash looked up but couldn't get a clear image of the individual standing before him because of the setting sun behind the man's back; all he could see was someone tall and ramrod straight, almost of military bearing.

'Help yourself,' Ash replied, and felt the bench's wooden planks lift, then sag as the stranger slumped next to him with a heavy sigh. In profile, the man looked as though he'd been handsome in his younger days, with a strong aquiline nose and firm jaw, spoilt only by longish lank hair that fell over his high forehead, its strands of grey easily winning against the blackness of youth. He wore a long, thick drooping moustache which, and despite its overgrown style, didn't detract from the man's military demeanour. In his day, his new companion might have been a member of the Queen's Guard, so erect and proud was his comportment. Ash guessed him to be in his mid-to-late seventies.

The straight-shouldered man squinted his eyes towards the mellowing red sun and said to Ash without prompting, 'They got it all wrong, y'know.'

Ash felt as though he'd just walked into a conversation in mid-sentence. He kept quiet.

The man shook his head slowly, as if regretfully. 'They didn't get the picture at all; thought I meant to batter her to death, as if I'd waste time on that silly bitch. Y'know, she ran naked in the street and into the nearest pub she could find, screaming blue murder, telling 'em her husband was trying to kill her.'

He gave a little dry chortle.

'No, it was Sandra I intended to murder, and I did so. But out of rage,' he added, as if that made the offence forgivable. He turned his head directly towards Ash, and the parapsychologist sat as if mesmerized. In fact, Ash *was* mesmerized. There was something familiar about this tall man and his story. If Ash was right – and he had a good memory for these things – it was one of those news items that never went away, was revived and speculated on every decade or so. And all because it had never been fully resolved. Ash was much too young to remember it himself, but he'd heard about it.

A *cause célèbre*. Almost folklore.

So Ash was patient and listened, even though not quite sure of the events that were being related to him. Besides, he already had some notion of the kind of people who resided in Comraich.

'Not often we get fresh blood here,' the lank-haired man observed, studying the investigator tip to toe. 'On the run, is it? Damnable lonely place Comraich, you'll come to find, even when full of guests. Always good to greet a newcomer, someone perhaps, who'll listen to my side of the story. Others here don't seem to care.'

Interested, Ash pressed him with a recollected detail. 'You mentioned Sandra. She was the kiddies' nanny, wasn't she?'

'Yes. Yes, of course. Here they think I've forgotten, keep feeding me pills, the odd injection, do you see? And hypno, mustn't forget the hypnotherapy. There's a joke in there somewhere, but I can't think what it is for the moment. Anyway, I don't always swallow the pills, hide them under m'tongue; spit them out after. So sometimes I get really clear flashbacks, remember nearly everything. I've been at Comraich for, oh, six or seven years, but often it feels like yesterday, y'know?'

A bit longer than that if I've got it right, thought Ash. *A few decades ago, if you only knew.*

'You said they'd got it wrong. Who was that? The police? The newspapers?' he prompted again.

'Yes. Yes.' The second 'yes' was drawn out, as if the man were sending his mind back in time. 'It was Sandra Rivett I wanted. She was married to a merchant seaman then, but they'd decided to split up, so she lived in a small bedsit in Clapham when she wasn't at the house. In Belgravia, it was.

You know the police discovered she kept a full-size picture of a naked man over her bed. Flighty little thing.'

He slowly leaned forward, elbows on knees, head in his hands.

'I got it wrong, too, do you see? Thought she was up for it. But she laughed in my face when I tried it on. I wanted her nice little round body, so different to my wife's bony backside. We were downstairs in the basement dining room when I made my move. At first, she was upset, then she started to laugh at me. That's when the red mist descended. I'd already spent years listening to my scrawny bitch of a wife complaining about my gambling – they used to call me Lucky, my friends did, and usually, I was. Ran out of luck that evening though.'

He gave another weary sigh. 'So I clobbered her. Sandra, I mean. I can't remember what with, but suddenly she was lying dead at my feet, her eyes staring straight into mine like a dead mackerel's.' He gave a little shiver.

'And that was the moment the cow chose to come downstairs. Wearing a dressing gown, I believe. She'd either just got into the bath or just got out. Wouldn't bloody well stop screaming when she saw what I'd done. So I went for her, almost laid her out, grabbed the dressing gown but she struggled out of it and ran screaming into the street.'

Ash could feel a chill seeping through him.

'Lucky' hadn't seemed to notice. 'Well, that was when I knew my number was up. Fortunately, I had good friends. Nobility sticks together, y'know. We hide our scandals. Oh, if you knew how many secrets we shared. Anyway, got a friend to drive a car I was borrowing at the time; he took it down to Newhaven and left it there, about a mile from the marina to make the rozzers think I'd skipped the country. Meanwhile, I was on a different route entirely. Acquaintances of great influence, people who knew and honoured my forebears, spirited me away by private plane to this place. And in this place,' he said with a devitalized sigh, 'I remain.'

He looked sightlessly into the distance, his face creased

with regret. 'Miss the kiddies, y'know. Frances – *Lady* Frances – must be all of fifteen by now. Then young Lord Bingham must be in his teens. Then my little sweetie, Lady Camilla. Don't even remember how old she was when I left. Sometimes I'm ashamed I stay here. Should I give myself up, just to get to see 'em, but it's bloody impossible to get out of this place. Believe me, I've tried.'

Ash realized the man had lost all sense of time: those 'kiddies' would be adults by now, probably middle-aged, or even older.

The man straightened and clapped his hands on his knees, the military sharpness about him regained.

'Well now, must get on, things to do. Ah look, we're soon to be joined.'

He motioned towards a figure that had just risen onto the crenellated walkway and Ash followed his direction. He immediately recognized the V-neck aubergine jumper and the longish gypsy-type skirt, the lush hair, its edges tinted ruby-red by the setting sun.

'Our beauteous Brazilian, our Amazonian Aphrodite,' his companion announced with pleasure and with something else – circumspection? 'She's my shrink, don't you know. Dr Wyatt. Delphine is her first name, which is appropriate because she's always *delving* into my mind. Sorry, weak play on words. Such a delectable woman, but out of bounds to the likes of you and me.'

Ash was puzzled. 'What makes you say that?'

'Oh well, it's just that I get the impression she belongs, if you know what I mean, to the abominable Nurse Krantz. Just a suspicion, mind. But . . . well, Krantz seems very proprietorial about her. But who can tell?'

The man rose abruptly. 'Another time, perhaps?' he said as he looked down at Ash, who was frowning, confused by Lucky's previous remark about the relationship between Delphine and the senior nurse. 'I can see you don't believe me,' the tall man said with a smile. 'It's only a suspicion, old boy.

229

Probably nothing in it at all. To my knowledge, though, our Brazilian beauty has never been involved with any man since she arrived here.'

Delphine was drawing closer and Ash could see there was a look of apprehension on her face.

Ash's companion was all briskness again, and he said hurriedly, as if wanting to be on his way before the psychologist reached them. 'We must talk again. You're a very interesting fellow.'

Ash almost smiled as he watched his apparently new friend walking away: throughout the conversation, Ash had hardly said a word.

By then, Delphine had reached the investigator's bench. She was smiling and Ash felt suddenly uplifted.

'I see you've met one of my patients,' she said, still smiling.

'Indeed I have,' said Ash. 'A rather sought-after individual, if I'm not mistaken.'

Delphine's face fell. 'You can't tell anyone—' she began.

'Don't worry,' Ash reassured her. 'Lucky's secret is safe with me.'

'Lucky' Lord Lucan? Ash smiled at the irony.

31

'You know, Lucan was a kind of legend in this country,' Ash told Delphine, as they sat on the bench seat facing the sea.

Shadows were lengthening as the sun began to sink below the horizon. It was getting chillier by the minute, yet neither of them was willing to leave the walkway. Ash found it hard to believe Lucan's insinuation regarding Delphine and Krantz; he also valued the psychologist's company too much to end their conversation just yet.

'Yes, I know the story. I was briefed on his history when I first arrived. Apart from sessions with me, he's undergoing hypnotherapy under Dr Singh. Dr Singh is our psychiatrist; have you met him yet?'

Ash shook his head. 'No, I haven't. I suppose you know Lucan isn't taking all his medication.'

With a smile, she gave a small nod of her head. 'Yes, we do. He still receives enough treatment to keep him passive though.'

'Passive?' He couldn't say he was shocked – at lunch Comraich's senior surgeon, the dandified Dr Vernon Pritchard, had listed the various sedatives that were administered to the clientele, but the fact that these residents were, in fact, prisoners, had only truly been confirmed by Lucan himself. And that was why Delphine sometimes wouldn't look at him directly, but would gaze off to one side. She wasn't comfortable with the deception. Then it dawned on him why she was so eager to tell him of the worthy work the hospital unit carried

231

out, perhaps to ease her own guilt and maybe prove her own self-worth.

Nearly forty years after he'd committed the crime, Lord Lucan was still on the run from the police who, presumably, were still after him. Then there was Douglas Hoyle, the financier who had cheated thousands out of their hard-earned savings and embezzled his own company. And the perverted Archbishop Carsely, with his proclivity for sexually molesting children.

He regarded Delphine Wyatt in a new light and suddenly, as if she'd read his thoughts, she turned not just her eyes from him but her face too.

Ash wasn't going to allow that to happen this time. Gently, he placed the palm of his hand against her cheek and drew her face back to him. Her skin glowed almost golden under the rays of the dying sun, and her eyes – which this time didn't evade his – were dark and lustrous, but also a little fearful. Such was the mysterious union between them – which he now realized both had felt when they first set eyes on each other – that she knew his mind and was ashamed, yet desperate not to be condemned.

'I was aware my father was an associate of the Inner Court,' she began to say as tears formed and glittered like tiny flames in the sun's reflection, 'although never in a high capacity, just as someone who was useful to it in certain ways which, frankly, I never understood. When he knew he was dying of cancer he wanted me to be secure, but he'd been bled dry by his second wife, my stepmother, whom I haven't seen since his funeral. I had already gained a medical degree, so before he died he arranged for the Inner Court to take over payment to further my studies as a psychiatrist. I owe the organization an awful lot and I don't mean that just in financial terms but for their overall generosity to me. This job, for instance. Once I'd gained my Masters Degree I joined Sunil – Dr Singh – here and we work in conjunction, practically as a team, although he is the senior partner, of course.'

To Ash it sounded almost as if she'd been groomed. He wondered just how far her loyalty to the Inner Court extended.

A single tear escaped and slipped down her cheek, leaving a glittering trail behind.

Ash moved in even closer as she continued.

'I was happy at first, although I missed my father very much. I truly thought this place *was* a peaceful sanctuary for people who needed it, and I was so proud of the work in the hospital unit, which is far more advanced than most other British hospitals; but gradually I came to realize that all was not what it seemed. The clients, the guests, the residents, all were used to wealth and luxury, but none can leave unless we can help them forget their past and be certain that they won't be recognized in the outside world.'

'What about youngsters, those like the twins, Petra and Peter? They can't spend the rest of their lives cooped up here.'

'They won't. They'll be cured – of all their addictions. Then parts of their memory will be erased and they'll be given entirely new personalities. We can do it, we've managed before.'

'You know Petra brought illegal drugs with her?'

Delphine raised her head in alarm.

'Those asthma inhalers she had. I'm pretty sure they contained cocaine, maybe even crystal meth.'

'I didn't know.' She sounded disappointed, saddened.

'Why should you? Junkies are cunning. But it's a long way to come for rehab.'

'That's only part of it. I can't tell you any more than that.'

'Of course, Delphine, I understand. But what about you? You surely can't spend the rest of your life in this place.'

She dabbed her eyes with a tiny lace-edged handkerchief. 'I don't intend to,' she told him. 'When I have enough money saved I'm going to leave, set up another practice, possibly abroad.'

'And they'd let you do that, they'd let you go?'

She smiled wanly. 'I'm sure you signed a contract before you came here. Well so did I when I joined, and it's watertight.

Any civil action they took against me would ruin my reputation as a psychologist as well as bankrupt me. I was made aware what would happen if they didn't want to let me go.'

'Sounds ominous.'

'Oh, they put it in terms that seem quite reasonable. But I don't think I'll have a problem in two or three years' time, after I've proved my loyalty.'

I wouldn't count on it, thought Ash. Everything he'd experienced so far at Comraich and the more he learned about it – guards and electrified fences to keep people in as well as out – told him the restrictions and the IC's power were formidable. And probably non-negotiable. Suddenly he felt an overwhelming fear for her – and for himself. His latent psychic ability seemed to be warning him.

Surprising even himself, he leaned forward and kissed her damp cheek. For a moment she went rigid, and Ash remembered Lucan's theory about Delphine's sexuality. But Ash felt in his very soul that she felt the same as him. He'd never felt so sure of anything before, despite his predisposition to cynicism.

And then she softened and moved her lips to his.

It wasn't a passionate kiss, it was a gentle one; yet it conveyed such feelings between them that Ash was almost overwhelmed by confusing emotions. Considering they had only just met that morning, and even though they had a near-death encounter in common – probably one of the most intimate experiences two people could ever share – their sudden, mutual closeness was almost mystical.

Ash drew away, just a little, remembering his fear of becoming too close to another woman; but the decision was no longer his to make. His arm slid around her shoulders and he was helpless to her embrace.

They kissed again, and this time the passion was almost impossible to ignore. He tasted her sweetness, and if a person could be lost to another's allure, then it was now.

It had grown dark, the sun was becoming lost to the

horizon, and he remembered the inconveniently approaching meeting with Sir Victor Haelstrom. Carefully, he raised his wrist to look at his watch.

'Delphine . . .' he began to say in a hushed voice.

She drew away just a fraction, joy and expectation combined in the look she gave him.

'I've got a meeting with Haelstrom,' he told her, slightly breathlessly. 'I'm sorry, truly I'm sorry, but I'm already running late.'

She cast her eyes downwards. 'It's all right,' she said, 'I know you've got a job to do.'

She studied his face again, looking for . . . what? he asked himself. Then he realized: *reassurance*. She was alone in the world. And now she served in this strange location, a castle that was both a prison and a refuge. Did she even have close friends in this huge place? Her patients couldn't be counted as such, but what about Krantz? He closed his mind to the association. What would a man like Lucan know about relationships, a man who had murdered his own children's nanny in a lustful rage? A patient who had blotted out long segments of his own life so that now he was not even aware of how many years had slipped by since his internment here. Locked away all these years, how could he so judge another's life?

'I should have been with Haelstrom ten minutes ago. Hope he's not strict on punctuality.' Ash remembered the dressing-down Haelstrom had given Derriman for being late that morning.

'I'm afraid he is.' Delphine placed a hand on Ash's upper arm, but not to keep him there. 'You'd better hurry.'

He smiled because of her concern. 'I take it he's a bit of a bully.'

'He can be. Then again, he can be charming too. It depends on his mood. And who you are.'

Ash was curious. 'He has a trace of an accent I can't quite make out.'

'Originally he was from South Africa. He left there many years ago, though.'

'Ah,' said Ash, as if it all made sense. Haelstrom was probably of Dutch descent, and when South Africa rejoined the Commonwealth in 1994, he obviously became eligible for a knighthood. *For what, though?* he wondered. 'He can be pretty obnoxious,' he said.

'That's who he is. But go, David, I don't want you to get into trouble on my account.'

Ash gave a small laugh. 'I think I can handle Sir Victor. Although there is something I need to get permission for. Babbage and Derriman were dead set against it.'

It was her turn to look curiously at him.

'I have to get down to the lowest floor. Specifically, I need to inspect the room or passage directly below the suite Douglas Hoyle occupied before he was killed.'

She became disturbed. 'That really is forbidden territory, even for me.'

He frowned. 'You don't know what's down there?'

'I do,' she said, then shook her head and her loosened black hair fell over one cheek. 'But even I'm not allowed in the sub-basement. Patients are brought up to me when necessary.'

Ash was thoughtful for a moment. 'I felt some kind of hostile force rising into Hoyle's room. It was so powerful it threw me back out the door.'

'David!'

'It's all right, it sometimes happens when there's a build-up of psychic energy. My guess is that there might be a kind of psychic epicentre below ground.'

'I'm not sure what you mean.'

'I guess I can only explain it by saying it's a meeting of strong psychical energies drawn to one area where ley lines cross or meet, and the force becomes so immense it breaks through natural barriers. Sometimes it's referred to as a telluric energy field – earth energy, if you like – a ley-line convergence, that can expand from its centre. I believe there's such an epicentre in the lower regions of the castle itself, or the rock beneath it.'

'Haelstrom won't allow you down there. It's where the dungeons used to be and, as far as I know, the door to the stairway is always kept locked. Only a few people are ever allowed access.'

'Sounds all the more intriguing.'

'I have another idea that might help you. From the shoreline below the cliffs there are caves, and at the back of one is a passageway that I think used to lead up to the cellars of Comraich. I was told that smugglers brought their contraband into the castle through it centuries ago, though I don't know whether it's true. If you like, I'll arrange for a park ranger to take you along the shoreline tomorrow and perhaps into one or two caves there. The biggest one is the obvious cave to explore. When the tide is out, it's easy to see, and there's a rough wooden stairway that zig-zags down to the shore in stages. It's a hard journey, especially on the way back up, but I did it once. And I was warned by Sir Victor never to attempt it again. The tides are treacherous, he told me, and the sea comes right into the caves.'

'Delphine, you don't know how important that could be.' He grinned at her and she shot him a smile, albeit a nervous one. He pulled her towards him again and she came willingly.

He could have cursed. 'Look, I really am late for my meeting with Haelstrom ... Are you okay if I ... ?' Ash gestured to his notebook and the shoulder bag. He put one into the other and his pen into one of the breast pockets of his field jacket.

'David?'

He stopped what he was doing to look directly at her, his eyebrows raised in query.

'Will I see you later?' she asked quietly. 'For dinner, maybe?'

He mentally cursed again. 'Dinner's out for me I'm afraid. I've got to explore the rest of the castle. I've only looked at the lower half so far, and there's a lot more I need to see before I start setting up equipment.'

Now her eyes clouded with anxiety. 'There are rooms there you won't be allowed to enter. Lord Shawcroft-Draker's apartment for instance.'

'I'll check with Haelstrom first. He can't keep too many places closed off to me, otherwise I can't do my job.'

'Let me help you.' It was almost a plea and he grinned.

He wanted to say yes, but he knew it would be wrong: sometimes he had to work alone to pick up 'feelings', 'sensings', and in company it sometimes wouldn't happen. It was pointless to explain: anyone not experienced in the phenomena wouldn't understand.

'I appreciate your offer,' he told her, 'but I usually work best alone. Besides, it can be cold, uncomfortable and even dirty work; it's not for you.'

If she were offended, she hid it well.

'And I might even make a vigil through the night if I find a likely spot.'

'You will be careful though.'

'Of what? Ghosts? They can't harm a living person.' It was a lie – there were many ways a spirit could inflict punishment – but he wasn't prepared to tell Delphine that: she looked worried enough.

'Okay, David, please just take care.'

God, he wanted to kiss her again, this time with even more passion, but there was no time. He finally stood and looped the bag's strap across his shoulder. 'See you later,' he said, walking away reluctantly.

He turned his head once before reaching the end of the walkway, and saw her still seated on the bench, her hands clasped in her lap, her face, in profile, looking into the sunset. His feelings towards her were not planned, nor were they really wanted. But they couldn't be ignored.

32

How could he have let it happen? he asked himself as he entered the castle through a door at the end of the walkway. After the death of Grace Lockwood, and even after Christina Mariell at Edbrook, who wasn't what she seemed, he'd vowed never again to have strong feelings for any other woman, no matter how appealing. Kate had been an exception, but that was more of a fondness between them rather than any great love affair. They had been drawn together by a mutual need for succour and comfort. Kate was an attractive woman, but their personalities were too different for a deeper relationship. Now he'd met Delphine, and his painfully constructed emotional defences had crumbled into dust. He was confounded, almost angry with himself. How could he have let it happen, and all in the shortness of one day?

He was afraid for Delphine as much as for himself. His track record for romance was disastrous!

Ash went through a narrow passageway leading to the grand reception hall, and the faint sounds of conversation grew louder as he approached the long foyer. He turned a corner and found himself among the chattering clients. The lengthy polished-wood reception counter was to his right, behind which the two young receptionists, Veronica and Gerrard, were keeping busy.

Several heads turned his way when Ash walked out onto the marble concourse and he couldn't help reflect on what a farcical lot the Comraich clientele seemed to be: so far he'd come in contact with a weirdly holy but perverted archbishop and his acolyte nun, and a missing lord whose sensational crime and disappearance had made him legendary throughout the world. Who would he find next?

With that in mind, he studied the faces he passed by a little more intently. Some guests stared right back, mainly with expressions of interest or annoyance at his presence. But most were complete strangers to him, although he *felt* one or two were familiar. Halfway along the hallway, where guests obviously met before cocktails and dinner, Ash came across one man he most definitely did recognize, but whose name he couldn't remember.

He was a bulky, rough-faced individual with a pockmarked face, who stared back at the psychic investigator with both suspicion and hostility. He had thick white hair and eyebrows that were still almost black above small, piercing eyes that were set so deep that they were almost in shadow, and they glared at Ash as if to challenge him.

Unlike the other clients, most of whom were decked out in smart evening clothes, this one wore an ill-fitting grey suit and a dull tie of indeterminate colour, his shoes an unpolished brown. He was stocky, but his paunch strained at the single button of his suit jacket, and his trousers were rumpled, as if he cared nothing for fashion or freshness.

Ash continued on to the reception counter. Veronica looked up as he approached and smiled.

'What can I do for you, Mr Ash?'

'Uh, I have a meeting with Sir Victor Haelstrom,' he said, leaning in towards her.

'Yes, sir. At half-past six.' The sweet smile was still on her lips.

'Yep. I'm running a little bit late.'

She consulted her own watch that, like a nurse's, hung down on the left breast pocket of her jacket. 'It's six forty-five. Sir Victor has already rung down for you.'

'Really? Did he sound cross?' He'd meant it as a joke, but Veronica's reply was earnest.

'Well, he didn't sound very happy,' she said. 'Shall I ring him back and tell him you're on your way?'

'If it helps. He's on the fifth floor, yes?'

'That's right, Mr Ash.' She was already lifting the phone, unseen beneath the counter top, and Ash wondered whether it was kept out of sight deliberately to stop guests thinking about the outside world.

Her message was brief and Veronica maintained her smile throughout the muffled but rasping response that even Ash could hear.

'He's expecting you,' she said as she replaced the receiver. He wondered if she was being ironic, but she gave no hint.

'Fifth floor, Mr Ash,' she confirmed again and pointed down the hall with the pencil she'd been holding during their encounter. 'You know where the lift is.'

He thanked her and as he turned away she said, 'Good luck?'

Ash did a double-take but she continued to smile in the same way.

As the investigator turned away, he looked again for the man who had been glaring at him with such hostility, but he had disappeared into the crowd. Ash still couldn't recall the name, but he remembered seeing his picture regularly in newspapers and on television when the war in Bosnia was at its worst.

He felt a sour taste in his mouth. Was this also the kind of person Comraich hid, hid and overindulged? War criminals whose appalling violations were so repellent, so brutishly inhumane to civilized society?

Ash shuddered. He was just beginning to understand the malign influences in this place.

A thought struck him before he reached the lift that would take him up to Sir Victor Haelstrom's apartment: was Delphine aware of the people harboured here? To him, she was an innocent, but was it possible for anyone, and especially someone who had worked here for several years, helping people, psychoanalysing them, delving into their deepest thoughts – was it possible to be unaware of who they were and what they had done? The notion that she was complicit in shielding them from justice shocked him.

As he pressed the call button and heard the elevator's heavy clunking racket, he wondered how many of Comraich's guests chose this means of transport to their rooms on the upper floors; not many, he reckoned, particularly those of nervous or claustrophobic disposition. Maybe many of the older residents were domiciled on the ground or first floors – the castle was certainly large enough to accommodate them. But then Delphine had told him there were two other elevators, one solely used by the medical unit, and presumably another roomier and brighter one for the guests and staff themselves.

While he waited, Ash took a moment to peek into the armoury close by: the ancient but well-kept and neatly arrayed weaponry was perfectly still. He stayed but a second or two, but none shook in any way and it came as a relief to him. He heard the *thunk* sound of the lift carriage arriving and walked swiftly to the heavy door, pulling it open with some effort.

Ash slid the safety door to one side, stepped in and stabbed at the button marked five. God, he needed a drink badly and, despite his resolution before the trip to Comraich, he certainly wouldn't turn one down if Haelstrom was the type of host who always offered a 'stiffener', even during a business meeting.

The lift trundled upwards and the investigator was nervously aware of every bump and the sharp screech of the thick hoist cables running on aged drive shafts and guide rails. The overhead light illuminated the mahogany interior so poorly he could make out only a dim half-figure of his own reflection in the car's age-mottled mirror. He felt uneasy, in a way stifled, despite the musty air coming through the safety door.

Above the safety door a gilded arrow moved past the floor numbers like the hand of a clock. Ash's room was on the second floor, which the pointer was only just passing, but what he was more interested in were the lower numbers. The castle contained six floors above ground, then three more below. Nine in all then, counting the as yet unseen lower basement. Yet the floor indicator showed only two subterranean levels; a third had plainly been chiselled off as if no longer in use.

His eyes went to the buttons in their perpendicular line on the panel beside the lift door and he saw that the bottom one was similarly disabled: covered by a welded metal strip, as if abandoned.

In the olden days, that floor was no doubt where the dungeons or *oubliettes* were, and he could understand if the underground prison was the castle's most neglected secret, but for a serious parapsychologist, it should have been a starting point for investigation, especially the area directly underneath Douglas Hoyle's room. Ash *had* to get down there.

It suddenly struck him that this very lift shaft might act as a conduit for the dark energies coming from below. The centuries-old misery, the torture, the violence and the hopelessness there could have leaked to the upper floors to cause the paranormal disruption. *My God*, he thought, *instead of weakening through time, the evil might have strengthened and been drawn up by some noxious ungodliness above.*

The small lift car juddered to an unsettling halt. Fifth floor. At last. Ash could hardly wait to step outside.

He yanked the iron safety door and for an awful moment, he felt it resist. But his hard tug succeeded and the door clattered open. Pushing – again, pushing *hard* – against the outer wooden door, he almost spilled into the hallway.

He took a deep breath and made an effort to stop his hands from shaking, then looked left, then right, in search of Haelstrom's apartment.

Just then a figure dressed in a long-tailed butler's coat came round a turning in the hallway to Ash's right. The man could have sprung directly from the pages of a P. G. Wodehouse novel, so aptly was he attired. The hems of his sharply creased pinstripe trousers rested on the tops of shiny patent leather shoes and he wore a grey waistcoat and a gleaming white wing-tipped shirt, the cuffs of which showed exactly one quarter of an inch below his black coat sleeves. His tie was of deep grey and neatly tucked into the waistcoat. His face was long with a high-bridged nose that suited him perfectly, and his fine dark hair was slicked back neatly, shiny and flat over his pate, its parting narrow and professionally straight in a style that might have come from a pre-war cricketer in a newspaper advertisement for Brylcreem.

Like the crusty gatekeeper at the faux entrance to the Comraich estate, this character too could have been hired from Central Casting, although Ash was sure both men were genuine enough.

'Could you direct me to Mr Hael— Sir Victor's apartment?' the investigator asked cordially, as the man approached.

'Certainly sir,' came the crisp response. 'You'll be Mr Ash, I take it?'

Ash nodded. 'Yes.'

'I act as manservant to Sir Victor and Lord Edgar,' the brisk-mannered stranger said as he reached Ash. He looked to be in his early sixties, and his five-foot-seven frame had a dignified poise which showed no condescension whatsoever. The investigator enjoyed such unassumed refinement. The man had heavy bags under his alert grey eyes, as though responsibility sometimes weighed too heavily on him.

'My name is Byrone,' he told Ash respectfully.

Ash found it difficult to hide a smile. 'Byrone?' he repeated.

'Yes, sir, and you're not the first to find it amusing. However, there's an "e" attached to the end of my name and, I'm afraid, the poet and I have too many differences to be compared.'

The butler's smile revealed a wry sense of humour. 'I believe you're a mite late, sir.' He lifted his forearm to consult his wristwatch. 'I was instructed to serve Sir Victor and your good self drinks when you arrived. I'm afraid you're already twenty-two minutes late for your appointment. If you'll follow me, sir, I'll get you to Sir Victor's door in no time at all.'

David Ash strode to keep up with the unexpectedly amiable butler and at the third door down, Byrone gently knocked twice.

'*Come in!*' Ash heard the irascible voice of Haelstrom through the wood.

Byrone gave the investigator a little wink as he turned the handle and smartly opened the door. The butler entered first and announced the investigator's name as he held the door open wider, his hand indicating the room beyond. Ash went through and saw Haelstrom sitting on the other side of a curved walnut desk.

'You're late!' The considerably larger man's cheeks were an unhealthy red as he glared across the room at the parapsychologist.

'It's a big castle,' Ash answered mildly. 'And I'm not even halfway through it yet.'

Haelstrom considered the reply for a moment, then grunted to himself. 'Take a seat.'

It was neither a request, nor an invitation; it was a barked order. And, although Ash was no rebellious hot-flushed youth, it was not a way in which he liked to be addressed.

While he paused, the butler, sizing up the awkwardness of the situation, said politely, 'Perhaps I can serve you drinks now, Sir Victor, while Mr Ash finds a comfortable place on the settee.'

The 'settee' in question was a long carved giltwood chaise longue for four with light green, striped silk upholstery and fluted, inverted baluster legs. The darker green cushions at either end set off the colour scheme admirably. As Ash crossed the apartment, he noted how tastefully opulent the whole room was. The windows, just behind Haelstrom's desk, were almost floor to ceiling and drawn heavy damask curtains made an imposing backdrop to Comraich's CEO.

To Haelstrom's left stood a lavishly carved Dutch walnut bombe cabinet resting on massive wooden lions' feet. Floral marquetry inlay decorated its drawers and doors.

A Queen Anne armchair covered in scrolled fabric sat somewhat discordantly before a huge plasma TV.

The high-ceilinged room was a veritable museum of fine pieces, and Ash, whose father had bequeathed him an appreciation of fine craftsmanship, looked round the room admiringly. He was rudely stirred from his musing when Haelstrom snapped, 'I haven't invited you here to appraise my furnishings. May we get on with the business at hand?'

Again, it was a direct order and again it was the tactful butler, Byrone, who saved the moment.

'Your drinks, Sir Victor?' Byrone reminded his master smoothly.

Surprisingly, the mention of drinks seemed to mollify Haelstrom, a sudden change of mood that Ash had already witnessed on his arrival that morning.

Haelstrom's glare mellowed, and although his smile seemed to scrunch his features disturbingly towards the centre of his huge head, his manner became courteous. Byrone, Ash pondered, certainly knew how to handle his boss. Maybe Haelstrom had a problem with alcohol and the butler understood how to please him.

The investigator casually took his suggested seat.

'I hear you like vodka, David . . .' Haelstrom began.

David? thought Ash. The big man's demeanour really had changed. For the moment, at least.

'I used to,' Ash replied cautiously. Haelstrom had obviously been fully briefed by Simon Maseby.

'Yes,' Haelstrom continued. 'Yes, well, now how do you feel about whisky?'

'Scotch or Irish?' he countered, though he had no particular preference.

Haelstrom smiled again, giving the investigator a crafty look. 'Japanese,' he replied.

Ash stared at him in surprise.

'There are two Japanese whiskies which have been favoured even above our own. One is a twenty-year-old Yoichi, distilled on the shores of the Sea of Japan. I'm not a Scot, so I feel no betrayal in recommending it.'

Haelstrom stood and came round to the front of his desk, leaning his ample rear end against the edge while folding his arms as if to give a lecture.

'Yoichi has a spectacular mix of smoke and sweet blackcurrant. An explosive aroma, it's said.'

He turned his head towards Byrone, who stood at attention by a beautiful drinks cabinet, its ornate upper doors open wide. Ash could see a vast array of bottled spirits in the shadows inside.

'But the one I want to recommend to you, David, is the world's best blend. This Suntory Hibiki's taste owes much to the variable climate where the distillers are located, which assists maturation and creates a purer whisky with a heightened aroma. The choice is yours but, as I said, I recommend you try the latter.' He looked pleased – if such a strained face could look so – as he waited for the investigator to make his choice.

Ash felt awkward: as far as Haelstrom knew, the investigator was supposed to be on the wagon. But what the hell, they both sounded terrific.

'Uh, I shouldn't,' he said, with an expression that endeavoured to be both faltering *and* doubtful at the same time.

His forced hesitation led Haelstrom to say, 'Of course, I could arrange a small absinthe, if that's your preference . . .'

Ash was startled, but thought quickly. 'Isn't absinthe supposed to be a little harsh on the system, let alone the brain?'

'I'm sure *you* could tell *me*.'

How the bloody hell did the man know about the absinthe in Ash's flask? Had his bedroom and luggage been searched in the investigator's absence?'

'The, uh, Suntory Hibiki sounds good. I suppose one wouldn't hurt.' He played out the game and if Haelstrom was wise to it, it didn't show.

The big man nodded at the butler, who was already poised,

with a crystal tumbler held in one hand. Byrone poured the exotic-sounding whisky, its top already opened as though he knew Ash would accept Sir Victor's suggested preference. He poured another for his master.

The butler brought the drinks over on a small silver tray, serving Ash first. Haelstrom raised his glass and the para-psychologist returned the gesture.

'Naturally, ice would be unacceptable,' Haelstrom said before taking his first sip.

'Naturally.' Ash's sip was considerably larger, and he found the other man's description of the Japanese whisky's qualities to be accurate. Both men allowed the subtle tastes to come through before Haelstrom said, 'Did you know the Japanese have gone crazy for wine, especially red?'

Ash shook his head, then tried another sip, smaller this time as the mix blossomed. He felt a pleasant heat descending into his chest.

'Yes, they heard that wine had great health benefits and now cannot import enough of the stuff. Wine exporters are reaping a fortune and their Japanese clients couldn't care less how outrageously priced it is.' Haelstrom held the glass up once more, this time to study the amber liquid, which the crystal motif multiplied into myriad pleasing images. Suddenly, he drained the glass and held it out to the butler, indicating a refill. 'Well, David, what do you have to tell me? What have you discovered so far?'

Ash placed the palm of his hand over the top of the tumbler as Byrone made to collect it. It had taken Ash an effort to refuse a top-up, but it had been a long day and he had a long night ahead of him. He felt Haelstrom's gaze.

Placing the glass on a small table next to the settee, Ash made a play of opening his shoulder bag that lay at his feet and taking out his notepad.

The big-boned man pulled over the Queen Anne chair and sat facing Ash. He was several feet away, but still Ash felt an almost overbearing discomfort which had more to do with the glint in the other man's tiny recessed eyes than his proximity. He waited while Byrone served his master another crystal tumbler of Japanese whisky.

'I'm waiting,' Haelstrom said impatiently.

Good-bye Dr Jekyll, hello Mr Hyde, Ash thought, but replied, 'Sure,' as he consulted his notes for rather longer than was necessary as his client's patience wore increasingly thin. Finally, he snapped the notebook shut. 'I've examined the lower floors up to the second, where my own quarters are,' he began. 'But I wasn't allowed to examine the lower-basement area for reasons that are not clear to me. Mr Babbage and Mr Derriman were adamant.'

Haelstrom just stared at him, voicing no opinion.

'Maybe we can come to that later,' Ash said uneasily. 'I've studied each landing and all the offices and public rooms. I've found cold spots, some of which might indicate some kind of psychic disturbance or presence.'

'What do you mean by "presence"? Ghosts?' Haelstrom's tone was distinctly belligerent, almost as if Ash had suggested an infestation of cockroaches.

'Not necessarily ghosts,' Ash answered, ignoring his client's brusqueness. 'Unnatural forces, images of real people now dead. Some of them are simply caused by draughts, though. It's a centuries-old building,' he added unnecessarily.

'You're saying?'

'Certain things – sounds, rappings, cold spots – they may seem like phenomena but probably have easily explicable causes. Wooden beams and floorboards contracting at night as the castle cools down can often sound like knocking, or floorboards contracting one by one can sound like footsteps. Cold spots can be due to small holes in the stonework, chilly air from outside sweeping through, sometimes a whistling draught can be mistaken for a creature *howling*. And Comraich is high on a clifftop with, I'm told, caves running beneath.

Subsidence, flowing underground streams, small animals such as bats, can also create noises or shifts in the atmosphere as well as rancid smells. And I haven't even mentioned vermin.'

'The castle has five cats to control rodents.'

'Well, there again, cats themselves can make noises in the night. I'm just trying to assure you that there are many common occurrences in buildings – especially large buildings with structural weaknesses, or resident animals and pets – which might cause concern if their unobserved movements are misunderstood.'

Haelstrom harrumphed in displeasure. 'Would you say a man splattered against a wall and hung there to die of, let's face it, fright, can be explained as a natural act?'

'Good God, no.' Ash leaned forward, wrists on knees, fists slightly clenched. 'Sir Victor, you obviously do have a problem here. Whether Douglas Hoyle was murdered by some unnatural force or someone human with incredible strength and an attitude problem can't be decided at this point. I have to look into it further.'

'You surely can't suggest a *person* did this to the poor man, killed him then used his blood as some sort of extraordinary Velcro to pin him to the wall.' Haelstrom's chortle at his tasteless joke was scornful and meant to be so.

'No, of course not,' said Ash, sitting back with a frustrated sigh. 'But that's precisely why I have to look around the level *underneath* Hoyle's observation suite. I felt energy emanating from there, energy so powerful it literally threw me bodily through the doorway.'

'Yes, I was told about that. Babbage assures me there was no trickery involved.'

That comment irritated the parapsychologist even further, but it took more than that these days to make him lose his cool. 'Can you think of any possible reason that I, or the Institute, should try to dupe you? I'm here to carry out a serious investigation.'

'For which you are being generously rewarded,' Haelstrom

came back at him, this time the one who leaned forward to rest his elbows on his knees.

'No, you're paying the respectable and highly respected Psychical Research Institute to discover whether Comraich is haunted or not. And I'm the best investigator you'll ever get. Now, there might be a practical solution that has nothing to do with spirits, poltergeists, demons or any other paranormal forces, and I've no intention of inventing them just to earn our fee, no matter how high it might be. That's between you and Kate McCarrick.'

'All right, all right,' Haelstrom murmured gruffly. 'Let's get on with it.'

Without chagrin, Ash told the big man, 'I need to see those architectural drawings I asked you for at lunchtime.'

'I'm afraid Derriman has found only two, one dating back to the 1950s, when extensive renovations were carried out, the second from sometime in the nineteenth century. The original plans unfortunately no longer exist. All others have been either lost or destroyed.'

He swivelled his head round to his manservant, who had been dutifully standing by the drinks cabinet, hands held behind his back, body straight. *Maybe the poor guy's never at ease in his master's presence*, thought Ash sympathetically.

'Byrone, go through to the drawing room and fetch the two rolled drawings that are lying on the desk there,' Haelstrom ordered before turning back to the investigator. 'The castle has a bloody history, d'you see? Many things have been lost to the past.'

But not the ghosts, Ash mused. They were not lost to Comraich.

Byrone quickly returned carrying two long rolls of paper, one an off-white vellum, the other yellowed like old parchment. He brought them directly to Haelstrom, who had been gazing at Ash without speaking. He indicated the investigator with a pointed finger.

'Give them to Mr Ash,' he said.

251

The butler crossed the room again and handed the drawings to the investigator before returning to his place by the drinks cabinet.

'Study them later, Ash, within the confines of your own room. I don't expect they'll be much use to you, but you never know – something might turn up. Perhaps a room that shouldn't be there, a wall so thick there might be a secret passageway inside. I wish you luck.'

Ash didn't bother to unroll the long scrolls there and then, but placed them carefully beside him on the satin seat.

'So far, you haven't told me much,' said Haelstrom, his displeasure evident.

'So far, there isn't much to tell,' Ash responded. 'Tonight I intend to go through the castle's upper regions, just to make the initial observation complete. I'll take some equipment with me, in case I find an opportune location to test. Tomorrow I can set up many more detection instruments, and I'll have to declare some parts of the building out of bounds, not only to your guests, but your staff too.'

'I'd like you to be accompanied by someone tonight – Babbage or Derriman. Only to guide you and keep you away from anywhere out of bounds.'

'That's not going to work. I have to have freedom of movement.'

'Yes, it's an awkward predicament, isn't it? Unfortunately, that's how it stands.'

'I take it that still includes the old dungeons.'

'It does, though I'm sure you wouldn't like it there, anyway.'

He frowned at Haelstrom. 'Just what have you got down there, Sir Victor? Is there something you're hiding?'

The question was put bluntly and belligerently, so Ash was surprised by the big man's reaction. Haelstrom laughed, and this time it was genuine, bringing tears to the corner of his small deep-set eyes. He beat the arm of his chair with the flat of his free hand, the other holding on to the dregs of the Japanese whisky.

Still spluttering, and with Ash just staring at him, Haelstrom managed to say, 'HIde . . . hiding from . . . you. That's very rich. Don't . . . don't you see it's for your own . . . your own good?'

Ash stiffened, his anger becoming hard to hold down. What made this thick-headed buffoon laugh so much at the suggestion that he might be hiding something from the investigator? Then it dawned on him. Comraich was hiding *all* its guests from the outside world – Hoyle, Lucan, the defrocked archbishop, the Serbian war criminal – but was it so obvious? Making a joke of the obvious? Was that why Haelstrom was laughing so much?

Whatever it was, Ash was quickly losing patience. 'Have you got someone *imprisoned*' – he used the word coldly, dispassionately – 'in the cells down there you don't want me to see? Is that the big secret?'

Haelstrom placed the crystal glass on a small side table and reached awkwardly into his trouser pocket. He drew out a wrinkled handkerchief, laughing in short fits now. He blew his nose noisily and it seemed to sober him a little.

'No, Ash,' he managed to say between gasping in breaths. Finally, his broad shoulders stopped shaking and he was in control once more.

'No, Ash,' he repeated, with scarce apology in his voice.

'Then what is it? You want me to make a thorough investigation, yet you're banning me from key areas.'

'I wasn't joking. It really is for your own safety.' His shoulders jerked as he suppressed another chortle. He did his best to regard the investigator seriously.

'You see, Mr Ash, underground . . . Well, underground is our containment area. It's where we keep our lunatics . . .'

33

Kate McCarrick sat alone in her office in the Psychical Research Institute and struggled to calm her own anxiety. Most of her staff had left for the night, so only a few other offices and the hallways were lit. She'd become used to the peculiar sense of loneliness that came with working late in a building almost emptied of other people. And sometimes, for her, it could be even worse.

That was when she had time to go through reports of hauntings that were sometimes horrific in their detail. Seasoned though she was, hardened to all things weird though she might be, there were times when Kate would rather be in normal company, particularly on late evenings like this.

She'd expected to receive a status report from Ash, but there had been no word. Kate had rung his mobile phone number, but there was no connection, not even a ring tone, and because she had no number for Comraich itself, she'd been forced to call Simon Maseby at his office.

Simon had assured her that all was well, that he'd spoken to someone at Comraich who told him David Ash had arrived safely and was already busy with his investigation. He had also explained that she couldn't reach David on his mobile phone because there was no signal, and no, he couldn't give her the castle's phone number because of the strict security there. Kate had almost flipped when she heard that. Why hadn't he told her all this before? Simon allayed her anxiety by telling Kate that he would be visiting Comraich himself the next day for an important conference. He would report back directly to her of David's progress. In fact, Sir Victor was hoping his initial investigation would be completed before the conference took place.

He'd finished by asking her whether she fancied a late supper. 'I really enjoyed last night – you still know all the right moves in bed.'

Kate had wanted to gag at that, but she only had herself to blame: she'd allowed the little toad to seduce her with hardly a fight. And what a miserable night it had turned out to be. She wasn't sure it was the alcohol or just plain bloody boredom. But regretting it now was no good; the deed was done, with no reward on her part.

'Fuck you, Maseby!' she'd said aloud, but only after she'd slammed the phone down.

Kate needed to be in touch with her investigator, mainly because she couldn't be sure of how well David would stand up to another ghastly haunting.

But Kate had other friends in high places and having contacted one in particular that afternoon, she might just find out a bit more about this rather sinister organization called the Inner Court.

34

On returning to his room, Ash found a surprise waiting for him in the form of a small silver-foil-wrapped package laid on his bed where he couldn't miss it. Beside it was a brief note: *David, thought you might miss your dinner tonight because of the work you have to do, so arranged for the kitchen to make you a sandwich for later on. Hope it's to your liking.*

It was signed D and with a big X for a kiss. God, he hoped it wasn't from Derriman.

He smiled to himself as he put the note back on the bed and picked up the package to sniff at it. It smelt like chicken and he realized he was hungry despite the good lunch he'd had.

He left it by the note on the bed and mentally thanked Delphine for being so thoughtful. The marked kiss, despite his self-imposed reservations, was a bonus.

Opening up his suitcase, he began assembling the equipment he required for his investigation that night. For this opening stratagem he needed only basic kit: a brushed cotton multi-pocket gilet, the type serious anglers might use (he slipped it on before his field jacket so that now he had more pockets than he would ever need, but it would serve as an extra layer during the cold hours). He'd be taking with him a Nite MX10 wristwatch with gaseous Tritium self-powered light sources that made the dials brighter than luminescent paint; a digital nightsight with a direct video output so that whatever was happening could be viewed on a tiny battery-powered television screen; another powerful torch, impact- and water-resistant, that used capacitor technology so that it took a mere ninety seconds to recharge fully; next came a folding steel walking stick, so it could be either hand-held or tucked away in one of the jacket's deeper pockets; and a fully automatic 'wildlife' infrared camera that could wirelessly transmit pictures to a remote monitor; finally, he picked a short LED torch with flood-to-spot beam.

Left in the suitcase were a set of ultra-powerful 12 km range walkie-talkies, a pocket monocular, and a fibre-optic flexiscope, used for inspecting nooks and crannies, or any fissures that might prove interesting.

These were all instruments that could come in useful for his night vigil, but there were other pieces of equipment he chose not to use on this initial surveillance, such as an electrometer (for measuring electromagnetism) which he often found too sensitive to the static in one's own body to be truly useful. The voice- or noise-activated tape recorder would be a must when he really got down to the job the following night, as would thermometers, barometers (for measuring atmospheric pressure), motion sensors, and other miscellaneous apparatus. Talcum powder, graphs, chalk, coloured pencils, transparent tape, cotton, were all standard paranormal search equipment, and all devices required for a psychic study, but again, unnecessary for this night: he still wanted to get a 'feel' of the castle, rather than exact proof of ghostly, nocturnal activity.

As an afterthought, he lifted out a thermal scanning gun which could measure cold spots from a distance of thirty metres.

Before leaving, he mixed an absinthe and water and downed it in one. *It's going to be a long lonely night*, Ash thought to himself as the drink momentarily warmed his chest. And the big question was, would he find ghosts roaming the hallways and chambers of Comraich Castle? Or any evidence at all of a haunting, and a particularly malign haunting at that? Outside the window was an almost full moon, the huge courtyard below washed silver, the gardens and woods a monotone grey that if stared at too long would induce all kinds of immobile images to the over-imaginative. But he wouldn't allow mental vagaries to take hold, wouldn't let his own fears govern his thoughts. He would come to this situation as he had others in the past: his professionalism would dictate his actions, former events of a similar nature wouldn't be allowed to feed his fear.

Now, after the drink he needed a cigarette; he really had given them up that morning. He was aware they were doing him no good, apart from settling his nerves sometimes, but today, determined to beat them, he'd deliberately binned what was left in the pack – three – before leaving for the airport, the cab already waiting for him outside.

In a way, he knew Kate had sent him on this assignment – an assignment that meant so much to the Institute, both in financial terms and with regard to its reputation – because she trusted him. She was relying on him completely. His breakdown was in the past, and he had to prove that, not only to her but to himself also.

Staring through the window, lost in his own thoughts, a movement suddenly caught his attention.

Two figures were walking across the silver-grey courtyard towards the castle gardens.

He squinted to see them more clearly, but the distance was too great. Curious, he snatched up the small telescope that lay among other paraphernalia he'd left in the suitcase and put it to his right eye. He was almost too late – the figures had reached the steps leading down into the gardens, where they would become hidden behind walls and raised flower beds, but he managed to focus the lens just in time.

Through the eyeglass, he immediately recognized Delphine, but the figure she accompanied, someone who held on to her as if finding difficulty in walking, was a mystery. A mystery made even more so, because this person wore a cowled garment, much like a monk's robe, the head well hidden beneath the pointed hood. Soon, both figures were out of view.

He checked the MX10 wristwatch: 8.16 p.m. The sedated diners on the first floor would probably be halfway through dinner by now, and most would shortly take to their beds: he reasoned early nights were likely to be encouraged at Comraich Castle, although maybe some would gather in the drawing rooms for discussions or a few hands of contract bridge, canasta or backgammon. Maybe the billiard room he'd been shown earlier might be in use, although the tranquillizers supplied so liberally by Dr Pritchard would no doubt soon have the guests heading for their rooms.

Moving the still-wrapped sandwich and Delphine's note aside, he spread out the 1950s plan given to him by Haelstrom as well as the second, older parchment, which contained a rough drawing of the castle's cross-sections. Sketchy and old though the latter was, it managed to give him a better idea of the ancient building's layout: storerooms, libraries, the chapel tower, the kitchens, the grand state hall (which was now the high-ceilinged dining room), the King's rooms (those now occupied by Sir Victor Haelstrom), the prison tower – that came as a surprise to him, for he'd assumed all the cells were contained in the lowest floors – the bailiff's room and even the toilets, cesspits and chimneys. He sought out the dungeons, but found to his frustration that the relevant portion of the drawing was missing. He wondered if Haelstrom had deliberately cut off the lower section before handing it over to him. The cut looked fresh.

Even the more detailed architectural drawings were vague, leaving the subterranean area mainly blank. One particular detail that interested Ash was an indication of a large door, with nothing to show where it led or what it protected. Well, tomorrow, if Delphine had managed to fix it with an estate ranger, he would be able to investigate the caves beneath the castle. He felt sure the epicentre for the apparent paranormal activity was somewhere below the building. He still couldn't understand why he wasn't allowed to inspect the lowest level. There might be lunatics down there, some of them dangerous, but presumably they were locked away in comfortable and well-guarded cells. What harm could he come to if that were the case? Haelstrom must be hiding something.

As Ash was poring over the plans the lights flickered and dimmed.

Almost immediately, they regained power and brightened. And brightened even more until they were practically incandescent and he had to raise a hand over his eyes to cut out the glare. Within moments, the lamp and ceiling light returned to normal, but the experience left him feeling uneasy.

He continued to study the plans before him. After a short while, he began to feel hungry. It had been a hell of a long day so far, and lunch had been hours ago. Absent-mindedly, he reached for the silver-foil wrapping containing the snack that Delphine had so sweetly had made up for him from the castle kitchens. The smell of chicken whetted his appetite even more. Picking up the pack, he began to unwrap it while still concentrating on the plans spread over the bed. And even though his attention was diverted, something alerted his subconscious, made him glance at the package in his hand. It didn't feel right; it felt as if something was moving beneath the silver foil.

He straightened up and began to unravel the soft wrapping.

'*Jes—!*' he cried out as he dropped the pack and jumped back in horror, slamming his shoulder blades against the wall behind him so hard that he fell to the floor.

35

The dining hall was almost full this evening and much of the soft-spoken conversation was about the new man who had arrived in their very own domain. There was an air of mystery about him. He'd come to Comraich to find ghosts, for most of them realized the castle really was haunted.

Their conversations, which might have been expected to be excitable, were subdued. Yet there remained an unease in the atmosphere that only the strongest of sedatives could cloak.

At the centre of the vast circular hall was the principal table, all other dining tables spread concentrically around it like a spider's web. And if that analogy suited, then Sir Victor Haelstrom, who, with others, occupied that middle point, could be likened to a blood-bloated spider sensitive to every vibration of the web's invisible membrane.

Dinner at Comraich was always served from 8 p.m. to 9 p.m. (the guests needed routine), with cocktails served, often with medication, at 7.30 p.m. in the long foyer at ground level. It was required that most guests be settled in their own bedchambers by 10 p.m., 10.30 at the latest, and sleeping peacefully by 11 p.m. Yet despite the various calming drugs administered to each guest throughout the day, there were always one or two who were night owls regardless. They could always relax and perhaps socialize in one of the drawing rooms overlooking the sea, or either of the well-stocked libraries. A good cigar accompanied by a brandy or two, usually with a mild narcotic in the brew, the taste disguised by the alcohol itself, or hot milk or cocoa spiked with a mild soporific could also be served. No matter what, the leisure hour always ended promptly at 11 p.m., when some late-nighters had to be helped to their beds.

However, for the past several nights running, *all* guests had been inclined to retire to their rooms as soon as dinner was over. None had the desire to walk the castle halls and corridors at night, and even the drawing rooms and libraries remained empty.

Haelstrom, still inches taller than his dining companions even when seated, looked at the empty chair opposite him at the table. He craned his odd-shaped head round, searching the restaurant.

'I don't see Dr Wyatt this evening,' he complained in his usual gruff manner, now looking directly at Senior Nurse Rachael Krantz, whose face reddened with anger as her hazel eyes flashed at the big man.

It was Andrew Derriman, seated on Haelstrom's left, who ventured an answer. 'I-I think she's out-outside, walking with . . .' he paused, then finished, 'with The Boy. Y-you know how he likes to be in-in the open air whenever he c-can. Dinner time is usually g-good for him. No sun, few, if any, people about except for a guard or two, and they ig-ignore him. It's one of his limited pleasures.'

'Not with this foolish ghost hunter, David Ash, then?' Again, he looked at Krantz, as if goading her. This time she merely looked away, but Haelstrom gleefully felt her tension.

It was Dr Pritchard who took the trouble to come to Ash's defence. Stroking his neatly trimmed goatee, he said, 'Stuffed prig though Simon Maseby might be, he certainly did his homework on your so-called "ghost hunter", whom, as a matter of fact, I checked out for myself through a contact at Edinburgh University that has its own unique Parapsychology Unit. Ash, would you believe, is a highly regarded member of the Parapsychologist Association, the international body for professional paranormal researchers. Full members must possess a PhD and have had a paper published in a respected scientific journal.'

'Am I supposed to be impressed?' Haelstrom retorted.

'Well, I am. You see, what parapsychologists attempt to do is apply scientific methodology to explain paranormal or supernatural occurrences. I think if anyone can do precisely that in these circumstances, it's David Ash. He's a man of substance and, I believe, academia. I think, Sir Victor, your mistake was bringing in this Scottish spiritualist – Mrs Glennon? – because you misunderstood the gravity of the situation. Too much time was wasted.'

Haelstrom didn't like his own judgement being questioned, no matter by whom. 'How am I expected to know about this kind of mumbo-jumbo?' he replied peevishly.

'You aren't, that's why you need advising.' Dr Pritchard became a little testy himself. 'Now David Ash has hardly any time at all to solve our problem before tomorrow evening.'

Everyone at the table was silent, including Haelstrom himself. Important members of the Inner Court were due to arrive from London for a central policy statement to be agreed. Everything at Comraich had to be sorted by then.

Kevin Babbage proffered his opinion. 'Even if the castle is haunted, ghosts – if you believe they're the souls of the bloody dead – can't hurt anyone. They're in the imagination, that's all. And thoughts can't hurt you. We can handle them easily enough.'

Dr Pritchard gave him a withering smile. 'Try telling that to Douglas Hoyle.'

'I thought Ash was only hired for a preliminary investigation,' said Rachael Krantz, her face still flushed from Sir Victor's sly jibe earlier.

'Then Ash will just have to contain any disturbances by his natural ability alone, certainly if he's as good as you suggest, Dr Pritchard.'

The senior surgeon almost groaned. Haelstrom just didn't get it, did he? Despite all that had happened so recently – *and* for several centuries past if one were to go back into the records of the old castle, as he had. Sir Victor remained apparently calm.

It seemed Haelstrom had decided to assert his authority again because of Dr Pritchard's rather louche observations; the big man with the frighteningly long-shaped head and odd facial features was used to absolute obeisance from his staff, no matter what qualification or honours they held. Ignoring the doctor, Haelstrom chose to turn his full attention on the psychiatrist, Dr Sunil Singh.

'It's been brought to my notice that Dr Wyatt is spending rather a lot of time with Ash. He shouldn't be distracted from his investigations.'

Various eyes around the table swung Rachael Krantz's way, perhaps expecting a few sharp words from her. They didn't get the sharp words, but the sharp looks from her were undoubtedly scarier. It was as if she were offering a challenge to her colleagues to speak. None rose to meet it.

Haelstrom's glare was still boring into Dr Singh, a good-looking, light-skinned Sikh with a day's growth of stubble on his chin. He and Delphine were used to sharing their patients and collaborating on individual cases.

'Tell me your assessment of Dr Wyatt these days,' he demanded bluntly of the psychiatrist.

Dr Singh gave a nervous grin. 'We get along very well despite, or maybe because of, our different disciplines, though they often overlap. Sometimes we disagree on the merits of Freud and his now fashionably discredited premise that sex is the root cause of all behaviour. Delphine often tends to favour Jung.'

'Is this significant?' Haelstrom replied impatiently.

Dr Pritchard answered for Singh. 'Nothing that's relevant to our discussions this evening,' he said smoothly.

Dr Singh's manicured hands were folded across his lap beneath the white Irish linen tablecloth. 'Delphine is also a great advocate of gestalt psychology and therapy using emotional as well as interpersonal meanings; she needs to examine the whole person and not just the particular signs and symptoms.'

'And that's a good thing?' None of it made much sense to Haelstrom. It was sometimes a ploy of his, deliberately allowing certain others to underestimate his cleverness. But in this case, he was genuinely uninterested in the psychological complexities of the human mind, whether framed in existentialism or Freudian psychoanalytic theory of the human id, ego, or superego. None of it changed the price of butter.

Haelstrom scowled as he sat back from the table so that a waitress could set his dinner before him. His grunt might have been interpreted as a thank you to the girl or appreciation of the fillet of beef he was about to consume.

The other diners around the table were all hoping the superbly prepared food would mellow Haelstrom's impatient and grouchy mood. Some evenings he could be delightfully entertaining or enthusiastically interested in the events of the day, while at other times he appeared to be a different man entirely, sharply disparaging, irritated by the slightest remark, hyper-critical of the behaviour or mistakes of others. Tonight was one of those times, and they all sensed it.

'Tell me, then,' the big man said to Dr Singh, 'how is Dr Wyatt progressing with The Boy?'

Everyone at the table turned their attention towards the psychiatrist, interested themselves in Dr Singh's answer.

His response was honest and unafraid. 'I think we all know there will never be any cogent advancement of his mind or physical condition. Delphine does her best, and I think he has formed a very strong attachment to her, but I'm sure Dr Pritchard would agree there can only be one eventual outcome. For which we can only wait. It could take years; it might be tomorrow.'

Dr Pritchard, deftly cutting the plump white meat of his sea bass from the bone, nodded in silent agreement.

'Dr Wyatt is an asset to Comraich, Sir Victor,' Dr Singh

assured him. 'She has great sympathy *and* empathy for her patients. I, for one, should hate to lose her.'

'So would I,' Pritchard agreed through a mouthful of succulent food. 'She would be very hard to replace. Especially as far as her relationship with The Boy is concerned.'

'Yes, yes, I'm not thinking of replacing her,' Haelstrom said tetchily. 'It's just the health of her special charge that worries me. What is his age now? Surely he's no longer a boy.'

'He's in his late twenties,' Dr Singh answered. 'Strictly, I suppose we should no longer refer to him as "The Boy". He's been here for so long now, though . . .'

Callously Rachael Krantz said, 'Why would anyone outside Comraich have to know of his death?'

Sir Victor Haelstrom regarded her with disdain. 'Because each year we have to provide proof of life, as we do for all our guests at Comraich. Benevolent or expedient our guests' patrons may be, but they are not foolish. Unless the guest's financial arrangements are funded by their own money, each year at an affixed time, we have to show a picture of our charge holding up that day's newspaper, the date and headline clearly visible, to the benefactor, much as kidnappers do with ransom victims. Even if, on that day, the guest is not particularly well, the set date is binding. But this, of course, is why our guests are so well looked after and kept as fit as possible. Which is why, Nurse Krantz, I find your suggestion extremely silly and without your usual perspicacity.'

Krantz flushed. 'I'm sorry, Sir Victor,' she said contritely. 'I agree, it was an idiotic thing to say.'

'Let's hear no more of it then.' There was no intimation of forgiveness in Haelstrom's tone. 'It looks like Ash will have to work very hard to produce results tonight. But then, how do we know the hauntings aren't already bloody over? It's only comparatively recently that they've begun; they could stop just as quickly.'

Dr Pritchard looked up from his meal and dabbed at his lips with a linen napkin.

Dr Singh stared across the table at his employer.

Senior Nurse Krantz looked distractedly around the room.

Senior Security Officer Babbage continued to tuck into his rolled fillets of lamb and seasonal vegetables.

And so it was left to the meek-mannered general manager, Andrew Derriman, who had hardly touched his pan-fried duck, to speak up. 'S-Sir Victor. Can't you f-feel it? It's . . . it's . . .' His quiet, almost whispered, words fell away as he gazed around the room as if to find something tangible, something that perhaps he could point at. The others at the table also began to search the room with their eyes, but they were all looking for something that had no substance, something that was just a sensation. A foreboding.

Eventually, even Babbage stopped eating and looked up.

'C-can't you feel it, Sir Victor?' Derriman persisted. 'It's i-in the air itself. Something dangerous. No, no, something frightening, here in this room with us. Like . . . like the building up of static just before a thunderstorm.'

Haelstrom looked at his general manager as if he'd gone mad. Then he began to feel the crackling tension too.

But it was only when a horrific scream from the far side of the dining hall froze him rigid in his chair that he felt the whole weight of the abomination about to come.

36

Sitting around the table that had attracted the attention of Sir Victor's party were six people. Each was prescribed a different cocktail of medication, but the regimens of all eight had two types of drug in common.

The older members were all prescribed AICAR, which boosted the body's ability to burn fat by fooling it into thinking it had undergone a long and beneficial workout without moving a muscle. Popularly known as the 'exercise pill', it was commonly used to fight obesity and muscle-wasting diseases, as well as to hold back the frailty of old age. Comraich, of course, had its own financial motive for improving its guests' longevity, for a living guest was a lucrative guest.

Its sister drug, the official name of which was GW1516, worked similarly, and equally well, although it required just a little actual exercise to boost muscle metabolism and so was reserved for the few younger guests at Comraich.

The second common factor among the diners at that particular table was that they all took antidepressants of some kind from Prozac to Fluoxetine (much the same thing), from Efexor to Cymbalta, from Alprazolam to Oxazepam – whichever suited each resident best.

The woman responsible for the ear-piercing scream that stunned everyone in the huge dining room was called Sandra Belling. Sandra was also on a beta-adrenergic receptor blocker which helped her block out the past. She was also being tested with a new, unlicensed drug called BDNF that was supposed to flood the mind with feelings of security and safety. The drug was now being given to her in a procedure being called 'targeted memory erasure'. Although not yet licensed in the UK, there were others at Comraich undergoing the same treatment.

Sandra had once been a seventies groupie called Fluff, a slim, long-legged blonde whose beauty had been legendary on the rock'n'roll circuit before booze and drugs and the trauma in her life had ravaged her face and body and tortured her mind. After several years bedding all and sundry, she'd finally embarked on a proper relationship with a world-famous rock star. Deeply in love, she fell happily pregnant, and nine months later the pair celebrated the birth of their daughter with a three-day heroin, cocaine and alcohol binge in a rented apartment in Paris, while the baby slept in her cot. By the time they surfaced from their doped-up alcoholic haze, the baby had starved to death.

The scandal had been suppressed somehow, thanks to the band's overworked PR and press agent. Their manager had quickly realized the band, already deemed the 'bad boys of rock', could suffer the ultimate collapse in sales and profile. So the guitarist had gone back to his narcotics, booze and gigs, while Sandra had attempted suicide twice, gone back to the bottle, and had threatened to confess all to the media. She was a loose cannon, and something had to be done. Fortunately, the rock star's lawyer had heard rumours of Comraich. A friendly High Court judge supplied him with a contact name and a deal was quickly struck. The annual fee was vast, but so was the rock star's fortune, and so it was that Fluff found herself swiftly interned in this superior refuge. For over thirty years she'd been kept docile by pharmaceuticals and hypnotherapy. Sandra had forgotten her daughter almost entirely now, although some nights she awoke screaming and had to be sedated even more heavily. Often she would claim a tiny naked baby with no face had been crawling on the bed towards her. And her vivacity had disappeared with her memories. These days she was more like a zombie, a bloated figure with ravaged features, ignoring her fellow-diners, staring at the food on her plate.

To Sandra's right was a stocky, heavy-set man with bushy eyebrows that almost joined above the bridge of his nose, wearing a plain grey suit, dark-blue tie and white shirt, filling his mouth with filet de boeuf. His name was Oleg Rinsinski and he'd once been a Russian billionaire and, prior to that, a senior KGB officer. After Communism collapsed, he'd seized the opportunity to make himself rich, using money he'd been bribed with to buy into his country's lucrative aluminium industry as well as other more clandestine markets. Well versed in extortion, blackmail, violence, murder, deception and financial chicanery, his rise as a man of wealth and influence had been rapid. Before long, Rinsinski controlled most of Russia's thriving market in aluminium and had become a leading arms dealer.

He'd considered himself untouchable. However, he had underestimated the strength of the Russian mafia when he'd been found out in an elaborate double-cross he'd arranged with a European business partner – none other than Sir Victor Haelstrom. So he'd decided to spend the rest of it in the safety of Sir Victor's retreat.

It had been a tremendous and frightening decision for Rinsinski to make, for he had a wife and one son and, more important to him, two gorgeous Russian mistresses, neither of whom knew of the other, but who each provided particular sexual services. Yet in the end, Rinsinski had little choice: the Russian Mafia would eventually find and kill him. So he agreed to pay the price, both in financial terms and his way of life – wives or mistresses were not allowed, a rule that could never be breached, nor negotiated. Fear of death is generally greater than the pleasure of sex.

As he happily chewed his beef, what he didn't know was that among the various, fairly innocuous tablets he swallowed each day, he was also being fed Androcur – the anti-libidinal drug. So while he still appreciated the perfect figure of, say, a woman like the psychologist, Dr Wyatt, he no longer carried the desire to ravage her. But he enjoyed the sophistication of it all, living out the fantasy of his younger days when he was building his power. He smiled to himself, meat filling his cheeks, and thought: *not bad for a Russian peasant of farming stock.*

Sitting on Sandra's left was a man with a thatch of long fair hair. Unlike everybody else, his clothes were informal: dirty jeans with holes in the knees and old, once-white trainers. He was slim, hunched and small. It was impossible to gauge his years partly because his blond hair made him seem young, while the extraordinary mess that had once been his handsome face suggested the opposite.

This was Kit Weston, three times Formula 1 world champion. Men and women alike had universally worshipped the faultlessly handsome racing driver, though for different reasons, and he had revelled in their adoration and the attention of the media. Then had come that final crash.

Always a showboater, he'd taken one on-track risk too many and ended up at the centre of a fireball. The ace racing driver had suffered eighty per cent burns over his body as well as several bone fractures. He'd been put into a ten-day coma while the physicians worked on his burns – even his lungs were scorched. Later, when they brought him out of his coma, even the world's best cosmetic surgeons could do little to recover his film-star looks. The intense heat had so deformed his skeleton and his musculature that he could walk only in small, awkward steps, like a hump-backed toddler. Paradoxically, his yellow hair had regrown thicker and healthier than ever, like a fire-razed forest.

It had been his idea to let the public think he'd died. He couldn't bear to face them ever again – literally, because one of his once brilliantly blue eyes had become opaque and half the skin round his mouth had disintegrated, revealing brown rotting teeth. His request to be thought of as dead had to be scrawled on paper with a withered hand, for in the crash he had bitten off his tongue, leaving only a stump.

He would really have preferred to have died. Indeed, so far

as the public were concerned, he had, for he couldn't bear to face them again. Instead, he had used his fortune to consign himself to an anonymous living hell.

Thousands of fans had attended his memorial service, the mourning crowds (and thrill-seekers) spilling out across the graveyard and into the street beyond, for there hadn't been enough room for everybody in the little Warwickshire church where Kit had been christened and was now to be buried.

The self-absorbed person sitting next to Kit Weston was a very darkly black, rotund giant of a man with swivelling bulbous eyes and broad shoulders that seemed capable of supporting a ten-ton truck. His hair was thick around the sides and back, but had lost ground to a smooth and shiny scalp that reflected the sparkling light from the chandelier overhead. His name was Osril Ubutu, and he missed wearing his khaki-coloured uniform with its host of dangling medals and dazzling military ribbons, all of which were self-awarded, but had served to impress the armed forces formerly under his command, and the peasants in what he'd regarded as *his* country in Africa. It was said of him that he'd boiled the severed heads of his enemies and kept them in refrigerators, either as a grisly display to impress visitors or to be eaten.

He had overthrown his corrupt uncle's government. It had been a popular move. And the uncle had been forced from his palace never to be seen again in public. Some said that his arms below the elbows, and the legs from above the knees had been chopped off, and then each tooth in his head had been pulled out with pliers – the gold ones presented to Ubutu in a velvet draw-string bag – and that the usurped head of state was left to slither around the palace courtyard, drinking from puddles after the rains, and sucking at apple cores tossed his way.

Ubutu, seduced by his own power and stolen wealth, had soon become one of the worst despots the African continent had ever known and had developed a hunger for sex that almost equalled his hunger for food. It was Ubutu's perversions that his wives had feared the most, for at their worst extremes many of them had had been left either dead or appallingly maimed for life. Now he was in hiding, presumed dead, for fear that the now liberated people he had so savagely oppressed would reciprocate in kind.

On his arrival at Comraich he was immediately put on the routine of sedatives and then, unknown to him, put on a continuous and infinitely more potent treatment – the 'castration chemical' called Leuprorelin.

The last two members of this dubious company were two very elderly men who sat and whispered to each other in German. Both were in their nineties and both had used stolen wealth to flee their beloved Reich before the inglorious end to the Second World War, one said to have escaped to Egypt, the other to Chile. In fact, they had already made arrangements to journey to England well before the war was over.

Alois Brunner had been right-hand man to Adolf Eichmann, inventing mobile gas vans which were used to kill tens of thousands of Jews. Now he was in the later stages of Alzheimer's. His hand was shaking as he lifted the spoon with its gooey contents up to his thin-lipped mouth. A globule of dew hung from the end of his nose, and the trembling of his aged head threatened to shake the dewdrop into the food in the bowl of his spoon.

His companion was Aribert Heim, just a couple of years younger than Brunner, and he, too had played his part in the horror of the last war. A former doctor in the gruesome Mauthausen prison camp in Austria, he'd been aptly named Dr Death. He'd arrived at Comraich many years after Brunner, for after the war he had fled to Egypt, taking the false name of Tarek and raising a family there. He'd eventually fled to Comraich when he'd been tipped off that Israeli Nazi-hunters were on to him. His son Rudiger Heim, left behind in Cairo, had announced his father's death of rectal cancer in 1992 with medical records to prove it. But the Nazi-hunters hadn't been taken in by such evidence and continued their searches.

At Comraich, he and Brunner had become constant

companions, though he was worried about Alois Brunner, who had come to Scotland over six decades ago. Together they relished stories of atrocities they had indulged in during the war, murmuring and slapping each other on the back. They had chosen to share a suite, with a single bed each, and most nights they reminisced in whispers, just in case their bedroom was bugged (which it was) and chortled with the bedsheets held up to their mouths to stifle the sound.

Although the number of years between them was small, Heim was much fitter than the older man and his mind more alert. As a practising doctor all those years ago, he'd studied the work of fellow-German neuropathologist Alois Alzheimer. He knew, therefore, that short-term memory impairment might sometimes leave particular long-term memories intact. He, himself, had heard Brunner muttering stories of the Reich to whoever would listen, stories that could incriminate them both.

Uncomfortably for these two ancient Germans, there were several Jewish guests at Comraich. He'd personally been told by Sir Victor Haelstrom himself, no less. Brunner's half-whispered, wheezy words might be understood by a Jewish guest one day, and who was to say those same words wouldn't be repeated outside this refuge, and then what? Heim had ruminated on this vexatious problem for some time now, watching anxiously as his Nazi friend's mental health worsened each day. He'd come to realize, and not reluctantly, that something would have to be done before it was too late. Perhaps a soft pillow put over Brunner's face one night when he was deep in sleep. It was time for the old man to go anyway; Heim would be doing him a favour by making his death painless. Just uncomfortable for a minute or two.

He regarded his ex-Nazi colleague thoughtfully and was thoroughly sickened by the sight of the dewdrop on the end of Brunner's nose. So much for the Master Race!

*

Sandra Belling and her dining companions represented a fair cross-section of the type of guests to whom Comraich played host, nearly all runaways from different horrendous pasts, not missed and in some cases thought to be dead by the outside world. It was a conspiracy theorist's paradise.

The universal regimen of sedation meant that the dining room was hardly a hive of animation at the best of times, but as the scream emanated from Sandra Belling every other sound and movement in the room came to a fearful stop.

37

The pain caused by his back slamming into the wall behind him was nothing compared to the shock and disgust Ash felt when he stared at the writhing mass of maggots falling from what remained of the chicken sandwich Delphine had supplied him with for his night vigil.

The soft-bodied larvae spilled over onto the floor and Ash kicked out at the nauseating mess irrationally afraid that, once finished with their meal, the squirming maggots would find their way up his leg and eventually into his groin.

He yelled, giving vent to his stomach-churning anger as he pushed himself to his feet, back sliding roughly up the wall. Was this Delphine's idea of a joke? No, he rejected that assumption out of hand – it was something he was sure she would never do. The kitchen staff, then? But then again, maybe not: none of them would have dared give someone of Dr Wyatt's seniority a silver-foil wrap of rotting meat and maggots.

Without further thought, he scooped up the living heap and strode hurriedly towards the open window, pulpy little grubs falling onto his wrist and onto the carpet as he went. Fighting his distaste, he threw the wriggling package out of the window without considering that somebody might be walking below. He shuddered, then examined the carpet and stamped on every maggot he could see.

He hadn't noticed in his barely suppressed panic – it wasn't the sight of the maggots that had horrified him so much as the thought that he could have absent-mindedly bitten into the sandwich – that the light from the lamp on the small table had dimmed. Ash headed for the bathroom and ran the tap before he shrugged off his jacket and scrubbed his hands in the tiny sink.

Suddenly there came a nightmare scream which escalated to another that was pitched even higher. Ash froze, cold water still running through his fingers. The sound had come from some distance away, but he knew its source.

The great dining hall ran beneath his room and he lingered a moment, trying to make sense of it: the sounds, the screams – for there were many more now – intermingled with others and so the noise was getting louder. Not bothering to wipe his hands or pick up his jacket, Ash dashed through the bedroom and into the corridor. Looking left and right, he saw he was alone, and without further hesitation he made for the oval staircase which would take him to the dining hall.

In his haste, he failed to notice the heavy door to the old-fashioned lift was open. But as he passed it, a big pair of coarse hands reached out for him from the lift's dim interior, the guard gate open wide, a foot planted in front to keep it that way.

Beefy fingers curled round Ash's neck, dragging him into the box-shaped lift.

He barely had a chance to see who was attacking him before a heavy fist smashed into his upturned face.

38

In the dining hall, there was complete chaos.

Sandra Belling had been shocked into a clearness of mind, shocked enough to be horrified in a way she'd never been before. Even the horror of finding her little dead baby, tiny lips bluish, cheeks hued purple, was nothing compared to this. Sandra was jolted out of her sedated haze and memory repression and she screamed and screamed, not only because of the wriggling maggots on her plate and the curling specks of larvae that dropped from the stocky man's mouth on her right as he chomped away on his beef, seemingly oblivious to the disgusting taste and the wriggling things tumbling from his lips and sticking to his lower jaw.

But when Oleg Rinsinski finally understood what he was eating, his scream, although of a lower pitch than Sandra's, was much louder. It bellowed through the room, but then only to join with all the other screams and shouts and sounds of retching. Men and women were fainting as they choked on their putrefied food and tried to heave it from their throats. Others were luckier, for they noticed their corrupted meals crawling with innumerable maggots before biting into them.

Sir Victor Haelstrom watched stupefied as the pupae developed, for the maggots were swiftly evolving. He was a lusty eater and had already consumed much of his beef, and the flies' eggs had turned to maggots extraordinarily fast – unthinkably fast – inside him, going on as quickly to metamorphose into young flies.

Haelstrom sneezed violently and a black stream of flies spewed from his nostrils, taking to the air in a united stream to soar around the room. Their instinct seemed to be to attack any human they found, buzzing around their victims' heads, landing on their faces and hands, deliberately invading eyes and ears, and even mouths. Where they found women in evening gowns, bare shoulders and arms, necks and faces, their attention was even greater.

On the dinner table where the two astonished ex-Nazis, Brunner and Heim, sat and where the disorder had begun, the older and more doddery of the companions, Brunner, staggered to his feet, his chair falling over behind him. The dewdrop that only moments before had clung relentlessly to the end of his nose at last fell, not onto the mixture on his spoon but into the mush-filled plate now covered in maggots and blossoming flies. The old German's eyes widened and he uttered a mewling sound and sprang to his feet, his spine straighter than it had been for twenty years or more.

His associate in secrecy, Aribert Heim, the erstwhile Dr Death, had his own problems with maggots and flies sprouting from his thin-lipped mouth. He too leapt up, swatting at the flies that swarmed around him. It was the same for everyone in the room as they ran chaotically about, crashing into each other, rolling on the carpet, fighting to get to their feet. Some collapsed with fear.

Those batting away the swarming insects, or swiping at them with table-napkins, were bent over, vomiting a mixture of maggots, flies and undigested food. It came like bile, but thick and moving, and the stink it gave off was cause for more nausea.

Kit Weston had crawled under the table, fortunate that he rarely ate much, although some maggots still spilled from his mouth. Through the gap between the edge of the tablecloth and the deep red carpet he saw the lower part of two legs wearing slacks over two-inch heels and he knew they belonged to Sandra Belling.

Sandra, still in her chair, was drumming her feet on the floor in fear and disgust, so Weston lifted the tablecloth with one tendon-tightened claw and reached for her waist with the other. There was still some strength in his arms, for not only did he take GW1516 but he exercised in his own limited way, trying to stretch those parts of his body which, like his hands, had shrivelled, withered and scarred over so restrictively.

Initially, Sandra pushed herself back into the chair, but then seemed to comprehend the scarred man's intention – which, for her, was the kind of breakthrough Dr Wyatt had been trying to achieve for years. After a brief hesitation, she allowed herself to be dragged under the table and Weston quickly pushed the tablecloth back into place to screen them from the worst of the mayhem beyond.

Luckily, Sandra hadn't touched her meal, but Kit Weston retched and retched as she thumped his back in sympathy. The sounds of screams, shouts and pounding feet went on all around them as they cowered close together in their gloomy shelter. Enough flies found their way beneath the cloth to require Sandra and Weston to bat them away with their hands. In the end, they both realized the best thing to do was to cuddle up close to the soft-carpeted floor like lovers.

Waiters and waitresses made for the kitchens, which astonishingly were free of flies or their pupae save for the few that found their way in when doors opened and shut. Chloe, the waitress who had served lunch to Dr Pritchard, Delphine and Ash earlier that day, sank to her knees on the hard tiled floor, sobbing pitifully, confused and frightened by the mayhem inside the dining hall. When a junior chef went to open the swing door to see what was happening for himself, she shrieked, '*Don't!*'

He didn't.

*

Osril Ubutu looked around him in wonder, his huge eyes wide with astonishment. He was used to flies, many, many flies. But never like this, not even around the carcass of a lion-killed antelope were there such flies as this. The upper section of the dining room had become a black, buzzing fog, swirling around the room like a flock of miniature starlings. The castle's restaurant was filled with an unwholesome stench, driving those fleeing into fresh panic. Some were fighting to get to the wide door, arms flailing, legs kicking, fists punching. Ubutu was no exception, though one man immediately objected to being pushed in the back despite the general commotion and he turned on Ubutu in a reflex response.

The blow that landed on the huge African's chest came from probably the most feeble man in the room: Alois Brunner. At any other time Ubutu would have found the situation funny, but this was not the time for laughter. For the briefest moment he peered down at this pygmy who'd had the temerity to strike the king, then, with his huge hand, he swiped the fool away from him. The frail old man went down without a cry and the side of his face smashed against the edge of the table, the one under which Sandra Belling and Kit Weston were entwined.

Brunner had grown weak with age and soft with all the luxury and easy living at Comraich. Some years earlier he might have struggled to his feet again, perhaps a little dazed but ready to retaliate. As it was, the blow knocked him practically unconscious and he tipped up the table, exposing the two guests hiding underneath for a second. Fortunately, the table tipped back, just with fewer plates, cutlery, condiments, glasses and minus a central flower arrangement. Once more they were in shadow and they remained there.

Beneath the table, it briefly crossed Sandra's terrified mind that the old Nazi was playing hide-and-seek, peeking under the tablecloth skirt to find them, but she soon realized his eyes were semi-closed and his mouth wide open.

In fact, the prone German's dentures had become dislodged inside his mouth as, in his barely conscious state, he'd sucked in air, which in turn sucked in the false teeth so that they became stuck sideways at the top of his throat. He rolled onto his back and suddenly his eyes popped fully open. He stared at the hall's high ceiling, blinked, and continued to gaze upwards. Sandra couldn't help but watch as the German's chest rapidly rose and fell, his lungs desperate for more air than they were getting. Then she saw something that was an even more nightmarish scene. She couldn't turn away from this sight, no matter how much it frightened her. She was held spellbound by the influx of hundreds, thousands, millions, of small black flies that poured *into* the German's open jaw, a mini-tornado that soon became a fierce whirlpool sinking into the man's mouth, choking him, sucked in further as he struggled to breathe, so that his chest heaved and his body thrashed, until his whole face was covered in a glittering mask of tiny moving insects that funnelled their way via the gaping hole of his mouth to fill his lungs.

Aribert Heim left his old comrade lying prone on the floor, the newly formed flies feeding off Brunner's wide, staring, dead eyes, and already laying soft larvae on the exposed flesh. The gestation period was ridiculously short, and very quickly the German's corpse was populated by a fresh generation of crawling maggots.

39

Ash huddled in the corner of the dimly lit lift, blood sluicing from his lower lip, his head spinning from the vicious blow he'd taken. He felt rough hands drag his shoulder round so that his attacker could see his face. Those same hands gripped his shirt beneath the gilet to haul him to his feet, and a coarse wide grin peered into his.

'You think I am stupid?' Ash's assailant demanded in a low, heavily accented voice. 'You think Lukovic doesn't know?' He slammed Ash back into the corner again, but this time left the investigator standing.

Dazedly, Ash looked into his attacker's brutish face. Who the hell was he?

Then he recognized the heavy-set man who had glared at him in the reception hall earlier. Karadzic's general: Zdravko Lukovic. The Serb shook Ash violently, his beefy hands gripping the front of the investigator's shirt.

'Who send you? British? Americans? Muslims?'

His spit dampened Ash's face. The investigator shook his head and tried to speak. 'Look, I—'

'No lies! I know your face. You come for me, yes? You are here to murder Lukovic.'

Zdravko Lukovic had been waiting for the day to come – despite the promises that he would be protected for his betrayal of his leader Radovan Karadzic. They would hide him somewhere safe, they'd said, and he would live the rest of his life in comfort, they'd promised him. Just tell them where 'The Butcher' was hiding. He'd told them.

But Zdravko Lukovic trusted nobody and kept a wary eye out for everything. And because he refused to take any of the pills they handed him each morning in a tiny paper cup (the staff weren't to know that he stuck the tablets to the side of his mouth with his tongue, spitting them out later when he was alone and flushing them down the lavatory) he was never truly sedated, although he pretended to be. The shots they gave him – and no, they wouldn't tell him what they were for, nor what the syringe contained – he couldn't avoid, but they seemed quite innocuous to him, with a mild effect unless sometimes he stood up too quickly and so suffered a short bout of dizziness. Maybe they were meant to stabilize his high blood pressure.

Unfortunately, because he refused the calming tablets, his paranoia grew greater by the week, although he hid it well. However, by now it had become more serious, a mental malady that was not so easy to hide. And of late – and this might have something to do with this strange new atmosphere in the castle (although he'd never made the connection himself) – he was becoming even more suspicious, sure that his enemies had tracked him down.

This was why Lukovic eyed any newcomer with suspicion. This was why he'd attacked today's newcomer to Comraich. Lukovic was not only paranoid, but psychotic too. He would kill anyone he suspected sent there to kill him, before they got him.

Now he had hold of the first would-be assassin and the man's death would send out a message to anyone else who wanted Lukovic dead. One by one as they came for him he would deal with them in the same way until those who wanted Zdravko Lukovic dead would eventually abandon the idea. And he, Lukovic, guest of Comraich Castle, would demand financial reparation from Sir Victor Haelstrom himself for breaking the promise of total protection, twenty-four hours a day, seven days a week.

His forearm was beneath Ash's chin, like a length of hard

wood, pushing against his throat, choking the life from him. Ash looked into Lukovic's gleaming, narrow eyes that projected pure hatred between the heavy lids. The man was immensely strong, pinning him into the corner of the lift as easily as if he were a child. The investigator's heels drummed against the wood panel. His head was already reeling from lack of oxygen. Ash was trapped and he knew that unless he broke his attacker's hold, he would choke to death.

Lukovic maintained the force against Ash's throat with his right arm, while his left held Ash's right wrist hard against the polished wood panelling.

In sheer desperation Ash pushed his free left hand into his assailant's snarling, brutish face. He thrust two stiffened fingers directly into the madman's right eye, wincing as they passed through the half-closed lids and pushed against the repugnant softness of the eyeball itself. Then beyond, his fingers slithered over the white globe until they reached harder matter behind.

Lukovic screeched as blood gushed from the ruined eye socket, a sound amplified by the limited confines of the lift, and instinctively yanked his head backwards. But the tips of Ash's gore-sodden fingers had curled behind the eyeball, and when Lukovic pulled his head back the eyeball popped as though sucked out and dropped against his upper cheek, held there only by thin bloody tendrils.

The Serb's yowls of pain and panic became even louder, easily competing with the noise from the dining room one floor below. He released Ash and staggered backwards, a gush of blood spurting across the small lift.

Ash gratefully drew in several heaving breaths, restoring life to his own flagging body. The other man was throwing himself from side to side in the lift, screaming and bellowing all the while, dangerous as a wounded bull.

Ash needed to get out of there, but just as he braced himself to rush past the weaving, outraged, agonized man, the safety door expanded shut with a loud *clank* like a guillotine. He fell back in surprise. How . . . ?

There was no time to think. The sharp sound had startled the other man too. He stopped his bellowing. The front of his suit was a maroon mess, as was his right hand and lower arm. He'd lowered that hand, dropping it to his side. He stared at Ash with his single hate-filled eye; the other still lay on his bloodied cheek, held there by red tendrils, its pupil looking downwards as if at something it could see lying on the floor.

The good one just glared at Ash with venomous spite and, incongruously, the investigator wondered if the dangling eye still had sight, for it remained connected to the socket. What would it be like to see in two different directions at once? How would a brain handle that?

Then, the blood-soaked man lifted the palm of his blood-free hand towards Ash. Lukovic lunged towards Ash and the investigator ducked, hurling himself into the corner behind the stumbling, enraged Cyclops. Lukovic whirled round fast, for apart from being immensely strong, his years of combat had taught him to endure even when wounded, and to make the enemy suffer. His large hand caught Ash's shoulder, but the investigator was swift and determined to avoid a wrestling match with an adversary whose strength was bound to over-whelm him.

He half turned, then drove his elbow back towards Lukovic's injured and exposed face, smashing it as hard as he could and crushing the dangling eyeball. The roar from the crippled combatant filled the air with an unbearable sound and the Serb used his whole body to push Ash against the mirrored back wall.

Once again, Ash was fighting for his life. Powerful arms closed round his back, and as he was pulled tight against the grunting Serb, bloody spittle lashed the investigator's face.

The bear hug tightened even more and Ash rose on tiptoe as his heels left the floor and his spine was pulled inwards. The breath left his lungs and tears were squeezed from his eyes like juice from a lemon. His mouth opened, but no sound came out as his body trembled with the unbearable pressure.

Ash felt his sight begin to dim. He tried to lift his arms but it was no use. Even as he looked into Lukovic's remaining eye he could see the cruel pleasure there. At least the encroaching blackness would take away the agony, unconsciousness anaesthetizing the shocking pain. As he began to slip mercifully away, he thought he heard the first crack of bone. It would be over soon. Surely he must be released from the torment before much longer.

But Ash didn't die.

As he emerged from the spiralling well of darkness into which he'd been almost lethargically sinking, the pain returned as if to welcome him back. He became aware of a terrible shaking. At first he thought it was a reaction from his own body. But it wasn't: it was coming from all around them, from somewhere inside the small lift itself.

The Serb still held him in his grip, though now almost tenderly. The pressure on his back eased and he almost swooned with relief. Slowly, his sight returned.

The big, Slavic face, still only inches from his own, looked around him in panic, the drooping red-veined, white mush of his dislodged eye swinging across the man's broad cheek. Then Lukovic gawped at the ceiling, where the lightbulb was glowing then paling, glowing then paling . . .

And all the while, the shuddering of the lift increased in violence. The metal safety door rattled, the walls vibrated. A thumping noise came from all around.

Lukovic's untouched eye looked at Ash, confusion fighting with fear. Ash, just as bewildered, could only stare back at him, while words tried to form in his throat, impatient to impart their message. A message of warning.

The lift cage juddered violently. Then again. The two men, face to face, could only focus on each other in dismay.

The wooden panels around them vibrated, the safety door clattered metallically while the heavy entrance door beyond remained sealed, unaffected by the lift car's convulsions.

Lukovic tottered back a step, his hands still gripping Ash

by his shirt. But it was the investigator who came to his senses first. Seeing the Serb's sudden loss of balance, he pushed him back hard, but the bigger man's grip on Ash's shirt took the investigator with him, and they both toppled to the floor. As they lay part-winded, part-paralysed with shock, the shuddering of the lift increased alarmingly. Then, suddenly, with a tearing screech, the lift plunged downward at tremendous speed into the seemingly bottomless shaft.

For a brief, almost pleasant moment Ash felt his body in free-fall; then their descent was arrested by a massive jolt, a seismic crash.

Lukovic screamed as the lift plunged into the pitch-black pit, which was not bottomless after all.

It was far worse than that.

40

Kate McCarrick looked across the candlelit table at the friend she'd known for – oh, for forty years at least, she thought. They had grown up together, had been playmates, living in a quiet avenue of semi-detached houses, a road of very few parked cars, where boys waited impatiently each season for the horse chestnut trees – council-planted in grassy areas along the wide pavements – to shed their prickly green-cocooned conkers.

'Glo', as Kate had always called Metropolitan Police Deputy Assistant Commissioner Gloria Standwell of New Scotland Yard, who sat on the opposite side of the restaurant's intimate round table and was now wearing a trim Jaeger black jacket and pencil skirt rather than her formal police uniform, had also collected conkers and delighted in smashing her opponents' to smithereens, which she used to do at least seven times out of ten.

But Kate knew her friend's secret, because she'd helped her soak the shiny brown nuts in vinegar and bake them in the oven for ten minutes so that the conker became a formidable weapon. Kate smiled inwardly.

Without doubt, her pretty friend had been a tomboy in those days, although she also loved playing with dolls and skipping and doing other girlish things. Their bond was tight, from their toddler years, through confusing, exciting puberty and later going on giggly foursome dates together with pimply adolescent boys only too pleased to be their escorts. That

289

was until Glo's socially mobile parents had decided to move up in the world and buy a much grander, detached house somewhere beyond the suburbs, opposite a large park with a lake so big that people actually sailed on it. It was a different world from Kate's, a world of drives, garages and posh cars. It was a place Kate had loved to visit for weekends and during school holidays. Not that she ever resented returning to her own more humble home. She envied Glo and her new lifestyle, but was never jealous; she loved her friend too much for that. Too soon, they had gone their separate ways, choosing different universities and making whole new sets of friends.

Kate had been surprised when Glo married early – she thought her friend too career-minded for that – but she'd happily attended the wedding as chief bridesmaid. Glo had joined the police force soon after leaving uni – no surprise to Kate – and her groom was a high-ranking police officer, which had also been unsurprising. Glo had risen swiftly through the ranks while still managing to bring up two children, a boy and a girl, and juggling the usual household commitments.

Her children were adults now, and Glo had divorced her husband. 'Irreconcilable differences' had been the reason given, but Kate wondered if her friend's superior rank had been the underlying cause of the rift between them. She also suspected Glo had waited for her son and daughter to come of age and so be able to understand and cope before she took such a drastic decision. On her visits, Kate had always noticed an undercurrent of tension between Glo and Tim, her husband, so when the break-up was announced, it had come as no great surprise.

She and Glo had remained in touch socially over the years, though less frequently than before, and their paths crossed professionally whenever the Met needed some help from the Psychical Research Institute. Kate felt Glo was embarrassed by the divorce. It was the one big failure in her otherwise successful life.

Now Kate smiled openly at Deputy Assistant Commissioner Gloria Standwell, the candlelight softening her friend's features and catching the short hairstyle that framed her face. Glo caught the look, raising her slim glass of Taittinger Nocturne champagne as a toast in return.

'It was good to hear from you after such a long time,' the policewoman said in mild reproach.

Kate sipped her wine before replying, 'Hope my call didn't give you too much of a shock.'

Glo leaned forward on the tabletop to give her response, which was spoken almost in a whisper, even though the Pimlico restaurant Kate had suggested for the meeting was the epitome of 'private'. Kate had been a client there for more years than she cared to count, and she often wondered just how many clandestine discussions had taken place within these hushed surrounds.

'It was the name you mentioned that was the shock,' Glo replied. 'The Inner Court remains top secret as far as the Met and the SIS are concerned. What do you know about it?'

'Well, I know it owns a perfect hiding place for those with lots of money to spend.'

'You've put me in a tricky position, Katie. You must already know there's nothing I can tell you.'

Kate had always been perceptive. 'That doesn't mean you don't want to,' she responded quietly. 'Look, Glo, I'm really concerned about one of my operatives who's on an assignment there as we speak.'

'Can I ask who?'

'David Ash.'

Gloria gave a wry smile. 'How is *he* these days?'

It was a pointed question, and Kate dealt with it easily. 'He's fine. I wouldn't have assigned him otherwise.'

The policewoman knew of her friend's casual on-off romantic involvement with Ash and Kate knew she thought he was too far on the good side of forty for her. Gloria understood Kate's anxiety for this enigmatic colleague of hers, a man the

Met had covertly used on one or two baffling cases. Gloria liked him a lot, even though he could sometimes be moody and withdrawn. He claimed not to be psychic, and if that were true, then he at least had some kind of genius for picking up vital clues that her colleagues had often missed.

'David is at Comraich Castle.' It was a statement, not a question.

Kate nodded, but kept silent as a waiter arrived to take away the empty plates that had held their *hors d'oeuvres*.

'Would you like to wait a little while before I bring your main course, mesdames?' the French waiter suggested tactfully, for he'd observed the two women were deep in conversation before he'd approached their table.

'Thank you, Vincent,' said Kate, smiling up at the waiter.

Gloria placed her glass on the table and leaned towards her friend. 'Now, tell me the problem and I'll try to help as much as I can.' Years of training had allowed her to discreetly examine other clients in the small downstairs dining room and, although it was dimly lit, she was satisfied there were no other diners of whom she should beware.

Kate also leaned forward on the table, the stem of her glass held loosely in her fingers. 'The problem is, I can't contact him.'

'And he can't reach you.' Again, it wasn't a question.

'You know about that? And the Inner Court?'

'We may need a while on this. First, I have to ask what *you* know about the Inner Court.'

'Don't go all policewomanly, Glo.'

'I'm not, I promise. But you've raised a very delicate issue for me. And it could be dangerous for you.'

Kate didn't even blink. 'It's David I'm worried about.'

'I can understand that. You still haven't answered my question, though. What do you know about the Inner Court? And who gave you the information?' she added.

'An old university friend. A man called Simon Maseby.'

'Oh, that little slimeball,' she said, leaning back.

Kate felt distinctly uncomfortable, having slept with said slimeball the night before. 'You know him, then,' she said flatly.

'Oh, the Met knows all about Maseby, although he's done nothing illegal as far as we can tell. But we are aware he's a go-between for the IC.'

Kate nodded. 'Simon was just a mite drunk when he told me a bit more about the organization than he probably should have after we'd signed the contract in my office.'

Gloria moved her glass of wine further away from her and leaned forward again. Her manner became more serious.

'Right. What I'm going to tell you could cost me my job and maybe even more, Katie. I'm only telling you because David might be in trouble up there.' She continued in an intense whisper. 'You're right to be worried: these people can be very dangerous.'

'That's very reassuring,' came the acerbic response.

'No. I didn't mean to worry you more, but I think you need to understand about this organization. But I must warn you, this information is strictly between us. It's only because I know and love you that I'm breaking the rules. I need your word that you'll never repeat what I tell you.'

Kate reached forward and laid her hand over Gloria's, where it rested on the tabletop. 'You know I won't, Glo.'

Gloria took another longer sip of the excellent wine and drew in a deep breath, as though she were about to plunge into an ice-cold pool.

Then she began.

'In this country we have layers of unelected elitist pecking orders under the monarchy with the Royal Knights of the Most Noble Order of the Garter, restricted to members of the royal family, at the top. Prince William took the title in 2008. You may have seen the coverage on the television news, where he wore a black ostrich-plumed hat and various bits and pieces including a garter strapped below his left knee.'

'And very fetching it was too,' put in Kate.

'Don't mock.' Gloria gave her a small scowl, which was spoilt by the immediate smile on her lips. 'All this pomp is important for the country's tourism industry as well as making the so-titled feel more important. Then there are the twenty-four Royal Knights *Companion* of the Garter, who are usually made up of former prime ministers, public figures, ex-cabinet secretaries, field marshals and public-spirited aristocrats with one or two industrialists thrown into the mix. Unlike Prince William, who is a Royal Knight, the Knights Companions' costumes are a little less overblown – *only* a little, mind – and the grandeur and ritual that go with them suits the wearers. But then, with the fancy regalia the chiefs in the Met sometimes have to wear, you'll hear no hypocrisy from me.'

Both smiling, they sipped at their wine together.

'Okay, now,' Gloria went on, placing the glass back on the table within easy reach, 'even more important and much more exclusive than the Knights of the Garter are the Queen's own personally chosen counsellors. This group is called the Order of Merit, whose membership is limited to twenty-four of the most illustrious people in the Commonwealth. Apart from each chosen member wearing a small blue and crimson cross with a tiny laurel wreath in the centre and an itsy gold inscription that says, "For Merit", there is no other regalia they're obliged to wear. Formal lounge suits and appropriate dresses for the ladies with the OM badge pinned to clothing is the only dress code required.

'When next they sit down for lunch with the Queen at Buckingham Palace it will be only the eighth time since its formation a hundred or so years ago that this exclusive coterie has met with the reigning monarch.'

'Who are the members – are they the Queen's favourites?' asked Kate, now intrigued.

'Oh, much more than that. Each one has a special talent or

skill that not only enables the Queen to keep the country sound, but also helps the Crown endure. And what an intellectually diverse body they are. They include the great mathematician, Sir Roger Penrose, the zoologist Lord May and Neil MacGregor of the British Museum, to name just three.'

'They seem a pretty dry lot,' said Kate. 'Not many jokes over the lunch table.'

'Don't you believe it. There are those from the arts present also. Men like Tom Stoppard and David Hockney. David Attenborough and Betty Boothroyd.'

Kate leaned back in her chair and almost whistled. 'That's one disparate and interesting lot. Can you imagine the conversations that go on?'

Gloria nodded, her expression remaining serious.

'And an interesting further point: Baroness Thatcher is the only ex-Prime Minister among them. Queen Elizabeth moved fast when Thatcher was ousted as leader by John Major and his cronies because she knew that the Inner Court wanted to bag her for themselves. The prestige, and perhaps legitimacy, it would have afforded the group would have been beyond value. Luckily, and shrewdly, Margaret Thatcher's loyalty remained with Crown and Country: she accepted the Queen's honour, not for the glory – the Order of Merit is far too understated for that, even if its influence is irrefutable and widespread – but because she bore no public malice towards the politicians who had betrayed her, and saw quite clearly where her allegiance lay: the people and their monarch. Sorry, I'm getting on my high horse, aren't I?'

'Well, you do sound like an admirer,' said Kate with a grin.

Gloria smiled ruefully. 'I am. She's a terrific benchmark for what women can rise to. Unfortunately, her downfall revealed the duplicity of the male of the species.'

Kate could only agree, although she remained silent. She had an idea that her companion had a lot more to say about the various powers in the country and Kate was reluctant to spoil the flow. Instead, she lifted her almost empty wine glass.

'Shall we top up before we go on, or ask them to bring our main course now?'

'I'm not in the mood for food at the moment,' Gloria told Kate. 'But don't let me stop you having more champers.'

The waiter was at his client's side before Kate could reach into the ice bucket. He waved the diminished contents of the champagne bottle in the policewoman's direction temptingly, but she declined by placing the palm of her hand over the top of her glass.

'Come on, Glo,' Kate chided, 'you're not on duty now.'

'Katie, as you well know, I'm always on duty.'

And you always were, thought Kate fondly. 'All right, perhaps a fresh bottle later, Vincent.'

As the waiter departed, Kate found her friend staring across the table at her, concern written all over her freckle-cheeked face. Kate raised her eyebrows questioningly. 'You're not having second thoughts about this, are you, Glo?'

'So far I've told you nothing you couldn't find out for yourself.'

'But now we're heading into deeper waters,' Kate commented. 'We really don't have to continue with this if it makes you uncomfortable,' she offered, while hoping fervently her friend would carry on in the same vein.

Gloria relaxed back in her chair. 'What the hell,' she said quietly. 'David Ash is important to both of us, and I know how worried you are about him. You're still not sure if he's up to the job, are you?'

Kate averted her gaze, fixing it on the glass in front of her. 'Is it that obvious?'

'I could always read you, Katie. And I know I can trust you. To tell you the truth,' Gloria responded, 'it's a kind of relief to talk about these things to someone who's not wearing a uniform or a Home Office pass.'

They both giggled at that, almost like they used to over silly secrets when they were kids.

Gloria straightened her spine, the pose somehow authoritarian, with only her familiar warm smile humanizing the image.

Kate nodded. 'Right.'

'Even more influential than the OM is another very secretive group of extraordinarily wealthy individuals known as the Multinational Chairman's Group, who together are so powerful they can influence government policies, both foreign and domestic. They lobby ministers to alter tax schemes, business incentives, as well as trade embargoes and such like. Governments are afraid of them because their world assets and resources can sometimes be used to destroy a country's economic system. Compromises are always sought, of course, because as well as individual countries facing financial crises, the pressure group itself can be damaged in the fallout.'

She deliberated for a moment, then said, 'You won't be surprised to learn that much of this is about corporate and individual taxation, particularly where international assets are concerned.' She paused again and then continued, 'Then there is the Bilderberg Group of businessmen and politicians which is similar in function, but far more open than the Multinational Chairman's Group. It has an unofficial annual conference to which a hundred and forty or so people are invited. These are mainly from North America and Western Europe.'

'So is this Multinational Group connected to the Inner Court in some way?' Kate asked, deeply puzzled.

'No,' came the policewoman's instant response. 'You might say that the IC is the very antithesis of the MCG. The Inner Court's machinations often involve corruption, undue pressure on rivals, questionable tactics – and blackmail. It's this last factor that gives them so much clout.'

'But why do you ... I mean, the law, how can it let them get away with it?'

Gloria frowned at the question. The powerful policewoman took a deeper sip of the Taittinger Nocturne before speaking. 'I'm afraid the law has to step warily as far as the IC is concerned, but SIS keeps continuous tabs on them.'

'But their obvious shenanigans can't be stopped?' Kate exclaimed a little too loudly. She realized the fine wine was beginning to have its effect on her and moderated her tone again. 'I mean, Glo, surely in this day and age, groups or organizations – whatever you'd call them – can't be allowed to get away with such practices?'

Gloria gave a soft sigh, but it was one more of solicitude than frustration.

'Perhaps I should take you back to the Inner Court's beginnings. It might just help you understand the predicament both the law and the Crown are in.'

Kate consented with a keen nod of her head. 'Go on.'

'Rather embarrassingly,' Gloria began again, 'no one really knows when the Inner Court first came into being, or how. It just seemed to evolve, and before anyone was aware, there it was, a secret order known only to the members themselves and the people they conspired with.

'About two centuries ago, a duke, whose name no longer matters, headed a group of notables, which offered its covert services to King George III, services that necessarily relied on guile, secrecy, influence, and occasionally, assassination.'

'And was the offer accepted?' asked Kate.

'Well, there's no existing record that it was declined.'

The deputy assistant commissioner gave Kate a moment or two to let her absorb what she'd heard thus far.

'Go on,' Kate urged again, though hesitantly, as if this kind of forbidden knowledge might somehow put her in jeopardy. But it was too compelling.

'Because the Inner Court was never officially acknowledged by the Crown, no connection could ever be suggested, let alone proved, not even to this day. Certainly, there may have been suspicions, but few would have been brave enough to voice them.'

'I'm sorry to interrupt,' Kate cut in apologetically, 'but why the "Inner Court"? Why did these people call themselves that?'

'We think it was because of its lack of faith in the country's judicial systems and means of commerce – much as it is today. It believed then, as it does now, that Britain should reassert itself as a significant world power.

'Its original motives were patriotic but, inevitably, too much secrecy lays the foundations for corruption, as does the quest for too much power and political advantage. Eventually, greed became the IC's cornerstone, and that began to erode their principles and distance them from the Crown as well as the government of the day. Yet the organization had already made itself indispensable to the sovereign state, and by then it knew where the skeletons were buried, so to speak.'

'Is the monarchy still involved?'

Gloria nodded grimly. 'You see, although there have been many hushed-up royal scandals throughout the ages, sometimes even minor characters – let's call them bit-part players – might easily have caused irreparable damage to the Crown's reputation. You remember the man called Michael Fagan?'

Kate searched her memory for a moment or two. 'Fagan. Yes, wasn't he the trespasser who got into Queen Elizabeth's bedroom, with the Queen herself inside? That was several years ago, wasn't it?'

'July 1982.'

'They put it down to a freak circumstance and failed security.'

'Oh, it was that all right. The Buckingham Palace chief of security was quietly moved on some time later.'

'But how could that harm the Queen's reputation? If anything, she was praised for her clear-mindedness and courage.'

'Rightly so. She acted perfectly, no panic whatsoever. But do you really believe a perfect stranger could break into the grounds of the Palace, and then into the building itself with so many guards and police officers protecting the place?'

'Well, I must admit that at the time I found it all a bit strange. So what was the truth, Glo?'

Gloria sighed uncomfortably. 'The Palace is well run, its head staff and guards are marvellous at what they do. Unfortunately, some of the below-stairs staff, valets, servants, many of them gay, are known to have little "jollies" from time to time to which both sexual partners and rent boys are invited. The Queen's Guard barracks, which are not far away, is a hunting ground to find fit young men who are only too eager for a good time. Don't frown, Kate. It's not unknown for the House of Commons and House of Lords to be used for similar frivolities.'

She paused. It was evident that Gloria was uneasy about telling her friend of these activities.

'You really can trust me,' Kate assured the policewoman quietly. 'I promise none of this will go any further.'

Gloria rallied. 'Now there's no suggestion Fagan was gay – he might have just been a friend of someone who thought a party in one of the staff's living quarters would be great fun. But here's the thing: Michael Fagan was never charged for breaking and entering, let alone entering the Queen's bedroom uninvited. He was later accused of stealing half a bottle of wine, but that was dropped when he was committed for psychiatric evaluation. In other words, he was let off with a slap on the wrist. I think that's because a deal was done. For his silence about the "below-stairs" shenanigans, he got off scot-free, more or less.'

Gloria sat back in her chair to give Kate time to digest the information.

'I remember asking myself what had happened to Fagan,' Kate said slowly. 'The result was all played down, very low-key, wasn't it?'

'That's right. It was thought to be the best policy at the time.'

'Rather than honesty?'

'Of course.'

It was a simple reply and, although Kate was adult enough to know that in government there were little lies and big lies, she hoped her friend hadn't become hardened to them.

'You told me you could give me *some* instances . . .' Kate let the statement hang in the air between them.

'Right,' the policewoman came back briskly. 'But I'll keep the next one short. There are more important things which involve Comraich Castle. Now, I'm sure you've heard of Paul Burrell, Princess Diana's "rock", as he liked to consider himself.'

'He was the princess's butler before her tragic accident in Paris.'

Gloria eyed her old friend in a way that made Kate shudder inside.

The policewoman said without a hint of irony, 'Let's not go down that particular road, shall we?' leaving the Institute's director wondering if the pun was intended.

Gloria was giving nothing more away, and the cold stare dissolved. 'Sorry. Yes, Burrell was her butler, but claimed to be much more to the late princess: general factotum, shoulder to cry on, the one who helped smuggle her various lovers into Kensington Palace, and most of all – her *confidant*. Yet when Diana died, Burrell was accused of stealing expensive gifts she'd acquired either on her travels, or from admirers. The police searched his home and found many of them gathering dust in his attic. He maintained Diana had given them all to him to keep for her.

'Thin story,' Gloria said, smiling a little, 'because if she's dead, who or what was he keeping them for? At any rate, he swore his story was true, but he was still put in the dock. His time there lasted no more than a week, and it soon became evident that some interesting, even salacious stories about the royals and their coterie were going to be made public by Burrell. In fact, his defence counsel could hardly wait to get started.'

'Ah yes,' put in Kate, 'this I do recall very clearly. The whole case against Paul Burrell was mystifyingly dropped when the Queen herself rang the court to say she now remembered the accused had once mentioned to her that Princess Diana had asked him to keep some items in store for her.'

'That was it. Most people had suspicions about the timing.

Burrell knew too many well-kept secrets concerning the royal family and, led by his own defence barrister, was prepared to reveal all in court. Metaphorically speaking, he knew where the bodies were buried. Both the Crown and the prosecutor were alarmed when they realized where his testimony was going and the case was hastily dropped. Ill-repute is not easy for the monarchy to deal with. Heaven knows, they'd had enough problems with Sarah Ferguson, Andrew's ex-wife and her various flirtations and business capers, which left her virtually bankrupt and her ex-husband to bail her out at least twice. But now, the family, or the "Firm" as they call themselves, have become vulnerable, even less respected by the anti-monarchists, and by many of the ordinary people. Only the Queen's outstanding personal and public popularity and reputation, along with that of the late Queen Mother, has maintained the standing of the royal family. She's aware that the monarchy has to modernize, has to live in today's world, otherwise it will sink. Her problem is how to do that, yet keep that royal mystique.'

'No mean task these days.'

'No, and our sovereign is ageing, although she rarely lets her weariness show. Incidentally, Katie, it's my firm conviction Charles will make a fine king, when and *if* he finally takes the Crown. Today's media enjoy bringing people down a notch or two, but believe me, he's a man of much capability and, more importantly, you might say, he has "soul". Yet he also has a spine of steel. Never underestimate him. He also has two terrific sons who, eventually, will help him carry out his duties.'

'We're kind of digressing, Glo.' Kate was impatient to get to the other, perhaps even more relevant matters that the policewoman was leading up to. 'I take it the Inner Court plays a part in all this in some way. Does it have some kind of hold over the Crown?'

'Oh, it would deny that completely. It has no power. What it does have is *influence*, and that's because its members know too many secrets of both the Crown and the Establishment.' Gloria drew in a breath.

'The first time royalty used the Inner Court was for a reason that most people would find unacceptable. This was the case of poor Prince John. It was shortly after the turn of the last century, when the British Empire was at its height. King George V and Queen Mary hadn't long succeeded to the throne, and the Great War was looming. One of their children, young Prince Johnnie, had epilepsy, which was considered an unacceptable abnormality then. Johnnie was an embarrassment to the Crown at a time when it needed to be seen as strong. The Inner Court had an isolated castle in Scotland and its members offered to give the young prince refuge there. The offer was reluctantly accepted and the boy and his nanny were sent to Comraich Castle, where he lived privately but in comfort until he died aged thirteen in 1919.'

Kate's eyes were downcast. 'A sad story,' she said.

'Well,' Gloria went on, 'the Inner Court then made itself useful in other ways too. That's how they got a grip on royalty in the first place.'

'What do you mean?' This Inner Court was becoming more sinister to Kate by the moment.

'Aah.' It was almost a groan. 'Let's just say that the organization has many informers – spies, if you like – some of them in the Palace. And, as they rightly say, information is power, as is influence.'

With a smile on a face that had lost its bloom, Gloria gave a shake of her head. 'You know, the current royals have sought assistance from the Inner Court too. There are no good guys here.'

'I can't believe Queen Elizabeth was ever involved in any skulduggery.'

Gloria merely smiled again.

After a beat, she said, 'I hate to shatter your illusions. But she's no fool and she must be tough as old boots by now, truth be known.'

She held up a hand to forestall the protest Kate was about to make.

'Remember,' she went on hurriedly, 'the Queen is surrounded by aides and knighted private secretaries and advisors and such. She has direct access to the top military brass, heads of national security, defence, and foreign policy. And there's Prince Philip, who remains as sharp as a razor blade, despite his age.'

'Even so,' Kate insisted, 'I can't see Her Majesty being involved in underhand practices.'

'Not even for the good of the nation?'

'Well . . .'

'Let me tell you about something that has always been dismissed as a foolish conspiracy theory. It happened a long time ago, I'll admit, under the morally impeccable reign of Queen Victoria. Since then the waters have been deliberately muddied, false claims have come to the surface, and fanciful stories have been perpetuated.'

'I'm listening.' Kate wore a look of tolerance.

'Jack the Ripper . . .'

'Oh, come on, Glo. All kinds of legends have been told about *him*.'

'And one of the more popular tales has a smidgen of truth to it, as they generally do.'

'One of Queen Victoria's sons, wasn't it?' Kate was mildly scornful. 'Or her own doctor? Certainly a doctor of some kind.'

Gloria surprised Kate by saying, 'You're closer than you might think. I could give you a list of suspects who've been named over the years: John Pizer, Walter Sickert, Aaron Kosminski and, yes, even Queen Victoria's surgeon, Sir William Gull . . . the list goes on. But all were false.'

'How do we know that?'

'Because the Ripper *was* discovered. Queen Victoria herself ordered further investigation to be called off and the gruesome murders ceased.'

'Then she knew who . . . ?'

Gloria nodded just once. 'Victoria had nine children, four of them boys. One of her sons – I think it was Alfred, but it's irrelevant now – was very interested in psychology and had studied the work of Sigmund Freud. He had an American friend called Henshaw, who was fascinated by both Freud and Jung. In his own country, the young American was referred to as an alienist, before psychiatry became more respectable. It's said Henshaw helped Victoria's son through mental and emotional turmoil and became a kind of mentor to him.

'But the reality was that Aaron Henshaw was himself a schizophrenic, who blamed East End prostitutes for luring his royal friend into sordid sexual practices. So he spent dark evenings wandering the dangerous streets of Whitechapel seeking out lone prostitutes. He accounted for seven victims in all.

'Fortunately or unfortunately, whichever way you look at it, he confessed to his royal friend, who was horrified. Henshaw let it be known he'd secreted away the damning case notes he'd made on Queen Victoria's debauched son. That was her personal dilemma.

'This was where the Inner Court offered its services. The alienist was taken to Scotland and ensconced in Comraich Castle, never to be seen or heard from again.'

'But he must have had relatives in America or friends in London, who enquired after him.'

'No doubt they did, but I can only guess they were fobbed off with a story that he'd been killed in an accident or from some unforeseen and rapidly terminal illness.'

Kate McCarrick sat back in her seat, took a deep breath and tried to relax. She wondered what she'd got David Ash into. Her friend seemed just as unhappy.

'The prince wasn't anxious about his friend?'

'Not until he heard of Henshaw's crimes,' the policewoman replied. 'And Queen Victoria was very domineering, don't forget, even with – *especially* with – her own children. As well as highly moral. Can you imagine her shock when she discovered the truth? Her first instinct was to have the alienist quietly assassinated. It was only at her son's bidding that she didn't, although who knows how long the Ripper was allowed to live on at Comraich?'

Kate noticed her friend's glass was nearly empty again and she thought another drink might just ease the tension. She was a little surprised when her friend, who was no great drinker, accepted the offer.

Kate rightly guessed that Glo had more to tell.

Much more . . . but it would take a little more time.

41

Ash felt the air rush from his body, but he also felt the life leave the man beneath him; the Serb general had unintentionally cushioned Ash from the worst of the impact when the ancient lift had crashed through to the second lower basement. This was Comraich Castle's secret heart.

Ash suddenly remembered Haelstrom's precise words: *Underground is our containment area. It's where we keep our lunatics . . .*

He groaned as he tried to move, one of Lukovic's dead arms locked around his back. Thick dust filled the air, making it difficult for Ash to draw in the breath that had been knocked out of his shocked body. The thick swirling particles also made it difficult to see clearly and the thunderous crash of the lift slamming into the concrete base of the shaft had momentarily deafened him.

Ash slowly managed to turn his head and could just make out the mangled wreckage of the lift cage around him, the twisted ceiling V-shaped to a point no more than a foot-and-a-half above him. The wooden outer door had blasted open, and through the mangled safety grille he could see that the base of the crumpled car had come to rest a couple of feet below floor level.

He began to choke on the cloudy billows of powdered dirt, his chest heaving, throat retching, and he pulled the muffler over his mouth and nose against the heavy dust. And all the while, the broken thickset man beneath him lay still and silent, chest unmoving, attesting to his brutal demise. Blood bubbled from the man's parted lips and his left eye remained open in shock, blood dribbling from both corners while the gore oozed from the open red hole which had once held his right eye. He was hit with the shocking realization that he had literally plucked a man's eye to save himself. Never before, even when fighting for his very existence, had he perpetrated such barbarity. He'd never thought himself capable of such savagery. And yet that was how he'd saved himself.

He began to understand.

There was some sort of pervasive evil in the castle that stalked the corridors, the passages and the hallways, infiltrated the rooms, the very ether itself corrupted and corruptive in some toxic way, the castle's evil past intruding upon the present. And he sensed its ungodly influence was at its most potent here in the lowest regions of Comraich. He'd felt it earlier that day, but not as acutely as he did now.

His ears began to clear, and gradually sounds emerged from the gloom: moans, wailings, shrieks – a mob of voices.

It's where we keep our lunatics . . .

Ash felt movement outside the smashed lift. Dirt still billowed, and as he peered into the blurring mists he caught sight of unsteady shadows. As the reverberations of the violent crash died away, the voices became more distinct.

And closer.

The safety door was bent and hanging loose, its iron framework unable to cope with the impact. If whatever was approaching had evil intent, Ash would be a sitting duck. He needed to get out of there, and fast. He hauled himself up into the dimly lit and cloudy corridor, lingering on one knee for a moment to take in his surroundings.

At first, and with the dust obscuring so much, the investigator could merely see spectral shapes in the long corridor, but as the air cleared he was able to make out moving figures.

He dragged himself to his feet. His legs felt quivery, ready to give way. He stretched out a hand towards the wall to steady himself.

Before him were the massed tenants of this subterranean floor, each wearing a white knee-length hospital gown. Despite the choking atmosphere Ash could smell their fetid, malodorous bodies as they advanced on him, the dust doing little to obscure the stench. He fought back his nausea as he took his hand from the supporting wall, standing almost erect to face them.

The pale figures crept towards him, their murmuring rising to a menacing pitch.

42

Kate McCarrick indicated that she and her dining companion were ready for their main courses. The waiter looked relieved; Kate knew that the timing for a three-course meal was important, and felt a little guilty as he quickly went through to the kitchen.

After they had eaten, the pair spent a while chatting over old times and absent friends, though Kate was anxious to get back to the night's main topic.

'Glo,' she said in a quiet but determined voice, 'tell me more about the castle. There's something you're holding back. What is it?'

'There are so many hushed-up stories, Kate. But there's one ... Well, it'll give you an idea of the Inner Court's compelling persuasiveness.'

Kate leaned forward.

Gloria was silent for a time, studying her friend before she seemed to make a decision.

'Okay,' she said finally. 'In for a penny, in for a pound.'

Then she began ...

'It's a bit before our time, but I'm sure you'll know something of it.'

Kate nodded encouragingly.

'It was one of the Second World War's greatest mysteries –

a mystery never explained, not even to this day,' Gloria continued. 'You'll have heard of Rudolf Hess, Deputy Führer to Adolf Hitler?'

Kate nodded again.

'And that, in 1941, at the height of the war, Hess flew alone in a Messerschmitt to Scotland and parachuted out, allowing the plane to crash?'

'Wasn't he on a mission for Hitler to make a peace agreement between Britain and Germany . . . to end the war between us?' Kate asked.

'Yes, in a way. But there was a secret motive, known only to Churchill and Hitler, plus a few others directly involved. The "motive" was never revealed and, to this day, remains a well-kept secret . . .'

Gloria hesitated again.

'I trust you, Kate. What worries me is what would happen to David should he uncover the truth.'

'But that was over seventy years ago: surely the truth of Hess's mission can't hurt anyone now?'

Gloria's smile was tight-lipped. 'You'd think not, wouldn't you?' Without waiting for a response, she went on. 'I've already told you how the royal family works and the lengths to which it will go. At that time certain members of the aristocracy, and one very important royal, were more inclined to align the country with the Third Reich.'

'Like Sir Oswald Mosley and his blackshirts?'

Gloria took another sip of her wine. 'Oh, he was a minor figure in the scheme of things. There were other richer and more influential people behind the scenes who felt Nazism, with its ideology of the exceptional individual, outweighed all precepts for the masses. They believed in racial superiority and the dangers of communism. They rejected liberalism, democracy, the rule of law and human rights. That the strong must rule the weak was their passionate ideology. Now,' she said, putting her glass down, 'there was one vital member of the royal family broadly in favour of a German–British alliance.'

'Edward, Duke of Windsor. Formerly Edward VIII. Abdi-
cated in 1936 to marry an American commoner named Wallis
Simpson,' Kate reeled off.

'I see you haven't forgotten what you learned at school,'
said Gloria with a smile.

'I've always found them an interesting pair. Enigmatic, even
now.'

'Quite. Anyway, fortunately for us, Edward's politics didn't
matter. But if Hitler *had* ever conquered England, he might
have put the duke back on the throne as a quisling king, with
Wallis the new queen.'

Kate thought about that for a moment.

'So,' Gloria continued, 'Edward and his new bride then
spent some time in Spain, where our own intelligence services
reported that they were feted by undercover German agents
and wealthy, like-minded high society. Flattery, right-wing
ideology and homage paid to the duke stroked his ego. It
wasn't long before he saw his abdication as premature and ill-
judged. Why shouldn't he be able to marry whoever he liked?
What right did the Church have to refuse to marry them?

'Churchill was worried by Edward's growing fraternization
with Joachim von Ribbentrop, the German ambassador at that
time and a close friend of Hitler. He knew drastic action had to
be taken. Edward was giving away too much information to
Germany and was encouraging the Nazi cause here in England.
So Churchill arranged for Edward to be offered the post of
Governor of the Bahamas during the Second World War, an
invitation that really couldn't be refused.'

Kate began to wonder where her friend was going with
this. She didn't have to wait long to find out.

'Have you heard of the Mitford sisters?' Gloria asked her
friend, leaning even further forward across the table, the pitch
of her voice dropping lower, so that it was almost a whisper.

'Of course. They were everywhere in the society magazines
and newspapers in the twenties through to the forties.'

'Oh, longer than that.'

'There were four of them, weren't there?'

'Six, actually, and one brother. Nancy, the one known for her wit and her novels, Pamela, the quieter one – though they were a little, shall we say, idiosyncratic? Then there was Diana, a fascist who married Sir Oswald Mosley and was imprisoned during the Second World War. Jessica, the complete opposite, a communist at one time and a fighter for social change, and Deborah, a socialite who eventually became Duchess of Devonshire. But the most interesting was the third youngest, Unity, who was besotted with Adolf Hitler.'

'I smell more infamy.'

'Oh', Gloria said, 'this is the real kicker.'

Her companion watched her intensely across the small round table which afforded them a quiet intimacy.

'Nancy Mitford, the writer, gained most of the attention, but it was Unity who earned the most notoriety by being an unadulterated fascist and more than just a devotee of Adolf Hitler. Unity was a zealous member of the British Union of Fascists and spent most of the thirties in Germany, where she met her hero and became part of his clique. She fell obsessively in love with him, though Hitler probably looked upon her as a mere dalliance. It was a tragedy waiting to happen.

'In 1939, when Britain and France declared war on Germany, the hopelessly lovelorn Unity took herself to the English Garden in the centre of Munich, put a tiny pistol to her head and tried to blow her brains out. The gun lacked the power to kill her outright, but the bullet lodged in her brain and caused irreversible damage. She was rushed to a hospital in the city, where she remained unconscious for several weeks. She didn't die, though it might have been kinder if she had.

'Hitler ordered a news blackout on the story and had Unity sent to a clinic in Switzerland. Some months later, her parents collected her and brought her home to England by ambulance. Unity was brain-damaged and virtually paralysed, with a mental age of twelve. Her fixation with Hitler was replaced by a religious mania ... probably the reason she refused an abortion.'

Kate almost spluttered into her raised glass. 'She was pregnant?'

'*Sssh!*' the policewoman hissed, quickly looking round the restaurant.

'I'm sorry,' Kate apologized, dabbing at her mouth with a napkin. 'You caught me by surprise. Are you telling me ... ?'

Gloria nodded. 'They weren't sure at the time – despite her sisters' wild reputation, it seems Unity was quite an innocent. But it is suspected that Hitler was the child's father.'

'*Hitler?* But—'

'*Keep it down, Katie, please!*' Gloria whispered across the table, this time with more emphasis, her face close to her friend's.

Kate raised a hand contritely and apologized again. 'Sorry, Glo, but this is *extraordinary*.'

'It is, and you're one of the very few people who now know of it. I have to trust you.'

Kate gave a small nod of her head. 'Of course,' she said, quietly and sincerely. 'So ... so if there was no abortion, what happened to the child?'

Gloria sipped some more champagne before speaking. 'As you might expect, Unity's pregnancy was in its later stages, so everything was focused on the harm she'd done to herself and the cause of the illness that was inevitably to follow.' She looked down for a moment.

'This is where it gets particularly interesting, Kate.'

'More?' Kate thought nothing else could surprise her. But a suspicion had arisen in her, prodding her subconscious like a half-remembered dream. They had started this conversation with Rudolf Hess, Hitler's deputy.

Gloria's quiet voice broke through Kate's thoughts. 'In those days, the press was not quite as intrusive as it is today, although suggestions that Unity might be pregnant were voiced by some. But she returned to England bundled in a huge blanket, so it was impossible to tell. She was taken to a very discreet Oxfordshire nursing home called Hill View Cottage. It was there that she gave birth.'

Kate took a sip of wine, fascinated yet increasingly bewildered.

'When Hitler heard that Unity had borne a son he was naturally delighted. He—'

'Glo, has all this got something to do with Hess and his flight to Scotland?'

'Hold on, I'm coming to that,' Gloria went on. 'As I was saying, Hitler was jubilant that he'd managed to make a woman pregnant, even if she were an English woman. And he thought the child might actually unite the two countries. And what a boy it would be. The son of the Führer, no less. Adolf Hitler's progeny. A true Aryan, a born Nazi. On top of that, the baby's mother was a genuine blue-blooded member of the British aristocracy.'

Gloria's account was so full of verve Kate could almost imagine the insane elation in the Führer's eyes.

'And so,' Gloria said with a tight-lipped smile, 'we return to his faithful deputy. Hitler decided it would be Hess who would fly to Scotland to uncover the truth and make the mad offer of an alliance if all was so. The Führer's clandestine supporters among the English hierarchy had informed him that Unity Mitford had been secretly taken from the nursing home to a secret location in Scotland.

'Many myths have arisen concerning Hess parachuting into Scotland and only one has any kind of credence. You see, it so happened that Lord Redesdale, Unity Mitford's father, had left his wife and taken himself and his parlourmaid – make what you will of that – to a tiny island off the coast of Mull in the Inner Hebrides, where he stayed for the rest of his life. So some people mistakenly surmised that was the obvious reason for Hess flying to Scotland.

'In fact, the truth was far more double-edged.'

Kate had already guessed. 'Comraich?'

'Comraich. The Inner Court had become involved. No –' she raised a hand to forestall Kate's next question – 'the IC was never on the side of the Nazis. The reverse, in fact. They were patriots, but only insofar as it validated them and enhanced their position.'

Kate took a large swig of wine as Gloria continued speaking.

'Comraich Castle agreed to take in Unity and her child. And, in fact, it was through the Inner Court's intrigues that word got back to Hitler that his and Unity's baby was clandestinely being cared for at the castle.'

'Intrigues? Why do you say that?' Kate asked.

'Because someone, probably Churchill himself, devised a simple yet cunning plan to end German hostility by telling Hitler his child was on British soil. However, it would never work if Hitler learned the full truth. Quite the opposite, in fact.'

Kate was confused. 'What do you mean, "the full truth"?' she said. 'I don't understand.'

Gloria smiled grimly.

'Because Unity's child wasn't a son, as Hitler had been informed, but a daughter. And even at such an early age it was obvious from the baby's over-large head and other physical attributes that Unity and Hitler's daughter was, and would always be, an imbecile.'

43

As the lunatics shuffled towards him, with hands dangling uselessly by their sides, Ash looked around for a means of escape. Behind him, at the end of a corridor, was a large, strong-looking wooden door, while opposite the lift was a cell door blown open by the huge pressure wave created by the antique contraption's accelerated arrival.

Still unsteady and finding it difficult to breathe, he staggered down the corridor to the wooden door. He fumbled with the large rusty doorknob above the empty keyhole, finally managing to turn it. Ash pushed hard but the door wouldn't budge. Praying it was merely jammed by age-old dirt, he used his shoulder to try to force it open. It refused his efforts. As the howling and wailing from behind him drew closer, he bent down to look through the keyhole to see if there was a key on the other side.

The lock was empty. Yet air was blowing through the keyhole, a draught with a hint of the sea. He pushed and banged at the door in desperation but failed to move it by even a fraction.

He turned in resignation to face the approaching horde.

There were more than fifty patients crowded together in the long corridor, the dust cloud still settling like stage fog around their feet. He could see their crazed faces. They looked like the walking dead.

One of the pack came forward, his hands raised towards Ash. Then another followed, hands and arms similarly outstretched, fingers bent like grabbing claws. A strange mewling sound came from the first man's mouth, drool dripping from his dusty-white, cracked lips.

Ash decided bravado was his only option.

Straightening up to his full height, he said in a commanding voice, 'Stop right there. I want you all to return to your rooms until I can get help.' He deliberately didn't use the word 'cells' in case it roused their undisguised resentment even more.

One or two halted and looked around, confused, but the rest continued to shuffle towards him. The nearest three were approaching in a loose triangular formation, taking up the full width of the corridor.

Ash did the only thing he could: he marched directly towards the trio, sternly warning them, 'Stand aside, make way, this instant!'

His logic was that these institutionalized individuals were more likely than not simply to do as they were told, and for a moment it seemed the ploy had worked. The leader came to a halt, dropping his arms and looking around as if bewildered. The second man did the same, although he was breathing heavily, taking huge gasps of dust-filled air so that his ample stomach constantly pulsed in and out.

But the third one was apparently even more aggressively insane than his two companions. He stood directly in Ash's path and, growling somewhere deep in his throat, pulled one bunched fist back behind his shoulder and aimed a punch at the stranger in their midst.

Ash blocked the wild-eyed man's fist with his forearm and then pushed him away hard, using both hands. The man fell heavily against the grimy, damp brick wall and Ash took advantage by plunging into the crowd jammed along the corridor. But he got barely three yards before they began to overwhelm him.

They yowled and keened, whined and shrieked, striking him, slapping him as he tried to protect himself from the worst of their hostility by covering his head and face with his arms. He fought hard, but there were just too many of them.

He felt himself going down and, half-panicked, he kicked out, only to be kicked back at, this time a woman's bare toes thumping into his groin.

He yelped with the pain, then smashed her with his fist, only adrenaline helping him endure the agony, turning it into numbing discomfort rather than unbearable pain. The adrenaline also enhanced both his strength and clarity of mind. He pushed, hit and kicked out, fighting with all his might, not caring if he struck man, woman or child, conscious only of the fact that if he didn't get away soon, he would probably be trampled or beaten to death.

With a superhuman effort he reared up, sending those trying to pull him back down into the clamouring mass. Brief images sped before his eyes – a woman with grey, matted hair spitting at him through long yellow teeth; a man whose wild beard and head of untamed hair hid virtually all his features save for the small, threatening bestial eyes; another man whose limbs were so thin it was a wonder he could even stand; a young girl, no more than nineteen, with black, deadened eyes, who might have been pretty had her mouth not been full of rotten teeth that snapped at him and tried to bite a lump from his cheek while her hand snatched at his crotch, whether with lust or loathing he'd no idea.

He was almost back at the lift now, but his attackers had the upper hand. Soon, he knew he would be dragged to the stone floor. Then he noticed the open cell door opposite the lift. If he could get inside, he might be able to barricade himself in until the security staff arrived.

But just as he'd made the decision and was pushing towards the open doorway, trying to ignore the punches and kicks and scratches he was taking, the hemmed-in crowd made a sudden surge forward which threatened to carry him with the flow back towards the big locked door at the end of the corridor.

Powdered concrete clogged his nostrils, yet the smell of mangled iron and twisted and broken cables from the crashed lift overlay even the rancid stink of the frenzied inmates. Ash knew that if he became trapped once more against that solid wooden door, he'd be done for.

He turned and smacked the nearest man's face, knocking him away. A restraining hand that had been holding Ash firmly was immediately gone. Next Ash drove his elbow into another crazy's chest; he fell away, but instantly an arm snaked around the investigator's throat from behind. Ash was at a loss to understand the inmates' hostility towards him. Maybe these people simply blamed him in some way for their own miserable torment and captivity. Judging by what he'd seen, their treatment was hardly humane.

But the unusual aggression was within him, too, and it drove him on. He kicked and lashed out at anyone who came within range. He would reach that empty cell at any price!

Broken teeth cut into his knuckles when he drove his fist straight into the open mouth of his nearest attacker, but he had no time to register his own pain as he swung at another who presented himself when the first collapsed onto the hard floor. This one was big though, towering over Ash and the others around them. But as the brute lunged, the investigator pulled a raving woman in between them, so hindering the giant just enough for Ash to take rapid steps towards the room he hoped might offer him refuge for a short time at least. The big man, whose head was completely bald and strangely pointed, his seething eyes staring out over bags of bloated skin below and under bushy eyebrows, tossed the woman aside; but as he did so, his grip on the material of her thin cotton garment ripped, and he suddenly became interested in her firm breasts. His smile was manic, matching his glaring eyes. He quickly lost interest in the fleeing investigator.

Ash watched in horror as the big man reached down for the half-naked woman, who must have been somewhere in her early fifties, yet still had the unblemished and puppy-plump body of a much younger person. She was lifted to her bare feet as the big man twisted her so that he was behind her. He gripped her with one broad arm around her shoulders and neck, while the big-knuckled fingers of his other hand reached between her legs. Other eyes had taken an interest and for a moment they forgot all about their quarry.

They dragged the poor struggling woman to the floor again, while the big man took swipes at those who wanted to join in. Shocked, Ash glimpsed soft writhing thighs among the scrum.

There was a time, no matter what the danger to him, when Ash would have tried to help the woman, but he knew he'd be no match for all these lunatics. This new, darker, more cynical side of his mind saw that this could work to his advantage, as it distracted those who were still trying to get him. He pushed, shoved, and heaved at the people in front of him, not really caring if anyone was injured in the process.

Then, suddenly, he was there at the open door, beyond which an inviting darkness seemed to beckon. One more thrust at a smock-wearing little man who staunchly stood in his way, and then he was inside. The first thing to assault him was an awful, nauseating stench, a mixture of body odour, dirt and the dulled scent of dried faeces. Nevertheless, gasping for breath, he slammed the door behind him, leaning his back against it, one hand searching for a doorknob that wasn't there. Of course, all the cells would be electronically locked, with no means of opening them from the inside. The crashing lift must somehow have triggered an automatic door-release system.

That was fine by Ash, whose main preoccupation right then was to keep the door shut. He imagined the banging and shoving at the door would start as soon as the crazies realized he'd got away from them, but for the moment he could only hear a confused clamouring. Was it too much to hope they'd forgotten about him altogether?

The cell was almost completely dark, the only source of light the faint glow emanating from a caged ceiling bulb. It was an awful place, a single room approximately twelve feet by twelve. It was little wonder the patients had been so anxious to get out. As his eyes accustomed themselves to the dismal gloom, he could just make out a cot-bed against the right-hand wall, a tiny table and chair and . . . and that was it. There was no other furniture; not even a rug for the concrete floor. No windows, no lamps, no other light source except from the grimy, low-wattage bulb in the ceiling. The smell was overwhelming and he almost gagged.

Ash reached into one of the long pockets of his field jacket and found the slim Maglite torch. He opened up its beam with a twist of its black barrel and slowly shone it around the walls. He expected to see something horrible, and he wasn't disappointed, for the grey-stone walls were daubed with hideous, noxious graffiti written in faded excrement and blood. What made the smeared daubings all the more sickening were their clumsy emblematic representations of Nazi swastikas and crude SS insignia.

He couldn't imagine who, or what, would make a person do this, or why the symbols hadn't been washed off. It made no sense, unless these inmates were left to live out their lives below ground with little supervision or observation, and no regard to their personal hygiene. It was cruel; wicked. Perverse. An extraordinary way to treat a fellow human, no matter how mentally unbalanced they might be.

Keeping his back firmly against the door, he slowly moved the light beam around the cell, suppressing the urge to gag from the stench that swept over him like heat from an opened oven. The unsteady beam of light – his hand was still shaking – picked out an open latrine in one corner from where the stink was fresh and even more atrocious. Rivers of excrement ran down its overflowing sides, while clumps of dark matter lay around its base.

There was something more that he'd almost missed. Ash jerkily swung the beam back to the spot.

Floating in the air above the ordure was a small, perfectly round orb. Obsidian, yet non-reflective, its absence of colour so deep it felt like a black hole capable of sucking in anything that came too close, never to release it again. Maseby had described the invasion of Comraich's main office by these things, and Ash had seen similar phenomena himself. Many researchers and sensitives claimed they were the souls of people who had passed over; but then the orbs, usually gold in colour or yellow, even orange, were generally assumed to be benign. He had witnessed them several times in his career as a psychic investigator. But this one seemed to give off a pernicious enticement, a subversive, ungodly lure. Even from where he stood he could feel its draw as it hovered two feet above the ground. He moved the light onwards and discovered at least a dozen more of the floating, pitch-black spheres. No wonder the very atmosphere down here exuded evil, and the room's stench was not just a physical manifestation but part of the corruptive foulness of the things themselves. He'd no doubt that Douglas Hoyle had occupied the room directly above this one.

Other orbs he'd seen had a tendency to shoot around the room excitedly, but none of these was moving an inch. It was as if they were aware of his presence. And waiting for him to make his move.

The brightness from the fully charged Maglite began to dim and he realized the threatening balls of darkness were somehow absorbing the very light itself. Just before the light disappeared entirely, he saw something – *someone* – shift in a far corner, and he heard a low sniffling sound.

Close to panic in the near-blackness, he slipped the torch back into his jacket and took out another gadget, a Minox night sight. Monocular and lightweight, its scope gathered and amplified the smallest amount of light to make objects clearly visible in the dark. And if there was no light whatsoever, an infrared light could be used instead.

The room was now pitch black, so Ash switched the sight to infrared. Through it, he saw in the corner of the room a figure standing with its back to him like a naughty schoolchild ordered there as a punishment. The black orbs were nowhere to be seen in this peculiar light, although Ash was sure they were still present and even multiplying, for the feeling of oppression in the cell had become almost numbing and his head hurt so much it was difficult to peer through the lens.

Ash blinked a few times to moisten his eyes, then looked through the lens again.

The figure stood, its smock open-backed, the drawstrings untied to reveal skinny buttocks and stick-like legs. The small figure shifted again, although its head remained bowed into the room's corner. It had been more like a twitch than a controlled movement, almost skittish, as if the person were afraid of him.

The mephitic odour that made the air seem so toxic, the childish daubings, the fascist ciphers and swastikas marking the walls, a still-moist pile of faeces in the middle of the floor, the cot-like bed with its stale, stiffened and torn blanket (even as he looked through the lens, a large black bug with too many legs crawled from beneath a tattered sheet) – all these nauseating elements combined to make Ash almost terrified. And those malign jet-black orbs, which he knew still lingered in the room with him. Somehow watching, somehow waiting.

When the thing in the corner finally began to move voluntarily, to turn towards him, Ash felt an overwhelming desire to be back outside, even if it meant facing the lunatic horde again. He could hear their muffled shouts, a high-pitched scream overriding all other noises, though they didn't appear to be trying to reach him.

The figure in the corner had now turned fully. While the red glow from the lens should have softened the effect, it was a terrifying sight.

And it began to come towards him.

'Oh, Jesus Lord,' he whispered to himself.

The creature's figure was slight and its legs stunted. He couldn't discern the sex until, through the tattered and torn, thin cotton smock he made out a limp hanging breast. The woman shuffled towards him rather than walked, a peculiar mewling noise coming from between her cracked dry lips.

But the true horror, which constricted his heart as if by a clawed hand, was the sight of her head.

It was huge, too huge for her to keep upright unless she held it between her long skeletal hands, the fingernails of which were worn to the quick. Ash had to force himself not to look away. Saliva drooled from her mouth down to her short neck, as there was no jaw to obstruct the flow. The top of her bulbous head was threaded with blue veins – some thick, some thin, some standing proud as though ready to burst through the stretched skin – which wove through sparse clumps of whitish hair.

Unconsciously he allowed the night sight to fall away, perhaps because its magnifying lens made her appear closer than she was. She was still close enough, though, and in the darkness Ash imagined her long, big-knuckled fingers reaching towards him. Then, suddenly, the room brightened. The massive head had sunk against her chest and the eyes, milky white pupils half-rolled into their lids, looked up at him balefully.

She shambled closer, a tiny mutant whose size bore no relation to the fear she was generating in his gut. Ash pushed his back hard against the door, unconsciously turning his head so he could see her only from the corners of his eyes, his heels off the ground as the balls of his feet dug into the bare floor. Logically, one swipe of his arm would have sent the creature flying back into her corner by the cot-bed, but reason was little help against such repugnant horror. Intuition became useless in the face of undefined dread.

With her body bent even more, the abomination reached up and touched his exposed cheek. And as her quivering, ragged-nailed hand felt him, sending uncontrollable shivers through his body, there was a tremendous crash against the door on which he leaned. It rattled the metal on its hinges and the door shifted, burst inwards, all but throwing him on top of the small, scraggy crone and the sparse-haired, horrid dome of her head, but he managed to throw himself aside just in time.

The lunatics in the corridor hadn't forgotten about him after all.

More light and bodies exploded into the room. The woman who had been menacing Ash stepped back, but not, Ash felt, because she was afraid.

The first man in, the big one with beard and hair that practically encircled his face, stumbled forward, but swiftly recovered, even when other gowned figures bumped into him.

Ash, who was half-crouched behind the now wide-open door, saw the hag stand erect, holding her weighty head up to face the intruders. The horde immediately fell silent and began to back away, out of the cell. Ash fell in with them, one step at a time, as if any sudden movement might arouse a fury in this tiny woman-beast who showed no fear of them.

Even in his steadily controlled panic, Ash realized his reaction was ridiculous. But maybe it was the orbs still floating – this time around her, either to protect her or to impart unknown powers – which the mad crowd now sensed. Either way, he would rather take his chances with them than stay in this room with her.

Ash saw the mutant was looking directly at him, and any courage he had left shrivelled inside him.

Dimly, he became aware of gunfire coming from the other end of the corridor and then the screams, not of pain but of fright. Babbage's men? Surely they wouldn't just open fire indiscriminately.

Now there were shrieks, more high-pitched screams, and much moaning. He guessed what was happening out there: Tasers were being used on the more hysterical cases, the guards herding them back into their cells.

He took his chance. The big man filled the doorframe, still backing away. Ash shoved him out so hard that the man bounced off the opposite wall. He pushed past and, perversely, was glad once more to be part of the mayhem outside.

44

'My God, Ash,' Haelstrom said with genuine concern. 'Were you in the lift when it crashed through to the basement?'

'I wasn't the only passenger,' Ash replied unsteadily. 'You'll find the dead body of one of your guests at the bottom of the lift shaft. A Serbian, I think.'

'Good God! General Lukovic?'

'He didn't really introduce himself properly,' Ash reflected sourly as he ran a dry tongue around his mouth and examined his clothes. Chalky powder still covered his lips. *What I need most is a stiff drink*, he told himself. *And then a bath or shower.*

Ash had been recognized by the guards and orderlies by his clothes (dirty and torn though they were). He'd been dragged roughly towards a rising staircase at the opposite end of the dark-brick corridor. At the top was another metal door, which was open, allowing even more guards and medics through to pacify – or at least, control – the patients below.

Ash had still been shaky and battle-worn and Haelstrom, who had been directing operations from the luxurious and state-of-the-art medical unit, had quickly gone to the investigator, eyeing his condition warily as he approached.

Ash knew one thing for sure, and that was that he wanted to leave this place. He'd had enough and seen too much. If only he could speak to Kate McCarrick; he was certain she'd find a way to get him home. But maybe not . . .

'I imagine you could do with a drink after what you have

327

been through,' said Haelstrom solicitously, as if he'd read the psychic investigator's thoughts.

Ash would have smiled wryly if his cracked lips hadn't been so painful. This time the big man wasn't trying to get him drunk. His genuine concern was evident in his gimlet eyes and the expression on his clenched features.

'What on earth was Lukovic doing there?' asked a bewildered Haelstrom as if to himself.

'Waiting for me.'

'Why would – ' Haelstrom began, then stopped. 'Let's leave that for now and get you tidied up, a drop of strong brandy first and then we'll have you fixed up in the infirmary.'

The CEO's tight suit jacket was unbuttoned, his tie was at half-mast, shirt neck open as if forced so by the flesh of his neck. More must have happened at Comraich that evening, Ash realized, remembering the faint, eerie screams he'd heard coming from the castle's dining hall before he'd made the dash to find out what was happening.

So what had *happened?* he wondered to himself, remembering his own nasty episode with the foil-covered sandwich.

'No. I'm okay. Just a few scratches and bruises, that's all.'

'I'd still like to have you examined,' insisted Haelstrom. 'I mean, you *must* have been injured in the lift crash alone.'

Yeah, thought Ash, *not to mention being almost throttled to death*. 'In fact,' he said, after swallowing to clear the dryness of his throat, 'it was Lukovic who saved me in the end. But I'll explain about that later. What I need right now is a shower, maybe a change of clothes, and a stiff drink to settle my nerves. Not necessarily in that order – I think the drink might come first.' To hell with pretending he'd given up the booze; no one would blame him after all that happened to him this evening. Hell, no – he'd been in what could have been a fatal air crash before he'd even *reached* Comraich. That alone could drive a man to drink!

Haelstrom was watching him with what passed for his version of concern.

'If you won't be looked over by one of our medical team,' Haelstrom urged Ash attentively, 'then by all means let's start with that brandy. Pandemonium has broken out in the castle this evening and I believe I need a strong drink myself. Apart from the inexplicable crash of the lift – perhaps it was age, wear and tear, who knows? – and then the attack on you in the containment area, well, we've also had a terrible incident in our dining room. With the help of our staff, some kind of order has been restored, and most of our guests have been sedated and taken to their rooms for the night. Regretfully, some have died. Heart attacks mainly; some crushed in the panic.'

Sir Victor didn't say what had caused the panic, Ash noticed, though if his own ghastly culinary experience was anything to go by, he could make a fair guess. Neither had he referred to the conditions in which the patients in the basement were kept. Perhaps Haelstrom was already in denial. Whatever the reason, it could wait. Right now, Ash needed that drink.

Later that evening David Ash was alone. Utterly exhausted. Extremely jittery.

Stoical by nature, he was nevertheless beginning to think that enough was enough. But what could he do? He should have tried to get hold of Kate somehow and check his legal position here. Malign forces had built up in this place, century after century. Were their powers unstoppable now?

He'd tried to explain to Sir Victor Haelstrom earlier, as he recounted his experience over a generous measure of Armagnac, his belief that dark spirits were using ley-line energy for their own iniquitous purposes, having been drawn to this place because of its egregious past, heinous events that possibly had acted as psychic beacons for dissolute spirits.

He'd half expected the big man to dismiss or debunk the notion out of hand, but as he'd told Ash in more detail all that had happened in Comraich earlier in the evening, Haelstrom had seemed to lose all his previous scepticism. Ash shouldn't really have been surprised. There could be no doubt by now to anyone that there were dark forces at work in this castle. And it was Ash's job to find out what they were.

Back at work while the rest of the castle slept, the investigator was sitting on a giltwood chair in a long, wide hallway, a galleried wall at his back, moonlight flooding through the windows in the opposite wall. Behind him were several portraits in oils and busts on plinths, some cast in stone, others in bronze.

He'd tried to convince Haelstrom to abandon Comraich, leave whatever malevolence dwelt within to itself, so that its strength might fade with time, becoming too weak to sustain its influence any longer. The violent history was probably the key element that had sustained the link between Comraich and these parasitic manifestations, but to put it plainly, someone here had reopened the 'door' of the netherworld to them.

'Someone in Comraich,' Ash explained, 'is acting as a conduit for spirits of ill-nature – whether consciously or subconsciously, I have no idea. But their strength is undeniable. My guess is that the woman I encountered in the cell is responsible for channelling the powers of these unknown entities from the spirit world.'

Haelstrom had blanched at this last remark. Ash had wondered then whether experiments were taking place here, especially upon those poor wretches in the cells.

He thought of the mutant woman, living in almost permanent darkness. Was her deformity the result of some gruesome experiment? And what of the mysterious black orbs, floating in her room, gathering around her frail, crooked body, as if to protect her? He recalled his feelings in there, the dreadful fear, the wish to flee the unknown. And her cell itself, he was certain, was directly beneath Douglas Hoyle's observation room. What manner of spiritual creatures had been sent to him through her?

Haelstrom had fixed him with his brow-shadowed eyes and

told him firmly that evacuating all the guests and staff from Comraich was not, and never would be, an option.

The big man's surliness had returned as he'd laid down the law. Ash had been reminded in no uncertain terms that he was committed to a non-negotiable contract to investigate the haunting of Comraich Castle. Haelstrom had demanded that Ash finish his investigations and present a full – a *full*, he'd repeated forcefully – report on what was happening in the castle and why.

Without another word, Ash had stood and walked to the door, where he'd turned and said, 'I'm going to give it one more night and one more day. You'll get your written report, but only when I'm back in London.'

Haelstrom had begun to bluster, but Ash had already turned on his heels and walked out the door.

45

When he'd left Haelstrom, Ash had gone looking for Delphine, anxious that she hadn't been caught up in the frenzy of guests, carers and guards, but she was nowhere to be found. He'd knocked on her door but there had been no response. He'd tried to return to the containment area, but found the heavy door to the stairs closed tight, an armed guard barring the way. Ash had then made for the medical unit, where an equally intractable nurse had refused him entry, though she did tell him she hadn't seen Dr Wyatt for an hour or so.

Ash had given up, gone to his room, quickly showered and examined his cuts and scratches. Incredibly, no real damage had been done, though he knew by morning some very large bruises would make their presence felt. His neck was red and sore where he'd been half-strangled. All in all, though, he'd suffered no lasting harm.

He'd showered and donned clean jeans and a worn-leather jacket over a soft-quilted gilet. He'd remembered to take the biker's dark muffler again for warmth later, then had taken the rest of any extra equipment he might need for the night. Into the leather bag now lying at his feet in the fifth-floor hallway, he'd tucked a Polaroid camera, his digital camera already inside. There were also reels of synthetic thread to stretch across doorways, stairs and passageways and surgical adhesive tape for making permanent seals. He'd added colour, black and white, and infrared film for his Nikon camera, these going into the gilet's deeper pockets. The tripod for this camera could be shortened or lengthened to a reasonable height, its minimum length used for the shoulder bag. A small DVD recording camera had also gone in. Batteries, flash bulbs, lenses and filters he carried in his gilet where he could reach them easily; a winding measuring tape in a leather casing would be useful to gauge distances and his last thermometer (his other four had already been set in likely places to register cold spots earlier in the day). Sound scanners, magnetometers and certain electric field measuring devices were, again, already in use elsewhere.

In truth, there really weren't enough instruments to spread around such an enormous building and he probably needed much more sophisticated equipment than he'd been able to carry in his big but limited suitcase: frequency change detectors, closed-circuit television monitors, electric field measuring devices, thermal heat scanners, anemometers, ventimeters and air meters (he'd the latter three, but needed more), and so on. But what he required most was a team of psychic investigators with walkie-talkie radio transmitters and receivers so that they could report back to him, enabling him to be situated at a central monitoring base controlling the searches.

Ghost hunting had moved on significantly since the time it took one lone investigator with minimal apparatus such as powder tape, greenhouse thermometers and the like, to do the job. But Kate and he had underestimated both the seriousness and the enormity of the problem at Comraich.

He retrieved one other item from the battered case; the flask of absinthe which he pushed into an inside pocket of his jacket. Ash couldn't resist taking a good swallow first. He rattled it beside his ear: it was almost empty.

Ash checked the luminous dial of his wristwatch: 11.15 p.m. Everything in Comraich Castle was quiet and still.

As he'd been setting up a movement detector camera in the

west corridor, one of the guards had informed him that security patrols would be monitoring the halls and passageways of the lower floors throughout the night.

Earlier, Haelstrom had shown Ash the devastation in the dining room. Even as they climbed the broad stairway, the investigator had heard what sounded like a hundred vacuum cleaners in use and had felt sea air gusting down from open windows somewhere above. Ash guessed that all the long windows must have been thrown open to try to rid the place of the fetid smell he could still detect. He'd shivered from the cold coming from inside the room and his eyes had widened as he'd taken in the scene.

All the tables and chairs had been moved to one side and ten kitchen staff were using industrial-sized vacuum cleaners – that was why the sound had been so loud – to sweep the floor clean of what looked like volcanic sand.

Ignoring the stench, Ash knelt down and collected a handful of the dark grey grains, more like dust than sand, he thought as he let it sift through his fingers.

'*They were flies before!*' Haelstrom had had to raise his voice to be heard over the din of the vacuums.

Ash had stood, looking at Haelstrom in bewilderment.

'*One minute they were flying around the room,*' Haelstrom had told him, his mouth close to Ash's ear, '*attacking people's faces, getting into their eyes and ears, and into their mouths!*'

He'd taken the investigator by the elbow. '*Let's get out of here so we can talk. Best let the staff get on with their job.*'

On the way to the lounge bar, Haelstrom had told Ash about the calamitous invasion of maggots – *crawling through the very food the diners were eating!* – and then hundreds – *thousands* – of flies that swarmed through the room attacking – *attacking!* – the castle guests. Ash was glad he'd thrown out his own infested food before the maggots had metamorphosed. Despite his experiences with the unnatural, he'd never come across a manifestation of this magnitude before and he was left almost breathless by the shock of it.

Now, as Ash continued his vigil in the long gallery, one painting in particular caught his eye: a bloodthirsty altercation between brutal-looking kilted warriors, some of whom waved claymores over their heads or stabbed into the exposed bellies of red-coated English soldiers while others slashed at their enemies with vicious-looking blades. He rose from his chair to examine it more closely. The head of one unfortunate Englishman had been almost severed, the wild-eyed terror on the poor victim's face brutally displayed in fine detail. Smoke fouled the sky, darkening the clouds as if to reflect the carnage below. Ash found the picture's realism almost too gruesome to contemplate for long and he moved onwards, hoping to find a subject that was mellower, more reassuring.

He soon found one, a depiction of three fine bewigged ladies peacefully concentrating on the lace-work lying across their laps while they chattered among themselves, perhaps waiting for their menfolk to return from a day's hunting – or even a savage battle in some faraway glen. Their skin was almost as white as their flouncy dresses, although their cheeks were crudely rouged, stained dark against the whiteness of their skin.

His musings were interrupted by the sound of soft footsteps in the long, draughty hallway. Ash peered in the gloom as the steps grew louder and a strangely familiar figure emerged from the darkness.

Cedric Twigg, whose vision was as sharp as ever despite the onset of Parkinson's disease, recognized the man standing alone in the moonlit corridor. He immediately straightened up and tried to walk normally, although he didn't entirely succeed: his left leg felt heavier than the right one, and tended to drag a little. The deep canvas bag he carried in one hand was feeling increasingly heavy. Before reaching the investigator, he wiped the drool from his chin with the back of his trembling free hand. His steps were still short, though, and his head continued to nod forward slightly, the muscles of his face visibly stiffened. The neurologist he'd consulted had warned him this might happen, and Twigg had realized he was to be one of those unlucky victims of Parkinson's for whom the onset of symptoms was rapid, barely affected by the Pergolide he was taking.

The other man – he recalled Ash was his name, supposedly some kind of ghost hunter – waited for Twigg to come to him. The assassin hoped the slight tremors that ran through his thin body were not too noticeable.

'Mr Twigg, isn't it?' Ash said as the killer drew near.

Twigg said nothing, noting Ash's glance towards the bag he was carrying.

'I'm David Ash,' the investigator tried again. 'We met on the plane, remember?'

Twigg, who had now reached Ash, nodded his head, a deliberate movement this time. 'We weren't actually introduced,' he said.

'May I ask what you've got there?' Ash pointed at the tight-zipped canvas bag, which Twigg was cradling protectively.

Before the assassin answered the question, he took a moment to appraise the ghost hunter, wondering how a man could become involved in such trivial nonsense. 'A package. I'm delivering it to someone,' he said softly. 'I'm sorry, Mr Ash,' he continued, 'but I don't have time to chat. If you'd just step aside, please . . .'

The other man opened his mouth as if to protest, but a sound from outside the castle caused them both to pause.

The noise was like . . . no, Ash didn't want to guess until he heard it more clearly. Stepping away from the galleried wall, he went across the hallway and opened one of the corridor's tall windows.

Twigg moved to join him, and both men stood and listened.

Ash remembered Gordon Dalzell, the chauffeur, remarking on the eerie sound that sometimes came from the woods at night since the wildcats had gained entry into the estate: like the babble of babies wailing. Caterwauling.

That must be what they were hearing now. Sometimes the pitch changed, became hissing snarls, nasty, vicious shrilling, and Ash thought he could hear the screeches of other, terrified, animals, even the agonized barking of deer. By the light of the full moon he saw black shapes rising from the trees in great flurries of wings as if the birds themselves were under attack. Growls, squeals, shrieking, animals baying, other creatures howling, all in the distance. He couldn't shake the dreadfulness from his mind. It sounded like a massacre was taking place in the darkly veiled woods.

He turned to see that Twigg was walking away, continuing down the hallway.

'Just the wildcats,' the shabby little man mumbled over his shoulder to Ash. 'Just cats hunting, doing what they do best.'

Ash closed the window against the gruesome, piteous racket. But even thus deadened, the sounds of slaughter troubled him more than he could say.

46

All-night vigils were usually boring affairs: no ghostly manifest-ations, no mysterious knocking, no unaccountable footsteps, no instrument malfunction. It was why parapsychology was so often ridiculed as a pseudoscience. Still, progress was being made. The discipline had been acknowledged by several aca-demic bodies in the UK, and there was at least one para-psychology unit, at a university in Edinburgh, and other institutions offered parapsychology courses as well as conduct-ing research into paranormal activity.

However, Ash knew that to most people the concepts of black streams (ley lines of negative influence), stage-one appar-itions (those that could be caught on camera while being invisible to the naked eye) and EVP (electronic voice phenom-ena) were little more than gobbledegook. Haelstrom had been too shaken to ridicule Ash's theories outright during their earlier exchange, but the investigator was still unsure whether the CEO was yet ready to accept his notion that some kind of psychic epicentre existed beneath Comraich.

The man, and his executive board of the Inner Court, whoever they might be, were, not surprisingly, unfamiliar with unearthly matters and discarnate forces: why else would they have approached the Institute in the first place? Equally, how-ever, they seemed to be overestimating just how much it was possible for Ash to achieve.

Ash found himself all but blaming Kate for not explaining the limitations of a psychic investigator to Simon Maseby at the very start. The huge fee on offer had perhaps blinded her to the reality of the situation. Or maybe she was just putting too much faith in her chief investigator's ability to solve such problems. Yet he couldn't find it in himself honestly to resent her, for he knew he was as important to her as she was to him. And clearly the true gravity of the situation here hadn't been adequately conveyed to her by Simon Maseby. He felt certain Kate would be trying to contact him by now, and probably worrying herself sick because there was no way she could do so.

The awful noise from the woods had ceased by the time Ash decided to make another inspection of his equipment sites, his hard boots echoing through stone halls. If a ghost were waiting, it wouldn't bother to hide: where would be the fun in that?

He strode down a passageway into yet another corridor; he checked rooms as he went, opening doors and looking in, avoiding the suites belonging to Haelstrom, as well as the area whose entrance was so much grander than any others, with giltwood, red-cushioned chairs with high backs on either side of the closed double doors, where beautiful paintings and skilful statuary abounded. Thick carpet here softened his footfalls and he hoped he wasn't spoiling Lord Edgar Shawcroft-Draker's neighbourhood with his working clothes.

Where the funny little man with the somewhat off-putting eyes had disappeared to, Ash had no idea; but this level was as complex and many-roomed as those below it, and no door bore a number or nameplate.

What a long and emotional day it had been. It was less than twenty-four hours since he'd left London, but it seemed like a week, so many things had occurred. Thankfully, nothing out of the ordinary was happening right now. He hoped. He wandered on, his route already mapped out in his head, for he'd studied the plans of Comraich beforehand. As insurance, in his gilet pocket he carried a nifty little gadget that acted as an electronic ball of string, plotting his course. To return to his starting

339

point, he merely had to tap a key and the route would reverse so that he could follow it back to base. It was perfect for complexly structured buildings, or even on a walk through the streets of an unknown city.

In a broad stone passageway somewhere near the labyrinthine castle's centre he came upon a large arched doorway with hinges and scrollwork of black iron and nail-head ornamentation in the shape of a crucifix. A plain architrave of venerable thick wood bordered the door. He assumed this was the castle's chapel. Ash thought he heard movement from inside and he stopped for a moment to listen.

A low continuous murmuring came to him. It sounded like an incantation, and he guessed the bishop and his acolyte were at their devotions. He hoped they were praying for deliverance from the evil that had assailed Comraich these past weeks. Deciding not to disturb them, Ash moved on.

He reached a narrow marble-topped console table on top of which was a delicately adorned vase filled with dead, sagging flowers. He stopped to examine the talcum powder he'd sprinkled around the base of the vase earlier to show whether the container had moved. It hadn't. A further sprinkling along the top of the console was similarly undisturbed.

Ash had set many such markers around the fifth floor, as well as all manner of other apparatus including motion-sensitive cameras, self-registering thermographs, sensitive static sound recorders, anemometers, ventimeters and air meters.

He checked them all, but nothing had changed. The thermometers confirmed something that had been puzzling him since he arrived: the castle was bone-numbingly cold, despite the fierce heat emanating from the many radiators he passed. Maybe it was always this way in the upper reaches of Comraich. On the other hand, maybe the 'uninvited', the uncanny entities, had stolen all the energy they could plunder and used it for themselves, gaining power from it. To the layman, it would sound absurd, but Ash was experienced enough to know this was an indication of a genuine haunting. Still he roamed, examining and testing instruments and devices, discouraged but steadfast, determined to find the epicentre of the paranormal activity. In his heart, and his senses, he knew it was there, beneath the castle. He resolved that the following day he would investigate the caves below the cliffs that formed the promontory on which Comraich was built. They were the key to all this, he was sure.

Strangely enough, Ash didn't feel tired. Far from it: the day's thrills, both welcome and otherwise, had stimulated his mind and body. He knew it was a trait that made him good at his job. He mightn't exactly appreciate all the problems that came his way, but he did enjoy solving them.

Ash opened a window and listened, but all he could hear was the crashing of waves against the cliff below. It was a raging violent noise, but it was a thousand times better than the pitiful cries of the animals preyed upon by the intruding wildcats. That was something else that puzzled him: why were the wildcats drawn to Comraich? What had brought them to this source of ungodly malfeasance?

The fresh sea air, although wild and tangy, refreshed his face and he let the wind blow over him, reviving his whole body and sharpening his mind. For a few minutes he remained there, the powerful breeze gusting into the corridor as if to sweep it free of malign infection.

Reluctantly, he closed the window again and, as he turned to walk down the corridor, he thought he saw something move in the shadows at the far end. He blinked, looked again, then dug into his leather jacket for the Maglite torch and aimed its bright beam at the spot. His mind may have been playing tricks, but he was sure he'd seen a hooded figure scurrying into the shadows.

'Hey!' he called out, expecting no response and receiving none.

Ash began moving swiftly down the corridor. He called out again, louder this time. All he heard in return was the echo of his own voice and the soft scuffling of feet up ahead, as if someone were climbing the steps of the tower at the end of the passageway.

Panting a little, he reached the tower's arched entrance and shone the light upwards.

The spiral staircase curled around a thick central shaft built of sizeable old-stone brickwork. He'd seen from outside that the towers had windows, so he presumed they also contained rooms and floors. Did the hooded figure inhabit one? More scuffling noises came to him, but the footsteps were slower now.

He called out again. 'Can I talk to you? I mean you no harm.' The faint sounds paused for a second, then resumed, fading as they went higher.

Ash had little choice but to follow, though he found the idea as appealing as venturing into a lion's den. He began to ascend the well-worn wooden steps, taking them slowly, cautiously, nervously. From above he heard the sound of a door opening and then closing.

Almost immediately he came to a landing. There was a door off it, but he was sure it wasn't the one he'd just heard being opened and closed. That sound had been soft, barely audible. Ash felt certain it had come from higher up.

His suspicions were confirmed when he heard more scuffling footsteps on the level above. Taking a mighty breath, he continued up the stairway. Round he went, his left shoulder scraping against the curving wall, aware that his haste was affecting his balance. Steadying himself by placing a hand on the central pillar, he held the Maglite in his left hand and proceeded more carefully.

Why had this hooded person fled from him? Ash had presented no danger. He'd merely called out, then followed. And why the strange garb? Another of the bishop's acolytes, maybe? Whatever, it was an eerie costume to see in the dead of night, but although it was stereotypical of reported ghost sightings, he'd never actually witnessed one dressed like that himself.

Another noise interrupted his thoughts.

It sounded like someone, or something, falling.

And then a guttural noise. A stifled sob?

Ash mounted the last few stairs to the topmost landing. As he faced the closed door through which his quarry must have passed, a chill ran down his spine, despite the sweat-inducing chase. Perspiration had soaked his entire body – the sweat of fear as much as exhaustion. He felt clammy, shivery, shuddery, and although a numbing sensation affected his body, he knew it was all in his mind. His mind, and the mood within Comraich itself.

Grimacing, biting into his lower lip to bring conscious pain that would help restore his own reality, he strode towards the closed door and, without hesitation, turned the handle and pushed it open.

There was a feeble nightlight near the base of the room's curved outer wall and in its glow Ash could make out the shapes of furniture – chairs, a sideboard, a free-standing cupboard, a table, a writing bureau and a bed. There were few other comforts.

A low snuffling noise brought his attention back to the bed and he was able to see a dark shape cowering beside it. He saw at the edge of his vision a light azure haze hovering over the crouching figure, so insubstantial that it was almost invisible and which vanished frustratingly whenever he tried to focus on it.

Ash realized that the Maglite in his hand was still pointing to the floor. He raised the torch and shone it directly at the quaking shape beside the bed. He moved the beam slowly, like a searchlight, afraid of what it might illuminate. His fear proved well founded when the cringing, brown-robed person lurched towards him.

Ash deliberately aimed the light full into the shaded cowl, and when he saw the face, the unremitting glare of the Maglite exposing all that had been hidden beneath the deep shadows of the hood, he felt his heart would stop.

Ash's eyes widened. He wanted to exclaim in horror, but all he could do was stare, his mind unable to make sense of what was before him. The torch almost slipped from his hand, perhaps a psychological reaction to something he really didn't want to see. He didn't waver, though, the light shining deep into the dark cavern of the hood revealing every hideous detail of the face, of the *thing*, that could no longer hide from him.

But eventually the sight proved too much, and Ash staggered backwards, hitting the doorframe with his shoulder.

And then he froze as he registered the sound of pounding footsteps on the creaky wooden steps below.

47

Kate McCarrick and Gloria Standwell pulled up the collars of their topcoats as they stepped out of the restaurant into the dark, narrow London street. It was drizzling rain, but the restaurant thoughtfully provided umbrellas for its regular patrons. Thus protected from the fine mist of rain, they set off in search of a taxi.

Kate was reflecting on all that had been revealed to her over dinner that evening and, desperate to know more about the Inner Court, was the first to speak.

'I understand how powerful this organization must be, but are they *directly* involved in politics?'

This brought a smile to Gloria's face. 'Oh, you'd better believe it.'

'For example?'

Gloria hesitated once more, then shrugged her shoulders.

'Do you remember back in the seventies, Kate, when you and I were just kids?'

'Oh yes,' Kate drawled, 'I remember them well, Glo, but I don't think we were much bothered about politics then.'

'No, course not. But you remember Harold Wilson, the former prime minister?'

'Vaguely, yes. Though more from what I've read since. He claimed MI5 tapped his phone, didn't he?'

'He did, and he was right.'

Although both women were huddled under the umbrella, they kept their voices low.

'Did they really imagine he was working for the KGB?' asked Kate.

They left the pavement to cross to the other side of the street. Kate noticed the reflection of the brilliantly white moon surrounded by silver-edged clouds reflected on the puddles. She wondered if it was as clear in Scotland, and whether David was looking at the same moon. As they reached the other side, with the drizzle beginning to ease, Gloria continued.

'If you remember, the country was constantly racked by strikes. The powers behind the powers that be—'

'Like the Inner Court?'

'Precisely. They were ashamed and embarrassed that Britain was being called "the sick man of Europe". We were slowly being stifled by the unions. Everywhere you looked, workers were on strike. Some union bosses were undoubtedly working for the Russians, and when the miners' strike forced Ted Heath out, the country was entirely on the rocks, so to speak. People couldn't get to work because of train strikes, the working week was cut to three days because we didn't have enough power to keep industry going – oh boy, we were in a *total* mess.

'Wilson won the 1974 election, but then other powers started to act. Wilson's name was smeared by the right-wing press and those behind it. They wrote about his mental health – implied he was going doolally – alleged he was having an affair with his private secretary Marcia Falkender, and so on and so on.

'What the press didn't know, however, was that plans were being laid for a military coup. Lord Louis Mountbatten would lead it. All major ports and airports were to be seized, as well as the BBC studios. The Queen would urge the public to support the armed forces, because the government could no longer keep order.'

Kate stopped dead and turned to face Gloria. 'I can't believe it! A military coup in *Britain*?'

'Seems impossible, doesn't it? But I can assure you, Kate, it was all deadly serious. Those wielding the real power felt the country couldn't be allowed to wither and die. And the Inner Court was in the thick of it, but on Britain's side, thank God. If the population had really known what was going on at that time, well, I think probably civil war would have broken out. Yet it was all kept under cover, although there were inevitably rumours.'

They began walking again, heels clattering on the wet pavement. Gloria glanced at Kate. 'I don't think it would ever have happened,' she soothed. 'The British are not cut out for mutiny.'

Kate sifted through her memory. 'What did happen to Wilson?'

'Forced out of office and replaced by Jim Callaghan. The usual reason: "ill-health", which actually did materialize later. He resigned in the same week as Princess Margaret announced her divorce from Lord Snowdon. The irony was that many suspected Wilson's resignation was timed to deflect attention from the royal family's embarrassment. In truth, the precise opposite was the case: Princess Margaret's announcement was meant to take the spotlight off the country's perilous situation.'

They had reached the end of the narrow street and, as they faced the busy main road Gloria said, 'The point is, that episode helped the Inner Court gain even more power within the political system, because it helped instigate a perfect campaign against both socialism and trade unionism.'

'I thought Margaret Thatcher was supposed to be responsible for saving the country from the unions.'

'But who do you think was behind her?'

'I don't believe it. Thatcher would never work with an organization like the Inner Court.'

'You must remember: this all happened very subtly. But the IC did make a huge mistake at first – it backed Edward Heath, the prime minister for a short time before Wilson.'

Kate could only smile in dismay yet again and shake her head.

But Gloria wasn't to be deterred; in a way, telling her friend of the machinations of government and industry was cathartic for her. She'd kept these secrets for so long.

She continued, 'The Inner Court knew about the idea of a European Community that was seriously being bandied about. In fact, they encouraged it.'

Kate laughed.

'You see, they wanted Great Britain tied with Europe because it would be very advantageous for their businesses, especially the armaments trade. A union of European countries would be marvellous for their organization. So they first helped Heath become prime minister in 1970. He was a buffoon but a very useful buffoon. The only thing they couldn't make him do was get married. Those were the days when homosexuality was still pretty unacceptable, particularly in politicians. But he was stubborn. So the rumour was started that he was asexual, though some of the young men and boys who crewed his yacht might say otherwise.'

A taxi came along, its for-hire beacon lit, but they let it pass. The conversation was too good to finish just yet.

'So,' continued Gloria, 'he was persuaded by the idea of a unified Europe, but needed the lie that it was merely a trade organization rather than a political one. It was the IC that advised him always to refer to it as a "common market", even though the Europeans preferred the term "community", because the public wouldn't then regard it as a threat to their country's sovereignty. Later, in his retirement, Heath pompously stated that the people were stupid to think the alliance was *not* politically motivated. Anyway, he lost the Conservative leadership to Margaret Thatcher, someone who appeared to talk plainly and honestly.'

The rain had stopped and Kate let down the umbrella.

'What about Thatcher? Was she also an Inner Court dupe?'

'Good God, no!' Now it was Gloria who was smiling. 'Obviously, she knew of the organization's existence and despised it. She would have nothing to do with its members and deeply resented our entry into the EU. The IC was aghast – here was somebody too strong to bend to their ways. She had become a liability, and they began plotting against her almost immediately.'

'And Heath?'

'He sulked right up to his death in 2005 as Thatcher led the party for the rest of his career in politics. Eventually though, after turning this ailing country of ours around, Thatcher was knifed in the back by her own party, in particular by Michael Heseltine, who wanted the premiership for himself and who struck the first blow.'

'Did the Inner Court orchestrate her defeat by John Major, then?'

'Not really. They were too busy getting Tony Blair into office. He was no more aware of it than Thatcher had been, of course, but he was an ideal candidate for them: so far right of centre that he might as well have been a Tory, a good worker – and networker – and with great stamina. The only problem was his wife, Cherie, a woman intensely disliked by some, and especially by the media. And, of course, he was very popular with the public. What the Inner Court would really have liked was for him to become president, first of Great Britain, then of Europe.'

'But what about the Queen?' asked Kate. 'You can't have a president *and* a monarchy, surely?'

'The takeover would be done in a subtle way and would take a long time, almost so the British public wouldn't understand it was happening. After all, most of those who voted to join the "Common Market" didn't really understand what they were voting for.'

'Surely there must be a way of controlling the Inner Court's influence?' Kate was aghast.

'Well, one of their plans hasn't worked out – *so far*. Tony Blair hasn't become President of the European Commission. However, he's still relatively young, so who knows?'

'Even with his track record: three wars in Bosnia, Iraq and

Afghanistan? Surely, despite the success in Bosnia, too many people feel he was dishonest in sending our troops into Iraq and Afghanistan.'

'Sometimes these things are forgotten. As I said, he's a comparatively young man still. But you'll notice both Blair and Brown were ignored when they left office – virtually all past prime ministers have been awarded the Order of the Garter. Normally it goes with, but after, the job. And Blair and Brown weren't even invited to Prince William and Catherine's huge wedding at Westminster Abbey, while dignitaries from around the world attended.'

Finally, Gloria raised her arm to catch the attention of a passing taxi. Before it pulled up, she turned to her friend. 'I'm trusting you with my career, here, Kate. If what I've told you ever gets out . . .'

'I promise. There's no fear of that.'

Gloria hugged her old friend, then turned to the cab which had pulled up beside them. As she settled into the back seat, she called, 'Thanks for the wonderful dinner – we must do it more often. But next time, my choice and my treat.' With that, Deputy Assistant Commissioner Gloria Standwell pulled the door shut and the taxi merged into the flow of traffic, leaving Kate with much to think about.

She was extremely worried for David Ash, and she damned herself for ever having persuaded him to go to bloody Comraich Castle.

48

'David! David, turn the light away from him!'

Delphine rushed past Ash, knocking him sideways roughly as she ran through the doorway and fell to her knees, her arm sweeping over the hooded creature's back as if to protect it.

Ash thought he heard a faint whimper as the hunched form on the floor huddled itself into the psychologist's embrace.

'Turn on one of the lamps – the light's softer.' Delphine's voice was calmer now, but firm, as she called back to the shocked investigator.

Numbly, Ash shone the torch around the semi-circular room and found the nearest lamp set on a small cabinet less than two feet from him. He quickly reached beneath the shade and switched on the lamp; the room was instantly bathed in a soft light. He looked towards the two figures crouched beside the small, comfortable-looking bed. Delphine's head was close to the cloaked figure's and she was making soft crooning noises to as she cuddled lt.

'I'm sorry, Delphine . . .' Ash began to say as he snapped off the torch, but she silenced him with a brief look back over her shoulder.

'It's all right, David,' she said, her voice still low, 'you weren't to know. Perhaps I should have explained, but there's been no time today.'

'Is . . .' he took a chance and guessed, 'is *he* all right? I didn't mean to . . .'

'It isn't your fault. But you frightened him more than he

351

frightened you.' She gently helped the figure sit on the edge of the bed.

She stroked his back gently. 'It's all right, Lewis. This is David, a friend of mine. He means you no harm.'

For a second, the bent figure looked past Delphine at Ash, who caught just a glimpse of one staring eye of the palest blue he'd ever seen. Even though pallid, there was a youthful clearness about it that told the investigator his first impression of old age had been wrong. The figure had seemed almost spindly as he'd chased after it. Apart from brightness, the eye was filled with the electricity of fright.

Delphine tenderly pulled back the hood so that Ash could see more of the trembling but docile young man. Now he observed the whole head and had to suppress the nausea that rose in his throat.

It was like looking at an X-ray, for the tight skin was translucent, almost indistinguishable from the skull. It was as shocking as it was pitiful, and the investigator had to force himself not to look away. Delphine sat on the bed next to the strange creature, who shuddered every few seconds, her arm around his shoulders, the other reaching across his chest to the top of his elbow so that he was embraced like a child.

'What –' Ash stopped himself. 'Who is he?' he asked Delphine.

The psychologist looked up at him, her expression showing no pity, just a firm pragmatism. 'His name is Lewis. He was here when I first arrived at Comraich. Apparently he'd been taken into the castle's medical unit as a baby. He nearly died, but the staff here managed to save him. Years later he was treated as a kind of guinea pig. You can see that his skin is more or less transparent. Imagine being able to see details of internal organs and blood vessels, or actually watch the effects of drugs and chemicals in a live patient. Mercifully, Dr Pritchard put a stop to such experiments when he came here. It took a while for Lewis to trust me – he'd received little sympathy from anybody else – but now there's a close affinity between us.'

'Does he . . . does he have a family; a surname?'

'Not that I'm aware of. I've know him for three years. Most people just call him "The Boy".'

She pulled Lewis's head down onto her shoulder and he leaned willingly. Her free hand gently stroked his hairless scalp.

'He's one of your patients?' asked Ash.

'Lewis is more than that to me. We're good friends. In fact, I'm one of the few people he comes into contact with.'

'I saw you earlier from my window, heading towards the gardens.'

'It's Lewis's favourite time of day. The sunlight's not too strong and there are few people about.'

'Does he still require medical treatment?'

She managed to shake her head, although her charge clung tight. 'Just a moisturizer, but he applies that himself. The doctors examine him once a year or so, but he's frightened of them and creates a fuss.'

'I'm not surprised,' said Ash.

'As you might imagine, with his condition, Lewis is extremely shy. And bewildered by it all.'

'What *is* his condition? Have they never discovered the cause?'

Delphine was quiet for a moment, then seemed to make up her mind.

'Lewis,' she said softly to the man in her arms, 'I want you to be brave for a moment. David is a friend of mine and he wants to be friends with you also. I know I'm asking a lot, but you must trust me. You know I'd never let anyone harm you?'

The strange man-boy – his age was impossible to guess – pulled his head away from his comforter's shoulder to stare into her face. Uncertainty was in his eyes (it came as a relief to Ash that the eye he'd seen did indeed have a partner, even if their tissue-thin lids seemed to render them unnaturally large) and Delphine smiled and kissed him on the forehead.

'It's all right, Lewis, I promise you. Now let's both stand, then I want you to slip off your robe.'

Delphine turned to Ash and he saw anguish in her expression, the distress a mother might feel when her child was suffering.

'His cloak is made of the softest cashmere, because any other material would be far too rough on his skin. At night, he wears a special silk gown.'

'Really,' said Ash, 'there's no need for him to—' but the youth was undoing the knot of the belt that held his cloak together, though he kept his eyes on the psychologist, as if seeking reassurance.

Delphine smiled encouragingly and helped him slide the robe off his narrow, limp shoulders. Then, naked but for silky white shorts, Lewis faced Ash.

Ash gaped, speechless, at what he could only think of as the apparition before him, who stared back at him nervously. The figure's limbs continued to tremble, but not from the cold, for the room was very warm. The investigator took in the wiry muscle behind the clear bones of the ribs and chest, the chambers of the heart pulsing, pumping life's blood quickly through the main arteries into the lungs, which showed as gossamer-like sacs. Taking up oxygen from the lungs, the blood was being siphoned into the left side of the heart, where the muscular walls were even thicker, darker. The process of observation was both fascinating and disturbing, perhaps something no layman could appreciate – the workings of the human body that no one should ever see.

'It's a shock, isn't it?' said Delphine. 'When I started at Comraich, I was briefed on some of Lewis's background and on his condition. I think it was a way of helping me bond with him and to become a kind of confidante and companion to him. I was told he'd been at Comraich for over twenty years. He was born prematurely at eighteen weeks, weighing less than two pounds.'

'Eighteen weeks? And lived? Is that possible?' Ash asked distractedly, for he was finding it difficult to take his eyes from the rarity before him.

'Of course he was expected to die – at that stage the chance of survival is no more than twenty-five per cent, even today. That he managed to pull through is little short of miraculous, considering his skin's abnormality. I'm told the best gynaecologist and obstetrician in the world were at the birth. Would you believe he measured just six inches?'

Ash was even more amazed. Whoever Lewis was, his parents must be either very rich or very important – probably both – to afford such care and then to maintain him at Comraich for nearly thirty years.

Ash couldn't help but continue to stare. He'd never come across anything like this before. The grey but solid bone structure, the strings of tendons and muscle like stretched rubber, the very living organs – God, the lengths and lengths of intestines. Again, he felt nausea rising inside him but he quickly controlled it.

Ash returned his gaze to the boy-man's transparent head. While the brain itself was partially hidden behind the bone of the cranium, Ash could see the nerves that sent impulses to different sectors of the brain, the ear canals, the epiglottis at the back of the throat, and the vocal cords inside the larynx, the muscles that moved his eyeballs. Then the fat muscle of the tongue itself, revealed whenever the jaw was opened. All this held within the grotesque, grinning *danse macabre* of the cruelly exposed skull.

For a moment, Ash felt he might faint, but he steadied himself as Delphine carried on talking.

'Even worse for Lewis, he has an epileptic condition known as Lennox-Gastaut syndrome, though we can control the seizures with medication, and he's also a haemophiliac, which is so dangerous because the merest cut to his body means it's almost impossible to stop the bleeding.'

Delphine had paused, hoping Ash was managing to compose himself.

'There are certain breeds of amphibians that have translucent skin like Lewis,' she explained. 'The olm, for instance, a blind South African salamander. Japanese scientists have created transparent frogs for medical study, allowing them to see details of internal organs and blood vessels. Organs of the frog can be studied throughout its lifetime and for instance, they're able to examine how certain chemicals influence bones. And of course, in the depths of the oceans are countless see-through species like jellyfish, sea-worms, sea snails, and octopuses which have evolved transparency as a form of camouflage. In the oceans' very deepest regions are species so sheer they're practically invisible, which is their way of coping with the immense pressure around them that would crush an unprotected human being or normal fish.'

The investigator's next question surprised her with its simplicity. 'How does he sleep? His eyelids seem like thin tissue. Does it make any difference if he closes them?'

'Not really,' Delphine answered. 'He just sleeps in a darkened room. Bright light is anyway uncomfortable for him; you'll notice all the lamps in this room are of a low wattage. Even when I take him for a walk in the evening he wears sunglasses. Naturally, because of his ultra-sensitive skin he avoids bright sunlight.'

'Do other guests know of him? How do they react?'

'They rarely see him, but after so many years, most have become used to him.'

Sympathy for the young man only just trumping his revulsion, Ash glanced around the room. He noted its spare plushness, the space hardly large enough to take much furniture, but what was there conveyed a sort of minimalist opulence – the bed with its silk sheets, the wall cabinets, loaded bookshelves, a wardrobe (though Ash couldn't imagine it contained much), a small, delicately carved table and lush chairs, as well as a beautifully cushioned armchair with curved arms and legs. There was an expensive-looking radio, but no television. And no mirrors.

Delphine was still speaking. 'Lewis's skin is missing two natural layers. The top layer, the epidermis, comprises a protective shield of dead skin cells right at the surface, and the layers below continually produce new cells and push them up to that surface. As the new cells force their way up, they continue a cycle whereby old cells are shed and renewed every fourteen to twenty-eight days. The epidermis loses somewhere in the region of thirty thousand skin cells every full day . . .'

It dawned on Ash that Delphine was drawing out her explanation so that he could adjust to the sight before him. He was still finding it difficult, but her method was slowly beginning to work. He was starting to see Lewis less as a freak, more as a dreadfully unfortunate man.

'Underneath these layers should be two others: the dermis, which is mostly made up of protein fibres known as collagen and which gives the skin its firmness, and beneath this is the subcutaneous layer made up of muscle and fat that protects the body from the harsh outside world. In Lewis, the last two are almost entirely absent, and no one here has ever discovered why.'

'But there must be other places Lewis could be sent to; specialists who could find out the reason, and maybe even offer a cure?' Ash protested.

Delphine almost smiled. Her efforts to humanize her patient to Ash were working: for the first time, David had used Lewis's name.

'Believe me,' she replied softly, 'Comraich has the means to bring in the finest medical scientists from anywhere, and Dr Pritchard has combed the world for someone who might be able to cure Lewis, but with no success.'

Ash slowly shook his head. The more he learned about Comraich, the deeper a mystery it became.

'How is it that Lewis can see? Doesn't he need something solid behind his pupils besides bone to reflect light rays back onto the lens?'

'If you used a ophthalmoscope you'd see he has a retina of over a hundred million light-sensitive cells at the back of each eye which register an image projected on to them and convert it into a pattern of electrical impulses, which are sent along an optic nerve to the brain.'

'I'll take your word for it,' Ash replied, loathe to make a closer inspection.

'As a matter of fact,' Delphine went on to inform him, 'Lewis has perfect vision, although strong light, sometimes even low sunlight, causes him pain. And flashing lights often bring on epileptic fits.'

Ash looked directly at Delphine. 'You've known Lewis for three years, you said.'

She nodded. 'I think he was one of the reasons my application for this job was accepted. I think they wanted a companion for him, as well as a therapist. I have to submit a detailed report on him every six months. Presumably it's forwarded to his patron, whoever that is.'

'But you must have discovered something more of his background over those three years.'

'How? Comraich *is* his background. Neither he nor I knows any more than that, even though we talk together for hours.' She smiled affectionately at her charge, and Ash couldn't help but be repulsed by the bare-toothed grimace Lewis returned, those long exposed teeth and their roots forming a ghoulish grimace rarely seen outside horror movies or a dentist's surgery. Ash inwardly shuddered, but noticed the tenderness in her smile.

'So is he . . . Lewis, is his brain okay?'

'Oh yes. He's not been as well educated as you or I, of course, and I suppose others might regard him as mentally retarded, but I know he isn't. It's Comraich Castle that makes him act the way he does.'

Then, mischievously, as if to lighten the mood, Delphine said to Ash: 'D'you want to *see* him speak? Actually watch his vocal chords work?'

'Uh. I'll take a raincheck on that. Too much, too soon, y'know?'

Delphine patted Lewis's arm gently. 'Now, young man,' she said in a no-nonsense voice, 'time you were in bed. You need your sleep.'

Lewis immediately walked to the wardrobe, pulled on a long silk nightgown and climbed into bed.

Delphine further surprised Ash by leaning forward and kissing Lewis's cheek.

'Good night, Lewis,' she said tenderly, like a mother to a five-year-old. 'Sleep tight.'

'Night, Delph. See you tomorrow.'

Ash wasn't sure if he was more startled by the fact that Lewis had spoken, or by the girlishly high pitch of his voice. He received another, pleasant jolt at the next sound from beneath the silky bedsheets that covered Lewis's head.

'Night, Mr Ash.'

He and Delphine quietly left the room, closing the door softly behind them.

49

After leaving Lewis in his lonely eyrie, Ash continued his vigil. But this time, it was different; now, he had a companion.

Both he and Delphine were exhausted – it had been a hell of a day, and this place, not to mention the people in it, were just mind-boggling. But the fact remained that Comraich was undergoing a terrible psychic storm that was dangerous to everyone in the castle, and he had to somehow convince Haelstrom to evacuate the building as soon as possible. The investigator felt sure that worse was yet to come. When it did, the consequences might prove fatal for many more of the castle's guests, especially those with weak hearts or other frailties.

Once again he visited all his equipment sites, with Delphine beside him. The psychologist looked tired and drawn. It was little wonder, considering what she had been through that day herself, though she had rejected Ash's urgings to get some sleep during what remained of the night. Yet still there was that prettiness to her face, that softness in her liquid-dark eyes and, he had to face it, he was very glad she was with him. She was not too tired to be interested in his ghost-hunting methods and the apparatus he'd brought, surprised that much of it was so simple. He explained that ghosts rarely hid themselves away; in fact, being found or contacted was part of their purpose, proof that they had the spiritual strength to manifest themselves, sometimes by materializing unexpectedly or by moving solid objects or even speaking. It made the spirits aware they could still enter this physical dimension.

Delphine's interest and intelligent questions gradually began to rekindle Ash's enthusiasm, and he realized some of his energy was reviving.

Soon his thoughts returned once more to the curious oddity he'd just seen. He wondered if Lewis might have attracted malign spirits. There was no doubt that he was sensitive, both mentally and physically: but *a* sensitive? Ash could only wonder what Lewis had endured during the years he'd been kept at Comraich. What was his secret? Delphine had denied all knowledge, though as his psychologist she should at least have been informed. He decided he would ask her later: with both of them exhausted, this was not the time to accuse her of withholding information.

After an hour checking his instruments, none of which showed any sign of disturbance, Ash decided to call it a night. He and Delphine returned to the third floor, where they lingered by Delphine's door, both of them weary yet tense, wired almost, by the castle's strange atmosphere, a kind of mood that was only in part to do with its chilly temperature. A patrolling guard passed them, a knowing smirk on his face as he wished them good night.

Delphine stood close to him, looking up into his face as if to ask a difficult question. He felt her warmth, but resisted his own feelings.

'I guess . . .' he began, but let the rest of what he was about to say hang in the air. He was going to suggest they should both return to their rooms and get some well-earned rest but, although she still faced him, her hand had found her door handle and she pushed the door open behind her.

'Delphine, I . . .' The huskiness in his voice was a mixture of weariness and desire. He reached round her and pushed the door open fully. He couldn't find words for everything he'd thought – *felt* – that day.

Before they went inside, she stepped into his arms and rested her cheek against his chest.

He closed the door behind them and wished fervently that

the bedroom doors had locks to shut out the world. He pulled her tightly towards him, her body small and slight in his arms so that he felt her fragility, and they kissed, softly at first, then harder, hungrily, her soft lips opening to him as his tongue met hers.

Delphine led him towards her bed and they both fell onto it. His mouth tasted her cheeks, her brow, and the delicate line of her neck. She uttered a small cry of passion when he pulled her hair aside and slid his tongue around her delicately shaped ear. His hardness was pressed into her and she moved her hips against him, parting her thighs slightly, arousing him even more, his kisses, matched by hers, becoming even wilder. Soon their hands began to explore each other's bodies.

Ash did his best to control his passion, but one hand soon cupped her breast over the softness of her cardigan, then slid inside the material of her blouse.

When his fingers brushed over her skimpy bra so that the tips of his fingers rested on the shallow lace trim, feeling the soft skin near the top of her small breast, she gasped. He paused, and she looked up at him, confused.

'Please, David . . .' she whispered. 'Please, don't stop . . .'

How could she know of the last two women he'd loved: Christina, who was not real, yet truly real to him, or Grace, whose agony he'd watched as her skin was torn from her flesh? Was he some kind of Jonah, deadly to any woman he came close to?

'What is it, David?' Delphine asked urgently, her passion barely in check. 'Why have you stopped?'

'I'm sorry, Delphine,' he spoke quietly and there was an edge of self-reproach to his tone.

His next words were spoken soberly. 'Delphine, I think I knew how I felt about you the moment you boarded the plane.'

Her eyes glistened.

'Are you sure?' she asked. 'We barely know each other.'

'I'm sure,' he said. 'But I just need to take things slowly. I hope you understand.'

As he turned to lie beside her, Ash sensed *she* was the one who needed help and consolation, compassion and support, and was angry at himself for his selfishness. What awfulness had she witnessed at this strange place? What dreadful experimentation had she discovered taking place within the confines of Comraich? She was obviously unhappy here, so why was she frightened to leave? He'd felt her doubt, her bewilderment, even when she was singing the medical unit's praises. He'd seen for himself the hesitation when he'd asked difficult questions. Was it the threat of what would happen to her should she desert the castle? Or did she stay because there was nowhere else to go? No, no, he reasoned. She was stronger than that.

Then was it concern for what might happen to Lewis should she abandon him?

As they lay side by side Delphine started to describe how, earlier that evening, she and Lewis had walked through the empty gardens, and how Lewis had been strangely reluctant to return to the castle. Then, when they'd heard the screams from the dining hall, Lewis had pulled her away from the building to the peaceful gardens, waiting there until all was quiet. Many hours later, when everyone had gone to bed, Lewis had allowed her to lead him back inside. While he'd made his way up to his tower room, Delphine had dropped by to check on a patient, then followed him up. Too late, alas, to prevent Ash from chasing after him.

They talked of the weird paranormal happenings at Comraich, and the terrible animal screeching that she too had heard coming from somewhere distant in the woods.

Ash told her about Lukovic, knowing the marks on his body would be obvious, and about what had happened in the containment area.

'I'm frightened, David,' she said. 'Frightened for you, for

363

Lewis, and for myself.' Delphine held Ash tightly and suddenly Ash felt the hesitancy between them evaporate.

All the fears and apprehensions that were *his* problems were swept away; swept away because, ridiculous though it might seem on such a short acquaintance, he knew he really did love her and would protect her – and Lewis, if it came to that – with all the power he had. It might prove insufficient, but in his lifetime he'd overcome some pretty grim situations. It had cost him, it had cost him dearly. But he'd learned that nothing was insurmountable or too overwhelming to come to grips with. He had twice lost women he'd cared for, but so what? He would make sure there was never a third time.

Gently, he pulled Delphine into his arms again, and she came willingly.

They lay naked beneath the bedsheets, having slowly undressed each other – the anticipation part of the thrill.

As they kissed, lips and tongues raising each other's passion, Ash slid his hand along Delphine's body from her hip, trailing into the dip of her waist, then up to her breasts, pulling his upper body away a little so that he could not only feel, but also see, those firm yet gently curved breasts, a dark aureola surrounding her pink nipples. The touch was exquisite, the sight beautiful. He ran his fingers lightly over them, feeling the raised nipple inside the palm of his hand.

She drew in a quick breath, then sighed with both contentment and expectation. His tongue moistened one nipple, so that she arched her back, pushing her hips against him. Without giving in to the desire coursing through him – he was so hard he felt it might burst – he breathed softly on her nipples, stopping occasionally to moisten them once more so that the air he exhaled stimulated her even more.

Delphine pulled his head tight against her breast so that he engulfed much of it with his mouth, his tongue still working tantalizingly. She moved his lips over to her other breast, and by now his manipulation was becoming wilder, so much more intense. Now it was her hand that glided down his lean body, over his chest, his stomach and then, even lower. Her delicate fingers encircled him and it was he who gave out a little cry of ecstasy. Steadily she stroked, more insistent, more strongly, until he forced himself to stay her hand before his passion overwhelmed him.

He chuckled at her look of surprise.

She smiled. 'Sorry,' she said, but he could see passion still burned within her, as a red flush spread like a bib over her light coffee-coloured chest, just below her throat and between her breasts.

He pulled her round so she was underneath him.

'David, please . . .' she gasped, for she needed him inside her more than anything else in the world.

Ash understood precisely what Delphine wanted, for he wanted the same.

Gently, he pulled away just enough to allow his fingers to roam her flat stomach, feeling her tense suddenly as they skimmed over the lower muscles of her abdomen. He reached the thick, black and wiry curls of her pubic hair, the edges so neat they looked trimmed, a smallish V-shape that seemed to point the way. His fingers ran through it and he felt her body tense.

He knew, and Delphine knew, that what was about to happen would affect their lives. Ash gave himself in to her submission. He dipped his fingers into the wet cleft between her thighs, and he was both surprised and delighted at Delphine's dampness, for her arousal was evident. Then, through his own desire to please her, Ash made a mistake.

His lips were kissing the elegant curve of her smooth neck and they moved down further, taking in the nipple of one breast, before moving across to the other. She moaned with the joy of it. He sunk lower and she arched her neck from the pillow, moving her face from side to side in sweet agony.

Ash sunk lower, moving his tongue into the dark thicket of curled hair . . .

And that was when she froze. He stopped, dismayed. She tried to push his shoulders away from her.

'Delphine . . . ?' He lifted his head to look at her face.

'I'm sorry, David. I'm sorry.' A tear formed in the corner of one eye and slid across her temple into the hair above her ear.

Ash couldn't understand, but then something occurred to him. He raised himself on one elbow so he could look into her eyes. 'Is it because of Nurse Krantz?' He'd put the question bluntly, but gently, with no trace of anger or even distaste.

She averted her eyes, turning her face deep into the plump pillow.

He'd made a guess, based on suspicion, because of the way Rachael Krantz reacted to him whenever they met, especially when Delphine was with him – the spite in her eyes, the straight firmness of her mouth, the chill of the atmosphere between them. Of course. It was jealousy, hatred even. But had she and Delphine . . . ?

He laid his head on the pillow and gently pulled Delphine's face round to his own. Ash was an excellent observer; he could easily read other people's moods, usually guessing rightly anything that was worrying them. It was one of the reasons he was so good at his job: his 'intuition'.

'What was it that made you stop, Delphine? What did I do that was so wrong for you?'

'Oh David.' She tried to turn away from him, but he held her face with the soft palm of his hand. 'If only I could make you understand . . .' She left the sentence unfinished.

Afterwards, they lay naked beneath the bedsheets, pleasantly exhausted.

'Delphine, I know it's none of my business, but do you want to tell me about Nurse Krantz?'

He smiled, and kept his voice soothing so that she would understand nothing else mattered between them. 'It's obvious she hates me, and I have a good idea why. What I don't know is what's happened between you. But, believe me, nothing you can tell me will make me love you less.'

There, he'd said it. Now it was up to her.

Her eyes widened and brimmed with more tears that made the pupils sparkle. She blinked and the tears spilled over, but there were no sobs, just silent weeping. Ash sensed the latent fear behind it.

'It's okay,' he told her. 'I promise, whatever went on between you two makes no difference to me. None at all.'

'It isn't what you think. Rachael and me.'

'You don't know what I think.' He gave a small laugh.

She went on apprehensively, still concerned at what his reaction would be. 'My father died after a long battle with cancer over a year ago. I was distraught on the day Rachael Krantz came to tell me he was gone and, in fact, had been buried two days earlier. I was . . .' Delphine shook her head, unable to find the right words. 'I suppose my feelings – my distress, alone, angry – all of it was overwhelming. I collapsed to the floor in a kind of faint. Next thing, I found myself lying on my bed. Rachael had carried me there.'

Ash could easily believe the sturdy senior nurse capable of lifting Delphine's slight figure.

'I awoke crying, crying like I never had before. I'm sure I was in hysterics and, of course, as a nurse, Rachael knew how to calm me down. She held me, one hand stroking my hair, her other arm around my back rocking me gently as she soothed me with comforting words. And I clung on to her, the thought of having no one left in the world to return my love frightened me. Rachael kissed my cheek, not in a sexual way, but tenderly, like a sister, protective and caring, and I gave in to it. And I allowed her kisses to continue, until they slowly became anything but sisterly.

'I didn't resist, David. She kissed me and I kissed her back, hard, desperately, *passionately*, because I had no one else to turn to and my grief had made me weak, physically and emotionally weak, and I had no resolve, nothing left. I only wanted to be loved. By anyone. Even Rachael.

'Soon her hand was inside my blouse and it felt like fire, but exquisite fire, as she touched my breast. For a moment I tried to stop her, but I was weak, drained. I had no strength left. Besides, I *wanted* her. Her hand moved to my waist and suddenly we were lying down, together, kissing . . .'

Delphine's head was now downcast. A little shakily, he had to admit, Ash touched her chin with his fingertips and brought her face up so they could look each other in the eye.

'Delphine, there's no shame in what you've done,' he said consolingly. 'You were in grief, bereft, confused. You'd just heard you'd lost your father, so how could you not look for some comfort, friendship too? A shoulder to cry on. It was unfortunate that it was Krantz who first told you and you were both alone in this room. Hell, Delphine, you're a psychologist – you should know. You're crazy to beat yourself up over one incident.'

'You don't understand,' she answered. 'That night I went back to Rachael's room, and we . . . we spent the night together. I was desperate – for company, or for something more, I don't know. Anything to push my father's death to the back of my mind.'

'And she took advantage of it.'

Delphine shook her head firmly. 'No, I can't blame Rachael. I knew what I was doing. The difference was, though, I never wanted – never *want* – to do it again. Rachael couldn't understand why I deliberately ignored her. She still doesn't, that's the problem.'

'Sounds as if it's Senior Nurse Krantz who's got the problem.' Ash grinned. 'Delphine, forget about her. And please don't worry, it makes no difference at all to me.'

And with that he drew her back towards him once again,

one arm encircling her shoulders. He kissed her lightly at first, and when she responded more urgently, he kissed her with greater force, all thoughts of Krantz gone, vanquished. All he could think of at that moment was Delphine, not just her body in all its beautiful nakedness, but her mind, her very soul, and she was reaching for him, her hand running over his shoulders, fingers running down his spine, further, slipping her arm over his hip to reach between them, finding him again, so strong, so hardened that she could no longer wait.

Delphine rolled over onto her back, her hand still holding him, slipping him into her and he helped, his own fingers touching hers and sliding himself in.

She gasped with pleasure. This was so different from Rachael, this was an act that made her senses reel and her mind swirl, affecting her whole being, mind and body, her heart included, so that she was soon breathless with the joy of it, pulling him in more and more, groaning every time he deliberately drew back, then giving out a small cry of bliss when he returned, plunging in again, each time harder, each time deeper. Every part of her body was awash with sensation. She quivered in surrender, every tendon tight, a tingling joy, so that she was lost in the uproar of her elation, the sheer rapture of her wholeness. Soon she began to feel an even greater surge, aware that it was happening to him too, her senses rising, building, until she thought she could take no more, yet *wanting* so much more. Her body became rigid as she arched her back in the euphoria sweeping through her until eventually – too soon, too soon, almost unbearable until the climax broke and was so exquisite in its torrent that she clutched at his hips to make the climax last and she almost screamed with the exhilarating thrill of *his* release into her until she shuddered, and shuddered again, the pleasure gradually calming itself, bit by bit, piece by piece, until she was left floating, coming down from some great height to slowly sink into a well of indelible gratifying glory that would stay in her mind forever, perhaps to savour, to revel in that remembered thrill for days to come. Maybe years to come. Or just until the next time.

Now Ash, too, was satiated and weak with exhaustion. Part of his joy was that he had enraptured and satisfied this perfect, entrancing woman, with her liquid brown eyes and a body so perfectly proportioned it could only be relished.

Still clutching each other, Delphine's head resting against Ash's shoulder, they murmured words of love before gradually falling into a calming sleep. They never heard the eerie night sounds of more animal screeches that came from the distant woods, nor saw the incandescent sparks that flew from the electrified fencing as deer and other small creatures tried, in vain, to escape the compound and the vicious, crazed wildcats in their new hunting grounds.

Oblivious, Ash and Delphine slept peacefully, bodies entwined, for it had been a long, eventful day.

50

Ash and Delphine were woken at the same time by the crash of the bedroom door, but the psychologist reacted faster.

Ash's bleary eyes opened to see Delphine next to him holding the bedsheets up to cover herself. She was wide-eyed at the furious nurse standing in front of the door she'd just slammed shut behind her.

'*You bitch!*' Senior Nurse Krantz shrieked. '*You bloody whore!*'

Ash pushed himself onto an elbow and looked at the white-uniformed nurse with alarm and bewilderment. *What the hell?* he thought, and then he recalled their conversation. Krantz must have got wind of their assignation from the smirking guard.

'Rachael,' Delphine said sharply, as if admonishing a recalcitrant patient, 'please get out. Get out now!'

'Can't you see he's using you?' came Krantz's shouted response. 'He's just a typical man who only wants one thing! Sex is all he's after!' She was pointing an accusing finger at Ash.

'Now wait a minute . . .' began the investigator, who had swiftly become perfectly clear-headed.

'*You bastard! Why couldn't you have left her alone? She's not for you!*'

'Krantz,' Ash said calmly as he sat upright in the bed next to Delphine. 'Delphine is not for *you*. No matter how much you might like to think so.'

'*Bastard!*' Another screech, but this time Krantz raced towards the bed, her arms flailing the air, headed for Ash.

He blocked the blows with his lower arms and had to admit, those blows *hurt*.

'Leave him alone,' Delphine cried out, leaning across him so that she took some of the wild punches on her arms. 'I love him, Rachael! Not you – I love David!'

While this was music to Ash's ears, he was getting a little irritated by the punishment he was taking as punches and slaps rained down. Finally, he'd had enough and he moved Delphine aside so that he could get out of bed, naked or not.

If Krantz was shocked, she didn't show it, but continued to hit out at him. Ash caught both her wrists and pushed her back, surprised at the strength of the woman. The curses coming from her wide mouth were now obscene, but succeeded in goading him into anger. He pushed her back hard towards the wall, letting go of her wrists so that she felt the full impact. As she strived to pull herself together to make another strike, the wind temporarily knocked out of her, Ash quickly pulled the door to the corridor open wide and grabbed her again.

'*Let me go, you bastard!*' she managed to scream at last.

'Sure,' he replied more calmly than he felt.

He shoved her into the corridor so hard that she rebounded off the opposite wall. Ash was conscious of other curious faces peering out to see what was causing the fracas.

But Krantz was not quite finished with him yet. With a yowl of hatred, she rushed at him again. This time Ash acted in a way he never had before.

He made a fist with his right hand, pulled it back, then let go with a punch that landed squarely on the bridge of her nose. Without further sound, save for the *smack* of the punch itself, Krantz went flying backwards, her shoulders hitting the opposite wall again, then sagged down to the floor. And there she sat, white-stockinged legs splayed, her hands to her nose from where blood poured as it swelled, able only to groan.

Ash swiftly slammed the door shut, grabbed a ladder-backed chair and stuck the top bar under the door handle. All the while, Ash was puzzled by his own reaction, for he'd never even raised his hand to a woman before, let alone punched one squarely on the nose. But as he chided himself, it occurred to him suddenly that Comraich itself was to blame: there was something lurking here in the castle's very ether, something malign that encouraged such violence. How else would he have gouged the Serbian's eye out in the lift only yesterday? David Ash felt disgusted with himself, although lingering somewhere in his subconscious was a perverse satisfaction and relief.

He went back to the bed where Delphine sat, bedsheet still drawn up to cover her nakedness, a petrified expression on her face. He paused as they both heard movement outside in the corridor. Suddenly, there was a thump on the door, as if Krantz had smashed her hand against it.

'*You bastard!*' they heard again, muted this time, then footsteps marching down the corridor, fading into the distance.

Ash sat on the bed, ready to calm Delphine, but if he was honest, to calm himself too.

Delphine dropped the sheet, and pressed against him, kissing his cheek, first hugging, then clinging to him.

'David, are you all right?' Her voice was filled with concern.

'Well, my knuckles feel a bit raw, but I think I'll survive. Nurse Krantz is going to have a hell of a bend in her nose though.' He grinned at her.

'Don't underestimate her, David. She can be a dangerous woman.'

'She'll fit in well with Comraich, then. I hardly need to state the obvious, but there's something extremely odd about this place. I'm not just saying it's haunted. I mean it's full of powerfully malevolent spirits. I've got to tell you, I don't want to be in this castle much longer.'

'You'd leave?' Delphine was dismayed and she drew back so she could look into his eyes.

He found her left hand and clutched it in both of his own. 'Not without you,' he told her simply.

She cast her eyes down and dark ringlets framed her cheeks. 'I couldn't leave here, David.'

He frowned. 'Why not?' he ducked his head so that he could see more of her downcast face. 'There's nothing here for you.'

'You're forgetting Lewis.'

Ash sat back.

'You might be perfect, Delphine, but you're not indispensable. Lewis would be taken care of.'

She shook her head sadly. 'No one could ever know him as well as I do. He depends on me, David. I just don't know how he would get by if I left. You see, you haven't seen the other side of Comraich. Nobody's free here, every one of our guests is monitored wherever they go.'

'Okay, then I'll make out a full report on this place, advising it should be shut down immediately.'

'They would never do that, no matter what you say. Sometimes I think Comraich is the heart of their empire.'

'Empire? Aren't you exaggerating a little?'

She gave a small, bitter laugh and shook her head. 'Do you really think you could go up against the Inner Court? Do you understand the vast wealth that is theirs? The contacts, the people – dictators, despots, wealthy Arabs, financial wizards who've taken a step too far. Then there's the disgraced politicians, not only British, but from all over the world, individuals who are supposed to be dead but with inside knowledge of the affairs of their own countries – the businessmen, the diplomats, the billionaires – people whose very existence would be under threat should it be discovered they're still alive because of the hidden knowledge they have, the contacts they hold, these failed ministers of state and business tycoons who have to hide because of their corruption. David, I thought you realized just how powerful the Inner Court is. The IC has power over life and death.'

'I didn't realize you knew so much about the organization,' Ash said, a little disappointed that she was not quite the innocent he thought. 'Are you part of it, Delphine?' The question was bluntly put, his mind almost numb to the prospect.

'No, David, I'm not part of it. I only know what my father told me long before he died. He said I should never betray the Inner Court because my life would be over. And I've learned things during the last few years that have truly frightened me. But the only reason I do stay is because of Lewis. I think if I left – if I was *allowed* to leave – poor Lewis would no longer have any future. Can't you understand that, David?'

'I understand you can't stay here,' he said. 'Look, once my assignment is over, we'll take him with us.'

'It would be impossible. We'd never get out the gates.'

'Then I'll do it alone and come back for you. I'll bring the police if I have to.'

She shook her head in frustration. 'Don't even think about it, David. It's far too dangerous, and if Sir Victor found out you'd . . .'

She paused.

'Yes?' he prompted.

'You'd be ruined.'

His shoulders slumped. 'Yeah, I'd forgotten that. My boss and I have signed pretty solid contracts. The whole might of the organization would come down on us like a ton of bricks. I'm not worried about myself, but for the Psychical Research Institute itself. It would break Kate.'

'Kate?'

'Kate McCarrick, my boss.' He raised his shoulders again, his back straightened. 'Okay, we're both trapped here for the time being, and Kate and I are contractually bound, so let's at least fulfil the contract. I've got an idea about the castle and where these dark forces are emanating from. I've got a feeling that events are about to reach a climax as far as these hauntings are concerned, and Comraich, guests *and* staff, might be forced to abandon the place completely whether they like it or not.'

Delphine smiled. 'Well, I can't fault your optimism.'

'I've got something in mind that I want to investigate before I put in my first report and recommendation,' he went on, ignoring her restrained amusement. 'We'll see how things go today and tonight and we might even find that the problem will resolve itself.'

It might – might *easily* – be a false hope, but right then, Ash had nothing else to offer.

51

The rocks along the seashore were slippery and lethal – a bruised knee or a twisted ankle was always a strong possibility. Ash cautiously followed one of Comraich's rangers, Jonas McKewin. He was a fit young man – in his early thirties, Ash guessed – and while somewhat brusque in manner, his grey eyes had a softness about them that tempered his attitude.

McKewin turned as the investigator let out a sudden curse. Ash's booted left foot was ankle-deep in a small pool of water.

'Have a care, Mr Ash,' the ranger advised unnecessarily. 'This shoreline is treacherous and not truly suited to sight-seeing.'

Ash grinned back at him. 'Yeah, I already got that impression.'

He pulled his foot free and balanced precariously for a moment on the rock he'd just slipped from. His hands stretched outwards to steady himself as he took another step forward.

'You'll get better when you're used to it,' the ranger told him. 'You'll see, you'll get more confident. Just don't be afraid of 'em.' He pointed around at the rocky beach. They set off once again, for this hadn't been the first time Ash had stumbled or had his boot slip off a mossy stone.

*

Ash and Delphine had earlier breakfasted together in the staff canteen, less sumptuous than the dining hall, of course, but the only facility available so early in the morning. The place had been buzzing with gossip about the previous night's invasion.

The glass-and-brick annexe was built on the west side of the castle, out of sight to anyone arriving at Comraich through the 'ruined' archway entrance, and the sea, rough and surly this morning, could be seen stretching out to the grey land mass that rose from it like a smudge on the horizon.

Before heading to the canteen, Delphine had, as promised, arranged for one of Comraich's khaki-clad rangers to show the investigator the cavern at the foot of the cliff on which the castle stood.

They had made love again after Krantz had left – less wild, more tender than in the earlier hours of that morning – which had left them comfortable in each other's arms. When Ash had removed the tilted chair from beneath the door handle, he'd half expected to find Krantz lingering in the corridor outside, one hand holding a blood-sodden handkerchief to her swollen nose, a meat cleaver or butcher's knife held high in the other, ready to bring down on whoever left Delphine's room first. Of course, it hadn't happened, Krantz hadn't been there, and Ash couldn't help an inward smile.

He'd returned to his own room and showered, wincing at the bruises that had bloomed overnight, then dressed awkwardly because of the stiffness of his entire body. He'd returned with his equipment bag to Delphine's room, where she'd been ready and waiting for him, wearing a heavy coat over her skirt and high-necked jumper, even though she wouldn't be accompanying him on this morning's venture. They had hugged and kissed in the entrance of her room, regretfully preparing for the day ahead of them.

*

The warm memory did little to dispel the wind chill coming off the troubled sea. It was freezing, causing Ash to pull the muffler up high under his stubbled chin. He began to wish he'd worn a thick woollen scarf too as he took a pair of black leather gloves from his pocket and slid them on. He carried a bright yellow hard hat at the ranger's insistence, to be worn when they entered the big cave that Ash had asked specifically to inspect as part of his investigation. McKewin had warned how easy it was to bang your head on the low roof, and the area was prone to rock falls.

As he picked his way across the slimy rocks, Ash noticed a long metal pipe, about a foot in diameter, that ran from the foot of the cliff face and into the sea.

'I take it that's an old sewage outlet from the castle,' he called out to the ranger, who was a few yards ahead of him. He reminded Ash of a mountain goat, sure-footed and swift.

Jonas paused for a moment to look around at the investigator.

'Aye,' he returned, 'it runs a long way out, as you can see. These are dangerous waters, Mr Ash, and every summer we have to warn swimmers not to go too far offshore. Mostly we tell 'em not to swim at all in the sea. Fortunately, it's normally too chilly to swim in these parts, summer or winter.'

As Jonas looked out, hands on his hips, booted legs set apart for balance, Ash could not but feel there was something noble in the man's stance. The investigator followed his gaze and could just make out the darker haze of the land mass in the distance.

As if reading Ash's mind, McKewin said, 'That's the Isle of Arran you can just about see. Beyond is Kintyre.'

'Like the song?'

'Aye. Mull of Kintyre. McCartney got it so right.'

'I can't imagine anyone wanting to swim around here, no matter what the season.'

'You'd be surprised. But honestly, it's to be avoided.' He pointed a finger at the angry tide, then lifted his hand to point a little further out. 'Y'see, just about twenty, mebbe thirty yards out there's a deep shelf, full of rip tides. Y'could almost walk out to it with your head just above the water. Then you'd step off the shelf and sink down further than you might imagine. The sea's black down there, it's so deep, and the currents could easily drag you off the ledge; then you'd be swallowed into the depths, your body probably never found again.'

'Just as well I didn't bring my trunks, then.'

The ranger grinned at Ash. His weather-beaten face became serious once more. 'Just don't say you haven't been warned,' he said with a false scowl. Then: 'Well, there's the cave you'll be wanting. You can see the opening easily enough from here.' Hard hat in hand, he waved it in the general direction ahead. 'Take no notice of the smaller ones: they go nowhere.'

Ash peered towards the large black cave entrance, which was closer than he'd thought. That was a relief at least, for the journey down to the rocky shoreline had been arduous enough, by short flights of zig-zagging wooden steps. With a mute groan, he wondered how tiring it would be climbing back up.

Clambering over the tide-dampened rocks and scrunchy shale, occasionally dipping a foot into trapped pools, also took some effort. He guessed those rough steps were kept in deliberate disrepair to discourage older ramblers from the castle making the descent. There were small crabs caught in shallow pools stranded by the outgoing tide, and bedraggled seaweed was everywhere, making the going even trickier as its slick strands endeavoured to trip him.

Ash and the ranger were near to the cave entrance when McKewin stopped again. 'Time for the hard hats, Mr Ash,' he said, fixing his own onto his bare head and buckling the safety strap beneath his chin. The investigator followed suit while the ranger regaled him briefly with the cave's colourful history.

'This particular cave is infamous for its smuggling and Comraich Castle was perfectly located for hiding contraband from the Revenue men. "The Running Trade", smuggling used to be called back in the day, and the Ayrshire coast was ideal because of its nearness to the Isle of Man, which legally imported goods for small duties to the Lord of Man. Manx smugglers traded mainly in port, claret, spirits and Congo tea, would you believe? But the game more or less came to an end in the 1760s when the Revenue seriously cracked down on it. The irony was that the laird at that time had switched to the slave trade.'

There was an edge of excitement in Ash's voice. It seemed that what Delphine had told him the previous day had been more than just hearsay. 'Wait a minute. You're telling me smuggled goods could be unloaded inside the cave, then carried up to the castle itself?'

'Aye. Stored away in the dungeons, most probably. A stepped tunnel was carved out of the rock. That was a long time ago, though.'

'Have you ever tried to get through it?'

'No. I think the last time anyone used it was during the Great War. After that it was just allowed to deteriorate. It's probably all fallen in by now. The ascent would have been too steep for most people, anyway.'

Ash studied the cave's large entrance with even more interest. 'Could boats actually navigate inside the cave?' he asked.

'Oh, aye. When the tide comes in, the cave is almost fully submerged, so the time has to be exactly right for unloading. Y'know, before the water level trapped the boats themselves. But with that deep underwater shelf just offshore, a large vessel could moor there while the contraband was rowed right into the cavern. There's even a kind of natural raised dock inside that came in handy for unloading. Tricky business, though, and, as I said, the timing had to be right. The story goes that many rowing boats, filled with smuggled goods, were trapped inside and smashed to smithereens when the sea was stormy. Many a man was found drowned in the cave, others just washed out to deeper waters. It's a bad place, Mr Ash. It's only fair to warn you of that.'

'But we're okay with the tide right now?' Interest had developed into concern. Ash had no liking for water.

'Oh, aye. The tide's on its way out at the moment. It's night-time you have to worry about, although it seems to go out again much more quickly than it comes in, but then there's no need to be caught inside, is there?'

Ash buckled the strap of his hard hat under his chin as he and McKewin approached the opening to the cave. 'Now watch your step here. It's filled with seawater when the tide turns, which makes everything very slippery. Mind your head too – the ceiling isn't even once you get towards the back; but that's why you're wearing a hard hat.'

The investigator took him at his word and slowly and carefully entered the capacious cavern, watching where he trod as well as keeping an eye on the ceiling height. The khaki-clad ranger already had his torch out and was shining it around the hollowed chamber. Ash took his Maglite from his shoulder bag and switched it on. Its powerful beam illuminated the cave considerably more effectively than the ranger's torch. He noticed the 'dock', a wide ledge about five feet above the shingle-and-rock floor, now eroded in several places. Ash aimed the light towards the rear of the landing stage and was excited to see a small opening, its ceiling so low that a person would have to crawl through the gap. As he swept the light across the broken stone walls, he saw that above them, just beyond the entrance, the rock sagged, as if ready to collapse at any moment. The sight made him uneasy.

'Seems like every year,' said McKewin, 'the cave shrinks a little more, the load above gradually becoming too heavy to bear.'

'Let's hope it holds a while,' half joked Ash. 'At least till we're out of here.'

'Oh, I think it'll stay this way for a century or more. Providing the ground underneath isn't shifted by an earthquake.'

'Earthquake?' Ash was surprised.

'It's not generally known, but the British Isles are hit by

thirty-odd earthquakes annually. Fortunately, most are exceed-ingly low on the Richter Scale, so unless you're in a particular region when one occurs, you'll know nothing about it unless it makes the news.'

Ash wasn't exactly reassured. 'Can I take a look back there?' he asked.

'Sure. It's safe enough if you take care. I'll not be far; they've asked me to provide an erosion report while I'm here. Just shout if you need me.'

Treading forward cautiously, shining the Maglite around the irregular sloping walls and vaulted ceiling that somehow seemed to turn the cavern into a miniature cathedral, Ash advanced. He was soon screwing up his face in displeasure. 'What's that terrible smell?' he called back to McKewin, who was busying examining the rock face.

'Ah,' the ranger called back, a grin on his red-veined face. 'You've got two kinds of smells the further you go in. One is a bit like an oyster tastes after you've swallowed it. Or so I've been told,' he added, his face wrinkled in disgust. 'Back there you'll be getting the smell of bat guano, acidic droppings that smell foul. It can be pretty thick the further you go, and you won't like the slime, either. But the bats themselves won't be a problem unless you wake them up. It'll be their hibernation time soon, so they'll be getting drowsy round about now. Just try not to panic 'em.'

Ash was on one knee, peering into the tunnel in front of him. 'Okay,' he yelled back, suddenly realizing there was no need to shout: the widening cave acted like an echo chamber. He lowered his voice. 'I'm going in now.'

'Right you are, but don't take all day,' came the reply. 'I've got things to do.'

'I won't be long,' he affirmed, before crawling forward on hands and knees, by-passing a crab side-crawling in the opposite direction. It was harmless enough, but Ash carefully avoided it. The whole interior was unpleasantly dank, but Ash was used to disagreeable locations.

The light showed the way clearly enough, although at one point the roof was so low he had to lie flat on his belly and squirm forward, all the while reassuring himself that if the bats could fly down this passage, then he must have room to crawl through it. Soon the smell was becoming overwhelming, but it was coming from ahead, where the cave must open out again. Using what space he had, Ash pulled the muffler up over his nose. He felt like a desperado in a Western B-movie, but the mask did little to filter the smell. He pulled himself along the lower section of the cave, grateful for the hard hat as he bumped his head a couple of times.

The claustrophobic length of the tunnel was mercifully short and, as he had anticipated, soon opened out to a larger chamber, its high ceiling pitch-black and its floor full of bat excrement. Resisting the urge to shine the torch upwards for fear of disturbing the roosting creatures, he moved forward, the gooey slime under his boots feeling like syrup, though at least he'd got used to its chemical smell. As he ran his light over the floor of the rough chamber, which was about fifteen feet square, he was surprised to find pieces of rotted wood, and other debris so mouldy he had no idea what it once had been, all littered around the ground. There were one or two remnants of open boxes, the wood black with rot. More shockingly, he saw human bones among the detritus. The bones of slaves who hadn't quite reached the end of their forced journey? How long had it been since the remains had been abandoned there, then scattered irreverently when more slave traders passed through over the years?

At last, the torch beam picked out a door-sized opening in the rock, almost opposite the narrow gap from which he'd just crawled. He saw the beginning of old, broken steps that led upwards, and he smiled tightly at the sight. This had to be the way up to the castle dungeons.

Cautiously, he picked his way through the mess in the chamber and reached the reinforced doorway. He shone the light upwards, following the cracked and broken steps.

Overhead, the tunnel had been shored up with stout timbers. From where he stood, however, it seemed that the tunnel ended in a solid wall after a dozen or so steps.

Dismayed, he collected himself and began to climb the uneven, crumbling staircase. What he had taken for the end of the tunnel was, in fact, the wall of a small landing, from which another set of worn steps led up, zig-zag fashion, in the same manner as the external staircase he and the ranger had just descended. Although the treads had been hewn from the rock, it looked to Ash as though the tunnel were a natural fissure, one that headed up, he hoped, into the sub-basement of Comraich Castle.

He began to climb again, using a hand against a crumbling wall when the going became less easy. As he pressed onwards, Ash felt his thigh muscles protest at the difficult climb. But soon he reached something that turned his stomach and the wide beam of the Maglite began to shake because of the trembling of his own hand.

52

The unpleasantness in Comraich the previous evening had suited Twigg, because the guests had been advised to keep to their suites while the matter was investigated in the clear light of day. As he made his way through the castle he passed only the occasional armed guard, who barely gave him a glance.

He wasn't in the mood to be civil to anyone, for the symptoms of his illness were even more evident this morning. He tried to control the tremors in his hands by carrying the package in both of them, pressing it against his midriff.

His expression had always been rather blank, something he'd developed to a fine art over the years, but today he could feel the muscles in his face stiffening unbidden. His limbs were leaden and he tried to avoid shuffling by consciously taking longer strides. But soon it wouldn't matter anyway, because this was the day when everything was going to change.

This was his time for glorious revenge.

Comraich and the Inner Court were not going to rid themselves of him so easily. He only wished Eddy Nelson were still around so that he, Cedric Twigg, could show his apprentice how to exact punishment against not just one individual, but a whole organization. Twigg planned to bring down that organization single-handed, or, at the very least, damage it beyond repair.

Had the muscles in his face been able to fashion a grin, then the assassin might have flashed it to the old guard at the foot of the reception area's broad, curving stairway who watched his approach with yellowing eyes. Placid Pat, as the amiable old watchman was known by all at Comraich, kept a concealed weapon about him at all times but was no hindrance at all. The venerable retainer had been part of Comraich's security for as long as Twigg could remember. He knew that the old man had once, many years ago, been the Reverend Father Patrick O'Connor in a little town near Sligo, close to the west coast of Ireland, where he was afforded much respect from his parishioners. Now in his dotage, he never seemed to leave his seat.

Twigg went by without responding to Pat's feeble wave of greeting. Instead, he concentrated on putting one foot in front of the other, doing his very best to walk in a straight line, hands tight against the package he was carrying. His purpose this morning was to examine the hole the crashed elevator had created, which he understood from gossip among the guards had breached the castle's very foundations. He reached the damaged ground-floor door to the lift shaft, which was now wedged half open.

As he poked his head through the gap he could smell dust and something far more unpleasant rising up the shaft. It was difficult to see clearly, for the shaft was deep, but the glimmer of light he could make out at the bottom probably meant that the car had distorted on impact, creating a space through which light from the containment area was filtering.

Twigg wriggled further into the opening, trying not to breathe in too deeply, but all there was to see were some dangling cables. He'd heard that one of the two passengers had escaped unscathed, while the other had been killed. It reaffirmed what he already knew: death was indiscriminate.

Twigg was sadly aware that he could once have shimmied down those cables to the sub-basement, then right up again once his purpose had been achieved. Not these days, though; his co-ordination was shot to pieces. Anyway, there was a different route he could follow that was so much easier, and he possessed one of the tough titanium cards that would open the necessary door for him.

Twigg planned to situate his device near the bottom of the lift shaft, so it would funnel the blast up to the castle's every floor. Since his illness had been diagnosed, he'd been stockpiling explosives at his woodland hideaway. The package he was about to place was the last of his cache. The rest had been sited throughout the castle in locations chosen to inflict maximum damage. All he'd have to do then would be to set the timers and wait for night to fall.

Afterwards, he would celebrate the destruction of Comraich with a nice cup of tea back in his cottage. Or he might finally open that special bottle of wine, a Château Margaux 1978 he'd been gifted a few years earlier as a bonus for a particularly important and tricky hit. And he would cheer every time he heard another, then another, and then another explosion, whooshing and rustling, ripping the castle apart, while the flames inside would gut it completely.

And he would watch it all from a safe distance, hidden inside the edge of the woods.

53

The sight that had stopped Ash in his tracks was nauseating. Completely filling the long straight stretch of tunnel ahead was the biggest mass of black cobwebs he had ever seen. There was no way round it, nor any way to gauge its depth, but the prospect of entering the sticky black mess was formidable. Horrific.

More horrific still was the thought of the number of spiders it must have taken to weave this dust-clogged, tangled monstrosity. What size must they have been, and for how many years had they worked to construct this black furry barricade, strong and thick enough to deter any explorer from venturing further. *How could one get through it?* he asked himself. *Would it burn ... could it burn? How do you burn dust?* Petrol. That would do it; but how effectively, he had no idea.

He took a swift step backwards as the huge cobweb stirred. Almost slipping on the slick, sloping tunnel floor, he realized that a breeze must have blown through the mass, causing it to billow slightly, giving the alarming impression it was rolling towards him. Again he shone the Maglite directly into the curled and drooping web, only this time he narrowed the beam, intensifying and lengthening it.

The light still failed to penetrate far, but he thought he detected movement inside the matted coils that had nothing to do with the air currents blowing through the zig-zag tunnel. No, there were *things* inside that dark, dusty mesh, some bigger than others – some static, others slowly crawling.

Steeling himself, although his instinct was telling him frantically to back off, to get away, Ash took a cautious step forward, and then another, keeping the narrowed beam of light on one of the larger black creatures he'd glimpsed sitting, *waiting*, in the tangled web. It still wasn't clear enough to see properly, and he debated with himself whether he really wanted to see. But Ash was no coward, and inquisitive by nature, so he advanced even closer across the greasy floor.

He came to a stop less than two feet away from the tunnel-blocking mass. He raised the Maglite to shoulder height, pointing into the jumbled skeins, all joined by the dust and undulating gently in the soft wind that blew in from the sea, and put his face even closer to the giant cobweb.

By squinting and looking straight along the fiercely concentrated beam of light, he could see more clearly the dark form he'd glimpsed earlier; it was twitching under the glare of the torch. Ash realized it was not a spider but a bat, still moving feebly, ensnared in the web. From the depths of the web, creatures were creeping towards it.

Ash was aware that spiders rarely hunted in packs, nor – and this was the really frightening bit – were they usually prepared to take on a creature much bigger than themselves. Ash shuddered. Though it was almost blind, the bat was obviously aware of what was happening around it and could sense the movement of the dusty silky strands. Ash, though he had no love for bats, felt pity for this one, which must have been trapped since the night before, or even longer. At least it wouldn't be long before it died, of either exhaustion or fright.

If he was to continue his progress, Ash had to find out how long and how tough the giant web was. Did it fill the rest of the tunnel, or could a well-protected person walk right through it? He rummaged through his bag and brought out a bundle of glow sticks. These were usually used when no other light source was available, or for testing the depth of wells or deep pits.

Ash picked out one pellucid plastic tube, a stick-like container in which two chemicals, hydrogen peroxide and phenol, were isolated from each other. A green fluorescent dye was also in the tube and this would glow brightly when the chemicals mixed. Ash bent the stick, breaking the vial inside, and shook it vigorously, then, stretching his arm back, he flung it as hard as he could into the maze of dirt-draped cobwebs.

It was so dense that the tube of fluorescent green light didn't travel far, so gave no indication of the length of the blockage, but it revealed more dark shapes inside the massed web. Many, many more dark shapes.

The nearer spiders froze under the muted glow, but others started to appear from their lairs in the darker parts of their tangled realm, attracted by the vibrations made when the stick had landed.

'*Dear God!*' Ash cried as he stumbled backwards again, barely managing to keep his feet. There seemed to be *thousands* of them, fat-bodied and with thick, hairy legs. The shiver that ran up Ash's spine reached his shoulders and made them shudder involuntarily.

How far down the passage in the rock did this abominable blockage run? He desperately needed to get directly beneath the castle itself, for that was where he was sure the psychic phenomena originated, but there was no way he was going to try and push himself through that lot without a tough biohazard suit. Maybe if he had a flame-thrower . . . He doubted Comraich would keep such weaponry among its armaments. He thought of soaking the massive web in petrol and setting fire to it, waiting while it burned to nothing before proceeding in stages. That might work. But Haelstrom would never allow that.

'*Mr Ash!*'

The hollow sound that echoed off the walls of the long tunnel made him start and spin round.

It came again: '*Ashashashas . . .*'

Of course. He'd been gone some time and the ranger was becoming anxious.

Ash called back, sure that the sound of his voice would

easily travel through the twists and turns of the original smugglers' harsh route to riches.

'*Can you hear me, Mr Ash?*' the ranger's echoing voice demanded, now with less urgency.

'*Yeah, I can hear you!*' Ash yelled back.

'*I was worried about you.*'

'*No need. I'm on my way down right now.*'

The investigator picked up his shoulder bag and looped it across his chest. With one last look back at the hideously thick, gargantuan barricade of webs draped with dirt and dust, Ash widened the beam of his Maglite and started making his way back to McKewin. He had to crawl through the shallower parts of the tunnel, where the rock looked to Ash as if it were burdened by its own weight. It surely couldn't have been like this at the time of the 'Running Trade', for it would have made movement of goods nigh-on impossible. As he squirmed through the claustrophobic section that led back to the main cave, the smell didn't seem as bad as before and he realized he'd become acclimatized to it.

At last, and with relief, he could see daylight up ahead. One last bit on hands and knees and then he was back at the cave's entrance. The park ranger ambled up to him, his own torch aimed at the ground to watch his footing.

'Glad you're back, Mr Ash,' he said amiably. 'Thought for a moment I'd have to come and find you.'

'Yeah, sorry about that,' Ash responded, somewhat breathlessly. It was good to get sharp sea air into his lungs once more, even if the chill had a bite to it and was slightly tainted by the dank atmosphere of the cave.

'Did you find what you were looking for?' McKewin asked.

'Not really. I could only get so far.'

'Aye, well, the tunnel's been there an awful long time. I take it you won't be going there again.'

'Guess not,' he said.

'Well, nothing wasted. At least you had a chance to see what nobody else has for a hundred years.'

Ash started to walk on, to get out in the fresher and more invigorating sea air, cold though it might be, but the ranger didn't move.

'I see you brought a little friend back with you,' he said wryly.

'Sorry?'

McKewin pointed to the investigator's right shoulder with his torch.

Ash turned his head to look, and almost yelped when he saw the huge, hairy spider with its eight furry legs.

With a snappy flick of his gloved hand, McKewin swiped the spider off Ash's suddenly rigid body. The ranger smiled benignly as together they watched the furred, brittle creature scuttle away and lose itself in the rock-strewn floor. Ash wished he'd had the chance to crush the life from it with his heavy-duty boot.

The hike back up the rickety wooden stairway was arduous, but far easier than ascending the tunnel had been. When they reached the top, Ash leaned both hands on bent knees and tried to catch his breath. Annoyingly, Jonas McKewin still looked fresh, ready for more.

'You okay, Mr Ash?' the ranger enquired solicitously. Ash looked up at him suspiciously, but there was no hint of mockery in his tone. The park ranger was aware of how tough the climb could be on anybody not used to such exertions, and the investigator had managed *two* ascents that morning, the first tougher than this last one. Ash straightened and drew in a long, beautifully sweet breath of fresh sea air before giving an answer.

'Yes, thanks,' he replied. 'I'm fine now.'

'Was it any help to you, the cave?' McKewin looked genuinely interested.

'Not really,' Ash replied. 'I was hoping for more . . . in fact,

I could *feel* there was more inside the tunnel the higher I went, so it was a shame the way was blocked. I'd have liked to have climbed a bit higher.'

Ash handed back the yellow hard hat, which he'd taken off with relief as soon as they were outside the cavern.

'Well, I'm sorry about that,' said McKewin as he took the headgear from him.

'Not your fault,' Ash was saying needlessly. 'It was just an idea I had. It probably would have led to nothing.' *Except a giant dirt-draped tangle of spiders' webs*, he thought to himself.

The ranger tucked Ash's hard hat under his arm.

'Thanks for your patience,' Ash commented.

'That's okay, Mr Ash. It was only when you'd disappeared so long in there I got a mite worried.'

'Yeah, I'm sorry, I—'

'Mr McKewin!'

They both turned to see another ranger approaching them, a man older than McKewin, red-faced and rather portly.

'Marty . . . ?' McKewin wore a puzzled frown as the khaki-clad figure reached them, somewhat winded.

'Y're to come right away, Mr McKewin!' he urged in a broad Scots accent. Marty took in Ash, the 'ghost-buster' with a curious frown, then turned back to McKewin.

'There's trouble in the woods.' He looked again at the investigator, as if he might in some way be responsible. 'It's a slaughter, man, a bloodbath. I've ne'er seen anything like it. I was on m'usual mornin' rounds checkin' the boundary fence an' such, when I came upon it. It was sheer bliddy butchery. The deer . . . och, those poor bliddy deer. Some had tried to get through the fence and were fried for their trouble. They must've went at it again an' again, hurtin' 'emselves more an' more till it or the cats killed 'em. Others were just mauled to pieces. Squirrels, foxes, all kinds of smaller animals torn apart, their bellies open an' still steaming with heat. I ran – I didn't waste any time lookin' for details – I just bliddy ran. When I couldnae find you in the office, I went straight to the castle. Sir

Victor's organizing a task force to go in, an' y're needed promptly.'

'So that was the cause of the ruckus last night,' Ash put in.

'Y'heard it goin' on?' said Marty incredulously.

'I heard something, but it was very late.'

'Aye, and we're early-to-bed, early-to-rise folk, so we couldn't have known.'

'Then you missed quite a lot that was going on in Comraich last night,' Ash told him.

'No one alerted *us*,' Marty said quickly, as if to absolve the rangers of any blame.

'The important thing now,' McKewin said gravely, 'is to sort things out quickly and quietly.'

'I'm nae sure aboot quietly,' said Marty, chastened by his chief's tone. 'Sir Victor's even organizing the guards now as well as the rangers. They're armed, but waiting for you tae guide them.'

'Right, let's be off.'

With a brief nod towards Ash, he took off quickly towards Comraich, Marty struggling to keep up with him.

Ash waited for a moment or two, getting the last of his breath back, looking out to sea as he did so. Dark clouds were gathering ominously over the horizon.

54

As he crossed the wide concourse outside Comraich Castle, Ash could see no activity. He had a mind to chase after Jonas McKewin, but realized he'd probably only get in the way.

The air was dry so far, but if that sky-filling dark mass of clouds gathering over the horizon was headed this way, a storm would be arriving before long. He passed the steps that led up to the castle's entrance, intending to inspect the estate's formal gardens. Delphine had told him that guests would be confined to their rooms until the chaos of the previous evening has been thoroughly investigated. Obviously, Haelstrom hadn't wished to endanger his high-paying residents unnecessarily.

Just beyond the steps to the entrance he came upon two parked cars: the sleek, black Mercedes-Benz that had brought him to Comraich and an equally sleek black Jaguar saloon. Gordon Dalzell was busy wiping down the Merc with a chamois leather while another, taller man with receding black hair was hosing down the Jaguar. Both men were wearing identical overalls, and both looked up from their activity as Ash approached.

'*Dè an doigh*, Mr Ash?' Dalzell called out cheerfully, his grin revealing a fine display of white teeth. 'Are y'settling in okay?'

Ash approached. 'You expecting more pick-ups today, Gordon?'

'Oh, aye. Busy day today. S'why the cars have to look spotless for our VIP visitors. I heard there's been a spot of bother, even more so than before?'

'You were here?'

'Ach, we helped clean up the mess those weird flies made last night. The strange thing is, there were no signs of them this morning. I mean, the cleaners do a pretty damn good job, but y'ken, there were bound to be one or two the cleaners missed, but they couldnae find one today, not even in the vacuum machines themselves.'

He lowered his voice when Ash came even closer. 'This is rumour, mind, but I was told that when quick autopsies were carried out on those people who'd died from the attack, not one fly or maggot was found inside 'em. Y'know, some guests were supposed to have choked on 'em when the flies blocked their windpipes and even got into their lungs. But nae, all corpses were empty of the bliddy things. *Now what d'you make of that?*' Dalzell's words were louder with the question.

Ash shook his head non-committally. He noticed the chauffeur's companion had turned off the nozzle of the hosepipe which trailed around the side of the ancient building and was moving closer to the conversation. The man, was medium-tall with sad hazel eyes set in a comfortable, lived-in face with a ready smile. His dark hair was thinning. He looked interesting, as if he had a lot of stories to tell, and the investigator gave him a brief nod hello.

'Y'havenae met my other half yet,' said Dalzell, his cheerful grin lighting up his shrewd blue-grey eyes. 'Graham Hamilton – he used t'race cars, y'ken?'

'Oh, I see . . .' Ash had been taken by surprise.

Dalzell laughed at the investigator's baffled expression. 'We're not all Screaming Marys, y'ken. We don't even call it a marriage: it's a civil partnership, and that's how we care to think about it.'

'Sorry, I didn't mean . . .' Ash struggled to speak through his embarrassment, ashamed at his naivety.

Hamilton spoke up and he was smiling too. 'We heard you had problems yesterday evening.' His accent was faint, a slight lilt, almost like McKewin's.

'If you mean an unscheduled journey in a lift shaft with a very abrupt end, then yes. Could've been worse, though.'

'Gordon told me you were a nice fellow. I'm glad you're all right.'

Dalzell was wringing out his chamois leather into a plastic bucket at his feet. 'Y'need to watch yourself in this place, Mr Ash.'

The investigator wasn't sure whether to take that as a threat or a warning. Dalzell was difficult to read.

'David!'

All three men turned to look back at the castle steps down which Delphine Wyatt was running. 'You have to help me, David,' she said in a rush as she reached Ash.

'What is it?'

'Petra and Peter. They've gone missing.'

'I thought everyone was confined to their rooms till the fuss was over,' said Hamilton, giving her a concerned look.

'Yes, that was the idea,' Delphine replied. 'But you don't know Petra. She's a force of her own.'

'Wait a bit,' Dalzell jumped in, anxiety also in his tone. 'I saw a young couple headed into the woods earlier. I caught sight of the girl – pretty thing, if she knew how to dress properly. She was with that young guy. Looked alike, the pair of 'em.'

Hamilton cut in then. 'Aren't the woods supposed to be out of bounds for the moment?'

'Yes,' said Delphine, 'until some kind of task force – wardens and guards – has been sent in.'

'Ach, I heard a whole bloody army's going in,' said Dalzell. 'I heard there was some kind of massacre of the park animals. I don't know—'

'Wildcats.'

They all turned Ash's way.

'The wildcats you mentioned yesterday,' said Ash, looking directly at Dalzell. 'They've obviously gone blood mad.'

'Aye, it's in their genes all reet. Should've all been exterminated long ago. Nasty predators, they are.'

Delphine looked up imploringly at Ash. 'David, I've got to go and find the twins. If they get lost in there then God knows what will happen to them.'

'Right,' said Ash, 'what are we waiting for?'

Delphine gave him a wan smile.

'I think you should stay here and let the wardens and guards take care of things, Dr Wyatt,' said Hamilton doubtfully.

'You know I won't do that,' the psychologist told him firmly.

He shrugged and held up his hands as if in surrender.

Dalzell dropped his leather into the bucket. 'I'll go and see what's going on. They should soon be ready to send in a proper force t'deal with those monster cats.'

'I think it's already on its way,' said Ash. 'Jonas McKewin has just been summoned to lead it.'

'How long since you saw the twins, Gordon?' Delphine asked urgently.

''Bout ten, twenty minutes,' Dalzell replied, screwing up his face as if it would help him remember.'

'Twenty minutes? Anything might have happened in that time. Oh God!'

Ash grabbed her arm before she could rush off. 'No need to panic, Delphine. The cats aren't going to attack again so soon after last night's carnage.'

'Don't be too sure,' warned Hamilton. 'There's something mad about the wildcat as a species. They're like foxes – never satisfied until they've killed all the chickens in the coop.'

While Dalzell went scooting up the steps and into the castle, Ash and Delphine hurriedly crossed the gardens to the edge of the forest, where they paused for a few moments, both of them hesitant in front of the shady trees.

Delphine cupped her hands to her mouth. *'Petra! Peter! Can you hear me?'*

They listened, and for the first time that morning, Ash became aware that the woods were entirely silent, as if all the birds and animals within were either hiding or had deserted the woods for their own safety. The stillness was eerie.

Delphine turned to him again, her anxious face looking up at him for reassurance, but Ash could offer no such comfort.

The investigator raised his own hands to his face and called more loudly, *'Petra! Peter! Come out now! This is no game!'*

They waited in silence but heard no sound, human or otherwise, in response.

'Delphine,' he said quietly but firmly, 'I want you to go back to the castle. There's no point in both of us searching for them. I'll bring them to you as soon as I find them.'

'No,' Delphine replied, equally firmly. 'We go in together or I go in alone. That's the end of it.'

'Okay, then,' Ash reluctantly conceded. 'But promise me you won't go dashing off into the trees. Stick to the path and walk slowly. Listen out for any noise, anything at all; it might just lead us to them.'

Her smile was still wan, but he could see she was grateful for his clear thinking, as well as his company. Together, they walked down the wide path into the woods, both looking around warily. The deeper they went, the deeper the shadows created by the forest canopy became. They froze each time they heard a rustling sound, and moved on only when they were sure it was just the stiff breeze coming off the sea causing the leaves and undergrowth to rustle.

Further on, they paused to listen again. The trees around them were closer together now, and the path had dwindled to a narrow track. Ash had no idea how far they had come, but he sensed that they were now too far in for anyone back at the castle to hear them. The trees, missing much of their summer foliage, suddenly seemed sinister, their thick branches twisted and gnarled, thinner branches like crooked fingers beckoning them on.

'Should we call again, David?' Delphine was clinging to his arm, undeniably afraid.

He stole a moment to kiss her cheek and she huddled even closer to him.

'I'm worried we'll attract some unwelcome attention, but I suppose there's little choice.' He kept his voice low. 'Let's shout one more time, but both of us together. If there's no answer, we'll have to try a different area.'

Together, they shouted the twins' names as loudly as they could, keeping it up for over a minute, listening intently when they were done.

After waiting in silence for another minute, they glanced at each other and Ash gave a small nod of his head. Their next shouts were loud enough to wake the dead, though Ash fought to keep such notions at bay.

'*Petra! Peter! Petra! Peter!*'

Loudly though they'd shouted, the silence was louder still.

'Sh-should we split up? We'd cover much more ground.'

Ash looked down at the frightened psychologist. 'Are you kidding?' He smiled at her. 'D'you really imagine I'd leave you all alone in *this* place?'

Delphine tried to hide the relief in her voice. 'I just thought maybe—'

'Don't even think about it. We're sticking together. Haven't you seen those low-grade horror movies? You know what happens to people who search alone: one gets a meat cleaver through the skull, then the other finds his or her head spinning round in the washing machine.'

She gave a tiny, nervous giggle. 'There are no washing machines in these woods.'

'And no heroes, either. We'll stick together.' He hugged her tight and felt little tremors running through her body.

And he thought: *No, never again. I swear by all the saints in*

Heaven, I'll never lose you. Not like Juliet, who drowned when it should have been me. Not like Christina, the ghost. And not like Grace . . .

And now Delphine. What would become of Delphine if he cared for her? No, he didn't just care for her. There was no doubt in his troubled mind that he loved this beautiful, intelligent woman beyond all else.

Sensing his shift in mood she peered anxiously at his face. 'Do you want to go back, David?' she asked, mistaking his sombre expression for unease.

'God, no.' He was sure she would go on searching alone if necessary. Returning to the castle without her was not an option. 'Let's try leaving this main path,' he said, glancing around. 'There are lots of smaller trails, so we might get lucky.'

Delphine was reluctant to leave the original path to venture deeper into the woods, but she knew he was right. She, herself, had never wandered this far into the forest before – it was too dense and too easy to get lost in. She guessed whatever Petra and Peter had in mind, they'd want complete privacy.

Ash and Delphine veered off when the path next forked, taking the narrower branch to the right, proceeding with caution and care, trying to make as little noise as possible. Seen through the leaftops, the sky now had a darker hue, as if the blanket of cloud held plenty of rain which it didn't yet wish to share with the world. It was creepy, the forest being so quiet, nothing stirring, no birds suddenly taking flight, no scuffle of undergrowth to betray a startled animal.

Ash's legs were beginning to feel weary – they'd had plenty of exercise already that morning – but still he traipsed onwards, leading Delphine by the hand. Then she stopped dead and he regarded her in surprise.

'Did you hear that, David?' she whispered, holding on to his hand tightly.

He listened.

'I don't think . . .' he began to say before a noise made him listen more intently.

It sounded like . . . like . . . a giggle. A girl's unwary giggle.

Ash felt Delphine readying herself to call out again and he put a straight finger to her lips.

'Wait.' This time it was he who was whispering. 'Let's see if we hear it again.'

They did. Definitely a girl's unselfconscious, schoolgirlish laugh. Which seemed to change to a long drawn-out sigh.

'Let's get closer,' Ash murmured quietly. 'We don't want to attract any wildcats that might be around.'

'If that is Petra,' Delphine whispered back, 'it won't matter. She'll make enough noise to attract them anyway.'

Ash knew the psychologist was right when a long deep moan came from somewhere ahead. And then a man's cry, and for a moment the investigator thought the twins might be under attack. But no, he reasoned. That wasn't fear in the man's voice, it was ecstasy.

'Come on,' Ash said to Delphine urgently, making no effort to keep silent any more. 'It's the twins. We'd better get to them before anything nasty does.'

They pushed their way through undergrowth and low branches, going only a short distance before they saw a splash of bright colour that definitely was not vegetation. Hurrying their pace, no longer caring about the noise they were making themselves, they finally came to a small clearing.

And there were Petra and Peter.

The girl's short, shimmering skirt was pushed up by her brother's hands clenched around his sister's hips, revealing pale, shapely thighs. The dark boots she wore emphasized the whiteness of her skin, her knees bent slightly to accommodate Peter's thrusting between them as he pressed her back against a tree trunk. Her tiny white panties were puddled around one ankle, dragging in the mud and the dead, golden leaves that littered the forest floor. Her jacket was unbuttoned, as was the blouse beneath it.

Of Peter, Ash and the stunned Delphine could see only his humping back, skinny-legged jeans shoved down to his bent knees, his head pushed into his sister's left shoulder. Petra's face was plainly visible, her mouth open in enraptured bliss, eyes half-closed and glazed between the lids.

When she caught sight of the investigator and psychologist standing at the edge of the clearing, her eyes opened fully in surprise, yet she didn't call out or bring the lovemaking to an embarrassed halt. Instead, she kept on thrusting herself against her lover so that he would sink further into her, bringing her exquisite joy to its natural orgasmic closure. And all the while, until the final, draining spasm, her open eyes were locked on Delphine's.

Already feeling like a voyeur, Ash turned to the psychologist, who was obviously sickened by the brazen display. Ash remained speechless; it was Delphine who screamed at the copulating twins.

'Petra!'

Only then did the girl alert her brother. She emitted another giggle.

Her twin froze, and at least had the dignity to pull away and stand, quickly zipping up his jeans and buckling his belt before turning to stare almost fearfully at the psychologist and her companion. He didn't seem to know quite what to do next, and smiled sheepishly (but not ashamedly, Ash noted).

As the girl was deliberately and slowly pulling up her panties, obviously putting on a show, Ash looked away, curious about the clearing they were in. Pouting because of Ash's apparent lack of interest, Petra did up the buttons of her blouse and jacket, while Delphine took long strides towards the twins without bothering to disguise her disdain, forgetting one of the first lessons of her profession: never let the patient be aware of the psychologist's disgust, no matter how repugnant the client's confessions might be. From the corner of his eye Ash saw Delphine and smiled to himself at the psychologist's stern, schoolmarmish, reprimand.

'Petra, we had an agreement before I brought you here,'

she was saying. 'You promised me you and Peter wouldn't do this any more.'

Intrigued to see what would happen next, Ash turned to watch the trio. Delphine was close to the twins, Petra's face turned away from her. Peter had the good grace to look red-faced at the ground.

'I thought you brought me here to stop me topping myself.' Petra replied crossly, still avoiding the psychologist's steely gaze. The young girl's face was set in a sulky moue.

'We'll have to talk about this later,' Delphine told them both. 'Peter, I'm particularly disappointed in you.'

'Maybe it's our parents you should be disappointed with,' the angry retort came back from the good-looking but petulant youth. He buttoned up his jacket. 'Come on, Petra. She's no right to talk like this to us.'

'But, Peter,' Delphine cried, 'I'm only trying to help you. Both of you.'

'If enjoying yourself is a crime, then the law should be changed,' Petra put in moodily, scowling at Delphine.

'It isn't just that you're committing incest,' the psychologist tried to explain. 'The consequences could be horrendous.'

'What?' Peter sneered scornfully. 'You're scared we'd produce a mutant like the one you're always trying to hide from everybody?'

Delphine was nonplussed for a moment. 'You shouldn't speak of him in that way,' she said after a few beats. 'He's no more a mutant than you or I, but his illness has made him a recluse. And anyway, I'm not going to stand here and talk about another patient with you. He's entitled to his privacy.'

'Then why don't you give us ours?' Petra said quickly and angrily.

'Oh, Petra, you know why. You both know we can't let you do this.' Delphine's voice was soft now, as if she pitied the twins.

Ash decided it was time to step in. 'Look, I don't know if

you're aware of it, but there are dangerous animals roaming these woods. They've already been on the rampage; it's why this area is out of bounds.'

'What kind of animals?' asked Peter, looking worried. He turned to his sister. 'I told you I'd heard wildcats had got into the estate,' he hissed.

'You're right – wildcats,' Ash said. 'And it seems they're killing and maiming anything they come across. So I suggest we all go back to the castle, right now.'

'Cats don't bother me,' Petra said scornfully.

'These would,' Ash told her drily.

Delphine cut in. 'I think it would be safer if we all left together.'

'We don't need you to protect us,' Petra grabbed her brother's hand. 'Come on, Peter, if they want us gone, let's go!'

'*Wait!*' Delphine tried to stop them, but they were off, running with the energy of youth.

Ash knew that, in his present condition, he would never catch them up, but Delphine was in far better shape. He turned to her and held her by the shoulders. 'You go after them, Delphine. There's something here I want to look at.'

She shook her head fiercely. 'There's no way I'm leaving without you. Can't we wait for the guards?'

'It's so hidden away, I have a feeling it's not meant to be found, especially by outsiders. The guards might not be too pleased with me.'

'What is it, David?' Her beauty was not diminished by her frown. He saw she was determined to stay by him no matter what had caught his interest.

'Okay,' he said with a resigned sigh, 'come with me, but remember, try not to make much noise. We don't want to attract the wildcats.'

Taking her hand, he led her across the small clearing to another one, which could just be seen between the trees and undergrowth. She grasped his hand in fear. He wished he could make her see sense, but there was no doubt that he felt better in her company. They crept forward and Ash cleared the undergrowth that was in their way. He was astonished by what they found in the larger clearing, where the grass was cut neatly short and there were plants and colourful flower beds around the yew-bordered perimeter.

Embedded in the grass were a series of foot-wide metal plaques. All were set in tidy rows, equally spaced, in strict symmetry. Rows and rows of them.

Directly across from where they stood was a narrow dirt track, rough, but accessible in a car.

'David,' Delphine whispered, in awe rather than trepidation.

He moved closer, taking her with him.

'I think it's a garden of remembrance,' he told her quietly. 'This is where Comraich brings its dead.'

55

'My guess is that every dead guest of Comraich is cremated, and their ashes laid to rest right here, within the estate,' said Ash.

He watched as Delphine moved to the first row of metal plates and knelt to read one.

'But . . . but look, David . . .' she said, pointing down at it, 'there isn't a name, or even a date.'

He knelt beside her and ran his fingers over the six numerals embossed on the bronze plaque, then glanced at the others close by. 'Seems like they all have a row of six numbers on them.'

'Then perhaps it isn't what you think it is after all.' Delphine was searching a wider field, squinting to sharpen her vision.

Oh, it's what I think it is, all right, thought Ash as he carefully wandered among the memorials, assiduously avoiding treading on any out of respect, even though there was just plain charcoal and ash beneath the metal. Reducing dead bodies to basic chemical compounds, gases and bone fragments by high-temperature vaporization wasn't his idea of a celebratory send-off, but then, he supposed, being shut in a box in your best suit wasn't exactly fun, either.

Delphine had caught up to him. 'I've never seen this kind of thing before,' she told him nervously.

'Well, there's usually a choice when you're cremated. Your ashes can either be planted like these, with a commemorative plaque, or they can be immured in a solid wall, scattered over a rose garden, buried at sea – whatever you like, within reason. I doubt any of these . . .' he waved his arm around to cover the area '. . . had much say in the matter, though.'

The investigator had noticed that the closer he and Delphine got to the rearmost rows, the less worn the metal was, the sharper the inscriptions. These were obviously the latest additions, although the numbers continued to puzzle him.

Then another thought came into his head. Uncannily, Delphine had the same idea.

'The numbers . . .' she said excitedly.

'. . . are codes,' Ash finished for her.

He reached into his coat's deep pocket to pull out a dog-eared notebook and a pen. He began to copy the numbers on the plaques, laying them out as they were in the field.

Delphine chewed her lower lip in thought. 'They must have a file on every person laid to rest here for their own records. It has to be run like a business . . .'

'A business that raises millions every year for Comraich and, of course, for the Inner Court itself. And think of the information and secrets brought here by guests—'

'All those skeletons in all those cupboards—'

'Blackmail,' Ash said. 'Some of those skeletons might even bankrupt major companies. Hell, they could probably bring down governments, if the IC chose. Influence. No wonder the Inner Court is big on that word. *Influence* is their power.'

'So that's why – ' she stopped abruptly, as though she'd shocked herself.

'What, Delphine? What aren't you telling me?'

'David, every guest here is given the "truth drug", sodium pentothal, to make them confess everything they know regarding colleagues and enemies alike.'

Ash was horrified. 'You were aware of that and didn't say anything?' He hadn't meant it to sound like an accusation, but what else could it be?

'I didn't realize, David.'

She stared into his eyes, and the hurt he saw in them made him want to bite off his tongue.

'I mean, I knew what was happening, but when I expressed my doubts I was told it was done as a kind of detoxification of the individual's mind, and that no records were ever kept. As a psychiatrist, Dr Singh was responsible for that. He sometimes gave me information that might help me enable patients to overcome their inner demons, or resolve their anxieties, but that's all.'

Having scribbled a good selection of code numbers, Ash stood and capped his pen, putting both it and the notebook back into his jacket. He faced her, now expressionless.

'David?' she said, as if appealing to him to believe her.

He grinned and pulled her into his arms. 'I'm a pretty good judge of people,' he told her gently. 'Although I have made some mistakes in my time.'

His mind seemed far away. He held her tightly and nuzzled his face into her raven-black curls. 'Not with you, though, Delphine. Everything I feel about you is good.'

She rested her head against his chest and he could feel her relief. But she could feel his heartbeat begin to race as his grip tightened even more. Her body stiffened with apprehension.

Outwardly calm, his voice low and even, he said, 'Delphine, I don't want you to look round or make any sudden moves, but you remember that dirt track we saw . . . ?'

Mystified, she started to turn her head, but his voice was sharp, though still low in tone.

'No,' he said. 'Don't look now, but there's one of those wildcats standing in the middle of the track watching us.'

She did as he asked and kept the side of her face tight against his chest. He felt her tremble and she sucked in a breath.

'What are we going to do?' she asked in an unsteady whisper.

'Well, it's a pretty mangy-looking specimen, about as big as a medium-sized dog, and at the moment it's just curious. Looks as if it's been in one hell of a fight . . . Uh-oh.'

'What?'

'It's been joined by another.'

Delphine stirred her head, lifting it from Ash's chest, but continued to avoid looking behind her. Then she became even more rigid in his arms.

'David,' she whispered, frightened.

He'd already guessed what she was going to tell him.

'There's another three prowling by the bushes.'

Ash risked a look and almost swore when he caught sight of the three predators. Their gingerish hair was matted, patchily caked in dried blood. One was limping heavily. All three were prowling back and forth, sizing up the two humans, assessing the risk to themselves.

Pretty bloody minimal, Ash thought. How did you fight off a pack of blood-crazed creatures that were as large as dogs, especially when you had nothing to defend yourself with? The creatures made no sound, merely observed them.

He looked again at the dirt track and saw with mounting horror that three more cats had joined the pair already there. It was as if they knew they had plenty of time, and were relishing the contact that would soon come. Ash felt that he and Delphine were being treated like trapped mice, and part of the fun was the anticipation of the kill.

Another solitary cat appeared from the undergrowth that ringed the wide burial place, its green, slanted eyes looking directly and wickedly into the investigator's.

This is not good, Ash told himself.

When Delphine spoke, it was difficult to catch her soft, quavering words.

'David, what are we going to do?'

'Maybe they're just curious,' he said, doing his best to sound reassuring.

He felt her shiver.

'They're probably just toying with us,' he quickly added. 'You know, cat-and-mouse stuff.'

'Cats always kill the mouse in the end.'

He could find no answer to that, and he noticed several of the wildcats had crept up to the boundary line of the neat rows of plaques.

'Seems pointless, just standing here waiting,' he coaxed her, 'so how about we walk off slowly, *very* slowly, give 'em nothing to get excited about.'

'Ailurophobia,' she responded.

'Sorry?'

'Fear of cats, that's what it's called. Ailurophobia.'

'That's good to know.' His smile was grim and he guessed this was Delphine's way of coping: imparting pointless knowledge. 'Will you be setting a test later?' He kept his voice light, hoping banter would take some of the fear away – his own as well as hers.

'When I was little, I wanted to be a vet,' she told him, her own voice somewhat quavery. 'I always liked cats then.'

'Tell you what we're going to do.' Ash saw one or two of the mean-looking wildcats had encroached onto the grass, delicately padding between the plaques, leaving the dead undisturbed. 'We're going to walk away very, very slowly, and get back among the trees. Now, they might leave us alone, or they might begin to stalk us. I don't think it'll be a sudden rush – they haven't sized us up yet – and because they're wild animals, they could be more scared of us then we are of them.'

'I don't think that's possible.' Her arm slipped into his as they prepared to move off.

'Of course, there's one other thing I could do.' More and more wildcats were appearing from beneath the undergrowth and between the trees. *Christ*, he thought, *there's a whole army of them!*

Delphine was peering up at him, expecting an answer.

'I could,' he said hesitantly, 'I *could* rush at them, maybe scare 'em off.'

'David!' She was shocked at the idea. 'Don't you *dare!*'

'Don't forget, they're not used to humans. To them we're an unknown quantity. At least it might give you the chance to run in the opposite direction.'

'I won't let you do it. It's stupid and I won't allow it. We'll walk away as you say, and they'll leave us alone.'

He gazed down on her, and even in such a desperate plight, Ash could only feel her guileless inner spirit. But he grew steadily more angry at the thought of the woman he loved being raked and torn by long claws, bitten by ravenous teeth ... He almost ran at the predatory creatures anyway, but Delphine's common sense prevailed. Their only chance was simply to walk away.

'Come on, David,' she pleaded, afraid he might still go through with his plan, 'let's start walking away *together.*' She emphasized the last word.

They both turned from the creeping beasts and, without haste, as though taking an almost leisurely stroll through the memorial plaques, they started walking.

The wildcats watched them leave.

And then, equally leisurely, they began stalking their quarry.

With Delphine clinging to his arm he could feel her tremors growing worse. They had travelled some distance back into the woods, with the sharp-clawed, sharp-toothed bestial felines trailing them languidly, both hunters and hunted equally aware that an attack was coming, the outcome of which was a foregone conclusion.

Ash saw a moving flash of colour in the trees on the left of the path they were on. They had been walking slowly for some minutes by now, and he feared time was running short. He knew the savage climax would come soon. The wildcats were stalking them ever closer, and it was as if he could actually *smell* the tension in the air. Each stiff step seemed hard won; each sudden rustle or snap of a twig might mean the assault had begun.

Yet they held their resolve, forcing themselves not to run, nor even walk faster, keeping their pace steady as if unconcerned about their deadly entourage.

Another flash of orange, to the right this time, and Ash guessed he and Delphine were gradually being outflanked. A trip, a fall – even a sneeze, in the eerily quiet forest – could set the cats off, and the investigator was only too well aware that they had to find some kind of sanctuary soon, or it would be all over. Ash determined that he would protect Delphine with every last ounce of strength in his body, yet there really could be only one outcome for both of them: they would be torn to shreds.

Ash spotted a stout branch lying in the grass beside the rough path and, without breaking step, he stooped and picked it up. He thought he heard a strange snarl from behind him, and then an elongated hiss. The time was coming.

The evil he sensed in Comraich Castle also dwelt in these woods.

'Delphine,' he whispered, although it sounded too loud in the quietness around them. 'The cats will attack any moment now.'

She turned to him, that small movement too swift, an interruption in their evenly paced stride.

Ash winced as he heard a chorus of hissing from both behind and around them.

'Stay cool,' he urged her. 'When they come at us, I want you to run. Run as fast as you can and don't look back.'

Thin, helpless tears trickled down Delphine's cheeks. They both knew their situation was hopeless: there were at least twelve wildcats, more joining them all the time, openly stalking them, starting to divide their forces, some to rush at David, the others to chase after her. All cats had incredible speed, and these were true hunters: they would bring her down in seconds.

'I've told you, David,' she said decisively, 'I won't leave you.'

Although touched by the determination in her voice, he was exasperated. 'You've got to try and get away. It's your only chance.'

The big scabrous beasts were drawing in, arrogantly bold, but still a little wary. One was now creeping along beside Ash, its mangy scarred head low to the ground, shoulder muscles bunched, its haunches high and quivering with power. Its tail twitched from side to side like a silent metronome.

'David, I'm staying with you,' Delphine repeated. 'We'll fight them off together. Who knows? They might not even attack. We may be able to walk straight back to the castle.' They both knew it was a forlorn hope, though Ash couldn't help but admire Delphine's optimism.

He looked sideways at the wildcat that had the nerve to come closest and, hesitating for only a moment, the investigator flicked at the animal with the branch he carried to see whether it would make it back off. He was well aware that such an experimental manoeuvre could also provoke an attack, but the situation was desperate.

In the end, it did neither. The creature hissed and its front paw struck out at the offending stick, although not violently; it was as if the cat merely thought it an irritant, perhaps even a plaything. It padded along, gracefully for such an unkempt specimen, keeping pace with its prey. Then, suddenly, the noises increased.

The pack began to make strange snarling sounds, unearthly wailings and hissing, curious choking sneezes as if clearing their throats of fur-balls, then raising their heads and sniffing the air. Ash wondered whether they could smell his and Delphine's fright.

Ash decided he'd had enough. The animals were going to attack sooner or later and now, as far as he was concerned, he'd prefer that it was sooner. The investigator stopped in his tracks, bringing Delphine to a halt beside him. He released himself from her clutching arm and turned towards the predators, noting that they were now surrounded.

'I'm going to force their offensive, Delphine, only it'll be me attacking them, not the other way round. You never know – they might be surprised enough to run away.' He gave a short humourless laugh at the thought that the cats would be scared of *him*! Holding out the thick branch to its full extent, he slowly waved it round in a wild circle, as if it might intimidate these wild beasts into breaking the circle.

Delphine had been looking around frantically, and suddenly her grip on Ash's arm became even tighter.

'David, I think we can get out of this. Look . . .'

'I'm a bit busy here,' he said, not daring to take his eyes off the wildcat he was facing. He wondered if perhaps she was in the first stages of hysteria.

'Look, there's a wall over there,' she said.

Her steady tone told him she wasn't the hysterical type. He glanced across quickly. 'I suppose if we had something solid at our backs we'd have a better chance of defending ourselves,' he conceded.

'No,' she implored. 'It's a very old walled garden. I often bring Lewis there. There's a summerhouse inside,' she told him, her voice reverting to a whisper. 'It's big and it's strongly built. We might be safe there.'

Ash could have kissed her.

'Right,' he said through gritted teeth. 'I'm going to smash this one's head in first, create some chaos. I want you to make a break for the garden as soon as I do.'

He was again aware of Delphine's reluctance to let him face the wildcats alone. 'This time I mean it, Delphine. It's our only chance,' he told her.

Nodding her head, she squeezed his arm again for reassurance.

Okay, you scrawny bastard, Ash thought, adding impetus to the blow he was aiming at the cat. *Time to meet your Maker, whatever perverse clown it is!*

Yelling loudly, Ash brought the heavy length of wood hard down, trying for the creature's evil (somehow *grinning*) face, but the beast's reflexes were acute and it managed to avoid the full force of the blow. Nevertheless, the end hit the wildcat's shoulder and it squealed as it jumped back a couple of feet in the air.

For a brief moment there was a stillness in the forest, broken only by the injured animal's mewling. Ash pushed the psychologist and she was off, running wildly through the brush and trees towards the wall she'd glimpsed, hoping one of the four entrances was not too far away.

Then, all was confusion as the other cats launched themselves at the crouched investigator. He used the branch to swat them away, their pained screeches deterring others briefly, but they soon gathered around him again. He took the fight to them, which not only surprised the cats as he'd hoped, but caused several to retreat into the undergrowth, while others had to gather their nerve again.

Swinging the rough staff like a baseball bat, and continuing to shout and yell, Ash caught one mid-air, sending it flying against another blood-crazed savage and amazingly, a skirmish broke out between the two. Many of the wildcats – and there were many more than he'd caught sight of following himself and Delphine earlier – were distracted by the fray and some joined in. He felt a searing pain down his left leg where one cat had darted forward and clawed him all the way down to the top of his boot.

He yelled in pain, but managed to kick the animal away. Another jumped and bit into his upper arm. With his free hand, Ash grabbed the fur on its neck, breaking its hold. It was heavy, but adrenaline had given him extra strength. This was primitive combat. He tossed the cat into its brawling fellow felines, whereupon it immediately joined in the fracas.

Ash quickly realized this was his chance. While many of the animals had become involved in the general melee, the few he was left to face seemed to have become more wary of him.

One approached and stood only three feet away from him, its haunches raised, quivering shoulders low to the ground, evil, slanted, yellow eyes looking straight into Ash's. He could feel its venom, its cunning as it prepared to lunge at him.

The investigator struck first. Taking one step forward, he brought the branch down hard between the beast's slanted eyes. He felt rather than heard the crunch of the wildcat's skull splitting, as the reverberation ran up the branch and along his lower arm. The animal dropped instantly, its companions sniffing its corpse, a little more wary of their foe. This two-legged animal was more dangerous than those they had slaughtered and maimed the night before.

The wildcats slowly backed away, but didn't leave. He saw they were slyly regrouping, and that the skirmish among the other wildcats was dying down.

Then he heard Delphine scream.

The investigator looked in the direction she had fled. She'd got further than he'd thought possible, but now she was bent over, a wildcat clinging to her back, tearing her coat with its claws and using its back legs to try and bring her down. As he watched, another cat jumped onto her shoulder and tried to sink its fangs into her neck. Fortunately, her coat's thick collar was protecting her, but it wouldn't be long before they brought her to the ground.

Out of the corner of his eye, he caught sight of a wildcat springing at him. Holding the branch like a baseball bat, he swiped at the creature while it was still in the air. It flew several feet, tumbling and screeching wildly as it landed on the back of another of its cohort.

Ash felt teeth sink into his lower leg, just above his ankle. This time he held the stout branch vertically and plunged it down into the creature's exposed head. It dropped to the ground lifeless with hardly a squeal. Surprised, Ash watched as the other wildcats pounced on their prone companion and bit into its unmoving body, tearing out lumps of flesh to chew on.

This was his chance. With one last strike at an advancing cat, knocking it to the ground, Ash bolted after Delphine, leaping over fallen branches as he ran, barely breaking pace. Most of the wildcats sped after him, spreading out between the trees as they did so in a flanking manoeuvre. It was this that gave him an edge, for their instinctive hunters' ploy made it just a little harder for any of them to get ahead of him. Delphine's screams forced him to run faster, dodging trees and high brush with a skill he never knew he possessed.

It took only seconds to reach Delphine, who was bent double trying to dislodge one wildcat whose claws were now entangled in her hair. He grabbed the animal under its belly and literally tore it off the terrified psychologist, its claws ripping away some of her hair. He tossed the surprised beast at the tall, brick wall close by, stunning it, then turned on the one still hooked into Delphine's back, front and back claws raking through her coat and the thin clothing beneath. This time, Ash struck the animal's arched spine again and again until it could stand the pounding no longer.

Snarling and hissing, the wildcat let go of Delphine and fell to the forest floor. Its spine broken, it dragged itself away on its belly, making small mewling sounds. The semicircle of wildcats waited until their wounded comrade collapsed before pouncing almost as one on the defenceless creature. Easier meat, Ash recognized wryly.

What manner of species were these that they would turn against their own with such brutal, dispassionate savagery? He couldn't help but wonder if all Scottish wildcats were like this, or if this particular pack – an unusual phenomenon in itself – were influenced by the malign forces that perhaps had drawn them to Comraich. With horror, he watched the defenceless creature as it pitifully tried to crawl away from the frenzied mob, while its companions gorged themselves on its belly and hind legs. These were not just hunters, thought Ash, but were scavengers too.

Delphine was now leaning against him, and he could tell

she was hurt, although all tears were gone. He also realized how very close they were to the old stone wall. Walking backwards, taking Delphine with him, and brandishing the tree branch that had served him well as a weapon so far, he whispered to her, never once taking his eyes off the swarming wildcats, 'Have you found a way inside?'

Several wildcats on the fringes of the teeming mass were beginning to take a renewed interest in them. Their strangely bushy tails were risen and twitching stiffly from side to side.

She replied to him softly, her voice less quavery. 'I think we can make it. The doorway in the wall on this side is just a bit further along.' She guided him backwards so that he could keep an eye on their pursuers.

The commotion was dying down and a few of the cats were moving away, obviously content with the meat they'd already consumed. But others were stirring, starting to stalk Ash and Delphine once more.

The investigator's boots crunched on the gravel.

'The path goes all the way round the walls, the entrance is midway.' Delphine was anxiously pulling him along somewhat faster than before.

'Don't panic,' he told her gently. 'Let them stalk us for a while, but if they break, we break too, okay?'

'Okay.'

Ash could tell the wildcats were readying themselves to renew their attack. It was as if he had some kind of psychic link with the creatures. Somehow he knew they finally intended to finish the hunt.

He was ready a second or two before the wildcats were.

'*Run, Delphine!*' he yelled as the animals began to charge. '*Run like hell and don't look back!*'

56

For a brief moment it felt as if he'd entered a portal to paradise with the Devil's own demons at his heels.

Although Ash had no time to ponder the metaphor, the image flashed through his mind nevertheless because the beautifully maintained walled garden was filled with colour, even so late in the season. The contradiction of being chased by snarling, hissing beasts into such a tranquil haven was not lost on him either.

Ash had roared at the cats, challenging them to take him on, pounding the gravelled pathway with the wooden staff to deflect their attention from Delphine. He'd laid some of them out with the makeshift club, but each time he disposed of one, another took its place. Finally, Ash had had no choice but to follow Delphine and hope that she'd managed to reach safety. His arms had grown leaden and the length of wood felt heavier with each strike. Taking one last swat at the horde, he'd run after the psychologist as fast as his tiring legs would allow, the wildcats in close pursuit.

He'd reached the entrance to the walled garden just as the claws of the nearest animal began raking his jeans. Delphine was waiting inside the arched door, holding it open just enough for him to get through. He'd squeezed in, then tried to slam the stout door shut, but the wildcat had managed to get its head into the gap. It screeched in pain, its gaping mouth revealing vicious pointed fangs. Ash turned swiftly and kicked at its head, then used the staff to shove it back out, allowing

Delphine finally to close the green-painted door. There was no bolt, but the sturdy old latch would hold off the creatures for a while.

Now he had time to think.

Ash rested his back against the thick wood and felt the fierce but ineffectual thumps as the wildcats threw themselves at it from the other side. His knees were slightly bent from both exhaustion and relief and Delphine slumped into his embrace. He dropped the bloodied tree branch and held her with both arms, quickly scanning the interior of the walled garden. Stone paths skirted the flower borders, cutting through them in neat symmetrical lines. Although his chest was heaving as he gasped for air, he held Delphine tightly, listening to the yowls of the wildcats as they scratched the wood just inches from his head, frantic to get inside and at their prey. He saw three more entrances to the walled garden, one of which was directly opposite them, and another to his left; both of those had doors that were shut, but to his right at the end was a wider entrance with no door at all.

He groaned aloud.

Delphine pulled away so she could see his face.

'Are you hurt badly, David?' she asked.

'No, no,' he assured her. 'Just scratches, mainly. I groaned because of *that*.' He pointed.

'The main entrance? I hadn't forgotten. That's why I said we'd need to hide in the summerhouse.' She pointed with a shaky finger.

Ash realized that, although his eyes had swept the whole place, he hadn't properly taken in the large yet elegant pavilion that almost dominated the garden. It looked Victorian. A solid sandstone base supported an intricate, white-painted metal frame and glass panels, all rising to a grand sloping roof and geodesic dome. It resembled a huge, elaborate conservatory or greenhouse as much as a summerhouse.

'We're not safe here,' he said to Delphine. 'The cats will soon find that opening.'

She nodded in agreement.

Their faces shot upwards when they heard a hissing sound from above. A wildcat had used a nearby tree to reach the top of the wall and was now glaring down at them, spittle drooling from its jaws. It was quickly joined by several of its companions, though all seemed reluctant to make the leap down from the wall. Ash picked up his makeshift cudgel and brandished it in their direction to let the beasts know what they were in for should they do so.

'Okay,' Ash said, speaking to Delphine without taking his eyes off the menacing cats, 'we're going to walk slowly towards the summerhouse, nice and steady, just like before.'

Ash walked backwards, his club at the ready as Delphine grasped the back of his ripped coat and led him along the path.

The cats remained on top of the wall, watching them.

'We're nearly there, David,' Delphine whispered. Ash noted the tightness in her voice. 'There's a side entrance almost in front of me. We don't have to go all the way round to the front.'

'Great,' he said encouragingly. 'Now, just open the door slowly and—'

From behind him came a gasp. 'Oh God, David, *it's locked.*'

His attention momentarily distracted, Ash failed to see the first wildcat positioned to launch itself from the wall, but he was in time to see it run down the path and leap towards them. In an almost reflexive movement, Ash swung the club using both hands and caught the creature's flank so hard it careered away from them, hit a stanchion of the summerhouse, then dropped to the stone pathway where it squirmed in pain. Ash hoped he had smashed its ribs or spine, but now the others were loping forward – there had to be at least six of them. Several dropped off the wall as they progressed, landing gracefully on the inner path where, without pause, they resumed their fluid chase.

'The main door!' Delphine cried. 'We can get in that way!'

Unless that's locked too, Ash thought.

They fled round the corner of the building, the wildcats

close on their heels. Ash and Delphine reached the main double door and the psychologist desperately pushed down one of its handles, practically crying out with relief as she found it unlocked.

Ash followed her inside, slamming the door shut just as two cats jumped at them. Mercifully, the glass in the door held fast, though a small crack had appeared in the pane. The pack scratched at the glass, hissing and making a strange, guttural growling sound more like dogs.

Ash gripped Delphine's wrist and moved away, eyes on the doors, silently praying they would hold. He led her into the sum- merhouse's interior. It should have been spectacular inside, for there were many species of flowers, plants and shrubs, all displayed in carefully arranged rows, with minor trees and long- leaved ferns in terracotta tubs. The whole place should have been filled with vibrant living colour.

But every single plant was dead and drooping.

Flowers, trees, ornamental shrubbery all hung limply, de- void of colour except for a rotting, uniform grey.

And the smell, which Ash and Delphine hadn't noticed at first in their fear-fuelled escape, was almost suffocating in its pungency. (It proved to Ash how other senses could be muted when adrenaline was racing round the human body, for the smell now that they felt safer was truly overwhelming.)

Delphine's cupped hand went to her mouth and she leaned forward as though she was about to vomit. Ash put the palm of his hand on her back to comfort her, although he was feeling nauseous himself. He'd smelt the stink of the dead before, although it was usually rotting flesh that created the odour. This was equally disgusting, though. The perspiration he'd exuded during the chase was turning into icy droplets. He shivered and Delphine stood straight, now apparently recov- ered, although her lightly tanned skin hadn't altogether lost its pallor.

'Here,' he said to her, pulling the biker's muffler over his head. 'Wear this like a mask. It might take the edge off the smell.'

He helped her put it on. Despite their dire circumstances, he couldn't help but smile as her large deep chocolate eyes looked up at him over the mask. She looked like a beautiful terrorist.

She shivered and hugged her arms. 'Why is it so cold?' she asked, pulling the muffler down again so that she could speak. 'My God, I was in here only yesterday with Lewis and everywhere was vibrant with colour. David, what's happened to the flowers?'

He knew that sometimes malign forces could generate such a ruinous metamorphosis as this by their mere presence, their intrusion and influence on nature catastrophic, but if he told her that, she might just begin to treat him as a patient.

Instead he dug into a deep pocket of his coat and brought out the pair of gloves he'd worn on the beach.

'Here, put these on. They're a bit big for you, but the leather will protect your hands if the cats find a way in. Now,' he said, 'is there anywhere in here we can lock ourselves in, a store room or something like it?' He quickly surveyed their surroundings, assessing any weaknesses. A building constructed mainly of glass wasn't exactly a fortress, although the white-painted iron framework would certainly hold. Several rounded pillars rose to the sloping glass ceiling to help support its weight, and there were seating areas where guests might contemplate the beauty around them, a beauty that had degenerated overnight to a decayed, rancid ghastliness.

Delphine was shaking her head, 'No, there's no store room.'

'Okay. In that case, we need to arm ourselves with something more effective than a lump of wood. Where do the groundsmen keep their tools?'

She looked at him blankly, her fright blocking her thoughts. Then: 'Wait – there *is* a place where gardening equipment is kept.'

'Show me.'

Delphine led him to the rear of the summerhouse. As they walked between two rows of decaying succulents a shadow passed over their heads. Above, they saw a feline shape walking casually across the angled glass.

'They're jumping from the wall onto the roof,' Ash murmured, for he could see that this side of the structure reached to within feet of the enclosing wall.

Another shadow appeared as a second wildcat made the leap.

'I hope that glass is strong,' commented Ash as he hurried Delphine along.

Other cats on the ground continued to throw themselves at the double front door, and as he glanced back the investigator saw that the original crack had grown a good deal longer. Meanwhile, an ever-increasing number were prowling along the incline of the roof.

They hastened through the lanes of corrupted plants and soon reached a five-foot barrier, beyond which Ash could see a neat array of gardening implements. Even better, they all looked unused, as if arranged purely for display. All were highly polished with sharp, stainless-steel cutting edges and sturdy wooden shafts.

Ash quickly made his way round the barrier. It was his turn to shiver at the coldness of the place: sweat that had trickled down his lower back when trying to escape the vicious pack of predators was now like ice water running down his spine.

He briskly inspected the implements that were to become his weapons and found he had a wide choice. There was a sharp-edged hoe, a spade with a wide polished stainless-steel blade, a border fork, a pair of long-handled shears, plus smaller items equally useful in closer combat: a weeding fork, a pruning knife, a small axe and an evil-looking brush hook.

There was a sudden shattering of glass from above and a wildcat dropped through the roof to land a matter of feet away. Ash grabbed the long hoe and rushed the wildcat before it had a chance to fully regain its senses after the fall. He dug the hoe's blade into the animal's exposed neck and its hisses turned to squeals as the sharp edge cut deep. The cat squirmed on the floor, and when it turned onto its back the investigator struck the exposed belly. Abruptly, its squealing stopped, yet the mangy cat still writhed on the glass-littered tiled floor, the hoe's blade embedded in its stomach, blood arcing from the fatal wound.

He hurried back to where Delphine stood behind the screen, and noticed she'd had the good sense to find herself a weapon: a long-handled patio knife, lethal and effective-looking with its shiny curved blade and wooden handle. Even before Ash could get to her there was another crash from behind. He whirled round to see that two wildcats had fallen through the roof, their combined weight too great for the glass to support.

Both had plummeted through and landed among shards of glass, which didn't seem to worry them at all. Only slightly stunned by the drop, the wildcats appraised Ash with mean, evil eyes. With the long-handled hoe still lodged firmly in the first cat's belly, the investigator needed another weapon. He snatched the stainless-steel border fork from its mount, its four sharpened prongs gleaming.

'I may need your help with these two!' he shouted to Delphine, who was crouched on her haunches behind the screen.

She was on her feet instantly, the lengthy patio knife with its curved blade clutched with both hands.

'What shall I do, David?'

He had no time to answer because the two wildcats were streaking towards them, making that curious hissing-barking sound as they came. The first one was dealt with easily, for as it leapt at Ash he merely held the fork before him and allowed the cat to impale itself. But its companion was only a split second behind and it went for the investigator's lower legs. Ash hollered with pain as the animal's deadly teeth pierced just below his knee. With the first cat in its death-throes on the end of the fork, Ash had no weapon. The pain of the jagged teeth and the animal's raking claws was so intense that Ash almost screamed.

Luckily, the wildcat was too concerned with its injured victim to notice the other enemy. Delphine smashed the long, hooked blade down on the beast's spine, the knife piercing so deep that she had difficulty pulling it free again. The blow should have ended the creature's attack on Ash instantly, but this was no ordinary cat: so blood-crazed was the animal, it continued to tear into the investigator. Despite her own horror, she plunged the curved knife down hard again, this time aiming towards the cat's ferociously twitching neck and shoulders, feeling the point of the blade sink in before raking it across the raging creature's furred back.

Ash tottered backwards, his shoulders hitting the display board of gardenware, the dying animal's jaws locked around his leg.

'*Oh, Jesus . . .*' he moaned as the pain hit its peak and threatened to bring him down. He grimaced and tried to prise open the wildcat's immense jaws.

'Oh David, David . . .' Delphine uttered as she knelt and tried to help him.

'I'm okay. Honest, I'm okay.' Ash winced as he worked his fingers into the creature's mouth. 'It feels like a bloody bear trap,' he murmured, and groaned again. The tough material of his jeans had saved him from the worst it, although blood still seeped through the largest of the tears.

Meanwhile, the cat, its life ebbing away, continued to hang limply from him, its bushy striped tail swishing weakly like a lazy sweeper's brush.

Above them, dark four-legged prowlers continued to move over the glass roof, casting shadows like illusory ghosts. Instinctively, the wildcats were searching for another way in, reluctant for the moment to repeat their companions' unintentional descent.

With a great effort, Ash finally managed to pull the wildcat's jaws apart. Relieved, he kicked the now-dead body. Then, with Delphine half supporting him, he glanced back towards the structure's main doors. He could see that the original crack in the lower pane was becoming even bigger, with other fissures splaying from it like lightning forks. The pack was still eager for blood, undeterred by the violent deaths of the three already inside.

'That glass is about to break!' Ash yelled to Delphine, pointing at the door. 'We have to block it with something!'

She looked around desperately. 'The plant tubs! We could push one in front of the glass!'

Delphine was right, thought Ash, but the clay plant holders were filled with earth and he wondered if he and Delphine had the combined strength to slide one across the floor. He limped to the nearest tub and tried to push it. It barely moved an inch.

As quickly as his injured leg would allow, Ash returned to what he now thought of as his weapons store. He selected the small axe and the wicked-looking brush hook. He told Delphine to take a pair of extending shears and a spade that looked as if its pointed blade would be capable of decapitation. Both of her utensils had long handles, so she could keep the cats at bay while he engaged in closer combat.

So armed, they made their way back towards the main entrance. On the way, Ash scooped up a conical plant support, a plastic-coated wire spiral like an open-sided funnel. He had an idea of how he could use it, although it would require some luck.

Their appearance at the entrance doors spurred the wild-cats outside into a fresh frenzy of bloodlust. They threw themselves at the panes of glass indiscriminately, although one burly creature – Ash wondered if it was the leader of the pack – concentrated on the cracked pane, seeming to recognize the weak point, using its oversized head to assault the fractured area again and again.

Suddenly, the glass shattered entirely. Ash just had time to push the conical plant support, broader end first, over the newly created hole. The cat raced straight into the plastic-covered wire, its claws, which were now very much in evidence, flailing through the openings at Ash, who held the wide end firmly in place so that it both covered the broken window and made an effective snare, albeit one that allowed the frenetic cat's razor-sharp claws to reach through and scratch him painfully from time to time.

Other wildcats were trying to worm their way through and Ash knew his makeshift solution wouldn't last for long. Using his knee and one hand to brace the wire cone against the door, he scrabbled around the floor with his free hand, reaching for the chopper. It lay just beyond his grasp, but Delphine saw his intention and picked up the heavy implement, placing the handle in his hand.

Ash raised it high, then brought it down on the beast's unprotected neck as a butcher might chop a leg of lamb. The animal's screech filled the summerhouse with the dreadful sound of its death call.

For a moment, the other wildcats backed away, and blood gushed over Ash's hand and wrist as the mortally wounded animal struck out in its agony. Then it convulsed once more and was still.

Ash staggered to his feet. The other cats, momentarily stunned, watched him with predatory eyes. He glanced over his shoulder at Delphine; her mouth was open in shock, but there was scant time to comfort her, for the creatures threw themselves into action again and several windows crashed inwards. The killing of the larger wildcat had galvanized a new-found strength in the pack. Their furious energy had set them hurtling at the glass building, several ignoring the main doorway, instead shattering their way in further along the structure.

'Get away, Delphine!' Ash shouted at her as even more wildcats fell through the glazed ceiling. 'Get behind the partition!'

She hesitated, reluctant to leave him, but when he yelled 'Go!' as loudly as he could, she started to run back towards the tool display. With the steel shovel she swatted away a cat that was in mid-pounce and it fell to one side, its jaw shattered.

Ash found himself vulnerable on two fronts, the cats taking their time now they knew their prey was trapped. The chopper was still lodged deep in the big cat's head, but he swiftly stooped to pick up the vicious-looking brush hook, its shiny curved blade as deadly as a machete. Sensing movement behind him, he swung round, still crouched, and cut through the underbelly of a pouncing wildcat. Gore splashed the surrounding lifeless grey plants and curled flowers, the smell of spilled blood blending with the decay's own pungent odour.

Ash stamped and hollered roughly, the cat which had outflanked him before cautiously backing away, ready to spring again. The investigator had only one plan as he waved the long hook and made as much noise as possible: to attract the attention of all the wildcats that had found their way inside the pavilion. He didn't know how Delphine could escape the slaughter, the bloodfest that surely must follow, but he knew he had to give her the chance. And if giving her that chance meant his own death, then so be it, for he was not afraid of dying, although he would have preferred a cleaner end. But however death arrived, he would be ready, for he'd seen its face before and remained undaunted.

Something heavy fell against his back, and he felt claws digging into his neck. He spun round, weaving the brush hook to and fro, trying to dislodge the animal. He had a vague vision of Delphine disappearing somewhere at the back of the summerhouse, and he thanked God for that, for all the attention was now on him, the wildcats' instinct telling them that he was the one to deal with first, the greater threat.

Two more cats jumped on him, and although the one on his back was crushed when Ash fell, the gnashing teeth of the others were only inches from his face. It was hopeless, he was growing weaker by the second, his adrenaline drained, his will weakening. All he wanted now was to get it over with, the sooner the better.

431

And then, over their howling and spitting and snarling, came another sound, barely discernible at first amidst the clamour, but growing ever louder.

The wildcats became aware of it too, their attention distracted sufficiently at least for Ash to throw one off and begin to deal with another whose jaws were wrapped around his wrist. And above or amidst the commotion – he couldn't be sure, for his senses were reeling – came the sound of . . . ?

An engine? Ironically, the purring sound of an *engine*!

He managed to get onto his knees and from the corner of his eye he saw Delphine drawing close. The wildcats scattered before her. In her gloved hands she held the long handles of a rotovator, pushing it before her as she made her way towards him.

He could see it was a lightweight machine, for Delphine was able to lift it to mash into the limbs or stomach of any cat that was within range. As she approached him through the milling, now thoroughly panicked animals, anything caught in the rotating blades was instantly torn apart. Paws, legs, even heads and lumps of furred flesh like the clods of earth for which the machine was originally intended sprayed messily in all directions.

She slowed as she neared him, becoming more cautious. Ash helped by pulling the wildcat round to face the rotovator, its jaw still locked on his arm. There was a scream as the sharp tines bit into its hindquarters, followed by an explosion of blood and fur as the crazed animal released its grip on Ash and tried to crawl away from the devastating machine, leaving a thick trail of shiny blood after it.

Ash scrambled to his feet as the wildcats scattered, terrified of the small but deadly machine. He limped to Delphine's side and together – Ash wielding the brush hook and Delphine pressing on with the rotovator, sparks flying each time the blades touched the tiled floor – they moved backwards. The wildcats began to regroup outside the summerhouse, and more

432

shadows appeared on the glass roof, but at least now they had the means to deal with them.

Then the machine began to sputter and cough. It gave one final hiccup, then shuddered to a halt.

'Oh my God,' cried a horrified Delphine, 'There must have been hardly any petrol in its tank.' She looked into Ash's eyes. 'I'm sorry, David. I didn't think . . .'

'Looks as though it's back to plan A, then,' he said with a grim smile, bending to pick up the shiny new spade she'd been using earlier.

'Take this,' he said as calmly as he could, even though the adrenaline was again coursing through his veins. 'Get behind me, back to back. They're still scared, so we'll walk out together and pray they'll stay that way.'

The plan worked until they reached the main entrance. Outside, however, the wildcats, sneezing and spitting, gathered around them, gaining confidence in numbers, although keeping their distance for now. Their haunches were raised, their fur bristling and their heads close to the ground, and Ash realized they were preparing their final attack, ready at last to finish the hunt.

Suddenly, Delphine dropped the shovel, turned and threw herself into Ash's arms.

'It's no use, David,' she wailed in despair. 'We can't fight them all off and we can't run.'

Ash knew she was right. The wildcats had them at their mercy. He squeezed her tightly, ready for the worst.

'I love you, David,' he thought he heard her murmur into his chest.

His free hand went to the back of her head, fingers working their way through the dark curls of her hair. He'd made up his mind. He was not going to allow this beautiful woman to die of a thousand cuts, bites, and slashes. No, he would never let anything like that happen again.

As the skulking wildcats crept nearer, he gripped the long-handled brush hook firmly in his right hand. They were both about to die, but he could at least make sure that, for Delphine, it would be comparatively painless. And then he would fight these beasts until his own death, taking as many as he could with him.

He readied himself to push Delphine away so that he'd have room to slash her throat as hard and as deep as possible; she would be dead before she even realized his intention.

Behind her back, Ash raised the long curved blade.

57

It would be over so quickly. Yet Ash hesitated.

Despite the alternative of allowing Delphine to endure the torture of vicious claws and gnashing fangs, it was almost impossible for him to be her executioner. But he had no choice. He spun her round and the raised blade hovered for a second. The wildcats were already sprinting at them; the leading animal sprang at her and Ash knew it was now or never.

He raised the brush hook to administer the killing blow, but as he did so the beast's body virtually exploded in mid-air, its high-pitched shriek lasting but a moment. Blood and chunks of flesh splattered over Delphine's back as she fell against the investigator, who now clutched her tightly once more, the long blade resting in his hand behind her as he tried to understand what was happening.

Then he recognized the stuttering sound of automatic gunfire as the confused, panic-stricken animals tried to scatter, clawing at each other in their haste to escape. The guns were relentless though, bullets bursting through them, several cats' bodies being tossed into the air by the force. Many tried to flee, yet still were caught in the barrage of gunfire. Others stayed still, paralysed by fear, and were carefully picked off by sniper fire. The luckier ones ran towards the rear of the walled garden, where they quickly dispersed into the avenues of plants.

Ash, clutching Delphine to him, looked up as the source of

the barrage became apparent. Advancing towards them was what seemed like an army of black-and-grey-clad guards in well-drilled units of eight, each group of four pausing to kneel on the ground and blast off a volley of destruction while those behind remained on their feet, raising their Heckler and Koch G36 assault rifles to their shoulders, well clear of the guards kneeling in front, who fired off twenty-five rounds apiece. The rear quartet would then advance and kneel as the others stood behind them. The pattern repeated over again until every visible long-clawed creature lay dead on the ground. A number of the guards walked among the bodies with pistols, dispatching any wounded animals they found twitching on the paths.

Ash pointed at the roof of the summerhouse, where several wildcats still lurked. 'Up there!' he shouted over the general din, but he needn't have worried, for those cats left behind on the glass roof had already been spotted. The marksmen, all of whom were exceedingly well armed, their equipment including handguns, two-way radios, bullet-proof Kevlar rubberized vests, small but tough-looking shields, black Kevlar helmets attached with goggles and a torch fixed on one side, roared as they came, and three or four stopped close to Ash and Delphine and sprayed the glass roof with more bullets. The summerhouse was quickly reduced to a mass of shattered glass and lifeless bodies.

One of the fearsome-looking guards came to a halt beside them. 'Y'look like you've been through hell, laddie,' he said loudly, appraising Ash first and then Delphine. 'I'll have two of my men escort you back to the castle.' He indicated two dark-uniformed figures emerging from the ruined summerhouse.

'No need,' Ash assured him, without quite controlling the shaking in his voice. 'We can get there by ourselves.'

He'd thought he was being helpful, but the Scottish guard snapped, 'Y'll do as I tell you.' He then stalked off, going after his men who were disappearing through the open entrance to the walled garden.

'Well,' Ash said to Delphine, the ghost of a smile on his

scratched face, 'no point in arguing. I only hope those twins of yours made it back.'

'Ach, aye,' said a new voice at his shoulder. 'Y'need nae worry y'selves about those two.'

Ash turned to see the smiling face of the yellow-haired chauffeur, Dalzell. His 'other half', had just arrived too, and both were still in blue overalls.

'Hello again, Gordon, Graham,' said Ash. 'You don't know how good it is to see you two.'

'Dear God, man, y'look as if you've been in the wars,' Hamilton said with genuine sympathy.

'You could say that,' Ash acknowledged.

Delphine spoke up, and the investigator could feel her trembling against him. 'You said Petra and Peter were all right?' she asked Dalzell.

'Oh, aye, they're fine. Came out the woods giggling, the pair o' them. Lord knows what they'd been up to.'

'Thank God, they're safe,' the psychologist breathed.

'They said they'd left you in there,' added Hamilton. 'Said y'were making your own way back.'

'We got distracted,' Ash told him, remembering the bronze plaques. What did the figures on them mean? He felt they were important.

'We were worried that you were mebbe lost in the woods,' said Dalzell, with a more sombre face than usual. 'Or worse. When we heard what we thought was a scream coming from some way off in the woods, we realized it was worse.'

Hamilton continued: 'Gordon ran to the edge of the trees—'

'I didnae go in though. I listened, hoping I could get a rough idea of where the racket was coming from,' Dalzell interrupted.

'—and I rushed in to the foyer where the guards were assembled for their briefing.'

'But it was only when we all were outside that we heard more screams and the smashing of glass, which directed the guards to the old pavilion.'

'Thank God for that,' said Ash. He felt Delphine going limp in his arms and he held on to her. Her pallor had returned, and her long eyelashes fluttered as if she were about to faint. Ash hoped she hadn't realized what he'd intended to do with the brush hook as the wildcats prepared for their final, fatal attack.

And he also wondered whether he would have carried out the deed. He remembered again his eye-gouging tactic on the Serb who had tried to kill him in the lift. Was there something about Comraich and its estate that was inspiring such savagery? Would he have acted so coldly towards Delphine in any other place, even though he thought he was sparing the psychologist an agonizing death?

There was something very dark in Comraich that brought out cruelty in those who stayed there. And what had called to the wildcats? What had brought such evil creatures here from the Highlands?

'Dr Wyatt looks as if she could do with a large brandy,' remarked Hamilton.

'I'll get her back to the castle,' the investigator told him as Delphine began to droop.

But Delphine snapped her eyes open wide and stood gamely upright. 'I'll be okay,' she said. 'I suddenly felt overwhelmed, that's all. I'm all right now.'

'No, you're not,' said Ash firmly. 'Your face has nasty scratches. Look at your arms.'

They all inspected her arms and saw the tears in her clothes.

'We'll escort you, Dr Wyatt,' Dalzell assured her. 'We need to get you to the infirmary and have your injuries looked at. You too, Mr Ash.'

'I can't argue with that, Gordon.' Ash looked round at the two armed guards, who could not help but look sinister in their dark uniforms. 'Though I guess we'll be safe enough with our minders.'

Yet more than just reason told him he shouldn't go back to the castle. His intuition – his sensing – was active again.

58

It was all harsh light and gleaming chrome in the high-tech medical unit of Comraich. Ash and Delphine did not have to walk far to reach the infirmary. They'd walked through the gardens, both still wary, even though they were escorted by armed guards and had the two chauffeurs with them.

Ash and the psychologist were still in a state of shock, and both knew exhaustion would soon set in. One of the guards had radioed ahead that they were bringing in two 'lightly injured' (*Well, that's a matter of opinion*, mused Ash) people, and to their surprise, they found Dr Pritchard himself waiting for them at the top of the steps to Comraich.

'Dear, dear, what a bedraggled sight you make,' said the senior doctor, sympathetically light-hearted.

There were several guests seated in the comfortable armchairs and sofas that furnished the hospital unit's waiting area, some of them, Ash noted, looking particularly well medicated.

Downstairs in the small hallway on the lower ground floor, an anxious-looking Senior Nurse Krantz was waiting by the reception counter. The investigator was ashamed to find he had to stop himself grinning at the large wedge of white gauze taped across her broken nose. He wondered how she'd explained it. There were dark patches under her eyes where bruises were beginning to announce themselves. She glowered briefly at him, but her main concern seemed to be for Delphine.

After the dull grey daylight, the unit's bright fluorescent

lighting hurt his eyes and he noticed Delphine was holding one hand flat across her forehead, as if afflicted with a headache. She still clung to him with the other hand.

'Migraine coming on, Delphine?' said a concerned Dr Pritchard. When she nodded he said, 'We'll get that seen to before we examine those nasty scratches.'

The other patients in the treatment area either moved or sat like zombies, providing Ash with an uncomfortable reminder of his experience in the containment area. There was something special about Comraich today, a feeling of . . . what? Just a feeling, he told himself silently. Maybe he was still traumatized by their narrow escape from the wildcats.

'First thing for you both,' said Pritchard, 'is to get you cleaned up. The showers are down the hall, Mr Ash, and you'll find a robe there to slip into. Your wounds don't look too serious. But one never knows. Have you had a tetanus jab in the past few years?' Ash shook his head. 'No? Then the sooner we give you one, the better. We don't want you coming down with lockjaw, do we? No, most certainly not.'

He stopped to inspect Ash and Delphine again, neither of whom had uttered a word since they'd entered the medical unit.

'Oh, I very nearly forgot,' said Pritchard to Delphine. 'Your migraine. I'll give you something strong, chase the pain away before it gets a grip.'

'It *is* getting worse,' Delphine admitted.

'Nurse Krantz,' said Dr Pritchard, swinging round. 'Will you give our psychologist some ergotamine tablets she can dissolve under the tongue? I don't think we need an aerosol inhaler, because hopefully this will be a one-off. Not quite like using a sledgehammer to crack a nut, but we want to stop the migraine before it worsens.' He passed this last remark on to Delphine, who was frowning, from either pain or anxiety.

Dr Pritchard delicately touched her scratched cheek. 'I'm aware of how you feel about addiction, but I assure you I only want you to use the ergotamine once, twice at most, just to see if it's suitable for your present problem.'

Ash flinched at this. 'You're using her as a guinea pig?'

Dr Pritchard bridled at Ash's censure. 'Not at all, Mr Ash,' he said quickly. 'We've enough patients here to conduct trials from time to time if we so wish.'

Yeah, thought Ash, *but do* they *so wish*?

Krantz had returned with the pills and, still scowling at Ash, she handed one to Delphine. The psychologist slipped it under her tongue. Ash couldn't help noticing how shaky her hand was.

Dr Pritchard had apparently noticed the same. 'Before you shower, I'd like each of you to take a sedative.'

Ash raised his free hand to ward off the doctor's offer. He didn't fancy being medicated by Pritchard, no matter how eminent he might be among his peers. 'Sorry, I've a lot to do this afternoon. I can't afford to be half-asleep.'

'You won't be,' Dr Pritchard insisted. 'I only intend to give you a low dose of clonazepam. Oh, you might feel somewhat tired for an hour or so, but you should rest for a while anyway, after what you've been through. And I'm only asking you to take one, just to relax you a bit. Surely you can't object to that?'

Ash looked at Delphine, who immediately reassured him. 'Dr Pritchard is right, David. We both need something if we're to get through the day.'

'Well, if you're sure,' Ash said doubtfully.

'That's settled, then,' said Pritchard quickly. 'I also want to take a look at the bruising around your neck, Mr Ash, to make sure there's no permanent damage from your unfortunate lift journey last night.'

The investigator thought he could detect weariness in the senior physician's voice, and realized that the past twenty-four hours must have been tough for him, too.

Ash put his fingers to his throat. It did feel sore, he had to admit. But considering the size of the hands that had endeavoured to choke the life out of him, that was hardly surprising.

'Now, a good warm, relaxing shower and then I'll see you individually in my consultation room. All right? Good. I'll see you both a little later.'

Dr Pritchard walked off, an affable man, but obviously a stern professional if needs be, thought Ash. The hospital staff almost stood at attention as he strolled by.

'I'll show you to the showers,' said Krantz brusquely. Her damaged nose made her sound as though she had a bad cold and Ash had to stop himself chuckling.

She glared at Ash as if she knew what he was thinking, then turned on her heels.

Ash and Delphine exchanged a conspiratorial grin, then rose to follow her.

59

Later, lying on the soft-quilted bed in Delphine's room, both of them still wearing spotless white bathrobes, they began to relax. The clonazepam they'd taken, together with the refreshingly warm shower, had induced a wonderful languidness, despite the morning's ordeal.

The cuts, wounds and lacerations they'd suffered when fighting off the wildcats had been cleaned thoroughly with antiseptic, which, Ash had to admit, had stung almost as much as the claws that had caused them. Maybe Senior Nurse Krantz had been a little too . . . enthusiastic. It was understandable, he supposed. Dr Pritchard had asked another nurse to deal with Delphine's treatment and Ash wondered if the senior doctor was aware of their little love triangle, mischievously enjoying the awkwardness of the situation.

After their showers, they'd followed the senior nurse to Pritchard's comfortable and surprisingly unpretentious office, where Ash and Delphine had settled themselves on a cushioned sofa. Curiously, no awards or certificates of achievement decorated the walls. Ash had been forced to reappraise the stylishly attired doctor whose skills were apparent without with the need of framed certificates. He was sure the doctor was genuinely qualified; Kate's research would have uncovered any deceit in that area. Maybe the absence of diplomas had something to do with Comraich's secrecy? His greeting was friendly, although he was strictly the professional physician this time.

He took Dr Wyatt into his examination room, closing the

door behind him. Krantz, left alone with Ash, had decided her services were no longer required. With a sneer that only worsened the effects of her broken nose, she left the office, glaring back at the investigator before shutting the door completely.

She was one to look out for, thought Ash reflectively. With the dark mood he could clearly sense descending upon the castle, he knew anything could happen in the next few hours. The atmosphere, both inside and out, was growing steadily more oppressive. Before long, he sensed, all hell was going to break loose. He felt no remorse for his assault on Krantz, and that was not like him, whatever the circumstances. He'd yesterday also killed a man. Okay, he'd been defending himself, but even so, something had touched him in this place, something malign and savage; something he had no control over.

Dr Pritchard was soon finished with Delphine and wore a benign smile as they returned from his examination room.

'All done,' he announced, 'with no lasting damage. There will be some discomfort for you to endure, Delphine, but the wounds are superficial.' He turned to face the investigator. 'I've given her a foil of Triptans that might help if the ergotamine has little effect; with luck, they will ward off a migraine cluster. If not, we'll try some nerve-block injections. Now, then, it's your turn, Mr Ash.' He indicated the open examination room door. 'After you. I want a good look at those hands and the bruising you took last night.'

The examination was brief but thorough. 'You'll live,' said Pritchard when it was over, grunting his satisfaction. 'I'll give you some painkillers with the sedatives.' He held up a finely manicured hand to block any objection. 'Just some more clonazepam, which will settle your nerves, and some dihydrocodeine, which is a strong painkiller. They might make you drowsy for a while, but that will soon wear off. Dr Wyatt has agreed to them; usually, getting her to take an aspirin is hard to do. But she trusts me, and I hope you will too.'

Now, relaxing on Delphine's bed, they'd finally found a little time for each other.

'Thank you, David,' she said eventually.

'For what?' he asked, running a finger down the long lapel of her bathrobe.

'For saving me from the wildcats.'

'When I could've fed you to them as a diversion, you mean?'

She smiled and he pulled her lapel open a little further, just enough to expose one breast.

'But you're frightened of this place, Comraich, aren't you?' Her expression was serious despite the internal glow she felt just being close to him.

At that moment he was more concerned with her soft, even subtle, curvaceousness. Her body was pleasingly rounded, but not voluptuous – Delphine was too slim and small-boned for that.

Incongruously, a thought occurred to him. 'What will happen to the twins?'

She frowned and looked away from him.

'Why did you ask me that?'

He hesitated before speaking. 'Sorry, but I'm just intrigued. They're too young to stay here for ever.'

She sighed, as if already defeated by the actions of her incorrigible patients. 'Probably chemical castration for Peter,' she answered despondently.

'What?' Ash was shocked. 'Surely there's a better way. A vasectomy, the pill for Petra?'

'That wouldn't stop them having sex, and that's the underlying problem. It isn't simple lust. Both of them are attractive; they could find any number of partners. No, there's a reason they behave as they do, and I intend to try my best to find out what it is. The twins' parents are very wealthy and famous. They could never live with the scandal.'

'What sort of parents are more worried about their own reputation than their children?' Ash said scornfully.

'I can't name names, you know that, but the public outrage would be immense. Comraich is their children's last hope. Both Petra and Peter have attempted suicide when they were separated.'

445

'So, unless you can cure the twins, a more drastic approach will have to be taken? Is that legal?'

'The letter of the law isn't always followed at Comraich. Peter will be told the tablets and injections are to relieve some other condition.'

'I'm sorry, Delphine, but that just can't be right.'

'You don't understand the full power of the Inner Court. But that's why I want to get to the root of the twins' problem before such a drastic step is taken.'

'And if you fail – what then? A lifetime of chemically enforced celibacy in Comraich?'

'God, I hope not! They're too young for that. I'll try to change them by redrawing their moral boundaries. Try to make them forget what's made them feel this way.'

'Brainwash them, you mean?' Ash was aghast.

'It's complicated. Comraich's medical unit has treatments that can bring about precise but benign memory loss. They've discovered that particular proteins can be removed from certain sections of the brain where memories are stored. The Americans, who first introduced the theory, call it "targeted memory erasure". The technique uses drugs to wipe out specific memories permanently. Of course, I've simplified the explanation, but that's the basic principle. Counselling and other methods are used to locate the problematic memories so that the drugs can be used to eradicate them. Although it's a relatively new procedure, the results here have proved positive. If they used that on the twins they would completely forget their time here and perhaps, eventually, even the loss of their birth mother – or at least their devotion to her – which I believe is the root of their problems. But, frankly, I don't want that to happen, David. I want to cure them purely psychologically, no matter how long it takes.'

His attitude softened: he could see she only wanted the best for Petra and Peter, for all her patients. She was the good side of the IC.

'Delphine,' he asked with real concern, 'I realize that we

spoke about it before, but could I ever persuade you to leave Comraich?'

She caught her breath. 'There are reasons I have to stay. For a start, I have a binding contract with Simon Maseby Associates.'

'No such contract would be valid in the eyes of the law. They are doing things here which I'm sure are illegal.'

She smiled thinly. 'Whether the contract is valid or not, if I were to break it, the punishment would be harsh. And I do mean harsh. I'd be treated as some kind of pariah – no, worse: a traitor – by the Inner Court. I'd never work as a psychologist again. Also, I promised my father. I had to. He was dying and wanted me to be under the protection of the Inner Court. He made me promise to stay at Comraich because of the security it would give me.'

She looked so contrite, so close to him on the bed, that he wanted to enfold her in his arms and take her anxiety away. Instead, he said, 'I still can't understand why you would make yourself a prisoner for life to the Inner Court.'

'Oh, but I'm not. I can travel to wherever the mood takes me. I could explore the world with no financial limitations. All Comraich asks of me is that I'll always return, and never speak of the castle or the Inner Court to the outside world.'

He realized now with certainty that, when she'd spoken previously of all the admirable and innovative work the hospital unit was involved in, she'd been partly justifying her actions to herself. The thought made him uneasy.

'David, please, I'm not a prisoner,' she insisted. 'But if I did decide to leave, they'd use that same targeted memory erasure to make me forget I was ever here.'

'That's what you've agreed?' he asked, even more concerned for her. 'Surely such precision can't be possible.'

'You'd be surprised how advanced our medical techniques are.'

'And you'd let them do that to you?' he asked incredulously.

'If necessary, yes. I'd wait until the treatment is more

advanced, even routine, but as I said, it's already been shown to work.'

A single thought occurred to him, but he left it unsaid. Instead he said, 'You mentioned before that you could never leave Lewis.'

She looked down and played with the cloth belt of her bathrobe. 'I'm the only one who really cares for him. And he depends on me for so much. I couldn't leave him here alone.'

'But he has carers, surely?'

'I'm the only one he trusts. From the moment I arrived there was an affinity between us. And, of course, I have other patients who need my help.'

Ash winced as he moved on the bed.

'Are you still in pain, David? I can prescribe a stronger painkiller for you.'

He didn't bother to tell her he'd taken only two of the eight dihydrocodeine tablets that Dr Pritchard had pressed on him, the other six still in the silver-foil pack tucked into his bathrobe pocket. The two tablets had blunted the edge of the stinging, but he would take more only if absolutely necessary.

Delphine raised her hand tenderly to his cheek, studying the scores across his face. 'Poor David,' she said quietly. 'The cuts will soon heal, though, and your bruises will fade with time.' Her gentle touch stopped roving, her fingertips lingering at an old scar on his left cheek. 'How did this happen?'

Maybe the pills had loosened his tongue, for he found himself telling Delphine something that he'd only ever explained to Kate when the wounds had been fresh. Now something made him want to relate the story to Delphine, a woman he'd come to love so swiftly that his emotions were in turmoil.

He told her about Juliet, how his father hadn't been able to save his older sister from drowning and how her ghost had returned to haunt him, blaming him for pushing her into the water. How that had led him to become a parapsychologist in an attempt to prove that there were no such things as ghosts, and how all he'd proved was that spirits of the dead did exist, and that some had evil intent. A woman – another ghost with stronger powers of manifestation – had given him the short scar on his cheek when he'd thought the haunting was over.

Delphine didn't question him, and he wondered whether his confession had been wise. Would she now think he was crazy? Was the compassion in her eyes merely a psychologist's acceptance of a patient's self-delusion?

Nevertheless, he went on to tell her of Edbrook. How he'd been lured to that old manor house eventually to discover its inhabitants were ghosts – ghosts in league with his dead sister who'd joined them to torment him further. And how, despite charlatans who exploited those who truly believed in the realm of the spirits and the paranormal, he had discovered more evidence that the spirits of the dead were real.

Ash decided not to tell Delphine of the ghosts that roamed the village of Sleath in the Chilterns, where he'd lost one he'd come to love through unearthly powers that some might call malign spirits. It was too soon. He needed her to believe in him totally, before he could expect her to believe everything he might say

'There's genuine danger here, Delphine,' he said sombrely, still toying with the lapel of her robe. 'This is why I want to get out of Comraich now. And why I want to take you with me. Lewis as well, if that's what you want.'

She was stunned. 'You know I can't do that. Besides, the entrance is too well guarded.'

'I saw a loading bay on the bank of monitors in Babbage's office,' he said. 'Delivery vehicles must be coming and going all the time. We could probably slip out that way unnoticed.'

She shook her head vehemently. 'The goods entrance is the best-guarded section on the estate, although you'd never know it just on sight. The guards are dressed in normal working overalls, but their weapons are always near to hand. Didn't you notice how many cameras there are? The trades-men's entrance is the most monitored area of all.'

'Then what about the shoreline? We could follow it round until we found safe ground, a coastal village, or somewhere with a telephone.'

'No, David.' She was adamant. 'You were down on the shore this morning. You must have seen how difficult it is to walk along it. The further you go, no matter in which direction, the rocks and pools get worse and eventually you reach cliffs that rise straight from the sea. On top of that, there's a watch-tower at each end of the beach.'

The psychologist gave a tiny, hopeless sigh. 'It's just impossible, David. Don't even think about it.'

He took a new tack, ignoring her pleas. 'Comraich is bad, Delphine. I've never felt so definite about somewhere in my life. I believe the castle is an epicentre for something evil . . .'

'Oh, David!'

'I'm not joking, Delphine; this is real. Sometimes where ley lines cross, occult powers can gather and create all kinds of havoc. You've seen for yourself what's happened here. The poltergeist mayhem in the ground-floor office before I came, the lift suddenly crashing, the bizarre killing of Douglas Hoyle, my God, the maggots and the flies just last night. And all the things that brought me here in the first place.'

He paused to draw breath, and when he spoke again, his voice was low, steady. 'Remember how the jet that brought us here suddenly lost all power, how it was nearly dragged down just as it passed over Comraich? Surely you can see what's happening here? Even the wildcats, drawn south from the Highlands. And,' he finished, 'I'm sure you can feel the oppressive atmosphere outside. It's as if the air itself is filled with a kind of static.' To illustrate the point, he placed a flat hand about an inch above her head; strings of her hair suddenly stood erect as if she'd received an electric shock.

She was silent. He was right. But to leave – even if they could – was impossible.

'If you feel so strongly about it,' she said with such a sad

450

face that Ash already knew he'd lost the argument, 'you should go alone, David. By yourself you might just have a chance.'

Doing his best to remain patient, he said, 'Delphine, weird things are happening at Comraich, and they're going to get weirder. I've never felt so sure about anything in my life. This ... this wickedness is becoming prevalent among the people here. It's like an infection passed by one to another, and then another. Why did that man, Lukovic, try to kill me last night? I didn't know him and he didn't know me. And why would I react with such uncharacteristic violence? Look at what I did to Nurse Krantz. Gradually, we're all becoming infected, Delphine. Soon we'll be unable to trust anyone. D'you want to be here for that?'

He was staring hard into her face, and now she crumpled. 'David,' she pleaded, 'I can't leave Lewis to whatever may happen. Please, you go. Don't worry about me – or Lewis; I'll take care of him – but you must go. You'll have more chance on your own.'

As the tears formed in her eyes, he pulled her to him, and slid his hand into her open robe to feel the arch of her back.

Delphine said, 'Please, David,' and he knew it wasn't a rebuttal; it was the opposite and said in earnest. He could see that she wanted him as much as he wanted her.

After their lovemaking was over, he recalled something Delphine had said that had been nagging at him ever since. If the IC wouldn't let Delphine leave without erasing her memory, then surely they would never allow him to leave either, with all the knowledge he now possessed.

Or had the intention always been that he would never leave Comraich Castle at all?

PART FOUR: THE CURSE

60

She had no idea how long she'd been in this dungeon. She was aware this dim, shadowy room was beneath a castle called Comraich – she'd been told that at some point long ago and it had stayed in her memory, a rare light in a rolling sea of blackness. But most of her memories of growing up, of becoming a woman, were murky and obscure. When she had first bled she had thought she was dying. She was aware she was different from the women, the nurses, who had come over the years to hose her down as she cowered in a corner of her room, her only home, laughing at her shrieks of protest – they never used warm water, just that cold, cold, heart-stopping jet of freezing, germ-killing liquid.

She shivered at the thought, the white powder that had been thrown over her by the handful, being told between angry laughter that it was for her own good, it would 'kill off the lice' that weaved their way through the sparse hair on her head as well as through her matted pubic hair and the thick bushiness of her armpits. Somehow she was always aware when the time was approaching for the forced disinfection, although she did not know how, for time was a meaningless concept to her, and she would busily search her own body for the tiny things that inhabited her, feeling the small creatures, her only companions, grubbing for them, then popping each one into her almost toothless mouth, cracking their tough little bodies with her gums before swallowing. By now, she found them tasty, as well as a diversion during her long, friendless internment.

She knew she was abnormal, both of body and of mind, for she had been cruelly mocked, chided, tormented, by her so-called carers – although never by the doctors in their white coats and skin-brushed clean hands – and she could compare their untarnished and perfectly shaped forms with her own.

She vaguely remembered also so many, oh so many years ago, when time did have some relevance, for she had been taken from her room – a spotlessly clean room furnished with a comfortable bed and chairs – and the doctors and nurses had worked experiments on her body and mind. They'd always seemed disappointed at the end of them, though still rewarding her with something sweet and lovely to eat. Neither the experiments nor the sweet rewards happened any more. After a while – how long, she did not know – she had been taken to a horrible, cold room below the towering castle, and there she'd stayed, ignored and alone from that day on.

Only two events from her past had remained in her poor sick mind. Once, when one of the male nurses had interfered with her body, her cell door closed so that no one would hear her screams of protest. He'd appeared to take strange pleasure in what he did, even though she knew she was ugly and malformed. The man was physically sick afterwards, vomiting onto the stone floor of her cell, his body bent, hands stretched out against a wall to support himself, his broad shoulders heaving, his throat retching. It disturbed her. Finished, he'd dashed from the room and she had never seen him again.

During the following months her belly had become swollen and her menstrual blood had ceased to flow, though she couldn't fathom the reason behind these frightening changes to her body.

On the day the baby was born she was hysterical with fear, but no one came to help her, for it had been a long time since her last cleansing and nobody else had noticed the bump in her belly, lost in the voluminous gown she wore. Through intense pain, unbearable pain, she gave whatever help she could to the little thing that had finally emerged between her legs to lie there, covered in slime, faeces, and blood, stillborn and silent. Exhausted, she had held the tiny, slick body in her arms, not knowing what to do with it. She had passed out, and when she had regained consciousness, it was gone.

The second event she could remember, though only vaguely, was when she had been taken to a room with bare concrete walls and laid in a bath half-filled with a silky kind of water. She recalled floating on the strange fluid while all kinds of things were attached to her: wires to the upper part of her head, tubes pushed into her nostrils and fixed to her arms – glucose to sustain her, they'd said. When the room's light was turned off, she found herself in total darkness, although she could sense she was still being observed. They laughed. 'Don't worry,' they said, 'it will all be over in three months.'

Strange and bizarre thoughts began to enter her mind after the first few weeks of complete sensory deprivation: a symbol, black and white and red, both awesome and iconic, somehow aesthetic, yet instilling cold fear in her heart.

She was not conscious of its meaning, nor what it represented, yet it was vivid to her. As time passed she found herself first in sympathy with it, then empathizing with it and then, finally, understanding it. Other bewildering, hazy and indeterminate emblems drifted in and out of her subconscious, a place in the mind where she now lived. An evil silver depiction of a skull and crossbones; a kind of embellished angled cross, two letters, SS, sharply defined like lightning strikes.

Further messages formed, risen from the subconscious but not yet defined, only sounds of voices shouting a phrase that was difficult to distinguish for some time. Eventually, those indiscernible voices became as one, swelling with power and rectitude. 'Sieg Heil!' they bellowed. 'Sieg Heil! Sieg Heil! Sieg Heil!'

But other presences were beginning to creep in: sinuous shapes that slithered into her worldless darkness – her only province, her universe, her cosmos – into the recklessly engaging void that was now her mind. These creatures of the mind's id – one of the three parts of the psychic apparatus and the unconscious source of powerful psychic energy – played and schemed in her brain, only thinly attached to the corporeal, fusing with her collective memory of bygone eras, of atrocities, attaching themselves to these evocations for purposes of their own.

In this woman's deranged mind they had found the ideal conduit that would help them return to the physical dimension.

61

Cedric Twigg hobbled on through the castle, desperately trying to keep his trembling hands steady by clutching the bulky satchel tight to his chest. He licked off the drool seeping from the corner of his mouth. Word had soon got around about the wildcats roaming the woods, but apparently the problem had been cleared up that very morning. The guests were intrigued, but thanks to upped levels of Lithium freely administered, even last evening's frightful event had dulled in their memories. Besides, a proper authenticated ghost hunter, a parapsychologist no less, was already here and on the case. Time was now short, Twigg realized. But it had taken him months to plan and avail himself of the highly dangerous materials and technical equipment required for his farewell to Comraich Castle and all the people therein. And tonight, with the bigwigs assembled for their gathering, was uncommonly fortuitous.

He knew that, as his condition deteriorated, his masters would soon realize he'd be of no further use to them, and so would find their own means of guaranteeing his future silence. He wondered briefly if they would have chosen the now defunct novice, Eddie Nelson, to execute him, and the thought raised a stiff smile.

Over the past couple of months Twigg had had no trouble acquiring the materials he needed – radio control switches to activate the bombs, timers and initiators, ammonium nitrate fertilizer, diesel fuel and, of course, various parts to make improvised detonators – all of which he bought from contacts in London and other cities. It had been a busy time for him, time that became even more precious when he learned of the date that the important Inner Court hierarchy would be attending Comraich for an extra-curricular summit-meeting.

The penultimate bomb, which was of particular significance to Twigg on a personal level, had been well hidden inside one of the castle's towers and was meant for someone who he truly believed was a monster. With all the excitement last evening, the assassin had found it relatively easy to sneak into the tower. The incendiary device would set alight all of the tower's interior wooden structure, primarily the floors and spiral staircase, making it impossible for the occupant of the highest room to escape. *He – it – would be sent crashing down into the fiery Hell from whence it had come!* Twigg sniggered.

Now virtually every bomb was in place. Only one more little trip to the castle's sub-basement was left. As he proceeded, Senior Nurse Krantz appeared from the other doorway to the special care units. 'Mr Twigg,' she snapped. 'What are you doing in this part of the castle?'

He was pleased to see the plaster and padding across the obviously broken nose, as well as the dark purple and yellow bruising beneath her eyes. He'd never liked her – nor she him.

'Sir Victor asked me to take a look at the lift-shaft damage,' he lied, before adding another lie. 'I used to be an engineer years ago and I think he wants a professional assessment.'

She sneered behind the mask concealing her injured nose. 'You? An engineer?'

He struggled not to giggle, for her voice had that blocked nasal sound, so different from the harsh, crisp quality of her usual tones.

'I've done many things in my time, my dear, so I'd appreciate it if you wouldn't hinder me.' He hoped she hadn't noticed the slurring of some of his words and decided to keep the conversation as brief as possible.

'Where's your pass?' she snapped. 'Nobody goes down to the lowest level unless they've got one from Sir Victor.'

Twigg reached into his raincoat pocket and produced a dark titanium key-lock card. 'You're aware of how busy everybody is today preparing for tonight's meeting, and Sir Victor is no exception. In fact, he's busier than anybody else, so rather than waste time writing me a pass to show to anyone who should get in my way, he issued me with this.' He waved the hard metal card at her as back-up.

As a matter of fact, it really was Haelstrom's key-lock card, which Twigg had slipped into his pocket over a year ago after the big man had carelessly left it lying on the corner of his desk. The funny thing was, Haelstrom had admitted to no one that he'd lost his key-card to the sub-basement, as if he might look a fool for mislaying it. Instead, he'd merely ordered a fresh card to be made without informing anyone as to the reason. Vanity, Twigg supposed. Sir Victor obviously did not want his employees to know he could be stupid enough to lose anything of such importance.

Senior Nurse Krantz continued to study Twigg suspiciously. 'What have you got in that bag?' she demanded, pointing at the satchel he was holding so close to his chest.

The assassin was growing impatient, for he was having difficulty containing the symptoms of his illness. He licked away the drool that was beginning to gather on the side of his mouth and stiffened his neck to stop the slight but constant nodding of his head.

'My tools!' he all but shouted. 'Tools to help me assess the structural problems the crashed lift may have caused!'

Although Twigg was a strange character who had very little verbal contact with lower members of staff, his anger was something new to Krantz; dour and unfriendly though he might be, nobody had heard him raise his voice before, and now it shook her.

It had been a bad morning for her, having had to explain the injury to her face. She wasn't sure if her story of slipping over and hitting a stone wall as she toppled was believed. But she'd caught the smirks passed between junior nurses and the

461

medical team. To add to her ire, Twigg said, 'If you'd like to check with Sir Victor on this busiest of days, I'm sure he'd appreciate your call.' His speech was a little unclear.

It was a bluff, but one that Twigg found usually worked where confusion and nervousness were involved.

Instead of declining the suggestion, Nurse Krantz merely turned on the heels of her white brogues, and stomped back into the initiation and special care unit: many of Comraich's clients were under observation in there, complaining of nausea and stomach pains (not to mention severe mental trauma) after last evening's terrifying incident. Krantz was far too busy to be wasting her time, let alone Sir Victor's.

'Don't be too long,' she growled over her shoulder at Twigg, which was said only to have the last word.

The tall guard, who had been observing this heated exchange, immediately stepped aside so that Twigg could slide his metal card down the coded doorlock slot. Although almost twice the size of the small, bald-headed man, the guard instinctively knew there was something dangerous about him. Maybe it was Twigg's cold, unblinking, protuberant eyes. Or maybe the guard had watched too many Halloween movies.

'Would you like me to accompany you, sir?' asked the guard, holding his chunky stun-gun across his chest. He wasn't happy – he didn't normally go down there where the lunatics were caged (especially since the cell doors had become unreliable, allowing the loonies to roam the long corridor outside their cells) but felt it was his unpleasant duty to make the offer.

'No, I'll . . . I'll be f-fine.'

'Sorry, sir?' The words had been difficult to understand.

'I said I'll be all right on my own,' Twigg snapped back, his irritation forcing his voice to be clearer.

'Very well, sir,' the guard came back with. 'I'll just go with you to the bottom of the stairs to make sure it's clear.'

The guard, Grunwald, entered first and Twigg followed him

down the stairway. If Comraich's upper floors were palatial, then the castle's lowest level was the antithesis. The stone walls smelt, and seeped water, the edges of the steps themselves were worn and bowed. And the muted wailing soon came to their ears as they descended. A rat – a rather large one – scuttled across their path at the bottom, disappearing somewhere into the darkness. All the ceiling lights were protected by mesh ironwork covers, and pools of water gathered in the indents of the concrete flooring.

The guard, who also wore a Glock model 34 sidearm, magazine capacity of seventeen rounds, as well as two flash grenades on the left side of his broad chest, nevertheless felt nervous in this dingy, underground domain that looked as if nothing had changed for centuries apart from having dim ceiling lights and code-lock doors. Even the foul air, musty and oppressive, somehow seemed old. But it was the soft moaning and muffled wailing coming from separate lock-ups that spooked him mostly.

'Right, sir,' he said, brisk with the need to leave this rotten place, 'corridor's clear, but if you need help there's a red alarm button inserted in the wall on the right-hand side. I'll be off then.' With that he took to the stairs once more, two at a time on the way up.

Twigg shuffled down the corridor, clutching his satchel as might Shylock a bag of silver. He ignored the indistinct cries and whispers that came from behind the doors, although he sensed some of the cause of their anguish: it was as if something unbearable but invisible had entered the confines of Comraich Castle. Some of the more impressionable staff had told him they'd seen small black orbs floating around down here. Portents of death, they said. If so, their arrival would not be unexpected by him.

He continued what was becoming an arduous journey along the dank corridor and occasionally felt eyes watching him from the slots in the cell doors. Yet no one tried to attract his attention by tapping on the glass, or calling out to him. He found that strange, given the dire atmosphere here in the very depths of the historic building.

Spotting what he was looking for directly ahead, he attempted to speed up, but his legs refused to obey him. He was also finding it difficult to breathe in the close environment, as though the air were somehow thicker, even cloying. He thought he could detect the faintest aroma of the sea, but it didn't seem to help much. Finally, he found himself at his destination.

The spot was marked by debris, dust and large pieces of rubble, masonry mixed with loosened iron reinforcing rods, dangling cables and other lengths of bent metal rails and chunks of stone. The pile of detritus virtually blocked the corridor and he carefully set the heavy satchel on a clear space before clambering over to the other side. The lift car was destroyed, its walls buckled and twisted, but as he leaned forward and peered upwards, he noticed a large hole had been smashed through one side of the lift, with another hole further up creating a sort of chute from the lift's bowed roof and crooked floor. He had to look away quickly as fine floating particles of dust irritated his bulbous eyeballs. He blinked several times to clear them.

It would take months to clear the blockage and install a new lift. No difference to him. If his plan worked as it should, then ultimately the whole place would be destroyed. Twigg turned away, eager to get on with his job.

Stumbling back over the debris, he reached for the satchel and lifted it cautiously, warily, paying the device he'd carefully assembled the respect and attention that was its due.

The C4 explosive inside the cardboard box had already been primed, its timer already counting down. There would be no need for concealment, for here, among the rubble left by the crashed lift, it would never be noticed in the few hours before its detonation.

Cedric Twigg smirked at his handiwork and the thought of

the consequences that would soon follow. Behind him was an old but strong-looking wooden door. With luck, the blast would rebound from it and direct the explosion to where it would cause the most damage among the castle foundations.

Unnoticed by him another door, the one opposite the lift, had opened while he'd been going about his work. Just a couple of inches. Just enough for a pair of crazed, slitted eyes to follow his progress.

The door quickly closed again and Cedric Twigg stood back to admire his own skill and cunning as he slapped his hands together to rid them of dust.

62

Grim-faced, Ash descended the broad, sweeping staircase, both furious and mystified by what he'd discovered. His equipment, which he'd left in strategic positions around the building, had been destroyed.

He'd kissed Delphine lingeringly before leaving her room to change into fresh clothes. He'd felt aroused once more, even so soon after they'd left her bed, and her smile had been warm and almost mischievous as she'd sent him on his way with an admonition that they should both get back to work. The thrill in her eyes had been still evident, though.

He'd gone to take the morning's readings and found every one of his sensors smashed to pieces. He was both angry and confused. Could any of Haelstrom's people have been responsible? If so, why? What purpose could be achieved by such wanton destruction? Or had the supernatural elements somehow found a channel, a conduit to enter the very depths of this wicked place, entities drawn here by something or someone? He recalled the crazed woman in the castle's lowest dungeon and the floating Stygian orbs in her dank, ill-lit cell. The possibility could not be ignored, yet the people who governed Comraich seemed strangely reluctant to acknowledge the danger they were in, or give him free rein to deal with it. The time had come for Haelstrom to tell him the full truth about the ancient castle. He'd asked Ash to give him a progress report, so this was the perfect opportunity.

The old guard who sat at the bottom of the stairs barely gave the investigator a second glance as he passed.

From behind the reception desk, Veronica looked up in surprise as the investigator strode by and knocked loudly on the manager's office door. She thought he looked tired, and was about to give him her warm smile and ask him how he was today, but on seeing the scowl on his brooding yet decidedly handsome face, decided not to do so. Besides, there was a lot for her to be getting on with. She'd been told to expect the arrival of many important visitors throughout the day for a hastily called conference, preceded by some sort of banquet that Gerrard was arranging.

Ash banged on the door again and Derriman's voice came over the small intercom, sounding both mechanical and tremulous at the same time. 'Yes, who is it?' The investigator guessed that Derriman was also having a bad day.

'It's David Ash,' he responded. 'Here to see Sir Victor.'

'Oh yes, Sir Victor mentioned he'd sent you a note. I think you're a little late.'

That should please the big man, Ash thought to himself and said, 'You'd better let me in, then.'

There was a buzz and the office door swung open an inch. Ash pushed it wide and marched directly towards Haelstrom's closed office door, ignoring Andrew Derriman's outstretched hand as he rose to greet the investigator. He knocked once with the heel of his hand, then barged straight in without waiting for an invitation.

'You're either in serious trouble here, or someone is playing nasty games,' he said before the surprised CEO could utter a word.

Haelstrom, seated behind his large cedarwood desk, looked briefly at his computer screen and then back up at Ash, the long, flat cheeks of his face already reddening before he'd even spoken.

Ash stepped forward, resting the knuckles of his slashed hands on the desk, and looked into the big man's compacted scowl.

'You're late!' Haelstrom growled at the investigator, who remained leaning over the desk.

'Bloody right I am.' Ash sensed that an overbearing man like Haelstrom, despite his contrary periods of politeness, had to be stood up to rather than pandered to. 'I've just been to check out the equipment I'd positioned around the castle. I was going to analyse the results for my report. The trouble was, I had nothing to analyse. Every piece of the equipment was smashed beyond repair.'

He studied Haelstrom's peculiar tight-featured face, staring into the small inset eyes. Haelstrom glared back at him.

'What are you implying?' he demanded, pushing his chair back as if to rise and tackle the angry investigator.

'What I'm *saying* is there is someone – or something – here in the castle who has deliberately destroyed my equipment. Either you've got a human saboteur, or Comraich is in as bad a paranormal situation as I've been warning you.'

Ash stood straight, hands off the desk. 'My advice to you, as before, is to evacuate the building immediately, or deal with these demons yourself. There's nothing I can do! If it's supernatural, it's gone too far and you should have called me in a lot sooner.'

'You know perfectly well we can't ask all our guests to leave Comraich. And besides, tonight there will be a banquet for important members of the Inner Court, followed by a crucial meeting. We can't do without you now, Mr Ash. If you leave, you'll have broken our contract and I will take appropriate action.'

Before Ash could speak, there was a knock on the door behind him. The general manager poked his head through nervously.

Haelstrom's features scrunched together again. 'What is it, Derriman? Can't you see I'm busy?'

'It's the memory stick you wanted,' the thin, stooped man persisted, entering the office and holding up a small flash drive. Ash noticed he still wore the wide sticking plaster across his brow, now somewhat grubby. He imagined the nurses had been kept rather too busy lately to tend to minor injuries such as Andrew Derriman's cut forehead.

'Memory stick?' asked Haelstrom gruffly.

'Yes. You remember? The file on Hoyle? You wanted it completed today.'

Derriman stretched his arm across the desk and the investigator caught sight of the device. A row of numbers was stamped along one side.

Haelstrom turned away and walked across his office to a neat row of grey metal cabinets. Their drawers were long and narrow, Ash noticed, much like safety deposit boxes, except these compartments were only deep enough for a memory stick. Each bore a different letter of the alphabet. Haelstrom unlocked the drawer marked H, deposited the stick and locked it again immediately.

H for Hoyle, thought Ash. He could have cursed out loud as he realized the significance. He had with him the other numerals he'd written down from the isolated clearing in the woods. If he could match the numbers from his notebook to the computer files, he could find out who was in that odd, eerie graveyard – discover some, at least, of Comraich's secrets. His fingers closed around the notebook in his pocket. He could have grinned, but maintained a sober expression as he found Haelstrom staring hard at him from under his bushy eyebrows.

He spoke over Ash's shoulder to his office manager. 'That will be all, Derriman. I assume everything's there.'

'I think you'll find the file includes all the pertinent points, Sir Victor,' Derriman replied meekly, already backing away to the door.

Haelstrom brought him to a halt just before he could escape. 'Mr Ash, here, is accusing somebody of destroying his equipment.'

'I'm—' Ash began, only to be cut off by Haelstrom.

'He's accusing us of vandalism,' the big man interrupted, sitting once more, seemingly enjoying the game. 'Would you know anything about that, Andrew?'

'Of-of c-course not, Sir Victor,' Derriman stammered. 'N-none of our people w-w-would have interfered with Mr Ash's instruments.'

'There you have it, Mr Ash. An honest answer from an honest man, one whose loyalty is never in doubt. After all, what would we gain?'

He leaned his elbows on the desk before him and turned his bellicose face towards the investigator. 'Now then, I only say that because of the exceptionally unusual experiences of the last few weeks, particularly the dining-room incident last night, a plague of biblical proportions. So, to spoil your chances of uncovering the mysteries surrounding Comraich would hardly be in our own interests, wouldn't you say? Precisely. It would be both peculiar and self-destructive on our part. I'm of the opinion that nothing now can be done to expurgate the problem before our conference later this evening. I cannot postpone it, because it would inconvenience too many important people. A problem of timing, you see. There will be twelve members arriving and all will be leaving in the morning, unless a certain decision has not been agreed, in which case the meeting will continue tomorrow until a consensus has been reached.'

He stared hard at the investigator. '*So.*' He underscored the word. 'So what I expect of you, Ash, is to do all you can to *control*,' he emphasized once again, 'these, these . . .' He was lost for a description. 'All right, then, let's call them spirits, who are creating such havoc at Comraich. Do what you can to lessen their power, make use of some kind of liturgical mumbo-jumbo if you wish. Voodoo, exorcism . . .' Haelstrom tailed off, apparently out of ideas. He was virtually imploring Ash now. 'There must be something . . .'

Ash sighed. 'I'm no witch doctor,' he said caustically. He disliked Sir Victor Haelstrom intensely, but he'd never let antipathy impair an investigation. Nor did he like to fail a client, however obnoxious. He felt his own professionalism was at stake.

'Look, there's hardly anything I can do to stop what's happening. I thought my job was either to find the cause – be it that ghosts were haunting Comraich, or something else. With most of my instruments ruined, I can't give you an answer either way. I've advised abandoning the castle until it's left in peace . . .' He held up a hand to ward off the big man's protests. 'And I understand that's impossible. But it might just be that the unearthly influences have used up their power with last night's attack. To conjure up such a potent manifestation as the maggots and flies would have taken up so much energy on their part – we can hope it has depleted their strength.'

Haelstrom appeared to see that as a welcome sign. His face lit up expectantly.

'Wait, wait,' the investigator cautioned him. 'I said *may have*. We just don't know yet how strong these forces are. I believe they're being channelled into our world by someone or something, here.' He did not add that the something might be the very fabric of the castle itself, the evil that had existed here through the centuries. The killings, the tortures, the outrages, even the wicked plotting of the cruel minds that had dwelt here – dark deeds and bloody savagery that might still resonate to this day. Although Haelstrom's scepticism had vanished, he might have baulked at that possibility.

'This is what I suggest we do,' Ash said, and he could see

he had the big man's full attention now. He would go along with any idea the investigator proposed as long as it didn't require the evacuation of the castle.

'Yes?' Haelstrom prompted, eager to clutch at any straw.

'Well, it would seem likely that there are malign spirits here that actually seek to do Comraich and its tenants harm – whether or not it was they who ruined my equipment. That being the case, we can only fight against these entities in a physical way.'

'So, your proposal?' he said impatiently.

'We keep the guests tranquillized, maybe even comatose.'

The big man nodded once, but said nothing more.

'Then we use your guards, position them all over the castle, secure the building. Even spirits can be intimidated by the living.' Ash shrugged, as if finished.

'That's it? Use our own guards to fight off these unearthly beings?'

'That's what I'm saying,' Ash replied.

'It's not much of a strategy, is it?'

'It's all we've got.'

Haelstrom looked around the investigator as if surprised. 'Derriman . . . you're still here?'

'Y-yes, Sir Victor.'

Ash turned to look at Comraich's general manager; he'd also forgotten the tall but timorous man was still in the room.

'Have you anything to add?' Haelstrom asked impatiently.

'Well, well no, not exactly,' came the reply. 'But, but I did wonder about something Mr Ash has told us.'

Ash raised his eyebrows in surprise. Perhaps Derriman was not altogether timid, for his last words were bolder than usual.

'Then speak up, man,' growled Haelstrom, his features screwed into a fearsome frown.

'I seem to recall that Mr Ash mentioned that these wraiths, if that's the right word, were being "channelled" through someone or something already here at Comraich. Is that correct, Mr Ash?'

'Yes. Like a conduit, a paranormal channel. Or the corruption may have already been entrenched through generations of inhumane practices that have taken place here throughout history.'

'But still brought forward by this mysterious someone or something.' Derriman was becoming more confident as he spoke.

'That's right,' Ash agreed.

'And you think it's being drawn from below.'

'Get to the point, man,' snapped Haelstrom.

Nervous again, Derriman looked past Ash at his boss. 'Sir Victor, the people in the . . . the cells in the sub-basement? The containment area?'

'What about them?'

Derriman gave several quick, nervous nods of his head. 'The woman in the last cell?'

'I've seen her.' Ash swung round to face Haelstrom again. 'The one whose cell is filled with graffiti drawn in excrement and blood.' He drew in a breath. 'Who is she?' He wheeled round again, knowing he'd receive no honest reply from Haelstrom. 'Who is she, Andrew?'

Comraich's general manager began to stammer again, this time his words incoherent, all the while peering past Ash at his boss, who remained behind his desk, his odd features still bundled into a taut frown.

'What is he trying to say, Sir Victor?' Ash said determinedly. 'Just who is this woman? When did she come here and who pays for her keep, such as it is?'

Haelstrom ignored the rebuke, yet suddenly seemed resigned, his shoulders actually sagging so that, unexpectedly, he looked smaller to Ash.

'She came to Comraich when she was just a baby, a few months after the war with Germany had begun. She was still in arms, I don't know how old exactly. God, it was long before I came here. I wasn't even born. I don't know the whole story.'

'I think you do,' Ash pushed quietly. Derriman had closed the door again and was hovering in the background.

Haelstrom peered up at Ash, some of the harshness return-ing. 'Client confidentiality, Mr Ash. Client confidentiality,' he intoned again.

'You need my help? I need more information.'

The big man sighed in resignation. 'All right, then, take a seat and listen closely. There isn't much I can tell you from my own knowledge, just an archive report I've read.'

Ash pulled a chair nearer to the desk and said nothing more that might cause the big man to close down.

'She has remained at Comraich since the day she was secretly brought here. In all her lifetime she has never left, not even for a day.'

'What's her name?' The question was put bluntly but softly.

'That I cannot divulge under any circumstances.'

'Was she always insane?'

'Mr Ash, she was abnormal from birth. Now they would call it Down's syndrome.'

'Down's syndrome children are generally happy individu-als,' said Ash.

'She wasn't. She always liked to be solitary, threw tantrums when she was approached unless it was someone bringing her food.'

'Has she always been locked away?'

'I'm not sure. Certainly since before I arrived here. But her confinement is as much for her own protection as anything else.'

This time Derriman spoke up. 'The archive report said she was never expected to live more than five years. It was a great surprise that she passed twenty, but somehow she has now lived more than seventy years.'

'Christ, she looks a hundred!' exclaimed Ash.

Ash was flustered. *What kind of parents would have allowed her to live her whole life like this?* 'She had a nanny?' he asked. 'A wet nurse; someone to be with her, play with her, comfort her?'

Haelstrom cleared his throat gruffly. 'Over the years, she's had several companions. But in my experience she has always been difficult to deal with and most of the time wanted nothing more than to be on her own.'

'Surely she hasn't always been alone in that cell, three floors below ground level?' protested Ash, aghast.

'She was placed there after she went completely insane. By then, it was actually dangerous to go near her. She posed a threat to the other guests.'

Derriman piped up again. 'Doctors here did try to help her, and she was visited by people in authority for some time following her arrival.'

'So at what age did she become totally insane?'

'Fifteen years.'

'Fifteen years of age?' Ash was incredulous and infuriated.

'As I said,' answered Derriman, 'the doctors at Comraich did try to help with her symptoms. Eventually though, they had to calm her with drugs. They also tried some experimental treatment.'

It was as if his blood had frozen. He felt numb. 'What kind of treatment?'

'Mainly sensory deprivation. It seems rather barbaric now, like electro-convulsive therapy, but it was thought to be a promising avenue at the time. She was left alone in a pitch-black room and placed in a shallow bath of saline water. But then she went into a deep coma from which she could not be roused.'

'Surely she wasn't left in that dark room?'

'The experiment lasted for three months, I believe. At the end of it she was taken to one of the smaller hospital rooms. Still she could not be woken, although the brain was functioning, so some kind of mental activity was going on. She dreamt, David. She dreamt all the time. The doctors could see the constant movement of her pupils under her closed eyelids. The coma lasted for three years. When she finally awoke she was still quite insane and soon there was no alternative but to put her in the containment area, where she has remained ever since, a danger to herself and others who tried to help.'

Derriman looked across at Haelstrom questioningly. 'Shall I say about . . . ?'

The big man glowered from behind his desk. Finally, he said, 'I suppose it can do no more harm, and yes, it will put Ash fully in the picture regarding the woman's insanity as well as explaining our . . . well, our revulsion of her. Tell him.'

Ash turned to Derriman, who wore a look of both sadness and discomfort. The investigator, intrigued, waited for him to begin.

After several moments of thought, the slightly stooped man began to speak. 'When she was in her late teens, she had a child. Nobody knows who the father was; perhaps another patient or a perverted guard.'

Derriman, obviously a sensitive soul despite his status in this strange and questionable establishment, gave a spasm-like shiver. While he waited for the man to continue, Ash noticed Haelstrom staring down at his desktop, a look of disgust drawing his pinched features even tighter.

Derriman took in a long breath. 'Nobody even noticed her pregnancy beneath the shapeless gown she wore. It would seem that she gave birth entirely on her own in the dungeon.'

At last Derriman had finally admitted that the sub-basement was a dungeon rather than a euphemistically named 'containment area'. The investigator did not look, but he imagined Haelstrom was cringing behind his desk.

'Don't stop there, Andrew,' Ash urged. 'What happened to the baby?'

The manager straightened his shoulders as if bracing himself to continue the shaming story.

'We think it was stillborn. She was found in her cell later when food was brought to her. Apparently she'd bitten through the umbilical cord to separate the baby boy from her own body. It looks as though she liked the taste, and went on to eat the child's placenta. But that isn't the worst of it. When they were found, great bites had been torn from the infant's legs and abdomen and she had just started to devour an arm.'

Ash almost gagged, but fought back the rising nausea.

Sir Victor Haelstrom took up the story. 'As Derriman has indicated, the child was a boy, probably born prematurely and certainly not fully developed. Officially, it was born without eyes, just empty sockets in its skull, although a confidential report on the matter suggested that the deranged girl had sucked out the eyes herself.'

Ash was reminded abruptly of the fight with the Serbian and his own vicious act of self-defence. He shuddered at the thought.

Haelstrom finished. 'The poor wretch,' he said, and Ash was not sure if he referred to the child or the young girl who had given birth to it. Had she even understood what was happening?

It was Derriman who resumed quickly, as if to complete the telling of the squalid episode without delay. 'I'm afraid after that, from what we can gather, she was almost entirely neglected. Nobody wanted to go near her, you see; for example rather than being bathed, she was hosed down with water.'

'Good God,' Ash rasped in a low voice.

'She receives no treatment now. An annual report on her is sent to the Ministry of Defence – I've no idea why – but apart from that, she might as well not exist.'

He shrugged his shoulders and raised his hands, palms outwards as if that were the conclusion of the old woman's history.

Ash was numbed. 'What . . .' he began. 'What about her parents? She must at least have legal guardians?'

He caught the look of alarm that passed between Haelstrom and Derriman. It was Haelstrom who spoke. 'That's no concern of yours.' The big man was becoming ever more irritated with Ash's interrogative manner, but he wasn't giving up just yet.

'But there must be something in her background, her heritage. Her bloody genes, for God's sake!'

Haelstrom rose to his feet, his big frame looming over the desk. 'That's enough! Your job, Ash, is to sort out these hauntings at Comraich, nothing more. I suggest you get back to work.'

Ash was not one to be intimidated. 'When I was in her cell yesterday, I saw Nazi insignia – swastikas – on the wall. How do you explain that?' he persisted.

'Enough!' Haelstrom roared. 'Derriman, please see Mr Ash out.'

Ash shrugged off the tentative hand that pulled at his elbow.

'Don't you understand?' he yelled back at Haelstrom. 'Those black orbs floating around her. The years she spent in a coma, followed by more isolation, have somehow enabled her to psychically draw terrible elements back to Comraich, elements I believe have visited, even manifested themselves in the castle years, maybe centuries ago. Derriman's right! The woman is the source of your problems. Her warped mind has summoned them back again, her insane mental energy their conduit. During those decades of neglect they've been gathering strength and they are now ready to strike.'

He shook his head in exasperation. 'Don't you see? Douglas Hoyle. His suite was directly above her cell. He suffered the full force of the spiritual corruption that had lain dormant for so long in Comraich Castle.'

'Then what are you suggesting, man?' Haelstrom stormed back at him.

'That it's already too late.' Ash's voice had dropped in tone.

Haelstrom stared back and, for the first time, Ash saw true panic in those small shadowed eyes.

63

Placid Pat was in his usual seat at the bottom of the grand, curved staircase, his eyes closed, head nodding, arms folded across his chest as if he were sleeping. But he wasn't; he was deep in thought. For behind Pat's friendly and helpful exterior was an Irishman of deep sorrow and humbled soul.

He made not a sound as he rested there, nor did there seem to be much movement, apart from the gentle rise and fall of his chest, and occasional change of position, perhaps a shifting of a foot. Remorse and guilt had lived with him for many years, refusing to leave. Pat knew it would ever be so, right up until the hour of his death. After that? How would his spirit deal with eternal damnation?

'O'Connor.'

Pat started at the sharp manner with which his surname was uttered. Many years ago, Father Patrick O'Connor would have been spoken to gently, with veneration even. But then, that was many years ago, when he was priest of a small town but a few miles from Sligo. He lifted his head and his eyes sprang open, his body immediately at attention even if he did not stand up, for he'd recognized the voice.

His chief, Kevin Babbage, Comraich's head of security, was striding towards him through the lobby, tough boots clattering on the marble floor. Babbage had a rough way about him, and a rough temper to go with it. Pat was not afraid of him in the least, although he was sure to remain respectful because he was, after all, his boss.

The stocky security chief came to a halt directly in front of the old guard.

'Sleeping on the job again?' Babbage said it more in resignation than anger.

'Ah no, Mr Babbage,' Placid Pat replied with due regard. His Irish accent was still noticeable, even after all these years away from his mother country, a country to which he could never return. 'Just resting my eyes and my brain a little. Sure, yer know well I'm always alert even if'n I don't look it.'

Babbage didn't dislike the old man – in fact, shrewdly, he thought there was more to O'Connor than he let on.

'I need you to be especially attentive, Pat. There'll be a lot going on today and tonight and I want you to be on your toes.'

'More than what went on in the woods this morning? The wildcats and such?'

'No, nothing to do with that, but we're expecting some very important visitors this afternoon and this evening. Everything has to be in order.'

'With the drama last night, Mr Babbage? And you expect everything to be *normal*?'

'I know, I know. There's been some weird goings-on.'

Jaysus, you got that right, thought Pat, slowly nodding his head.

'I want you to report anything unusual you see happening. Anything at all and right away. Use your radio, don't try to come and find me. Okay?'

'Sure, I'll do that all right. Incidentally, I noticed the quare feller actin' strange-like earlier. He was headed for the medical unit, but there was something funny about the way he walked, y'know?'

'I take it you mean our Mr Twigg?'

'Aye, that's the one. There was somethin' odd about his manner. Also, he was carryin' a big heavy bag to his chest, and when he returned sometime later, I could see the bag was empty by the way he was just swingin' it in one hand.'

'Yes, a few people have mentioned he's not quite himself

lately. But I don't think it's anything to worry about. He was probably just taking something down to forensics for analysis.'

Like somebody's head, Pat considered quietly to himself, and only partly in jest. Though he'd said nothing, Pat had guessed Twigg's deadly function long since. He knew the type. He hadn't been given that cottage in the woods for nothing, either.

'Look, we've got more to worry about today than Cedric Twigg,' Babbage insisted. He raised his thick wrist, which had strands of black hair peeping from his shirt cuff, looked at his wristwatch and cursed. 'Half four. Most of the damn day gone.'

In the distance, they heard the familiar sound of rotor blades. 'First guests arriving,' he said, then swore again. 'I need you to be on the alert when they come through the lobby, Pat. I mean I want you on your feet, just till they pass by. Soon as they've checked in, you can rest easy again. Try to stay awake, though, will you?'

'Right, y'are, Mr Babbage. No worries here.'

The security chief turned to go in the direction of the huge control office, where the landing helicopter would be shown on the monitor screens.

'By the way, Mr Babbage, sir . . .'

Babbage stopped, looked round at the old white-haired guard, irritation plain on his face.

'What now, Pat? I've got a lot to do.'

'Well . . . it was just that I wondered if you'd noticed anything about the light this afternoon?'

Babbage frowned. 'O'Connor, you think I've got nothing better to do . . .'

Pat ignored the rebuke. 'Look, see. Don't you think it's kind of yellow?'

Babbage looked about him, up towards the lobby's high windows, then down towards the half-open, oakwood front doors. There was a funny colour coming through them, he thought, but what the hell did that matter?

'It isn't unnatural, not this late in the afternoon,' he said testily.

'Not in October, sir. I've been outside, looked at the sky. It's as though a mist was blowin' in from the sea.'

'Then that's it. A mist from the sea.'

'But there's no wind. Not even a breeze, y'know? It's giving me a creepy feeling today.'

Babbage gave a short laugh. 'You're dreaming, man. Fussing over nothing.'

Pat sighed resignedly. 'Still, there's a strange atmosphere about the place.'

'For fuck's sake, Pat. I've got enough on my plate. Now just get on with your duty and don't let me catch you falling asleep again.'

Patrick was about to tell Babbage he'd not been sleeping before, but thinking. Thinking lots of strange things.

It was too late anyway: the security chief was already marching off.

The latest visitors to Comraich had been received by Sir Victor and Mr Derriman and taken to their suites. Pat wondered how many more were due to arrive. Four had been flown in by helicopter earlier in the day, then a further three had been driven in from Prestwick Airport; another, who had been unable to take the private jet, was making his own way. Four more were expected, and these would be flown in by the larger, grander helicopter, from London's Arms Fair directly to Comraich Castle in the early evening. Apparently, individual business commitments had delayed all four, otherwise the whole group of conference attendees would have already been here.

Together with Lord Edgar Shawcroft-Draker and Sir Victor Haelstrom, they would be gathered for the important meeting, perhaps with Andrew Derriman in attendance but only to answer any question relevant to his position. Pat knew from experience that no minutes of the meeting would be taken, that everything said, planned, and agreed upon would be kept entirely secret, nothing would go on file or be recorded. Only a majority consensus would be counted.

Pat knew of this because beneath his tranquil manner lay a keen and inquisitive mind. As Father O'Connor, he'd been a strict but kindly priest, easy on those who confessed grave sins, yet rigorous in upholding the laws of the Church. Perhaps some thought him too unerring in his duty to God, but in those days the local priests ruled their parishes and generally their influence was stronger than the rule of law. Father O'Connor was a handsome young man and that, with his kindly but authoritative manner, attracted more than one young girl and even some parishioners' wives. Many would have bedded him, then begged God's forgiveness afterwards. He was only too aware of his appeal, understanding their temptation. His own temptation was immense, for several of the girls had that dark-haired Irish beauty about them, with their high cheekbones and their green almond-shaped eyes and their firm jaws that were extremely pleasing to the eye.

But Father Pat also believed in his God and it was a miracle of faith that saw him through, despite his frustrations.

He was also respected by the men who *truly* knew him, for he could be a hard man too. Because he'd yet another enduring belief, and that was for the reunification of Ireland. It wasn't enough to live in the Republic; he desired more than anything else to have his country whole, with no partition between North and South. Among other values, this was the most important taught to him by his dada. His father who had died from a British soldier's bayonet piercing his back.

While he did not hate the Brits, nor the Proddies in the North, he had no conscience about them, so consequently no pity when he shot at them or played his part in blowing them up. Although the Troubles had been lauded as a religious conflict, in his heart he knew religion played only a small part; it was all to do with territory under one nation, and only by ridding the land of Ulster Protestants could that come about.

Those who fought with him knew him to be fearless and fierce. As long as the children were always protected.

In the summer of 1979, Lord Louis Mountbatten was visiting his holiday home in Mullaghmore, a small seaside village between Bundoran in County Donegal and Sligo. Many men of the IRA lived in Sligo, or visited in the holiday season, and the Garda Síochána warned Mountbatten that he was risking his life if he continued to spend time there.

Mountbatten had once held the highest rank in the British military and was mentor to the young Prince Charles, who revered his brave great-uncle. Mountbatten ignored the cautions. And on that fatal summer's morning, he decided to take his thirty-foot wooden boat into the bay for some lobster potting and tuna fishing, oblivious of the fact that Thomas McMahon of the IRA had slipped onto the unguarded boat the night before and attached to it a fifty-pound radio-controlled bomb.

It was decided that Father Pat would be given the honour of triggering the explosion. What Father Pat had not been told was that Mountbatten would be accompanied by an old lady of eighty-three years, and three children: fourteen-year-old twin boys and an Irish youth of fifteen working as a crew member.

The operation went exactly as planned, Father Pat detonating the bomb at precisely the appointed time. One of the twins was killed outright, the other maimed for life, the elderly baroness dying some time later from horrific wounds. Lord Louis was blown unconscious into the sea, where he drowned.

But it was the Irish youth's death that caused Father Pat the most grief when he learned the full truth of what he'd done, and soon, along with that mind-wrenching sadness, came the grieving and guilt for his actions on that fine, bright day.

Thomas McMahon was arrested as he tried to slip back across the border, but although convicted for murder, McMahon never gave away the names of his fellow conspirators.

Eventually, Father Pat had had a complete mental breakdown. Guilt had led the priest to the very brink of madness, as he was faced with the evil inside his own soul. It took him on the path to Hell, then abandoned him, leaving him to find his own way back.

Why the shame should have governed his mood and his actions then, he wasn't sure, for in the past he'd assisted the terrorist organization in all kinds of atrocities. But those killings had never involved children, especially Irish children. Thoughts of the lad's horrendous death tormented him during sleep and in his waking hours. He even grieved now for Mountbatten, an old man of seventy-nine, out for a pleasant day's fishing with his family. What glory was there in killing such as these?

Finally, he could endure the guilt no more, and he'd begged an audience with his archbishop, to whom he'd confessed his crimes against a foe he could no longer hate.

The archbishop naturally viewed the matter most gravely, but ordered the priest to keep quiet about his association with the terrorists. He also prescribed repentance, but alone in the privacy of his own house and not in his parish church before his faithful flock. Meanwhile, the archbishop would consult with an authority in the Vatican to determine a course of action. The priest was to maintain his silence until then.

A month later it was settled and the priest was informed of his punishment. Father O'Connor would be exiled to a secret location in Scotland. His parishioners were to be told he'd taken up a post in South America at short notice.

And so it was that Placid Pat, once known as Father Patrick O'Connor, found himself seated at the bottom of the grand, red-carpeted stairway in Comraich Castle some thirty-odd years later. It had become a routine that numbed his soul and quietly suppressed his guilt, while never quite extinguishing it.

Until recently.

Until a weird, oppressive atmosphere had begun to descend upon the castle. Or perhaps that peculiar oppression had *ascended*, risen up from the depths of Hell itself.

Earlier that day, he'd watched a complete unit of guards

being assembled and briefed about the wildcats that had recently plagued the woodlands of Comraich. He'd witnessed the horrific incident with the maggots and the flies in the dining hall.

Then there was Twigg. Something bad about that man, Placid Pat could feel it in his bones.

And earlier, the ghost hunter, David Ash, dashing down the stairs to storm into the office. Then his departure, still grim-faced and his eyes burning with fury.

Yet there was someone else troubling Pat's guilt-stricken mind – two people, in fact – who had troubled him for the past few months. He knew a lot about them, for although Pat was not much of a talker, he was a great listener. He'd witnessed the comings and goings from the perspective of his own personal purgatory in the great hallway lobby. And recently, he'd observed the castle's complex moods worsen. It seemed to him that everyone, guests and staff alike, was becoming more frightened by the day. And he thought he knew why.

64

David Ash too had witnessed the faint yellow hue of the sky
outside the castle, and had felt its oppression.

It might have been a mist drifting in from the sea, except
there was no breeze to carry it inland. This was no sea mist,
either: it was a pollution of the air itself. And somehow, it
lingered inside the castle also, so that the brightest of interior
colours were muted and dulled. The fabric of the curtains and
upholstery glowed less vividly, as did the glorious tapestries
depicting ancient battles and hunting scenes, their colours now
insipid.

Ash was growing more anxious by the moment. Instinct
told him that a calamitous event was building that would
manifest itself a lot sooner than later. If Haelstrom were to pay
no heed to his warning, then so be it, though the investigator
didn't want to be around to witness whatever occurred later.
But he would not leave without Delphine, and there was one
other thing he had to check out first.

He thought about his ruined equipment. Either the spirits
were intent on destroying any evidence of their presence, or
someone, someone *human*, did not want him to succeed in
identifying what it was haunting Comraich.

His job here now seemed futile, perhaps even finished.
He'd warned Haelstrom and Haelstrom had declined to act.
Ash had done all he could. Now he only wished to be as far
away from Comraich as he could get.

Outside, the yellow hue of the sky had deepened further.

Shadows inside the castle were becoming denser and longer, the gloom steadily settling into the ancient building.

He did not want to be here when nightfall came.

He tried Delphine's room first, knocking quietly on the door. When there was no response he knocked more urgently. Finally, he turned the knob and went in.

The room was empty.

With the fuss that had gone on, the sedated guests had all been confined to their rooms, bringing an eerie quietness to the halls and corridors. But that didn't mean that none would require treatment. Perhaps her office would provide a clue.

Ash hurried from the room and set off down the corridor leading to the grand stairway. He shuddered as he passed the ruined lift shaft, two yellow lengths of warning tape criss-crossing the outer door to prevent anyone opening it. Passing only one armed guard, Ash took to the deep-red carpeted stairway, two steps at a time.

At the sound of his muffled footsteps, the old, white-haired guard, in his usual position at the bottom of the stairs, peered round and gave the investigator a gently suspicious look.

Ash stopped and asked him abruptly, 'D'you know which is Dr Wyatt's office?'

The old man watched him for a few seconds, his pale eyes seeming to search Ash's face as if in an effort to read his mind. Finally, he raised a thick-fingered hand and pointed down the long lobby area.

'Y'll find it four doors down on the left, sir,' he answered politely.

'Thanks,' said Ash and was off immediately, striding purposefully towards Delphine's consulting room.

This time Ash walked straight in without knocking. He found himself in a small anteroom containing a two-seater sofa opposite an empty reception desk. Through the open door opposite he saw Delphine working at a desk. She looked up in surprise and her face lit up in a smile of welcome.

'David,' she said, beginning to rise from her chair.

Marching into the consulting room, Ash returned the smile with interest, kissing her hard on her lips and pushing her back into her seat.

The consulting room was decorated with easy-on-the-eye watercolour landscapes, the largest of which portrayed a brook running over smooth rocks and widening out into a pleasing stream. (*Of consciousness?* he wondered.) The walls were painted light pastel blue and a tall potted plant stood in one corner, with a vase of late flowers placed on a small coffee table.

She sighed after his lingering kiss. 'What brings you here?' she asked with a puzzled expression. 'I was just finishing some paperwork, then I was going to find you.'

'No secretary today?' he asked.

'All non-essential staff have been asked to stay in their quarters. With all that's happened, many are too frightened to work anyway. Haven't you noticed the terrible feeling of oppression that's descended upon the castle? I suppose it could just be an emotive reaction because of all that's happened here so recently.'

'Happened so far, you mean.'

'Do you think there will be more?' Her eyes were wide and scared as she tilted her head up at him.

'We have to leave, Delphine. After what happened to us this morning, I half expected you to be resting, or being treated in the medical unit.'

'I wasn't badly hurt by the wildcats. You took more punishment than me.'

She'd lifted one of his scratched and scored hands off the desk where it had rested. She tenderly kissed his fingers.

'It's okay. The painkillers haven't quite lost their effect yet.' The soothing creams and anaesthetics they'd used on his injuries, especially the slashes across his face, had in fact mostly worn off now, but he didn't mention that to Delphine. He hoped the scars would fade in time.

'Delphine, I'm serious about leaving. It's darkening already and we should get out before it all starts happening again.'

'What do you mean? The hauntings?'

He nodded. 'I'm sure it's going to peak tonight, and I don't want to be around. And I don't want you to be around, either. You have to come with me.'

Her eyes cast downwards, she said nothing for a while. Raising her head again she said, with just a hint of defiance in her voice, 'We've discussed this. For one,' she said earnestly, 'we could never get out of the grounds. The exits are too well guarded.'

'We'll find a way. Most of the attention will be *inside* the castle tonight.'

'And two,' she continued as though she'd not heard his words. 'I can't leave Lewis. He—'

'Then I'll carry him on my bloody back,' Ash interrupted, frustrated.

'You don't understand, David. Comraich is his home. What would the outside world make of him?'

For that, Ash had no immediate answer. Even if they did make it, poor Lewis would be regarded as a freak. He'd be used as a guinea pig, a phenomenon, something to test, carry out experiments on. And he could never leave wherever they kept him; he could never walk the streets, face the sun, enjoy the cities because everybody would be staring at him. At least here he could walk the grounds, the gardens, the woods.

'I'm sure we'd find somewhere that—'

'No, it's impossible, David.' Delphine had made that sound like the last word on the subject, leaving Ash dismayed and disappointed – yet he understood her refusal.

An idea came to him. 'What if we went to Lord Edward Shawcross-Dexter, whatever his name is, directly? Pleaded with him to let us go?'

'Lord Edgar,' she corrected him. 'Lord Edgar Shawcroft-Draker.'

'He sounds like a man of influence.'

'Oh, he is. But Lord Edgar is also very unwell.'

That gave Ash a moment of pause.

'He's dying,' Delphine added.

'God . . .'

'Mesothelioma. It's a very rare and incurable cancer. Sir Edgar has a massive tumour in his stomach and others in his right lung and neck.'

No wonder the man looked so grey, Ash thought with a shock.

'It's the reason for the conference tonight. It's to elect his successor as head of the Inner Court.'

Ash glanced down, gave a tiny shake of his head. When he looked up again, he said, 'Why didn't you tell me he was dying?'

'Was I supposed to? It's a confidential medical matter, and as a doctor myself, I shouldn't have even mentioned his condition to you.'

'I'm sorry. It really is incurable?'

'I'm afraid so. It's only medication that's holding the disease at bay. Without the drugs, I think he'd be dead by now.'

'How long d'you think he'll last?' Ash genuinely cared, even though he distrusted this powerful man and his clandestine organization.

'Who can tell? It could be three months, it might be tomorrow. That's why the conference can't be put off.'

'But if Shawcroft-Draker is on his last legs . . . I'm sorry . . .' he held up a hand in defence, 'I didn't mean to be so blunt, but if the thought of dying has mellowed him somewhat, then he just might be receptive to our leaving. All three of us – you, me, and Lewis. He might even let us use the jet.'

'Oh, David, for someone so pragmatic, you're being foolishly optimistic.'

'And *I'm* known for my pessimism,' he said wryly but with a genuine smile. 'Look, let's take a chance. If we can get to see

Lord Edgar, and I explain that the situation at Comraich is getting worse, he might listen. After all, that's why I was hired in the first place. My credentials are sound.'

She shook her head despondently. 'I don't know. I think they overestimated what you could do in the first place. Besides, he'll be preparing for tonight's conference.'

'So we know where he'll be at present – in his suite on the fifth. D'you have any idea of who will take over? Haelstrom?'

'I think Sir Victor would prefer to get back into the business of selling arms to foreign buyers. The Inner Court's main clients over the years have been the Emirates and African states. He'd already earned his honorary title and efforts had to be made to ensure he didn't lose it.'

'Efforts by the Inner Court, of course.'

'Of course,' she affirmed. 'He needed to be out of the spotlight for some time, so here he is.'

'Naturally. I bet he hates it.'

'I'm sure he does.'

'So.' He took a long breath. 'Will you agree to my plan?'

'Appealing to Lord Edgar? You're going to do it anyway, aren't you?'

His silence gave her the answer.

'I thought perhaps you could stay with Lewis while I saw Shawcroft-Draker. Then, if he agrees, I'll come and get you. If he doesn't, I'll come and get you anyway and we'll make our way out without his help.'

She seemed resigned to the idea.

'One other thing,' he said.

Delphine closed her eyes for a moment. 'Nothing dangerous, David, please,' she pleaded when she opened them again.

'Is Haelstrom's office empty? You said most staff had been confined to quarters, and I imagine he and Derriman will be welcoming the conference delegates.'

She nodded apprehensively. 'Sir Victor will, certainly. I don't know about Mr Derriman.'

'Can you get me in?'

'Why, David?'

He told her about the memory stick Derriman had brought in, and the six numbers stamped on it.

'I need to get into that cabinet, Delphine. Nobody will know of your involvement, I promise you.' His smile was closed-lipped and wide, with little humour. 'Will your key card get us into the office?'

She nodded slowly.

'Then what are we waiting for?'

'Suppose Sir Victor isn't receiving the delegates? Suppose he's in his office?' said Delphine.

'Tell you what, we'll ask the old boy sitting by the stairway if he knows where Haelstrom and Derriman are. If either is still in the office, we'll forget it.'

He kissed her forehead, and then her lips as a kind of reassurance, and she returned the kiss fully. His senses heightened, it felt as though he were melting into her and he was reluctant to pull away.

Finally, he did so, leaving them both breathless.

Without another word, he led her by the hand through the empty outer office and into the lobby. As she turned to close the door behind them, Ash noticed someone in a smart dark blue overcoat entering through the castle's main doors. The man closed the big door and came marching across the lobby, well-shined shoes clacking against the hard marble floor. He was towing a small, wheeled suitcase behind him. One of the tiny wheels squealed noisily in the silence of the long, almost empty lobby.

The slicked-back black hair, grey at the temples, the expensive silk tie and stiff-collared white shirt. The smug look on his clean-shaven, puffed-out face.

'Oh, no,' Ash groaned. 'That's all I need.'

65

Simon Maseby waved energetically at Ash, a gesture the investigator declined to return.

'Be with you in a moment,' Maseby called out as he reached the reception desk. 'Same old room, I take it, Gerrard?' His voice sounded hollow in the long hallway.

'Yes, sir, the usual one. Aired and ready for you to move straight in.'

'I assume the others have already checked in?'

'Seven so far, sir. The rest will be arriving shortly.'

'Jolly good. And Sir Victor, Mr Derriman – where will I find them? In the office?'

The sallow-faced receptionist gave a polite shake of his head. 'Oh no, sir. They'll be in the reception room with the other new arrivals at the moment.'

'And Lord Edgar?'

'In his suite, preparing for the conference, sir. Dinner will be first on the agenda, after the welcome cocktails.'

'Hmn, looks like I need to catch up,' Maseby said briskly.

'There's no rush, Mr Maseby, sir. Cocktail hour always overruns.'

'Indeed it does,' replied Maseby, giving Gerrard a knowing wink. He then turned his attention in the direction of Ash and Delphine, who were waiting near the centre of the lobby.

He marched straight towards them, one hand already outstretched for Ash to shake, which the investigator reluctantly did, noting the soft clammy feel of the other man's grip;

when he'd first met the dapper consultant, his handshake had been dry and firm. Perhaps he had uncomfortable thoughts on his mind this evening. Maseby immediately turned to Delphine.

'Dr Wyatt. It's a pleasure to meet again. I doubt there's any psychologist as pretty as you in the whole of the kingdom.'

She smiled limply at his patronizing remark, but before she could say anything, he'd turned back to Ash, his manner abruptly altered.

'I hear you're not helping much with these alleged hauntings,' he said, a frown barely furrowing his smooth forehead. Ash wondered if he used Botox.

'That's not quite true,' Ash answered calmly, determined not to let Maseby get under his skin. 'I've established that the hauntings are real. I've advised Sir Victor that he should evacuate the castle.'

'Come, come, that's a bit over the top, isn't it?' the consultant sneered.

Ash shrugged casually, and was pleased to see a spark of annoyance in the other man's sharp little eyes.

'Then I think you should come up and give me a verbal report while I change for cocktails and dinner.'

'Can't do it.'

'I'm sorry?' Maseby bridled. 'What d'you mean, you can't? I insist.'

'You can insist all you like, but right now I'm too busy. Maybe later?' he added, fairly sure that everybody would be 'too busy' later that night, though he wasn't planning to be among them.

'Well . . . well, if that's the best you can do, so be it,' Maseby blustered. 'But you can be sure I shall be reporting your attitude to your superiors.'

'So be it,' Ash said firmly, throwing Maseby's own words back at him.

The smartly dressed consultant turned sharply away from Ash and Delphine and quickly strode to the curved staircase.

He mounted the steps two at a time, not acknowledging the old guard's salute as he passed by.

Placid Pat couldn't have cared less: his mind was on other things.

66

The ex-Reverend Father Patrick O'Connor had been in a sour but reflective mood all day. All the comings and goings: watching a collection of guards being briefed on their mission to clear the woodland of wildcats; the return of the two foolish young people as well as the so-called ghost hunter and the lovely psychologist; the hurrying and scurrying of maids, servants, waiters and cleaners, preparing for tonight's jamboree.

But *Jaysus*, that fat, black despot hiding from an African country he'd brought to its knees, hundreds and thousands starved to death or killed horribly by his own militia, a clutch of war criminals and the so-called businessmen, cheaters and liars, even *God damn them*, rapists! All living in luxury in this haunted grand abode. Oh yes, he knew it was haunted, always had been since he'd arrived more than thirty years ago, but this time haunted *fiercely*, the Divil finding his own spinning their lives out in undeserved luxury for an impossibly high fee. But in the end, the Divil will out. It was a true saying, all right.

On the doorstep earlier, he'd wondered about the yellow sky, a *dirty* yellow sky smeared with sin but now turned to the deep blue that came with nightfall. The moon had become sallow as the hours drew onwards, as if that same yellowness of sky had been drawn into it. And even the smell of the old castle had changed, for a strange acrid pungency wafted through the halls and passageways.

All day he'd brooded, thinking back to when he was a priest, where the flock of his parish in the little town came to him with their problems and to confess their sins. Honest, God-fearing people who laid aside feuds and differences for that blessed morning, the men always wearing their finest suits, the kids with their faces and necks scrubbed clean, women in their nicest frocks, their Sunday best, hardy folk who paid true homage to their maker. Sure an' all, the men might get drunk and rowdy on a weekend night, but when Sunday came along, they still attended service despite groggy heads and lumps and bruises marking their Saturday night's entertainment.

The counselling he gave to humble, husband-beaten wives during the week, explaining to them divorce was a grave sin in the eyes of the Church. But since then he'd had plenty of time to think. Why should women be treated so? Had Christ ever said that leaving a cruel husband was wrong? Were the eyes of the Church the same as the eyes of God?

And then there were the lasses, so happy and filled with life. How many had come to him fallen from grace, pregnant by a lad who'd said he loved them? Was it right that they should not cross the Irish Sea to find an abortionist? Who was he to judge, a sinner himself? A *murderous* sinner. A *grievous* sinner.

And as the long day had slowly passed, as the very air in the castle became ever more tainted with evil, his thoughts turned again to the grievous sin that was being continuously committed by another man of the cloth, one of his own faith: Archbishop Carsely.

He could not exactly know what corruption the deluded man imposed on poor Sister Thimble every day, but it showed in her eyes, the darkness around them evidence of the torture she was undergoing constantly. Pat was sure that sexual depravity was involved. Yet there was no sign of remorse on that pompous cleric, even though his sin was evident in the good sister's expression. It couldn't go on. He would not allow it to go on.

He felt the weight of the gun beneath his zipped-up gilet,

and his plan gathered pace. His frustration in his brethren's failings had increased recently, and it had crossed his mind that other forces might be working on his subconscious, teasing him with lascivious thoughts of what Archbishop Carsely and the nun were up to. They had been growing worse, and now Placid Pat felt broken and confused. But, above all, he was filled with self-righteous fury.

Something had to be done, the artful voices in his head told him. *The false bishop was shaming all Catholics, including himself, who was paying penance for his own sins in this strange purgatory.* Carsely's debauchery demonstrated that there was no contrition in the prelate's heart.

The man must accept his punishment now, on this very day. And it would be administered by the Reverend Father Patrick O'Connell.

His fingers reached to touch the weapon concealed in its shoulder holster.

67

Delphine slid her key card into the reader on the main office door and waited for the faint buzzing that would inform her of the lock's release.

The door opened and she pushed through, Ash following close behind. While Delphine was still scanning the room, Ash placed an ear against Haelstrom's door and listened for several moments. By the time she joined him, he was convinced the room beyond was empty. He relaxed and tried the brass doorknob. It wouldn't budge.

'What now?' Delphine whispered anxiously.

Dipping his hand into a pocket on the inside of his jacket, he produced a small, buttoned-down leather wallet.

'Tools of the trade,' he told her. 'Sometimes necessary.'

He opened out the wallet pocket to display both sides arranged with a selection of thin metal sticks. Ash knelt and placed the lockpicker's tool-case on the floor, each instrument kept in a separate holder. He slid one out that was slightly thicker and stronger-looking than most of the others. Its end was angled at about forty-five degrees, its shaft a little wider for easier handling.

'We call this the wrench,' he explained to her in soft tones. 'And this,' he showed her another, thinner metal stick, with a curved end coming to a point, 'is the pick.'

He held both instruments up to the door lock. 'Looks like a pin-and-tumbler lock, so it shouldn't be too difficult,' he said, sliding the wrench into the key opening. This was followed by the pick, which he pushed further into the keyhole, using the lever wrench to support it as he twisted. 'There are five pins inside which I need to push up till they click – you'll hardly hear the sound, but I'll feel the release of pressure. I'll do two at a time, leaving the one at this end for last.'

It took but a few seconds before he twisted both appliances and a small but audible click told them the door was open.

Ash hesitated, still holding the wrench and pick in place. He looked up at Delphine. 'You don't think this door has an alarm, do you?'

She froze, having no answer, and he grinned as he gently turned the knob and pushed the door wide open.

'Okay, so I checked it for a contact strip when I was in here earlier,' he said, still grinning. She frowned back at him chidingly. Cautiously, they entered, and although they both knew the room would be empty they breathed a sigh of relief when it proved to be so.

'You'd make a good burglar,' Delphine commented as she looked about her.

Ash pointed beyond Haelstrom's broad desk at the slim grey cabinets that lined the wall. 'Right. This is where the fun starts.'

They walked around the desk, the investigator sweeping his eyes across its surface in the vague hope of finding the keys to the filing cabinet, but seeing only the usual office clutter. He tried the cabinet drawers anyway, but they remained firmly shut.

'You don't think Haelstrom could have left his keys in a desk drawer, do you?'

'I doubt it,' replied Delphine going back to the desk. She pulled at each of its drawers but none would budge. 'Can you pick the locks? On these filing cabinets, I mean.'

'No. I don't have the patience. But they don't look too tough to me.'

Ash went to the cluttered desk and picked up a metal ruler, smacking it lightly against the palm of one hand.

'I'm hoping this'll do the trick.'

Still tapping the ruler against his open palm, he inspected the curious, custom-made units. He reached inside his jacket for the notebook in which he'd written down the numbers from the graveyard.

'Which cabinet to start with?' he wondered aloud. He showed Delphine the sets of numbers in his notebook. 'Can you find any connection to them?'

She studied the numbers, then looked at the cabinets again. She looked between the two twice more, before finally saying, 'You've made a mistake in what you've written down. Look, where at the start of the figures you've written an 8, it should have been a B. See there, on that cabinet there's a B just above the handle.'

Ash forced the tough steel ruler through the thin space between the narrow drawer and the frame of the cabinet. It took some effort, and for a moment it seemed the plan wasn't going to work. Then, its lock suddenly breaking as he and Delphine used the ruler as a lever, the drawer flew out several inches. Triumphant, they paused to inspect its contents before pulling it out as far as it would come.

Row upon row of stamped memory sticks lay inside like dominoes, their markings plainly visible. There were still several empty spaces, obviously waiting to be filled by fresh arrivals.

Ash consulted his notebook and removed a stick bearing a matching number. 'Okay, let's plug this one into the computer and see what comes up on the screen.'

Delphine took the flash drive from him and went over to the computer, putting on her glasses as she did so. Meanwhile, Ash browsed through the other sticks in the cabinets, checking codes against those he'd hastily scribbled into his notebook, then turned to look over Delphine's shoulder. When she tried to access the file, a box appeared requesting a password for access.

She twisted to look up at Ash. 'I was afraid of that.'

'Me too. I suppose it would be too simple for Haelstrom to use his own name? He's self-important enough.'

'I'll try, but I doubt it.' Delphine tried SIR VICTOR HAEL-STROM and a number of variations without success. 'No, that's not going to work,' she said, staring at the screen. 'Much too easy.'

'Yeah, it was a silly idea.' Ash rested a hand on her left shoulder, as if lending support. 'COMRAICH?'

She typed it in, three ways, one in caps, next in lower case, lastly with only an initial C. Failure.

Unwilling to be beaten, she began to try random words: COURT, GULFSTREAM, REFUGE. All wrong. Her shoulders slumped, but REFUGE had given Ash pause for thought.

'Not REFUGE. But try . . .' he started to say, but she was ahead of him.

'SANCTUARY,' she said, feeling a buzz of excitement.

But it was wrong, yet again.

'This is hopeless, David. We could be here all night long and still not come up with the correct password.'

But her last attempt had jogged something in his memory. Somebody – he couldn't remember who – had given Comraich Castle another name.

'Sanctum.' He stood straight, staring into space as if trying to remember more. 'Inner Sanctum, that was it! But just try SANCTUM.'

She did and instantly the screen faded to black, then came back with the words PASSWORD ACCEPTED.

He bent over and hugged her and Delphine smiled when the once-blank screen was suddenly filled with information:

BETTERFIELD, BERTRAM: B61074
ARRIVAL: 21st JUNE 1886
DECEASED: 7th FEBRUARY 1906
APPROPRIATE PARTIES INFORMED
BODY CREMATED: 8th FEBRUARY 1906

There followed a truncated life history, but what interested Ash and Delphine was the reason for Betterfield's incarceration at Comraich for twenty years. It seemed he – although British through and through and thought to be a champion of British imperialism and trade at the time – had secretly been an agent of Germany, which had been trying to break Britain's trading and manufacturing dominance. Betterfield had helped in Germany's struggles to gain power and territory in Africa.

So, confidential arrangements were made with the Inner Court.

Well, there was some justice in that, reflected Ash as he skimmed through the more formal notes displayed on the computer screen. When questioned by senior security figures, Betterfield had collapsed and confessed all. Ash wondered what interrogation methods were used in those days. Pretty brutal, he imagined.

Bertram Betterfield agreed to disappear from society – he was warned that it was only because Queen Victoria herself would not sanction his execution that he remained alive. Ironically, the fortune Betterfield had accumulated went to help pay for his unwanted stay at Comraich.

'And so here he died eventually,' said Ash, stretching his shoulders after leaning over the computer for so long.

'Shall we try some more?'

Ash shook his head. 'I'd like to find someone more recent, or at least a person we might know of.'

He returned to the filing cabinets and studied his notebook again. He picked one at random.

'There's one here that looks as if it has seven digits, which should be more recent but I'm guessing that rather than eleven, as I've put down, the middle has worn away and it should be an M.'

He forced open the 'M' drawer with the ruler, reached in and brought out a memory stick at random. Delphine removed the first stick and inserted the one Ash handed to her.

'Fingers crossed,' she said as the request for a password

was demanded on screen. 'Let's pray it's not a different password every time.'

She typed SANCTUM again and smiled as access was granted.

'Holy Jesus . . .' breathed Ash as the name came up, blasphemy not usually part of his dialogue.

> MAXWELL, (IAN) ROBERT
> orig. JAN LUDVIK HOCH

'We've hit the jackpot, Delphine,' Ash said in awe.

'Robert Maxwell – the newspaper magnate?' Delphine swung back to look at the screen.

'He was a publishing tycoon, his only rival as a media giant was Rupert Murdoch, and Murdoch won out in the end. Eventually, they say, Maxwell committed suicide or died of a heart attack after fraudulent financial deals he'd set up to bolster his collapsing empire began unravelling. He'd even dipped into his employees' pension funds to shore up his newspaper empire. Look at the screen

> MAXWELL (IAN) ROBERT
> orig. JAN LUDVIK HOCH
> BORN: CZECHOSLOVAKIA
> ARRIVED COMRAICH: 6th NOVEMBER, 1991
> DIED: 9th AUGUST 1996

Ash was shaking his head. 'This can't be right.' But he and Delphine read on, discovering more about the man.

> On 5 November 1991 it was reported that Robert Maxwell had fallen from his yacht the *Lady Ghislaine* while cruising close to the Canary Islands. When his body was recovered three days later it was almost unrecognizable, bloated and damaged by fish. A hasty autopsy by a Spanish pathologist concluded that death was caused by drowning. The body was quickly cremated. The official story was that he had

suffered a heart attack and had fallen unconscious into the sea, although many believed it was the suicide of a man in ruin both financially and politically. Maxwell was also rumoured to have been assassinated by Mossad agents.

'So far,' murmured Ash to Delphine, 'all in the public domain. Maybe he *was* killed by Mossad. Israel's secret service is highly regarded among intelligence agencies worldwide, but it's never been known for its subtlety.'

He pointed at the next piece of information as Delphine scrolled down.

'No, look, there it is,' he said, quickly reading through the fresh lines that came up and giving Delphine a summary. 'It was the Inner Court working with our own security forces that had Robert Maxwell kidnapped by the Special Boat Service. He knew so much about so many people in so many countries that it became a race to take him out first when his business empire started to crumble. He was left vulnerable; all those government officials and businessmen had washed their hands of him.'

Ash rose for a moment and stretched his aching back. 'He'd stolen as much as £400 million from his companies' pensions investments. It looks like the Inner Court and the British government struck a dodgy deal between them. If the SBS could secretly capture him and hand him over to the IC, all his secrets could be dragged out of him using sodium pentothal—'

'And other, more dangerous drugs I wouldn't care to name,' Delphine cut in.

'Right,' said Ash, 'the ideal solution. Then he could be left alone to live out his days here, sedated by lithium, or whatever.'

'But the body pulled from the sea three days later?'

'It could have been anyone of the right age and build, some down-and-out or drunk who wouldn't be missed. There was never a proper post-mortem and the corpse was quickly cremated. No one ever made a proper identification.'

'That's horrible.' Delphine was shaking her head in disgust.

'It's a wicked world.' Ash leaned over her again as more type came up.

'Jesus,' he whispered again in wonder. 'Would you look at this.'

The psychologist's eyes widened when she read further. 'Maxwell's eventual death on 9th August 1996 was the result of suicide . . .'

'I suppose he couldn't stand the idea of being cooped up, no matter how luxurious the prison.'

The next line came up and they both gasped at what was displayed onscreen.

'. . . following an overdose of yew-tree berries.'

'Yew berries? How—'

Delphine stopped him. 'Yew seeds are toxic. A lethal dosage would be fifty to a hundred grams. I'd guess he wandered through the woods one day, perhaps part of his exercise regime. Found himself among the crematorium plaques and assumed that one day this was how he'd end up, far from the public eye and, of course, his precious sons and daughters. Whether he cared for his wife, who knows? He'd left her in 1991.'

'So he chose his own way out,' said Ash, a trifle sadly. 'He must have visited the area over the weeks, each time collecting and taking the berries back with him to the castle, hiding them in his clothes, which would be easy enough . . . He was a self-made man from what was then Czechoslovakia, who used to claim – or boast – that he never wore shoes until he was seven years old. He fought in the Czech army, rising to captain. Something of a hero if you believe what he said. In a way, his nemesis was Rupert Murdoch, who managed to outwit him in taking over two big-selling newspapers – the *Sun* and the now defunct *News of the World*.'

Delphine suddenly became anxious. 'David, we've been in Sir Victor's office a long time . . .'

'You're right. We don't want to push our luck. Let's get

going.' He hastily took a handful of memory sticks from each of the drawers he had broken open and stuffed them into his jacket.

'I've no idea who we've got, but I imagine some of the names will interest the police. Maybe even puzzled historians.'

'Surely you're not thinking of showing them to the authorities. My God, it could bring the Inner Court down if it were exposed! You – *we'll* – be in terrible danger if Sir Victor finds out.'

He returned to her and kissed her cheek. 'Exactly. In any case, something tells me tonight Comraich Castle will be a risky place to be. That's why I'm so keen for us to be gone.'

She stood, slipped her spectacles inside her coat pocket. 'But how?' she pleaded. 'How are we going to get away from here?'

'Like I said, I'll go to Shawcroft-Draker and explain the situation to him. Not that we've pilfered Haelstrom's special files, but, first, to warn him he needs to evacuate the place, and second, if he should refuse, I'll ask his permission for just us to leave.'

'He'll never allow that.'

'We'll see. Don't forget Maxwell's memory stick,' he said.

She handed it to Ash and it joined the others in his jacket. 'Now let's go!'

As they walked back through the main office Ash noticed that, even though no window was open, the papers on the desks were moving, as if touched by a breeze. Ash frowned and paused. He could feel a faint rumbling beneath his feet.

It's beginning, he thought.

68

Delphine carefully closed the main office door, then looked up and down the reception hall. It was still and silent, like some vast underground cavern.

'David,' she said, touching his arm, 'Placid Pat's gone.'

'The old guard? Yeah, I noticed.' Maybe Placid Pat had felt the underground rumbling too and had gone to investigate.

'He rarely leaves that spot,' said Delphine, indicating the empty chair. 'Occasionally, he might patrol the building, but not at this time.'

'Let's move away from here,' Ash suggested. 'I don't want anyone wondering what we're doing. So far we've been lucky and I don't want to push it.'

They began walking down the hallway, the sound of their shoes echoing off the walls and high ceiling. Ash couldn't shake off the feeling of being inside a cathedral, only there was nothing holy about Comraich Castle.

The investigator drew Delphine to a halt, peering around to make sure there really was no one else to hear him.

'Delphine, d'you mind if we drop by your office?' he whispered.

'No, but why?'

'I'll tell you inside.'

They were already close to her room. Once they were inside the anteroom, he closed the door softly behind them.

'What did—' she began, but he cautioned her with a rigid first finger to his lips. 'Let's go through to your office.'

509

She shot him a doubtful look. Her thoughts were easy to read and he gave her an innocent smile. 'Don't think it's not on my mind, but this will be less fun.'

Looking mystified, she unlocked the door to her consulting room, where Ash almost collapsed on her comfortable couch.

'Delphine, I don't know about you, but after yesterday's near-fatal plane journey, the episode with the flies, last night's vigil, the sea caves this morning, and then those bloody wildcats, I'm just about all in. Now something tells me that tonight things are going to get worse around here. Whether we stay or leave, I can get through it, but . . .'

'But you'd like something that could help keep you going.'

He turned his palms upwards, managing a tired grin as he lifted them from his knees.

'I noticed earlier that you had a drugs cabinet in this room, and I thought if you had any Benzedrine or something . . .' He looked sheepish.

'I'm against amphetamines of any sort,' she said. 'But I do have something that might help you, though it certainly isn't Benzedrine. Times have moved on, David.'

She took a bunch of keys from her bag and opened the metal cabinet. 'A company in America came up with a drug in tablet form whose effect in some ways replicates Ritalin. Originally it was part of a group of pharmaceuticals used to treat narcolepsy, even Alzheimer's.'

She stretched her body, standing on tiptoes to reach a small carton on the top shelf.

Still seated, Ash asked doubtfully, 'Isn't Ritalin used on overactive kids?'

Delphine turned back to him and laid the cardboard box on her desk. 'Not in the way you think. Ritalin actually improves attention, memory and cognitive flexibility, so it helps control those who suffer ADHD.' She held up the box. 'This is Modafinil. Like caffeine, it stimulates the central nervous system. It'll keep you awake all night, maybe longer, and it will concentrate your mind, but I've got to warn you, too much and it'll mess with your circadian cycle; you'll act as if night is day, and vice versa. Do you really want this, David?'

Her concern was touching, yet undoubtedly the night ahead was going to take a lot of endurance. 'Yeah,' he said. 'I'm afraid I do. And I think you might need some as well.'

'This is highly unethical. I could be struck off if it got out. You should go through a proper medical examination and counselling first.'

He reached out a hand to take the box, but she withheld it.

'I'll give you a strip of ten, which is far too many, but you may have to share with me.'

He grinned as she opened the box and took out a silver-foil blister pack, then leaned across the desk to give it to him. He took the foil, glad she lived in the real world.

'Don't worry, I won't abuse it. I'm not made that way.'

'Yet you drink absinthe.'

That shook him. 'How . . .'

'Sir Victor had your case searched before it was taken to your room.'

Ash sat back on the couch, bemusement clear in his dark blue eyes. 'And he told you? Why?'

'He wanted me to keep an eye on you. Maseby said you were once virtually an alcoholic.'

'So that was it? You've just been keeping an eye on me?'

She hurried round the desk and sat close to him on the couch. With a gentle hand, she turned his face towards her. 'I would never have spied on you, David. You must understand that. What happened between us was more than just attraction – there was no ulterior motive on my part.'

Ash was silent for a moment and then his body seemed to relax. He pulled her close and kissed her hard on the mouth, and she kissed him back.

When she finally pulled away she said breathlessly, 'I love you, David.'

'After two days?' There was neither cynicism nor mockery

in his response, only wonder. 'You don't know enough about me,' he forced himself to say.

'We both did a lot of talking earlier this morning. I don't need to know any more to love you.' She suddenly looked uncertain. 'Have I been too blunt? If I have, I'm sorry. I'm just being honest.'

He nuzzled her cheek. 'You can be as blunt as you like if what you said is true.'

'It is. I've no doubts.'

'I feel the same, Delphine.'

'I know you do.'

'Bloody psychologists,' he said quietly.

They kissed again, their embrace tight.

Remembering their plight, Ash gently eased her away. 'We've got things to do. Like get as far away from this place as possible.'

Her eyes had been closed in the joy of the moment, but now they snapped open, although she still acted as if in a daze.

Ash was serious. 'I want you to go up to Lewis's room and stay with him while I talk to Lord Edgar. Get him ready to leave and pack any medication he needs in your bag.' He tore the strip of Modafinil in half and handed one side to her. 'Five each, okay? Perhaps you can give one to Lewis, if it won't react badly with any other medication he's on.'

'It shouldn't, but I have to be careful. The medication he takes already is what he needs to stay balanced and to prevent any seizures.'

Ash put his strip into a pocket. 'Okay, you'll just have to use your judgement.'

'I don't know, David. It all seems so ... so drastic. And unbelievable.'

'Oh, you'll believe before the night's out. I can feel – *sense* – the pressure growing. Can't you?'

As if on cue, the ceiling light in the consulting room suddenly flickered, then dimmed. The investigator felt the floor beneath his feet begin to tremble once more.

Delphine clutched him tightly. She looked round the room and saw the softly rendered landscapes on the walls begin to tilt. One of her framed diplomas dropped to the floor, the glass shattering.

'Come on, we haven't much time,' Ash told her, pulling her to her feet.

'Is there a staircase to the fifth?' Ash asked as they began walking away from the front lobby.

'Yes, off the old armoury, but we can take the lift. The newer one used by the VIPs.'

'No.' Ash had no desire to be trapped inside *any* other lift, no matter how grand it might be. 'We'll take the stairs. It'll be safer.'

She looked at him quizzically, but followed.

As they approached the armoury, he sensed a familiar vibration coming from the room ahead.

He grabbed Delphine before she could step over the threshold. She looked at him in surprise, her eyes wide, and he pointed into the room.

'Look at the weapons.'

She did, and gasped.

All the ancient pieces – the swords, the pikes, the axes, and more – were bristling on their well-organized installations; a low thrumming sound came from their battle-worn metal as the lethal instruments of conflict quivered on their mounts.

'David . . . ?' Delphine whispered.

'It'll be all right. I don't think it's strong enough to release them. Not yet.'

'What isn't?'

'The dark power rising from beneath this castle.'

'David, we can't go in there! It isn't safe!'

Suddenly he had a flashback to Grace, flayed in front of his eyes as he lay helpless on the ground. He was afraid for himself, but more afraid of what might happen to his new love. He would not let the forces of evil take her from him this time.

'We have to go back,' he shouted above the noise. 'We'll

use the grand staircase to get up to the next floor, then double-back on ourselves.'

They turned together and, holding hands, ran back down the marbled hall, the curving staircase just ahead of them. Ash saw the big wooden entrance doors at the far end and wished he could just keep running, take Delphine away from this evil place. But he knew they had things to do first. As they took to the broad curving staircase he noticed the old guard's seat was still unoccupied, and that the two receptionists were no longer behind the long counter.

In fact, Comraich appeared to be empty, as if Haelstrom had finally heeded his warning and evacuated the whole building.

But in his heart, David Ash knew it was not so. In fact, the castle was filling with entities presently without form, elementals with one purpose in mind.

To destroy Comraich and everyone in it.

69

Placid Pat finally reached the fifth-floor landing and sat awhile in the empty chair he found there to get his breath back and give the muscles in his legs a rest. *That's what you get at my age*, he told himself, *when y'sit on a bloody chair all day and y'get no exercise. Weak legs and haemorrhoids.*

He'd been content to wallow in his own guilt for decades without conversing with the Lord, and in truth he'd been too ashamed to try. They hadn't let him confess his crimes to the Garda, and even in the confessional box, his bishop had not forgiven him his sins, nor even ordered penance, but had merely sat behind the wooden latticework screen contemplating how to distance the young priest from the Catholic Church. The time had come for things to change.

The source of anger for Placid Pat's woeful existence nowadays was watching defrocked Archbishop Carsely while the poor, sweet-faced Sister Thimble followed in his wake, her lips moving silently as she passed the wooden beads of her rosary through dainty fingers after each repeated prayer. Pat had no doubts at all that she was praying for the soul of the man she followed. The man who abused her.

But although it was commonly accepted among the castle's staff by now that the relationship between the cleric and his acolyte was an unholy one, no one had prevented its continuation; no one, to his knowledge, had even tried.

Until now, for he, the once Reverend Father Patrick

O'Connor, had determined to stop this disgrace to his Church, to his religion, on this very evening.

Stiffly, he rose from the chair and made his way towards the chapel. He heard voices coming from one of the fancy staterooms further along the red-carpeted passage and he made an effort to lighten his steps, already deadened by the lush carpet. He came upon the slightly open door from where the hum of voices came, accompanied by an occasional eruption of laughter: the VIP conference delegates upon whom all the staff had been instructed to make a good impression.

But what a wrong time to have them visit. Strange things were happening in the castle. What would be on the agenda at the conference that night? Would they be discussing these supernatural events? Might they even see some at first hand? Pat thought it highly likely.

For now, however, other concerns were more pressing. Placid Pat knew that carrying out God's will by bringing an end to Archbishop Carsely's debauchery would be a righteous retribution for his own sins.

As he crept past the door he peeked into the stateroom and glimpsed some of the men inside, standing straight and immaculate in their formal evening wear.

Let them drink their champagne or expensive brandies, let them enjoy themselves before all hell breaks loose.

Pat moved slowly through a warren of passageways and corridors until finally he reached the arched double doors that led to the castle's chapel. He put his ear against the crack between them and listened. He could hear recorded music, a hymn that was only vaguely familiar. He thought he heard a woman's feeble cry. With no further ado, Placid Pat pulled his Second World War Colt .32 ACP revolver from its shoulder holster, a reliable enough weapon for an old warrior who had never used it yet and would probably never use it again. He held it with the barrel pointing upwards as he pushed through the doors and stepped into the intimate chapel, crouching low, knees bent, both arms stiff and extended, hands curled round the nickel-finished grip, the pouched tip of his right index finger poised to pull the trigger.

He almost dropped to his knees when he saw the figure, a statue of the Virgin Mary, the Immaculate Mother of Jesus, looking down at ex-Archbishop Carsely and Sister Thimble from a pedestal by the side of the altar with its high, arching stained-glass window behind, the colours muddied by the darkness outside. Instead, he approached the pair boldly, heedless of the noise he was making.

The nun was facing away from him, bent over the first pew. Carsely was standing directly behind her, his hands around her waist. He glanced at the guard, took in the revolver, but didn't stop what he was doing; if anything, the threat seemed to give him renewed vigour. Sister Thimble's habit was pushed up above her pale rounded buttocks and she gave a tiny scream of pain as Carsely thrust himself hard into her. For a few moments more, so greedy was he for satiation he ignored the old guard, moaning in his ecstasy, perhaps the added danger increasing his perverse pleasure, and rammed himself even further into the nun, as blood began to trickle down her plump white thighs.

Pat too groaned aloud, though in despair at the pagan barbarity that was taking place before him in all its profanity and filth in the very House of God.

'Oh, dear Mother of God . . .' he moaned in painful anguish.

Sister Thimble, her dishevelled habit ruffled around her waist, heard his distress and slowly swung her head round towards him.

And the lascivious, lewd grin she gave the guard, her mouth filled with blood because in her own ecstasy she'd absently bitten into her lower lip, caused him to fall to his knees, the gun shaking in his hands.

The wild, excited pleasure in her eyes seemed to be inviting him to join in the fun. And when she smeared the blood around her lips with her tongue, he felt a wave of bile rise into his throat and spill onto the short centre aisle.

70

Ash and Delphine were both breathless by the time they'd run through the first-floor landing, passing the great oval dining room which was now spotlessly clean and free of people, past two of the castle's five libraries and several relaxation areas, every one of them equally empty and strangely soulless, despite their sumptuousness. On the way, Ash had spotted those dense black orbs floating through the halls, either singularly or in groups, as if exploring the castle. So dense were they, so deeply black, that they appeared to absorb the light itself. A grey haze like obverse halos shimmered around their darkness as the light was drawn in.

Delphine slowed, as if fascinated by them, and Ash had to grab her hand and almost drag her along. Even with the exertion of running he could feel the cold spots as they sped through them, the chill dragged along behind like dust from a meteorite's tail before falling away to ebb back into the infinite bleakness that was their source.

And now, trying to regain their breath and their energy, they stopped by an elegantly framed set of lift doors the colour of matt gold.

'This . . .' Delphine drew in another breath. 'This lift can take us up to the fifth floor.'

'No, I told you: we need the stairs.' He stood for a moment, panting. 'I think it's time for my first "fix". Won't you join me?'

He took the blister pack from his pocket and popped a

Modafinil tablet into his mouth; Delphine followed suit –
reluctantly, it seemed to Ash – and together they hurried
onwards.

Soon they reached a far less elegant section of the building.
Here there was no plush carpet or grand portraiture, just a
long, narrow corridor, the ceiling lights dim, though from low-
wattage bulbs or the oddness of the castle's oppressive atmosphere it was impossible to tell. They continued their journey to
the rear of Comraich Castle and every time they passed
beneath a ceiling light, it flared brightly, then shattered over
their heads, causing them to duck before hurrying on.

When the first bulb exploded, Delphine gave a small
scream of surprise, her free hand reaching up to brush thin
shards of glass from her hair. But they continued on, each
lamp flaring, then detonating with the sharpness of a gunshot,
leaving the corridor behind them in darkness.

'Where to now?' he asked as they reached the end of the
corridor.

He saw that Delphine was shaking, visibly trying to keep
herself under control. She pointed a trembling finger. 'The
tower. We've reached a corner tower. This is the staircase used
by maids and porters when they're working this side of the
building. At the very top is Lewis's apartment.' She was taking
small gasps of air.

'You okay?' He slipped a hand behind her neck, his fingers
reaching through her lush black hair.

She nodded vigorously, swept into his embrace for a
moment, and said, 'Let's – let's go on. Lewis will be frightened
on his own tonight.'

The lights on the stairs had dimmed almost to nothing, so
Ash brought out the Maglite. 'Take this,' he told her. 'You lead
the way.'

As they climbed they passed tall vertical slits through which
archers used to shoot their arrows. Ash peered out of one to
see the calm sea sheeted in silver from the full and now
magically bright moonlight. *So much for Frankenstein and his*

pal Dracula, thunderstorms with boiling clouds and forked light-ning, he thought. The pill was obviously kicking in.

They reached the fifth-floor landing and they took a few moments to rest with their backs to the curved stone wall. Still catching his breath, Ash took Delphine by her upper arms. 'Time to split up,' he said. 'Make sure Lewis is all right. I'll come and get you both after I've had a few words with Edgar Shawcroft-Draker.'

She was confused and her dark eyes looked to one side in the way he found so endearing. 'I've told you before, make sure you call him *Lord* Edgar,' she admonished.

Her words of warning caused him to smile. 'I'm not very good with titles.'

He gave her a little push towards the next flight of stairs, but for a moment she resisted.

'What if he doesn't agree to our leaving? What if he wants to keep us here?'

'Then I'll have to persuade him.' This time his smile had no warmth.

'David, you have to be careful,' she pleaded. 'These aren't men from the Rotary Club.'

'I know. I'm only too aware. But I sense something in this man, *Lord* Edgar Shawcroft-Draker. I see a lot of regret in his eyes.'

'You felt that from just a brief glimpse?'

'Yes. Do you think I'm right?'

'I've had some time to study him. He talks to no one except Sir Victor and Derriman, and naturally his butler, Byrone, and he won't let me get near to him or speak to him alone. He's a sick man, David. His illness seems worse every time I see him. But that doesn't make him weak in the mind: he's still a strong leader.'

'Believe me, I'm sure you're right. But if I can convince him—'

She broke in abruptly. 'What if you can't?' she asked again.

'As I said, I'll try to convince him. And if he still says no, then we'll leave anyway. It'll just be tougher. Now look, you must go . . .'

His last words were firm, brooking no more argument. Again, he guided her back to the rising stairway. 'Keep the torch on all the time. The batteries are fully charged, so it should last a good while. Now go!'

A quick peck on the cheek, and then he sent her on her way. He watched until she'd disappeared round the bend in the spiral.

Ash felt a new freshness rising in him and wondered if the pill was working so quickly because pumped-up adrenaline was pushing the drug faster round his system. No matter: it helped, whatever it did. He began to make his way along the castle's passages, trying to remember the route to Lord Edgar's quarters, and soon found himself face to face with a familiar figure.

71

'Mr Ash?' Byrone said in surprise as he turned a corner and almost bumped into the parapsychologist.

'Mr Byrone! I— uh . . .' stammered Ash.

'No need for the "Mr",' the manservant said with the easy grace born of many years' servitude. In one hand he balanced a cloth-covered tray, the cloth entirely hiding its contents.

'May I help you, Mr Ash? You look lost. If it's Sir Victor you seek, then I'm afraid he is extremely busy at the moment entertaining some very important arrivals. I imagine he'll be busy well into the night.'

You can bet on that, Ash thought.

'As a matter of fact, Byrone,' said Ash, 'I'm looking for Lord Edgar's suite. I have some urgent business with him that can't wait. *Mustn't* wait.'

Byrone blinked at the investigator's sudden challenging tone – or perhaps at his impertinence. 'His lordship is resting at the moment, and I have instructions not to disturb him. You are perhaps aware that he is not in the best of health.'

Ash was becoming impatient. 'I promise you,' he said evenly, 'what I have to say is of the utmost importance to the health of both Comraich and everyone in it. I can't express how vital it is for us all . . . especially today's "very important arrivals".' It did no harm to gild the lily.

Byrone paused and thought. Then he said, 'I'm afraid you will have to take the matter up with Mr Derriman.'

He made as if to walk away, but Ash deliberately blocked

his path. He wasn't fooled by the butler's appearance, for Byrone was stockily built and his nose looked as if it had taken a few knocks in its time. For all Ash knew, the manservant could have been a hired minder, there to protect his master as well as serve his needs. He might even be armed.

Whatever, he would take on the man without hesitation if the lives of Delphine and Lewis were at stake. Ash tensed his muscles in preparation.

If Byrone noticed, he gave nothing away, merely eyeing Ash closely as if making up his mind.

'Vital, you say?' he asked, unflustered.

'Absolutely. It's quite literally a matter of life and death.'

'Ah, death.' Byrone smiled wearily, and although Ash expected him simply to turn on his heels and walk away, he continued speaking. 'Look, sir. I'm on my way to administer his lordship's medication and I'll explain the situation to him. Then he can make up his own mind. I do know he is intensely interested in your findings. But I warn you, Mr Ash, if you intend to hoodwink him with parapsychological babble, then the consequences for you will be severe.'

'Is that a threat, Byrone?'

'Why yes, sir. What else would it be?' said the butler amiably.

Ash smiled inwardly. *This could turn into quite a tussle*, he thought, seeing the smartly clad retainer in a new light. 'Okay,' he said, 'I promise nothing but truth and honesty. After that, it's entirely up to Lord Edgar. I'm just doing my job.'

'Very good, sir. In that case, please wait here.'

Ash sat down in a floral tapestry chair and watched as Byrone disappeared round a corner, holding the tray at shoulder height like a waiter.

And as Ash waited impatiently, he felt something run over his foot. He just caught sight of the brown rat scurrying along the skirting board, before it disappeared into the shadows from which he had so recently emerged.

72

Senior Nurse Krantz was suspicious.

Other duties had taken her away from the medical unit's reception desk, so she had no way of knowing whether that creepy stunted little man, Cedric Twigg, had returned from the containment area in the sub-basement – the 'dungeons', as she privately referred to the place. She'd asked the nurse who'd sat in for her (a rather plain, skinny girl in her twenties who Krantz had taken to her bed only a week or two after her arrival some years ago), but had been met only with a shrug of the girl's shoulders. The senior nurse was not about to put her own life at risk by going downstairs to see whether Twigg was still around – after all, it was a full moon that night and, though there were those who thought the connection was a myth, some of the nutcases definitely were affected by the lunar cycle. And that – along with so many extraordinary things happening in Comraich lately – was only *one* reason she would not go down there alone any more. She was well aware of how despised she was by patients and medical staff alike. And somehow she instinctively knew that danger was abroad that night, something in the heavy atmosphere of the castle. Everything felt strange, as if there were static in the air, the oppression that often preceded a thunderstorm. Yet still she was curious. Had Twigg truly obtained permission to enter the restricted section on his own? Had Sir Victor really lent the shabby little man his own key card? It didn't seem likely to Senior Nurse Krantz.

What to do? If Twigg was still downstairs, what could he be up to? She did not trust the shifty, bald-headed man. Could he be involved in some kind of mischief? She'd never heard of him carrying out any kind of structural assessment before. Besides, she was well aware of what the Inner Court really used him for, and it was another reason to be somewhat timid around him.

Krantz decided she would find the security chief, Kevin Babbage and pass the buck on to him. Her mind made up, she quickly took to the stairs that would lead her up to the castle's ground floor.

She stomped her way to the lobby, wondering what the tiny black orbs with their graduating charcoal haloes were. She blinked several times as if to clear black floaters in her pupils. There were dark-garbed guards racing here and there, as if none of them knew where they were going, or what was happening. Neither receptionist was behind the long counter. It appeared Placid Pat had also deserted his station.

Krantz marched to the hefty door of the control centre and rapped loudly.

'Yes?' The voice came from a tiny speaker on the door frame.

'It's Senior Nurse Krantz. I need to see Mr Babbage.'

There was a buzzing sound and the door clicked. Krantz pushed it open and stood on the stepped platform that over-looked the enormous room. Sitting before the banks of TV monitors were three men, frantically stabbing at keyboards in an attempt to make clear the identical snowy, dazzling displays that were each meant to show a different area of the castle. Elsewhere computer screens were filled with lines of scrolling gibberish, fax machines spewed blank paper and even the television news broadcasts had become nothing but shadowy double-images of voiceless newsreaders. Water coolers bub-bled and a jet of steam whistled upwards from the coffee machine. Not even the phones were working.

Security Chief Kevin Babbage stood in front of a whiteboard, looking as if he would be tearing his hair out had he not been sporting a buzz-cut.

He noticed the red-haired nurse standing on the platform by the door, a wide-eyed, dismayed expression on her face as she surveyed the chaos.

'What the hell d'you want, Krantz?' Babbage bellowed across the room. 'Can't you see I've got enough problems?'

Nevertheless, he stepped away from the whiteboard and hurried through the desks to reach her. If there was more trouble, it seemed that he didn't want others to overhear it.

'What's wrong?' he snapped as he swung round the steps' metal rail and came up to the platform.

'I'm sorry, Mr Babbage,' Krantz answered promptly, not at all intimidated by his brusque manner, 'but I saw that man Twigg on his way down to the sub-basement some time ago, and as far as I know, he hasn't yet returned.'

Babbage scowled. 'And you've been waiting all this time for him to reappear?'

'No, no – I've been busy. I've only just found out.' Her own response was equally fierce. 'I thought it strange, though, that he should have his own special key-card. He told me Sir Victor had given it to him so that he could carry out a structural assessment, but I can't imagine that, can you?'

Babbage ran his hand across his bristling hair as he eyed the chaos below, then capitulated. 'Okay, okay, I'll take a look with you. You seen Derriman around?'

'He's probably upstairs having cocktails with the bigwigs.'

'Yeah, that sounds about right. Come on, then, let's see what we can find. I'm getting nowhere here anyway.'

They left the ops room and Krantz had to trot to keep up with the security chief's pace.

In their haste, they failed to notice the small orbs now above their heads, floating like miniature black balloons near the hall's high ceiling, gathering together and swallowing the light around them, eventually becoming one huge seething blurred shadow.

73

Ash's patience was practically exhausted when he heard footsteps approaching from the direction Byrone had taken earlier.

'Thank you for waiting, Mr Ash,' said the manservant as he rounded the corner, now minus tray.

'Did you know you've got rats running round this part of the castle?' said Ash as he stood.

'Alas . . .' (*Now there's a word you didn't hear often these days*, thought Ash) 'it's a common problem in old buildings, sir. Ours find their way up from the dungeons below.'

Another man who called the sub-basement what it really was. Ash decided he liked that.

'They rarely come this far up, though,' the butler explained. 'We have some very hungry cats to keep them away.'

'Really?' he said. 'As a matter of fact, I haven't seen one cat inside Comraich since I've been here.' *Though I saw plenty outside this morning*, he thought.

Byrone paused a second. 'Now you mention it, sir, I haven't seen the castle cats recently either. Not for a week or so.'

'Since the wildcats found their way onto the estate?'

'Hmn, yes, I suppose.' The manservant took up his stride once more. 'Anyway, Mr Ash, you'll be pleased to learn that his lordship has agreed to see you. Kindly follow me.'

Ash followed the butler down a long, wide corridor. Byrone, at first a couple of strides ahead of Ash, slowed so that soon they were walking shoulder to shoulder. 'I've given his lordship his medication, but you might find he will tire very quickly,' the butler said in a hushed voice. 'If he does, you'll have to leave.'

'I thought he had an important meeting tonight?'

'That he has, Mr Ash, which is why he must rest before it begins.'

'And the dinner he's supposed to attend before that?'

'I fear he may have to excuse himself. But we'll see how it goes. All I ask is that you do not tire Lord Edgar more than necessary. May we agree on that?'

Ash had no wish to exhaust a dying man, but he needed to obtain his permission to let Delphine, Lewis and himself leave the compound. He felt sure they wouldn't make it out without that permission.

'I'll try to keep it brief,' he said, 'but there are things about Comraich he will have to know.'

Byrone gave him a hard stare.

'Only for his own good and that of his guests,' Ash hurriedly added. He had already decided that obtaining permission to leave would be his main aim. If Shawcroft-Draker wanted to hear more, then so be it: he'd get the full story. But the parapsychologist was only too well aware of how much a non-believer would, or could, accept.

They had arrived at Lord Edgar's door. The manservant tapped lightly, then opened it and stood aside so that Ash could enter.

The investigator was surprised by what he found. Unlike the lavish grandeur of Haelstrom's suite, Lord Edgar had opted for splendid simplicity, with admirable and exquisite furnishings and decoration, ornamentation sparse but pleasing. It was a large room that overlooked the sea, the high windows' heavy drapery drawn back to reveal the dramatic clifftop view, the waves below rippling with the reflections of the clear moon that dominated the stars in a black sky.

Outside, he could see the castle battlements, though how an enemy could hope to scale this part of the cliff face with its almost vertical precipice was beyond him.

The large room's simplicity was perhaps evidence of its occupant's own clear and uncluttered mind. But as Ash looked around for his host he saw that there was no one other than himself and Byrone present.

Ash was standing near an uncluttered desk with a leather-inlaid top. There were a few documents neatly stacked on one side, a crystal paperweight and a silver letter opener, but what caught Ash's attention was a sealed white envelope resting against the paperweight. In fine script it simply read: *The Inner Court.* It was placed so that anyone entering the room would notice it immediately.

Then a dry, low voice sounded through an open door on the far side of the room. 'Please show our guest through, Byrone.'

The manservant led the way, this time entering before the investigator. 'Mr David Ash, my lord,' Byrone announced, stepping to one side to give Ash his first proper view of the grey man he'd seen on his arrival.

Lord Edgar was seated facing the door in a comfortable-looking high-backed armchair, just to the right of a warming log fire. The laird of Comraich was even thinner than Ash had remembered. Instead of the grey suit and tie he'd worn before, the thin man had a thick green and black tartan blanket pulled round his narrow shoulders like a shawl. Below that were grey check trousers, and on his feet, black loafers. Flames from the fire gave the right side of his face a rosy glow, but the flesh on the unlit side was pale and sickly-looking.

Yet, despite his evident frailty, Lord Edgar Shawcroft-Draker appeared in good humour. 'Forgive me if I don't rise to the occasion,' he said with a fleeting smile, 'but I hope a handshake will suffice.'

He held out a hand that trembled slightly as it reached out from the blanket, for a moment exposing a woollen jumper over a rotund stomach.

Ash stepped forward and took the proffered hand, which felt as dry as old parchment; he was conscious of the effort put into the other man's grip, and the investigator held his hand firmly but without undue pressure. Lord Edgar let his long skinny fingers drop back under the blanket.

Lord Edgar indicated the twin of his armchair on the opposite side of the fireplace. As he seated himself, Ash noted that, although the fire was in full flame, the heat it threw out was far less than might be expected.

Noticing the parapsychologist's puzzlement, the old man leaned forward confidentially. 'I'm afraid draughty old castles keep in precious little heat, even in the summer months. We do our best to keep the guests comfortable and warm, but up here at the building's summit, as it were, and on the top of a promontory over the Irish Sea, it's almost impossible to conserve warmth.' He relaxed back into his armchair.

It's going to get a lot colder before the night's out, even for the guests below, thought Ash.

The elderly laird was speaking again and the investigator was relieved the reedy voice was loud enough to hear without a struggle.

'In high summer, it's very pleasant to take a stroll along the battlements and to breathe in good, life-giving, unpolluted sea air.' With his head, he indicated a pair of French doors. 'I have easy access, you see. The doors lead directly onto the battlements. Usually, in autumn or winter, we draw the curtains closed to help keep out the draughts, but on a night like this, I love to watch the rising moon against the velvet blackness of the universe behind it, with a whole galaxy of twinkling stars. Unfortunately, it's something you rarely see these days in most of Britain because of light pollution.'

The old man fell silent, but before Ash could speak, he seemed to rally once more.

'Now, Mr Ash, may we refresh you with a drink? I'm sorry that we don't have absinthe, but I'm sure Byrone can find you something – er, if I may say so – something better for your health.'

Christ, does everyone know? thought Ash. He wasn't really surprised, but why should his liking for absinthe be significant?

Byrone, who had been standing discreetly nearby, came forward. 'What would you like, Mr Ash? A nice single malt would keep the chill off your bones, if that will suit.'

Scotland? Whisky? What could be better if absinthe was off the card? 'Single malt, please. I'll leave the distillery to you.' He wondered if they knew his absinthe had run dry. Perhaps there would be a fresh supply waiting when he returned to his room.

'Very good, sir. And your lordship. Shall I prepare your special now?'

'No, I don't think so,' Shawcroft-Draker said slowly, as if he were thinking on it. He suddenly gave a half-smile. 'Bring my other preference for the moment, Byrone. I'm rather interested to hear what our parapsychologist friend has to say.'

'Very well, my lord. I'll return directly.' With that, the butler disappeared into the larger room.

'So tell me, Mr Ash,' Lord Edgar began when they were alone. 'Have you discovered anything of special significance in the history of Comraich Castle so far? Do you know of its violent past, of the curse that was laid on it? That certainly must be of interest to you, especially with regard to the aberrant, even surreal incidents that have occurred here recently, no?'

'You're referring to when the family of one of the ancient lairds was thrown from the battlements down to the rocks below, I take it? I've heard some of it.'

'With the gorier bits left out, no doubt.'

'What I was told seemed pretty ghoulish to me. Whether or not that has something to do with the haunting at present, I couldn't tell you. But without doubt, there's evil shadowing this place.'

They were suddenly interrupted by the soft *whumph*, *whumph*, *whumph* of a helicopter slowly descending outside, a sharp beam of bright light preceding it to the landing pad. The noise soon abated after the machine touched down.

'Ah, the arrival of the last of the Inner Court members.' He allowed a small sigh. 'A long journey, I must admit. I hope our members aren't overtired for tonight's conference, but it was the only way to get almost everybody in one place, in view of their business commitments.'

Byrone returned with a silver tray bearing two fine crystal tumblers. He served the host first, Shawcroft-Draker's shaky hand reaching out from beneath the folds of the tartan blanket for the glass of murky-looking liquid. The butler then brought the tray over to the investigator as Lord Edgar raised his glass in salutation.

'You know,' he began, 'clinking glasses used to be one of my small pleasures – it makes a special contact with another person, a toast to each other's health, you might say – but alas, nowadays I'm usually too weary to make the effort.'

Ash stood and closed the gap between them.

'All the best, your lordship,' Ash said genuinely as his tumbler met Lord Edgar's, and there was indeed something pleasant about the sound the two glasses made. The laird smiled in appreciation.

As the investigator returned to his seat, he noticed that the butler had retreated to the shadowy side of the room. Ash also noticed that on top of a magnificent credenza lay the tray that Byrone had carried in the passageway when he'd first encountered him. The distinctively patterned cloth covering the silver tray was now rumpled, exposing what looked like a syringe.

Suddenly there was a dull thud and the windows vibrated.

'What was that?' Ash commented.

'Sometimes the sea makes the most extraordinary noises . . . anyway where were we?' Shawcroft-Draker murmured almost to himself. A telling moment, a geriatric delighted he hadn't quite lost his memory. 'Ah yes,' he went on, his voice not as querulous as before he'd sipped his oddly murky drink. 'The curse! The Mullachd, to use the old Scottish word for it.'

'Yes, the driver who brought me here from the airport mentioned how the Laird McKinnon's wife and daughters were thrown from the battlements, and he laid the curse as he jumped after them.'

'Unfortunately, it was far worse than that. If he'd not allied himself twice with the English he might have lived on to a hearty old age.'

Lord Edgar fell silent, was lost in contemplation once more, reflected fire dancing in his eyes beneath drooping lids.

Ash was forced to stir him. 'It was an English king who declared an end to the hostilities, wasn't it?'

'Revenge was sought, my friend. The poor Scots had been defeated twice by the English king, Edward II, but when Edward III came to the throne, he was weary of pointless battles and allowed Scotland its independence. Laird McKinnon was no longer in favour with the new king – in truth, Edward could not care less about him – and that was when the clans took their revenge.'

The old man slowly and sadly shook his head back and forth, as if he were seeing the atrocity acted out before him.

'The usurper laird, who had fought alongside the other clans, laid claim to the castle for himself in the end. He was a wicked, evil fellow who gave a damn for no one, not even God. He had the defeated Laird McKinnon and his family hauled up from the dungeons to this very part of the castle. The fire in the hearth was well lit and a long knife inserted into the burning logs, so that its tip was made red-hot.'

Had the room grown darker with more shadows, or was it Ash's own keyed-up mind imagining?

'There were two daughters, one aged thirteen, called Finella, the other sixteen, with the sweet name of Leanne, though the family history tells us she was the feistier of the pair. Anyway, out on the battlements, beyond this very room, McKinnon was forced to watch both his daughters, young as they were, tortured, abused, and finally raped by the malicious new laird's untamed warriors. This arrogator was appropriately named Laird Deahan, which he relished, because translated into English it means Demon.

'Can you imagine that Mr Ash? To be forced to watch both his young unblemished daughters tortured and abused with a red-hot knife, raped in front of him, innocent children, whom he loved above all else – the barbaric acts against them, their struggle despite fear and incomprehension, being ravished by the roughest of clansmen. And then to see them thrown off the battlements to the rocks and sea far below.'

Ash wasn't enjoying this, as Lord Edgar might have realized, for his heavy-lidded eyes constantly sought out the investigator's, as if to measure his sensibility. But Ash kept his face a still mask, without a hint of any emotion, which perhaps encouraged the head of Comraich Castle, for the chronicle became even more gruesome.

'By the accounts we have of that diabolic day, Laird Duncan McKinnon fought like a wild man. It's told he was a man of massive strength. We cannot know how many of his foe it took to immobilize him, but eventually his strength was gone and he succumbed.'

The gaunt man's voice remained firm, though to Ash he appeared more withered by the minute. Despite his stated abhorrence, he seemed to be enjoying the hideousness of his account.

'McKinnon was pulled to the flagstones, compelled to kneel and witness a further appalling violation against his family, for now it was the turn of his poor hysterical wife, Elspeth, wailing for their lost daughters. She too was stripped, though to be humiliated rather than abused. She was made to kneel only feet from her tightly held husband. Her hair was pulled back to expose her neck to an axe-wielding barbarian.

'God only knows what was running through the broken laird's mind at that point.'

Ash sniffed at his whisky before putting the glass to his lips, pretending to appreciate the aroma of the liquor while trying to detect any hint of poison. Both Lord Edgar and Byrone were watching him pointedly and Ash had no choice but to hope for the best. He took a sip, allowing it to roll around his mouth, then swallowed. Liquid fire ran down his throat to rest for a while, seeming to expand in his chest. It was exquisite.

But so too, were some poisons when mixed with other, stronger flavours. *What the hell*, he thought, and took another large gulp. Oddly, it made his senses keener.

'I see you enjoy our special Scottish brew, Mr Ash,' said Lord Edgar, genuine pleasure in his smile. 'And you should. It's a sixty-year-old Macallan single malt; you're also supping it from a Waterford crystal tumbler which is the finest of receptacles from which to taste it.'

'Two – the Macallan and the glass – of the very best,' Ash readily agreed, pleasing his host.

'Where were we?'

Lord Edgar grunted with satisfaction and continued his story. 'Just as Elspeth was about to be decapitated, the fearsome tormentor, Laird Laghlan Deahan, became dissatisfied. Perhaps McKinnon had not yet shown enough grief; certainly he had not begged for the life of his wife nor even his daughters. There were no pleas for mercy, not even from Elspeth, who merely wept in despair. McKinnon himself refused to show weakness.

'So Deahan decided something more drastic was required to cause his sworn enemy to submit, perhaps even to swear worthless allegiance. He ordered the naked Elspeth to be laid on her back against the hard stone, her arms and legs spread-eagled. As she lay flat, exposed and shivering, the castle's conqueror ordered that her four limbs should be severed from her body, one at a time so she could anticipate the pain that was to come. You would think she would be dead, or, at least, in a faint, before the last limb was severed, wouldn't you? But no, the record tells of her screams for her daughters and her husband, for God to take her quickly, to end her suffering. And Duncan McKinnon could only watch until eventually all that was left on Elspeth's torso was her head; then it, too, was finally removed from her body. Before his wife's dismembered corpse followed his daughters over the battlements, that head, with its long grey tresses, was brandished in front of him, the eyes still half-open so he could see right into them. Were they accusatory, blaming him for all they'd lost because he'd chosen to fight three wars with the English against the Scots, his own people? Would the brain inside that severed head have still lived on a few seconds more without its body? There are some physicians who claim it could, but who's to know? Would that have left an energy behind for us to experience today? You're a parapsychologist, Mr Ash: What do you say?'

Ash took another sip of the whisky before he spoke, trying to dilute his abhorrence of the tale just told. He waited for the heat the single malt had created in his chest to subside before answering. 'I think all legends eventually become exaggerated,' he said. 'I hear some pretty gruesome things about many ancient manor houses, and especially castles, much of the time in my line of work. It doesn't necessarily make them true, but I do know that certain inhuman activities can create a mark that lives on with the property. Such excesses as you have described can send out resonances so intense that they are recorded into the buildings' very fabric. Given time – and it could take hundreds of years – they may fade away of their own accord. You could say, like a battery running down.'

'An understandable reaction, Mr Ash. I mean, from you.'

'I've studied these phenomena for many years,' he said, placing his hand over the tumbler as Byrone approached with the bottle.

'I'm sure you have many interesting tales, Mr Ash. But let me finish the story of the Mullachd, if you'd care to hear its ending, of course,' the present laird of Comraich Castle said, regarding Ash as if immensely interested in his reaction.

'I do dislike unfinished legends, embellished or not.' Ash had the feeling that this wily old man was testing him for some reason that he couldn't fathom.

'Then you will be interested in this. Laghlan Deahan was not yet finished with the unfortunate Laird McKinnon. While two strong men held him down, the Demon pushed the red-hot blade into McKinnon's left eye. And as the man screamed, the searing blade was pulled free, and slowly inserted into the other eye. Yet although McKinnon writhed in agony, still he never once pleaded for mercy.

'They pulled him to his feet and made ready to haul him down to the castle dungeons to live out whatever life remained for him in complete darkness and tormented by memories. But somehow – whether because McKinnon possessed incredible strength and fortitude, or because the pain and torture had ignited in him unnatural powers – somehow he broke free of the men holding him to stagger to the very edge of the battlements.

'Leaping into a crenel, he turned back to face his tormentors and he screamed his last defiance at them. The curse. The Mullachd.

'He told them that the castle, so hard fought for, would never be left in peace, that it would eventually be consumed by the same fires that had eaten away his own eyes.

'Then, before anyone could reach him – though personally, I imagine that no one tried too hard to do so – Laird Duncan McKinnon leapt to his death on the rocky shoreline far below.'

Shawcroft-Draker had lost himself for a few moments, for he gazed unblinkingly into the flames of the fire as though seeing images there of the legend he had just recounted. He'd related it with such unabashed and graphic detail it was as if it gave him distorted pleasure.

After a few quiet moments, the old man, the head of Comraich Castle, forced his attention away from the unwarming blaze and turned it on the psychic investigator.

74

Placid Pat raised his head, although he remained on his knees in the small aisle that led to the chapel's altar. From outside came the sound of the helicopter settling on the castle's helipad as its searchlight lit up the tall stained-glass window behind the statue of the Blessed Virgin.

He stared at Carsely, committing perverted sin in the very house of God, and the corrupted nun he sodomized in front of God's altar, the scene now lit like a ghastly kaleidoscope.

Shaking, Placid Pat raised the pistol. Carsely lifted a hand and his voice boomed out as, even now, he continued his penetration.

'*Noooo!*'

Pat pulled the trigger anyway. The *click* of the hammer echoed through the chapel. But the gun didn't fire.

Pat quickly checked the safety catch and tried again, but the result was no different. He pulled back the slide to see if the bullet was actually in the chamber. It looked fine. It looked menacing. It looked good to go.

Releasing the slide, he tried one more time and still nothing happened. The debauched pair's fear turned to laughter. Carsely thrust his hips in and out again.

'It's God's will, you know!' Carsely shouted, mocking him.

In frustration, Pat bowed his head and prostrated himself before the altar. The pistol lay discarded near his spread right hand. Tears fell onto the thin red carpet that led to the altar steps.

With blurred vision he saw the shape of the nun still bent over the length of the first pew, the ex-cleric continuing to mount her, still laughing derisively at the humbled figure lying no more than twelve feet from them. The nun beneath him sniggered.

But when the blast came from somewhere beneath the confined pulpit, she lost all sound, and when the flames that instantly followed engulfed them she no longer heard, nor saw, nor felt anything. She swallowed flames that seared her throat to boil her lungs as her priestly lover melted into her.

Placid Pat had seen enough explosions in his time to know that he was witnessing the effects not of God's wrathful vengeance but of a concealed incendiary device. He watched in horrified resignation as flames flew down the aisle towards him. Within seconds, he had become part of the inferno. Pieces of burning timber fell from the vaulted ceiling, everything made of wood exploding into fire around him. He lay spread-eagled, his mind screaming with the agony of burning.

At least he was facing the altar.

At least his burning arms were stretched out as if in supplication.

And at least all pain, all remorse, all guilt was evaporating as he lay dying in the furnace that had once been the holy chapel of Comraich Castle.

75

The timing wasn't great, but Ash knew he had to get round to the subject of his and Delphine's departure. (It seemed best not to mention they wished to take the young man in the tower too at this particular juncture.)

Before he could speak, the old man held up an emaciated arm.

'Byrone,' Lord Edgar rasped, 'I think I should take my other medicine now, don't you? I'm sure it will give me time to finish my discussion with Mr Ash.' He looked at the investigator. 'Would you mind popping into the other room?'

Ash rose to his feet and took himself and his drink to Lord Edgar's office. He was pondering how someone could tell a tale of such gory terror – and not without enthusiasm, as Lord Edgar had done only minutes ago, when Byrone appeared at the door.

'His lordship is ready now,' he announced, a puzzled expression on his long face.

As he followed Byrone into the smaller room, Ash wondered what kind of 'medicine' the butler had administered this time – he had already decided that the frail old man had been sipping morphine earlier. Byrone went to stand by the sideboard, where the cloth-covered tray still rested.

Lord Edgar Shawcroft-Draker gave Ash that queer half-smile that the investigator was becoming used to as Byrone filled another glass with murky-looking liquid and handed it to the laird.

'I assume, Mr Ash, that you have many questions to ask about the Inner Court and Comraich Castle.'

God, there were so many questions Ash wanted to ask Lord Edgar, even though escaping Comraich was a priority.

'Well . . .' Ash began slowly, picking up as he went along, 'I was wondering how you knew so much of the, uh, bloodier details of the Mullachd? It's almost as if you were there.' It was a crass remark, he knew, but over the years the parapsychologist had learned that flattery was the best way to gain a person's trust.

What he got from Lord Edgar was a desiccated chuckle. 'It was written down, young man, as near to the actuality as dammit. You see McKinnon employed a young scribe, whom Laghlan Deahan forced to record the events. The Gaelic account was translated into English for King Edward III and bound into a book. Copies of both are in Comraich's private library.'

Ash sipped his whisky, relishing the smoky taste. He wondered how well it mixed with the Modafinil.

Shawcroft-Draker appraised him. 'The curse is common knowledge. What we cannot understand is why the castle is now apparently being haunted after so many years of peace. We had hoped you would pinpoint the source of the hauntings and so advise us how to end it.'

'I'm no exorcist. I told Maseby and Haelstrom that.'

'No, but I understand you are skilled in the alleviation of such problems.'

Ash said nothing.

'Many important people have lived out their lives at Comraich, mainly in serenity. But now we are at a loss as to what to do.'

'That's easy. Evacuate the bloody place!'

'Please, Mr Ash, don't take me for a fool. You're fully aware that would be impossible. For many of our guests exposure would mean immediate incarceration – in many cases, for life.'

'Is it any different here?'

'Call Comraich a prison if you will, Mr Ash, but I doubt you'll hear any so-called prisoner complain.'

Ash decided it was time to bring the conversation round to requesting safe passage for himself and Delphine. 'Speaking of prisoners, Lord Edgar—' but the old man interrupted him.

'I'm sure by now that you've recognized several infamous faces. General Lukovic, for one,' he added with a wry smile. 'I understand he inadvertently saved your life. A stroke of luck for you.'

Only then did it strike Ash just how lucky he was still to be alive. First, he'd walked from the crashed lift almost unscathed; then in the containment area the guards had arrived just in time to prevent the patients there tearing him apart; and that morning he and Delphine had been saved from the wildcats with seconds to spare. Then there was the password to access the computer files, and how easily SANCTUM had popped into his head. He'd never believed in guardian angels, but it was as if there were something here working in his favour. Whether it was luck, or something else, somehow he felt he wasn't entirely on his own. Anyway, if luck was on his side, he might as well push it.

'We have others like Lukovic,' Shawcroft-Draker was saying, 'but we at Comraich do not judge, we simply listen.'

'And use what you hear for blackmail, of course.'

'Nothing so crude, Mr Ash, although I admit our guests and their knowledge are often very advantageous for us.'

'What about Robert Maxwell? How was he "advantageous" to you during his time here?'

Lord Edgar stiffened and scrutinized the investigator with heavy, weary eyes.

'How on earth did you discover that?' His tone was more curious than threatening.

Ash realized he was doing himself no favours; the more he knew, the less likely Lord Edgar was to let him leave.

'I didn't,' he said, backtracking. 'It was just a lucky guess. I'd never believed the story that Maxwell either had a heart attack or jumped overboard. But he needed to disappear, and this would have been the ideal place.'

'Very perceptive, Mr Ash.'

Lord Edgar suddenly sat straight, as if making a positive effort to regain his authority. Ash was aware that Byrone was watching from the sidelines.

'Unbelievably perceptive, in fact,' he continued. 'It seems you have "guessed" rather too much about Comraich. I would imagine Dr Wyatt has been of some help to you in that regard. Perhaps I should tell you everything; that might help your deliberations as to our problem here. However, it need not be a problem for much longer.'

Ash frowned, perplexed. Was Shawcroft-Draker hinting that Ash would soon no longer be a problem? That sounded ominous. Nevertheless, Ash was intrigued as Lord Edgar continued to reveal more than Ash could have ever imagined of the secrets of the Inner Court. He was horrified by Comraich's grisly roll call of criminals and despots who'd spent or were spending their last days at Comraich while the world thought they'd dropped off the face of the earth. And yet, it was fascinating.

The most intriguing story concerned Rudolf Hess, Deputy Head of Hitler's Third Reich, and his solo flight to Scotland during the height of the Second World War

'You may have read of the famous Mitford sisters? Particularly Unity Mitford, who became obsessed with Hitler, and, unfortunately, fell in love with him.'

Lord Edgar leaned forward in his armchair again as if to take the investigator into his confidence.

'Or,' he said quietly, 'of Hess's solitary foray into Scotland. You see, Unity Mitford, entranced by Hitler, fell pregnant by him. When war was declared, she shot herself in the head at the English Gardens in Munich. She failed, but the bullet did enter her brain. The family brought her home and immediately sent her away to a secret place where she gave birth to Hitler's child.'

Ash was grey with shock, but managed to remain still and expressionless.

'Now the great irony.' Shawcroft-Draker was still leaning forward in his seat, grimacing. 'The baby was *not* a boy. Hitler's dreams of siring a male heir to follow in his own footsteps were dashed. The child was a girl!' The lord weakly slapped his knee as though he thought the outcome was greatly amusing.

'Not only that, the great Führer, leader of Germany, and most of Europe at that time, had not only fathered a girl, but it was apparent that she was abnormal!' His voice had risen in near-hysteria, but Ash remained unmoved. 'She was abnormal, dear boy, with a misshapen head and was, as the doctors and carers were soon to discover, feeble-minded too. Can you imagine Hitler's shock when the news got back to him? Which Churchill made sure it did.'

'Churchill *knew?*'

'Indeed.'

'Did she die?'

'No, she has lived in Comraich ever since.'

Ash gasped. 'Of course. In the dungeons. That old disfigured woman is Adolf Hitler and Unity Mitford's daughter.' It wasn't a question.

Lord Edgar merely nodded his head.

Suddenly, Shawcroft-Draker clutched his stomach and bent forward, a grimace appearing on his face. Byrone hurried over to his master, looking full of concern.

'I'm all right,' Lord Edgar assured him. 'Not yet, not *yet.*' He'd emphasized the words as though the two men shared a secret pact. Ash studied the room, particularly the high French doors that opened onto the battlements. He was looking for a fast way out should the necessity arise.

And instinct told him it wouldn't be long before it did.

76

From the edge of the woods, but where he could not be seen from the castle or by the guards patrolling its perimeter, Twigg had watched the large Augusta 109 helicopter settle not far from the smaller Gazelle, its landing light cutting a clean beam through the night sky. Earlier in the day, he'd heard the arrival of the other helicopter, bringing more important members of the Inner Court all the way from Canary Wharf and Biggin Hill. No doubt the passengers it had disgorged on touchdown were tired, thirsty and hungry after the long journey. Their smart suits may have been a little rumpled after such a tedious trip, but he was sure they'd swaggered self-importantly into the castle lobby where Sir Victor Haelstrom would have greeted them at his most obsequious, the more acceptable side of his Jekyll and Hyde personality.

Now four passengers disembarked. Twigg saw the long and thin Andrew Derriman, a worthless streak of piss to his mind, hurry from the castle to welcome the late arrivals. Haelstrom was probably now in one of the small state rooms, drinking with the visitors who had arrived much earlier.

Set before the assassin on the scattered leaves was an array of battery-powered detonating equipment that would set off a series of explosives expertly concealed. He'd hidden a number of bombs and incendiaries around the place – oh, so carefully hidden – which, when they blew, would set off a series of chain reactions to create utter chaos and destruction.

The placement of the explosives on the helicopters had

been easy enough. Earlier, as Twigg had watched, a fully uniformed guard had escorted the VIPs into the castle (fear of more wildcats on the prowl had made sure the new arrivals were well protected) and had soon returned to watch over both helicopters, or in case any Comraich guest capable of flying such machines decided they'd had enough of their confinement. Twigg had waited in the trees until he saw the guard amble off to pee. And that was when the assassin had his chance. In the Gazelle, Twigg had planted a timer-ignited bomb: a rectangular wad of brick-red Semtex 10 inside a small box, easily hidden, to be detonated at his convenience. It hadn't taken long, and nobody had come along to ask him what he was doing inside the machine.

Twigg sniggered to himself in recollection and gazed lovingly at the detonator that would start the sixty-second countdown. In the castle below, the explosion would be devastating.

He would wait a little while longer for the IC senior members to rush for the bigger helicopter, and when the Augusta 109 had risen into the night sky, Twigg would create a glorious airborne funeral pyre by exploding the machine in mid-air.

This time, his snigger induced a bubble of snot from his nose as it turned into barely suppressed laughter.

77

The light from the slowly dying fire was as ineffectual as its heat, creating curling, wraithlike shadows around the room. Ash couldn't help but think these weaving, ever-moving dark shapes were like gathering phantoms. They were growing stronger and denser by the moment, and it was difficult to see Lord Edgar's face. Byrone had taken a seat by the wall after tending to the laird, which surprised Ash, for the butler wasn't the type to sit in his master's presence unasked. The room was very dark in that corner, though, and Byrone was merely an indistinct shape in the shadows. Ash noticed that even the light from the lamp on the small occasional table had dimmed to a faint glow, so the adumbration made everything nebulous, lacking in definition as if the darkness that hovered around them were closing in.

Lord Edgar's chin now rested on his chest, and just as Ash thought he had dropped off to sleep, the slumped figure suddenly rallied, lifting his weary eyes to the investigator's. To Ash, the man appeared to be in pain as he picked up the glass of medicine and sipped at it. Ash wondered again at what else besides morphine was in that glass. The long French doors rattled against their frames as a stiff gust of wind suddenly threw itself against the cliff face and battlements.

Ash felt the chill wrap itself around him, and the shadows further encroached upon the fading firelight, cooling even while the logs in it continued to burn. The two men could have been enclosed in their own private world, from which the silent figure of Byrone was excluded.

compelling to reject. And such a man would be asked to pay a very high fee indeed.'

When Shawcroft-Draker paused for a moment, Ash jumped in. 'Hold on. "Such a man"? You *are* talking about Gaddafi, aren't you?'

'Of course not,' Lord Edgar snapped back. 'Gaddafi is already here.'

Ash quickly subdued his shock.

'However, I believe Gaddafi is far too great a risk for even Comraich. It was to be my main thrust at the conference later tonight that we must dispose of Gaddafi ourselves. We already have access to his fortune. He put his complete trust in us once he knew his surviving family would be provided for.

'It's too risky for the Inner Court, don't you see? We know that MI6 is only too aware of the succour we give to certain rogues, but if they found out we were sympathetic towards someone as genocidal as Gaddafi . . . well, they would regard us as enemies of the state. It would be tantamount to having offered Saddam Hussein sanctuary during the Iraq crisis. No, the Inner Court's own survival depends on its actions; there are lines we must never cross.'

'But all the other evil war criminals, financial miscreants and deposed dictators you pamper here – how can that be tolerated by those in authority?'

'Yes, how indeed? But then you're not taking into account our knowledge. Believe me, knowledge is a great power in itself.'

'As I said earlier: blackmail.'

'Point taken, Mr Ash. We could even break the monarchy, should we choose so to do. That's a first-class reason to leave us alone, do you not think?'

A moan came from across the room and both men looked in that direction. The swirling shadows seemed even deeper to Ash.

'Are you all right, Byrone?' Lord Edgar enquired.

'For the moment, my lord, for the moment,' came the muttered reply.

Lord Edgar returned his attention to the investigator, who was baffled by the exchange.

'I can sense your confusion, Mr Ash, so let's make the most of whatever time is left. You see, I believe acceptance of our prospective guest would mean the certain ruination of the IC.'

Ash waited patiently for Shawcroft-Draker to continue.

'I expect you've heard of a certain Robert Gabriel Mugabe,' said the laird.

'*Mugabe* wants Comraich to take him in?' Ash said incredulously.

'Oh yes, my friend. Even though his prostate cancer will probably kill him soon enough, he actually fears assassination. Ironic, wouldn't you say?'

'Illogical, certainly.'

'He has seen the uprisings elsewhere in the world and knows that eventually it will happen in Zimbabwe. He's afraid of what the rebel forces would do to him, and so he would rather live out the rest of his days in secure comfort. With the billions he has stolen from his own people, he can easily afford that.'

'But you object to his acceptance here.'

'Precisely. We might be able to keep one assassination quiet, but two would multiply the risks enormously. Mugabe would be an unnecessary problem that in my view would prove insurmountable. Our whole organization would be jeopardized.'

'So at tonight's conference, you'll veto the idea.'

'Tonight it will no longer matter to me.'

Even more puzzled, Ash said, 'Does that mean you'll let me leave Comraich?'

'Soon you will be on your own, and then you can do whatever you like. Yes, you'll be free to go, and I sincerely hope you make it.' The old man wheezed in a deep breath and Ash saw that his shoulders were trembling and his head

551

unsteady. Then he said something Ash found even more surprising: 'Corruption has a limited shelf life, as many of our moguls and politicians eventually learn for themselves. And, dear God, I'm so weary of it.'

'You could end the Inner Court, though, couldn't you?' Ash said urgently, yet knowing it was hopeless.

'Sometimes I wish I could; but corruption breeds more corruption. No, there are too many secrets, too many secrets . . .'

Lord Edgar's head suddenly slumped to his chest and the investigator thought for a second the old man had gone. He laid his almost empty glass of whisky down and knelt before the laird, ducking his head to look into the troubled face.

'Lord Edgar . . . ?' He gave the man's bony knee a gentle shake. To his relief, the laird gave a muffled grunt and peered about him with half-open eyes.

'Did you think I was dead?' he asked the investigator, who remained on one knee. Lord Edgar smiled, just a wisp of a smile, but a smile nonetheless. 'Would you . . . would you do something for me? Would you please go over to Byrone and tell me how he is?'

Mystified, Ash rose and walked across the room to take a look at the butler. The curling shadows almost seemed to clear a path for him.

Byrone was rigidly still, leaning slightly to one side. It was a miracle he hadn't fallen off the chair, thought Ash. He realized in shock that something was not right, and felt the butler's neck for a pulse. There was none.

He went back to Shawcroft-Draker.

'He's dead,' he said, quietly and tonelessly, like a doctor who'd had too many patients die on him that week.

Another weak smile. 'That's good, that's grand,' Lord Edgar murmured.

As the investigator made to return to his own chair, the laird grabbed Ash's wrist with surprising strength.

'Byrone chose an easier way than I.'

Ash crouched on his haunches so that he could hear Lord

Edgar a little more clearly. 'You mean he deliberately took his own life?'

The grey man nodded his head awkwardly.

'He took the easier way, and quite right too. He had little to repent, apart from forty-odd years of duty to me. He chose pentobarbitone, a fast-acting barbiturate, with a little something extra. I think he waited until he was sure I'd come to no harm from you.'

'He thought I might hurt you?'

'He – we – couldn't be sure how you would react to what I've told you. For myself, I picked a harder and slightly slower method of dying. A method intended for you, originally.'

Ash was duly shocked, but then, his murder was something he'd practically expected, even more so after this conversation with Comraich Castle's overseer.

'You needn't worry, my boy,' said his lordship, and his cheeks had begun to hollow, the bones above them becoming more prominent. The parapsychologist was certain the dying man did not have long to live. Creases in Lord Edgar's face had deepened even more, engraving his already wrinkled countenance with a fresh criss-cross pattern of dark lines.

'Can I do anything for you?' Ash urged earnestly. 'Shall I fetch Dr Pritchard?'

'No, no . . . the deed is done, and can never be reversed, as they say. Nothing now can hold back the poison inside my body. If you could pass me what's left . . .'

Ash quickly reached past Shawcroft-Draker for the glass. He put it into the dying man's trembling hand almost tenderly and helped lift the tumbler to his thin lips.

'At least it isn't dulling my senses as much as I feared,' said the Laird of Comraich. 'Although by now it doesn't do much to dull the pain, either.'

Ash changed position and sat at the laird's feet. 'Maybe you should have taken the same way as Byrone.'

'He was such a loyal servant. I'm pleased he died quietly and, I hope, peacefully.'

'Why didn't you choose the same method?'

'Curiosity, I suppose.'

Ash's face was impassive.

'So what were you planning to use to kill me off?' Ash indicated the now empty glass.

'Saxitoxin. The effects of that take thirty minutes after ingestion to begin working. It presents all kinds of severe symptoms: tingling, a floating sensation, muscle weakness, vertigo, respiratory failure, paralysis, and finally cranial nerve dysfunction. All very unpleasant and exactly what is beginning to happen to me. Undetectable in an autopsy unless you know exactly what to look for. I'd chosen it especially for you.'

'Thanks a lot,' said Ash grimly. 'What were you going to do with my body?'

Instead of answering his question directly, the older man went off at a tangent. 'We knew you'd been an alcoholic, but then we were made aware of the reasons behind your dependency.'

Kate must have told Maseby about Grace, he thought.

'So that's why I've been offered drinks all the time, right from the journey here onwards.'

'Correct.'

'You got one thing wrong. I'm not really an alcoholic. Yeah, yeah, I know most alcoholics say that, but I only drink hard liquor for particular reasons. I think if I told you, you'd quite understand.'

'I'm sure I would; I know your history.'

'So, your plan was to find out from me the reasons behind Comraich's haunting, get me drunk on your doctored whisky and then ask if I'd like a tour of the battlements, during which I'd "accidentally" fall over the edge. Should my body ever be found, all the autopsy would reveal would be a very fine single malt, which would convince everyone my death was a drunken accident.' *Everyone but Kate McCarrick*, he thought to himself.

Ash sat back in his armchair opposite the dying man.

'You're very astute, Mr Ash.'

'It's still an elaborate way to murder me. Why poison me if you were going to throw me off the cliff anyway?'

Lord Edgar was drawing in shallow, rapid breaths. 'The Inner Court is meticulous with its plans. We couldn't know what fight you w-would have p-put up if not poisoned first. That was Sir Victor's idea.'

Wouldn't you know it? thought Ash. He saw that the drug was beginning to work on the man opposite him, whose thin hands clutched the chair's arms. He realized Shawcroft-Draker wouldn't be capable of coherent speech for much longer.

Leaning forward in his seat, his wrists resting on his knees, Ash asked in a grim voice, 'Why the change of plan? Why did you take the poison rather than give it to me?'

The laird lifted his head and peered down his nose at the investigator as if he didn't know who the man was. But then he seemed to gather himself and Ash realized that the symptoms were arriving in spasms.

'You might call it an epiphany, Mr Ash.'

The investigator was surprised at the old man's clear diction.

'When I learned my cancer was incurable, it set me to thinking about my life and how I'd used it. How I'd used people. I think the decision was made the moment I saw you when you first came to Comraich. I realized you were a comparatively young man with many years of life ahead of him. It was then I made the decision about my own life, and for the first time I realized how I'd abused it by protecting and giving succour to so many criminals, despots, and even dictators who were forced to run and hide from their own countrymen, stealing all the wealth from their people while babies died of disease and malnutrition.'

A shudder ran through him and he weakly lifted a hand to let Ash know he was still all right.

'Would you like me to get you more morphine?' Ash asked.

'No, that's very kind, but it can do no more for me. I just wanted time enough to explain my loathing for all I've done.

I'm afraid that you're my stand-in confessor in Byrone's absence. Many a night since my illness was diagnosed we've spent in this room discussing the error of our ways.'

He shook his head while maintaining a faint smile.

'We served together in the Second World War – he was my sergeant – and have known each other since. He was a friend, more than just a butler, although he never once stepped over the line. Even when I told him I would end my life in my own way, rather than let the cancer take me, he did not try to deter me. Far from it – he asked permission to die with me. How's that for loyalty, eh? A passing breed as far as this world is concerned.'

Lord Edgar suddenly bent forward, holding his head in both hands as if to quell the dizziness. Anxiously, Ash stretched forward too, ready to catch him should he fall. Inadvertently, the ailing laird had allowed the blanket to fall away from his shoulders, and the tumour in the old man's stomach seemed to rest on his bony upper thighs like a football.

Shawcroft-Draker covered himself again, although his movements were slow and awkward.

Ash hoped the laird would last a little longer, for there were still questions the parapsychologist wanted to ask him. He pulled his armchair closer, virtually in front of the fire, though its meagre heat posed no danger.

There were many questions Ash might have asked, but just one was uppermost in his mind: the identity of the almost transparent young man now waiting with Delphine.

'Lord Edgar, can you tell me who "The Boy" is?' said Ash.

78

Oleg Rinsinski lay back on the light blue Bio-Electro Magnetic Energy Regulator mattress with a big grin on his coarse, brutish face, eyebrows a thick black shagpile across the top of his nose, heavy-lidded eyes closed and yellowing stunted teeth showing through thick lips. He resembled a typical James Bond villain with his heavily stubbled chins. His hero in 007 movies always tended to be the villain of the piece. It was a great shame the recent Bond movies no longer had such stereotypical baddies. If only they made films where the bad guy who wanted to rule the world won. Now *that*, he could clap for.

And the girls: where were the Ingrid Pitts nowadays, the real women, who you just knew were frisky in bed, but could always keep up with the bad boys' violence? There should be a shrine somewhere for Ingrid Pitt, somewhere he could lay flowers to celebrate her life. If he had someone like Ingrid to watch films with, he'd be a happy man. Because *she* was a man's woman, especially in those vampire movies she was so good at.

Naked and alone on the blue magnetic mat that was supposed to cure all his ills, he smiled while he thought of lovely Ingrid.

The ultra-thin filaments were already beginning to vibrate slightly, arousing him. By rights, there should have been a nurse with him to regulate the intensity, but he'd tried so often to get into their little panties that they all refused to stay in the room with him after they had set the controls.

Rinsinski forced his hairy, naked body to relax on the narrow bed with its healing mattress. A smaller, thinner mattress, was tied tightly across his chest and stomach with straps, restricting his movement. Before long he could feel a gentle tingling sensation all over his gross body.

When he'd first used the device, a doctor had told him that the magnetic therapy machine was good for stress and skin disorders, as well as arthritis, asthma, gout, osteoporosis, infertility, multiple sclerosis and tinnitus, all of which he believed he suffered from.

But today, he'd had to insist on using the machine. He was sure it also had a calming effect. He really needed that, especially after last night's drama in the dining room. All guests had been ordered to stay in their suites for the time being, but Rinsinski was not a man to take orders. They'd finally given in, and one of the nurses had rigged him up.

After a while, dreaming of Ingrid, he began to doze – until the tingling sensation began to feel a little too intense, and then, rather uncomfortable.

Bellowing for a nurse seemed to be of no use – probably all cowering in their open-plan hutches, he reckoned. Still, they should have been able to hear him, even if the door was closed.

Growing impatient, Rinsinski tried wriggling his hirsute body to loosen the ties that now seemed tighter than when they were fitted, as if they'd shrunk and become as rigid as metal straps. The first serious pain he felt was in the big toe on his left foot, where he'd always complained he had gout. It intensified. Then, something strange: the big toe on his right foot began to tingle and hurt just as much. Still nobody answered his yells.

He struggled against the straps, but they only became tighter. He suddenly smelt burning. He lifted his head from the pillow and peered down his stocky body. Although it was difficult to see beyond his barrel chest and the smaller mattress that lay over it, he could just make out the top edge of his right foot. The skin there was smouldering. He checked the other side and that was beginning to smoulder too, a thin stream of black smoke rising from it.

This time he roared in Russian, then broken English, but still no one came to his aid.

He thrashed his head from side to side, frantically attempting to heave his body, buck his thick legs. But he could not move. It was as though he actually *were* magnetized to the mattress, which was becoming hotter by the moment.

'*Help!*' he cried desperately. '*Help me at once!*'

His cry was louder than ever, yet no one came.

'My God,' he moaned as tears began to blur his vision and to run down the sides of his thick-featured face.

Suddenly, hope! He could hear someone rattling the doorknob from outside. But the door was not opening.

'*Please!*' he begged. '*Please someone – help!*'

It was growing so hot beneath him, as if the ultra-thin filaments inside the melting mattress were red with heat. He tried to move a shoulder, but the searing plastic stuck to his skin, stretching strings of the stuff rising with his shoulder, then drawing him back like elastic so that he lay there, stuck. And the smoke was thickening, making him cough.

Someone outside was banging on the door and calling his name, but faintly, as if they were several rooms away. Yet there was no lock on the door, no windows to smash. *No one to help him*.

But they must, and quickly. He knew what was about to happen.

And it did.

The two mattresses, one beneath him, the other tied around his chest, broke into tiny flames, and those flames rose and danced, around him and above him where his chest hair had already singed away. And soon, all the hair on his body began to flame like a miniature forest fire.

He screamed, he twisted and turned, tears drying instantly on his jowly face. There were thumps and bangs and kicks on the door as staff tried to reach him, but they couldn't break in even though there was no lock on the door. And the smoke rose from him as his body roasted and steamed, curling in the air like mocking spirits.

He imagined he could see ugly, delighted faces within the smoke while he cooked. Juices sizzled from his now hairless body as though he were a pig roasting on a spit.

His fat and the meat on his bones became liquid and finally burst into one great blaze. Although he screamed, the agony was momentarily gone because all the nerve endings of his neural system had burned away. But then the torment rekindled as the vicious heat found the inner nerves, nerves deep within places normally protected by flesh and bone, so that his half-choked piteous cries rang out only weakly.

As he approached death he knew there was no longer any point in screaming. It was too late now, even if the door were to be broken down.

And as his black-hearted soul fled like someone from a crazy man wielding a bloodstained axe, his final visions were not of his wife and children but of lovely, luscious, sex-goddess Ingrid. Maybe she would even be waiting for him at the golden gates, for Oleg Rinsinski in his vainglorious mind had no doubt that he was heading heavenwards.

79

'"The Boy",' Ash repeated. 'The young man called Lewis,' he urged, anxiously pushing the conversation along before the older man expired.

'Ah.' Lord Edgar managed a thin-lipped smile. 'Delphine still gets it wrong after, what? Three years?'

'I don't understand.'

'His name is *Louis*, pronounced Louie. Always has been. She just mispronounced it to begin with and we never corrected her: less chance of anyone putting two and two together, d'you see? Does that give you a clue?'

Ash shook his head.

His lordship gave the chair's arm another thump, and it seemed to Ash that dust curled from it. The room was growing darker by the minute, encasing the two men in a shrinking cocoon of dim light. The doors leading to the battlements rattled against their frames once more. By now he could see only the dead butler's shined shoes and the part of his trousers that almost covered his ankles; the rest of his body, still sitting in the chair, leaning at an awkward angle, was lost to the shadows.

Shawcroft-Draker suddenly began to wheeze again; he pulled a white handkerchief from beneath the tartan blanket and held it to his mouth.

'Can I get you anything?' Ash asked gently.

'No, that's very kind, but really, no. I don't think my life will extend much longer and I *should* like to tell you of Louis. Even if I've left nothing much behind to be proud of, at least Comraich has taken care of him all these years.'

'By keeping him in a tower room, allowed out only at night when others can't see him?' Ash suppressed his anger, remembering how frail the man before him was.

'That was necessary, I'm afraid. You've seen his skin, how translucent it is. Before Dr Wyatt came here, he hardly ever left the tower, he was so ashamed. For twenty-odd years he never had a friend, someone he could talk to. Dr Wyatt's arrival at Comraich changed all that. A bond developed between them.'

'Then she knows who he is?' Ash had leaned further forward with the intensity of the question. Had Delphine not trusted him enough to confide in him?

The other man might have scoffed: Lord Edgar's pained breathing made it difficult to tell.

'My boy, even Louis doesn't know who he is. Perhaps *he* felt Delphine might be able to tell *him*.'

'But you know.'

'Yes, yes, of course I know. And I think it's time he knew too. After all, he must be, what, nearly thirty by now.'

'And . . . ?' the investigator urged impatiently, for he, too, was aware that the Laird of Comraich did not have much more life in him.

Ash thought Shawcroft-Draker was choking at first, and half rose to help. Then he realized the other man was laughing through his wretched discomfort.

'I'm . . . I'm sorry . . . Mr Ash. I don't mean . . . to mock, but if only you knew . . .'

'So tell me.'

'I will, I will. But . . . but let me tell you in . . . in my own . . . way.'

They both waited, the glow of the fire diminishing by the moment in the surrounding darkness, as a candle might slowly die. The moving shadows of the room ate into the space between them.

'Of course, you remember Princess Diana . . .' Lord Edgar began, and Ash felt a sudden, extra chill run through him that had nothing to do with the coldness of the room, nor the wind that rattled the windows so fiercely.

The Laird of Comraich fell quiet again. Ash guiltily hoped he hadn't lost him, not at this crucial point in the story. Then the old man began rubbing his wrist, dislodging the tartan blanket to reveal the unsightly tumour once more. 'Strange sensation,' he said as he continued to rub his lower arm. 'Sort of prickling, burning. Tingling too.'

'Princess Diana,' Ash reminded him.

He ceased all movement. 'Diana. Yes. Lovely girl. But, you see, she'd begun to rebel quite early in the marriage. Originally, she was forced to wear unfashionable dresses and rather silly hats. It was only later, once she began to use her own designers, that we realized how gorgeous she was. Five feet nine and beautiful with it. Flawless skin, beautiful eyes – moviestar looks, if you like.'

He swayed in his chair. Only the arms prevented him from rolling off. 'Give me a moment,' he murmured to the investigator, and Ash watched him as he tried to control his balance.

The Saxitoxin was taking its toll, Ash realized, and wished there was something he could do to help the man.

'You may recall,' he continued softly, 'that at one time, early in the marriage, she threw herself down the stairs at the Palace as a protest. She tried it again, some time later, and it was discovered she was pregnant. She'd had her first child and longed for another. She—'

'I recall many people assuming Prince Harry's red hair meant that she'd taken a lover . . . a guardsman . . .' Ash interrupted.

Lord Edgar spluttered and clung to the arms of the chair.

'What dreadful minds we have,' he croaked, once his coughing settled. 'Everybody – *everybody!* – seems to forget that Diana's brother, Earl Spencer, had red hair before it turned grey. The colour was in the Spencer genes, for God's sake!'

Despite himself, Ash grinned and held up a hand in surrender.

Lord Edgar leaned forward so that their faces were even closer and he did not have to raise his voice to be heard.

'Please listen, and try not to interrupt again. Time is short ... So, as I was saying, when Diana fell down the flight of stairs for the second time – this would have been in 1983 – she was eighteen weeks pregnant. The fall induced early labour. Imagine the shock. She'd told no one of the pregnancy.'

Delphine had told him that Lewis had been born at eighteen weeks. The conclusion was inescapable: Lewis – *Louis* – was Diana's child!

'But it was the baby's condition that shocked them all – or frightened them, if you prefer,' Lord Edgar continued.

'Louis' skin: so fine it's translucent,' said Ash.

'It's transparent. Let's not prevaricate. All the baby's internal organs could be plainly seen. Louis was a freak of nature. Can you imagine how the royal family felt about that? William and Harry have never been told, of course. Obviously Her Majesty and Prince Philip were called, but only they and the Prince of Wales were aware of all the circumstances.'

Ash opened his mouth to speak, but the Laird of Comraich stopped him with a weary, trembling hand.

'Please! No more interruptions. I can feel myself fading and I want you, at least, to know Louis' birthright, no matter how unsightly his condition.'

The investigator hung his head and listened.

'Impossibly, the child wasn't the first to suffer such a curious physical abnormality, but in the past no baby born with it had been allowed to live. There were congenital problems for the boy, naturally: brain haemorrhage and heart disease were strong possibilities. The baby weighed less than one and a half pounds. He was so delicate, they say he resembled a newborn bird. He could be held in the palm of one hand. The attending physicians advised that the baby should be allowed to die naturally, but the Queen and Prince Philip decreed that such a decision could be made only by the baby's parents. Diana was heavily sedated, and an immediate decision was required, so the boy's fate was left solely to his father.

'Many things – cruel things – have been said and written about Prince Charles, a lot of them inaccurate. But I can tell you, he's a very spiritual person, a man with *soul*, and deeply philosophical. He was aware of the problems the monarchy faced should the matter become public knowledge, and, of course, he knew the child would face a terribly difficult life.

'But Charles is no murderer. The baby was placed inside an incubator to keep him warm, and a ventilator used to help him breathe. Premature and abnormal the child might be, but while there was a chance he could live, Charles's uncompromising stance was that everything possible must be done to help his son survive.

'When he was asked to name the boy, without hesitation he said Louis: a small tribute to his great-uncle who had been murdered by the IRA just four years earlier.'

Ash listened in awe. Delphine really hadn't a clue who her patient and friend was.

'Of course, this was all done secretly. The baby's true identity was never revealed to the medical staff who managed to keep him alive.'

'And you – when did you discover who he was?'

'As head of Comraich, I was informed of the child's parentage when he arrived, though of course I was sworn to secrecy. Even Sir Victor isn't privy to the secret and never will be, unless . . .' Lord Edgar struggled to draw in a breath, 'unless he is chosen as the new head.'

Another hold you have on the royal family, Ash thought to himself.

'Remarkably, the baby survived. You might even say "miraculously".'

Another notion struck Ash. 'Has Prince Charles ever visited his son?'

'So far as the prince is concerned, his son is dead. Within

days of his arrival we were instructed to inform him that the boy had died of complete renal failure. He agreed that the body should be cremated here. He had no wish to attend, nor would it have been wise to.'

'Instructed by whom?'

'By the highest authority, Mr Ash.'

Ash could see he would get no further with that line of questioning, and time was running short. 'But Diana . . . ?'

'Oh, she was told the baby had died within minutes of the birth. The sedatives were very strong, so strong that, when she was finally allowed to come round, she could scarcely remember the incident. Perhaps she didn't want to remember. In any event, Diana never referred to the occasion ever again, I'm told.'

Ash was purposely blunt, angered by what he'd learned. 'So there's no official evidence, then, that Prince Louis exists.'

Shawcroft-Draker appraised Ash coldly. 'There *is* evidence, and it's in a deposit box in the vault of my private London bank, Coutts. Along with other items—'

Perhaps there would come a time when Ash would remember that, but at this point his thoughts were too much in turmoil to give it any particular significance. Once again, the old man swayed in his chair, his hands clutching the armrests tightly.

'Vertigo,' he told the investigator. 'Just another effect of the Saxitoxin. My brain is acting strangely too. I think I'm going to a bad place. Perhaps Byrone will be waiting for me, although he was a better man than I.'

Ash knelt before Lord Edgar once more, gripping his upper arms to steady him. *Christ*, he thought, *he's dying in front of me.*

Lord Edgar's movements slowly began to stiffen, as if he were collecting himself. Their faces almost level, the Laird of Comraich peered at Ash with fading, watery eyes.

'If I had known,' he said, catching his breath, 'I think I would have taken Byrone's way out. It must have been more pleasant than this, don't you think? Or I could have asked Byrone to put a bullet in my brain.'

He groaned aloud and it seemed to Ash that the shadows around them were closing in even more rapidly, becoming frenetic, feathery wisps of darkness reaching into the soft cocoon of light.

'I . . .'

Lord Edgar Shawcroft-Draker was attempting to speak, but now his words were thin and so quiet that Ash had to put his ear to Lord Edgar's mouth.

'These ghosts, Mr . . . Mr Ash, those that you . . . came . . . to investigate. They have visited me before, you know. Generally . . . in my sleep, but not . . . but not always. They . . . they have shown me my future. They revealed to . . . me . . . the Hell . . . the Hell that they have come from. The same . . . Hell that waits for . . . me. And it's ugly . . . it's abominable, abhorrent . . . a hideous place. I was glad . . . so glad . . . you came to me tonight. You see, by telling you . . . telling you . . . these secrets, I might save . . . save myself . . . at least from some of these horrors. Do you think it . . . possible? Mr Ash? Have . . . have I redeemed myself in some . . . in some small way?'

His eyes searched Ash's, as though he might find the answer there. Perhaps even some kind of absolution.

Ash saw the old man's eyes losing their focus. He was fading, Ash realized, waiting only for an answer, some spark of forgiveness – from him, of all people.

'I'm afraid, d'you see? I'm terribly afraid. Please forgive me my sins, won't you?'

'I'm sorry, Lord Edgar, I'm not a priest,' he said quietly.

Then Lord Edgar's head slumped forward, and the life finally left him.

Despite his revulsion for all the dead man stood for, Ash felt that he should somehow pay his respects, but he was never given the chance. From somewhere in the castle – it sounded close, it had to be on this floor – came another loud *boom*.

Suddenly, the fire lashed out at Ash from the hearth, the heat causing him to utter a cry of fear rather than pain. He fell to the floor and he saw that the dancing shadows were backing away, as if they too had been scorched by the unexpected torrid flames. He rolled away from the fire, but realized that it had retreated to the confines of the hearth and was burning brightly, throwing out as much warmth as it had when he'd first entered the room.

Byrone's corpse fell to the floor with a thump, and Ash began to pick himself up. He looked towards Lord Edgar, and saw he sat upright still, but with his head resting over the low back of the armchair, his neck exposed so that his Adam's apple protruded like a gruesome lump ready to be sliced in two, and his cheeks had sunk into deep shadows. The eyes were not fully closed, but they were dull, and the laird's mouth had opened wide. His chair had caught alight, small fires burning along one of its arms.

As Ash staggered to his feet he heard the door to the outer room crash open. Then heavy footsteps strode across the floor with a familiar voice shouting. *'The chapel's on fire, your lordship. An explosion! And there has just been another in the corridor outside! We must get everybody out!'* Filling the smaller room's doorway was the huge figure of Sir Victor Haelstrom.

Then came a sound so frightening that it made Ash momentarily shrink into himself.

It was the bellow of Haelstrom's terrible rage.

80

When Kate McCarrick awoke she found herself already sitting up in bed, the covering blanket fallen to her waist. She wore only a sheer nightdress, but her body beneath it was layered with a fine film of perspiration.

Her eyes were open wide but unseeing in the dimness of her bedroom. It took a second or two for her consciousness to catch up with her, for her mind was momentarily blank. Then the terrors reached her again.

She'd been dreaming – no, she'd been in a nightmare. Yet as much as she concentrated, she could glimpse only brief images. Most were of David. He was in danger. He was in terrible danger. Kate raised her knees under the covers, her arms going around them, forehead resting on top. She tried to remember, but as with most dreams, this one was elusive, so that all she could capture were feelings: feelings of fear and horror.

Something bad, something vile, was happening in Comraich Castle, and David Ash was caught at its centre.

She pushed away the bedclothes and walked across to the large plate-glass window overlooking the city. She needed to see the signs of normality, the lighted windows, the night-time traffic, shadows of people walking the pavements – the testimony of life itself.

Kate was familiar with unaccountable manifestations and sensory illusions, but this sensing in her own mind was different, somehow more solid, a feeling she could almost touch.

And it was because of David's psychic gift, although he always scoffed and denied it. Yet lately – for the past few years, in fact – his repudiation of it had faltered, become less certain, as if he were finally beginning to admit to this sixth faculty, although he referred to it as a strong 'intuition' rather than a psychic capability.

She thought – she sensed – that his own mind was sending out signals of distress, even if he would not acknowledge it himself. There was something awful inside Comraich Castle and, frustratingly, there was nothing she could do to help him. Kate cursed herself for deciding to have an early night after the last two lengthy dinner dates she'd had; perhaps in deep unconsciousness, the subconscious had been reached, setting her dreaming of such diverse amalgams as fire and water.

Perhaps there was just one small thing she could do. Even if it would probably have little influence. She hoped her friend Gloria Standwell would not be annoyed for being disturbed at home at this time of night.

Kate reached for the phone on the bedside cabinet.

81

Haelstrom paused in the doorway for five seconds only. First he stared at David Ash, then the body of Lord Edgar Shawcroft-Draker; he ignored Byrone's corpse altogether.

As Haelstrom bellowed, Ash had no time to recover before the dark figure was pounding towards him, huge arms stretched forward to grab the startled investigator. Ash was caught in a crushing grip and both men went flying across the room so fast and with such force that they crashed through the long French windows out onto the battlements, where the wind sweeping up from the sea tugged at their clothes and hair.

They fell, such was their impetus, and Ash took the brief moment of reprieve to roll away from the other man, whose beefy hand clasped wildly, trying to catch hold of the investigator again. But Ash was quickly on his feet while the heavy-set Haelstrom struggled to his knees, still bellowing, still scrabbling at windblown air.

The light from the full moon was bright and lit up the lengthy crenellated battlements, bathing the walkway in its clear silver glow. The wind whipped at Ash's hair and in the distance he could see the silvery-white foam of rushing waves. It gave him a sense of how high up the flagstone walkway was and a chilled shiver skipped through him as he remembered the McKinnon family's fate. For some reason Haelstrom appeared to be harbouring similarly murderous intentions.

He waited no longer. Haelstrom's cumbersome body was

still bent over and winded and his massive head offered a target too good to ignore. The investigator aimed a booted foot directly at it, kicking with all his might.

Haelstrom roared in pain and went staggering into the wall, fortunate not to fall through one of the open crenels. He remained hunched. Kicking was not Ash's preferred way of fighting (in fact, he would not choose to fight at all), but he'd had no choice. Haelstrom was capable of crushing him like a bug and both opponents knew it.

If he could daze the big man sufficiently, Ash reasoned, he might just get the chance to escape. He pitched himself at Haelstrom once more and caught him on his fleshy thigh with his left boot. Haelstrom howled, but the pain seemed to spur him on rather than discourage him. He stood erect, despite the injury to his leg, and swiped his arm backwards at the investigator. The back of his big, chunky fist caught Ash on the temple, knocking him back across the walkway. He remained on his feet though, and met Haelstrom's limping run towards him.

The two men collided midway across the flagstones, and because Haelstrom was both taller and much heavier, Ash took the worst of it. He grunted as Haelstrom sent him spinning backwards to come up flat against the wall opposite the battlements. Left breathless, he did his best to dodge Haelstrom's next drive at him, but the big man's fist smashed down hard into the angle between neck and collarbone. It felt like being hit with a sledgehammer and Ash tried to ignore the shocking pain by dodging round the older man and bunching his fist, punching hard into the other man's kidneys. It was a good blow, a telling blow, and Haelstrom arched backwards, giving Ash another opportunity to strike.

He drove his fist into Haelstrom's massive head, striking a cheekbone and almost breaking his own knuckles. He winced and stepped back to regroup, sucking at his bruised knuckles and tasting blood – his own blood – while Haelstrom staggered, still on his feet.

The big man, his features curled into a sneer, held out his massive arms, curved like a Sumo wrestler's, legs apart, feet firmly planted, as if ready to force his opponent out of the *dohyō*. There was no doubt in Ash's mind that the boundary of the hypothetical circle extended over the edge of the battlements and he took up a crouched defensive position. He considered making a run for it, but his left leg, raked the previous day by a wildcat's claws, was now throbbing painfully; besides, Haelstrom's bulk took up almost the whole width of the walkway.

His opponent began to close in. Soon, he would make his rush. Ash feinted one way and then the other, but his opponent was ready each time. On the third attempt, the investigator tried a different tack: he deliberately ran at Haelstrom, head lowered to smash directly into the surprised man's stomach. Haelstrom staggered back a few feet, but that was it. All Ash had done was put himself in reach.

Ash suddenly felt his feet leave the ground as Haelstrom crushed the breath from him and lifted the helpless investigator towards the outer wall. He thought his spine might break at any moment and he wheezed as he tried to draw in more air. It was hopeless: the other man was too powerful and his grip was like steel, clamping his arms tight to his sides. He felt a sudden jarring as his back and his head hit the wall. Haelstrom abruptly changed position and grasped Ash's lapels, drawing him towards the edge, and Ash suddenly found his head and shoulders were hanging over empty space, the wind rushing up to meet him from the base of the cliff six hundred feet below.

Oddly, he was struck by how clearly he could hear the waves dash themselves against the rocky shoreline; it was as though all his senses had become more acute, sharpened, and every detail of Haelstrom's queerly featured face, twisted in a snarl above him, stood out.

Was this what it was like for everyone who died violently? Was everything suddenly rendered in high definition and perfect surround sound? He could even see the pores in his opponent's face in the strong moonlight, the hairs inside the man's small crooked nose, the bubbles of spittle on his lips.

Then Ash felt his body being tilted further over the foaming abyss, tipping beyond the point of no return.

He prepared himself to die.

82

As Kevin Babbage and Rachael Krantz descended the stone stairway to the dungeons, the smell and the floating dust assailed their nostrils. The security chief was beginning began to regret his decision to accompany the senior nurse on the expedition. Although there'd always been a stench of excrement, urine and general body odour coming from the cells, it had never reeked as badly as this. Beside him, Krantz reached out to touch the wall to steady herself, for the light was bad here and the steps were worn from centuries of use. Her hand came away wet with slime and she brushed her fingers against her white uniform.

As a precaution, the security chief had ordered the containment area guard, Grunwald, to keep the heavy self-closing safety door behind them open just in case there was trouble and Babbage and the nurse needed to get out fast. As he had put his weight against the iron door and wrinkled his nose as the foul air came up at him, the sentinel's relief that he hadn't been made to go with them had been all too clear.

Not generally a nervous individual, Babbage couldn't help but be aware something was very wrong about Comraich Castle lately, and it wasn't just the maggots and the flies. No, there was a definite oppression hovering over the place, far worse than ever before. Even the ceiling and wall lights were low, as if the generators weren't working properly. And it was *cold*, so bloody cold that several people were wearing topcoats even in the operations room. He could see the vapour from his mouth each time he breathed out.

When they reached the bottom step, Babbage undid the two buttons of his jacket in case he needed his gun in a hurry. He turned to face the long dingy corridor. It was difficult to see things clearly down here, even though the ceiling lights were just about working. He was going to have those generators checked out again.

He felt Nurse Krantz at his side.

'Look,' she said, pointing a finger at the end of the corridor.

Squinting, Babbage peered into the shadows, seeing only rubble and dirt caused by the old elevator's crash.

'I can't . . .' he began, then stopped when he saw a shape, a woman wearing an inmates' smock. She was holding something clutched to her chest.

'It's her,' prompted the senior nurse. 'Her. The madwoman. The cell locks must have failed again.' The red-haired nurse clucked her tongue in annoyance. She started forward, but Babbage held her back.

'Just hang on a minute.' The security chief went to the nearest cell door and gave it a shove with his hand. The door was locked and he peeked through the wired glass observation panel. It was even darker in there, but he could see the figure of a man lying in a foetal position on his cot.

Meanwhile, Krantz had tried the door opposite and found it shut tight. She, too, looked through the letter-box viewing window. The room looked empty, but as her eyesight adapted to the semi-darkness she realized there was someone sitting curled up in one corner of the cell. It was a man, for he wore thin, pyjama-style trousers. His forehead was lowered to his bent knees, hands and lower arms tucked into his lap. She gave the wired window a sharp tap with her fingernail and when the inmate looked up to see her, his wide eyes were crazed. He sent a shiver through Krantz and she was *used* to handling the crazies.

She gave a start when a hand touched her shoulder.

'This one, too?' asked Babbage.

'What . . . ?'

'The door,' he replied tensely. 'Is it locked?'

'Oh. Yes. Yes, there's an old man in there, curled up in a corner. He can't get out.'

'Nor the other one.' The security chief turned his head to seek out the figure that Krantz had spotted a minute ago. She was still standing there, staring at them, black orbs floating around her.

'How the fuck did she get out if all the other cell doors are locked?' Babbage wished he'd brought his flashlight with him: this permanent gloom was giving him the creeps. In fact, the whole fucking castle had been giving him the creeps for weeks now.

'Okay,' he said quietly to Krantz, only partially hiding his nervousness. 'Let's put her back before she starts getting excited.' He walked on ahead and Krantz hurried after him, pushing at doors along the way, making sure they were also locked.

Babbage came to a halt unexpectedly and the nurse almost bumped into him.

'Look. That thing she's holding,' he said edgily. 'What is it?' He had a nasty feeling about what the madwoman clutched to her flat chest so tightly.

'It's just a box.' Krantz's voice was brusque: she'd been dealing with the idiocies of patients like this for more years than she cared to remember. 'She probably picked it up from the rubble.'

When the nurse started walking towards the crazy woman, Babbage noticed it was not really a box at all. It was covered in dust, but there was something odd about it. He could just see dusty wires on its top and a small nub.

He looked into the wild eyes that stared up balefully into his own. Baleful because the size of her head, which was too big to be supported by her skinny neck, meant that her jaw rested on her chest and her black, slanted eyes, pupils dilated from the darkness she constantly lived in, couldn't possibly look anything other than baleful.

And Babbage said in a kind of low moan, 'Oh no, oh no . . .'

For that small nub on the top of the object that appeared to be a simple box was suddenly glowing red.

Experience told him instantly that what she held in her thin, clawed hands was a time bomb. *A time bomb? So that's what that creepy little bastard Cedric Twigg had been—*

Rachael Krantz, who was marching forward to deal with this mentally disordered crackpot, was stopped in her tracks by Babbage's moans.

She looked over her shoulder to see the horror on his face, then back at the old loon holding the box. A box with a red light on it. A red light that flicked on and off three times as she watched, then—

The deafening explosion vaporized Hitler's daughter instantly, then seared the skin off Senior Nurse Rachael Krantz's bones, and threw the burning shreds of Security Chief Kevin Babbage down to the far end of the corridor in a rich boiling cauldron of flame and flesh before diverting up the stairs to consume the guard and then roaring its way onwards.

Soon after that explosion, which had literally shaken the castle to its foundations, there came the booming of many more.

83

The desolate hunched figure that had once been a colonel and tyrant roamed the round room in the tall tower, wearing the traditional robes of his people because they would not let him bring his military uniform with him (nor any of his mistresses!), venting his fury at empty air, kicking chairs and breaking furniture, smashing fine ornamental vases on the carpeted wooden floor.

Once they called him a monster, those infidels of the Western media – but *never* to his face, *never* in his presence. Politicians, diplomats, interviewers, those in opposition – especially *those* cowardly scum – not even royalty, had ever called him a monster to his face.

But now, physically, he *was* a monster. To escape the unjustifiable wrath of his own people he'd endured painful cosmetic surgery in a Marseilles clinic. They'd advised him he would have to look considerably different if he was ever to go out into the real world again unrecognized. But not this, never this.

He stopped to hold his hideous head in both hands for a moment, for the pain in his temples was excruciating, the ache developing gradually over a period of weeks so that now it had peaked and become unbearable, causing his eyes, over which his brow extended so far they were almost hidden beneath bone and shadow, to flow with tears of pain and self-pity. There was something wrong with this place called Comraich Castle, something indefinable but clearly evil; sometimes he thought the ghosts of hundreds of thousands of his own people had followed him to this cold, lonely place just to torment him, while others had already been waiting here so that they could taunt him with constant whispers of: *Lockerbie, Lockerbie, Lockerbie* . . .

The Inner Court's plan to help him flee the uprising against him, which he'd finally realized he could never win, was clever and skilfully executed. Like all dictators he had employed body doubles, men who so closely resembled their chief that they were often used as decoys. He'd had two of his own lookalikes surgically refined, so cleverly that even his own bodyguards could not tell them apart.

In those last days of the revolution one doppelgänger had been sent from the beleaguered city of Sirte to the leader's hometown of Bani Walid in a small convoy of military vehicles. The rebels would have no doubt as to whom they'd captured, for even the double's dental records had been substituted for the dictator's in case there was ever a post-mortem.

Meanwhile, the Inner Court had insinuated the real despot into a group of 'legitimate' businessmen whose private aircraft was about to depart from a small airstrip near Homs, concealing him in a compartment under a short row of seats.

As he reflected on all this, a shocking sound came to his ears: an explosion, a sound he knew only too well. Then another, and another, this one so huge that the tower, his eyrie, shook to its very foundations.

He panicked. Had subversives followed him to his secret hiding place, his haven of safety, his promised and highly priced refuge? Surely this could not be so! But then came even more explosions, some distant, some closer. And then one that was closest of all: beneath his very feet, the floor jolting suddenly, causing him to fall to his knees.

To his relief, the floor did not fragment: it and its covering carpet remained intact under him. Soon, though, he smelt smoke and felt the carpet on which he belatedly prayed for forgiveness begin to grow warm and smoulder, until soon the heat and the smoke became insufferable.

He scrabbled on his hands and knees to the door. The doorknob was hot to the touch. Pulling himself up, he yanked it open, throwing part of his robe over his head for protection, and ran out onto the small landing at the top of the spiral staircase.

He screamed, but his cries were lost in the chaos. No one could hear him. No one came for him. He was crying, sobbing, his throat already painfully parched because of the smoke rising in curling mists that seemed to contain figures, some of whose faces he recognized. Those men and women he'd had executed as enemies of the state. The choking swirls now billowed into other familiar faces, all of them gloating, grinning sickeningly before morphing into others, many of whom he either did not know or had forgotten during forty years of torture and death, but all of whom knew him.

Howling, he rushed back into his apartment, unaware that flames from the room beneath were eating away the flooring. As he reached the centre, the fire flared up from below, feeding on wooden boards and beams, hungrily consuming the lush carpet under his feet.

As he looked down in dread, the flames erupted with an immense roaring bellow, providing a wide portal through which Colonel Muammar Gaddafi plunged from this world into the very depths of Hell.

84

Haelstrom was gripping Ash so tightly that he was about to pass out, but even with his senses fading, the investigator heard the terrific *boom* and then felt the whole building shake and tremble before the effects of the explosion settled. His fingers gripped tightly, holding on frantically to the stone battlements on either side of him to prevent Haelstrom pushing him onto the sea-soaked rocks below.

He felt the big man's hold on him weaken as Haelstrom was distracted by what sounded like a roar of thunder somewhere deep in the castle.

Suddenly, adrenaline pulsed through Ash and everything became acutely clear to him again. As Haelstrom's huge head turned away from him, searching for the source of the explosion, the investigator pulled himself back from the brink with the help of the thick stones he was pressed between. Before Haelstrom had even realized it, Ash had dived past him to crash on the walkway's flagstones.

Haelstrom twisted his neck further to see Ash sprawled on the ground behind him. Now, he turned his whole body round to face the investigator, who was on one elbow, beginning to rise. Their eyes locked, and through Haelstrom's look of vicious contempt, Ash could also see confusion. The huge man reached forward again and took a first step towards the exposed investigator.

'Leave him alone, you bastard!'

The shrieking voice seemed to come from nowhere. Both

men swivelled their heads to look in the direction of the French windows they'd smashed through minutes earlier.

If Haelstrom had looked confused before, he now appeared totally perplexed.

And so was Ash as he took in Delphine standing just outside the broken doors, poised in a marksman's semi-crouch, legs apart but planted firmly on the ground, knees slightly bent, and her arms stretched forward holding something in her hands, pointing it directly at Haelstrom.

Something that looked like a pink tube of lipstick.

It was a weird tableaux in the moonlight: the huge figure of Haelstrom, the bright moonlight behind him casting an elongated black shadow across the flagstoned walkway, Delphine poised like a slim female gunslinger, and beyond her, just inside the shattered doors, shards of glass glinting under the light, the figure of Louis, dressed in his long cashmere robe and soft shoes. He stood perfectly still and Ash could only guess how frightened and disorientated he must be feeling.

But the lipstick that Delphine, her tan face whitened by the moonlight, was pointing at Haelstrom was possibly the most bizarre element of the freeze-frame.

Ash's gaze returned to Haelstrom, who had a stupid grin on his face, the small features pulled together in the centre of his massive head.

'Don't be silly, girl,' the big man growled and took another step, this time towards her. 'You can't frighten me with—'

That was all he got to say.

Delphine's thumb pressed down and two wires shot out from the weapon and clung to his bulk. He screamed with sudden shock and his whole body juddered in the moonlight as the Taser sent 50,000 volts into him.

Haelstrom staggered backwards across the walkway, the shock not enough to knock a man of his size unconscious, but the pain of it sufficiently excruciating to empty both his bowels and his bladder. His legs came up against the crenellated wall and he sat down hard in one of the gaps in the battlements before, unable to stop himself, tipping back through it and over the cliff edge.

They heard his scream, terribly loud at first, then fading as his bulk disappeared into the night, stopping only when he hit the wave-battered rocks below.

Trembling, Ash scrambled to his feet and hurried over to the small figure of Delphine, who now stood with shoulders slumped and head down. She dropped the weapon and practically threw herself into Ash's embrace.

'Oh, God. David . . .'

Her body was trembling more than the investigator's as he held her tightly against him.

Her drooped shoulders spasmed as she sobbed. 'I never meant to kill him, David, you must believe me. I only intended to disable him for a while. When he went for you . . .'

Another wrenching sob brought a halt to her words.

'Delphine, he was going to kill me. You saved me from a ruthless, evil man. I didn't have a chance against him.'

'When . . . when I saw him trying to push you off the battlements I could only think of using the Taser in my shoulder bag. Dr Singh and I always carry one in case we ever need to subdue a violent patient. I . . . I've never had to use it before.'

'Just don't ever forget and use it on your lips.'

He felt, rather than heard, the small laugh that came from her, and then she clung to him even more tightly.

Other muffled explosions were coming from different levels of the castle, although none as powerful as the first. They heard faraway screaming, a man's screams, and looked at each other in dismay.

'What the hell's going on?' Ash said, to himself more than to Delphine. 'Those sound like bombs. Is the castle being attacked?' He sensed that these explosions were man-made rather than supernatural. They weren't necessarily part of what was coming, but they couldn't help but make it worse.

There was equal questioning in her frightened eyes.

'Lewis and I heard an explosion coming from somewhere on the fifth floor, I think. Did you hear it?'

Ash remembered the loud *boom*, and how the fire in Lord Edgar's hearth had flared outwards, its rekindled heat scorching his face. That must have been caused by the explosion that had Haelstrom rushing into the laird's suite to warn him.

'That's when I brought Lewis down. I didn't know if we should wait any longer in his room, and I was worried about you. The door to the suite was wide open and I could see through to the battlements. I was even more anxious when I saw Lord Edgar's body slumped in an armchair, and Byrone's on the floor.'

Through all the confusion, the fight, the fear, Ash's mind was suddenly more alert. He gripped the psychologist by her elbows. 'Delphine. I know who Lewis is. We have to protect him. We've got to get him out of here.'

She looked at him in bewilderment. 'I don't understand . . .'

'No need to for now. Is that Taser thing still workable?'

'No, it needs to be recharged from the mains.'

'We don't have time to wait. Something awful is happening to Comraich at this very moment.'

He hurried her back through the opened doors to Louis, who was standing very still in the semi-gloom, the robe's cowl pulled over his head so that his face was in shadow.

'Are you all right, Lewis?' Ash leaned forward a little to try and glimpse the young man's – *the young prince's* – countenance.

'I'm okay, Mr Ash. But are you all right?'

Ash smiled at the exiled prince's concern and answered more brightly than he felt. 'I'm fine. But we have to leave Comraich Castle, d'you understand? And right away.'

Louis held on to the psychologist's hand. 'Delphine explained to me why we have to go away, but I'm a bit confused.'

'When we're clear, when we're far away from here, some-where peaceful where we can talk, I'll tell you all I know.'

'Everything?'

Ash's smile was warmer now. 'Everything,' he promised.

Another explosion shook the room, although it sounded as if it came from a lower floor.

Delphine spoke quickly, as though fully aware that time was running out. 'David, Louis suffers from epilepsy. He has the Lennox-Gastaut syndrome, to be exact, which means he can have a seizure and drop to the floor at any time. I medicated him with Inovelon while we were waiting, so he should be okay if his adrenaline doesn't run out of control. I thought I should warn you.'

'We'll be fine,' he said.

'You know he's also a haemophiliac. If he cuts himself, he's likely to bleed to death unless we can stem the flow promptly.'

Christ, thought Ash. 'Anything else?'

There was a certain wryness in his voice that almost made Delphine smile, despite her terror.

'I'm guessing you don't want to hear about his eating problems at this moment.'

Ash could not help but grin. 'We won't stop for a menu on the way out then.'

Delphine stood on tiptoes to kiss his left cheek and caught his small wince of pain.

'Your cheek's burned,' she said anxiously.

'Scorched, but nothing serious. Let's get a move on.'

With that, they headed to the hallway, Ash leading with Louis in the middle, still clutching Delphine's hand.

85

The biggest blast so far, the one for which Twigg had used C4 explosives, had rocked the whole building and sent flames shooting in every direction, charging along the dungeons' corridors, scorching the walls and blowing open cell doors at random to roast some of the cowering inmates inside while others had been left untouched.

After obliterating Kevin Babbage and Rachael Krantz, the blast had coursed through the 'welcoming suites', where it found easier material to burn, so that most of the lower ground floor was quickly ablaze. Only rancid, sooty air and searingly hot, blackened walls were left in its wake.

But Twigg had given his device destructive energy to spare, much of which made its way straight up the old lift shaft, escaping through the hole in the carriage's buckled ceiling and shooting onwards to the upper floors, with flames spilling out at each level, destroying everything they could feed on.

Doctor Vernon Pritchard did not look quite as dapper as usual. His bow-tie hung loose around his neck, soon to fall off completely, the top button of his shirt was undone, one pointed collar rising over the lapel of his blood-smeared jacket, his shoes were of indeterminate colour under the powdery dust that caked them. Dr Pritchard was shaken, an unusual state for him to be in.

A deep gash on his high forehead caused by flying glass had bled profusely, and he was presently resisting a frightened nurse's attempt to staunch the blood with cotton wool, all she could find in her panic, despite the fact they were in Comraich's medical unit.

The problem was, Comraich's medical unit was in flames.

Exasperated by her clumsy attempts, he took the bloodied swab from the nurse's hand and brusquely told her to go and find any patient needing help. He dabbed at the cut with the antiseptic-soaked cotton wool, then held his own silk handkerchief to the injury. It wasn't long before the handkerchief, too, was saturated red.

All around him nurses and porters were helping those patients who could walk or be pushed in wheelchairs towards the stairway doors, which were hanging off their hinges. So far he'd seen no patient on a trolley and guessed his medical staff were only picking out the easier ones to help. Partitioned offices were burning, and flames were beginning to lick at the suspended ceiling panels. Soon, he quickly realized, the whole ceiling would be alight.

He spotted the Indian psychiatrist, a brilliant young man, if sometimes a little arrogant.

'Dr Singh!' he called out over the clamour of raised, frightened voices and the occasional screams. 'Get as many patients as you can up to the lobby, and then outside if necessary.'

Sunil Singh was carefully guiding an old man on two walking sticks towards the wide stairs that led to the upper floor.

'I will do my best, sir,' he said, 'but there are so many patients too sick to move.'

A nurse tugged at Pritchard's sleeve. 'Should we use the lift, sir?'

'No. Only as a last resort. You know the fire drill. Lifts should never be used in a burning building.' He was leaning close to her ear so that he didn't have to shout. 'Do your best with the stairs for the moment.'

Someone shrieked as part of the false ceiling dropped down

from its metal framework. The fire was beginning to take hold and other explosions could still be heard.

As Dr Singh brushed by with the almost doubled-up old man, Pritchard stopped him. 'Dr Singh, you could have saved five more viable patients while you've been helping this one. If there are those that can't be helped, leave them!'

'But . . .'

'No. You have to learn that there are those who can be saved and others who are just unlucky. Make your choice for the greater good!'

Even in the panic and confusion, Pritchard managed to make his advice sound like an order.

'Very well,' Singh conceded. 'But will you help?'

'No. There are others below in greater need. I'm going down to the containment area.'

'Is that wise? The explosion came from there.'

'We cannot let the poor devils burn to death just because they're feeble of mind. Nurse Krantz seems to have gone missing, so you must do your best to help as many patients as you can.'

With that, Dr Vernon Pritchard rushed to the far end of the landing outside and in the quickly fading light made his way down to the sub-basement, where the fire seemed to have burned itself out. Thus encouraged, he continued on his way.

As the fast-moving fire from below drove onwards and upwards it found timbers, tapestries, and paintings to consume. When it arrived at the long, high-ceilinged lobby it joined forces with other conflagrations ignited by Cedric Twigg's slyly placed incendiaries.

Guests were rushing down the carpeted stairway, panicked into disobeying the strict instructions they had received to remain in their rooms. Both guests and staff were trying to escape the burning building as quickly as possible.

Among the crowd descending the broad stairway was Andrew Derriman, dressed in a smart dinner jacket, the expression on his long face even more anxious than usual. He was almost lost in the crush, but managed to push his way through, determined to bring some order to the chaos. The bust of an ancient nobleman suddenly fragmented inside its niche in the curved wall, shards of marble flying outwards like shrapnel to kill or maim those who were closest. Derriman had to duck as a chunk sailed over his head, but others in the vicinity were not so lucky. One man had his nose sliced off by a particularly sharp fragment while another was knocked over the balustrade onto the marble floor below, breaking his neck in the fall. Others were crushed to death, though few would mourn their passing.

'Kit! Kit! Where are you?'

Sandra 'Fluff' Belling had run down the smoke-filled corridor to Kit Weston's room. After the frightening and inexplicable attack of millions of tiny flies in the dining room, during which the ex-racing driver had done his best to protect her with his own disfigured body, Sandra and Kit had gone back to his room, where they'd lain on his bed and talked until dawn, baring their souls. It had been Sandra who had done most of the talking, for the hunched-up little man with the thatch of yellow hair that fell over his forehead to hide his ravaged face had only the stub of his tongue left. She had never confessed the full truth of her baby's death in that Parisian hotel bedroom to anyone at Comraich, and doing so now had formed a bond between them. When Sandra had heard the explosions her first thought had been of Kit.

The corridor was packed with milling guests, all unsure what to do. She could see the ceiling was filling with rolling smoke and pushed and shoved her way down the corridor to Kit's quarters, keeping an eye out for him as she went. The fire bell sounded, briefly adding its clamour to the noisy confusion before suddenly falling silent.

She'd looked back to see the landing at the far end of the corridor was now aflame. And as she'd reached Kit's room she'd seen the orange glow of fire at the opposite end of the corridor. If it really took hold – and it looked like it had – they'd be trapped.

Her hammering on Kit's door having produced no response, Sandra barged her way in.

'Kit!' she cried again, for she could not see him. Something was wrong with the lights. They'd been flickering all evening, but by now they just glowed dully, hardly giving out enough light to see by.

'*Kit, please! Where are you?*' she shouted in terrified frustration. Then she heard what sounded like a moan coming from the floor on the other side of the bed. She raced round the end and saw him hunched into a ball in the far corner of the room.

Kneeling, she touched his shoulder and tried to pull him round to face her. Like a recalcitrant child, he pulled away and bunched himself even tighter, his hands round his ankles.

'*Kit, it's me! It's Sandra,*' she pleaded.

The only response was another moan and a small shifting of his body.

'It's Sandra, Kit. Don't you remember? We talked and talked.' She tried to keep her voice steady so as not to frighten him further. 'We have to get out. The castle's on fire!'

'*'Ire!*' he cried, and suddenly she understood. Kit had smelt the smoke, heard the screams and explosions. He was reliving the nightmare of his final crash.

'We have to leave, Kit.' She tugged at his body, and once again he flinched. Smoke was entering through the open door as if chasing Sandra. She thought she saw hideous figures contained in the billowing blackness, unclear shapes twisting and writhing, shapes that were a sickening parody of the human form, creating faces that grinned at them. Somewhere, she thought she heard a tiny baby crying. The baby she had allowed to die.

'*No!*' she shouted defiantly. '*You can't do this to me! I've paid the price too long and now I know it can never be repaid in full. But I won't let you take him as well!*' She put her arms round the cowering Kit and pulled him to his feet. 'Listen to me,' she said, taking his ravaged face in both hands. 'The building's on fire . . .' she'd tried to say it calmly but firmly, and yet still he shrank away from the word, ready to sink back into the corner. She hauled him back up. 'Not this time, Kit,' she said. 'This time you've got me, and this time nothing – *nothing!* – is going to take you away.' Sandra hugged him as if he were her dead child.

Two days ago she would, like Kit, have given herself to the flames, even welcomed the pain as punishment for what she had done; but now she had a person's life in her hands, a chance to redeem herself.

She led Kit around the bed, ignoring the spiteful fumes billowing about them, but when she saw heavier smoke gushing through the open doorway with a flickering orange glow behind it, she came to a stop.

'Wait, Kit,' she warned, kicking the door shut while propping him up. 'Kit, the corridor is on fire. We can't risk getting out that way. If I open the door again, the flames will be drawn in. We have to try a window.'

Kit Weston looked at her with those cornflower blue eyes for which he'd been so famous. The fear in those once smiling eyes was shocking.

She led him back across the room, which was quickly filling with smoke, causing them to cough uncontrollably. Sandra got him over to one of the room's two small-paned sash windows and attempted to open it, though she knew the windows in all guest suites were fixed shut to prevent suicide (*escape?*) attempts. To her surprise, Kit tried to help her, though his strength was even less than hers and they soon gave up.

'We'll have to smash it!' she shouted to him over the rumbling noise of the fire. They clutched each other even tighter as yet another explosion shook the castle.

Sandra fought her way through the floating phantoms in the smoke-filled room, picked up a straight-backed chair and, warning Kit to move away, hurled it at the window. The glass broke easily enough, but the wooden framework was left intact, the openings too small to climb through. She went to swing the chair again.

'Let m me try,' she heard him say in his strange mumble that few could interpret. He hefted the solid piece of furniture, then proceeded to attack the wooden frame. It took several attempts until one vertical bar splintered, then broke. After that, the rest of the framework was comparatively easy to pull out, albeit at the expense of several lacerations from the glass fragments that remained lodged in the woodwork.

Sandra moved her mouth close to his ear so that she didn't have to shout, then said calmly, 'Kit, we are going to have to jump. We're on the second floor, but there's a soft lawn, and I'm going to make us a landing pad.' She quickly gathered up all the bedclothes and pillows and dropped the soft bundle out of the window. Kit soon got the idea and almost disappeared in the swirling smoke as he grabbed the cushions from the sofa and armchair, then more pillows and thicker blankets from the linen cupboard, taking all that he could carry back to Sandra so that she could add them to the pile. Fresh sea air came to them through the broken window and they swallowed it greedily.

It was time to jump.

'You go first,' she told Kit.

He shook his head determinedly and pointed at her. 'You,' was all he said.

She saw that determination had replaced fear in his blue eyes and decided it would be folly to refuse. 'Okay,' she replied. 'But you follow immediately,' and she waited until he nodded his head. Meanwhile, the smoke had become a churning fog all around, and it was as if spectral hands were reaching for them, trying to detain them until the flames licked into the room; but the vaporous spirits had no substance and no apparent strength. She sat on the window ledge, said a silent prayer and pushed herself into the void.

Sandra screamed as she fell, landing heavily but uninjured on the pile of soft furnishings and bedding. Quickly rolling off, she looked up to see Kit hanging on to the window ledge by the tips of his fingers before letting go. He landed with a loud cry, clearly shaken but otherwise apparently unharmed.

Within a moment, Sandra was by Kit's side, quickly checking on him to make sure no bones were broken. When their eyes met in the bright moonlight, they both grinned. Then they turned as one and staggered away, supporting each other while more explosions shook the castle behind them.

In the containment area Dr Pritchard could see no sign of fire itself, only the evidence of its passage. The walls were blackened and powdery dust floated in the air, creating a yellowish fog that raked his throat. He squinted into the gloom, his bifocals lost somehow in the mayhem of the medical unit, but still nothing would come into sharp focus. Were those figures he could see in that mist of powder and dust? He didn't really register their lurching presence until he'd cautiously wandered down the blast-blown corridor and found himself among them. His intention had been to open any cell doors that were still locked and lead the occupants to safety, for Dr Pritchard had always taken the Hippocratic oath he had sworn as a trainee very seriously indeed, despite his generally insouciant manner. He knew his duty, and had always performed it to the best of his ability. The right thing to do in the circumstances was obvious. However, down in this darkened pit for lunatics, his intentions were far from clear to the scramble-minded tenants, whose psychological state had been made even more egregious by the shock of the explosion.

Dr Pritchard imagined that many would have been deafened by the blast, the unnatural silence confusing them further. Although most of the cell doors had been blown open, some remained crouched in their cells, afraid to venture out, though many had been emboldened by the fact that freedom was at last at hand.

What Dr Pritchard could not know was that the sudden heightened functioning of their flawed minds had left them more easily accessible to beings no longer of this world, spirits that had not yet found their place of peace in the beyond. The mentally ill patients of Comraich were even more susceptible, more exposed to malign influences that had travelled from the darkest regions of another dimension as if responding to the clarion call of evil itself. The liberated feeble-minded 'patients' had by now become vessels for malicious spectres drawn to Comraich by the allure of one mad woman who had welcomed them in, endowing them with power on the physical plane.

Dr Pritchard had decided to make a swift exit, Hippocratic oath or not, but before he could move backwards and away from the mist wherein the shadowy figures stirred, he was confronted by a huge figure that had come forward from the crowd. A strong, thick-fingered hand suddenly encircled the doctor's throat, squeezing tightly, blocking his ability to breathe, foul and clogged though the air was. Pritchard tried to speak, tried to reason with the patient, but the hand only compressed his throat further. He felt other hands scratching at him, and he half recognized some of the perpetrators, for he'd spoken with them often over the years, but now those same faces, always insane, had become somehow ... altered. Their countenances had become subtly demonic, the features slightly exaggerated, noses too long, teeth too pointed, brows jutting so that their maniacal eyes peered out from deep caverns.

As he struggled to free himself, a strange conjoined mewling sound came from their drooling mouths, so similar in pitch and tone that it could have been one voice, only it was too piercing, too cacophonous, too raucous, to come from any individual.

The noise drove into his head and caused him even more pain than the ever-tightening grip on his throat.

And suddenly he was almost lifted off his feet to be pushed, shoved and half-carried into the nearest black hole that was one of the dungeon cells. Others crowded in from behind, while still more were inside, as if waiting. The huge figure slammed the door closed and the mewling rose to a crescendo as more and more bodies piled on top of him.

The stridency of his screams reached the ears of medical staff and patients upstairs as the frail and the sick were led away to supposed safety on the upper floor. These people stood unnerved for barely a second before moving onwards, shuffling away from the various fires that had broken out.

Not one of the medical staff – doctors, nurses, therapists, or porters – suggested going down to the dungeons to find the cause of those terrible, ear-piercing and piteous screams that might have been made by new arrivals to Hell.

And those who did manage to escape the burning of Comraich would hear those screams in their mind every night when it grew dark. Every night until they, themselves, passed away.

Osril Ubutu was tonight dressed in full East African tribal dress and his figure dominated the circular VIP drawing room on the castle's fourth floor. He would have preferred to have worn his buff-coloured army uniform, with its shoulder epaulettes and the chest decorated with its myriad military medals.

Early in the evening, he'd knocked on doors of various suites and in his booming voice had invited each of the occupants to join him in a drink. Most agreed that a good stiff measure was what they needed, for some of them had already become virtually immune to their lithium regimens. Yes, a strong snifter and cheerful gossip would keep thoughts of hauntings and other such nonsense away for the rest of the night.

And so several of his fellow VIP guests had accepted the despot's invitation. With his great booming voice, Ubutu was certainly the centre of attention in the drawing room that night, for despite his ogreish appearance in his voluminous white cotton *kanzu*, he was gifted with immense charisma, and he had many interesting – and brutal – stories to impart.

At first, the laughter was quite nervous, but as time wore on and more guests joined the gathering, and as alcohol and medication mixed, the laughter grew more raucous as the tales told by Ubutu became more outlandish. Then, halfway through a particularly gruesome story involving a novel use of garden shears, a distant explosion had caused the crystal chandelier to vibrate and tinkle.

Ubutu and his intrigued listeners looked around in puzzlement, then further, closer blasts caused them to freeze on the spot. But when the biggest explosion thus far rocked the whole room, causing some guests to fall to their knees, the real panic began.

Some of the men ran towards the open French doors, which suddenly slammed shut and refused to open again, despite the efforts of several beefy shoulders.

Osril Ubutu stood stock-still in the middle of the room, the chandelier continuing to rattle above him. His heavy-featured face was set in a mask of horror, for it was *he* who had not wanted to be alone on this night, *he* who had truly believed the castle was haunted by the spirits of the angry dead. Because he'd already experienced the fury of the demons, the ghosts of those he had killed – they'd visited his dreams in the past, in his own bed, in his own palace. And he had consulted witch doctors, who had purged him with foul-smelling mysterious herbs that burned slowly on earthen fires, as they danced around him, ululating and chanting. But the nightmares and waking visions had resumed, if anything more strongly than before. He'd known then that the last witch doctor who had attended him would join the ranks of the decapitated others who had displeased him and whose rat-nibbled heads now lay in the palace cellars.

But Ubutu had never felt such trepidation as he was feeling now. He anticipated with fear the spiritual vengeance of every person he had ever murdered, executed, or tortured.

His gaze revolved towards an elderly but distinguished-looking lady with elegantly coiffured grey hair sitting nearby. She had left his company minutes before and now silently quaffed a dry sherry from a long narrow glass. Her exquisite jewellery failed to sparkle under the shifting light.

Ubutu didn't know what had made him turn to look at her. She seemed oblivious, lost in her own world of sherry and anti-depressants.

When she noticed he was staring at her she shifted uneasily in her red-cushioned giltwood chair, one of many set around the circular room's outer wall. As they stared at one another, Ubutu felt something emanating from him. Something bad. Something that even he was scared by.

And then, to the dictator's astonishment, the woman's high-piled hair ignited. As if unaware, she continued to stare back at him unperturbed. He watched with interest, wondering whether she would scream when the fire reached her scalp, but before it could do so, her whole body burst into flames. They burned blue at first, but as they rose into the air, cocooning her still-seated figure, they turned yellow, then yellow and orange. Yet still she did not move, as if paradoxically frozen, her blank expression plainly seen through the column of thin fire.

Others in the room began to notice and gape. And as they did, Ubutu switched his gaze to the empty chair next to the woman, and was not entirely surprised to see that it too ignited, and then the next one and the next. Slowly he turned his body through three hundred and sixty degrees until, one by one, every giltwood chair around the perimeter of the drawing room was ablaze.

The burning woman's husband had rushed to help, but he could only watch as her stiff body charred and the delicate sherry glass melted over her blistering fingers. The heat turned her black and parts of her fell away to burn on the floor. Finally, her charcoaled body toppled stiffly from the chair to scorch the rich carpet.

As Ubutu glanced at the man he screamed and dropped to his knees, his clothing already burning. The dictator looked up and the long window hangings lit up as one, flames searing the walls and rolling across the ceiling. The exalted throng, glasses of alcohol long-since discarded, desperately tried to reach the windows, hoping to make their escape around the balcony, but were beaten back by the flames. People all around the room were falling to the floor, coughing violently from the heat that burned their throats, for these strange flames produced no smoke. The lucky ones suffocated as oxygen was consumed by the flames' prodigious greed. The unlucky ones became part of the fire that Ubutu was spreading like a contagious disease, their expensive lounge suits quickly vaporizing into fiery tatters. The room soon became one huge conflagration.

Tears flowing from his heat-irritated eyes, Osril Ubutu could only stand rooted to the spot and watch the blazing demons as they danced around him. He snarled at their taunts, tried to spit into their phantom faces, but his mouth and throat were far too parched to raise any saliva. Instead, he roared defiantly like the lion he knew he was.

Then eventually, realizing even a lion such as he could not defeat these devils, he let out a mighty warrior's cry. He saw that his *kanzu* had caught alight at the hem and the fire was about to engulf him, so he ran forward through the inferno. He dived straight through the flames that masked the French windows, smashing the melting glass. Ubutu, now a blazing ball of fire, flew over the low balustrade outside and plummeted towards the treacherous rocks far, far below.

His booming warrior's roar accompanied him all the way. And so did the demons in his head.

86

'Which way?' Delphine asked anxiously, trying not to clutch Louis' hand too tightly in case she bruised it.

'The tower stairway,' Ash answered on the move. 'We can get down to the ground floor that way. But we have to make a stop so that I can collect some gear that might help us.'

They hurried on, flinching each time they heard a fresh explosion and the vibrations ran through their legs. He could sense that these explosions were definitely man-made. Ash asked himself who the hell could have set bombs. Someone taken by the idea of destroying the ancient curse? Or just somebody who had a grudge against Comraich? Whoever, this person knew his stuff: it sounded like Comraich Castle was going to be demolished and anyone trapped inside would be crushed or burned to death.

They turned corner after corner, found themselves in smoky hallways and passages, and Ash would have been lost in the maze had it not been for Delphine, who always seemed certain of which direction they should take.

The grey acid mist hung from the ceilings, acrid-smelling and ominous. On several occasions they passed large rooms that were completely ablaze. The castle was fitted with an elaborate sprinkler system, but for some reason it had failed to trigger.

Finally, and to Ash's great relief, they arrived at the tower's spiral staircase.

'Better if we go in single file and keep to the right-hand wall where the steps are widest,' Delphine said.

Smoke was being drawn upwards, the round tower was acting as a chimney for the fires below. Soon, all three had streaming eyes, but Ash, leading, kept them going. He could hear Louis' hacking coughs and he hoped the young man's frail body would not give up. Ash tried to maintain a steady pace, giving neither Louis nor Delphine time to be overwhelmed by all that was happening. Fortunately, bright moonlight shone through the slitted windows, giving them some help in seeing the way through the smoke. However, it was growing darker the lower they went.

'Delphine,' Ash called back. 'Have you still got the Maglite I gave you earlier?'

'In my bag.'

'Can you pass it to me? It's getting harder to see down here.'

Down they travelled, the smoke becoming denser. They dreaded each turn in case fire was blocking the way. Going back up would be pointless.

Louis' coughing was becoming worse and Ash stopped for a moment. He dug into the pocket of his jacket and pulled out a clean white handkerchief. 'Hold this over your mouth and nose,' he told the young prince. 'It might just help a little.'

The cowled figure nodded and obeyed. Delphine drew out a smaller handkerchief of her own and followed suit. With a grunt of satisfaction, Ash continued the descent and for the first time realized he was limping. Adrenaline had veiled the pain earlier but now, each time he stepped on his injured left leg, it felt like a hot rod of iron had shot from his heel right up to the knee. He tried to ignore it but couldn't help wincing a little every time he put his left foot to the floor.

Smoke drifted upwards and occasionally the investigator saw a blackened orb amidst it, the smoke itself seeming to curl into fiendish faces, too vague to focus upon but there all the same, though never for longer than a moment or two. The malevolence that was inside Comraich Castle had acted as a catalyst for evil spirits; a kind of gateway, giving the incorporeal

601

phantoms a semblance of fluctuating form. A doorway had been opened up, allowing entities through, and he prayed – *literally* prayed – that it could be closed again, but only after the wraiths had been banished to their rightful dimension.

Finally, Ash, Delphine and Louis found themselves on the castle's second floor. Ash debated whether to leave Delphine and the prince to wait for him, but decided they would be safer together.

'Keep low and follow me,' Ash told the others. 'Try and stay beneath the smoke.'

Bent double, the smoke haze flowing only an inch or so above their heads, they stumbled along the corridor. Ash turned to see Louis gripping Delphine's hand, doing his best to keep up. At the far end of the corridor, the main landing was an inferno.

They reached Delphine's room and came to a halt. 'Bring anything you might need,' Ash instructed. 'Not too much, though! Maybe just some scarves and the muffler. Soak them with water and tie one around your lower face, making sure you cover your nose. Do the same for Louis. Oh, and you'd be better swapping those high heels for something more practical, too.'

'I'll change into my boots.'

'Perfect,' said Ash. *And just as sexy*, he thought.

'David.' Delphine's narrowed, smoke-irritated eyes stared into his own. 'You've been limping all the way. Are you hurt?'

'It's where the wildcat clawed me, I think. Believe me, I'm covered in bruises all over, so this injury doesn't matter much – it's company for the rest. Look, take back the torch in case you and Louis need it.'

He extended his arm, the Maglite in his fist.

'*Louis?*'

'Lewis is really Louis. I'll explain later.'

She looked puzzled, but to Ash's relief didn't press him for an explanation. She refused to take the Maglite: 'There's a full moon out tonight and it always shines directly into my room.

Besides, the lights still seem to be working, even if they're only dim.'

'Okay. Be as quick as you can and meet me in my room. You know which one?'

'Oh yes.'

He smiled, despite the danger they were in. He opened the door to her room and peeked in to make sure it was safe. She'd been right about the moonlight: everywhere inside was bathed in soft silver light, although it made the shadows deeper.

He gently pushed her and Louis through. 'Don't be long.' With that, he was off, bending low and limping, his left hand running along the corridor's wood panelling. It felt warm to the touch and he was conscious of the fact that the whole castle would go up like a tinderbox once the flames took hold. At least he hadn't heard any more explosions for a while and he could only hope there would be none.

Ash reached his room and opened the big suitcase still on the luggage rest at the end of the rumpled bed (*no housemaid today, then*).

The first item he took out was a large waterproof Maglite, heavier and more powerful than the one he'd just offered to Delphine. Next he drew out a handful of light sticks, the kind he'd used in the tunnel beneath the castle. He had to dig deep to find the last object, though he hoped he would never have to use it in anger: a combat knife, the foot-long blade partly serrated on its top edge.

Satisfied, he transferred the items to his shoulder bag. As he surveyed what was left of his ghost-hunting equipment he wryly reflected there was no need for it now; ghosts were undoubtedly present in Comraich. They had found their 'window area', their 'magnetic' human presence here in the castle – the old woman in the cell opposite the lift three levels underground, the offspring of Adolf Hitler and Unity Mitford. The investigator was sure that she was the conduit that had drawn these sub-beings into the castle, though of course all the wickedness that had taken place there had only served to enhance the attraction of Comraich, as had the fact that it was built on a ley-line junction. And on top of that, there was the centuries-old curse – the Mullachd. It must have played its part too. So far as the spirit world was concerned, it was a perfect storm.

Ash pulled the strap of the bag over his head and across his chest and clipped the combat knife's leather sheath to his belt. The door opened and Delphine and Louis entered, both still ducking from the thickening smoke in the corridor.

Ash grunted his approval when he saw the two of them were wearing soggy wet scarves that revealed only their frightened eyes.

'Which way do we go?' Delphine asked in earnest.

For one fleeting second, an idea passed through the investigator's mind, but he dismissed it almost as quickly as it came to him. 'There might have been a chance to jump from a window, especially if I lowered you down as far as I could by hanging out, but I don't think Louis would make it.'

'I don't think I'd make it,' Delphine scolded him with a brief smile. 'Have you seen how high up we are?'

'Just a thought.'

He went to the open door and peered out both ways. The fire was really taking hold at the far end. Flames were beginning to roll along the ceiling, an almost mesmerizing sight in its awesome beauty: the colours, the curls, like a fiery torrent of water. Within the turbulent smoke that came off the flames were many black orbs. As they raced through the smoke, they bobbed and weaved, pulsating, preparing to form a fuller shape, an apparition, a stage-four manifestation. Ash sensed some had made that transition already.

Although the orbs were unclear and like wispy streaks as they tore along the corridor, Ash could just make out monotone, malformed Scottish warriors, indistinct claymores raised in insubstantial fists, a hint of colourless kilts over incomplete legs. He snapped out of it when he felt the psychologist by his side.

'Oh dear God,' he heard her say in a breathless whisper. 'Those black orbs: they're like the ones that invaded the office a few days ago.'

He realized with relief she could not see all that he saw.

'We'll go back the way we came,' he said over the rumbling sound. 'The spiral staircase should get us to the ground level at least.'

'It will,' she said, handing him the sodden muffler. He quickly pulled it over his face, then turned to them both. 'Stick close behind me. We'll have to move faster than before.' He glanced up at the corridor's ceiling as if to make the point.

The rolling fire was almost over their heads.

87

Andrew Derriman clawed his way through the mass of struggling bodies at the bottom of the grand stairway, aware that he had to bring some order to the panicking mass of staff and guests. Why were the emergency ceiling sprinklers not in operation? The main alarm had hardly sounded; had that been sabotaged too?

The beleaguered general manager finally pushed his way through the fallen bodies. The path to the castle's main entrance was blocked by fire and the hall was rapidly filling with people. Before long there would be a deadly crush. He saw Veronica and Gerrard, still at their station though looking somewhat bemused behind the long wooden reception counter.

'Veronica!' he called cupping one hand around his mouth. 'Open the counter flap and the office door, then take them through to the side exit. Try to keep them calm! Make them form a line, two by two.' Although scared, he had not stuttered once.

All around Derriman people were picking their way between prone bodies. He directed them towards the counter, the varnish of which was beginning to bubble. He held up an arm to block the heat and saw that the flames were only a short distance from the end of the counter.

'Hurry, please hurry! There's a way out through the offices back there – Veronica and Gerrard will show you. But please don't panic, there's plenty of time!'

The last assurance was a lie, but it didn't matter anyway: guests were already scrambling over the hot reception counter, barging their way through. Derriman had stopped to help those who had tumbled down the stairs, but he was soon knocked sideways by those still on their feet. He fell awkwardly, skidding across the marble flooring. As he lay there, supporting himself on one elbow, he surveyed the mayhem before him.

Derriman understood their alarm, but the Comraich clientele, by most standards a fairly refined bunch, had turned into a scrabbling, screaming mob that cared nothing for their fellows. A man fell screaming from a landing above and Derriman closed his eyes so that he would not see him hit the unyielding marble floor. But he could not ignore the wet sound as the body landed, nor the sharp crunch of broken bones.

The sheer racket from the panicking guests made Derriman want to block out the noise by putting his hands over his ears, but then a thought reared up in his mind: *Lord Edgar! Was he safe?*

Despite his lordship's dire medical condition, the proud old man had always treated Derriman with respect, no matter how much the castle manager nervously stuttered and stammered in his presence.

The VIP delegates had been enjoying pre-supper cocktails in Comraich's highest, most sumptuous drawing room when the first explosion had occurred. He and Sir Victor had hastened to the explosion's source and had found a small inferno raging in the chapel.

Sir Victor had sent Derriman back to the seriously startled Inner Court guests to reassure them and to take them down to the ground floor for safety's sake, while he, Haelstrom went off to tell his lordship of the fire. So Lord Edgar should have had both Haelstrom and Byrone to take care of him.

But then had come other explosions, seemingly from all over the castle, and the VIPs had insisted they leave Comraich immediately, not just because of the danger, but because they did not want to be around when the emergency services or, worse still, the media arrived. If the fire truly took hold, then the blazing castle would be seen for miles around, and although it prided itself on its self-sufficiency, Comraich's own fire-fighters were hardly equipped to deal with a conflagration such as this.

Derriman and the VIPs had soon become caught up in the chaos, confusion and panic on the lower floors. It seemed every guest and staff member was headed for the main staircase, where their evacuation had soon become a shambles. He could only hope and pray Haelstrom had reached Lord Edgar in time to bring his lordship down by the tower stairway.

The image of that spiral staircase brought another reminder: The Boy would be alone in his rooms at the top of that tower. *My God, has anyone thought of him?* Leaping to his feet, the tall stooped man ran the palm of his hand across his forehead, and the sticking plaster that was still there. Should he leave The Boy to die in the fire?

Derriman had never considered himself a particularly good man, but he certainly couldn't let the poor young man die alone in his room. Of course, he might already be dead, but what if Derriman could have saved him but failed to do so? The image made him shudder. He would never forgive himself. It might be stupid and it might be a pointless thing to do, but there was only one *right* thing to do. He'd done his best to get the Inner Court members out, and now it was time to come to the aid of someone unable to help himself, even if it meant sacrificing his own life.

Derriman turned away from the mayhem, from the ugly, self-serving crowd, and started to run down the long marble hall towards the tower stairway.

88

Delphine let out a small scream as a rat brushed by her foot. Ash turned at the sound, taking care not to blind the others with his powerful torch.

'Rats,' he said calmly, 'deserting the sinking ship. They won't harm you – unless you block their way.'

There were more of the creatures running and slithering over the steps nearer to the centre stonework.

'It'll probably be worse the further down we go. But don't be afraid – they're as scared as we are and only want to get out of the burning building without the likes of us getting in the way.'

The smoke was curling up the spiral staircase, becoming thicker the nearer they got to the ground floor.

'Just try not to slip,' he warned Delphine and the monk-like figure of Louis. Ash noted with alarm that the black orbs travelling within the smoke were multiplying. Some of them were shimmering, trying to manifest themselves into more human form. He realized now it was the spirits who had ruined his surveillance equipment, not any malicious humans. He'd half suspected that Nurse Krantz had been the culprit. A woman scorned, and all that.

Ash came to a halt once again: he really didn't like these twisting shapes inside the flowing, curling smoke. He hoped neither Louis nor Delphine could see them yet.

'Are you all right, Louis?' he asked patiently.

The hooded head nodded just once and the wet scarf over his mouth muted his reply. 'I'm okay, but is it much further?'

'Almost at the ground floor, I think. A couple more turns.'
He almost added 'your highness', but stopped himself in time.

They continued their downward journey, with vermin
accompanying them all the way. They came to a stop when
they finally reached the ground-floor landing, while the rodents
continued their journey down into the castle's deeper regions.
Smoke swirled down the long, marble-floored corridor, billowing up to blacken the high, moulded ceiling, while below was
all hazy smog. Through the wide entrances to the rooms along
the hallway they could see the glow from fires within. Tapestries, timbers, drapery, furniture and the carpet on the broad
staircase – all were ablaze. At the far end of the corridor they
could make out human figures rushing through the unsettling
murk of smoke, while flames shot out from other open doorways.

The investigator grabbed Delphine's arm and she winced
at his urgent strength. 'Are there any other exits on this floor?'
he shouted above the din. 'Small access doors, windows,
anything we can escape by?'

She shook her head emphatically, one arm pulling the
hooded figure of Louis close to her. 'All the windows are
barred. There are side exits, but they're always kept locked
and I don't have keys!'

Christ, Health and Safety would love this place, thought Ash.
'Let's see what lies further down. Those people must be
heading somewhere.'

Taking Delphine by the elbow, he let her hold on to Louis,
who was shaking, his shoulders hunched. Ash hurried them
along, conscious of the fact that within minutes the whole of
the entrance lobby would be completely consumed by fire.

Delphine fell and the investigator knelt on the floor to help
her up while Louis pulled beneath her shoulder to assist. With
a feeling of deep dread, Ash felt the marble under his knee and
realized the floor was warm. He laid a flat hand against it and
it felt warmer still. God only knew what was happening in the
medical unit below.

On their feet once more, all three moved forward as before, dodging flames that spat from doorways on either side as if there were dragons within. Ash kept to the centre so they were out of reach. It seemed foolhardy to be racing towards the conflagration at the far end of the hall instead of away from it, but it seemed to be their only option. He expected another explosion at any moment, but mercifully none came.

Briefly, he wondered who might be responsible for the bombing. Not an official body like the intelligence services or the military, surely? Too many innocent people had died. No, it had to be someone with both insider knowledge and a grudge against the Inner Court. But then, how could someone like that gain entry into a place so heavily and proficiently protected by enough well-armed guards to fight off a small army? Maybe this was the final act of some ongoing vendetta: the discovery and destruction of this prestigious inner sanctum.

He was certain he was overlooking something obvious, but for the time being he was more concerned with how they could escape from the castle than with who was trying to destroy it.

They had passed the larger lift and were nearing the older, destroyed one. Just before it was the wide entrance to the armoury. Ash came to a skidding halt, holding back his companions as he did so.

Nearly tumbling to an untidy heap, but supported by the investigator's waning strength, they looked questioningly up into Ash's deep blue eyes, which was all they could see of his face because of the mask he wore. By the look of those eyes, they could see he was perplexed, thinking of something beyond the mayhem before them.

'Stay behind me,' he told them, pulling down the now-dry muffler from his mouth to be heard clearly.

'David, where are you—?'

But he'd left them and cautiously approached the wide entrance ahead.

Ash had felt it just in time – a vibration that he remembered from before when he'd peeked into the armoury while waiting for the lift. It grew stronger the closer he came to the room. If the display area had felt dangerous before, his instinct was telling him it was even more so now.

He stood to one side of the armoury entrance, using the stone wall as a shield, then gingerly edged his head round to look into the room.

The fine arrangement of weaponry was quivering on the fixtures, the clacking and thrumming rising and growing louder at his presence. A ten-inch Dragoon pistol fell to the floor with a heavy *clump*. A circular array of short-bladed sabres fairly rattled in their mounts. A long pike with a vicious-looking metal point toppled and bounced against the hard floor. It was as though an immensely powerful magnetic field were ripping them from the walls. From the corner of his eye, he saw an object hurtling towards him and he pulled back just in time as a thick-bladed knife broke free of its mount and whisked past his head to clang against the opposite wall, chipping out a piece of stone before bouncing back to the floor.

Delphine and Louis were now right behind him. He held out an arm to prevent them venturing further and they stared in awe as the archaic weaponry rattled against the walls.

The investigator slowly pushed his companions back, and the thrumming sound grew softer the further the trio backed off.

'What is it, David?' Delphine asked. 'What's making them vibrate like that?'

'You might call it poltergeist activity, but I think it's stronger than that,' he told her. 'My guess is that it's telluric energy – "earth energy" is another name for it. Its tremor comes from a force beneath us, although I do seem to have some weird attraction for it. God knows why: maybe I'm a trigger of some kind. Let's just say my presence induces paranormal agitation. It's a bit complicated. I'll try and explain if . . .' He realized he'd chosen a bad word. '*When* we get out of here. But there's no chance of getting past this entrance without being killed. We'll have to find another way out.'

Suddenly Louis raised a loose-robed arm and pointed towards the entrance lobby. Ash followed his direction and saw someone emerging from the smoke-haze which now filled the whole area.

'*Mr Ash!*' a voice called. '*Dr Wyatt!*'

'I think it's Andrew Derriman,' said Delphine, trying desperately not to choke on the smoke fumes by taking in shallow breaths.

Ash saw that Delphine was right. The general manager of Comraich was rushing towards them and he was going to pass by the armoury!

'*Derriman, stop!*' Ash shouted as loudly as he could, holding up a hand of warning.

But Derriman was either too overwrought or too confused to heed the investigator's words.

He was only just past the entrance to the large armoury room when an ancient iron axe tore itself from the wall and flew straight at him as if hurled by a powerful warrior. Its edge, blunted with age but an effective weapon nevertheless, buried itself in the side of his head.

Ash watched horrified as Derriman staggered and turned, yet did not quite fall. He looked directly at Ash with a puzzled, almost comical expression, as if to ask what had just happened. Then the gash in his skull began to bleed, and more antique weaponry flew at him from every part of the room. He only had time to utter a short but sharp shriek before he toppled to the floor, his body a grotesque pin-cushion of blades, swords, spears, double-edged claymores and other death-dealing weapons of old, as brutally effective now as they had been centuries before.

But it was only when an iron mace, its round head embedded with inch-long spikes, smashed into his face that death finally relieved his agony.

89

Aribert Heim, the evil Nazi doctor who had caused the deaths of hundreds of thousands in the abhorrent Austrian concentration camp Mauthausen, left his suite on the castle's fourth floor. He'd flinched each time another bomb had gone off somewhere in the building, hiding in the rooms which, until so recently, he'd shared with his Nazi colleague Alois Brunner.

Strangely, although pleased to have the place to himself, last night Heim had felt very alone. And afraid.

Heim had decided to stay in bed until the fuss was over, pressing his hands hard against his ears to block out the screams and shouts, the pounding of running feet. He would have been content to lie there all night if necessary, with his bedclothes pulled over his head, hands clamped against his ears, but there was a bigger problem. Even with the door closed and his head beneath the sheets, the acrid smell of smoke reached him.

The castle itself was burning.

Hastily clambering into his dressing gown and slippers, he warily stepped out into the corridor and walked towards the source of the most calamitous sound: the fourth-floor landing. He reached the rail above the broad, curving staircase, and peered over to see guests and staff alike struggling against one another to descend, even though great plumes of smoke billowed up from below. Down there, at the very bottom of the oval staircase, he could see an enormous flickering orange glow, which suggested the fire had taken hold. Why were these stupid people running in that direction?

Like lemmings they fled, not away from the fire but directly towards it.

Perhaps there was an exit the conflagration had not yet touched. Certainly, the front doors had to be caught in the blaze. A side door, then. There should be one through the offices behind the receptionists' counter. But he was definitely not going to join the throng below, tied in one huge knot of arms and legs.

Even the Jews had gone to their deaths peacefully, and the only sound that had come then, muted through the gas-ovens' metal doors, was the wailing. That dreadful sound came to his ears now, even over the screams and bellows of distress as people below fought each other to get clear of the collapsed heap of humanity spreading from the stairway and swelling out into the lobby like a spillage of oil.

But he, Aribert Heim, would not lose his dignity by joining them, frightened though he was. No, the best way to avoid a panicking crowd was to walk away, find another escape route. This is what he would do. This would show the *Dummköpfe* the honourable way to act by using his brain, which was still sharp, even if his body was a little feeble. He would escape the fire as he had escaped the Allies.

The smoke was growing thicker on the fourth floor as he returned the way he'd come, so much so that a dense layer of blackness permeated the ceiling, its languid, wafting underbelly drifting halfway down the walls. He tried to control his strained coughing by stripping off his dressing gown and tossing it over his head and shoulders, leaving him in blue-striped pyjamas, his body bent over to avoid the smoke. Meanwhile, his eyes were streaming tears, though they were caused by the astringent fumes and not apprehension or terror. He squinted up at the darkened smoke-filled ceiling, where he was sure he could see shapes like little pitch-black balls, some of them pulsating.

And something much worse.

Heim uttered a small cry as he quickly pulled the dressing gown back over his head, drawing in stinging fumes as he was forced to take a deeper breath. He was sure the smoke was forming into hands, clawing hands of no real substance, which tried to reach down to him. *Just my imagination*, his once-clinical mind told him in an effort to banish the fear. But he was quite clear about the images his blurry eyes had taken in. Stumbling on, he passed the door to his suite, but did not linger: it would be foolish to take shelter inside. Besides, he'd another goal in mind.

After falling once, feeling inexplicably frail, and having picked himself up, he finally arrived at the destination he'd been aiming for as the corridor abruptly widened into an ornate hallway. He'd reached the grand lift.

With some trepidation, Heim pressed the call button to summon the roomy lift to him, wondering if anyone else had thought to use this particular method of reaching the ground floor. Heim was satisfied the only danger lay at the front part of the castle, where he had seen for himself the flickering orange glow in the swirling fog of smoke near the bottom of the oval staircase. There must surely be other stairways towards the back of the building.

His tired old legs could barely support his weight these days, and tonight – probably because of all the excitement and dread of late – they were more exhausted than ever. He wouldn't be able to walk down some ancient stone stairway; more likely fall down it and break his neck.

Anxiously, the German pushed the call button again and waited impatiently for the *ping* that would tell him the lift had arrived.

Meanwhile, the smoke around him grew progressively heavier. He doubled up almost to his knees, a raw cough raking his throat. There was pressure on his chest. He waited. And waited.

There were shadows all around him and several were

almost tangible. He tried to ignore them, but held the dressing gown tightly around his head, peeking out occasionally to check that the lift hadn't arrived unheard. When at last it came, he rushed to the slowly opening doors, thrusting his fingers through them in a vain effort to hasten the process. But the doors took their own time and in his efforts, his dressing gown slipped down his back to the floor.

He tried to squeeze through the opening sideways, and as he did so he ripped a button off his blue-striped pyjama jacket; it sprang across the hallway to land on the floor by a giltwood settee.

He practically stumbled into the capacious car, coughing and spluttering and wiping tears from his eyes. He barely registered the lift doors closing far more rapidly than they had opened, almost slamming shut.

The smoke haze inside the lift was like heavy smog. When his eyes adjusted themselves, although still somewhat blurred, he realized he was not alone.

In fact, the lift was crowded.

Crowded with people, all of whom had their backs to him. And oddly, they all, as far as he could tell in the gloom, wore the same blue-striped pyjamas as he.

When he blinked a few times to improve his vision, he realized their garb was tattered and grimy, torn in places and hanging loose from their bodies as if three or four times too large for them. And the blue stripes were darker too. And wider.

Heim tried to suppress a cough so as not to bring attention to himself, but he couldn't hold it back. His throat was too raw, his mouth too dry. The choking cough escaped, followed by another, then yet another. Hand to his mouth, he tried to muffle the coughs, but still they were piercing within the confines of the packed, descending lift. He couldn't remember pressing the Ground Floor button when he'd entered.

At last, they began to turn towards him: skeletal faces; sunken, haunted eyes; cheekbones that jutted over deeply hollowed cheeks; and jawbones that almost pierced their skin. The clothes they wore had no buttons, and the material was so threadbare and rough that he wondered how they could survive in the cold.

For the lift interior was very, very cold, so much so that the haze had become an icy mist. But none of them appeared to notice. They just stared as Aribert Heim, Dr Death, looked at them and shivered.

And not only from the cold, for even after so many years he remembered some of those emaciated faces with their shaven heads. He was hallucinating, that was all, he told himself; the past brought to life by his own panic. But now the ghosts that he, Aribert Heim, had created all those years ago shuffled towards him. And even as they fell upon him and began to pulverize his face, he still believed it could only be in his imagination. There were no such things as spirits of the dead. No matter how they stamped on him or beat him, tore his clothes away or stuck their skeletal fingers into his chest and yanked out his heart while it was still beating, he knew, *he knew*, without a doubt, this was all unreal, hallucinatory, impossible to be true.

But he did feel the horrendous pain.

And he did suffer a dreadful death, despite what he refused to believe.

90

Delphine screamed and buried her head against Ash's chest to shut out the sight of Andrew Derriman's thin body being cut to pieces, even as it lay on the stone floor.

The weapons still flew from the walls and into his prone body. It didn't seem to be enough for the cruel spirits controlling them that he was dead. Ash, his arms protectively around Delphine, wondered if this was meant simply to violate the fallen figure further, or to torment them, the onlookers. Derriman's corpse flinched each time it was hit, but Ash knew this was because the relentless weapons were cutting into nerves and tendons. There was no life left in the poor man's body.

Would they soon start to fly from the armoury and begin to attack beyond it? Meanwhile, the cries of hysteria and the *crump* of the growing fire came to his ears. It was difficult to see anything clearly beyond the armoury entrance, for the smoke was denser and the glow of the fire had reached a great height. All he could make out were blurred suggestions of milling figures. There had to be a way out down there somewhere, otherwise those people would be running down the hall to get away from the flames, but any attempt to reach the entrance lobby would result in certain death from the flying weapons. One thing was sure: they couldn't remain where they were.

'We have to make a move,' Ash said as an iron club struck the side of the armoury entrance.

Delphine's horrified eyes peered up at him. Louis merely

619

stood close to them, straight and still, as if mesmerized by the activity inside the armoury.

'David, where can we go?' Delphine asked, and he was relieved to find a steadiness in her voice. If she cracked, it would make things even more difficult.

'We follow the rats,' he replied, as calmly as he could.

They retraced their steps and took the spiral staircase down to the medical unit entrance. And that was where the stairs ended.

'Oh Christ, I was afraid this might have happened.' Ash made the effort not to sound too desperate for the sake of Delphine and Louis. 'These stairs won't take us any further.'

Where the staircase should have been they could now see only a pile of rubble.

'The walls must have collapsed in the explosion,' he said.

'Look!' Delphine pointed. 'The rats. They're heading *into* the medical unit. Perhaps they can lead us out of here.'

Ash went to the open medical area doorway. He quickly scanned the scene and soon realized what was wrong. Somehow, confused perhaps by the twists and turns in the dimness of the spiral staircase, they'd missed the door to the upper floor of the medical unit and had emerged lower down.

'I think we've come further than we thought,' Ash said, turning to Delphine.

She came close to him, bringing Louis with her. 'Of course! You're right – this is where the welcoming suites and observation rooms are. The stairs haven't collapsed; they were never there in the first place.'

Ash gazed into the second lower level, taking in the separate fires that burned fiercely inside, melting plastic curtains where some after-care patients had been housed. Further along, the suites were all burning. The heat from the unit caused the investigator to shield his face with his lower arm, while Delphine attended to Louis, pulling up the dried-out scarf she'd wrapped around his neck and lower face. She also pulled the hood forward, for it had fallen back a little in their rush. All that could be seen now were his disturbed, shadowed eyes.

He was trembling, but so was she.

Ash suddenly spoke up, clearing smoke from his raw throat. 'You know, I think I've got an idea where those vermin are heading. There is a way out from down here, though I don't know whether it's passable.'

Delphine's brow was furrowed and her eyes glinted with tears from the smoke. 'What are you talking about, David?'

'Feel that breeze?' he asked her. 'See how the flames are inclined towards us? There's a draught coming from some-where, and I think I know where. In fact, I'm bloody sure. It's the old smugglers' tunnel that leads up from the sea caves.'

Even as they spoke, three large rodents scurried past them, running into the blazing area ahead.

'They prove my point. They're headed for the old lift shaft, where the carriage blasted through.'

'How can you be sure? We might be running straight into disaster.'

'Not if those rats' natural instinct for survival is right. Rats will only desert a sinking ship if there's somewhere for them to go, somewhere to swim to, even if it's just a lifeboat full of sailors.'

Despite the torrid heat, Delphine shuddered. She took hold of Louis' hand. 'Okay, Captain Bligh. If you think we can get through those flames, we'll certainly give it a try.'

Ash grinned at her before pulling the muffler back over his nose and mouth. 'We have to hurry and keep low!' Ash shouted over his shoulder. 'We mustn't stop for anything,' he added. 'See, through there, where there's a gap between the flames. Look at the rats, see how they're using it?'

She nodded, fearfully watching the vermin scuttling through the second basement through a corridor of fire.

'Let's go!'

Ash grabbed her hand and sprinted towards the clearer

lane ahead, and such was the strength of his grip that she had no choice but to follow. She held Louis' hand firmly, but he kept up with her, all three bending low once they were further into the fiery alley.

Delphine almost tripped over something lying on the ground but Ash gripped her hand tightly, as did Louis. Between them they kept her upright and resumed their journey, their clothes beginning to smoulder in the heat that licked at them from either side.

Ash kept them moving and, far from proving a hindrance, Louis helped Delphine, steadying her when her legs threatened to give way again, changing hands so that he could maintain his grip on her and help her keep her balance. The heat was becoming unbearable, but still Ash dragged them along, his body growing weaker, each step like treading through molasses, the pain in his left leg worsening. Then suddenly, the area had opened out and the flames receded. Beyond, they could see the half-partitioned office cubicles, all of them deserted, all of them burning.

Their respite was due to the shaft of the larger lift. Air must have been coming down it, for somehow breathing was easier. They rested for a moment until Ash, who was bent over, hands on his knees, trying to get some oxygen into his lungs, noticed Louis' plight: his robe was smoking badly and when Ash laid a hand on it, the material was hot to the touch. The exhausted investigator rubbed the robe down, resisting the urge to smack at the worst of the smouldering material in case he damaged the delicate skin beneath it. As Delphine recovered some of her energy, she helped him. Soon the robe, though warm to the touch, was free of threat, and they all rested, both Delphine and Louis aware that Ash would soon cajole them into running again.

It was then that Delphine noticed the naked body lying on the ground, halfway out of the lift as though he'd tried to crawl out when the doors opened. Why was he naked? The lift's interior would have been like an oven during the descent.

Perhaps he'd torn his clothes off because of that? The doors would have tried to close repeatedly as he attempted to crawl out, hitting him time and again until the mechanism had broken with the body wedged in the middle.

She pointed at the prone body and Ash looked round to see. He went over to the lift and studied the reddened corpse. The old man lay on his stomach, his head sideways on the carpeted floor. His eyes and mouth were wide open as if in mortal shock. Ash had rarely seen such a ghastly expression: it looked as though he had been frightened to death.

Inside the lift car lay a bundle of clothes that looked like torn, ragged striped pyjamas.

Ash felt Delphine by his side.

'My God,' she said, her words almost lost in the crackle of splitting wood and glass, and the softer crumping of the fire itself. 'His face! It's unrecognizable. Should we pull the body clear?'

Ash saw blood seeping out from under the man's chest. It flowed smoothly like thick dark oil, the flames reflected in it as it pooled smoothly over the carpeted floor.

'No, leave him as he is,' Ash said. 'There's nothing we can do for him now.'

The oxygen was depleting steadily, consumed by the hungry firestorm, and the air was becoming too thin to breathe. He reached into his jacket pocket and pulled out the pack of Modafinil that Delphine had given him earlier. With shaking hands, he pressed through two tablets and popped them into his mouth. Swallowing was almost impossible without even saliva, let alone water, to wash them down. Somehow he managed, although he felt the tablets lodge somewhere in his throat.

'David . . .'

He saw that Delphine was having trouble breathing too. She'd ducked low where just a bit more air was available.

'You . . . you shouldn't take . . . too many of those,' she gasped.

'I'm going to need them. I think . . .' He drew a deep draught of air. 'You should take some too.'

She shook her head and he could only shrug. He glanced at Louis to see how he was and gawped in surprise.

The prince – whom Ash could regard only as a boy, despite the fact that he was in his late twenties – was standing erect only two or three feet away. He was perfectly still and also perfectly calm. For some reason, he'd thrown back his hood, although he still wore the soft scarf loosely over his face so that only his eyes were showing beneath the perfect roundness of his bald pate, the skin only tissue-thick over the skull.

But it was those eyes that fascinated Ash, for instead of flames reflecting in them, he could now see that his almost colourless eyes had become a gentle but intensely deep azure, soft and yet barely dominating the darkness behind. There was a peace in them that was entirely out of context with their situation. Ash tried to remember where and when he'd witnessed that same blueness before, but couldn't. It was impossible to pin down, but he was sure he'd seen eyes of that colour and expression somewhere else.

Ash rose and stood closer to him. The gentle but striking blueness in those large, enigmatic eyes immediately vanished.

Louis said, 'We must hurry. That way.' He pointed ahead. The inferno further along the unit appeared impossible to navigate, but since it was towards the point where Ash had intended to take them, he did not argue.

Delphine was by his shoulder again. 'David, did you see his . . .'

'. . . eyes? Yes. I thought it was just me. Listen, we have to go in that direction. Look behind us, the path we just took a minute or so ago.'

Delphine turned her head and saw that the section for observation and recovery was now one massive inferno, with no central path left to work their way through. She turned to look at Ash and Louis again.

'But how can we go forward? We're trapped.'

'Maybe not,' Ash replied. 'We're near a corner; let's see what's round it.'

Without another word, he pulled the cowl back over the prince's head then, grabbing both Delphine and Louis by their elbows, he hurried them on. He had to admit to himself that he'd been about to give up until the phenomenal colour in Louis' suddenly deep-blue eyes had somehow spurred him on. He trusted the feeling of hope it had given him.

'No stopping for anything!' he yelled, clear in his own mind that they had no time to waste if they were to survive.

And turning the corner, both he and Delphine gasped a dry cry of relief.

91

Ash, Delphine and Louis stood before two thick, transparent plastic doors, above which a sign announced: INTENSIVE CARE. Beyond them, the way seemed clear, the flames as yet only licking at the white-painted wall that stretched away further than they could see, its paint beginning to bubble and form peeling brown patterns.

They watched more vermin come round the corner, then turn right at the thick plastic barrier. It seemed that they were running directly into the flames that lapped at the wall separating the intensive care unit from the observation rooms. Ash moved closer and saw that a tunnel of air had been created between the wall and the flames, leaving a few inches clear at the bottom. Its torrid heat was apparently something the rats were ready to endure if it meant escape, though how the creatures knew this was beyond him. As far as he could tell, the area on the other side of the scorched wall was as yet untouched by fire, but Ash reckoned that within minutes the wall would be consumed by the flames, followed by the ward beyond.

He rushed Delphine and Louis through, elbowing aside one of the plastic doors that was already starting to melt, wrenching his jacket free as hot, sticky, plastic strands glued him to it. Mercifully, it was still sufficiently solid to mute the intensity of heat and smoke as it sprang back into position.

Ash stared down the long narrow ward with its cot beds, medical apparatus, transparent tents, and other less easily identifiable hardware, trolleys carrying cylinders of oxygen, an abandoned blood-pressure cuff lying on a chair, drip-feeds standing by evacuated beds, their contents spilling onto the floor. Further down the ward were several cots whose white sheets concealed what were obviously corpses.

It was incredibly hot in there and when he breathed a wheezing sound came from his throat. They had to move along quickly if they were to get by the fire which was threatening to engulf the ward. As he looked back to urge Delphine and Louis on, he was surprised to see them standing at a bedside.

Surely they hadn't found a live abandoned patient? Even with the best will in the world they couldn't hope to take anyone with them. He hurried across and peered over their shoulders.

On the cot he saw an elderly man with white hair and hollow cheeks. The dark hole of his gaping toothless mouth suggested the man was very dead indeed. Ash sincerely hoped so, for Delphine was pulling off his oxygen mask.

She handed the transparent plastic mask to Louis.

'Take two or three deep breaths of this,' she instructed as she inspected the oxygen cylinder nearby and made sure the gas was flowing.

Louis did as he was told and his chest rose and fell as he drew in the pure oxygen.

'Deeper,' said Delphine. 'Fill your lungs and hold it there for two or three seconds.'

Once again, the prince followed her advice.

Delphine glanced at Ash. 'I hope you're not squeamish,' she said.

Ash was taken aback: the thought of using an oxygen mask taken from a dead body that had probably been diseased was pretty repulsive.

'You're next,' she informed him. 'This will make you feel much better.' He was about to take it when he saw the exhaustion in her tender eyes.

'After you, Delphine. You're nearly out on your feet.'

She didn't argue. Taking the mask from Louis, she took in

at least eight deep breaths. When she'd finished and handed the mask to Ash, he saw some of the sparkle had returned to her deep brown eyes.

Ash followed suit. God, she was right. He felt more lively already. Pure oxygen was what they had all needed. But if they were to survive, they had to get moving again.

All done at six huge breaths, Ash tossed the mask onto the bed. While not quite a new man, he undoubtedly felt more spirited. Maybe the pills he'd taken were kicking in too.

'Now we go,' he said sternly, brooking no objections.

Together they hurried down to the far end of the ward, passing melting plastic doors on the right, smoke seeping through. *What was beyond the doors at the end?* he pondered as they ran, the shoulder bag banging against his hip. *Well, if a bag worked for Indiana Jones, it could work for me.* Ash laughed, then realized he had taken in rather too much oxygen, and too deeply. He was a little light-headed. He focused himself: *What if the fire was impassable beyond the door at the end of the unit?*

They would soon find out. As Louis was about to push through the double doors Ash grabbed his sleeve. He could easily make out the orange glow beyond the semi-transparent doors.

Again he elbowed one plastic door aside.

The instant rush of heat was almost overwhelming, but he saw there was space beyond to continue their escape. Urging his two companions through, he allowed the toughened plastic door to slap back into place.

'*Keep moving!*' he yelled as the other two waited for him. They skirted the fire and kept close to the warm stone wall on their right.

Delphine suddenly stopped, bringing Louis to a halt beside her.

'*Can you feel it?*' she cried over the crackle of the fire and collapsing timbers. '*There's air coming from somewhere ahead!*'

It was as Ash had hoped: they were close to the old lift shaft.

He ushered them onwards, moving faster now they had some much-needed encouragement and with their lungs recently filled with pure oxygen.

At last they reached the point Ash had been aiming for since they'd left the armoury. Before them stood the lift's heavy wooden outer door, half-open as if left that way by the last person to use it, but in fact blasted aside by the huge explosion from the subterranean dungeon. Ash and Delphine, gripping onto the side wall, peered down into the blackness of the shaft and felt a clean breeze flowing upwards.

The investigator reached into his leather bag and pulled out the hefty, long torch. He shone its beam into the pit below, grimly aware of the heat at his back. His heart lifted as he smelt more than just dust and soot in the rising draught: there was a hint of sea air in the mix.

'Look, Delphine, can you see it?' He pulled her closer to him and held her firmly as she leaned into the shaft and saw what he meant.

'The top of the old lift!' she exclaimed. 'It's battered and bent but there's a hole on one side we can slide through. D'you think the big explosion, the one that shook the building, was planted down there?'

'Yep,' he replied, almost light-heartedly. 'Someone – God knows who – placed a bomb in the rubble left after the lift car crashed through the ceiling. Come on, we've got to get going. I'll lower you onto the top of the lift – what's left of it; then I'll lower Louis so you can help him drop the rest of the way.'

He handed the long torch to Louis, saying, 'Keep the light on Delphine, help her see around and below.'

Louis took the Maglite and aimed its powerful beam into the shaft.

Without hesitation, Delphine let Ash take her by the wrists and help her over the ledge of the opening, then gently lower her into the drop.

'Okay?' he called down to her, now on his knees to get her closer to the lift's buckled top.

629

'Just scraping my feet on something. I'll be all right if you let me go.'

'Sure?'

'Sure.'

'Okay.'

He was almost at his limit and he cautiously let her wrists slip through his hands, hanging on to her until her fingertips slipped past his own.

'Didn't even have to fall,' she called back when he finally released her. There was a hollowness to her rasping voice. All three had raw throats from the smoke-filled air. 'The roof is misshapen enough to form a kind of slide. The metal is hot but manageable.'

The explosion must have blown upwards through the already buckled roof of the lift carriage.

'Ugh!' he heard her groan from below. 'Rats down here. They must have jumped over the edge or climbed down the walls. Right now they're looking at the hole I'm standing over. Think I'm making them nervous.'

He almost grinned. 'Stand back and let them through. We'll work better with them out of the way.' Ash became serious again. 'If you block their way, they'll attack. Otherwise, they're peaceable.'

'You know a lot about vermin!' she called.

'With my work in old buildings I see a lot of them, although never quite so many. Don't worry, they're usually harmless.' *Except when they're not*, he thought, but chose not to say.

With the torchlight opened to its widest beam, he and Louis watched as Delphine edged herself as far from the dented hole as possible. They saw the agitated rodents flow like a bristle-haired stream, scuttling through the almost V-shaped opening.

'You next, Louis,' Ash said, looking up at the prince. 'Drop the torch down to Delphine and she can use it to help us see.'

Louis did as instructed and the psychologist caught it deftly. She shone the light back at them.

Turning away from the sudden glare, Ash spotted more

vermin gathering in the corner behind Louis. They leapt over each other to get away from the heat, while those at the front watched Louis and Ash warily.

'Right, your turn, Louis. Climb over the edge and hold on. I'll take your wrists and lower you. Delphine's down there waiting to catch you if you fall, so don't be afraid.'

Louis did as he was asked and, out of the corner of his eye, Ash caught sight of the rats tentatively crawling forward. The prince was hanging over the edge and, noticing how weak his grip was, Ash immediately grabbed his thin wrists. They felt weird to the touch, oddly soft and supple, the bones beneath the skin like sticks coated in thin rubber. Ash felt that if he squeezed too tightly they would snap. The investigator lowered the boy gently. When he glimpsed Louis' upturned face, the huge balled eyes, the clearly visible veins, muscles, tendons and teeth, he almost recoiled in shock before suddenly becoming aware of the fluid forming in Louis' tear ducts as he saw the investigator's horrified expression.

Ash was ashamed. He was treating Louis like a freak, as so many others would if they escaped Comraich.

It was the first time he'd been able to examine properly the prince's grotesque – how he hated himself for even *thinking* that word – mask of a face, bright reflections of fire dancing over the contours of his fine vellum-like skin. Louis struggled to free himself, clearly despising, even hating himself. Ash sensed the prince's misery, but grasped the thin wrists more firmly.

Ash felt something scurry across his back, then onto his arm, using him as a kind of ladder. He felt another rat run over his shoulder on the other side to scurry down his arms, digging its sharp claws in for grip, passing over his hand and on to Louis' thin, naked arm, the robe's loose sleeve having slipped down.

'Delphine!' Ash shouted. 'Catch Louis if you can. It should be easy – he's as light as a feather!'

The psychologist scrambled from her refuge on the corner

of the lift's buckled roof. She looked up with the torch and screamed as a dozen rats fell onto her. Still she held her arms up to receive Louis, while managing to keep the flashlight cupped into the palm of her hand.

Ash finally released the robed figure and Delphine had him in her arms almost instantly, steadying him as he turned into her embrace.

'Now get back to the corner! Both of you. I'm coming to join you!'

With rats clinging to him, and the fire behind scorching his back, Ash slipped over the open doorway's edge and dropped down onto the lift's roof. Other, smaller creatures were throwing themselves over the edge like lemmings. As he landed with a thump that shook the lift carriage, nearly upsetting the balance of Delphine and Louis, the terrified rats rained down on him. Nearly losing his footing, he hit out at them, knocking the creatures away; they seemed content to slither down through the jagged hole and disappear into the darkness.

He scrambled his way over to his two companions, finding Louis locked in Delphine's arms. She kept the torchlight's beam angled downwards so that Ash was not dazzled.

Ash put a light hand on Louis' shoulder. 'I'm sorry, Louis,' he said quietly.

Louis turned, the hood back over his head. 'That's all right, Mr Ash. I do understand.'

Delphine looked at Ash with a concerned expression, but he simply shook his head. Louis' voice, although mumbled awkwardly, had been so forgiving – and truly understanding – that Ash wanted to turn him round and enfold the slight figure in his arms. What must this young man have been through all these years? Someone to be scrutinized, studied, prodded and have electrodes fixed to him just to discover how nerve systems worked, how blood moved through the body, how food was digested? What next for him should they all survive and then escape the Comraich estate? The media would go wild, questions would be asked in Parliament, Charles would be reviled once more. The monarchy would be compromised.

Even if they reached the outside of the castle, Ash had little doubt the small army of guards would be ordered to hunt them down, and if necessary, shoot all three of them. That way there could be no evidence nor any witness. Delphine, a young recluse, and David Ash, had been burned to nothing, the authorities would be told. Kate would be told.

They heard constant *thunks* as the rats dropped from the opening, two of them on fire as they fell.

Licks of flame were beginning to shoot from the doorway above.

'We have to find our way out through the dungeons,' Ash said. 'Let's hope there's no welcoming committee left. Delphine, d'you still have the smaller torch I gave you?'

'In my bag.'

'Use it while I take the larger torch. Remember to keep the beam open wide. Narrow it if you need more concentrated light.'

With that, the investigator took back the hefty Maglite and shone it into the sloping roof of the lift car. Without hesitation, he slid into it, almost losing control as he plummeted down. Fortunately, it was a short trip: within a moment he was crouching on debris left by the earlier explosion. He pointed the beam wide along the length of the corridor and took in the scorched walls and battered cell doors. It was lucky there was not much that would burn here, for the blast had travelled on, finding old timbers and more inflammable material to ignite.

The smell was awful, and soot and dust soon covered the part of his face that was unmasked. He'd heard somewhere that sometimes the centre of an explosion was often left relatively unscathed as the blast blew outwards, so although he stood among ruins, it wasn't as bad as he thought it might be.

Tentatively, he swung the light beam round and took in the doorway close to him, the door itself blown across the cell's small chamber. It was the dungeon where Hitler's daughter had been kept. It took but a few strides for him to climb across the rubbled corridor and shine the Maglite into the empty room, its sparse furniture merely cinders: there was no charcoaled body that he could see. He wondered what had become of the mad old woman.

Stepping back, he shone the powerful torchlight towards the other end of the corridor which was almost lost in a fog of dust and smoke, the aftermath of the explosion. His heart skipped a beat as he made out the movement of figures in the churning clouds.

Of course. The inmates. For some reason they had moved to that end, perhaps intending to use the stairs to escape their confinement. They must have been released from their cells when the bomb blasted down the corridor and up the lift shaft.

Now he could just make out several of the figures lingering over something dark that lay prone on the ground. But some of the blurred faces began looking towards the new source of light. He heard their low murmuring and then shouts, cries of alarm. They fought each other to get away, either panicked by the light or fearful of retribution. Again he tried to make out the figure lying face down near the steps and although he could not identify the person, Ash saw that he did not wear the usual baggy smock of the sectioned patients.

Ash had a terrible thought: Was the recumbent body – obviously dead – someone who had made their way here to set the patients free and lead them to safety, but who the inmates had turned on and killed? Ash shuddered. Either way, he didn't want to spend more time in their company than he had to. It was time to get moving again.

Ash felt a breeze on his face that was strong enough to ruffle his powder-dusted hair. It blew the soot and other smells of the explosion away from him and towards the far end of the corridor where the milling inmates were, lost, frightened and dangerous.

But his interest was in the opposite end of the dungeon

corridor, and the thick wooden door that had permanently sealed it, almost fatally trapping him during his earlier run-in with the containment area's inmates. He swung the Maglite towards it and smiled when he saw that there was hardly anything left of the door, just fragments of wood thrown into the tunnel beyond, and twisted iron hinges hanging loosely.

Water dripped like huge tears off the secret tunnel's ceiling, and it trickled down the mossy walls as if in a grotto. Where it came from, he'd no idea, though he guessed there must be a whole network of cracks and fissures running through the cliff face. There were broad puddles on the uneven floor, but most of the invasive water flowed in narrow streams at either side of them along the two walls, following the tunnel's descent, which he felt sure would lead to the big sea cave hundreds of feet below shoreline.

'David?' Delphine's concerned voice came from the top of the lift car. 'Are you all right?'

'Never better,' he responded. 'It looks like we have a way out. Help Louis down and I'll catch him at this end.'

'Is it safe?'

He glanced into the tunnel again, using the torch, its beam set at its widest angle. There was a line of vermin making their way along the sloping floor of the passageway so patiently cut and maintained by smugglers and slave traders centuries before.

'The rats seem to think so,' he called back, 'and as I said, they're born survivors. Let's move, Delphine, before the whole bloody castle collapses on top of us.' *And before the dungeon people notice where we've gone.*

He heard Louis slithering down the short, rough metal chute and caught his legs as soon as they appeared. Ash gently lowered the prince, and again it came to him how slight and frail Louis was. Ash feared it would be difficult getting the exiled prince down the winding, slippery smugglers' tunnel.

And he didn't even want to think about the monstrous web that he knew lay across their path.

92

It was heavy going. More than once one or other of them slipped on the damp and greasy tunnel floor, strewn with mossy rocks that had dropped from the rough-cut ceiling. In places, whole sections of wall had collapsed, forcing them to climb around or over.

A couple of times they all slid off their feet, particularly when the descent became steeper, and both Ash and Delphine did their best to cushion Louis' fall. But their efforts were not always successful: once Louis fell so heavily that they were unable to catch him; yet he never cried out, even though the stone floor must have hurt his delicate skin. Luckily, his cashmere robe, light though it was, saved him from the worst scrapes. At one point, where there were no steps, was a stairless slope so slick and steep that they all slithered down together. Delphine gave out a small shriek, but Ash, who had been in the lead, was able to turn and soften their landing by spreading his arms wide and catching both of them before they jarred against the base.

On they went, masks lowered but breathing in musty stale air that was occasionally relieved by the salty, sea-blown draught from below. After ten minutes Louis was becoming more and more unsteady on his feet, one arm often reaching out to balance himself against a wall.

'I think we need to take a break, David.' Delphine's voice sounded hollow and echoed in the tunnel. 'Louis is all but done in.'

Ash was reluctant, but he knew she was right. At one stage he might end up carrying the prince, but his leg was still painful and he would sooner delay that moment for as long as possible. They had reached a set of rough-hewn steps and the investigator motioned for them all to sit.

'You're right.' He looked back at Delphine on the step behind him. She looked more weary than frightened. Her face, with her scarf-mask dropped, looked grimy and anxious, the dirt on her skin emphasizing the whites of her eyes. She noticed he was studying her and she smiled a smile so radiant that all anxiety seemed to drop away from her.

Louis was behind Delphine. Ash stretched back and put a hand on the robe-covered knee. He wasn't surprised to find Louis trembling, and although his strange face was hidden in the shadow of the hood, the investigator knew his expression would be one of fear.

'You going to be okay, Louis?' he asked quietly, shaking the young man's knee gently to comfort him.

'Of course I will, Mr Ash,' came the response, resolution in his tone.

'Please, call me David.'

What would happen to the monarchy when the truth about Louis was discovered? Ash could have wept for him. A poor, unfortunate son who had been turned away out of fear of public opinion.

'David,' said Delphine, 'I've just had a thought. Move over, will you?'

She shuffled down the steps to share the one he occupied.

'What is it?' Ash's mind was still elsewhere, his reaction automatic.

'What if there's no way through to the cave on the shoreline? What if the roof has fallen in further on?' She gripped his arm.

'It certainly isn't blocked completely, the draught is too strong for that. But anyway, what choice do we have? We can't just sit here; when the castle collapses it could take the whole cliff with it, us included.'

He sighed, but could not look away from her imploring eyes. He decided that now probably wasn't the best time to tell her about the mass of cobwebs that dammed the tunnel from wall to wall, ceiling to floor.

Meanwhile, the rats scurried by them, leaping down the steps in a constant, bustling line. They seemed to be in a tearing hurry. Maybe they knew something he didn't.

Ash, Delphine and Louis continued their long, hazardous descent, becoming accustomed to the cave-water stench, their masks covering their faces again. Ash led the way, lighting up the tunnel with the wide beam of the Maglite, then Louis, and finally Delphine.

A few cobwebs had begun to appear now, although gossamer thin, hanging from the ceiling. Ash brushed them away with a flick of the long-barrelled torch, dreading what he knew lay ahead.

Even this far below the castle they could feel an occasional vibration followed by a small roof fall of dust and pebbles, an indication of what was going on in the building above: burning timbers falling, stonework collapsing. It perhaps wouldn't be long before the whole structure would crumble in on itself. If that were to happen, Ash feared the zig-zag tunnel they were in might collapse with the impact. Here and there wooden crossbeams held up the sagging roof, while other stout-looking stanchions propped up crumbling walls; but these supports were themselves ancient and rotting in places, bending from the strain in others. Just how much longer could they do their job with all the pressure bearing down on them from above?

He endeavoured to keep Delphine and Louis moving as swiftly as possible, but the going was as rough as ever. Then the Maglite's beam picked out the obstruction he had feared most. Before them lay the huge tangled cobweb, black with centuries of dust and matted in places where water had dripped from the ceiling.

'*Oh God!*' Delphine cringed.

Louis stood as if paralysed.

Ash washed light from the torch over the sickening mass, looking for weak spots, but so dark and interwoven was the web it appeared as solid as the rock that surrounded them. He watched a stream of rats disappearing eagerly into the mass via a small hole at floor level, but, as far as he knew, rats had no fear of spiders. He concentrated the beam of light so that it penetrated further into the huge cobweb. There were things moving inside, some of them fat and bulbous, working their way through the strands, searching for food. His flesh crawled as if the furry-legged creatures were actually on him. Smaller spiders also crept through the mass of entwined strands but well away from bigger ones, for whom they might provide an alternative meal. He'd never heard of cannibal spiders before, but then never had he come across a web like this.

Delphine was pointing her own smaller torch at the horrendous mass before them. 'There's no way I can go through that, David. I'm . . . sorry, I'm . . . s-sorry, but I just can't do it.'

Ash turned to face her. 'We've no choice, Delphine.' He tried to keep his voice calm but confident. 'It can't extend far' – *how did* he *know?* – 'and we'll be on the other side in seconds. I'll cut a path through and you and Louis can keep close behind me.'

'No, David!' She was panicking. 'Those big things, as big as crabs – what are they?'

'Only spiders. They can't harm you,' he added.

'You don't know that! I've never seen spiders as big as those – how do we know what they're capable of?'

'Well, we can't stay here and we can't go back. Eventually, we'll have to make our way through. We can move fast. Our clothes will protect us.'

'Speak for yourself. Louis only has his robe and I'm wearing a skirt. None of us has gloves. Why can't we just wait here until it's all over?'

The ceiling settled above them, sending down small rocks and dust as if right on cue.

'Don't you see?' Ash almost pleaded. 'Apart from the dangers up there, the tunnel's unsafe. We've been lucky so far, but if we don't move on from here...' He left the sentence unfinished.

'I-I can't!'

He heard a note of hysteria in her voice and he pulled her in to his chest. The Maglite was pointing at the dripping ceiling.

'Delphine, you've got to trust me. I'll get us through this. And there are a few tricks we can use.'

Her tear-blurred eyes looked up at him, despairingly unconvinced. 'Tricks?'

'D'you have your glasses in your bag?'

The question confused her for a second, then she nodded her head in comprehension.

'Good. Put them on, for a start – they'll protect your eyes.'

Delphine rummaged through her small leather shoulder-bag and drew out a brown spectacle case. She quickly snapped it open and her fingers took out the black-rimmed glasses.

Ash smiled; rather than making her look donnish, she seemed more vulnerable. 'You'll be in the middle, between Louis and myself. If that's okay with you, Louis,' he added, looking in concern at the robed figure.

Louis nodded his head, the movement barely visible inside the hood. 'Of course,' he murmured nervously.

'Okay, we'll keep it tight,' said Ash. 'A Delphine sandwich, right?'

She managed an unsure smile.

'But first...' Ash opened the flap of his weathered shoulder-bag and yanked out a clutch of glow sticks. He gave three to Delphine; she looked up at him expectantly and Ash was aware that just giving her something to do was at least holding her fear in check.

'Now, I want you to crack them and hurl them into the web as far as possible. Let's give the bloody spiders a scare while lighting up the place for ourselves.'

He did exactly what he'd told Delphine to do, cracking the sticks and allowing the chemicals to mix and create coloured lights. Red, lime green, yellow – a dazzling display. Pulling his arm back, he tossed the first stick as hard as possible into the tangled mass. Delphine followed suit.

'Good!' Ash encouraged. 'Keep 'em near the middle so we'll have a path!'

Soon the great mass was lit up like a Christmas tree. It would have looked quite pretty, except for the exposed silhouettes of the creatures scuttling in confusion through the interlaced silken horror.

When she saw them, Delphine backed away in dread. 'I can't!' she screamed at Ash.

'We're not done yet,' he responded calmly, shining his torch on to the line of vermin running along the base of the wall, passing fearlessly into the flossy barrier.

Kneeling, he grabbed the long tail of a passing rat, lifting it into the air at arm's length as it squealed and thrashed. He flung it as hard as he could into the tangled mesh. Pausing momentarily, the fat black silhouettes suddenly moved fast towards the entangled rodent. Ash had no desire to watch the fierce battle that ensued between three huge spiders and the terrified animal, the attackers rushing forward through the mesh of their own creation, nipping at the rodent, then backing away to allow another to perform the same manoeuvre. He guessed there was venom in their bites.

Meanwhile, he'd grabbed another rat and, as it protested and wriggled in his hand, he placed the torch on the tunnel's wet floor, pointing directly at the other rats to blind them. He snatched at another with his free hand, this time holding it by its shoulders, avoiding the frenzied gnashing teeth, while the rest scattered. He jumped up and threw the squirming animal deep into the tangle then, still holding the first rat by its scaly tail, he swung it in a wide loop over his shoulder and launched it straight into the feverish storm he'd already caused inside the terrible barricade.

As much as he cared for Delphine, he knew he had to be strict with her.

'Hands around my waist,' he ordered as he dragged her back from the position she'd retreated to. 'Pull yourself tight against me, and pull that scarf over your head and cover as much of your face as possible. Your glasses will protect your eyes but let me be your guide – don't let go of me whatever you do.'

He beckoned Louis closer.

'Louis, you're going to bring up the rear, keeping as close to Delphine as possible. Take her torch. Pull your scarf up over your nose and the hood around your face. Remember, you're bigger than the spiders are.' Ash indicated the struggling beasts behind him with his thumb.

Turning, he widened the Maglite beam a little and backed closer to Delphine. 'Remember, keep against my back as tight as possible. That goes for you, too, Louis – stay as close as you can to Delphine. If you see anything coming towards you, try and blind it with the light.'

Ash reached under his jacket and drew the combat knife from its sheath. Hauling in a deep breath of foul air before pulling up his biker's muffler, he held both the weapon and the torch out in front of him.

With one last cry of 'Hang on tight, here we go!' he pushed his way into the huge black web.

93

Ash slashed with the knife in one hand and thrashed with the long-barrelled torch in the other, cutting a surprisingly difficult path through the compacted mass. He hadn't realized just how tough the major strands forming the foundation would be, for they seemed to become more impenetrable the further he advanced. Nevertheless, he fought his way through, his strikes becoming more desperate as he advanced. Progress was slow, but never once did he moderate his attack. He could feel Delphine shivering behind him, her covered head pressed against his shoulder blades, and he could only hope that Louis was just as close to her.

'Keep it tight!' he yelled to encourage them, web strands getting into his eyes, forcing him to keep them narrowed. Something ran over his scalp, too light to be a rat. He shook his head vigorously, unsure whether he'd dislodged it from his thick hair. Veils of gossamer gauze floated down to land on his head and shoulders, but he pushed on, clearing his eyes with the back of his knife hand.

He suddenly spied something monstrous racing directly towards his face, a large creature with a swollen, pale body, definitely not a rat. It was – with its bloated skin, eight fast-moving thick hairy legs and seemingly myriad eyes – an unwelcome host. It looked as if it were so full of blood it could almost burst. Whether it could see or sense him Ash was unsure, for it must have spent most of its life in total darkness; or did the many eyes allow it some kind of advanced vision?

These thoughts flashed through his mind in an instant – and almost by instinct he thrust the blade of his knife straight into the creature's grotesque face, flicking it off in a quick movement so that the weapon would remain free and lethal. He eyed with distaste the thick gooey substance left on the serrated part of the blade.

'We must be nearly through!' he shouted, hoping the others would believe the lie. 'We're doing fine!'

There was a frantic scuffle to his left and he felt Delphine cling on to him even more firmly. He risked a glance and saw in the light of a lime-green glow stick another rat doing battle with two oversized spiders, their bodies locked together as they sank down through the web. He silently wished the rat good luck, deciding he preferred the rodent to the repellent arachnids.

Ash continued to thrash and slash, stopping only to toss more glow sticks along the way. The spiders were now coming in greater numbers – more than he could flick aside or stamp underfoot. He reached into his pocket for another glow stick and his heart sank when he clutched fresh air and realized he had thrown the last of them. The way ahead was becoming darker, despite the strong beam of his torch, and for a moment it looked as if they'd come up against a solid wall, but he attacked it with even greater ferocity as spiders continued to claw at his head and face. The knife cut as if through butter, but the big Maglite became easily entangled and he had to yank it free constantly, slowing their progress. *Thank God for Modafinil*, he thought, as he trampled on the lower sections of the web as if it were long thick grass.

He glanced down and saw one of the vile creatures was about to run up his leg. He stamped on it hard and felt the sickly *squelch* as its bulging body burst. Dirty green liquid and blood shot from it.

He felt Delphine clutch at him more tightly.

'Don't worry, we're nearly there!' he shouted over his shoulder again, and this time it was no lie, for he could smell the sea even more strongly and, in spite of the web's thickness, the salty breeze was stiffening, coming straight off the waves. He took one more swipe at the tangle in front of him and was relieved to see the way ahead was easier, the strands not quite so knotted.

'Hey, I think—'

With a short cry, Delphine slipped and fell, clutching at his legs as she went down. He spun round, grabbing her shoulders, and looked up at the robed prince.

'We're almost there, Louis!' he shouted. 'You can easily get through. Take my knife. We've passed most of the spiders!'

The young man did as instructed, bravely plunging into the web ahead, although he would rather have helped Delphine back on her feet.

Ash returned his attention to Delphine. 'Are you okay?' he touched her forehead with his own.

'I-I'm sorry. One of those things was coming at me and I lost my footing. God, I lost my nerve, too!'

Ash saw a huge spider two inches from her outstretched hand as she tried to sit up. Carefully avoiding her fingers, he brought the heavy Maglite down hard and squashed the creature flat. Delphine shuddered at the sound and quickly looked away.

He quickly hauled her upright and she immediately pointed at something creeping around his exposed neck.

'What is it?' he asked.

'It looks like a long centipede, only fatter and a sickly greyish-yellow colour,' she replied with a grimace.

Now he was aware of it, he felt the multitude of sharp little legs on the skin of his throat. Somehow, the lapels of the old field jacket he wore, the collar of which he'd turned up to protect his neck, had come loose in the fray. Delphine, disgust on her grimy but determined face, reached up and plucked the creature off him. Ash felt its legs resisting, digging into his flesh, but with little hesitation the psychologist gripped the freakish creature more firmly and pulled it free, leaving a double row of pinpricks on Ash's neck. Praying the creature's claws weren't poisoned, she threw the predator away.

Ash threw one arm over her shoulder and brought Delphine as close as possible to him. Together, they ducked their heads and continued forward along the path Louis had cleared, only occasionally looking up to see whether anything frighteningly fierce was in their way.

The cobwebs began to thin and a few seconds later they were free. It was like emerging from some kind of hideous cocoon. The struggle had made them sweat profusely, and they now stepped into an ice box which instantly froze the perspiration on their skin.

Louis was waiting in the darkness a few yards further on. Ash turned the torch beam on Delphine, starting at the top and working the light down her body. He flicked off any clinging spiders and cobwebs he found with his bare hands, then gently turned her round so that she was facing away from him. Her back was covered in spiders, but fortunately no supersized horrible ones, and he quickly disposed of them.

Satisfied he'd done his best, Ash handed the torch to Delphine and she proceeded to do the same for him. When she'd finished, Ash did what he'd been wanting to do for what seemed like an eternity. He embraced her. He lifted her chin with the knuckle of his finger and kissed her full on the lips.

When he pulled away, he looked deeply into her eyes and said, 'I love you, Delphine.'

With that, she was in his arms, kissing his face all over, despite the dirt that stained his skin. Her eyes brimmed with tears, this time from emotion rather than fear.

'I love you too, David,' she told him softly.

It was only after more kisses that they remembered the third member of their party. Ash took the long Maglite from her and turned it on Louis.

He stood stock-still, just a short distance away, further down in the tunnel.

As if paralysed, Ash and Delphine stared at him in horror.

94

'Lucky' Lord Lucan casually strolled from the burning castle, keeping to one side of the panicked guests, now joined by equally panicked Comraich staff and guards. There was pushing and shoving all around him, mingled with screams and curses as everyone crammed through one of the building's narrow side doors.

To his knowledge, there had never been a fire drill at Comraich and he certainly did not want to mix with the common breed the castle was taking in as guests more and more often these days. He liked to stick with his own kind. Unhappily, there seemed to be increasingly fewer of them as the seasons went by.

Many of the male guests were wrapped in expensive dressing gowns or shivering in silk pyjamas, while the few women wore fur coats over their nightwear. He himself wore a smart Savile Row dark blue topcoat with a half-velvet collar and lapels over age-old winkled pyjamas, and an equally venerable cardigan. The fire's flickering reflection could be seen in the toecaps of his rarely worn patent leather shoes. Lucan had witnessed one of the Comraich guards smash the butt of his gun into a guest who had objected to being shoved roughly through the fire exit. The man had dropped like a stone, to be trampled where he lay. Lucan had avoided that sort of thing by quietly sidling against the wall.

The escape from Comraich had been as undignified as it had been ungentlemanly and he wondered if it had been like this just before the *Titanic* sank. With the fire roiling at their backs, getting ever closer, and the hallway past the back reception offices being so narrow, people had been squeezed far too closely together. It was inevitable that order would break down, he supposed, and soon become a matter of looking after number one.

At least he was finally free of the inferno and breathing in the night sea air. It was brisk, though, and he drew his shabby cardigan tighter, buttoning up his topcoat and pulling the lapels around his neck. His long hair blew wildly in the strong wind that raced up the cliff face from the irate sea below.

Instead of walking round to the concourse to join the mingling guests and staff who had escaped and were now looking up at the blazing castle, shivering and wondering what to do, he turned towards the walkway overlooking the sea, where there was a row of cannons and several benches for him to choose from. As he mounted the stairway to the walk, the moon, bright and silvery above, shone like a blank silver coin.

No sooner had he sat down than a castle door below the level of the walkway burst open and a large group of dinner-suited men belched forth from the ancient building. These must be the VIPs who'd been congregating in Comraich that evening. He noticed, stretching his neck backwards and sideways, that the queer little fellow Mabee or Maseley, something like that, was leading them. They were agitated all right, no doubt about that, but there was no panicked flight here, just a general bustling quick march. And why not? These men had no fear of being burned alive: they had their own personal escape route.

None noticed him on his perch above as they spoke in an anxious huddle with the strange little Marsbey fellow. Lucan listened to the crackling of the conflagration inside the castle for a while as he gazed out over the silver-streaked sea.

Then he heard a different noise: the sound of a helicopter warming up, followed quickly by the muted blares of far-distant sirens.

This, he thought, was turning out to be an exciting night.

95

'Oh, Louis . . .' Delphine almost moaned.

Ash caught her arm before she could rush to the lonely figure waiting there, as if frozen in shock, afraid of what might happen if he moved.

The investigator took the torch from Delphine and widened its beam so that it was softer. He turned it back onto the exiled prince.

Spiders, large and small, covered the brown robe he wore, two of them on the side of his hood. Most of them were perfectly still, but some crawled across his slight body. In his right hand he still held the combat knife Ash had given him.

Ash began to walk slowly towards him, keeping the light as steady as his suddenly dry voice. 'Louis, it's going to be okay. Just stay where you are and keep very, very still.'

He could feel Delphine walking with him, just behind his left shoulder. The Maglite was held in his right hand.

It was slightly awkward to reach him, the floor uneven and slippery. 'Hold your nerve, Delphine,' he whispered to the psychologist, who was as yet unsure she was free of the creatures herself. She was aware of tiny movements over – and *under* – her clothing. 'If you make a dash for him, he'll panic.' Ash almost slipped but managed to steady himself as well as the light. 'I don't want to arouse those things.' His voice was low, a murmur, no more than that.

With horror, they watched as a large, hairy-legged spider,

with two venomous-looking pincers, crawled around from behind Louis' lower leg to come to a rest on his ankle.

Ash was relieved when the young man did not react: it was as though he were in a trance, overcome with fear, afraid to move. *A good thing in the circumstances*, the investigator thought to himself as he slowly approached.

'What are we going to do?' murmured Delphine.

Ash held up his free arm to stop her. 'First, let's see exactly how bad it is,' he whispered back. She looked up at him, baffled.

It wasn't long before she understood though.

They were very near to the motionless robed figure now, but Ash was making a wide berth of Louis while playing the light on him all the time. Still, the prince remained rooted. Delphine half expected Louis to lose composure at any moment, perhaps to swipe the creatures away, or perhaps to turn and run screaming down the dark, seemingly endless tunnel. She followed Ash round, wondering what his tactics were going to be.

'Don't get too close, Delphine, we don't want to get them agitated,' Ash whispered even more softly as she trailed him.

'Oh, dear God!'

They were now behind Louis, and while there had been several kinds of creatures fixed or creeping over his front, the back of his robe was glutted with spiders of all shapes and sizes, two of them extraordinary grey-white monsters with discernible blue veins beneath their thin-skinned, bloated abdomens.

With Louis covering their rear as they'd pushed their way through the giant web, more spiders of different species had dropped on and clung to his exposed back. Incongruously, considering the circumstances, Ash had a flash of insight into their ecosystem: with very few insects flying into the web, these spiders ate each other, the larger ones obviously picking on the small. As if to give evidence of this, he watched a large spider ensnare a much smaller one, paralysing it, then proceeding to devour it at once rather than cocooning it in silk for a later feast.

It turned his stomach, but not as much as the number of these hideous creatures crawling across Louis' back.

'God, David, what are we going to do?' came Delphine's urgent whisper again.

Ash already had a plan, but had taken time to walk around Louis to assess the problem.

'Louis,' he spoke quietly. 'Listen to me, but don't move just yet. First, hand me the knife.' The young man did so and Ash returned it to its sheath. 'Now, I'm going to remove a spider on your ankle. Don't worry; I'll just flick it away. You won't feel a thing.'

Ash hoped.

Returning carefully and slowly to Louis' front once more, he knelt at the young man's feet. *Only fitting*, he told himself with a certain grim acerbity, considering who the young man really was.

Without hesitation, but with sure accuracy, he swiped the Maglite at the creature perched now on the prince's instep and knocked it away before it had a chance to act. As it rolled awkwardly on its back, fat, hairy legs waggling in the air, Delphine deftly put the low heel of her boot through the struggling arachnid and pressed down hard. Taking her foot away from the gooey mess left on the tunnel's damp floor, she wiped the sole of her boot against a small rocky projection. Ash was impressed by her calmness.

He stood and peered closely at the hood. As he spoke, he tried to ignore a bristling spider on the material a few inches away from Louis' exposed cheek.

'Louis . . .' he began as if in hushed confidence. 'Louis, there's no belt to your robe: is it buttoned from the inside?'

Ash sensed the surprise and confusion going on inside the cowl's shadowed interior.

'I'm serious, Louis. Can you tell me quickly?'

It was a curious Delphine who spoke for the young man. 'It's popper studs all the way down. That's how Louis wanted it made – not *too* monk-like.'

'Many?'

'Poppers? No, just a few, ending near his knees. The hem was supposed to reach the floor, but again, Louis didn't want it to restrict him too much.'

'And is the robe loose? It looks like it.'

'Yes.'

'Good. That may add to our advantage. But I'm going to act soon. Those creatures on the material are confused, I think, but they're beginning to get curious. Anything could set them off. We don't want them getting inside.'

Delphine shuddered as she realized what Ash was about to do.

'Stand clear,' he told her, giving her a quick glance. 'Right, Louis, in a moment I want you to lean forward.'

The hood tilted forward an inch.

'Slowly,' Ash continued. 'Just bend over a little. It's not going to be very dignified' – he was struck by the notion he was talking to royalty – 'but it'll be the best way. Try to remain still once you're leaning forward and leave the rest to me. I'm going to move very fast and lift the robe up from the hem and bring it right over your head, hopefully trapping the little buggers inside.'

He'd deliberately used the word 'little'.

'Okay, ready?'

The slim form, which seemed larger because of the loose, voluminous robe, bent forward slowly.

'That's fine, that's enough,' Ash told him, trying to sound confident as he warily moved around Louis, careful not to surprise the spiders, which he noticed were becoming restless.

'I'll count to three, Louis, then I'll pull the robe over you. We can easily deal with any laggards.'

Adjusting the Maglite to its most concentrated beam, so

bright it was difficult to look at it directly, he stretched out his arm and gave it to Delphine.

'Hold it so it shines at the floor, then the moment I say two, shine it full onto the robe – move it around a second or two and hopefully blind or dazzle the bloody things. Remember, they're used to living in darkness.'

She took it from him and nodded, her body trembling.

'Keep it down!' He hissed and pointed at the tunnel's rough floor, for nervousness had made her forget what he'd told her. 'Ready? Count of two for you, three for me.'

Ash wiped his sweaty palms against his thighs. 'Here we go. One-two-three!'

He'd squatted to grip the hem of the robe, his arms wide apart, and in one swift movement he lifted the material and stood, pulling the garment over Louis' head, hood and all. Keeping the bundle closed, he tossed the whole piece as hard and as far as he could back into the huge cobweb. The creatures that had dropped out scattered and Ash trod on any that came near.

The dark bundle hung limply, but well within the web.

Delphine rushed forward to hold on to Louis – now naked apart from his white shorts and soft sneakers.

'We're not quite finished.' He nodded at Louis' transparent skin on which there were still a few black, scuttling things left. Delphine drew in a sharp breath, her hand up to her mouth. Ash grabbed the torch from her and backhanded the dazed spiders off the young prince's flesh as gently as he could. It didn't take long and the investigator was sorely relieved when it was over.

Except it wasn't quite over.

Ash glanced down at Louis' white boxer shorts and frowned. 'I'm sorry, they'll have to go too, Louis.'

'But . . .' His eyes looked appealingly into Delphine's.

'You can wrap my scarf around your waist,' she said, sympathizing with her patient and friend's shame and vulnerability.

Ash shrugged off his thigh-length field jacket and helped Louis to put it on. He thanked the investigator and smiled gratefully, even though the material must have felt almost unbearably rough to him. Meanwhile, Delphine did something clever with her scarf, turning it into a sarong that covered Louis' exposed legs. Ash retrieved the Maglite from Delphine and shone the beam down the slanting tunnel ahead.

He tried to remember how far they still had to go but it was all a blur. It couldn't be that far, surely? He didn't think he'd climbed that far from the entrance cave when he'd been here before.

Delphine's arms were enfolding Louis, supporting him. The prince was exhausted and shivering – on this side of the web the breeze had become almost a gale, funnelled up through the tunnel from the large cave below. At least the air with its tang of the sea was refreshing.

'We'll take Louis between us,' he said to Delphine. 'You take his left arm, I'll take his right, so I can show the way with the torch's wide beam. Delphine, you can still use the small Maglite, maybe keep its light low to the ground so we can watch where we tread.'

The chill made him shudder. Louis must be really freezing with only my battered jacket to keep off the worst of the cold, he thought.

'Do we have much further to go, David?' asked Delphine, more out of concern for Louis, although the deep chill ran through her as well.

'I— uh . . . I don't think so. Hard to remember.'

'Any more nasty surprises?'

He shook his head, then paused. *Maybe*, he thought.

'Come on,' he said, 'let's just get out of here.'

96

Like every other guest at Comraich, Petra and Peter had been confined to quarters earlier that day. He'd sneaked along to her room, bringing with him the stash of drugs he'd bribed a guard to supply him with on a regular basis. If the nervous guard had ever been discovered in the transactions, the ex-military man had no illusions: he would have been summarily executed and his body thrown into the castle's furnaces, so Peter had had to ensure the bribe was too big to ignore.

In his sister's suite, they spent the rest of the day and what was to be the rest of the night naked in her four-poster bed, making drug-fuelled love as never before following their long period of enforced celibacy. By the evening they were in a pleasant haze in which they'd talked, explored each other's bodies again, garbled profound inanities and finished the last of the cocaine Petra had brought with her to Comraich in the modified asthma inhaler. During all this, they'd kept their parched throats moist with three bottles of Chablis that Petra had liberated from one of the empty drawing-room bars.

At one stage they thought they'd heard the distant sound of running boots and someone giving the bedroom door a thump and shouting words neither of them understood. That made them laugh, anyway. Together, in each other's arms, they dozed off to peaceful, then exciting, places, where dreams were reality and everything else was fiction. So senselessly stupefied were they by night-time, the muffled explosions meant little to them. Not even the great *boom* that shook her bedroom had any effect other than to disturb their faraway state of mind, causing Peter to turn over in bed and cover his ears with a pillow.

It was the smoke drifting in under the door that started to rouse Petra. In her surreal waking dream, the black smoke became demons with huge black, slanting eyes and hairy snouts for noses and sharp claws for hands. They circled the bed, those angled eyes on her and her sleeping lover. They grinned slyly and drooled from their rough lips, giving her lascivious looks, swirling claws pointing at her naked breasts as if to touch them. Yet these grotesques were made only of smoke and could have no real impact on her bare flesh.

Whatever sense she still had told her that, although the demons were imaginary, the smoke was real enough. For it raked her throat and reddened her eyes with its irritation.

From somewhere in the castle she thought she heard a scream. And then another. And the heat in the room was becoming overwhelming.

'Peter!' she cried, pushing vigorously at his shoulder.

He stirred but did not wake.

'Peter!' This time it was almost a scream and it half brought him to his senses. His survival instinct managed to cut through the murkiest of thoughts. Blearily he sat up, looking around at the drifting smoke. The bedroom was hot.

'Oh, fuck,' he croaked, 'the castle's on fire!' He turned to his sister. 'Why didn't anyone come for us? Why aren't there fire alarms?'

'Maybe they're not working,' she said falteringly.

He glanced over at the door where the smoke was now billowing through.

'Oh God, oh God!' His eyes went towards the window, and Petra's gaze followed his.

'Why are all the fucking windows barred?' he shouted, as if it were her fault.

'You told me yourself. It's to stop anyone on this floor getting out.'

'Or throwing themselves out!' He realized the bars in this case were for her; she'd tried suicide twice before.

He leapt from the bed, dragging the bedclothes with him, leaving his sister completely exposed. For a moment, his head whirled and he reached out for a bedpost to steady himself.

'What are you going to do?' wailed Petra, her knees drawn up, hands around her ankles.

'I'm gonna see if we can get out!' he hollered back, shuffling to the door, holding the dragging bedclothes to his waist.

'No, Peter. Don't! It's too dangerous!'

'Well, we can't bloody well stay here, can we?'

It was rare for him to shout at her so angrily. Petra recognized the panic in his voice. He was scared for them both. He put his hand on the brass doorknob and jerked it back instantly.

'It's hot!' he cried, backing away a little. *But there is no other way out*, his fervid mind told him. He wrapped the blanket around his hand and reached for the doorknob once more.

'No, Peter, no!'

But it was too late. As he pulled the door open, the flames reached in like red-gold talons and grabbed hold of him, the bedclothes catching fire almost immediately. Then they swelled in, a rolling mass engulfing him completely.

His hair on fire, his flesh blistering, roasting and spitting as the juices ran, he turned back to his wailing sister, naked on the four-poster bed. Bizarrely, and perhaps because she was still in a drug haze, she could see his pale blue eyes as the fire lapped around his body. They stared straight at her. His mouth was open, and before he swallowed flames, she was sure he called her name.

His blazing arms, blackened in parts and red-raw in others, reached out to her, the one person he'd truly loved and who knew all his secrets, as he knew hers. He staggered to the bed and Petra realized what her beloved brother wanted.

Peter craved her comfort, for she was all he had – *had ever had*.

And she did not back away. Instead, she opened her arms as a mother would to console an injured child. Then, as a ball of fire with a blurred and blackened image of some creature within that might once have been a man, he fell upon his sister.

And, screaming with the pain of it, Petra wrapped her arms around her brother. And then her legs as she drew him in.

97

'I could cheerfully shoot the guy who wrote those bloody horror books about rats,' said Ash mildly.

'Why did you read them, then?' Delphine kept up the false tone of cheerfulness that Ash had adopted for the benefit of Louis, as all three stopped on the brink of the large cave.

'They looked interesting.'

Louis was between Ash and Delphine and was visibly shaking as he took in what lay before them.

'And were they?'

Ash could just discern the psychologist's own anxiety in her reply.

'Well,' he replied, 'kind of. But a little bit too much information about what rats are capable of, especially when they're excited.'

The trio had left the giant cobweb behind, much to their relief, following the tunnel's zig-zag turns without further mishap, finally finding themselves on the slippery stone steps that would take them to the sea cave. Delphine had wrinkled her nose at the foul acidic smell that came their way before they had reached the last step.

'It's only bat dung,' Ash explained, 'but the bats themselves won't harm us. Anyway, they're probably outside hunting. For insects, not humans,' he added quickly. 'No vampires here.'

However, as the three of them stood on the last step, Ash surveyed the cavern with horror. For this was the place the rodents had chosen for their own sanctuary, instinctively aware that the tide was washing into the sea cave, the waves too powerful to swim through. The nasty surprise that Ash had anticipated had materialized: the vermin – and there were thousands of them – filled the space before them, waiting out the storm and blocking their path.

Mostly, they appeared calm, but because of lack of space some snapped at those that tried to squirm over them. They made squealing noises like children at play, but soon the noise abated as the stiff-furred, grimy animals bedded down for the night. Soon, however, they would need to eat, and the only food available was of the two-legged variety.

'David,' Delphine whispered so as not to disturb the sea of vermin blocking their way. 'What do we do?'

Louis peered round at the investigator as though expecting him to provide a solution. He cut a crazy-looking figure in Ash's olive green field jacket, below which protruded his stick-like legs through which the shadows of his bones could be seen. He was shivering violently. The investigator, who was somewhat shaky himself, fervently hoped the shock would not bring on the prince's epilepsy.

'The only way is onwards,' Ash answered resolutely. 'Ever see that Hitchcock film, *The Birds*?'

Louis looked bemused, but Delphine nodded her head just once.

'Remember the scene at the end?'

This time there was no reaction from Delphine.

'It's a beautiful scene,' Ash continued. 'The hero opens his mother's front door. It's a great shot full of quietened birds, the town in the near-distance, and gulls and crows as far as you could see. The hero has no choice but to get his family and girlfriend far away from there before the birds attack again. It was full of tension, because although the enemy, the birds, appear to be dormant for the moment, the menace is still there.'

'David . . .' Delphine was becoming impatient in her anxiety.

'Okay. So the hero has to get his mother, girlfriend, and a

young girl – his niece, I think – to walk through the birds to reach his waiting car. They get into the car and very carefully drive off, expecting to be attacked at any moment.'

He paused.

'What happened to them?' Delphine asked eagerly.

Ash shrugged his shoulders. 'I don't know. That was when the credits rolled.'

Delphine groaned. 'That's not funny, David. What are we going to do now? How much longer before they turn on us?'

I wish I knew, thought Ash.

A few of the rodents looked their way uninterestedly. Most had hunkered down, apparently content for the moment. Yet Ash could feel the frisson in the air, as though aggression could break through at any time.

In reply to Delphine, Ash said quietly, 'We'll do what the characters in the movie did, only without the car: we'll just walk through them. Unless you can think of a better plan.'

Delphine could think of no other plan, so nodded her assent once more, but this time with an audible sigh. Ash reached around Louis and drew the psychologist to him and she came willingly, aching for his comforting embrace, wishing she had his determination.

As for Ash, he held her tightly, pushing his cheek into the comfort of her hair. He would not lose this one. He would not lose this woman he loved and who he knew, beyond doubt, loved him in return. Past heartaches, tragedies, had to be pushed back to the furthest corner of his mind lest he endangered her without thinking. He would not allow anyone or anything to take her from him. Ash kissed her cheek and tasted a tear that had trickled from her eye.

'I promise we'll get through this together. You, me and Louis. We've come a long, difficult way, and this last hurdle is all that lies between us and the sea cave. Just trust in me, okay?'

Her lips were trembling, and her smile was unconvincing, though she was obviously trying hard.

'I do trust you, David. You know that.'

'Good. I needed the encouragement.'

Reluctantly, he let go of her and looked at Louis, whose peculiar face was not easy to read.

'I trust you, too, Mr Ash,' he said in his strangely high, melodious voice. 'I'll do anything you say, sir.'

Mr Ash? Sir? My God, thought the investigator, *Louis is a prince of the realm*.

'I've said before, how about you call me David?' Ash said, smiling, the only response he could think of.

'All right . . . David.'

'That's better.' Ash realized they had to make a move. It was frigidly cold and the wind coming in off the sea was whistling harshly through the tunnel on the other side of the cavern. Even if the rats left them alone, he wasn't sure that Louis would survive the night in such conditions. He remembered the narrow passageway he'd had to negotiate to reach their present position from the cave, the rock ceiling low and sagging. There was always a chance that the explosions in the castle above had created more subsidence, or even triggered a rockfall, trapping them there. Still, they would have to face that problem when they reached it. For now, the rats were bad enough.

He motioned the others closer. 'Right, we're a team now, and together we're going to work carefully through that crowd of rats just as though they were sunbathers on a packed beach. They won't attack unless we annoy them by stepping on their tails or paws. If only one of them kicks off on its own, try to ignore it. Boot it away but don't try to take on all of them. Keep it personal.'

Ash looked directly at Louis and realized he no longer reacted to those odd, transparent features.

'Louis, I'm going to carry you across.'

He held up a hand to ward off any protests.

'You're a haemophiliac, Louis,' Delphine put in. 'If you get bitten by a rat, we'll never control the bleeding down here.'

He saw the sense of it even if he did not want to consider himself a burden. He accepted with a nod of his head.

'You've got a choice,' Ash said good-humouredly. 'I can hold you in my arms, carry you over my shoulder in a fireman's lift or give you a piggy-back. You decide.'

'Piggy-back,' the exiled prince said right away, and Ash was again reminded more of an excited boy than a man nearing thirty.

'That's good. Delphine can carry the big torch to light our way, and you can hold the smaller one for extra light.' He took in both of them. 'Now, if you see any particularly nasty specimens looking our way with blood-lust in their eyes, shine both torches at them – concentrated beam, Delphine – and try to dazzle them. They might flee, or they might be mesmerized, whatever, but it's up to us to keep going.' He turned his back to Louis and handed the Maglite to Delphine. With his knees partly bent and elbows stretched sideways, Ash said to Louis. 'Hop aboard. Make sure you've got a good grip on me, and shine the light just a little ahead so Delphine and I can see where to plant our feet.'

With that, the investigator took one tentative step off the stone stairs, waited to see if it caused any disruption among the so far passive vermin, and when it didn't, followed up with the other foot.

Before long, and comparatively easily, they were halfway across the chamber. The rodents were aware of them all right, but other than some rising to their haunches and sniffing the bat-dung-scented air with twitching snouts, they squealed but did nothing to delay them. Ash sneaked a quick look up at the rock-and-root-formed ceiling. There were hardly any bats visible on the periphery. But just as he looked down again he heard sounds coming from a smaller tunnel on the far side of the cavern.

Suddenly the vermin were quivering as one as they, too, looked towards the opening. Ash could feel the tension change to something stronger. It was as if an electric current were bouncing around the high cave.

The noise grew louder, like an approaching tube train, and then thousands of black and brown flying mammals burst through the opening, returning from their nightly insect feast. The squealing and squeaking sounds coming from both the bats and the unnerved rats filled the chamber with echoes, the cavern's acoustics amplifying the clamour several times over.

Mayhem quickly ensued as the flying creatures swooped over and down at the intruders on their territory while the rats jumped up at the bats, bringing some down by chance rather than skill, hordes of them tearing the fallen mammals to bits while their enraged fellows dived at the vermin on the ground, their deadly fangs burrowing into the rats' throats.

In all the chaos, Ash saw that Delphine had been shocked into stillness and he had to shout at her to make her act.

'The opening, Delphine! Make for the opening where the bats came in!'

With Louis still on his back – Ash had carried heavier backpacks than him – he nudged into Delphine to bring her out of her stupor. She took one look at him and understood what he wanted her to do. She focused on the black hole from where the flying creatures spewed and began edging towards it.

'There can't be many more bats to come through. When the stream stops, we'll crawl out!' Ash hurried her along, kicking out at any rat that was taking too long a look at him. Nevertheless, he felt several nips at his trousers that tore through to his flesh.

'Louis, put your head down against my back!' he shouted over his shoulder. The prince, who had been knocking swooping bats aside with the metal torch, obeyed. A group of rats scattered at their approach and revealed the dulled white bones Ash had seen on his first trip into the cliff's inner cave. He saw Delphine stop in shock when she was confronted by human skulls.

She was soon distracted when a bat landed in her hair and became entangled. With a screech she reached back with her free hand and tried to smack the struggling animal away. It was a hopeless gesture though, for the more the small creature struggled, the more it became tangled in Delphine's lush black curls.

Just a step or two behind her, with Louis desperately clinging to his back, Ash reached forward and grabbed hard at the frenzied, fluttering ball of fur, feeling its birdlike bones breaking under the pressure. The investigator pulled the bat away from Delphine, wrenching some of her hair from its roots as he did so. The bat's squeal was so thin and high-pitched it was lost in the prevailing cacophony, but it was the feeling of tiny cracking bones that stayed with Ash.

Delphine turned to him and he could see she was bravely trying to hold back tears of either fear or pain – probably both. However, this was not the time for hugs and sympathy.

'Run!' he shouted at her. 'Just ignore everything else and run. We're nearly there!'

And so they did, swatting away excited, vengeful, winged and four-legged rodents. Some rats leapt up at the flurry of erratic, flapping creatures, which were easier to deal with than the big humans making their way across the chamber. Some of the bolder rats jumped up and bit into Ash's and Delphine's clothing, most only tearing the material, although some slashes and bites struck home.

Ash watched proudly as Delphine, who seemed somehow now emboldened, angry even, kicked, punched and swiped the animals out of her way. It also made his progress easier, burdened as he was, albeit lightly, by the young man on his back. After two minutes that seemed more like two hours, the three of them reached the opening, which was now mercifully free of bats.

Ash put Louis gently down with his back to the entrance, placing his own body protectively in front of him. Delphine flattened herself against the rock on the other side of the opening. Again, Ash had to shout to be heard over the night-marish noise.

'Delphine! You go in f—' He stopped as he caught sight of a winged creature bearing down directly on him. Ash instinctively lashed out with his fist, punching the fluttering creature square on, knocking it to the ground where it lay twitching until two rats jumped in to tear it apart.

Ash started again over the din of creatures behind them. 'You go in first, Delphine. You'll find the roof is low at one point, but you can easily crawl through. Then you'll reach the big sea cave.' He remembered the park ranger, Jonas Mc-Kewin, telling him that if the weather was bad outside, the bats wouldn't leave home. It wasn't yet morning, so Ash reasoned they must have been caught in a sudden storm out there, and had headed back to the safety of their roost.

'Louis, I want you to stay behind Delphine. I'll bring up the rear.' He returned his attention to the psychologist. 'Use the torch at its narrowest beam. Any more bats come back in here, dazzle them with the light.'

'But aren't bats blind?' shouted Delphine, anxious to leave the huge cavern.

Ash shook his head. 'No, not all, that's a myth. But if they really want to, they can easily get by us: that's why we're going single-file.'

He took the smaller Maglite from the prince and gave him a cheerful, reassuring grin, despite the madness going on behind them. 'Okay, let's go. Delphine, I think the weather's pretty bad tonight, so don't expect the cave to be homely.'

She climbed in, waving the light before her. Louis and Ash swiftly followed, as keen as Delphine to get away from the noisy chamber. The psychologist soon reached the point at which the tunnel was at its lowest and she pushed herself along on her stomach, avoiding two small crabs as she did so. They scuttled away from her in their comical but creepy sideways walk. And then, over the sound of air rushing past into the inner depths of the cliff, Ash heard the welcome noise of crashing waves and smelt the strong, salty aroma of the sea.

In front of him, Delphine turned her head and shoulders to cry, 'We're there! We've made it to the cave!'

Ash grinned. *Thank God for that!* The sticky ooze they'd had to crawl through and the stench that had gone with it made him want to vomit, as it had earlier that morning.

'You hear that, Louis?' he called ahead. 'We're almost there. But take care when you get into the cave itself – it sounds like a stormy night out there.'

Louis did not reply, but quickened his pace, using his elbows to speed himself along.

Finally, they emerged from the shallow opening and were immediately drenched by sea spray. Although the water was cold, it was cleansing, washing away some of the grime and muck from their clothes and faces. God, it *was* cold, though!

Delphine and Louis had already moved further along the stone ledge that had been used to unload smuggled goods. Carefully, he eased himself around the rocky projections and stepped over the gaps where bits had broken away. Reaching Delphine and Louis, he hugged them both, kissing the psychologist on her now salty lips and Louis on the forehead. They were both shivering, chilled to the bone.

He switched off the smaller torch and exchanged it for Delphine's larger one. 'Put it in your bag to keep it dry,' he told her. 'We'll use the bigger Maglite for now.'

A wave came crashing into the open cave and washed onto the ledge, drenching them all the more. Ash groaned to himself. They had to get the shivering Louis out of the cave and up onto the top of the promontory. Somehow they would find a refuge there, and with all the confusion that must be going on by now, they might even find a way out of the Comraich estate.

Another wave boomed into the cave and they clung together to resist its pull as it receded. A nasty thought worried

Ash. Was the tide still rising? What if the cave filled right up, perhaps even to the sloping roof?

He looked around desperately for a higher place on which to wait for the tide to turn, but there was nowhere, nowhere at all, that they could reach.

'David!' Delphine's sharp cry made him turn to her. 'It's Louis. Look, he's bleeding!'

This made matters a whole lot worse. The haemophiliac prince could easily bleed to death while they waited for conditions to improve.

'We have to find out where he's been cut,' said Delphine, firmly taking control. She began undoing the buttons of the field jacket that Louis was wearing and Ash helped her get him out of it. His strange body was bruised virtually black in places. But then Ash saw the blood spilling from the prince's soft, pellucid, lower leg.

'His leg!' he shouted.

The cut was on his calf, about halfway up, and in itself, it did not look too serious. But on Louis, it could prove fatal.

'We must stop the flow!' Delphine shouted, bending on one knee to examine the wound more closely. 'A rat must have bitten him when he was on your back.'

'Or slashed him.' Ash was pulling the muffler over his head. Quickly twisting it again and again until it formed a tight band, he told Louis to step into it.

'It'll be too loose.' Delphine had already tried to stem the flow with her damp scarf, but Ash knew what he was doing as he pulled the improvised tourniquet up to a point just above the wound.

'Delphine, d'you have a pen or anything like that, in your bag? Something that will help tighten the material around his leg.'

'Will the small torch do? It has a longish barrel.'

'No, we need something strong but thinner.'

She opened her bag and pulled out her Mont Blanc fountain pen.

'That'll do it.'

Ash snatched the pen from her hand, slipped it between the circle of material and the flesh of Louis' calf and began to turn it clockwise. It immediately tightened around the leg to cut off the blood flow and Delphine again pressed her scarf against the slash itself. For a moment, the bright red fluid slowed to a trickle as Ash shone the big torch on it. They waited. And waited. The blood wouldn't stop oozing. Louis suddenly slumped against the rock face.

'We have to lie him down,' said Delphine, 'and hold his leg higher.'

Ash gently began lowering the exiled prince, until Louis' bare back rested on the cold, wet ledge, where there was hardly room enough for two of them, let alone three. Delphine held Louis' leg up and again they waited, praying the flow would begin to slow and eventually cease.

Ash saw quickly that was not going to happen. Since his sister had drowned, the investigator had been mildly hydrophobic, but as much as he feared the water, he began to consider jumping into the sea and swimming along the shoreline to the wooden steps that would take him up the cliff, where he might be able to find help. Surely someone from Comraich would be able to contact the Coast Guard and paramedics. He probably wouldn't make it, though he would certainly give it a try.

'There's only one thing for it,' he said, and began to unlace his heavy boots.

'No, David, no!' she pleaded. 'You can't—'

But then the next huge wave roared in, and everything changed.

98

A wall of water exploded into the cave, filling every part, foam brushing even the high stone ceiling and sweeping Ash, Delphine and Louis from their precarious perch on the ledge. Ash heard Delphine scream, the sound immediately lost under the tumultuous fury of the crashing sea.

As they were washed away, Ash just managed to catch hold of a jutting piece of rock with his fingertips and for a moment the water swirling around the cave lifted him high enough to get a better grip before submerging him entirely. He clung on underwater, the enormous wave swirling around him, threatening to break his grip before finally receding.

Underwater, the light from the large torch, which was still on full-beam, as it sank, illuminated the water as it was drawn towards the cave's once-gaping entrance. Ash thought he could see the dark shape of Delphine struggling to reach the surface and, further ahead, a smudge that could only have been Louis fighting against the current that was drawing him out of the cave.

The only chance he had of reaching them was to swim underwater, but first he needed to fill his lungs with air. He kicked up to get his head above the surface and catch a breath. It was difficult. The turbulent water threw his body around as if he were in a giant washing machine, but as soon as he'd taken the biggest breath of his life, he dived back under, pushing himself off the rock face below the water to give himself impetus, using his arms and hands to take him down into the murky depths, the faithful Maglite still giving off its glow.

He could feel the current sucking him out of the cave as it retracted, and he went with it, using the undercurrent to drag him along. He had to reach Delphine and Louis.

The investigator was well aware he was no great swimmer, but his instinct for survival took over.

Suddenly the glow from the torch dimmed, replaced by a different kind of light. When Ash surfaced again, there were rather than rock, clouds above him, but far to the east, allowing the pure bright moon dominance over the night sky. And although the savage winds were stormy and incoming waves were silver-topped, there was no rain. He was surprised to see most of the rocks on the shoreline were above water. He realized the route into the sea cave was much deeper than the shore on either side of it, which explained the ferocity and volume of the tidal waves, for they had unimpeded access.

Treading water in the broad trench as its current drew him ever further out to sea, Ash looked around for Delphine and Louis. There was no sign of them, so he dived again, salt water stinging his eyes and the moon's bright reflected rays soon lost in the gloom.

When he resurfaced, he caught a glimpse of Delphine only a few yards away. *Thank God!* He went under once more and swam to her, placing his hands under her arm and pushing upwards. Within seconds, they were face to face, trying to tread water.

She gasped in relief and briefly enfolded him in her arms. Not far away there was a rocky boulder jutting above the surface and he pointed towards it in an exaggerated motion. She nodded furiously, and they swam to it together. He pressed his cheek to hers as they clung there.

'Did you see the prince anywhere?' he shouted, and even in her frightened state she looked baffled.

'Louis,' he cried quickly, hoping she'd think she'd misheard him in the howling wind. 'Where did you see Louis last?'

'I . . .' She spluttered water, hanging on to the rock for dear life. 'I don't . . . I don't know. He . . . was swept away from me!'

Ash remembered Jonas McKewin warning him how dangerous the currents on this part of the coast were.

Then: 'David! Look! Over there!'

She was pointing at a spot thirty yards or so away. If the moon hadn't been so bright, she would never have seen the small white head that suddenly appeared on the rolling surface of the sea. Ash spied it too, and now had to resist the surge that was trying to suck them out to sea. Could the tide have turned so quickly and so dramatically? Louis would soon be dragged beyond reach.

'Delphine, I'm going after him.' His mouth was close to her cheek. 'I want you to stay here.'

She caught at his arm.

'You'll be safe if you can just hang on here. I think the wind's dying down. Look at the waves – they're much smaller.'

As the previous incoming surge retreated from the shore, they were both lifted higher in the water and were able to grab a better purchase near the top of the sea-washed boulder.

Delphine clutched at him again. In the moonlight he could see not only her concern, but her exhaustion too. If anything, she looked even more beautiful. In the silvery light her skin looked so pale, like smooth porcelain against the raven-black hair that framed her face with limp curls, her eyes wide, begging him without words to stay safe.

Christ, Ash wanted to sit there until help came or the tide had gone out completely. But he couldn't let the young prince, who'd never lived a normal life, simply drown.

'Promise me you'll stay here,' he urged. Her eyes opened once more and he could see resignation in them.

Without another word, Ash pushed himself from the rock and started swimming urgently to the last place they'd seen Louis. The current was now helping him, and for every wave that tried to send him back, the tide took him out further and more swiftly.

He thought he glimpsed something just above the surface a few yards ahead but he couldn't be sure, it disappeared so rapidly. He could do nothing for Juliet now, but maybe he could save Louis; maybe they needn't both die.

Then, in the bright moonlight, he just caught sight of Louis sinking below him. As he dived down everything went black and he felt himself being sucked deeper by the current. The prince was gone, completely out of sight. Yet another memory flashed before him of his morning walk along the shoreline: McKewin had said there was a deep sea shelf about thirty yards out with dangerous rip tides. He felt an urge to swim for the surface again, but he suddenly realized something very odd was happening below him.

Although the deep water was so dark, something lighter was slowly filtering through. As it grew stronger he saw the silhouetted shape of Louis, his arms straight out to each side of him, legs together, head unmoving. It was as though the young prince were enacting a kind of crucifixion.

A subtle blue light, gradually gaining in strength, shone behind Louis. It radiated through his naked flesh, revealing his bones and organs like an X-ray. The sarong was gone now, and Ash noticed that the makeshift bandage he'd made for the young man's slashed leg had worked itself loose and was floating away. A small trickle of darkness curled from the wound like a thin stream of smoke that was soon absorbed into the seawater. Then, as he watched, the bleeding stopped altogether. Steadily this wondrous, somehow gloriously peaceful blueness spread under the water like a soft, gently billowing cloud, its edges undefined, vignetted. Even the strong rip currents did not move it. It floated below like a sublime ethereal haze and Louis was sinking towards it. Ash remembered the blue in Louis' eyes earlier, and the faint azure light over the prince's cowering figure when Ash had first encountered him in his room.

This was the same pure shade.

As the prince slowly sank, he resembled an exotic creature from the deepest oceans, whose diaphanous nature allows them to withstand pressures of many tons, their flimsy bell-like shapes roaming the deepest oceans like divine aliens.

Ash at first thought that Louis must be dead, for he could clearly see his lungs were flat against his ribcage. Then the prince slowly and gracefully revolved as he floated downwards. And Ash, whose lungs were at their limit, saw Louis smile up at him, his face wondrously beautiful in its peacefulness.

Ash sensed Louis' smile was a message – a sign that all was well, that his death was but a return to one whose love had brought him to her, to be now cherished. His mother was reclaiming him and would love him in some other, sublime place.

Ash watched in awe as Louis sank into the most beautiful blueness he'd ever seen. The incorporeal soft-hued mist slowly enfolded him, enveloping Louis, and he was soon lost from view in the azure haze.

The investigator was mesmerized, and knew he had witnessed something truly glorious. Nevertheless, his lungs protested for lack of air. Although he was deep below the surface, he swam up unhurriedly, without panic, for he *knew* he was protected. As he did so the brightness below faded. He looked back over his shoulder, just before he surfaced. There was nothing below him now but a black void.

Mother and son had vanished.

99

Now that was utterly peculiar.

Way out to sea, Lord Lucan saw three small lights headed straight for Comraich. *What in the blazes?* he asked himself. *Can't be bloody aeroplanes, not that close together.*

He was distracted by shouts and the nearby clattering of a helicopter's rotors landside, where the castle's helipads were. He looked over and saw the larger of Comraich's two helicopters readying itself for take-off. All was perfectly clear in the moonlight. Lucan tutted at the behaviour of the so-called VIPs, who were physically pushing and shoving, fighting to get aboard the flying machine. He heard their shouts of rage and indignation and the crackling of the fire inside the castle, even over the sirens – which now seemed quite near, perhaps from just inside the compound's gates. One man ran shrieking out of the small side door, his back, arms and hair alight, but no one helped him.

Lucan turned back to the helicopter. It was actually rising into the air with one of the dinner-jacketed VIPs hanging half-in, half-out, with someone in the passenger seat next to the pilot – it looked like that oily little fellow Maseby – doing his best to dislodge the poor panicky bastard, who fought like a demon.

He had no chance. The chopper was all over the shop with displaced passengers upsetting the machine's balance. It must have been at least a hundred feet in the air before the unfortunate chap fell with an ear-piercing scream, which lasted about three seconds before his body splattered against the ground.

All rather exciting, thought Lucan.

Then came the biggest thrill of all.

The fancy helicopter, three hundred feet in the air, had just turned to head out to sea when it exploded spectacularly in a great bloom of yellow and red fire edged in black. Burning wreckage tumbled from the sky, together with flaming human body parts.

Lucan wondered if he'd be deafened for life from the thundering boom of the explosion as he went over to the walkway's crenellated wall to watch the helicopter's wreckage drop to the rocky shoreline below. Burning sections were scattered all over the rocks.

It was then that something further along the shore caught his attention – a small light flashing on and off.

Cedric Twigg sniggered, a hand to his mouth, though no one would have heard him from where he hid just inside the woodland watching his handiwork. His plan had worked perfectly.

Comraich Castle was blazing brightly, the flames encouraged by the rough winds blowing up from the sea. The sounds of walls crumbling and floors falling in were music to his ears. Those who'd survived the explosions and the inferno now stood like zombies before the conflagration, frightened for their lives.

The explosion of the helicopter had been the tour de force, such a wondrous demonstration of one man's mastery of his art – a magnificent firework display in the night sky, outdazzling the moon and stars.

But now he could hear sirens approaching. Police? The sounds were close enough to be inside the compound. He sniggered again as he collected his detonators and other items, throwing them all into his large holdall.

Oh, one more thing. He'd almost forgotten after the wonderful pyrotechnics. The Gazelle helicopter was still to blow. Might as well wait to finish off the show.

100

Ash dragged in air and seawater at the same time.

Spluttering, and choking, he tried to keep his head above the choppy surface, treading water and trying to swim breast-stroke at the same time. He was desperately tired now. The amazing uplift in his heart and his spirit from what he'd witnessed in the depths beyond the shelf was wearing off. Struggling against the ferocious current that tried to carry him further out to sea, he prayed for another miracle to help him reach Delphine and safety.

With his strength ebbing away, a miracle of sorts did occur: his hands knocked against something hard, not rock but ... *metal.* Ash kicked wildly against the undertow and his hands scrabbled frantically to gain a purchase on what proved to be a metal tube just beneath the surface.

In an instant, he knew what it was, for he'd observed it earlier. The long pipe that led down from the castle to the shoreline and then on out to sea – the sewage outlet.

Ash could have cried with relief as he mustered all his reserves of energy to pull himself along the pipe, fearful of losing his grip and afraid his hands and arms would become too exhausted with the effort.

He continued, foot by foot, each time he went under forcing himself up again, using the tops of the wind-blown waves to propel him along. He knew he could reach the higher part of the rock-strewn beach and might be able to stand or drag his feet along soon. With luck, the tide would have receded sufficiently by then to enable Delphine to walk to the shore.

But the sea was not yet done with him. It drew him back, and for a moment he considered how easy it would be to allow his body to float away, slowly to drift into the depths as Louis had done. As Juliet had been forced to do. The temptation almost overwhelmed him: to be somewhere peaceful, away from this world and its troubles, to be among friends again, to see Grace maybe waiting for him . . . But no! The vision of Grace succumbed to that of Delphine, and that vision gave him the strength he needed to fight onwards, onwards, nearly there . . . onwards . . . onwards . . .

His mind was beginning to wander due to utter, helpless, hopeless fatigue. It was undermining him – not just the muscles in his arms and legs but also his consciousness. Thoughts that should have sustained were faltering. Strength was finally seeping from flesh and sinew. His mind was closing down with his muscles. He felt himself slip below the water, but it didn't matter because his lungs were becoming too relaxed to take another breath. The water was like a soft bed. If he could just lie here for a while—

Something, someone, grabbed his hair and pulled roughly. The pain was excruciating, but only for a moment, for another hand reached under his armpit and tugged hard. He was floating now in the right direction and his knees scraped soft shingle and hard rock on the shoreline.

Ash reared up and drew in so much air his lungs might have exploded.

Other arms lifted him and, half-delirious with weakness, he saw faces, familiar faces . . .

Ash lay against a smooth shore boulder, his boots in a shallow rock pool. His vision was still blurred and he had to blink several times to clear it, unsure whether his eyes were filled with seawater or tears. Finally soft hands, *kind* hands, took over and wiped his eyes and then his face. He looked up to see the wind blowing Delphine's lush black hair around her cheeks as she smiled at him. He could just about summon the energy to smile back at her, and something in their mutual gaze told him she would never go away. She kissed him and he lifted a weary hand to stroke the back of her neck beneath the thick curls.

'David,' she whispered, close to his ear. 'Louis . . . ?'

'He's gone,' Ash replied just as quietly. 'But trust me, Delphine. He's in a better place.'

When at last she pulled back he could see other figures around them.

Mercifully, the chill wind had abated somewhat, so voices did not have to be raised, although the small gathering of soaked people huddling together still felt compelled to speak loudly.

'Sorry I nearly had to pull your hair out,' said Gordon Dalzell, 'but it was the only part of you I could reach. Otherwise, you'da drifted right back out again.'

'How did you know? Where we were, I mean?' Ash asked, the effort of forming a coherent question almost too much.

Another figure came forward, the moon behind him. 'Well, y'can thank Dr Wyatt for that. She saved your life, as well as her own.' The voice belonged to Graham Hamilton, Gordon's business partner and 'other half'.

Delphine held up the slim Maglite. 'When you left me on the rock I thought I'd lost both you and Louis.' She bowed her head, but Ash knew it wasn't the time to tell her of the awesome miracle he'd witnessed under the sea. 'I couldn't see either of you and I wanted to swim after you.'

'I'm glad you didn't.' Ash would never have been able to stand losing someone he loved so very much. Not again.

'Then I remembered the torch: it was still in my little bag.' She held the thin Maglite aloft. 'First I used it to sweep the sea in the hope I'd find you. But you were both gone.'

He saw a tear glistening on her cheek.

'Then she used her brains,' interrupted Graham, as if afraid

679

that the scene might turn mawkish. The wind blew again, so Ash had to strain to hear the words. 'Dr Wyatt shone the torch up to the top of the cliff – not at the castle, obviously.' Graham's grin was broad in the moonlight.

'Will y'nae stretch it out too long,' Gordon reprimanded his partner good-humouredly. 'We're getting awful cold down here.'

'Well, she not only tried to signal the people up top, but she used Morse code. How's that for good thinkin'?'

'SOS is so simple,' said Delphine. 'My father showed me how when I was seven years old.' She was wearing Gordon's jacket, which was much too big for her.

Graham continued. 'An old boy, one of the guests I'd seen around for years, was on the castle walk, and I went up t'see if he needed any help. Instead, he just pointed down to where this little light was shining an SOS in Morse code. At first, I thought it might've been a survivor of the helicopter explosion.' He noted the perplexed expression on Ash's face. 'There's a lot to explain, but dinnae ask me now. Anyway, I saw Gordon and we got Mr McKewin to bring us down.'

Ash saw the head ranger standing on the fringe of the gathering.

'So, with some difficulty . . .' Gordon glared at Graham. 'We managed to make it down here to the shore. We were lucky the tide was on the way out or we'd never have made it to Dr Wyatt to get her back here.'

Not to be outdone, Graham interposed, 'Anyway, we got to her and despite looking like a drowned rat – sorry, Dr Wyatt – she insisted we search further out. We saw nothing but rough waves until eagle-eyes here' – he pointed at the ranger again – 'spotted you clinging to the sewage pipe. But it was only when you were further in that we could reach you.'

He seemed satisfied with his story.

Ash heard the *whumph-whumph-whumph* of helicopters hovering and looked up. He could make out the castle on the top of the promontory: behind its burning windows and balcony doors there was a complete inferno, and even as he watched, part of a wing collapsed with a grinding roar audible over the combined sounds of the sea, the wind, helicopter blades – and gunfire.

'What . . . ?' He looked around at the others.

It was Gordon who answered. 'Scotland Yard's Metropolitan Police, the Serious Organized Crime Agency and the SAS, along with the Strathclyde Police Force, of course, have joined together to lance this bliddy boil on the backside of the United Kingdom. They're havin' somethin' of a set-to with Mr Babbage's men. Why they've chosen to intrude at this time, well – it may have something to do with you, Mr Ash. It became known to them that you were never gonnae be allowed to leave this place alive.'

'Me? I didn't realize I was that important.'

'Let's just say the authorities have had enough.'

'Then it's the Inner Court they're after?'

Gordon looked at Graham, who shrugged.

'It means y'gonnae have to sign the Official Secrets Act, but I don't s'pose y'll mind.'

Delphine was watching Ash in a state of perplexity.

'And I'm afraid, Dr Wyatt, they'll put you through the wringer as well. But I'm sure Mr Ash's word will go a long way concerning your involvement.'

Ash began to protest, but Graham put up a hand. 'Don't worry, she's already been thoroughly investigated and the word is she's in the clear. Believe me, there's gonnae be a mighty upheaval over what's happened here tonight and what's behind it all. I wouldn't be surprised if Dr Wyatt and y'good self, Mr Ash, will be invited t'leave the country together for a few months until it's all sorted out. After a full debrief, that is. You know what spooks are like.'

'Oh,' put in Gordon against a backdrop of gunfire, shouting, screaming, and helicopters coming in to land, 'and I think your leave of absence – your holiday, let's call it – will be all expenses paid. As long as you understand that there are one or two things you must remain completely shtum about.'

'We'll see,' replied Ash, his mind beginning to function normally again.

'Oh, I'm sure you can drive a hard bargain, David,' said Graham, grinning from ear to ear. 'You've done the country a great service, I believe, even if others might, er, take the opposite view. But nothing will prevent tonight's activities getting out and y'kin be sure the media will be all over it.'

'And by the way,' added Gordon, 'your boss, Ms McCarrick, will receive a hefty donation to the Physical Research Institute, as well as double payment for your time. T'be honest, David, I think you've hit the jackpot.'

Ash was unimpressed by any financial reward that might be offered as compensation, but he was interested in the reasons behind it. 'This all sounds as though it was planned. Something else has been going on here, hasn't it?'

'Oh, aye,' said Graham, now deadly serious. 'Well, that is, the Inner Court has been known to the authorities for generations. As for Comraich, it also served its purpose for both good and evil associations. Let's say it saved much embarrassment for certain high-ranking individuals.'

'Wait a minute.' Ash looked intently first at Gordon and then Graham, his mind so concentrated that he hadn't noticed the wind had become even milder, the waves calming themselves, although the seawater remained choppy. 'You two ... You're only a pair of chauffeurs, for God's sake. How do you know all this?' He looked from Gordon to Graham again.

It was Gordon who answered. 'Basically, the story I told you in the car was true, except that our chauffeur business was set up not in Edinburgh but in London, where we got to drive some very important people. Government people. But we missed Glasgow and moved back up. We were fine until the business took a downturn some years back, and that was when that greasy squirt Maseby popped his head in the door with an offer we could hardly afford to refuse. But we asked for time to think on it ...'

Dalzell broke off as a heavy rumbling noise reached them

from above. They all looked towards Comraich up on the clifftop. Huge walls were falling inwards, the fire totally out of control despite the jets of water from fire-fighters' hoses.

'Ah, the end of an era,' it prompted Graham to say almost woefully.

'Yeah, and we've done our bit. Mebbe they'll give us our retirement benefit now.' Gordon gazed up at the ruined castle, fascinated by the lights, sirens, shouted commands, and again, the faraway crackle of heavy-duty machine-gun fire.

Hugging Delphine close to him, in part to warm her, but mainly because he wanted her there in his arms, Ash said gently, 'Gordon, you haven't finished your story.'

'Oh aye. Well, the very next day we got another visitor, this one from MI5, who made us an even better offer to report everything going on here to them. Swore us in, made us sign the Official Secrets Act, all of that. So we've been spying here ever since. They know pretty much everything that's happened here.'

'But how did you communicate with them?' asked Delphine.

'That was easy enough. We often had to go into Glasgow or up to Edinburgh and we had a special number to ring. We were warned we'd be under surveillance by one of Kevin Babbage's men for the first few months, which was true, but we became trusted soon enough.'

'Also, we had dead drops,' added Graham.

'Aye.' Gordon grinned at Ash. 'Just like in the films. No doubt y'remember when I brought you here and we stopped at the Electric Brae.'

'Now that *was* scary,' said Ash.

'Gets plenty of tourists. Well, y'remember I left y'on y'own to get the full illusion? In fact, I'd gone off to our dead drop, a kinda' hollow spike thing which you push into soft ground. It's big enough t'tek notes or even rolls of film, and has a lid t'keep everything inside dry. It wasn't far away from the car but off the road in a bushy area. That day I just had to let the powers that be know you'd arrived safety. As well as about the problem with the jet before y'landed.'

'Who planted the bombs in the castle?' Delphine wanted to know. 'Was it you two?'

'Good God, no!' Gordon exclaimed, genuinely aggrieved. 'We dinnae do that sorta thing. And it wasn't the SAS or SOCA, either. No doubt they'll find out in time.'

Ash shivered, feeling the cold and damp working into his bones again now that the adrenaline was draining from him. 'So what happens now?' he asked, looking at Jonas McKewin, who was discreetly making his way over the rocky shoreline, his retreating figure clear in the moonlight.

They followed Ash's gaze.

Gordon chuckled, but it was Graham who spoke. 'T'tell the truth, we honestly don't know. I wouldnae thought they could keep a story as big as this secret, even if they served every news editor in the country with a D notice, or whatever they call it nowadays. And never forget the power of the internet. McKewin there, for example, they'll catch up with him sooner or later. His helping us find you down here will go in his favour. With so many big fish to fry, I doubt he'll even get to court. My guess is that many workers here will receive long suspended sentences, to be invoked only should they be tempted to speak out about Comraich.'

'But will it involve the Inner Court itself?' Ash wondered aloud. With Lord Edgar, Sir Victor and Andrew Derriman all dead, what other names would be connected to the IC?

He looked at Delphine, and her sad face remained pale in the moon's sheen. Pale and pure. Like Louis'.

And that was one story, Ash promised himself, which would never get out.

Never.

Because as far as he was aware, apart from the Queen and Prince Philip, only he, David Ash, a commoner, knew the full truth of the prince's life, and he alone knew its end.

101

'Lucky' Lord Lucan, his frayed half-velvet collar pulled up around the fine, long strands of his hair, walked with shoulders hunched against the chill of the night along the road leading out of the estate. Every time he saw headlights or heard sirens coming his way, he stepped over the verge and into the trees where he couldn't be seen by the many and varied military and police vehicles sweeping by. There were even fire engines bowling down the road – six of them, he'd counted so far.

He squinted back at the orange glow in the sky and knew the castle would probably be burned to the ground.

Ah well, game's up for Comraich, he thought to himself. And who knew, perhaps the Inner Court, itself? What a fuss there would be among the aristos. He'd learned as a young lad what kind of skeletons were hidden in the closets of grand folk such as himself. These days, though, he hardly missed the friends of his own ilk, the gentry, as they used to be called, the upper classes. No, he no longer missed them. He didn't miss anything of his old life. Except its freedom.

Ah yes, he missed his freedom.

He stumbled back over the verge and into the trees and was amazed to see three rather fine-looking luxury coaches hurtling down the road towards the glow in the sky. Undoubtedly these would be for the guests at Comraich.

Chuckling to himself, he took to the smooth tarmac again. There was still the sporadic sound of gunfire back there, but it was obvious the guards on the estate's gates hadn't shown much resistance, for not a peep came from up ahead now.

At last, sure the action was all behind him, he took to the middle of the road. The moon threw a long shadow before him – his own shadow – and as he passed the blockhouse near the wide-open metal gates, he stiffened his nearly eighty-year-old body and threw back his shoulders as if at attention. His head was erect and his eyes stared straight ahead, as was only befitting an ex-lieutenant of the Coldstream Guards.

And in this bold manner he marched across the threshold and out into the open roads of Scotland, a lonely, solitary figure.

In his heart he knew he would never return to Comraich.

102

On the way back to his cottage in the heart of the estate's woodland, Cedric Twigg grew tired. He'd abandoned his big bag with his detonators and timer equipment a long way back.

He'd slouched through the undergrowth and had strayed from the secret narrow path leading to his cottage, so that currently, although headed in the right direction, he was a little lost. Through the trees behind him he could hear the clamour of gunfire: soldiers or police discharging their weapons and shouting at the guests and castle staff to stay where they were. He'd blown up the small Gazelle helicopter on its landing pad before it had even taken off, killing both pilot and passengers. That had warned the army choppers to stand off and sweep the area with their powerful searchlights before landing, trying to find the perpetrator. He froze each time a beam of light shone through the trees, but the many conifers here made a thick canopy and he was sure he hadn't been seen.

Stumbling onwards, tripping over exposed tree roots every so often, he was determined to make his way back to the one place he'd feel safe. His breathing was shallow and sharp, barely filling his laboured lungs. His limbs trembled in a worrying way. Not far now. He'd soon be home. Must remember to get his tools of the trade down from the loft and bury everything in the woods. Dig a nice deep hole. Certainly wouldn't do for them to be found and the cottage was bound to be thoroughly searched. He didn't plan to spend however long he had left in some stinking prison cell.

His nose twitched. Cat's piss? No, more than that. Whatever it was, it was coming from the direction in which he was walking.

Twigg had to stretch out an arm and rest his aching body against a solid old cedar. He tried to steady his breathing, drawing in great wheezing breaths that hurt his throat on their way to his lungs. Wiping the sweat from his brow, he wondered how much further he had to go. Shouldn't be far now, should be quite near. Unless he'd been walking round in circles. *Don't be so bloody daft!* He knew these woods like the back of his hand.

There! There was the bloody path. Not four yards away and he hadn't noticed it until now. It was the excitement of it all. Blowing up the bloody castle! How he wished he could go back and watch it fall in on itself. What fun that would be! Too dangerous though. Might get caught. Best be getting back to the cottage.

He staggered onwards.

And glory be, there it was, just waiting for him to come home to it. Nice little white house, nice little path leading to the stable-style front door . . . the *open* stable-style front door.

Hadn't he locked it when he left earlier with his holdall of goodies? He always locked up when he went out, surely? Perhaps the thrill of the day had got to him, causing him to forget his usual routine. It was this bloody illness, that's what it was. Taking over his body. Medicine and pills were inside the cottage – they'd soon calm him down.

But was that a light shining from the windows? And the bloody windows were open! He can't have missed that. This wasn't like him at all.

Warily, the assassin approached his charming little woodland home.

The smell of cats grew stronger the closer he got. He wished he'd taken a pistol with him. He tried to step lightly when he reached the crazy-paving path up to the front door, but his legs were clumsy, his balance a bit askew. Slowly, not because of his Parkinson's but because he was beginning to feel some kind of dread, he walked – shuffled – cautiously up to the open door.

He paused on the doorstep.

And peered inside.

Lit by just one inadequate oil lamp, the interior was cast in gloom and shadows.

As Twigg squinted into the shadowy room, with moonlight shining through the tops of trees behind him, he began to make out shapes. For some reason, his tremors became a constant trembling as the shapes became more evident.

Now Cedric Twigg was not a cowardly man – his profession did not allow for that – but this night he suddenly knew true fear and it weakened his bladder. The shapes occupied the top of his small square table, while more squatted on the stairs leading up to the first floor. Two sat on a hard straight-backed kitchen chair, and more lay sprawled before the hearth of the unlit fire. From each one there came a contended purring which sounded more like a pleasurable snarling. One or two of the big cats prowled the room, their thick bushy tails waving in the air.

All watched him with evil yellow eyes.

He took one reluctant step into the feline-crowded room to see something even more strange. Someone – or some*thing* – occupied the lumpy old armchair by the hearth. And it was watching him. Watching him with only one eye.

A sane person might have turned swiftly and headed off back into the woods as fast as their legs would carry them. But an assassin, by definition, had to be somewhat insane even if it was their own dark secret.

Twigg took two further steps into the room for a closer look, because he could not quite understand what his eyes were telling him.

For, sitting in his lumpy, threadbare armchair, was someone who couldn't possibly be there.

What hair Twigg possessed prickled and suddenly it was as

if his body had forgotten to tremble any more. In his shabby old raincoat, he stood stock-still as his beady, bulbous eyes took in the . . . the *person*? . . . in his own favourite seat.

Eddy Nelson, his apprentice, his *dead* apprentice, looked up at Twigg through the one eye the wildcats had left in his face. Holding up his dislodged jaw with one slashed hand to what was left of the upper part of his face he said, 'Ayo, Ce-dic.'

Twigg staggered back a step. The dead man's expensive blue suit hung in tatters, smeared with quicklime and dirt from his freshly dug woodland grave.

'Sh . . . shudna dunnit, Ce-dic,' the mutated rasp of a voice complained, Nelson working the gore-dried mandible as a ventriloquist would move the jaw of a dummy.

Twigg found he'd nothing to say in response. Instead, his gaze roamed down to the corpse's open belly, where entrails and intestines were hanging out of a great gash of a wound. Nelson was trying to hold back all he could of those silvery tubes and strings of meat which glistened dully under the poor light from the oil lamp by the dead man's . . . feet?

They were shoeless and sockless and toeless as well. Just lumps of mouldering meat, which made the speechless Twigg wonder how this man, now slightly shrivelled and withered, had got himself to the cottage. Had he dragged himself across the woodland floor? Or walked awkwardly on the stumps? And had he dug himself out of the shallow grave, or had the wildcats returned to exhume him?

At the thought of the wildcats, Twigg became more aware of them. They were prowling around him now; one of the biggest, with mangy, dirty, bristling hair, was on the table nearby, ready to launch itself at him.

'Mu . . . my . . . frens,' Nelson announced with what might have been pride.

The stench of corruption and cats' piss was almost overwhelming, making the assassin feel faint. And the trembling had returned, although it was more like shuddering now.

His big mistake was turning around and trying to make it

back through the door. Not that he had any other choice, of course.

The wildcat leapt at his half-turned figure and landed squarely on Twigg's head, its long claws digging into his cheek for purchase. Twigg cried out, which proved to be the signal for every cat in the room to pounce.

The form in the armchair started to laugh, a peculiar grating, jarring, empty sound that paused only when the ragged corpse of Eddy Nelson, real name Nelson Eddy, clumsily dropped his jaw onto the floor, as the frenzied wildcats pulled Twigg down and rapaciously tore him to pieces.

The last thing Twigg saw was the lime-stained jaw streaked with dried blood, for it had landed just a few inches from his beady staring eyes.

And the last thing he heard over the sounds of the screeching, squealing cats was Nelson's hoarse guffaw of a laugh as the dead man tried but failed to keep the rest of his guts inside his open stomach.

103

Prince Philip, Her Majesty, Queen Elizabeth II's royal consort, impatiently paced up and down the lush carpet in what was commonly known as the Balcony Room of Buckingham Palace. It was where numerous royals had stood happily, if a little stiffly, waving to the crowds who always turned up in their thousands for every important celebration or state occasion.

In his pacing, the prince paused for a moment to look down the Mall. He always stood back a little from the tall, draped windows, because he knew that with the Union Jack flying, signifying the Queen was at home, the forever optimistic crowds from all over the world invariably gathered at the palace gates, yearning to catch a glimpse of any member of the royal family, never thinking they were sometimes watched in return. The mere shadow of a figure would send the tourists into a frenzy.

He looked back across to where his wife sat in a small gilt chair reading through a leather-bound report, the cover impressed with the royal crest in a gold motif. Queen Elizabeth favoured being closer to the people she served whenever there was trouble on the horizon, for the public's faith and adoration always imbued her with strength.

The prince continued his pacing, hands held loosely behind his back, worried by the anxious frown on the monarch's usually unflappable countenance. He wouldn't disturb her while she was reading.

The report contained a necessarily shortened version of events that had recently taken place at Comraich Castle. It seemed that it now lay in ruins, razed almost to the ground. The report also apparently included some previously unknown details of that bloody mysterious Inner Court, the bane of so many royals and dignitaries over the decades. What was to be done? What was to be done about *them*? Prince Philip frowned in angered frustration.

At last, his wife raised her eyes from the report and removed her reading glasses. She sighed as he approached and handed it to him. Now it was her turn to wait patiently and silently while he quickly scanned the pages.

In his early nineties, she thought her husband still cut a fine figure of a man. His back was once ramrod straight, but these days, his shoulders were a little rounded as if the years of high office weighed upon them mightily.

Queen Elizabeth said not a word while he skimmed through the report from the Home Office.

Finally, he closed the leather-bound primary transcript and dropped it contemptuously onto a nearby table. He looked across at his wife, who could only respond with a resigned expression.

Prince Philip walked back to stand by the long glass-panelled door that overlooked the Mall.

'Fuck them,' he said quietly. 'Fuck them all.'